THE
OCEANS
AND THE
STARS

A SEA STORY, A WAR STORY, A LOVE STORY

THE
OCEANS
AND THE
STARS

THE SEVEN BATTLES AND MUTINY OF *ATHENA*,

PATROL COASTAL SHIP 15

MARK
HELPRIN

THE OVERLOOK PRESS

New York, NY

Library of Congress Control Number: 2023935978

ISBN: 978-1-4197-6908-5
eISBN: 979-8-88707-076-6

Printed and bound in the United States
10 9 8 7 6 5 4 3 2 1

ABRAMS The Art of Books
195 Broadway, New York, NY 10007
abramsbooks.com

For the United States Navy

They that go down to the sea in ships, and occupy

their business in great waters; These men see the

works of the Lord, and his wonders in the deep.

Psalm 107

Sailor take note

Of the bright and the deep

And the vast embrace

Of the oceans and the stars

Contents

Prologue

Hampton Roads, Winter

Snow falling upon water makes a sound so close to silence that no heart exists it cannot calm. It fell across the Chesapeake and in the harbors and inlets and far out to sea, surrendering to the waters with the slightest exhalation and a muffled hiss. Though few are there to see it, in winter this happens often.

In the construction and maintenance of warships in Virginia's Tidewater, now veiled in steady snow, engines throbbed, cranes swivelled, and barges plodded over black waters. The spacious anchorage of Hampton Roads is ringed by naval stations, air bases, and shipyards making up the largest concentration of naval might in existence. Interwoven with civilian cities and commercial waterways, this sinew of steel is a world of its own. Even so, its powerful present cannot overwhelm images that upwell from the past: the sails of the French fleet in surprising bloom off Yorktown; the *Monitor* battling the *Merrimack*; and within living memory the Battle of the Atlantic, when ships burned offshore and corpses washed up on the sand.

From these docks and quays millions left for the World Wars, half a century of Cold War, Korea, Vietnam, and the Middle East. And for the scores of thousands who did not return, the flat coast of Virginia was the last they would ever see of their country. In summer and from war to war, as their ships passed by, young sailors would fall in love with girls on the beaches even though they could hardly see them.

None of this can be erased. Absorbed in their tasks, people do forget, but ofttimes spectral images suddenly appear. Across the water in the vast shipyards, cascades of sparks rooster-tail from the darkness of a cavernous shed or beside a massive hull. As if descended from the flash of guns, they seem to escape the underworld so as to insist upon the eternal presence of battle. And a warship headed out, as in uncountable times before, can arrest a watcher onshore as the ship speeds toward harm's way across the world and far from home.

Sailors find it hard to explain how they were changed by the sea; how even on a carrier, in the company of five thousand souls, they came to know the ocean's loneliness, and how war at sea unaccountably bound them to all others in every age who have sailed in fighting ships.

The Navy's stories are different and differently understood. Nonetheless, the stories unfold, and must be told.

*

At 0700 on 21 January, crowned by pier after pier of steel-gray ships of the line, Naval Station Norfolk was covered in deep drifts after a great and unusual snowstorm. In an emptied helicopter hangar at the edge of the long base runway, a court-martial was about to be called to order. Specially installed to provide heat as much as illumination, klieg lights shone hot from temporary rigging. At the outset of the proceedings Navy brass had assumed that civilians and press would crowd the hangar. They never did, at least not as imagined, and on the day the findings would come down no one was present other than the principals. Outside, sailors passed by, oblivious of the trial within. The public had long lost interest, and the press, which had been reassigned to cover a sparsely attended presidential inauguration amidst driving snow the day before, were trapped in Washington by hangovers and closed roads.

At its extremities, the cavernous building was dark, but its center was as colorful as a field of wildflowers. Sixteen in all, the national ensign and the flags of the Navy and various fleets and commands stood behind the dais, blindingly lit. Everyone was in dress uniform.

Because the charges included two capital counts, they required in addition to a military judge (in this case an admiral) twelve officers ranking higher than the defendant. Accordingly—as the accused was a captain—thirteen admirals walked in and took their places. The president of the court was Admiral Porter, of four stars, soon to retire, the dean of the Navy, and loved by all ranks. An unlit pipe was cupped in his left hand.

The admirals were expressionless and grave. The cut, insignia, ribbons, and devices of their uniforms added to their genuine authority. Most had a lot of gray in their hair. Some had nothing but gray.

At the prosecution table, trial counsel drummed his fingers as he and his numerous assistants scanned the panel, but at the defense table sat only defense counsel and defendant. Despite recent wounds and surgeries, the defendant's military posture was straight and strong. Whatever the verdict, his expression would remain the same and he would neither move a muscle nor blink.

As there was much that he loved, he had much to lose. But the prospect of death made love full and intense, and love that was full and intense made it possible to face death with equanimity. Although it takes some doing to know this, nothing could be more true.

Now, in a blaze of light and color, after the unprecedented snow that had streamed down upon the halyards, the masts, the stays, and the whitened decks of a mile-long line of ships, Stephen Rensselaer, Captain, United States Navy, awaited the capital verdict with less apparent anxiety than even those who would hand it down.

I

The Origins of United States Ship *Athena*, Patrol Coastal 15

Patrol coastals 1–14 were named after phenomena of the weather—
Cyclone, Whirlwind, Firebolt, Typhoon, *etc.—but not 15, the* Athena.
*She was of a different design, one of a kind, and, like her namesake,
the first and last of her class.*

Captain Rensselaer's Dream

Stephen Rensselaer was named after the famous and sometimes infamous Hudson Valley Stephen Van Rensselaers of earlier times. But years before Annapolis, and perhaps why he chose the Naval Academy, he came to associate his first name with that of Stephen Decatur, the youngest captain in the Navy's history and the hero of the Barbary Wars, whose life was heroic but whose death was not. Neither the Barbary pirates nor the British were able to kill Stephen Decatur. Rather, he died at his house across Lafayette Square from the White House, after a duel occasioned by his opinion in a court-martial. Politics are more dangerous than battles at sea, and when a sailor leaves Washington for a theater of war, he often breathes a sigh of relief.

Bravely then, when Stephen Rensselaer was assigned to four years of Pentagon staff duty he made the biggest investment of his life, stretching to buy and furnish the top floor and roof terrace of a large Federal townhouse in Georgetown. He added a few English and American pieces from the same period and before, all of which, like the house itself, had the inimitable patina of survival.

The longest wall was lined floor-to-twelve-foot-ceiling with bookshelves symmetrically graced here and there by lighted nautical paintings and a river study of misty terrain in rural nineteenth-century France. Framed in gold and glowing beneath their lights, the paintings were portals to another time. On the street wall, between two triple-hung old-glass windows, was his ceremonial sword, spotlighted by cold-blue halogen beams that flashed against its silver.

Decked in teak, the roof was his alone, a quiet place in which to read in the open air. From here he could see a plain of roof gardens visually broken by brick chimneys, colorful chaises, green umbrellas, and rickety grills. Though the treetops and church spires that rose amidst all this danced in waves of heated summer air, in the fading blue dusk of winter they became black and austere against the snow. His neighbors may have wondered why he didn't have a garden. Had they asked, his answer would have been that because he would have to go to sea he didn't want to raise plants he would betray. Had a neighbor volunteered to take care of them—the low walls separating rooftops were easy to cross—he might have added that abandoning something can be more painful than never having had it.

*

Long before *Athena* ever set to sea, before she was fitted out in the Bollinger Algiers yards across from downtown New Orleans, Rensselaer returned to his house in Georgetown on a cold night early in the fall. Freed of summer blur and haze, every light in Washington sparkled.

He and a lieutenant serving under him in Rensselaer's own capacity as an aide to the Secretary of the Navy had had dinner in a seafood restaurant on M Street. They were unable to talk shop in a public place, although such strictures are frequently ignored, especially in the densely surveilled Barnacle on Capitol Hill, where senators in their cups give away to half a dozen intelligence services more secrets than Aldrich Ames ever could have. Were that place swept for bugs, a hundred entomologists would have to sort them out. But because the lieutenant and Rensselaer had little in common other than secrets, to the recently divorced Rensselaer's embarrassment the conversation consisted of him giving career and family advice to a blissful young newlywed.

In the restaurant, old wood and a hundred gem-like bottles behind the bar in pools of light were bathed in the murmur of conversation, the sounds of cutlery settling upon china, and the sparkling crash of ice in silver shakers or tumbling into glasses. As intended, it was both tranquil and exciting.

"Our apartment is up on Wisconsin, Captain. It's near Whole Foods, which we go to only sometimes. Too expensive. We're near the park. It's not bad. We're just starting out."

"Right."

"What would you say?"

Rensselaer was half surprised and half trapped. "About what?"

"About being married, sir, starting out."

Rensselaer took a deep breath. "It's . . . it's a wonderful time. But you'll have to be careful. Depending upon your assignments, you can be at sea so much she'll learn to live without you. If she's sharp, she'll understand that aboard ship the weight of the missions and the near-constant activity

3

make the time pass more swiftly than for someone who doesn't have the same pressing demands. So you might be moving on separate tracks, and at different rates."

The lieutenant hadn't thought of things that way.

"Let's say, for example," Rensselaer went on, "that she has depleted much of her energy in pursuing a highly advanced education, and then she finds herself teaching infantilized college students offended by everything and expecting the world to honor their inflamed sensibilities. So . . . she's watching everything go to hell around her, teaching below her level, self-censoring, under pressure from the administration. When she comes home, like everyone, she needs to share her daily life. She needs to be comforted. But the house is empty, and where are you? You're in the goddamned Sunda Strait trying not to collide with a supertanker some moron is driving in the wrong lane. Needless to say, the loneliness is extremely difficult for her.

"Is she going to ask you to resign your commission? Like me, you began as an eighteen-year-old midshipman at the Academy. You've spent your adult life in the Navy. You have a calling. If she asks, you probably would. But she's considerate, and she doesn't, so she begins to resent you, and she feels guilty about her resentment. Meanwhile, you're apart. The enforced separation becomes ordinary and natural. When you come home, the tensions are laid bare and you fight. Which only makes things worse when you're away.

"It doesn't have to be like that, but unfortunately it often is. You have to work hard for it not to be."

"Okay. Then that's exactly what I need to know. How do you do that?"

"I didn't."

"Oh."

Because the restaurant was packed, only now did the waitress arrive, rushed and holding her pad. She was beautiful enough to shock the two naval officers out of their previous conversation.

Uncharacteristically, and to relax himself after what for him had proved to have been a somewhat difficult discourse, Rensselaer ordered a scotch with his meal, and the lieutenant followed suit. The lovely waitress appreciated very much that, without the slightest hint of predation, they appreciated her. And then, pressed just right, and for those who didn't have to wear it, the uniform was an advantage of sorts.

So she brought single-malts in cut-glass tumblers three-quarters full and three times what they expected. "What's this?" Rensselaer asked.

"My hand slipped," she said with a slight smile as she turned to leave.

"Evidently twice," the lieutenant clarified. "If we don't finish them she'll be deeply hurt.

"Never get over it."

"You think?"

"I'm sure."

"I don't react so well to alcohol. And look at all this," Rensselaer said, swirling the scotch in the glass.

"Give it a try, sir."

*

Perhaps because Rensselaer had spent many years on rolling decks and in yawing passageways, when he walked home even Carrie Nation wouldn't have noticed anything amiss. He got up the stairs rather well, but in the enormous, book-filled living room he lurched a bit as he approached a credenza laden with photographs in silver frames. Here were several iterations in black-and-white of his mother and his father, and in the center two 8x10s in modern color: one of a woman who, he knew, was ravishing, brilliant, and sweet; and, the other, a wedding photograph of a couple passing beneath a canopy of raised swords. Brides are gorgeous. She was especially so. He opened a drawer in the credenza and put the two color portraits in it, with a clatter, face down. Then he closed the drawer. Had he been younger he might have cried, but he hadn't cried in decades.

While lighting a fire, his movements were exaggerated by the alcohol as it grew in effect. These were slightly and pleasantly involuntary and, he thought, somehow perfectly . . . *Italian*. When he stood up he walked backward without looking and crashed into his chair.

Fearing that he would not feel very well in the morning, for the next two hours he stared at the flames, his emotions simultaneously anesthetized and intensified, until they and the fire burned down and all that was left were forge-like coals that seemed to breathe as they pulsed red and then became dark crimson in exhalation before turning to white ash as light as snow.

In the two hours until the fire was safe to leave—fire at sea is as dangerous as incoming water, and in this regard sailors are habituated to be more careful than most—he surprised himself with disorganized thoughts as wild as had been his movements before he fell into the chair: deep, beautiful, musical thoughts as impossible to retrieve as the will-o'-the-wisps of flame over wood or coals, which sometimes made half-circles in the air and fled up the chimney like sprites. Such was alcohol for someone who, before his divorce, had rarely drunk it.

Just as he was rising from the chair, the phone rang. He straightened irritably, walked to his desk, and answered. It was the night duty officer. "Good evening, sir. The secretary"—that is, Freeland, Secretary of the Navy—"would like you to be here tomorrow at o-six-hundred. "I just received the call, sir."

"Very well."

Hurriedly, Rensselaer hung up, brushed his teeth, set his alarm for four thirty, undressed, and threw himself into bed. Despite his agitation and what seemed to him an unnatural beating of his heart, he fell asleep almost instantly. And, eventually, he dreamt.

*

Dreams are the natural art of every soul. A preview of freedom from mortal constraint, by impossible juxtapositions of suppressed desires they reveal what in life is hidden by trouble and necessity. And they can be prophetic.

Other than in combat, the national ensign—that is, the flag—is not flown at night from the gaff of a United States ship. Nor would its colors be recognizable in moonlight, much less in the monochromatic light that barely escapes a solid layer of cloud. But in Rensselaer's dream, the *Athena*, which he had never himself seen, was no longer in the Algiers yards but forging through the Indian Ocean. Quietly rising and falling in perfect rhythm as if on a sine wave, she was alone on the dark sea, the ensign lofted and straight-pressed by the wind. Though it was night, even if it was dimly lit and by memory alone he could see its colors, and the white foam unfurling brightly from the bows. Like music, a ship in motion is a beautiful thing purely in itself, but also for what the eye sees. And, like music, it speaks to the soul.

As if a bodiless spirit, he watched while suspended in air off the port side. Knowing it was a dream and yet believing it still, as if he were a lookout he heard himself reporting to the bridge that he was at "bearing zero, niner, zero, position angle ten, movement of contact tracking that of the ship." He knew they couldn't see him. Nor did they need to. The darkened bridge was crowded with men in light so dim it took an hour for the eyes fully to adjust.

Absorbed in their jobs, now and then speaking quietly and formally, they stood their watches in expectation of both nothing and everything.

Constant surveillance and readiness made them alert to the tranquility and emptiness of the sea and wedded them forever to the smooth pitch of a ship riding forward on wind-driven swells. Minor changes in weather, wind, sky color, water, and cloud loomed large.

Major changes were exciting enough to overwhelm the senses. From Rensselaer's vantage point in the dream, the motion of the ship, almost like that of a living thing—a horse in smooth canter, or a dolphin blending the curve of its back to the roll of the waves—seemed purposeful, conscious, and sad.

There she was, at three-quarters ahead whether in sunlight, rain, storm, or under the stars. Smaller than even a frigate, she was far from land, separated from the fleets or any ship that might have sustained or protected her. Her color was darker than even the sea, which when the moon is imprisoned by cloud has at best a barely visible wash of silver.

A surge of affection and admiration overtook Rensselaer as he watched the flag stiffly oscillating within very narrow bands, but sometimes, with changes in the wind, snapping like a whip. Though *Athena* proceeded as if hurrying to a destination, in the absence of a visible coast or another ship she appeared only to be chasing infinity.

Unlike a yacht, she was not smooth of aspect but roughly faced with guns, missiles in boxes, towers, radomes, antennae, and other accoutrements of war. He watched the unceasing roll of waves rebuffed by her bows, their luminous foam hushed down into the deep.

The sea was speaking to him in silence. Its message was: as your spirit rises to fill the place of appetites and illusions, take stock and be comforted, for all time is lost in the oceans and the stars. You've left behind the things of life on land that shield you from a truth the sea will not let you forget—that you are first and last a spirit, that you are alone, and that this can be borne.

THE WEST WING

Rensselaer crossed west on the Key Bridge early in the morning when the traffic was light, the wind was cold, and the ducks on the Potomac still slept, their heads tucked beneath their wings. To supplement his midday hour at the gym he almost always walked from Georgetown to and from his work at the Pentagon.

Like all politicians, Freeland, the Secretary of the Navy, was deliberately inscrutable, unpredictable, and unreliable: you couldn't know what he was really about or where in his eyes you stood. His thinking was mainly a form of calculation, and people were nothing more than either encouragements, accessories, or impediments to maneuver.

As he crossed the bridge, Rensselaer thought back to a hot day in June the year before, in Freeland's Mercedes convertible with his personal aide, an irresistible, underemployed redhead known to all—despite her discretion, intelligence, and fluency in several foreign languages—merely as "Rusty." She was driving him back to Georgetown from the secretary's estate in Middleburg, where several of the staff had been summoned to work on a weekday when Freeland wanted to stay near his horses, his helipad, and his pool.

To avoid the crowded main arteries, she took the back roads. Many of them were very old, and their white macadam unfurled leisurely amid the huge trees and horse fences of great estates. The Michelins on the Mercedes rolled steadily along the hot pavement as the sun shone down on Rusty, moistening her skin and liberating her perfume, which, Rensselaer imagined, she had applied to her low-cut, seersucker sun dress as well as liberally to herself. She was not unaware that her presence was having an effect upon her passenger.

"Is something wrong?" she asked. The question was loaded.

"No."

"Really? You've been staring at me," she said, shifting gears, and responsibility.

"I was looking at the road."

"You were turned toward me, and you had a sort of dinosaur look, like you wanted to eat me."

"I was looking at the road . . . on the *left* side of the car."

"Uh-huh."

"And, besides, there's the Navy Secretary with the estate, the car you're driving, the horses, the ships, and the Savile Row suits."

"Him?"

"Yeah, him. You never leave his side. He's handsome, rich, formidable."

"He is formidable," she confirmed. "No question. And he's as wealthy as a cat."

Rensselaer thought for a moment. "He's what?"

"He's as wealthy as a cat."

"That's something I've never heard."

"It's an expression. Everybody says it."

Rensselaer closed his left eye skeptically and as if looking through a loupe. "Where are you from?"

"Chicago."

"In Chicago, people say someone is as wealthy as a cat?"

"In my family they do. You say, 'Oh, he's as wealthy as a cat.' But I'm not his girlfriend. Or his mistress."

"Everyone thinks you are."

"That's the way it's supposed to be. He's gay."

"Oh," Rensselaer said. He had had no clue.

"It shouldn't get in the way, but he doesn't want to complicate things. It would ricochet around the fleets."

"Yes, it would ricochet around the fleets."

"Most people close to him know, but he just wants to get on with business."

"So, you . . . ?"

"I live with my boyfriend. He's at State."

"I see."

"At the Pakistan Desk."

"And he doesn't mind that people think you're Freeland's mistress, or whatever? I admit that I did."

"No. He knows I'm not, and he's supremely confident: I love him for that. Jealous people get left. Jealousy repels, trust attracts. He calls me Trusty Rusty. I know it's stupid, but I like it."

In Georgetown when she stopped to let him off, the smell of good leather and her perfume rose in the heat of bright sun flooding into the car, and Rensselaer was enveloped in a kind of hallucinatory red. But that was that. Even had their ages been better aligned and she were unattached, after the divorce he could hardly imagine himself, at his age, finding someone else and starting over. She put the car in gear, pulled out, and drove back toward the Key Bridge, where before dawn as the ducks slept in the cold wind rippling the water below, he remembered this.

*

On his walk to and from work he passed through Rosslyn, with which he felt a linguistic kinship in that Rosslyn wasn't spelled Roslynn and Rensselaer wasn't spelled Renseleer. Both names managed an unexpected double *s* to begin with, and then to do without the expected double letters at or toward the end—*e*'s in his case, *n*'s in Rosslyn's. The best part about Rosslyn was its name. Otherwise, like so many cities, it looked like a bunch of discarded appliances.

He had Arlington Cemetery and its almost palpable spirits entirely to himself. It didn't open until eight, but he knew the guards, and when he was in uniform they let him pass. Twice a day he walked the length of this ground and experienced a devotion more genuine and powerful than any that might be sworn absent the many long lines of graves that validated it. To swear allegiance to and defend the Constitution was a wonderful thing that brought as much feeling as something of primarily intellectual import might.

But no matter the oath, those who had lived and died in service of it were what made it holy, not just as an article of faith but as a story of doing. It was to these men, and women—some of whom, and increasingly so, were soldiers, sailors, airmen, and Marines; and others who were the wives who waited—that his love and gratitude radiated, only to echo back as if somehow they had answered.

For the chain of command did not stop at the president. Hardly so. It rose far beyond him, to the people and the history of the United States, to the principles and stories of the living and the dead—nothing disappearing, nothing ever to disappear, at least in the lives of the faithful. The guarantors of this were those who lay silently beneath the elms as Rensselaer passed by.

*

Though he had to report sooner than usual, he was early even so, and he paused on a hillside amid the long rows of patriot graves and the massive trees risen from this hallowed ground as if to be their constant and devoted guardians. He would neither sit on a gravestone nor, because of his uniform, on the ground, so he stood in the wind and the rising sun, looking toward the Capitol as east light left the classical buildings on the Mall shadowed across their west facades.

Though saturated with history, Washington was less than four and a half of his life spans thus far: nothing compared to Jerusalem, Athens, or Rome. There was a lot to come, a lot to be weathered, and a lot to be done. Because the city was young, spacious, calm, and gleaming white, it promised the ideal. However. . . .

Only weeks before, his first assignment had been to sub for the Navy Secretary on a visit to a well dug-in senator perpetually hostile to defense, and naval appropriations in particular. "He's from Minnesota, and uses us as a punching bag to get the ice-fishing vote," the NAVSEC told Rensselaer. "He treats me like a waiter, so I'm sending you as a reminder that we're part of a separate branch. You're there to gather information so that I'll be prepared when I do show, which I won't. You're my representative. Be diplomatic. We'll have you driven over so you'll be fresh, but take your time and walk back so you can get the idiocy out of your system."

"You think that's necessary?"

"Oh, I do."

Rensselaer arrived at the Hart Building half an hour early and was kept waiting in the senator's outer office for another hour. He wasn't surprised. In government's treasured hierarchies, those lower down must always wait. This gave him plenty of time to scan the hundreds of framed photographs—Senator Hamburger with presidents, with the justifiably deceased leaders of his own party, and alongside a few foreign potentates who had conspicuously tortured expressions. He thumbed through the senator's spirited (i.e., ghostwritten) campaign manifesto, *Hamburger's Recipe for Minnesota.* It was published by a New York publishing house owned by a conglomerate that had a lot of business in areas to which the senator's committee assignments were highly relevant, and it fetched what *Publishers Weekly* termed "a rather high advance for a book that could have been written by a moth." To add insult to injury, the senator's political opponents went into bookstores and covertly shifted it to the regional cookbook sections, as if it were *Minnesota's Recipe for Hamburger*. And when the senator was accused of touching a woman's lower back, newspapers could not resist the headline, "Ethics Committee to Grill Hamburger in July."

For team spirit and uniformity, the senator made his long-suffering staff wear embroidered baseball caps, even indoors. Not exactly in tune with the times, and never having been in a supermarket, he offered a choice between two slogans: "Ice Fishing Isn't for Broads," and "Hamburger Helper."

The ceilings in Hart were pompously high to make up for the small offices necessitated by its pompous atrium. In the waiting area, a giant oil portrait served to inform Rensselaer that Hamburger had a tiny head and a pencil mustache. Eventually, the real thing said, "Have a seat, Captain. You are a captain, right?"

"Thank you, sir. I am."

"So where's your boss?"

"He had urgent fleet business, Senator. I can relay your concerns for when you do meet."

"That'll be in committee," Hamburger threatened.

"Sir," Rensselaer said, taking out pad and pen and trying to be as deferential as possible, "I'm ready to listen."

The senator looked up at the high ceiling as if to check with God. "When the *Ford* was off New Jersey—people are always trying to invade New Jersey, right?—I went out to it in a helicopter. I was supposed to be impressed."

"You weren't?"

"Why would I be? It's hollow. Twelve billion dollars and counting and it's as hollow as a barrel."

"If I understand you, sir, yes, there are problems with the EMALs and the munitions elevators, but they're not going to persist, I can assure you."

"That's not the point. It's *hollow!*"

"Hollow?"

"Empty, man. Just air. A giant, empty cavern. It's a fake."

"That's the hangar deck, Senator, where the airplanes are kept."

"Why not keep them outside, and fill the inside with something useful?"

"We can't keep them outside all the time. There's the weather. In extremis they could be swept overboard. Corrosion, being able to work on them. They need a lot of maintenance."

"So? Build shelters for them on the outside, up top."

"Sir, the flight deck has to be clear for launch and recovery. You know, when the planes take off and when they land?"

"Why not have elevators that would lower the shelters, then?"

"We do have elevators, only we lower the planes, and put them on the hangar deck, the hollow space."

"Wouldn't it be better to have pop-up shelters? The planes would be ready all the time, and they wouldn't have to squeeze into the elevators. Have there been studies of this method?"

"I don't think so. At least not yet," Rensselaer answered, feeling seriously unmoored.

"You go back and you tell your boss that the people of the United States of America are sick of spending twelve billion bucks a copy for empty shells full of nothing but air."

"I will."

When Rensselaer returned, he said to the SECNAV, "He's an imbecile."

"No kidding."

"A senator, a United States senator," Rensselaer added in disbelief. "How can that be?"

"Oh," the SECNAV said, amused, "you ain't seen nothin' yet."

Reflecting on this amid the dead of so many wars, Stephen Rensselaer naïvely resolved to be more assertive in the face of ignorant authority. There were plenty of fools in the Navy, but because their ideas were tested in flight, on the often wild oceans, and in their depths, it was not the same as in politics, the hollows of which were far deeper and darker than those of any ship, ever.

*

Before the secretary arrived, Rensselaer turned on the lights and sat down at a long table perpendicular to the secretary's desk, which was itself a table with a leather top. In back of the secretary's chair were ship models (one in a glass case), family photographs (divorced, with grown sons, he still kept a photo of his ex-wife), a complex government phone with more buttons than an accordion, and, partially hidden, a muscular shredder.

An enormous gold-framed painting of a clipper ship on a green sea covered the wall behind these. The office windows looked out at the modest capitals of the Pentagon's columns. The windowsills held several ceremonial swords on stands, and a sextant displayed in an open, mahogany box.

The Wall Street Journal, the *Times*, and *Washington Post* were laid out on the conference table. Rensselaer was about to review them for pertinent articles when the secretary came in, closely followed by Rusty. Freeland was white-haired, square-jawed, of medium height and build, in a tailored suit and red silk tie. Rensselaer stood.

"Anyone want coffee?" Freeland asked.

"No thank you, sir," Rensselaer answered. The walk in the air had banished what might have been a hangover. Rusty shook her head almost imperceptibly. They sat down, Freeland at the head of the table, his chair askew and his legs crossed parallel to the table's shorter edge.

"Last night," Freeland announced, "the president made known that he wants to see the Navy Secretary and the Chief of Naval Operations this morning at nine. So, we and the CNO will get there at eight, and wait. Have you ever been to see him, Stephen?"

"No sir, never met him."

"Or any other president?"

"No sir."

"By the end of their terms, most presidents are as jaded and as easy to irritate as a forty-year-old dog. They just want out, and who could blame them?

"He completely ignored our posture statement. I'm sure he didn't read it. Frankly, I'm not even sure he knows how to read. I do know that he wants larger ships because they're more impressive. They are. I'm fine with more large ships as long as we can have smaller ones too. But he wants to get rid of the small ones, if you can believe it, because they're *small*. Jesus Christ.

"He sprang this on the Secretary of Defense and the Joint Chiefs, who managed to talk him down somewhat. But maybe to save face or just out of belief, he wants some small vessels to sacrifice. He's decided to scrap the Patrol Coastals."

Now Rensselaer knew why he but none of the other military aides was there. "Having commanded a PC, you're coming along. Rusty, you'll take notes, and, of course, the president—like every president I've known—is made happy by the presence of uniforms and beautiful women. That's just the way things are. Sorry, Rusty, if he won't see through to your soul."

"That's all right. A lot of people don't see through to my soul, and, to tell you the truth, I'd rather the president wouldn't either."

"Got it," Freeland said. "And, Stephen, it's not just because you've commanded a PC and are an eloquent and expert advocate, it's because you'll impress the president with your academic credentials, because he has none—although tread lightly."

"Why would I even mention them? There's no reason. And he did go to—"

"Yes, he did," Freeland interrupted. "He was expelled for invading the president's office. Ironic, isn't it? And he got his degree in a special program that was kind of like work release."

"I didn't know that."

"Neither did the voters. The record was expunged."

"Yikes," said Rusty.

"I never said all this," Freeland told them. "Right? He's impressed by academic credentials, but he might be jealous, and then you'll be cooked. Certainly it's good that you were a SEAL. He loves the SEALs. They've got the best PR and the most movies. It's a crapshoot, but I want to try to save the PCs. So let's go. They have a coffee and tea service over there, with great cookies. On the way, we can get the etiquette straight."

*

It was always dramatic, cinematic, and slightly ridiculous when the secretary's motorcade rocketed out of the Pentagon's underground garage—four black SUVs with smoked windows and corkscrew antennae. He and his aides could have taken the Metro, which would have been faster.

Crossing the Potomac, Rensselaer saw in his imagination the capital waterfront as it appeared in 1900: sailing ships in the main, but steamships as well, small launches and schooners; heavy trade, busy wharves; boats to Boston, New York, and Philadelphia; seagulls that had followed clippers up from the bay; and in the sunshine, floating like a cloud, the Capitol dome, taller than anything on the hill, white and new, or so it seemed. He yearned not for the past, but for a country and a people that in understanding mortality and knowing austerity lived simply, modestly, and in tranquility. It was comforting that the water below was unchanged, still master of the world's surface, its memory of hundreds of millions of years unyielding and untouched.

"This president," Freeland said, "cannot be contradicted. You can suggest a counter to what he says by prefacing it with 'What if . . . ?' or 'I've been under the impression . . . ' or 'Do you think . . . ?' or 'Would you prefer . . . ?' But you don't interrupt him, or speak unless he calls on you.

"That president," Freeland contrasted, pointing to the statue of Lincoln as it looked outward between the columns and then disappeared, "was a brave genius. This one thinks he is. What one hopes for is that you can walk out of there with your head. He thinks he knows everything, and he's not friendly to defense. But no matter. It's always interesting to be in the presence of the commander in chief. Presidents, Rensselaer—and I've known a few—are divided into distinct types: those who understand that they are just men, and those who don't; those who loot the office of its honor, and those who bring honor to it."

"And this one?"

"No comment. You'll follow me into the Oval as my aide; Rusty will come in as the seductive note taker. I have no idea how many the CNO will bring. But the fewer people the better. When his chief of staff—or he himself—says, 'Thank you,' you get up like a rabbit. No, a pheasant. Bang! You're up. You say, 'Thank you, Mr. President,' and exit quickly. That's the drill."

The SUVs rolled in past the first White House checkpoint, after which the three with the security contingent peeled off to the right toward the Ellipse to park and wait. Before the gate dropped at the second checkpoint a uniformed Secret Service officer looked in the windows and asked if there were any firearms in the secretary's vehicle. Told there weren't, he took a step back, the gate opened, and the SUV drove into the rectangular parking lot known as West Executive Avenue, past limousines with flags, and hulking Secret Service SUVs exactly like the one in which Rensselaer was riding.

Then they walked beneath the kind of canopy one doesn't see very much these days even in New York where once they were legion, and after being greeted at the last checkpoint, ascended some cramped stairs into the West Wing Lobby. There they would remain for almost two hours.

16

Although the seating was not that comfortable, it was a lovely place in which to wait. Huge, museum-piece paintings lined the walls of a room of major if not palatial proportions, and the impeccable uniforms of the skinny, bored, young Marines who had to stand all day like cigar-store Indians lent a great deal of color. It varies from administration to administration, but White House secretaries are usually elegant and well turned out. The feeling is like going on a date in the days when there was such a thing as courtship, and when college girls came down the stairs to meet their boys they wore formal dresses and white gloves.

"As you'll see," Freeland said to Rensselaer, quietly, "everybody who waits here will be talking on a cell phone. I don't. I think it's rude, so I'd appreciate if you'd turn yours off."

"I already did."

Pleased, Freeland leaned back on the striped settee the three of them occupied. "I don't know why, but I'm twenty years your senior, Rensselaer, and you remind me of my father, who's ninety-five."

"That's a compliment, sir."

"It is. Believe me, it is."

Then they got a lot of reading done—newspapers, cables, and reports. When called to see the president they were confidently well prepared and informed. The CNO and two aides arrived on the instant, and they all proceeded at once, the secretary and CNO in the lead.

*

As they walked down the hall toward the Oval Office—for some reason they had been ushered in past the vice president's suite—Freeland noticed that Rusty was a little shaky. "Rusty," he said, "this is no big deal."

"That may be easy for you to say," she said tensely.

"We're not going to see Saint Peter," he whispered. "You're superior to the president in every really important way, and don't you forget it."

As they waited in the Oval Office for the president, the secretary and the CNO chatting, their staffs silent, Rensselaer wasn't thinking of or taking stock of himself, but he, a mere captain about to meet the President of the United States, would have had nonetheless every reason for equanimity.

Marines who have risen through the ranks and are older almost always have a lean and rugged look, which is not as common in the Navy. But

Rensselaer, having been a SEAL and forever bound to extremely high levels of fitness, resembled those tough Marine generals who never betray the slogan, "Every Marine a rifleman."

He had been in the military since 1985, when at the age of eighteen he had entered the Naval Academy. Now, at fifty-two, he stood six-foot-one. He was dark-haired, sharp-featured, clear-eyed—they were blue—and seemingly much younger than his years. Adding to every qualification earned over his career was the confidence derived from his great physical strength and endurance (for his age). This alone allowed him to care little for advancement and status, as if he measured everything in terms of surviving on an enemy coast.

He knew this strength would leave him. It was already beginning to ebb. Eventually, having paid little attention to position and career, on what would he rely? Nothing, but it didn't matter, because by the time strength was gone he would be old enough to have realized that ceaseless competition among men offers no elevation at the end, no immunity to suffering and death, no insight as to purpose or what comes when life finishes its reign.

So, absent plot or maneuver, his career had meandered to follow his interests, his talents, and chance. At age twenty-five, a lieutenant, junior grade, and a SEAL, he had deployed in the Western Desert of Iraq, tracking and blowing up Scud missiles from a mile away in a camouflaged trench, with a 50mm sniper rifle and one incendiary round shot into the fat, volatile, liquid-fueled body of the missile. Before anyone could hear the report, the bullet had arrived, the missile had exploded, and most of those nearby were dead. Nonetheless, at times the Iraqis swept in with helicopters and troops, and at times Rensselaer and his team had to fight their way out against disadvantageous odds.

At twenty-seven, a full lieutenant, he became an SWO (surface warfare officer), and served on several ships for five years, at the end of which, in 1998, he arrived at Harvard, where after four years he exited with a Ph.D. in government and a thesis on nuclear strategy—the same subject of his thesis at the Naval Academy as a Trident Scholar—and was promoted to lieutenant commander. The next year, in the Second Iraq War, he commanded a Patrol Coastal in the Persian Gulf—or, as the Arabs insist, the Arab Gulf.

In 2005 at age thirty-nine he was promoted to commander, and then served for two years as the XO (executive officer) of a destroyer, after which he was detailed to staff duty for two years under Admiral Johnson, the Director of Strategic Systems Programming. Following that, he spent a year at the Naval War College, exiting as a captain, taking command of a destroyer squadron for two years, and, at fifty, commanding an amphibious ready group, and then, at fifty-two, being assigned to the Secretary of the Navy.

He was of senior rank, expert in nuclear strategy, an experienced combat veteran and SEAL, and he had held numerous commands at sea. The doctorate, the War College, and his overall presentation made him a natural for his current position, which, it was understood, would be followed by virtually assured promotion to rear admiral, lower half, where he had been headed anyway.

The doctoral thesis had become a well regarded book, and he was known in the highest reaches of the Navy through his articles in the *Proceedings* of the United States Naval Institute. They were carefully done, beautifully written, and two of them had stimulated important policy changes.

But despite the fact that his uniform was bedecked with the Naval Special Warfare Trident and almost as many ribbons as the CNO's, including the Navy Cross, which the CNO lacked, and there he was, sitting in the Oval Office, soon to be an admiral, by his own lights and in fact he was a failure.

A late marriage had become a broken marriage with no children. The beautiful young woman sitting next to him reminded him of what he did not have: the completion, via union with such a woman, of something that he feared would always elude him. What he felt was sterility: not of achievement but of purpose. Nonetheless, he knew that it is hardly unusual to have lived and died in failure and puzzlement, and he knew as well that sometimes it is possible to redeem yourself in service.

*

Then the President of the United States walked in. Everyone stood, and the officers saluted even though their hats were at their sides and generally in the Navy one did not salute when uncovered. But it was the president. For a moment it seemed that anything could happen. And anything could, for there is no question that power is the reckless catalyst of great and improbable events.

With a rumble in his throat, the president fell arthritically into a chair at the head of two sofas in parallel like a giant equal sign, to which his visitors returned after he was settled. He used this chair for meetings rather than speaking from behind the *Resolute* Desk, because he needed a hearing aid and refused to get one. Being close to his interlocutors often gave them a thrill—unless they knew him. Various of his minions, familiar faces across the television channels and on the front pages of every newspaper in the country, stood around the room in languid poses. One, leaning against the wall, with his hands in his pants pockets, reminded Rensselaer of a cowboy.

Perhaps more than any of his predecessors, this chief executive had been elevated by fate. His father, a country doctor and member of the New Hampshire legislature, had saved the life of the governor's only daughter when the governor was a young state employee driving a snowplow. When one of New Hampshire's U.S. senators died in office, the man now President of the United States, who was then a lawyer in Hanover, was appointed to the Senate out of gratitude to his father the country doctor.

He won the next election, and the next, serving in the Senate largely at the behest of inertia. Without so much as a peep, he had consistently voted the party line and been conveniently absent for controversial decisions, and as he had virtually no accomplishments and a phobia of taking a stand, he decided to run for president.

Unlike any other candidate in the race, he neglected everything and put all his money on Iowa, where he won the caucuses by a stunning margin. Then he won New Hampshire as a favorite son and irritatingly familiar face (it was said that they wanted to get rid of him), and went on to sweep South Carolina partly due to his previous momentum but helped for sure by the fact that his wife—a former Miss South Carolina and a Ravenel—campaigned there while he was running around like a woodchuck in the Iowa corn.

Winning the first three primaries gave him great momentum, but he probably would have been knocked out by any one of his nastier, smarter, better-known rivals were it not for the fact that, while campaigning in California, a lunatic who thought his victim was Walter Cronkite shot him in the chest. For months he was touch and go in a coma. The entire country followed the medical reports like a soap opera, and as the primaries came and went even voters of the other party pulled the lever for him much as they might have clapped for Tinker Bell. By May it was all sewn up, just as he had been, though he didn't know it. Upon awakening (for him) on the twentieth of June and being told that he was the presumptive nominee, he said, "I am?"

All the money that lay unspent in the primaries was diverted to the general election. At the convention, he was brought out in a wheelchair as they played "Happy Days Are Here Again." With no sense of irony, the standing ovation lasted an hour. That fall he ran into a bit of a problem when his drunken driving convictions were discovered, but he won. And he understood, as did everyone else, that for better or worse God had made him president, for only God could have.

That isn't to say that he had no political skills, for certainly he did. And he had a ruthless side perhaps somewhat like that of Jack the Ripper. This had allowed one of his many detractors to tag him with the description, "cruel but stupid," a phrase that stuck to him relentlessly.

"I've got fifteen minutes and then I've got to greet the president of Babylonia or some shit," said the head of state. "I asked that we get rid of those little boats and get more big ones. And you say no. What's the problem?" He was irritated, drumming his fingers against the arms of his chair.

As unruffled as an English butler, Freeland said, "We can certainly do that, Mr. President, but there might be repercussions."

"Like what?"

"I've brought along Captain Rensselaer. He was a SEAL, he has a Harvard Ph.D., and he's commanded a Patrol Coastal. With the CNO's permission, perhaps he can comment."

The CNO nodded.

As suddenly as falling off the edge of a cliff one hasn't seen in the dark, Rensselaer knew he had been brought along as cannon fodder, or at the very least the big bumpers between a ship and a pier or wharf that are known as *camels*. Rusty had the same revelation, and was glad she herself was not to be sacrificed. Rensselaer was new at the SECNAV's, and could be replaced without much loss of efficiency.

"Who the hell are *you*?" the president asked.

"Stephen Rensselaer, sir."

"I like your shoulder stuff more than the Admirals'." The CNO's shoulder boards were gold and white with thin blue edges. A captain's was blue with four gold stripes and a star. "It looks more naval." The president turned to the CNO. "Frank, yours is kinda wishy-washy, almost effeminate. We should do something about that."

The CNO's lips moved very, very slightly, until finally he said, "Sir."

Turning back to Rensselaer, the president asked, "Rensselaer. Is that . . . that's Dutch, isn't it?"

"Yes sir, in origin. American since sixteen fifty-one."

"In the Hudson Valley."

"Yes sir."

"Aristocrats." This was not said in a friendly fashion.

"No, sir, not since seventeen seventy-six."

"Well, it tends to linger, doesn't it," the president declared quite nastily, and as if he had won the point merely by his rhetorical question.

"Not in my family, sir."

"Oh? Harvard?"

"The Naval Academy, sir, and then Harvard."

"As I said, it tends to linger."

"No sir, with all due respect. Where I come from, Columbia County, there are Rockefellers who are poor. One even died in Vietnam. My father was a foundryman upriver in Troy. My mother was a nurse. They weren't aristocrats, and neither am I."

Already, Rensselaer, the mere captain, had argued with the president.

"Okay," the president said, more animated than usual, which at first was received by everyone as something good. But he was stirred by anger. "So, you tell me, what's the downside of getting rid of the PCs?"

"Yes, sir. To begin with, PCs can go to vastly more contested areas in the littorals than can other ships. The PC is the smallest ship we have—"

"I know, that's why I want to get rid of them," the president interrupted.

"Yes, sir. Smaller than the PC are boats, which have neither the endurance nor the punch of the PC. The reason PCs can cover so much more area is that they have an eight-foot draft. The littoral combat ship, the next step up, has a fourteen-foot draft, and is a zillion times"—here he deliberately resorted to exaggeration—"as expensive. We no longer have the *Perry*-class frigates, but even their draft was twenty-two feet. And destroyers such as the *Arleigh Burke*s have thirty-two-foot drafts, sir."

"What about an aircraft carrier?"

"Thirty-eight feet, sir. The PC is cheap to buy and cheap to operate. It's a diminutive target. It's equipped for surface combat against the kind of small-boat swarms the Iranians have in the Gulf, and against low-flying aircraft and some anti-ship missiles. It's ideal for weapons interdiction, anti-piracy operations, and the protection—or destruction—of oil facilities such as drilling platforms and docks. It can infiltrate and exfiltrate SEALs, and sending it in harm's way is not, due to its low cost and small crew, a major risk."

"Captain, how much do you know about our black programs?"

"I know only the ones I know about, sir. If there are others, I wouldn't know."

"Directed energy?"

"I'm familiar, sir."

"As far as you know, do these PCs have the ability to bed down a directed energy weapon?"

"They do not. They have neither the electrical generating capacity nor the hull space."

"So?"

"I understand sir, but we're building an extension to the class—the *Athena*. She's bigger, with all-electric drive, and she's intended eventually to bed a small, directed energy weapon."

"You know, we're not going to be in the Middle East forever," the president said. "We're energy independent and exporting. That place is a hellhole. As far as I'm concerned, if the oil supply is interrupted we can fill in, the price will stabilize, and we won't have to pay for any more goddamned, two-mile-high, Bedouin office buildings built on sand."

Rensselaer said, "But you know, sir, in response to the recent decades of warfare in the Middle East, Germany and Denmark have shifted to more blue-water forces. Already there's a shortage of smaller-displacement warships in the Baltic, which requires them. If we scrap the PCs we'll have to build them again from scratch. But if we gradually shift to the *Athena* class we would have assets of great value for use in the Baltic and the South China Sea, particularly in the Philippine archipelago."

The president turned to Freeland and the CNO. "All right. Can we afford them?"

"No," the CNO said.

"But we can!" Rensselaer exclaimed, carried away by the truth and forgetting all other considerations. "It's not difficult. The Danes built their *Iver Huitfeldt*-class frigates for three hundred and seventy million dollars apiece. To build the equivalent ships in America would require double or triple that. But not if we take a lesson from them. How did they do it?" he asked rhetorically.

The president leaned forward, not out of interest but as if to say again, and newly imply, *Who the hell are you and how the hell did you get in here?* To do his job, or rather, to attempt it, the chief executive had to depend on hierarchy, delegation, and deference, none of which was present at that moment.

Rensselaer went on. "They asked their shipbuilding industry how they could do it, and heeded what was said. That is, pre-qualify shipyards, use international classification rules and civilian standards where possible, and provide very high levels of specifications. The navy rather than the contractors did the integration, they reused many components common to other ships in their fleet both for economy of scale and quick modular replacement. And to extend the lives of these ships, they installed double the electrical, cooling, and fiber-optic capacity needed at present. In short, they were smart, they worked hard, they weren't weighed down by bureaucracy. Let the line officers, the engineers, and the shipbuilders build the ships.

"Trying to get anything done through the bureaucracy is like drying yourself with a soaking-wet towel."

"Thank you, Captain. Russia and China are building up their blue-water navies. We have a limited budget. We're going to have to do without some things if we're going to build our three-hundred-fifty-five-ship fleet. I'm proud of that. When I go to rallies in Norfolk, Biloxi, San Diego, it's incredible. Really high energy. The biggest naval build-up since Reagan."

"Yes sir," Rensselaer said, though actually the naval build-up was at a slowing in the rate of decline.

Relieved, the NAVSEC and CNO thought this would be the end of it and were just about to break in when they had the painful realization that it wasn't. Without pause, Rensselaer followed on. "Mr. President, the truth is, the three-hundred-fifty-five-ship fleet by twenty forty-eight is sleight of hand."

For a moment, the only one in the room breathing normally was Rensselaer. The president's eyes narrowed like a boxer's. "Do you mean to tell me," he asked pointedly and threateningly, "that what my Navy Secretary and the CNO are telling me, and then what I tell the American people and the world, is sleight of hand?"

Rensselaer swallowed, looked down, and then looked up directly at the president. "Yes sir."

The president leaned far forward, as if to spring. "Let's hear it. And it better be good."

"Mr. President, you've done far better than your predecessor in regard to the fleet, but, still, the only reason that by twenty forty-eight we may have three hundred and fifty-five major combatants—if indeed we reach that number—is because of the drastic service-life-extension programs. That is, keeping ships long past their planned retirements. Specifically, the DDG-51 destroyers up to ten years beyond their thirty-five-year lives, seven *Los Angeles*-class attack subs from thirty-three to forty-three years, and obviously many more when you take into account that even the published plan, subject to realistic cost estimates, would leave us fifty-four ships short."

"Who said?"

"The Congressional Budget Office."

"What the hell do they know?"

"They know."

"It's still up to me, not Congress." This declaration terrified everyone else in the room, but they were used to it. The president went on: "I'm the commander in chief. I'm going to take care of the Navy."

Once again, Freeland and the CNO thought—hoped—it was over. But it wasn't, as Rensselaer added, quietly, and in full knowledge of what it would do, "And every year, Mr. President, Congress has appropriated more money for shipbuilding than either you or your predecessor has requested, sir."

"Jesus Christ," the president said. Then, turning to the secretary and the CNO, asked, "Where did you get this guy?"

They looked wonderfully sheepish and said nothing.

"Mr. President," Rensselaer interrupted, "the *Athena* is built. She's new, and has started fitting out. Are we going to just scrap her, sir?"

"Look, you have to contend with whatever small part of the Navy you have to contend with. I have to contend with the whole Navy, the whole Army, the Air Force, the Coast Guard, the budget, the Congress, the states, the parties, the electorate, every goddamned country in the world, and history, too. I have to have a different perspective, and I do. Give me that, will you?"

The president moved his head from side to side, looking down and letting out a kind of whistle. "I'll try to understand your concern, Captain." He glanced at his Patek Philippe.

"I know. I just want to make the most accurate case in regard to this particular decision, so that from your perspective you can appreciate the details closer to the ground. Because it's from the ground up that events take their course. And, Mr. President, you make a good case, but it's completely unconvincing."

"What?!" the president said, shocked. The feel of the room was as if a dozen crossbow bolts had crashed through the windows and lodged in the walls.

Rensselaer responded as if the president had actually asked a question. "Sir, I know you have all that responsibility, but having a farm of a hundred acres doesn't excuse planting one of them in brambles and poison ivy."

As the mere captain appeared to be speaking to an equal or perhaps a subordinate, the president's jaw dropped slightly. And then, as if an alien spacecraft had landed on the White House lawn, he said, "What the hell?"

And that was it.

"Thank you," the chief of staff said.

Everyone rose at once, repeating, though not quite at once, "Thank you, Mr. President."

As they were walking out, the president got up from his chair, looked over at the CNO and Freeland, and asked that they stay a moment.

"Who was that? What's his position?"

"He's my aide, Mr. President, newly appointed."

"And afterward? What?"

"Rear admiral, sir, lower half. Given his record he's past due for an important assignment. He's an unrestricted line officer with the Navy Cross and a C-level suffix for billet requirements—that is, a Ph.D. Under his belt he's got the Naval Academy and successful command of a Patrol Coastal, destroyers, a destroyer squadron, and an ARG. Sir, we need this kind of officer."

"Fine, but for the year that I've got left, I want him outta here."

"Sir?"

"The PCs will be retired without replacement or service-life extension. What do you call that, SLEP? Yeah. Strike the follow-ons to the new PC from the list. That'll be a little more money for other ships. But you can finish up the. . . ."

"*Athena.*"

"The *Athena.* Let my successor deal with that. It'll be soon enough. Meanwhile, put Rensselaer in charge of it, fitting it out, whatever is done with a new ship. And when it's ready, put him in command."

"Mr. President," the CNO said. "It would be unprecedented for a captain to command a PC. Usually it's a lieutenant commander, or, at most, a commander. A captain on the promotion list for admiral would be very noticeable. He'd almost surely resign."

"Well wouldn't that be tragic. The *Athena* is his baby, and he gets nothing more. Understand? I want to be very clear. Nail him to it."

A Streetcar Named St. Charles

New Orleans seems not to belong either to the United States, the Western Hemisphere, or, for that matter, Earth. Insanely dependent upon a Three-Stooges-designed system of badly functioning levees and pumps to keep the Gulf of Mexico, swamps, lakes, and mud from swallowing it, most of the city lies below sea level in perpetual suspension between life and death, which may contribute to the feeling that when there you can't be entirely sure if you're alive or dead. The inhabitants drink a lot, unnecessarily, as they can be perfectly drunk on the very air they breathe. Brushed by palm fronds, they drift through the darkness trying to find a bed on which to lie down—even though in New Orleans it is mysteriously possible to lie down while standing up.

Yachts, fishing boats, tugs, barges, tenders, and huge, ocean-going ships glide past the city, mute emissaries of the real world. They make their escape to the Gulf like people who file past the glowing oddities of an aquarium and are happy to exit into the daylight and open air. The city is corrupt, its luxuries are corrupt, its necessities are corrupt, its days are corrupt, and its nights are corrupt, but oh how easily they flow.

Shockingly and amazingly, not everyone there doesn't work. One who did work was Rensselaer, who managed to carry on even though the ethos of New Orleans is antithetical to that of the Navy. It is neither a humming outpost on the Arabian Peninsula, a busy European or Japanese port, nor a fixture on one of the three domestic naval axes, which run all along the East Coast from Maine to Florida, then, skipping like a stone past New Orleans (*pace* a naval air station), across the Gulf of Mexico from Pensacola to Corpus Christi, and up the West Coast from San Diego to Bremerton and the Hood Canal, swinging out like a davit to Hawaii and Guam.

Whereas the small contingent he commanded was quartered on the other side of the Mississippi, in Algiers, Rensselaer lived in the Garden District, traveling every day to and from the Bollinger Yard across to downtown New Orleans. The *Athena* rested for a while in a floating dry dock called *Miss Darby*, as it needed some through-the-hull work and corrosion-proofing. In his commute, Rensselaer never once saw another soldier or sailor in uniform, and never quite got over the way people stared at him. Although like everyone else around him he couldn't be sure that he was alive, dead, or in between, he did know that his career would soon be over. For he was in charge of a program that would be canceled after its first prototype, and he would then be assigned to command almost the smallest of the Navy's ships, the only one of its class, and of a type that he had captained fifteen years earlier. Perhaps like all kinds of failure, early retirement, unemployment, and aging, this made him intensely aware of purpose and mortality. He judged that he was done, that absent advancement, testing, and the possibility of great deeds, his life from then on would be quiet, uneventful, and haunted by regret.

*

Someone else in New Orleans who actually worked rather than merely survive on mystery and vapors was one Penelope Catherine Farrar, a lawyer. Not just a lawyer, but, especially ill-fitting to New Orleans, a tax lawyer. She didn't like the name *Penelope*. It had too many syllables, it was as sing-song as *calliope*, it sounded to her like the name of a pet, and some people pronounced it as if it rhymed with *cantaloupe*. Nor would she truck with the sobriquet *Penny*, just as, she said, she would have refused to have been called *Nickle*, *Dime*, *Quarter*, *Dollar*, or *Fifty-Cent Piece*. So from third grade on she was known as Katy, a name with which she had fallen in love after seeing a movie in which Katy was a beautiful and independent ranch girl not where Katy lived by the York River in Virginia, but in the snow-covered mountains of Colorado. There was even a song that went with the movie, and she remembered it for the rest of her life.

Four years younger than Rensselaer, at forty-eight her presence was remarkable. Everything that she was, conspired to possess her physical body as an electrical current possesses a wire. She was fairly tall, although because she was thin she seemed taller. Her features were finely delineated and extraordinarily engaging, as if much was compressed within her, waiting to spring out in a thousand observations, questions, recollections, and declarations that for some reason were kept in and, thus contained, agitated with constant energy.

She didn't need to think before she spoke, because she could think far faster than she could speak, and she had already thought so many things

29

through—habitually, seriously, even gravely. But she did think before she spoke, and, because of that, she was generally reticent.

However, when she did speak, it was usually so quick, sure, interesting, and economical that anyone who knew her always wanted to hear what she had to say. And when she did speak, the careful observations, deep thoughts, and striking analogies that had accumulated in silence would now and then break through her reticence in surprising and often inappropriate enthusiasm. People who are wonderful and lovely and worthy—but who can never believe they are anything but that—burst forth this way now and then, passionately uncontained, sparkling, and speaking fast, only to sink back into protective reserve.

When she was young, she had dyed her reddish-blonde hair completely blonde, and her time in the sun amplified its goldenness as it swept from her in a gorgeous mane. But as she grew older, and lost some weight as well, she allowed it to return to its natural color and no longer kept it long. Her face was not merely intelligent and entrancing, it was interesting and beautiful in a way that a man moved by profundity and grace would find deeply attractive.

Part of her appeal was a kind of potential energy that arose from the resistance within her of seemingly polar opposites. Yes, she could be as severe, precise, and as demanding as the once-archetypal spinster librarian. Given her command of the facts, it was difficult to cross her, and her natural authority could be off-putting. And yet she was capable, for example, of languidly positioning her svelte frame, half sitting on a table or a desk, feet on the floor while she leaned back slightly, both hands supporting her almost parallel to her back, as—entirely relaxed, but seductively alert—she surveyed the room with a magnetic, feminine mastery much like that of a leopard splayed upon a limb. You could not take your eyes off her, and you did not want to.

After her children were grown, her husband left her for his fatuous, perky secretary, who talked like a chipmunk and to whom Katy referred after the fact as "Beef Jerky, my former husband's secretary at Fatuous, Perky, and Chipmunk." That was hardly enough to dull the pain of finding herself, not Chicago-born, alive and alone in a Chicago winter. And if you say *Chicago* enough times, it makes no sense whatsoever. An estranged daughter was married and living in Boston. This child laid every fault of the world and in the stars on Katy, and Katy had loved her so. A son was a roughneck on the North Slope before he would go to graduate school in Geneva. Astoundingly, he took his father's side, another heartbreak. As the house was big, the memories bitter, and she was in perpetual shell shock, she wanted a complete change. So she sought a job in New Orleans, Chicago's opposite, and she got it.

The downtown skyscraper where she worked was entirely out of place and could have been in New York or San Francisco. Faced with red stone, it was actually quite attractive. Three male partners at the firm, two of whom were divorced and one widowed, were, according to their notions, in love with her. Educated much the same way as was she, they wore French, horn-rimmed glasses from Ben Silver in Charleston, and Brooks Brothers and Paul Stuart suits, and they were kind, wealthy, and capable. As she, too, was a partner, a match with any of them would have been comfortable—coming to work and leaving together, living in one of their grand houses, and spending a great deal of time in Europe, with a trip or two to Japan.

But she had already had what they offered, they were in many ways like her husband, and she thought that, more or less, her days were over. The time remaining would be a time of quiet, when, for the failure she thought she was, nothing challenging or exciting lay ahead. She had raised her children, had her marriage, matured in her career. What was left? Certainly not love. Not the kind of love that for the young is wonderfully giddy and all-possessing.

Neither she nor Rensselaer had any idea that the other existed.

*

Athena had to be guarded even before she was fully fitted out. No code books, communication software, scramblers, or operational documents of any kind were yet present, but certain physical assets and valuable secrets of design had to be protected.

She had come on her own power the sixty miles or so from Bollinger Lockport, where she had been built. With all-electric drive, she had in her generators and motors new materials of great efficiency and necessary secrecy. Both the generators and electric motors they powered depended upon the employment of new magnets, the types, weights, and placements of which were the source of *Athena*'s unprecedented power and, thus, potential speed. The *Cyclone*-class horsepower-to-weight ratio had been the Navy's highest, allowing the Cyclones to reach a speed of thirty-five knots in thirty seconds. *Athena*'s generators and motors, which occupied the same space as her predecessors' diesels, used demagnetization-resistant samarium-cobalt magnets of high coercivity, capable of operating at elevated temperatures and correspondingly higher speeds. These were coupled with neodymium-iron-boron magnets ten times more powerful than their ferrite counterparts. This substitution in the rotors, encasements, and generators created an enormous increase of power and efficiency.

In theory, *Athena* could accelerate to over fifty knots—comparable to the automotive zero-to-sixty—in about forty seconds. Not only would this subject the crew to perceptible G-force, the hull had to be modified to shed the concomitant drag and provide stability in high-speed turns. Unlike any ship in the Navy, *Athena*, like a boat, was designed to skid her stern in a fast turn.

Because of this, her propellers and external shafts had to be set differently and closer to the hull. Even the variable-pitch propellers themselves were of such novel design and placement that when she was up on the blocks they had to be shrouded from view. Other countries had supercomputers, but they didn't have the same postulates and assumptions programmed into them. One would have thought that, to protect these innovations, posting guards with sidearms was rather pathetic given that China had more than likely stolen every detail electronically. But even if you're dying of cancer you should still wash your hands before eating, if only out of habit and self-respect.

And then, the ship had to be protected against sabotage and theft as well. If Tiffany, fancy hotels, and shopping malls were guarded, so certainly *Athena* would be, too. And there was yet something else, a combination of pride and tradition that stretched back to the eighteenth century. Like a jealous lover, the Navy is possessive of its ships. Should people pay them too much attention, it wakes as dramatically as a dog summoned by hard rapping at the door.

Bollinger had its own security staff, but after the engines and propellers were installed the Navy had a sailor on the quarterdeck (before there actually was a quarterdeck) from 0800 to 1600, and two on each watch from 1600 to 2400 and 2400 to 0800. Taking into account redundancy and leave, this required a complement of seven, including a capable E-6 striker who served as senior master-at-arms.

After relocating from Lockport, the detachment took up residence in a house on Bermuda Street in Algiers, delighted to be only a short ferry ride from all the temptations of New Orleans. Rensselaer visited this house for formal and spot inspections. Acclimated to shipboard life, the sailors kept it in pristine shape. The beds were made so tightly you could bounce a quarter on them. Pots, pans, and kitchen counters shone. The garden was tended as if Luther Burbank had come back from the dead. And, purely from habit, the sailors painted the house, which pleased the landlady, a nonagenarian with a voice like a snare drum and a face like a bat, because she had become accustomed to beery and troublesome students. The E-6 was ambitious, and he ran their quarters as if they were on the flagship of the Seventh Fleet.

Someone like Rensselaer, who'd spent his entire adult life in the Navy, knew automatically—having had experience in so many of the ranks—how to find the perfect balance of authority and friendliness. He ate with his men often enough to get to know them, but it was always in a formal manner and it was infrequent. He treated everyone with great respect, but he kept his distance.

And although he could come and go as he pleased, he spent almost every day closely supervising at the yard. He knew every rivet, spacer, and plate. When he returned home, he devoted at least two hours to running, swimming, calisthenics, and weights, after which he had the strength only to eat dinner, do his required reading, and go to bed. In his first few months in New Orleans, he had made no friends, and reasonably expected that this would not change.

*

But it did. Late in December and early in January, New Orleans shares with much of the South a darkness that seems to make no sense. Like an eclipse at midday, it is contradicted by the mild weather, and the greenery of still-flowering trees and shrubs. Looking up through Spanish moss, you find it hard to believe that the sky is dark gray, the light sepulchral, and the wind still.

These days were most depressing for Rensselaer, when the lights went on even earlier than five and he could see them as he crossed the Mississippi from Algiers to the Canal Street Terminal. At least on the ferry he was moving smoothly ahead over the water, something that

33

always seemed able if not to bind up all wounds at least to hold them in abeyance.

As he walked up Poydras Street to St. Charles, which with its shining glass towers and five-o'clock spill-out of bankers and lawyers could have been in New York or Chicago—in Los Angeles they emerge in their automobiles from underground garages, vomited as if from the innards of the earth—it was quiet nonetheless in the persistent eclipse. The St. Charles streetcar was supposed to come every twenty minutes, but it never did, and in the almost silent twilight no one thought it would.

Katy Farrar had left her firm a few minutes earlier than usual. Now she stood on the northwest corner of Poydras and St. Charles, waiting patiently for the streetcar, briefcase hanging by a shoulder strap. Her posture was absolutely and effortlessly straight, her expression guardedly neutral. A tentative breeze slightly lifted her still-buoyant, reddish-blonde hair. She wore a conservative, navy blue suit and a single strand of pearls. The pronounced dip between the exquisitely defined tendons fronting her neck showed that she was both thin and strong.

At first and without attraction, Rensselaer noticed how motionless she was, how she held her position as others shifted from foot to foot, walked about, or slouched. Not her. This interested him. He admired it. What drew his eye and made him wonder was her strength, which, though she was beautiful and delicate, radiated from her.

Had he been younger and less worn he might have fallen in love as instantly as he was once wont to do. But not in late middle age, when, from the perspective of the young, things moved hesitantly in slow motion. And yet something stirred, something that—by necessity and from experience—he suppressed.

Several blocks away, the St. Charles streetcar approached through the dusk, its headlight not as strong as one might have thought, and its forward progress slowed as it jerked from side to side while rolling on. When it arrived it lurched to a stop as if it had bumped into something. Those who had been waiting boarded silently.

Rensselaer found a seat on one of the front benches, at the sidewalk side, Katy on the street side and across from him. She noticed his military uniform. The simple Navy windbreaker had such modest insignia, which she wouldn't have recognized anyway, that she thought he was of low rank. And in downtown New Orleans it would have been reasonable to assume that he was not, as he was, an unrestricted line captain, but someone who worked in a procurement office, perhaps ordering rolled steel, catfish, or sugar, for the fleets. But his face suggested something quite different, and in its way was very much like hers. Taking note of this, she averted her eyes. To her annoyance, however, she kept thinking of him. She cleared her throat as if to banish any thought of this man, and was temporarily successful—until, after a long run under overarching trees, the streetcar, which had been delayed by construction at Lee Circle, reached her stop. It was his as well.

He was ahead of her when he alighted upon the pavement. But as they turned toward the enameled green flank of the streetcar, they were standing close to one another when it began to slide south. After almost in lockstep they crossed St. Charles in the dark of evening, she went off to the left, he to the right, each now aware of the other.

*

Rensselaer's predecessor, a lieutenant commander, had been lucky in finding a place to live. Grateful to get out of his lease, he transferred it to his successor. Almost impossibly, the Garden District is quieter than the rest of New Orleans. And within its tranquility and calm are mazes of even further refuge.

Off one of the quietest, oldest, and most out-of-the-way streets, a long, narrow alley ran slightly up not a hill but a bump, dead-ending before it reached the next cross street. Three-quarters of the way down this alley, on the right, a sandy driveway cut through a plot of oaks and bayonet palms, curving sharply left after a run of about fifty feet. Around this corner, invisible until after the turn, was the little two-storey house where Rensselaer lived during his New Orleans tour of duty. It was sided in paint-worn clapboard, and its gray tin roof didn't lack for patches of rust.

You ascended to a covered front porch from which you could look out upon the sandy space meant for a car, had there been one. At night, no light from other houses penetrated the dense vegetation. And except for wind, rain, and birdsong, it was always silent. The first floor was one big room, a kitchen on one of it sides, fans above, and plantation furniture on the other: dark mahogany, bamboo, and rattan. No television, no fiber optic, no landline. The second floor had a bedroom and a bathroom. All the windows were screened and had storm shutters. Both upstairs and down were big wall-mounted air conditioners.

Almost every night in winter Rensselaer made a fire in a grill that stood in the sand beyond the porch, and barbecued chicken or fish in a slew of vegetables. He would frequently drink a beer while waiting for the coals, but water while eating. Then he read before sleep, which came at will, the result of learning to sleep by his own command in arduous conditions—under an artillery barrage, in enemy territory, in high, buffeting seas—because these were times and places when and where without sleep he would not have survived. He was able to find profound peace just before he slept, the very thing that allowed him to sleep so easily.

And here, especially with the sound of downpours, humid breezes, and leaves and the tin roof struck by steady rain, sleep was magnificent. He did wonder, however, if it would have been better—better than now, better than it had been for a long time—if the right woman were to be lying next to him, someone aware of what had passed and what was to come, knowing of love as well as its absence, knowing, as only a mature woman might, of defeat, redemption, and the sad beauty in the sound of wind and rain.

*

Their schedules were much the same, but because of unexpected events at work—an obstinate fitting on *Athena*, a delayed letter ruling from the IRS—they saw one another at the streetcar stop only about once a week. After a month, the first acknowledgment came, when he had briefly looked directly into her eyes (a thrill for them both), and she responded with the tiniest, shortest, slightest smile. Several days later, they nodded. Then she was gone for two weeks and he didn't think of her that often until she appeared again at the stop, and he discovered how pleased he was that she hadn't left forever. On the streetcar, looking straight ahead but turning his eyes so that he could keep her in view—a strain, and, he thought, ridiculous-looking to boot—he had a very strong desire, which surprised him, to dance with her. He longed for it.

To dance, that is, in a formal, prescribed fashion, to hold her and move gracefully to music. They would be brought together and yet held apart by gentle, civilized custom, in the exciting suspension between the perfect imagination that comes with falling in love, and the subsequent reality, whatever it may be. When he thought about dancing with her, gliding as the rest of the world blurred and he could see only her face and shoulders, he didn't experience the same sensation he might have felt had he been fourteen. And if only because he wasn't fourteen he was able to allow for the fact that, in one form or another, she might have had the same sort of thing in mind.

And she did—that is, to be held by him and to hold him—though, as a consequence of experience, she pulled herself back. And to be truthful, because although now it was warm enough for him to have shed his jacket and she saw the big square of ribbons and other decorations and insignia on his khakis, she didn't know (most people don't) that the eagle clutching arrows signaled the rank of captain, and still thought that he might be a military equivalent of the IRS officials who were her insufferable, natural-born opponents—an iguana-like species that lived on metal desks under fluorescent lights.

Despite this, by mid-March when *Athena* was beginning to come alive, each had observed that the other was without a wedding ring, was never accompanied, and seemed, across the ever-shrinking spaces that separated them, to be modest and wanting. Soon they began to say hello, and then, as April approached, they found themselves one day, for the first time, forced to sit next to one another. Because the seats were so narrow that the naval officer and the lawyer, Stephen and Katy, were compelled to touch, they, like the streetcar named St. Charles, were electrified.

*

"Hi," he said, so restrained as to be clipped.

As if standing on a high diving board, she hesitated, and then responded with "Hi," as almost a question, almost as if to ask, *Why did you say that?*

Seconds passed, until he said, "I'm not usually this eloquent."

"I'm not either," she said. "I don't know what came over me. And I didn't even have a martini at lunch. In fact, I never do. In fact, I've never had a martini." She had hardly intended to be so voluble. It had just leapt from her. But she wasn't embarrassed.

"That's the one with the olive."

"Right."

"I've never had one either. I've never had a cocktail. No one's ever even offered me one."

"Cocktails were something for our parents' generation. I was quite amazed to see the many types in a James Beard cookbook from the fifties, and also in *The Joy of Cooking*."

"People who go to bars still drink them."

"I wouldn't know. I don't go to bars."

"Or rock concerts," he said, not asking.

"Never been to one," she answered.

"Nor have I. May I ask, do you have a name?"

"Of course I have a name. Everyone has a name," she said, playfully, but, still, as if he were an idiot.

"But would you tell me . . . it?"

"Maybe. If you tell me yours."

"Rensselaer."

"That's not your first name."

"Last name."

"I won't ask why you're named after a polytechnical institute. I'm sure you've heard that one before. But did they name the polytechnical institute after your forebears?"

"My very ancient forebears."

"And you're in the Navy?"

He looked down at his insignia as if to confirm.

"What do you do in the Navy?"

"Across the river, in Algiers, I'm seeing along a new class of ship that's to have neither a twin nor descendants. Kind of like me."

"I think I see it from my window," she said, actually excited. "It's up out of the water?"

"It is, in dry dock."

"I see it every day. And I see you quite a lot, too, as you know. What rank is required to do what you do?"

"Underemployed captain. To put a captain in charge of a patrol coastal is a marked demotion. I blew it." He seemed to take pleasure in remembering.

"How do you mean?"

"I sidetracked into NSW—Naval Special Warfare, the SEALs—then to surface warfare, then graduate school, then to staff, and then, kind of late in the game," and this was what amused him, "I discovered after spending my life in the Navy that I couldn't respond adroitly to over-bearing authority. This is my last assignment. I finish the ship, take command for a short time, and I'm out. You?"

"I'm just a tax lawyer."

"What rank?"

"Partner. I should've been something else, but I blew it."

"Something else, like what?"

"A pilot. An FBI agent. A violist, maybe. I hate sitting at a desk."

"I'd very much like to hear your name." That was it. He was in love. Like a blind man, he had heard her voice, and that was enough.

She thought for a moment, weighing whether or not to tell him. It seemed to her that things were going too fast, which made her feel almost angry. But, still, she did tell him. "Katy."

"Katy what?"

"Actually, my name is Penelope, but I've never liked it. I go by Katy. Some people who knew me when I was young still call me Catherine, or even Penelope, although most of them have more or less faded away."

"Katy . . . ?"

"Farrar."

"Katy Farrar," he repeated. "It sounds like something out of Stephen Crane or Edith Wharton."

"A literary Navy captain."

"Why not?"

This embarrassed her, and she showed it, reddening beautifully. "I'm sorry."

He thought it was a wonderfully telling overreaction, and although she may have been, at least according to his first impression, perhaps the sharpest, most vital woman he had ever encountered, and still lissome despite her age—which he misjudged—he saw as well how intensely full of sorrow and self-doubt she was, how checked by sadness and regret that seemed to have neither origin nor justification. But of course how would he know? Unlike as in a less complicated flirtation, this spurred him on.

"Don't apologize," he said. "I'll tell you some lawyer jokes."

"I know them all."

"I bet you don't know this one."

"I'll bet I do."

"Oh yeah? A lawyer woke up after surgery and noticed that the curtains were tightly drawn across the windows. He asked the nurse why this was so. What did she say?"

"'There was a fire across the street, and we didn't want you to think you'd died on the table.' See? I toldya."

They came to their stop. After they disembarked, and the trolley pulled off, and they had crossed St. Charles, they reached the point where they would go their separate ways, only this time, instead of doing so deliberately as if the other did not exist, they turned, face to face.

Now close, and looking directly at her for the first time other than just briefly, he saw how beautiful she really was, and he determined to know her.

*

Because her office was on a very high floor and her view of the Mississippi as it flowed past the city was unobstructed, she kept a binocular within reach. When a large ship went by, or a yacht under sail, she would often pause from her work, swivel, raise the binocular, and by the trick of bright optics hover in the air above them, taking in all the details of crowded decks, billowing mainsheets, and wakes churning in white. The compressed visuals worked together with the intensified colors to make an unplanned work of art.

The day after she had spoken to Rensselaer, she aimed the binocular not at the river or distant flatlands, waters, and clouds, but at the shipyard. In the smaller of two dry docks, the *Miss Darby* (as it announced in large letters on its side) was the ship she now knew as his. Despite months to go, due to its long, thin, and businesslike shape it already looked like a warship. Now and then, people appeared on the open deck or on the wharf, and although she was unable to tell much about them from so far away, she knew somehow that they weren't Stephen Rensselaer (whose full name she now knew), that she would know him even at a great distance, that she would be excited—and feel it in her body—when she did see him, and that she was pleasurably driven to look for him.

At a knock on her glass office door, she turned and rested the binocular on her desk in a single, graceful movement, and gestured for the man on the other side to come in. This was Roger, one of the three partners who—

inexplicably to her—seriously sought her company, which, at their age, domesticity, and wifelessness, could only mean a yearning for marriage.

Katy Farrar didn't understand how anyone could be truly interested in Katy Farrar, if only because, having by her husband's account driven him crazy, she found it difficult to imagine another man letting himself in for what her husband, in agreement with her son, had claimed he could not abide. Incapable of putting anything back whence it had come, he felt reprimanded when she returned everything to its rightful berth, something which she could not help. A towel hanging at a jaunty, careless angle was an offense to symmetry, as was an uncapped toothpaste tube, or a folder on a desk that did not sit in parallel with the lines of the desk itself.

What was wrong with arranging things in a refrigerator by type, and, on the door shelves, the row of jars by height? It was effortless, well organized, and efficient. She was extremely well aware of how things were and how they ought to be. Her memory, her senses, and her eyes were easily and always alert. Contrary to what the detractors of such a personality might suspect or assert, nothing in her ordered precision stopped her from being daring, profound, witty, and . . . orgasmic. But he left, after which she assumed that anyone else would eventually do the same.

So there was Roger, standing in front of her, reasonable, undoubtedly gentle, not quite shy, with blond, thinning hair, a pinstripe suit, and an English bow tie. She had never been to his house, but she guessed that he had a lot of mahogany and cherry furniture, a tantalus, crystal glasses, dog-and-hunting prints, potted palms, and a marble hall. He radiated comfort, resignation, kindness, longing, and the Anglo-Saxon ability to be mildly intoxicated throughout the day, starting at just after noon. She liked him, and was tempted by his aura of relaxed oblivion, excellent tailoring, and lots of gin.

He stared at her. She lifted her head a little, as if to say, *Yes?* But he was frozen.

"What?" she asked. And when he didn't respond, she said, "Roger, hello? Talk."

"We're putting together the McLaren Petroleum Trust and, needless to say, there are some very complicated tax aspects. In the next few weeks, do you have time to look this stuff over, or can you recommend an associate who's good with net operating losses and depletion allowances? McLaren Oil is spread across eight fucking states and three countries."

Before she could answer, he said, his pitch noticeably rising and his speed increasing, "And I'm going out this weekend on the boat. The weather's supposed to be good and I've got new sails. I know that may not sound exciting, but they're so white and clean that on a blue day it's really something to behold. Blinding, really."

"I can look over the trust documents," she told him. "It shouldn't be a problem."

In answer to her silence, he ventured, with the timidity of sensing defeat, "What about this weekend? It would be really nice."

"Actually, Roger, I'm seeing someone. And—sort of coincidentally, I guess—he's making his boat ready, too. I don't think it would be a good idea for me to get on the water before he can take me. But it's kind of you to ask."

"I see," he said. "The invitation is always open. What kind of boat does he have?"

"I don't really know, exactly, but apparently it can go quite fast."

He didn't know it, but Roger was actually glancing at it as he tried not to stare at Katy.

"Sail?"

"I think it has a motor," she said, quite charmingly.

Roger felt the superiority of having a sleek sailing yacht rather than a cabin cruiser. "How big is it?"

"I think it's a couple of hundred feet."

"A couple of hundred feet!"

"Maybe two hundred?"

"Jesus. That's enormous. Two hundred feet?"

"Ya. It's big."

"Yes. Yes. Okay, well, I'll bring you that stuff, probably next week. Thank you, Katy. Thank you."

As he left, she thought, *Oh God. What have I done?* Perhaps at forty-eight she had no right to feel like she was seventeen, but she did. And she loved it.

*

She looked for Rensselaer every evening, and he looked for her. As they made their dinners, as he studied engineering and installation manuals, of which he was not fond, and she wrote briefs, of which she was not fond, they thought of one another. Especially before sleep, after they switched off the lights and lay in the dark, they imagined the other. They imagined making love, real love, because of love, and then they slept, hoping to dream.

Their schedules were such that they often didn't see one another for days, but one Saturday when it was unusually hot they each went out early in the evening to the market closest to them both, and he saw her holding an empty basket and staring at the fish counter. While she was still unaware of his presence, he said, from almost next to her, "How about some barbecued chicken instead?"

She turned, poker-faced, mastering her surprise. "It takes too long," she answered, "and when I do it, it's either undercooked on the inside or burnt on the outside."

"That's because your living doesn't depend upon it, but at the Who Dat? Barbecue, theirs does, so they've got it down, and you don't have to clean up, either. We could go. There's not much in your basket."

"There's actually nothing in my basket."

As they left the market together, anyone who had had to guess might have assumed that they were a couple. "What are you worried about?" he asked her, kindly. Although she seemed quite happy, she seemed pained as well, perhaps not on his account or on any account at all.

"I have to tell you, I can't read and choose from the menu while making conversation. I hate that."

"I know," he said. "It's like trying to converse while walking, when you have to move into single file when someone passes, or to avoid a dog on a leash, or at a narrow part of the sidewalk where tree roots crowd it. I'll tell you what. We won't say a word until we're seated, we've ordered, and we've had a moment of silence."

"Why silence?"

"So we understand that we don't have to speak if we don't need to. Your presence is enough, as it was months ago when I saw you at Poydras and Saint Charles—nervous and preoccupied, perhaps suffering from a surfeit of awareness, open, observant, sad, and beautiful."

She made no response, only wondering how it was that he knew her so well, although she never would have admitted to being beautiful.

*

When they had settled in, she inspected the silverware. "You know," she said, speaking rapidly, "most restaurants have dishwashers that don't reach the required sterilization temperatures. Ideally, things should be steam cleaned, although even in an autoclave not all viruses are eliminated, I've heard, and it's probably true." It was almost as if she were talking to herself. She was nervous. He knew it, and that it would pass.

They studied the menu. The waiter came and left. "Okay," he said, "tell me what I would have found if I were Sherlock Holmes, or if I had looked you up on the Internet, which I didn't."

"I didn't look you up either. It would be understandable but creepy."

"I think so. Young people," Rensselaer stated, "*meet* on the internet. How can they do that?"

"They don't rely on accidents, because we're so far from the belief that marriages are made in heaven. And they're used to ordering everything on the Internet, why not another person? But to make yourself available to the whole world like that is like putting yourself on the shelf at the supermarket."

"I suppose it's the descendant of the personal ad."

"Exactly. Do you like walks on the beach?"

"Me? No. I was a SEAL. For me a walk on the beach means a bunch of sweaty guys trying to carry a telephone pole."

"Well then do you love dogs?"

"I do. I don't have one, but if I did I'd buy him a BarcaLounger."

"If I had a dog," she answered, without the slightest pause, "you might not like him, because he wouldn't thank vets for their service."

Her quick return pleased Rensselaer no end. "I do admit," he said, "that it took some doing not to look you up."

"You wouldn't have found much. You really want to know?"

"I do."

"I see." She looked down, and then she looked back up, pleased. "I was born in and grew up in Virginia. When I was a little girl I was fat. I thought you were supposed to eat a big breakfast, so I did even though I hated it and it made me hungry the rest of the day. Then I ate only lunch and dinner and I lost a lot of weight, started running and swimming and lost more. William and Mary, class of ninety-three. I made a point of absorbing the pace of eighteenth-century Williamsburg, and it was easy to do that in winter when there weren't so many tourists, especially late in the day. You know, the college abuts the restoration. That was the heart of my education—the sense of time and the slow pace, the patience, beauty, and dignity. The modest aesthetic. What a pity it's gone, but we can't live in restorations, can we?"

"No."

"And then, then things changed. UVA Law School, ninety-six, Supreme Court clerk."

Impressed and delighted, he smiled. "For whom?"

"O'Connor. Marriage to a fellow clerk, whose name was Colt. I became Katy Colt (until I changed it back), and I followed him to Chicago, to Winston and Strawn, where I fell into tax because I didn't want to litigate." She paused, as if catching herself. "I have a fear of public speaking. It gets worse as I get older. I'm not really comfortable with people, but I guess I don't really mind that."

"How about people one at a time?"

"That I can do."

"When you speak," he said, "it floods out of you, as if speech could never carry all that you think. It's enthusiastic and joyous, and then you get quiet, as if embarrassed."

"Does it bother you?"

He slowly shook his head from side to side. "Not at all. The opposite."

When she looked down and wouldn't look up, he broke the silence that followed, by saying, "Katy." It was a beautiful name.

"Stephen?"

"Not Steve. I never wanted to be called Steve. It's like someone straining to lift a box."

"I prefer Stephen anyway. I don't know why. And Rensselaer?"

"Dutch seems a little odd to most people, I know."

"No quotas for you."

"I wouldn't take them."

"Nor would I."

"I sense that, just from the way you vet utensils."

"Which telegraphs what?"

"Skepticism. Independence. Shedding and defying what's commonly expected and assumed. And maybe a little OCD."

"Well, yeah," she said. "And this is the Big Easy. I've never liked easy."

"In navalspeak you'd say that running with the wind is exhilarating, but tacking against it makes you strong."

"As long as we're channeling fortune cookies, I'll see your metaphor and raise you one. In the end, salmon have to swim upstream, and they better know how, because to forget would mean extinction." And then she said, "I don't think I've ever knowingly met anyone of Dutch extraction."

"There are pockets mainly in Michigan and New York. Not Pennsylvania—they're German. On the Hudson when I was a child in school we learned the anthem of the Dutch West India Company. Really. I don't suppose they teach it anymore." Forgetting that it was his turn to offer, as she had, a resume, he asked, "You've never been here?"

"No, I find it almost impossible to go to a restaurant by myself. I hope you don't think I'm a nut, but I don't mind telling you that most of the time when I'm on a business trip, rather than sitting alone in a restaurant I have a picnic in my room."

"Everyone does that. I do it," he said. "When I was in France not long ago I used to get sandwiches and eat in my hotel room while I read the French papers. I'm either too self-conscious, or not self-conscious enough, to sit alone in a café or restaurant—if I can help it. Sometimes you can't, of course."

"But I'll bet you were never so shy that when there was no market convenient to the hotel you ate from vending machines."

"No, but . . . Katy," he said, moved by her confession, "I appreciate shyness. I appreciate it very much."

"You do?" Suddenly she felt that her growing infatuation was accompanied by something of greater weight.

"Yes, and since there are two of us here, we can relax. No one will stare at someone because he or she is sitting alone. And you said that sometimes people call you Katy."

"Yes."

"May I call you Katy?"

As her expression became a slight smile, she said, "You already do."

Even before the chicken, baguettes, and salad, the waiter brought iced and frosted glasses of achingly cold beer, which quickly relaxed them a lot further.

"According to you, you blew it," she said. "I did, too. I guess by this age almost everyone does, one way or another, even if they don't know it. "

"For a reason."

"What reason? I know mine."

"Then you go first."

She did. "All right. It's simple. As I've gotten older and the time ahead has grown shorter it's become very clear to me that most people . . . rather— most people or not—*I myself* have spent much of my life trying to gain recognition, prestige, and money in a kind of giant game of Chutes and Ladders, although I never played that game and I don't know if the analogy is correct. But not that long ago I just sort of stopped and let out a breath and said, what am I doing? Do I really care about this stuff? People kill themselves all their lives so that other people will regard them in a certain way.

"How many orchids are there in the Amazon? Trillions? They're beautiful. No one ever sees them, but they're there. Value is independent of recognition. It must be. If a tree falls in the forest, of course it makes a sound. What kind of idiot would think it wouldn't? A sound is not defined by its being heard."

"The idiot might say, what if there's no air?" he told her.

"I admit, in a vacuum forest there would not be a sound. Oh, and by the way, you should know, I'm forty-eight."

"I wouldn't have thought so, but it goes well with my being fifty-two. You look much younger. I'm not just saying that."

He went on. "I've come to pretty much the same conclusion as you. Certain things seem not to matter anymore, and others seem to matter a great deal more than they used to. I'm in New Orleans, where I've never been before, because I pissed off the President of the United States. Perhaps I flatter myself by thinking that it was because I don't have the disgusting, oleaginous skill, which some people so much admire, of attaining power by satisfying it. Because of that, I'm always at the edge of things and then cast out. It never fails, and the older I've gotten the more it kicks in. My father, too, was always at the edge of things, and easily cast out."

For a moment, she was speechless, as this described her as well. "I can tell you," she said, "that someone like that, and I'm exactly like that, *wants* to be cast out. Because to be in the center of things is illusory. Only at the edges is it real. At least that's what I think, what I've found, and what I feel. But you know, you're a captain and I'm a senior partner, so what does that say?"

"It says we haven't put in the time to be an admiral or a Justice of the Supreme Court. We chose a certain way."

She nodded. "True, and I don't believe that's an excuse."

"No. By nature," he added, "at sea—if you're at least somewhat reflective—you learn exactly that, because anywhere at sea is so far from the center, where power lies, where millions of people coordinate their wills and build giant cities, skyscrapers, bridges, railroads, dams . . . and ships. At sea you're pretty much alone even if you're stuffed into a steel vessel with hundreds or even thousands of other people. You look out, and the only thing there is the ocean, two-thirds of the world's surface, miles deep, mainly unexplored. All you see is a little of the top, and even that's too vast to comprehend. You're just on its edge, you feel very small, and, in understanding this, you're freed."

"When you're out at sea," she asked, "do you have a lot of time to read? I could see going through Gibbon or Victor Hugo in their entirety with all that time and no distraction."

"You're a real lightweight."

"Well, could you?"

"No, especially if you're in command. You never stop working and you're on-call twenty-four hours a day. Just running the ship properly can fill up all your time. You're responsible for its safe navigation, its readiness for combat, its propulsion, hotel systems, damage control, crew morale, personnel, training, diplomacy ashore, and a hundred other things. Just changes to the goddamned software are enough to drive you crazy. I delegate that to the kids, who live and breathe it. We go through continual training evolutions and drills, absorb new systems, implement new directives. There's so much paperwork and so many things to study that you just don't have the time to read at leisure, certainly not if you're the captain. Even my XOs hadn't any time, because they were burdened enough in studying for command."

"What's an XO?"

"Executive officer, sort of like a vice-captain."

"I thought that on the bridge you'd stare for hours at the sea."

"There's more or less continuous activity on the bridge, but you have moments. In the absence of mountains, rivers, cities, and trees, you look more closely at what there is, and you find that though it appears to be less, it isn't. You become keenly aware of the clouds. They and the colors of the sea are ever-changing, but clouds appear in three dimensions, stretching miles high, looming like mountains, or breaking up the sky into woolly skeins, or dots like sheep in the field. You know, how in England you can look across miles of green squares dotted with sheep. Actually, we do have a particular time for what can be an almost Zen-like practice."

"You do?"

"We do. Because before you stand watch at night you have to sit in the dark for half an hour to an hour. That's how long it takes the iris to open widest, so you can operate properly on the night sea. The lights on the bridge are red and low, and don't degrade night vision. You can't listen to the radio or anything, because you're bringing all your senses to maximum power. When you're ready to go to the bridge, despite the engine noise and the wind you can hear the ticking of someone's watch even if he's twenty feet away."

After a moment in which she looked at him as if she were registering a change within her, but then reverted to careful conversation, she said, "I don't think people give the Navy enough credit. Part of it's because it's out there, where no one knows what's going on, so it's easy to ignore."

"It doesn't matter. Eventually, everyone gets to a point where you don't need credit, even in the Navy. I'm there."

"I am, too. I see myself as old, with cats," she said, half teasingly, half testingly.

"I see you as young, with dogs."

He couldn't take his eyes off her as she spoke. He loved the fact that her skin wasn't as unblemished as a girl's but showed some effects of the sun, that in her face and even in her hands and most certainly in the way she moved and spoke there were signs of experience and coming up against things, and of a kind of weathering that showed strength, all of which he found admirable and attractive in so many ways, not least sexually.

"I should have cats—I don't, yet—because my husband threw me out and got a younger woman." She thought to herself, here it comes. This is where he'll know it's over. "That shook me up, and I think I'm still shaking. My children are gone; I never see them. Tax law isn't a life. Three guys—three—at the firm seem to be interested in me, but I'm past that. I'm not twenty. Sure, they're personable, somewhat educated, not just lawyers, and I don't think they ever beat their ex-wives. I mean, this is New Orleans, you have to watch out for all that Tennessee Williams stuff. I don't know why I'm telling you this."

"You're telling me this because we're sitting here together, so, obviously, I'm interested in you."

"Well, they are, too. I don't see how they can be. They could almost be identical triplets—fine Southern gentlemen, a little pudgy, who drink a lot, dress beautifully, and seem to have racehorses."

"Do they? And if they do, are the racehorses pudgy?"

"I don't know, but I'd be willing to guarantee that they have *pictures* of racehorses, within three feet of half a dozen single-malts and an ice bucket. Horses or dogs."

"Maybe they want what they don't have, a beautiful woman with great depth."

"I don't understand how that pertains to me, and I'm not being falsely modest. False modesty is disgusting."

He was about to speak, but she held up her hand, almost like a traffic cop. More than a little tipsy because she was unused to alcohol, she took a drink of the still very cold beer, and said, "I can drink beer, and eat anything, because I'm so thin. I didn't used to be this severe. You don't find that off-putting?"

"No. Look, no one ever sees himself properly. Mirrors and photographs distort. They don't capture the life of someone. I don't want to sit here flattering you, so let's leave it at this. I'm telling you, with no uncertainty and no ulterior motive—and then I'm going to stop—that you're exquisite. You're, as they say, drop-dead gorgeous. Finished." She tried to conceal that she loved this, but couldn't.

"If you say so."

"I do."

"But, again, what about you? Why are you single at your age? I apologize, if you're a widower, for putting it so roughly."

"Not a widower. My wife left me. I used to say it was because I spent so much time deployed. But I don't know. I asked too much, she gave too little. She asked too much, I gave too little. I can't speak for her, but I was too young and too self-centered. A bookie wouldn't have bet on us, but we couldn't see it."

"Did she love you?"

"Apparently not enough."

"Did you love her?"

"Oh yes."

"Do you still?"

Without hesitation, and soberly, Rensselaer said, "Not as much as I did."

"I've always thought," Katy said, "even before I was alone, that it would be impossible to start over. That just conveying who you are and the story of your life would take more time than you have left."

*

Remembering the feeling of ease in the Washington heat as Rusty had driven him in Freeland's Mercedes, Rensselaer spent the money to rent a black BMW convertible with brown leather upholstery and a steering wheel fashioned of what appeared to be rosewood. Speeding along in the open air with the sun beating down and the country sliding rhythmically by to music was precisely what he wanted when next he would see Katy. And when they did clear the outskirts of the city and suburbs they felt wind and sun, in air that smelled at times of cane, flowers, pine, and the burning of fields. He had never seen her sit back: in the restaurant and on the streetcar she was rule-straight and had edged forward while speaking. Here, she relaxed, her face to the sun and her eyes closed.

Then she leaned forward a bit and turned to him. "What's the song?"

"'Beast of Burden.'"

"I know, but isn't that . . . ?"

"Yes, The Rolling Stones. Sort of uncharacteristic."

"You'd think they'd been here," she said, and it was true. The ballad was languid but exciting, perfect for the moment and the wind waving the cane and grasses. Her eyes closed and her face turned again to the warm sun, she leaned back once again, equally content and excited. It was the seal set on the beginning, when you know you're really in love, and the world has changed.

The road was straight but narrow and often flanked by drainage ditches close to the pavement, so when he glanced at her it could be for only a second or two, and he did it again and again. He'd seen her in nothing but a suit. Now she was in a sundress, and he saw—as she knew he would—that her tanned shoulders and arms were firm and beautiful. When she opened her eyes, he said, "Most people who work in offices are pale, if not jaundiced."

"I have a garden," she replied.

"Is that what keeps you fit?" he dared, because it was a comment on her body.

"Swimming, running. Lifelong habit. I used to shoot skeet."

"Lucky skeet."

"They were," she said. "I didn't hit them. Except once. In high school I had a boyfriend whose father had a trapshooting field. In my first outing, when I had no idea what I was doing, I didn't miss any. No one believed I wasn't a practiced expert and headed for the Olympics. Neither did I, until after law school when I went out again and failed to hit a single one. I don't think I've ever recovered," she said, not exactly tongue-in-cheek.

The cane fields waved in the wind as the car shot down the straight, empty road. "I have to say," he told her, "that . . . the way you look away after you make an assertion; the way you clip your sentences, paragraphs even, and then lapse into inexplicable silence; the way you speak fast and intensely as it floods brilliantly and comes to a sudden stop. . . . You must run rings around the Southern gentlemen at the law firm. You run rings around me. And I'm beginning to think that you may have struggled all your life to contain and subordinate yourself."

"Because I'm a woman? I hope you haven't swallowed that."

"No no. Because you're you. There are certain substances, sodium for instance, that must be isolated from exposure to the elements because if not they react so fast they flare or explode. You discipline yourself to operate at the slower speeds and with the lesser intensity of everyone around you. When I first saw you, I thought, there's so much in that woman, so much life, so much to be told and said, like an actor who can't wait to come onstage and into the lights."

Her only response was a slight smile.

They drove in silence until they reached an airboat place, where he put the top up in case of rain. Even in shadow, Katy glowed from the sun and wind. With the air now still, he said, "You probably shouldn't have worn perfume. Mosquitoes."

"I didn't."

He was skeptical. "That wasn't a criticism. I really like it."

"But I didn't."

He leaned closer. "That's just you?"

"Just me."

He was still very close, and she hadn't pulled back. One kiss, intoxicating and full of promise.

*

The airboat guide was huge, bearded, baseball-capped, and tattooed. He wore green-mirrored sunglasses the color of a fly's eyes, in the shape, roughly, of a flying saucer. The first thing he said—to Katy, clearly with a fifth-grade boy's idea of shocking her—was, "Want some gator bits?" He held out a plate of barbecued alligator. "They're farmed, and they never know what hits'em."

"I've been eating way too much gator," Katy replied. "Breakfast, lunch, snacks, and dinner. Gator, gator, gator. I'll pass."

"She doesn't scare easily, huh?" the guide asked Rensselaer.

"No," he replied. "She's a waitress in an alligator restaurant."

The guide was now ready to take them out without the usual friendly condescension of guides who encounter what they often rightly assume to be helpless city people. His only clients that afternoon, they asked questions respectfully, and he answered seriously, about the draft of the boat, how far on sandbars and over matted vegetation it could shoot, its speed, its power, its stability. They sat in front of him and somewhat lower. Everyone put on ear protectors. Then the engine was started, the propeller engaged, and the aluminum boat came up to speed, going very fast over slightly wind-rippled, open water. The boatman made it weave from right to left and left to right over and over just for the pleasure of it, like a water skier repeatedly hopping a wake. This showed his passengers that the boat could heel and still remain stable, that it could slide through turns nimbly, that going fast was to be enjoyed.

Without warning, they made a sharp turn into a long straightaway deep in the swamp and then glided as slowly as a canoe. At first, the channel was banked by grasses and reeds. Then mangroves and live oaks rose on each side, and the light dimmed as they floated beneath branches from which hung enormous clumps of moss. For ten minutes they moved slowly down this alley of black water, imagining what it would be like at night, miles from any road or field, impassable, its own world as foreign to New Orleans as New Orleans was to the rest of the country.

Closer to open water, the boat stopped at a half-hammock in which quite a few alligators were waiting patiently for fish the boatman pulled from a bucket in the bow. Trained and relatively docile, made to grasp the fish three or four feet over the water, they rose so fast and their jaws snapped so quickly it was a wonder the boatman still had his hands. He didn't invite Stephen and Katy to feed the alligators, but he did fetch a baby one a foot and a half long and presented it to Katy, who held it level in both hands before her and studied it closely.

"Now you can just toss it in, ma'am," he said, and after a moment she did. They sped back over open water at high speed as the sun went low, herons took flight, and the boat weaved to the port and starboard of an imaginary centerline before it pulled up to the dock so adroitly that even a Navy captain was impressed.

"I guess we got sunburnt," Rensselaer said as the top of the convertible retracted. "It feels good. Irresponsible, but good."

As they pulled off, he asked, "Now what?"

"We could keep going," she said, "deeper and deeper, to see where the road leads. Maybe it ends at the open sea. There's not much of a hard line around here where the land ends and the Gulf begins. It's more like gears or fingers meshing, a compromise. I miss the clear line, but that's what makes this whole place like a dream. And to think that people come here to gamble and get drunk. They miss the point. It's the underworld. It's Hades. The water has corrupted the land, and the land has corrupted the water."

"A right turn will take us where we haven't been, left will return us to the city. What would you like?" he asked.

"How much gas do we have?"

"Three-quarters of a tank."

She pointed right.

*

An hour later in the dark they pulled up to a few buildings in what was almost a town—a combined post office, store, and gas station, and a restaurant from which music wafted out over several rows of pickup trucks. The slow, country music was seductive, and the smoke issuing from the vent above the kitchen was redolent of barbecued fish, meat, and shellfish.

He glanced toward Katy, but she was already out the door, and the way she walked was not the same as what it had been in the city. It was smooth and timed eagerly to the slow waltz from within, with several electric guitars, and a woman singing. Inside was a bar, dance floor, stage, and a dozen tables. As Katy entered, followed by Rensselaer, heads turned, but then turned back, and lost in the music the musicians and singer onstage didn't even notice. Rensselaer didn't order beer with his shrimp boil, because driving in the dark on the narrow, shoulderless road he had to be a hundred percent on task. She, however, had no such requirement.

Given the music, he was more nervous than she was, remembering how so early on he had wanted to dance with her. Two couples were on the floor, and another rising to join them.

Were he and Katy to dance they would hardly be alone or draw attention. She appreciated his hesitancy, and she, whom at first he had taken as the awkward, shy, damaged one, gave him an inquiring and daring look.

He was brave in every way except socially, but this was not social, it was love, and the music was enough to make anyone brave. So he rose and extended his hand to her, reaching across the table. Taking it, she stood, and they went out onto the floor.

"I don't dance well," she said, but without any care.

"Neither do I." They embraced, and started a languid waltz, seeing only one another. Except that, after a while, they imitated other couples when the women would separate for a few steps, still holding one of their partners' hands, twirl, and come back—all without letting go. It left them momentarily in a three-quarter stance, with him cradling her. They did this several times until they could do it perfectly, and she turned to look up at him, all her tension and doubt having fled, the sometime city brittleness of her movements, the checking of her steps, all gone, all gone in favor of the softer, more radiant person—her reddish-blonde hair having been made lighter by the sun and buoyant about her neck as she danced; her skin almost throbbing with sunburn and heat; her body lithe, graceful, and released.

That's when he said, because he couldn't help but say it, although it was so early, but he knew it was true, "Katy . . . I'm sorry, but I can't do anything but love you." It was quite so.

KATY AND *ATHENA*

As the first commanding officer of *Athena*, Rensselaer had the privilege of originating the ship's motto and crest, which the ship and its crew would own, and which would not change. For the crest he chose a gold-leaf-rimmed oval, with Athena seated at its center on a field of blue. She wore a flowing white gown, and, rather than helmeted, she was depicted in the style of an early twentieth-century Gibson Girl, so classically beautiful and gracious that the sailors would often stare at her.

As she was Athena, goddess, inter alia, of wisdom and strategy, a little owl peered calmly from the bottom folds of her robes. Until one was mesmerized by her face, most striking of all was that in her right hand she held an upright spear with a golden tip. Arcing around the top of the oval, also in gold, was the Greek, Ἀθηνά Πρόμαχος, or, "Athena Who Fights in the Front Line," which was written at the bottom of the oval in English, in white against the blue field, resting on the gold rim, descending and then ascending.

Per custom, Rensselaer worked with the Army's Institute of Heraldry, which did very well except that at first Athena was made to look like the centurion on the American Express card. Rensselaer's exchange with them went something like, "She's a woman. Make her like a beautiful Gibson Girl."

"A what?"

"Look it up."

"More feminine?"

"For sure. She's Athena. Yes, she's beautiful, but you don't want to mess with her."

It was a magnificent crest, and really it was all because he was in love with Katy.

Katy

They took refuge in the Garden District, lost in it and as separated from the continent and all its cares as if they were at sea. The vegetation that surrounded them had a life of its own: it moved in the wind, it folded and unfolded, furling at night and unfurling in the sun. Perpetually fragrant, it engaged in a duet with raindrops and strong breezes.

In the dilapidated and tranquil Garden District are corners where you can stand for an hour and no one will pass. At night, breezes and rain flow and fall as if to wash away the day. And when time no longer matters, it's easier to see and feel one's essence and that of another.

For good reason, from experience, and for the sake of her independence, Katy held on to her house and its garden. She kept most of her clothes there, her books, and other things, but almost every evening and every night she stayed with Rensselaer. They made dinner over an open fire as often as if they were Australians or Africans, who seem not to be able to do without it. They cooked not with charcoal but rather with the orange coals of wood at its most even heat, between the wild flame of the beginning and the senescence of the end. As the outside light disappeared, the coals would pulse, and the smoke of the wood and the grilling was calming. Never was a Rensselaer or a Farrar so content, they agreed, than at evening, outdoors, under a veil of semi-darkness, by a fire.

And then, lost and safe in the copse of thick leaves that registered each raindrop, they lay together before they slept. The rain came down, pattering on the leaves—you could almost hear them bend when struck—tattooing the tin roof, running musically along the metal gutters and rushing through downspouts and runnels like half a dozen wilderness streams.

"If it wouldn't ruin us," she said, "and it would, I would just stay here. I wouldn't go to work. You'd stupidly resign your commission just before retirement."

"I think there are people in these parts," he answered, "who've done things like that. You don't see them much, but when you do you can tell. They've let go, because they wanted to stay forever in what we've got right now. But they can't. Without the contrast, it's as if they're in the world of the dead. You can be an alcoholic, you can be a heroin addict, or you can stay forever in the Garden District."

"The attraction, the temptation . . . " she said. "It's true. But you wouldn't. . . . "

"No. I don't want anything I haven't earned, and we haven't earned this. There's more to do."

He turned away from her, switched on a bedside lamp, and turned back. She was exquisite in the nude, with the placid yet assertive dignity of a Greek marble. "Tell me about that." He loved to hear her speak. Even at ease, she was concise and captivating. Her eyes sparkled with the light of the lamp, and for a moment the rain came down really hard as strong, humid breezes forced their way through the louvers and cooled the room.

"My mother told me," she said, "that falling in love—and I suppose as we are in middle age we tend to doubt the very fact of falling in love—is like trapping moonlight in a box. If you open a box of moonlight in anything but bright moonlight itself, it evaporates faster than the eye can see. Love, she said, is like that. When you first fall in love you're in a kind of dazzling moonlight, and the world keeps the box full. Later, it can be like opening it in darkness, and nothing is in it—except that when the love is real it passes the test, and the dark room is miraculously lit in white by rays that love has privileged to last.

"When the *Athena* is finished and you take her to Little Creek, and then maybe the Middle East—God, I hope not—you'll be away for no one knows how many months. I have to stay here. I'll go back to work, in the life I had before you. The three Brooks Brothers, the suited suitors, will pester me, and the law firm will offer refuge and security. All as before. You'll be taken up by the excitement of the sea, your duties, your life before you knew me.

"That'll be the dark room in which we'll open the boxes to see if— contrary to what the world might say—the light is there. Then we will have earned it, it will be real, and anything will be possible."

Athena

Like every good ship, *Athena* was seductive and all-absorbing in the way of a woman, because she promised the flashes and ignitions of new worlds through new eyes. Fitting her out was somewhat like what a bullfighter does when ceremoniously donning his traditional costume, and picking up his sword with the knowledge that it was the fine, silver line between his life and that of the bull. Something there is that calls you fully awake when preparing for war. It lights up life so that you love it in a way that those who are forever safe never can.

First and last in her line, a ship like no other by dint of her birth, *Athena* was meant for daring. A one-off, she was designed to surprise, to risk—and to be expendable. The rake of her bows and the un-modern bristling of her weapons proclaimed this almost impudently. She was fast, and she was lethal. For those interested primarily in the story, it continues on page 70. For those who might be intrigued by the genius of this little ship, let us count the ways.

Athena's *Architecture*

Whereas the *Cyclone*-class patrol coastals were near-duplicates of British craft built for Egypt and Kenya, *Athena*, similar in appearance and purpose, was an American modification and design. Computational advances in fluid dynamics over the thirty-five years between the laying of the first Vosper Thornycroft keel in Britain and Bollinger Lockport's keel for *Athena* allowed her an extra six knots speed even assuming the same horsepower and screws as the Cyclones she would supersede. Perhaps most remark-ably, the new hull design and screw placement allowed something close to the skating turns associated with a boat rather than with any ship of *Athena*'s size. Her stern could slide without digging, reducing heel to ten degrees even in a top speed turn. Such maneuverability would be confounding to the informed and reasonable expectation of an opponent in combat.

She exceeded the Cyclones' 180-foot length by another thirty feet, and their twenty-five-foot beam by five feet. This gave her far more carrying capacity than her sisters—in fuel, armor, weaponry, and stores. Electric drive extended her range yet more, because the turbine generators turned at a constant rate rather than in fuel-guzzling surges. For example, the standard endurance of the Cyclones was ten days unsupported. *Athena* upped that to twenty-five days, depending upon crew size and how an extra 15 percent stowage in weight and 8 percent in volume might be utilized on each cruise.

The Cyclones had steel hulls with aluminum superstructures shielded only in part by one-inch steel armor. Their displacement at full load was 330 tons. *Athena*'s displacement was just short of 400 tons, and a great deal of it in comparison to that of the Cyclones was usable for additional load. This was attributable to metallurgical advances that made the armor lighter yet stronger, and to the use of carbon-fiber composites for non-structural interior components.

Designed for the standard Cyclone complement of four officers, twenty-four enlisted seamen, and nine SEALs, because of her increased size and carrying capacity *Athena* had more comfortable and private berthing spaces, a bigger cabin for the captain, and two officers' cabins. Nothing was lost to carrying capacity, however, in that the ship's balance and trim required lighter spaces in some areas, which were precisely where the more capacious living quarters were then situated.

Deployed mostly in the Persian Gulf, the Arabian Sea, and other areas of high heat, the *Cyclone* class was notably uncomfortable. Following on this experience, *Athena* was designed with better air-conditioning and more water—a distillation capability of six thousand gallons per day as opposed to four thousand—for longer, cooling showers to bring down the body's core temperatures elevated by the fierce Arabian sun.

Her Propulsion

Occupying the same volume as the Cyclones' four 13,400-horsepower diesels, *Athena*'s power plant (two generators and four advanced-induction electric motors with the samarium-cobalt and neodymium-iron-boron magnets) was able with less weight per horsepower to put out not 53,600 horsepower but 80,000 running at full load. This and the astounding instantaneous torques of the advanced-induction motors allowed unheard-of acceleration, and exceeded the Cyclones' maximum speed of thirty-five knots by fifteen, to more than fifty in a cooperative sea; that is, more than fifty-eight miles per hour. Due to the best horsepower-to-weight ratio in the Navy, this speed was reached in an astonishing forty seconds, speed and acceleration that by habit and observation no enemy would attribute to a ship of *Athena*'s size and appearance even if apprised of it. An enemy's training and tactics would then lock him into reactions *Athena* could counter.

Her Primary Armament

Her main armament was divided between a forward-mounted MK-46 30mm chain gun, eight short-range Griffin missiles, and, unprecedented for a PC, two Harpoon missiles, which allowed *Athena* to punch far above her weight. The gun, firing at 250 rounds per minute from a dual-feed, 400-round magazine, had an effective range of a mile and a half, and, depending upon the type of ammunition used, a maximum reach of more than two miles. Mounted forward of the bridge, it was directed by a low-light optical sight, a forward-looking infrared sensor, and a laser rangefinder. Its high-explosive, or armor-piercing, incendiary, or airburst ammunition, delivered at range, gave it impressive power.

A volley of accurately aimed airburst rounds, for example, could cripple or destroy an enemy patrol boat's communications and sensing systems, and kill everyone on deck. Following this, armor-piercing rounds might strike the innards, the magazines, fire control, and propulsion, and blow holes at the waterline. High-explosive rounds might shatter the bridge and the deck-mounted weapons. Illustrative of the gun's capabilities is that, hypothetically, mounted on the U.S. Capitol it could with a long burst reliably destroy a townhouse in Georgetown. Emptying its magazine on the White House, one-half the distance to Georgetown even if for many tourists too far to walk (especially in summer), it would by explosion and fire eventually turn the executive mansion into something like a plantation wreck out of *Gone with the Wind*.

Because the United States since the Second World War has suffered so few casualties at sea other than by accidents, many—not least sailors themselves—have come to believe that war at sea is clean and safe. It isn't. Ships are compact containers full of flammable fuels, volatile chemicals, and high explosives. The sailor may enjoy more comforts than the infantryman, but when his ship is in harm's way he can be blown to bits, exsanguinated from severed limbs, burned to death, or drowned in numbingly cold water—either trapped in the ship as it goes down or as part of it is inundated, or swallowed by the open sea.

The Griffin missile had a slightly greater range than the main gun, and delivered a single, high-explosive warhead of thirteen pounds either horizontally or in a power dive from above to exploit an unarmored deck or roof. Eight of these were mounted amidships for vertical launch. As an example of their destructive potential, straight on or in a downward trajectory, one would completely blow apart a cabin cruiser, or render useless, though not sink, a tugboat.

The Harpoon missile, of which *Athena* carried two, was something else entirely. A casual observer from the beginning of the Cold War into the first years of the twenty-first century would immediately see that Soviet and Warsaw Pact (then Russian and Eastern European militaries and their third-world client states) fielded warships—from heavy cruisers to motor torpedo boats—freakishly laden with a large number of missile tubes nearly monopolizing their decks. That is, they went all-in on missilery.

After the battleship era, Western vessels never looked as fierce. In fact, when below-deck VLS (vertical launch systems) were introduced, the ships took on the appearance of defenseless yachts. They were hardly so, but, nonetheless, smaller craft such as *Athena*, which hadn't the depth below decks or the volume to carry VLS, were not fitted with the bigger missiles carried by their Soviet-style counterparts.

NATO and allied navies concentrated instead on defensive means such as electronic jamming, misdirection, and kinetic interception, none of which required much space or weight, and created the capacity to bear a fuller spectrum of weapon systems, sustainment, and defenses. But precisely because the PCs had such heavy responsibilities in the Persian Gulf and frequently encountered much larger Iranian warships, the *Athena* class would carry two Harpoons.

Originally designed as a response to Egypt's Soviet Styx missiles' sinking the Israeli destroyer *Eilat*, until the *Athena* the Harpoon was not deployed on patrol coastals. Each a full fifteen feet long, not far from the Griffin boxes the pair was mounted amidships like crossed swords. A Harpoon weighed more than three-quarters of a ton (the Griffin only thirty-five pounds), and required a devoted fire-control system that was expensive and complicated. The Harpoon's range was sixty miles, far beyond *Athena*'s radar horizon, necessitating the use of an unmanned aerial vehicle to provide terminal guidance to target.

The Stalker UAV, the largest UAV *Athena* could carry without impinging on other requirements, had a recoverable range of 12.5 miles and a sacrificial range of twenty-five. With a good tailwind the Stalker's range could be doubled in the sacrificial mode, but with cross or headwinds both recoverable and sacrificial ranges were reduced. As the sacrificial range was the default and there were two Harpoons, *Athena* would carry two Stalkers, giving each missile the maximum effective range, in ideal wind conditions for its targeting drone, of fifty miles. Arriving at Mach 0.71, the Harpoon's nearly 500-pound, high-explosive warhead was enough to put a ship four times *Athena's* size out of commission or, with a lucky shot, send it to the bottom.

Such a ship, however, would have a more distant radar horizon, likely longer-range missiles, a faster surveillance and terminal guidance drone, and electronic countermeasures of its own. But given *Athena's* defensive capabilities, that was not the end of the story. She would carry eight shoulder-fired Stinger missiles for defense against low-flying aircraft, helicopters, and large drones. Every crewman was qualified with and issued an M4 rifle and a sidearm. The SEALs carried their own idiosyncratic, sometimes exotic, and ever-evolving weaponry, even in regard to knives, an arsenal which, as a lawyer such as Katy might have said, included but was not limited to such things as .50-caliber Barrett sniper rifles, light machine guns, various types of automatic rifles, sidearms, grenades, and even Claymore mines should they be needed in combat.

Her Secondary Armament

Athena's chief secondary armament was the .50-caliber Browning very heavy machine gun. She had six twin versions and two singles—two twins on the port side, two on the starboard, one each on the stern starboard and port sides, and a single-barreled .50-caliber on each of the bridge wings. With a cyclical rate of fire of 750–1,000 rounds per minute, and a maximum effective range of a little over a mile, this gun had so many different types of ammunition—nineteen and counting—that the gunners' mates labored to keep accessible the various combinations of ball, tracer, incendiary, armor-piercing, and practice rounds they had to load into their fourteen barrels, keeping in mind that, for example, a saboted, light-armor penetrator could pierce 1.34 inches of steel plate at 500 meters but only 0.91 inches at 1,200 meters, at a cost of $10 per round, whereas a saboted, light-armor-piercing *tracer* had somewhat different characteristics and cost $15 per round.

The effect the hail of fire these guns had at range was devastating, but at Rensselaer's urging, modifications were made to *Athena* to make it even more so. On both the port and starboard sides, where two twin-barreled guns were mounted, he installed two empty mounts, and each bridge wing had an extra mount. He made sure that in the box of tools and accessories flush against the bulkhead behind the guns were heavy, heat-insulated gloves, so that on command the crew on one side could detach and carry their weapons to the other side. (The stern guns remained fixed in place.) Thus, *Athena* was capable of a broadside of thirteen .50-caliber barrels at a prodigious rate of fire, spitting out bullets of varying and complementary function.

Supplementing the .50-calibers were three 7.62mm M-134 miniguns, one of which could be mounted at the bow of the SEALs' twenty-foot rigid-hull inflatable boat (RHIB) carried on and launched from *Athena's* stern ramp. Less than a yard long and weighing only thirty-five pounds, the minigun had an effective range of three-quarters of a mile and could spit out NATO-standard 7.62mm rifle bullets at the astounding rate of up to six thousand rounds per minute. That is, a hundred shots per second. The miniguns, too, had double mounts on each side.

Despite being the smallest ship (rather than boat) in the Navy, *Athena* was the only ship designed to accomplish by herself the ancient maneuver of crossing the T—bringing her full broadside to bear upon an enemy ship's bow or stern, where the number of guns was perforce limited. Long abandoned in modern naval warfare, it was resurrected to deal with Iranian small-boat swarming tactics, shore bombardment, or wherever concentrated kinetic fires were needed. The deadly mass of machine-gun fire was combined with the 30mm chain gun and two grenade launchers capable of lobbing 350 grenades per minute out to a mile. *Athena's* gun power was an example of how, at limited ranges, quantity can have a quality all its own.

Her Ordnance

As with all else, power was limited by its own appetites. At one point after Rensselaer and Katy knew that each was as in love as the other, when this had been professed, and then the wonderful shock and inimitable high of being in requited love took hold, they had gone out on a Saturday night to dinner and a movie, although during both they were almost oblivious of everything but one another. During dinner, their eyes had locked and rarely separated. Other diners noticed the upright, semi-hypnotized posture of newly obsessed lovers, the kind who were in love even with the pattern and drape of material as it is carried on the other's body.

The movie had many a scene with automatic weapons fired by impossibly muscular men, and impossibly thin women who could impossibly toss the impossibly muscular men into the air. Although Katy shut Rensselaer up during the movie, batting his arm as if they had been married for forty years—even that, he found wonderful—he explained afterward the popular misconception (like so many others, arisen in Hollywood) that automatic weapons had magical loads of ammunition which issued from them like water from a garden hose.

A garden hose, if connected to a municipal system, has a giant network of reservoirs, dams, and pumping stations that allows it to pour out water continuously. If supplied from a well, it has an aquifer, a pump, water lines, a pressure tank, and regulators. No such source of supply exists for the submachine guns and semi-automatic pistols in the movies, which, in real life, if set at the movie rate of fire, would empty—the Uzi or the M4, for example—in three seconds. Thus the need for one of the several types of fire discipline to husband ammunition.

In regard to this, a ship presents a multifaceted picture. It can carry immensely more ammunition than either the infantryman or the typical support unit that supplies him. Yet it lacks a continuous supply train, and when its magazines are emptied, something known as "going Winchester," it must seek underway replenishment or return to port. Thus, the more ammunition or missile reloads it can carry, the better. But as in balancing the ever-present conflicting demands required by offensive armament, armor, speed, and endurance, aboard ship all things are limited by weight and volume. *Athena* could not be as fast as she was and have the endurance at sea that she had, and yet simultaneously supply her weapons as fully as she might have had she existed in a world unbounded by limitations. Still, her size and displacement in contrast to those of the *Cyclone* class enabled her to draw upon greater reserves of ammunition, even if not upon stored missilery.

Whereas the Cyclones carried 2,000 rounds of 25mm ammunition for their big guns, *Athena* carried 4,000 rounds of 30mm for hers. At an average weight of 1.5 pounds, without either metal boxes or the breakable links that arranged it in belts, it weighed three tons. The Cyclone's 2,000

.50-caliber rounds became *Athena's* 10,000, or, at approximately 0.25 pounds apiece, 1.25 tons. Ten thousand—as opposed to 2,000—7.62mm rounds for the minigun weighed in at 625 pounds. And 4,000—as opposed to 1,000—grenades at half a pound apiece weighed a ton. All told, with belts and containers, *Athena's* ammunition load was almost seven tons.

This made her more vulnerable in terms of her magazines should they be struck, though less vulnerable in that she could defend herself with more than a little shock and awe.

Unlike as in other ships, 10 percent of each deployment's ammunition was devoted to live-fire practice, as nothing improves marksmanship like live fire.

Her Countermeasures

Other than armor, speed, maneuverability, intelligence support supplying a battle picture of the surrounding ocean or jagged littorals, and frequent practice in damage control, *Athena's* defensive measures consisted primarily of classified and arcane electronic warfare systems that could jam, redirect, and in other ways incapacitate hostile missiles. Non-electronically, incoming missiles were met with flares and metallic chaff launched in quick volleys: flares to seduce infrared seekers and chaff to confuse active-radar homing. Such things didn't always work, but when they did it was dramatic. An incoming missile—death itself moving fast—would as if suborned by conscience make a strange turn and dive into the sea. All forms of passive defense, however, were irrelevant to wire-guided missiles or aimed ballistic projectiles, whether anti-tank missiles or rocket-propelled grenades.

These latter weapons, of relatively short range, were best dealt with by suppressive fire. But RPGs tended to pop up as if from nowhere, the first salvo from skiffs or ships that, before such a surprise, presented no justification for attack. One defense against RPGs was maneuverability: were they launched from sufficient distance, were the screws already turning at a high rate, were the helmsman alert, and were the ship lucky. Maneuverability had little effect on a wire-guided missile unless the gun crews could react fast enough to kill the man guiding it. The solution, and last resort, was what the sailors referred to as the Hip Pocket, one of which was mounted amidships atop each side of the superstructure.

Originally developed for the Bradley Armored Fighting Vehicle, these were small and light. Always alert, they could sense the flash of an RPG launch and automatically slew to fire a two-foot-diameter cloud of .22-caliber pellets. Rensselaer planned to augment them with 12-gauge shotguns. An RPG stays within a tight window of approach rather than crossing in front of the shooter like a clay pigeon. To hit the clay, a shooter would have a second or less, but five or six seconds to hit an RPG. Whether either the Hip Pockets or the shotguns had any effect against a heavier anti-tank missile was an open and perhaps dubious question.

Her Navigation and Communication Systems, and Her Music

In Condition I (ready for battle, if not necessarily called to general quarters), Condition II (modified battle readiness situationally dependent), and Condition III (deployed readiness, i.e., not expecting but prepared), *Athena*'s bridge, bigger than a Cyclone's, would be active and crowded. Ten sailors or more might be at work, depending upon what was happening: what weapons might be fired and from where; if a translator were necessary; if the captain were on the bridge; if the incoming and outgoing officers of the deck (the OODs) were both there, briefing in transition; if someone were waiting for orders before going below.

So many systems required operation and monitoring that just to list them, much less gracefully integrate them into a holistic picture of the ship's status, environment, challenges, and potentials, might change the view of someone who from either prejudice or ignorance or both might think of a line officer not as the equivalent of a civilian professional but rather as something like Popeye's great-grandson.

To wit: surface search radar; navigational radar; video systems; Loran C; Omega; emergency indication radio beacon; depth sounder; speed log; WESMAR scanning sonar; Gyro Compass; magnetic compass; autopilot; anemometer; forward-looking infrared; six separate VHF/UHF transceivers; LOS/SATCOM transceivers; three separate cryptological consoles (in COMMS, not on the bridge); an infrared signal set; weapons and fire control consoles for the 30mm gun, the Harpoon missiles, the Griffins, and the Hip Pockets; two internal communication systems; engines and steering controls; lights; horns; hailers; technical reference books; shipboard management computers; logs; etc.

However, Rensselaer had learned from his command of DDGs (guided-missile destroyers) that integrated bridge and navigation systems had gone too far, and for no good reason, in the incorporation of touch screens and trackballs. Much like the new cars that required navigating a cursor across a computer screen to select options thereon rather than keeping one's eyes on the road and, without looking, adjusting the heat or the radio by turning knobs, the touch-screen throttles and trackball cursors of integrated bridge systems were absurd ways to drive a ship. On *Athena* the throttles would be physical levers, and the rudders would be moved by wheels.

On his way to New Orleans, Rensselaer had gone to Northrop-Grumman in Charlottesville and made himself so ubiquitous and insistent that just to get rid of him they agreed to retrofit *Athena*'s bridge system, as he requested, with old throttles, of which they had a large and useless stock. It didn't hurt that he was in charge of *Athena*'s fitting out, and that they didn't know it would be the last of its class, especially since he told him that he had had conversations with the Secretary of the Navy and the president, and that he had always recommended a very large buy of follow-on vessels. So although *Athena* had quite a few touch screens and trackballs, not a one was for ship driving, which would be done the old-fashioned way.

During his years of effort and by making use of a lifetime of connections in the Navy, Rensselaer added to such things both his own invention and his insistence on preserving the ability to navigate and maneuver without the aid of electronics. His invention, which he funded by convincing the integration contractors that it might be used elsewhere and thus be profitable to them, was a means of lengthening the radar and optical horizon of the *Athena* beyond the Cyclone's eight and five miles respectively to eleven and eleven. This he did by installing a telescopic mast that when extended was roughly twenty-six feet above the surface search radar and more than forty feet above the topside observation deck. At the top of the mast was an off-the-shelf commercial radar of the type one might find on a medium-sized yacht, and a ball mount for high-magnification, low-light optics. The three miles of radar and six miles of visual increase were mainly important in terms of situational awareness. Although this system required several laptops that further crowded the bridge, it could provide an extra ten minutes warning of, for example, an enemy speedboat approaching at sixty knots, or twenty minutes warning and maneuver time in the case of a patrol boat at thirty knots. In combat, twenty minutes is a lifetime.

And then, Rensselaer thought to knit all this together ineffably with music. He decided to install powerful, high-quality speakers at every combat station aboard so that in the fight music would coordinate reactions and make them more precise. He set very little store in his request to Washington to finance this, and, not surprisingly, the bureaucrats did not respond positively to a change order that included the sentences: "Bagpipes made the British Empire, and, before that, swept the Celts through France. Music focuses the mind and brings courage even to the mediocre heart." But Katy liked it, and other things as well.

To her satisfaction and heightened regard—as it illuminated something she found admirable in Rensselaer's character—he had always insisted that his crew navigate not only by the integrated bridge systems but with paper charts, chronometer, and sextant. Further cramping the bridge, and the cause in future of many bruises, was a chart table and maneuvering board. Should all the electronics fail, no officer or chief under his command would be unable to steer the ship, find relative-motion solutions, or vector for wind and currents. He had a genuine love for the maneuvering board, an erasable surface over a large compass rose, upon which true headings, multiple bearings, and vectored intercepts were plotted with precise, differently colored lines—just as they were instantly plotted on the flat screens of the electronic bridge systems, but on the maneuvering board only after careful consideration, calculation, and verification. Results came more slowly but more surely, as they included one's thought and experience. When at home Rensselaer would attend to his double-entry banking ledger, he did the calculations first mentally, and then with a calculator. The incidence of mistakes in data entry, though rare, roughly equaled the errors in his mental arithmetic. This habit of double-checking was extended into the use of the maneuvering board in conjunction with its electronic descendants.

Katy

Katy believed that patient and steady regard to tradition was the sign of something in a man that she could count on. The stately, plump, preppy lawyers smitten with her thought tradition was something you could buy, wear, drive, ride, sit on, or drink. Rensselaer's view of tradition, she understood, was as something for which you might die but that nonetheless was less likely to require your death than to save your life. This was, for her, beguiling and reassuring. It was strange, but she felt that both he and she would have been essentially the same had they lived in any era of history, never quite fitting in if only because they were quietly adamantine in regard to what they believed was beautiful, right, and true, and their conviction was thoroughly independent of the pressures, fashions, and disappointments of their life and times. It bound them together more than they had been bound to anyone else in all their lives.

At the beginning of May, Katy was at her desk quietly parsing the Internal Revenue Code in several thick volumes opened in front of her. Exactly the same sections were displayed on three computer screens, but she preferred paper and ink. She had to absorb parts of the code thoroughly before she then would turn to the regulations, revenue rulings, and court cases. The phone rang. She was concentrating so hard she almost didn't hear it. Still staring at the text, she picked it up and said, "This is Katy."

He loved when she answered that way. It was simultaneously so modest, confident, and poised. "This is Stephen," he said, affectionately.

She looked up from the open books.

"I need to meet you at our bench." He was referring to a quiet bench beneath huge oaks on a forgotten street close to downtown, where they often met for lunch.

"I had lunch two hours ago," she said. "It'll take some time to get there. Can it wait until evening?"

"It can't."

His answer and his tone made her nervous. "Now?"

"Yes."

As she left the office, rode down in the elevator—or, as Stephen insisted when it was going down, the "descender"—and headed out, she grew increasingly upset. Hardly noticing anything around her as she made her way to the meeting place, she remembered a recent conversation.

"When I look back," Stephen had said, "at all the struggles I've seen— they were never-ending—for recognition, position, wealth, prestige, power, fame . . . the stories they make were great and indispensable, but not their objectives. Were I magically made younger, I could see nothing but to strive once more, but now the tests, momentous actions, and touching scenes, stripped of sound and dimly seen, are little and diminished."

"I know," she answered. "The law is a system that can stumble upon the truth, but never seeks it directly. Tax law is just a game, like a psychotic, OCD-version of a pinball machine, and I play it all day. You know what's infinitely better? When I look out the window and watch the river and the clouds. And in the evening, the shadows, the wind coming up Poydras, the clanging of the trolley bell. There's more in those than in all my hours of work, maybe because they're just lovely and effortless. They have no ambition—the deep shadow, the luffing wind, the clanging bell."

"Katy, once I deliver *Athena* I'm done with the Navy, and I'll come back to you."

She walked fast toward the quiet street. A cool wind from a thunderstorm coming in from the west pushed her hair back and sometimes was strong enough to lift the lapels of her suit. Everything around her seemed to blur, and yet she was intensely aware of it and would never forget the colors, the midafternoon darkness of the oncoming storm, and the sound of normal things—traffic, the singing of the streetcar wires—that now took on new significance. Stephen was waiting at the bench, in his khakis, a duffel next to him. When he rose to embrace her, the embrace was the only thing that stopped the trembling that had begun when she saw the duffel.

"What?" she asked, although she knew. The west wind blew the newly fallen petals of a garden full of peonies down the street and briefly up in the air so that they looked like snow.

"The Iranians sank a tanker in the Strait of Hormuz, and as two PCs sped to help they were met by dozens of shore-based anti-ship missiles and swarms of speedboats. They fought like hell, it seems, but they were sunk, and before anyone could get to them, the small boats machine-gunned the survivors in the water. More than fifty men. It's probably on the news already. Right now, aircraft from Al-Udeid and the *Vinson* are attacking the Iranian coastal bases. We've lost a few planes. The whole Fifth Fleet is out in the Gulf. Ships are pouring out of Hampton Roads, San Diego, Hawaii, Japan, and Guam. It's suicidal for the Iranians, but they have a culture of martyrdom and they're going to stand up everything they've got.

"You needn't cry," he said, gently. "Millions of people have done this before."

"I haven't."

"I know," he told her. "Waiting is always the hardest."

She didn't have to say *I love you*. Nor did he. It was evident more than anything else. "When?" she asked, and then looked at the duffel. "Right now?" followed in protest.

"I got the call at the yard."

"But you've just finished builder's trials. You don't have the full crew."

"*Athena* did magnificently. With the wind astern we once made"— here he stopped to convert knots—"just shy of sixty miles an hour. And she can skid-turn like a speedboat. She's a great ship. I couldn't have a better one."

"You're taking her out . . . ?"

"She's at the wharf, ready to go."

"To the Persian Gulf?"

"To Norfolk, where we'll load stores, ammunition, and missiles, take on a full crew, and then head out."

"Have you left anything behind? Do you want me to. . . ."

"I dropped your things off at your house, but this is all I have. The rest is in Washington. When the tenant's lease is up, you'll see the house in Georgetown. You'll like it. Washington is your city probably more than mine."

She knew that at dusk she would watch *Athena* leave port and go down the river—not like a plane lifting from the runway and rising fast, but, rather, stately and slow. The stern light would take such a long time to fade into the darkness that it would come close to breaking her heart.

"Now, listen," he said, "this has happened so many times before, and each time it does, for the one who leaves, and the one who waits, it changes and deepens everything. It can be borne."

She closed her eyes and nodded. She knew what would come next, and that she would cry. He asked her to marry him. They embraced.

And she said yes.

NORFOLK

In late May's midmorning sun, *Athena* rounded Cape Henry in a sparkling heat haze that painted the beaches with a tinge of white which seemed to match the sound of crashing surf. North of Lynnhaven Roads she passed into the Chesapeake Bay. Then, running beyond Little Creek, the home port to which she would return within hours, she made for Naval Station Norfolk to take on ordnance.

Ships at this, the largest naval base in the world, tie up at fourteen major piers along which fighting vessels, with names that do not rhyme, often nest, nonetheless, two or three abreast. At evening, lights festooning the fleet shine like those of a city at Christmas. Some older sailors could remember gliding past a dozen aircraft carriers and fifty cruisers and destroyers lit up and busy, loading and unloading, fixing and welding, with sparks flying across their decks, cranes slewing, barges maneuvering and patrol boats darting.

Now far fewer ships were present, but the activity around them was ceaseless, and the streets of the base, running miles to the east, were crowded with vehicles. After they were supplied and armed at a frantic pace twenty-four hours a day, most of the ships would sally through the roads and set their courses for the Arabian Sea and Persian Gulf. Like the ground crews of fighter aircraft, the thousands of sailors on base felt a sense of urgency and responsibility that drove them to efficiencies seen only in war. Though nothing in this regard was ever spoken, across the silence between them and the sailors on board they felt a strong sense of brotherhood. As a ship left, those who stayed ashore would spare a moment from their duties to stand and salute.

When *Athena* found her assigned pier, the missiles, missile loaders, ordnance trucks, and cranes were waiting. In peacetime it was hardly unusual to wait a week or more to load armament, but not now.

In the Second World War, the carrier *Yorktown* was so badly damaged in the Battle of the Coral Sea that in normal circumstances its repair might have taken several years. But in light of the impending Battle of Midway, Admiral Nimitz ordered expedited work, which, he was told, would take ninety days. This he pared to three. With men and materiel flown to the ship as she limped home, efforts commenced at sea, and after she pulled in, the activity of the twelve hundred men assembled to receive her at Pearl Harbor began before the drydock had fully drained as they started work in water chest-high. Even Honolulu's electricity was diverted for their use. Three days later, leaving behind exhausted but proud seamen and engineers, the *Yorktown* steamed toward Midway.

In that spirit, though hardly at that speed, the Harpoons, Griffins, and tons of ammunition were loaded aboard *Athena*. As the frames for the Harpoons and canisters for the Griffins were already affixed to the deck, most of the job was not in their physical transfer, although that had to be done cautiously and by the book, but in testing connections and filling out forms. In five hours it was done. By that time, *Athena* had finished bunkering fuel, and at dusk she backed from the pier, pointed her bow northward, and headed for Little Creek, the amphibious base that was home to the Patrol Coastals.

As *Athena* left Norfolk, the lights strung on docked ships from stern rail to island or mast and down to the bow came on in star-like catenaries. While she glided slowly and silently by, north and east of the naval base the gentler lights of houses glowed safely along the shore, reminding the sailors and the soon-to-depart contractors who had taken the ship from New Orleans that this was what they were fighting for—these soft lights, these wooden houses set back from the beach, and the families at peace within.

*

As the ordnance was loaded onto *Athena*, a 757 took off from the civilian airport at San Diego with a SEAL detachment aboard. The six of them sat together in the back of the plane, radiating the physical power that was the gift of continual training. Their commanding officer, a Lieutenant Commander Holworthy, was disturbed that his group comprised six rather than the nine the new Patrol Coastal *Athena* could accommodate. They had trained as nine, but three were detached and sent elsewhere.

Before the flight, he had taken his men to an obscure hallway in the airport and led them through an hour of calisthenics. This was the only way they could justify their long immobility on the aircraft. Were civilians to do the same, their flights too would be more comfortable, the enforced rest a welcome recovery rather than an enervating ordeal. He would lead them in more calisthenics in New York before embarking for Norfolk, this time not in the hallway but on the tarmac, where they would guard the transfer of air cargo containers that carried their weapons and equipment.

After their exercise in San Diego they had watched it load, and would watch it again in New York. Their specialized and individualized arsenal of accessories—from night vision equipment, sniper rifles, and communications, down to boots, helmets, and uniforms—was worth well over a million dollars, could be dangerous in the wrong hands, and would in its absence slow and degrade their performance were they to work with new sets of uncalibrated and non-customized tools. So at JFK they would remain next to their two airfreight containers as they exercised.

Somewhere over Arizona the Bloody Marys arrived. Partly to thank the SEALs for their service (something the best of them always find keenly embarrassing) the steward didn't charge for drinks. On airplanes, Holworthy drank Bloody Marys. They had nutritional value, and vodka. Drinks in hand, blocking the way to the heads—which no one sought at the beginning of the flight anyway—the SEALs sat and stood in a group, speaking softly enough not to be overheard.

Holworthy was a sandy-haired Texan who looked like the soldier greeted by Eisenhower in the famous picture of his meeting with paratroopers before D-Day. He was unattached, impatient, and highly ambitious. As SEAL teams placed less emphasis upon rank and hierarchy than upon the inherent leadership that revealed itself in action, he felt always frustrated by detailed orders from above. "Irregular warfare must be irregular. Give us our orders," he would say to his men to illustrate his view, "and then fuck off."

"Where are we going *now*?" one of them asked, with some irritation. They were part of SEAL Team 8 at Little Creek, but had been detached to Coronado before assignment to newly bulked-up Seventh Fleet. Almost as soon as they had come to terms with this, they received word that they were headed back to Virginia.

"Does the war in the Gulf," Holworthy answered, "give you a hint?"

"Seventh Fleet is going in as well. Why are they bouncing us around?"

"Back to PCs."

"The PCs are all covered. There's even an excess. Isn't that why we were sent to Coronado in the first place?"

"It is," Holworthy told them. "But there's a new one."

"A new PC?" someone asked. "You're kidding. They're supposed to be phased out."

"It's a variant, upgraded, the first and last of its class. PC Fifteen, the *Athena*."

"Never heard of it."

"They didn't ask you. I'm told it's bigger, more comfortable—"

"Good," someone interrupted.

"Lots'a new stuff on it. And the CO . . . ready? Is a captain."

"Can't be. You can't be a captain on a PC. It's impossible."

"No. It's true."

"What'd he do?"

"He had an argument."

"With who?"

"The president."

"The president of what?"

"The United States."

"The President of the United States. That could be good, or it could be bad."

Holworthy continued. "I asked around at Coronado. He's supposed to be capable, sharp, and demanding, but he's had a lot of commands, and he leaves them scratching their heads and wondering what happened to them. That's according to the guys who were around when he was a SEA—"

"He was a SEAL?"

"Indeed he was. In the Gulf War, muppet—before you were born—he earned the Navy Cross."

Holworthy then went over Rensselaer's history to the extent that he knew it, and when he finished he said, "He does well and he always moves up, but he's one of those guys who's bound to come a cropper because he plays by his own rules. When they coincide with the Navy's— and that's a lot: he's Academy—he does brilliantly. But if they don't, it's as if there's no such thing as the Navy, never heard of it, or he's founding it on the spot."

"Kind of like guess who?" O'Connor, Holworthy's second, added. Holworthy, a lieutenant commander in charge of only five men, and only in the informal way of a SEAL detachment, was neatly analogous to Rensselaer, whose name O'Connor had yet to learn. And like Rensselaer, Holworthy was headstrong.

"The difference," Holworthy explained, "is that with his rank and the nature of his prior commands he's had far less room for independence. Two days ago, I bumped into a captain I met at West in February, and asked about Rensselaer, our new CO. 'Oh yeah,' he said, and smiled as he shook his head back and forth. 'You gotta understand, with Stephen, if there's a conflict between Navy regulations and what he calls—I'm not kidding, I swear—the laws of nature and nature's God, he'll say kiss my ass. He gets one choice billet after another, does exceptionally well, takes it to the edge, and is elevated two seconds before it all goes south. He was an aide to the SECNAV and on the selection list for rear admiral, lower half, when, in the presence of the CNO, the SECNAV, and the National Security Advisor, he more or less politely told the president to stick it. Admirable in some respects, but not something I'd recommend."

O'Connor dropped an ice cube he had in his mouth back into his Bloody Mary. "I just don't get how a SEAL with the Navy Cross could become a staff weeny."

"He's old. Officially, in the PT manual, they call someone in his late thirties a 'high-mileage SEAL.' This guy's got almost twenty years on that."

"But he was whatever he was and probably on the weeny track even before he got old."

"Look," Holworthy said, "he was kicked out. That suggests to me that he's not really a weeny."

"Why?"

"Because," Holworthy answered, "think about it. The dude abides. Weenies can't do that."

*

Bracketing *Athena* at Little Creek—her home port though she would remain abroad for most of her life—were two PCs, forward and aft. Preparing to sail for the Gulf slightly in advance of *Athena*, they were veterans seasoned by survival. Nonetheless, their past combats and their age weighed heavily upon them. Even their names, *Firebolt* and *Typhoon*, were subsidiary to that of *Athena*, a beautiful, wise goddess, forever young, who could toss lightning bolts and make storms. Although warships are made to fight, they are yet feminine, buoyant, and graceful in the waves and wind.

Athena had not a postage stamp of rust. In comparison to her sisters, she was blemishless and perfect. And she was bigger. When a beautiful woman is statuesque her beauty is magnified. Katy was most times more beautiful, and certainly wiser, than the young women in their twenties whom she and Stephen might see in a restaurant or a park, and though Stephen would not have lasted more than a day with any one of them due to their natural energies and endearing inexperience, he like everyone else was immediately influenced by their presence, as Katy was, too. Once it is lost, youth swells in value in a way that the young are incapable of imagining. *Athena* had exactly this advantage over *Firebolt* and *Typhoon*, and had they been alive it might have been observable and unconcealable.

Although much smaller than Naval Station Norfolk, Little Creek is itself enormous, and it too was bustling: ships preparing for deployment, vehicles busy on its roads, helicopters touching down and taking off, lights blazing everywhere, young SEALs swimming miles out in the surging swell, and not just in daylight. Some of *Athena*'s contractors had departed at the naval base, but others were now packing up. The civilian airport was nearby, and they would catch late flights out.

The rest of the crew was on its way in from as far away as Japan. *Athena*'s sudden activation had caught the bureaucracy by surprise, and sailors had to be swept up from all over—some who had been in transit, some waiting to be reassigned, some who had been suspect and in limbo for minor yet unadjudicated infractions now cleared by emergency order.

Rensselaer had protested that he hadn't time to shape his crew, and only by calling Rusty, who felt strongly for him, did he manage a little control. She had walked to the appropriate office and charmed the appropriate subordinate, who arranged to send *Athena* five supernumeraries so that in an effort to select the best, the captain would have five to reject.

Although Rensselaer returned to *Athena* every few hours to supervise the loading and stowage, he spent the two days after *Athena*'s evening arrival vetting the crew in an office a quarter mile from the ship. It hadn't changed since the fifties or sixties. An overpowered window air conditioner refrigerated the room and made a hypnotic sound, the desks and chairs were wood highly polished by twenty thousand elbows and ten thousand behinds, and a green linoleum floor was so cold that feet could feel it through shoes. Bright colors outside—blue sky, blue water, and a thickly leaved tree that moved in the wind—were attenuated by blinds that hadn't been dusted in half a century.

The crew sat on benches in the hall outside. Some slept after long flights, inevitably some of the younger ones played games on their phones, others talked or read newspapers, and one or two crazies stared at the fluorescent lights. They had come through the civilian airport or been disgorged from C-130s at the naval station airfield or NAS Oceana, and some arrived by bus from Mayport or by train from New London, etc. They stayed in a barracks with other sailors from different ships, all of whom were in the same boat. War seemed both close and distant. The closeness was due to a strong sense of unease; the distance, when the unease passed out of mind.

Officers were interviewed first. Of these, only one was extra. Rensselaer spoke first to his XO candidate, a thin, wiry, dark-haired lieutenant commander, quite a bit over six feet, with big, coal-black eyes and eyelids that were wide open, and closed only once every minute or so, not in a blink but for a couple of seconds. This, plus his muscular tension, was somewhat frightening. He was from Boston, he was Jewish, he spoke with a fairly heavy Boston accent, and he had been through NROTC at MIT, with a major in mathematics.

After naval formalities, Rensselaer said, "Have a seat."

"Thank you, sir." He sat, and stared.

"Um," said Rensselaer, who rarely if ever said *um*, "the first thing— your name."

"Alan."

"Your last name. Pronunciation."

"Movius, the way it looks. Mo-vee–us, as in the German, not the French." He pronounced the French exaggeratedly, drawing it out—"Moe-vieu-ze."

"Next question."

"Sir."

"You were the XO on the *Augusta*, and the captain transferred you out. Why? Your record has no explanation and you weren't due."

"The captain and I had a disagreement about the manner in which he treated a female ensign: staring, suggestive comments, calling her to his cabin at late hours to 'pick up papers.'"

"She couldn't handle it herself?"

"She could, and did. She was fully capable. She had it under control."

"So why did you . . . ?"

"All I did was tell him that if he persisted I would throw him overboard. And I meant it."

"He didn't bring you up on charges?"

"No, sir."

"Do you always speak to your superiors that way?"

"No, sir. Never. Except that once."

"I'm astounded that he didn't take action. What he did was wrong, but. . . . "

"He recognized that I had a special responsibility in regard to the ensign."

"Which was?"

"She's my sister."

"Got it." Rensselaer scanned the folder and turned a few pages, saying only, "Very impressive."

"Thank you sir."

"Tell me, if you had been in command of the boat that the Iranians captured in the Gulf a few years ago, how would you have handled it?"

"It wouldn't have been captured, sir."

"No? Even though the Iranian boat was faster and more heavily armed?"

"No."

"What would you have done?"

"I would have tried to outrun them."

"And if, with their superior guns with greater range, they had fired upon you?"

"I would have come about and closed range at high speed so that we could fire back."

"Even if you and your crew were grievously injured or killed?"

"Yes, sir."

"Why?"

Movius leaned forward as if facing an enemy, his eyes now protectively in a slight squint, his jaw firmed. "I would not surrender a United States ship, sir, period."

"You would fight?"

"Of course I would."

"The chief will show you to your quarters."

*

Rensselaer scanned the names on the list of candidates and glanced at their folders. To his surprise and delight, a dozen had once served on PCs. They had volunteered from the fleet and shore duty, he would find out, because they had a bent for deprivation and action. He knew also that the prospect of wide responsibility must have drawn them as well. On a PC, everyone had multiple jobs and was continuously learning and cross-training. This led to a feeling of autonomy and satisfaction (absent in the specializations on larger ships), something he planned to intensify to an unprecedented degree.

Among other things, he was going to make some of the crew auxiliaries to the half dozen SEALs *Athena* would take on from SEAL Team 8. The SEALs wouldn't like it at first, but he would challenge them to bring the selectees as close to their high standards as possible, and then, seeing it as a challenge, the SEALs probably would get to like it. Had Rensselaer not been a SEAL himself, he might not have known this.

He wanted as big a land force as he could muster, because he projected that it would be sent ashore to destroy shore-based anti-ship and anti-aircraft-missile sites, and bases for Iranian small boat swarms. There would be little downtime on *Athena*, and not just for the SEALs. Thanks to two treadmills, everyone on board would run six miles every day other than in combat. Thanks to swim calls when possible, everyone would swim a mile as often as could be arranged. And thanks to the SEALs, the crew, even the chiefs, who were older, would be pushed to their calisthenics and close-quarter-combat limits. Free time, he thought as he scanned the list, would be appreciated mainly as a chance to sleep.

Who was on the list? As on every American warship and in every combat unit, the names meant a great deal and they meant nothing, for although these names had originated all over the world they were now American, as unified as if in France they had all been Pierre or, in Norway, Sven. The list comprised those not already aboard, not including the SEALs, who would come as a unit: Armentrout, Di Loreto, Martin, Speight,

Velez, Pisecki, Williams, Harding, Holt, Rodriguez, Washington, Via, Rosen, Lanham, Movius, Pinafore, Josephson, and Rensselaer.

The first one he called was Di Loreto, not only because Di Loreto's hometown was Ossining, New York, on the widest bay of the Hudson, the river that was roughly the north–south spine of Rensselaer's own world, but because of Di Loreto's previous occupation in the Navy.

"What did you do in the eight years between Ossining High School and your enlistment?" Rensselaer asked, looking up from Di Loreto's record.

"I worked in my family's gas station, sir."

"I know that. It's here. But what did you do? Did you just pump gas and clean windshields?"

"Oh no, sir. People pump their own gas these days, except in New Jersey, Connecticut, and, I think, Oregon, although maybe not even there anymore. I've been in California for a while. I don't really know."

"And why not in New Jersey, or wherever?"

"Unions, I guess. They say because it's dangerous. Idiots."

"So what did you do?"

"I was a mechanic, sir. I started when I was, like, five. We fixed every kind of car. You know, one of those kind of shops, because the dealers are a rip-off."

"Every kind?"

"Every kind. Even when you could only get the manuals in German. We did engine rebuilds, trannies, electronics."

"So you had to teach yourself how many different makes and models?"

"A hundred?"

"And you could do it?"

"Yes sir."

"After you enlisted, you ended up with the naval Marine Mammal Program. How is that?"

"First as a mechanic, sir. Nobody makes the kind of equipment we use—used. Even if an order went through, the Pentagon might take two years to make it and it would cost a hundred thousand dollars. I could usually do it in two weeks for a coupla thousand."

"So you were essentially a fabricator."

"Yeah, until I got Lucy, my dolphin. She's in the Pacific now." Here Di Loreto showed emotion. "They're so smart, sir. They have feelings, and loyalty. After her time was up and we took her into the open sea a thousand miles southwest, she came back to Point Loma. She'd swim back and forth, squeaking a distress sound. She was angry and sad. You can tell that. I had to stay concealed, because she wouldn't have understood if she'd seen that I was still there. I'm telling you, I cried. They're a lot like us, you know."

"You trained her?"

"Yes sir."

"To do what?"

"I was in MK6, sentries. She would attach a magnetic device onto a hostile swimmer's air tanks. A buoy would pop up on the line to the surface. We made it so the magnet was so powerful that even if the swimmer took off his tank he wouldn't be strong enough to pry it off, even with a tool. Without his tank he'd have to surface. With it, we would know where he was even if submerged. The sea lions were even more amazing. I made stuff for them, but I didn't train them. They could sneak up on the swimmers and handcuff a buoy to their leg or arm. I helped build that, and maintain the stock."

"That's extraordinary."

"It is, sir. Underwater autonomous vehicles are never going to be half as good. It's a beautiful thing, to watch a dolphin help you—with all her heart."

"You can fix things."

"I can, sir."

"And you're a boatswain's mate as well, used to small boats."

"Yes, sir. That's all we had. Every day."

"You're hired."

*

Then a slight young man came in, as happy as a golden retriever and as innocent. His name was Pinafore.

"Sit down, Her Majesty's Ship."

"Sir?"

"Gilbert and Sullivan."

Pinafore looked behind him, as if to see them standing there. "I don't understand, sir."

"You've never heard of Gilbert and Sullivan?"

"No, sir. Who are they?"

"An English operetta composer and lyricist."

"Oh."

"'I am the very model of a modern major general,'" Rensselaer said, hoping to jar Pinafore's memory.

But Pinafore stared at Rensselaer uncomprehendingly. It was clear that he thought Rensselaer might be insane.

"Okay, Pinafore. What do you like about the Navy?"

"I love being at sea, sir, and being responsible for my job."

"Gunner's mate."

"Yes, sir. What I do makes me happy when I do it well, and I always try to do that."

"Fair enough," Rensselaer told him. "I couldn't ask for more."

Next up was a sailor named Via. To Rensselaer, he didn't look quite right. Something about him was feral, and he made no connection, not even looking Rensselaer in the eye.

"You were last on the *Vinson*."

"Yes sir."

"You volunteered for this."

"I did, sir."

"What did you do on the *Vinson*?"

"Airedale, sir."

"That's not what it says here."

"I was about to strike."

"Okay, but you didn't."

"No sir. If I'd stayed, I would have."

"So why here?"

"I want to kill Iranians, sir." He thought this would be appreciated.

"Do you?"

"Yes, sir."

"Why?"

"We're at war with them, sir, and, you know what they did."

"I know very well what they did, but I'm afraid I can't use you."

"Sir?"

"Pack up. Find something else."

"Why?"

"Seaman Via, we may be called upon to kill the enemy, and that we will do, but I don't want anyone on my crew who wants to do so. I've been around such people and they've never failed to fuck up. If you want to kill, it means you're flat, something's missing. I want people with depth. If you want to kill, you're likely to make the wrong judgment. Think about that."

"What I think, sir, is that in war you need people like me."

"No. Bloodlust doesn't win battles."

"Then what does?"

"Intelligence, ingenuity, courage, daring. Bloodlust is for criminals, not for soldiers, sailors, or Marines. Red dyes are the first to fade. Dismissed."

"Dismissed?" Via shot back, impudently.

"That's right," Rensselaer answered. "Hit the road."

If Via could have killed Rensselaer, he would have killed him then and there, and he showed it. But he couldn't—not just because of the law, but because Rensselaer was not so easy to kill.

*

Last up were the SEALs, six at once, high-testosterone. SEALs seemed permanently to have the air either of men who were still in battle or have just come out of it. They combined confidence bearing upon arrogance with wariness bearing upon paranoia. Extreme fitness, relentless training, and the knowledge that one can far transcend assumed limits are perhaps what make for their peculiarity.

Their dense musculature renders them one and a half times as heavy as they appear to be, they're only sort of in the Navy, they expect deference, they get it, they keep to themselves, and, as they are used to autonomy, they want their received orders to focus on the objective rather than the means.

Despite what they had heard, they were immediately comfortable with Rensselaer, because he had been and in some ways would always be one of them. Thus they had nothing to hold over him so as to establish their independence. At Little Creek they had been informed that in the Gulf War he had knocked out four missile-launching sites, that he had evaded capture for a week as an entire Iraqi company pursued him, that he had finally run out of ammunition and been taken, imprisoned, and tortured. And that then he escaped. Now he was a captain, although his assignment to such a small ship was hard to assimilate even in view of the scuttlebutt that in the Oval Office he had told the president where to get off. Which, of course, he hadn't.

Like Movius, the XO, Holworthy was a lieutenant commander. He led his five men into Rensselaer's temporary office and exchanged formalities. As there was only one visitor's chair and none of the SEALs would take it, only Rensselaer seated himself, relaxedly and unselfconsciously.

"You're the only organic unit I have," Rensselaer said, "and I'm grateful that you came that way. It'll do a lot in terms of stabilizing and breaking-in a new ship. I know you know your jobs, and I'll interfere as little as possible. We haven't gotten our orders yet, but you can probably guess their nature. In regard to that, I'm going to ask you to do something which hasn't normally been done, at least not in modern times."

They perked up, raising their already straight backs. "Sir?" Holworthy asked.

"In the time it takes to get wherever we're going, I want you to train as best you can a dozen men—whom I will pick but you can reject. Bring them up physically, in tactics, weapon handling, and CQC, so they can function ashore to supplement you."

Holworthy protested. "Sir, you know it takes years."

"Of course I know. I spent those years. But I also know two things. The most important lesson you learn in those years is that you can do what no one—including yourself—expects you can do. That's the first thing. The second thing is that I've just challenged you. Are you going to take the challenge or not?"

"Take it," Holworthy said. He couldn't have said anything else, as Rensselaer had known.

"Very well," he answered, addressing all the SEALs. "Make ready."

As they left, Rensselaer heard one say, "At least on a PC there's no sled." He was referring to the SDVs (SEAL delivery vehicles), upon which SEALs in scuba gear would ride submerged through dark, freezingly cold water sometimes for ten hours at a time. It was not a popular activity, but they could do it, and sometimes they did.

*

When the weapons, yet more ammunition, stores, and personal effects had been assimilated, berths had been assigned and claimed, watches established, checklists completed, systems vetted, decks scrubbed, stations established, the P.O.D. (plan of the day) posted, and after the crew had been given the last chance to contact families before embarkation, the ship was ready to come alive and sail to war.

Rensselaer had neither to strain nor to pretend sympathy with those, of whom there were many, with aching hearts. When leaving women and children behind, going to war seems only hollow, foolish, and dangerous. One's doubt and betrayal are physically felt in the perfect cross of sadness and fear. Having just spoken to Katy, the last thing he wanted was to lead his men into battle, or even to leave shore. He had told her that he loved her, and she had done the same. This was enough. Perhaps that which these men felt so strongly as to have to will themselves through their normal routines was a balance for the ennui and nihilism of those for whom life is meaningless. Rensselaer thought that if all such people had to bid goodbye to ones they loved—that is if they were in fact brave and fortunate enough to love—as they went off to war, ennui would disappear and irony, as it was stripped of its pretense of wisdom, would lose its touch. All he could think of was Katy.

And yet, when he began to speak, it was as if another person had arisen within him. He was like a ship pulling away from a city, leaving behind what had seemed so all-encompassing as to dwarf the vessel, which, magically, as it gained distance began to seem larger than the receding city itself, and then to become the whole world.

A June storm that, like *Athena* herself, had come up from the Gulf, had hit Norfolk. So a tent appeared at the wharf, close to the ship. Large enough to hold the entire crew and the naval officials seeing them off, it was white, with transparent plastic panels as skirts, and butter-colored, varnished poles. Wind-lashed rain blew open the flaps and skirts uncontrollably and, crossing from one side of the tent to the other, wet the sailors as if they had been on an open deck in squall.

After the base chaplains said their blessings and the commanders said their piece, it was the captain's turn to speak. He dared not do so with a heavy heart. The first days at sea would shift the polarities of his men, and his job was to begin this even before they boarded. He started in medias res, his approach surprising to his listeners.

"I have always believed," he said, as rain drilled upon the tent and the wind tried to lift it, "that women bear the greatest burden of war. It is they who must wait, they who are deprived of action, they who must have the patience of not knowing, they who hold the family together alone, they who may lose and yet must continue, they who, like Athena, have a tranquil wisdom that puts ours to shame. Throughout history, we have made the world, but we made it for them. For, unlike us, they have the gift of receiving it. The woman I love puts it this way: she says I'm like the cat that drops a bird at the feet of its owner. And that's her."

They laughed.

"It's true. When I was young, when I played sports or sailed on the Hudson, I always imagined that somewhere in the air a particular girl was watching. I wanted to meet her expectations, to be worthy of her. Countless hours were spent in striving for her approval and shaping my life, for her.

"This is what you know—even should you not know that you know it—and what you feel when you part from them and you question what seems so much like a betrayal. Is it really for them, for women, and children, that I fight? On balance, will they be better off? Or have I been swept up by the part of me that would go to sea and debark on an enemy's shore to seek and find combat? Is it that same self that also builds, farms, invents, and loves?

"You may not say it out loud or think it, but your soul is divided as it seeks both the comfort of the hearth, the primacy of love; and the compulsion to see beyond the horizon, the impulse to draw the sword. In quiet times you may feel longing and regret, but I hope to make your days so full and your sleep so deep that you'll have little or no time to ache for home. If you stow your love in the deepest, safest place you can find, you'll keep it alive, you'll elevate the chances that you'll live, and a long deployment will pass swiftly.

"I'll expect of you perhaps more than any commanding officer you've ever had. And everything that you deliver—and deliver it you will—will be not only for your country and our mission, but for yourselves: to keep you lean, honorable, alert, and alive. Who wouldn't want that?

"You'll leave part of yourselves behind, and as the coast recedes and the ship powers ahead without cease in every kind of sea, you'll exit the present and enter that timeless realm which binds together all men at war from every age. Though it's neither glorious nor always terrible, in it you'll be awake to life. What you feel, what you apprehend, the visions that will appear, the fusing of past and present, the transformation of your soul into that of the universal soldier—whom you will come to know, for you are he, and he is you—will mystify and remain for the rest of your life. You won't be able to explain what happened to you, and you won't dare say what you suspect. But here, in this lashing rain, with the sea we are about to cross lapping at the wharf as if to call us away, I'll say it for you. You will have been to another world, a world in which the presence and prospect of death gives to life an intensity and illumination you'll never again see. Be grateful for what is to come, and fight as you have never fought before—to live, and to prevail."

The crew received this in silence. Not a sound for about a minute. Then the soaking-wet band began the Navy Hymn, and as it played Rensselaer said, without bravado, and almost sadly—but strongly—"Crew of the *Athena*, bring the ship alive."

They rose, and in tight, successive ranks, ran to the ship, up the brow, and to their stations. *Athena* came alive. That was how it was done, always with speed. Perhaps it was to give the men the momentum that enabled them to leave behind everything they would fight for, and everything they loved.

II

Blue Oceans, Bright Stars

On the sea, small beauties are exaggerated. An albatross riding on the air pressure born of collapsing wave crests, skimming the surface over and over for a catch. Or when somewhere between ship and horizon a white flash appears—the silver of a leaping fish or the crash of a diving shearwater, much as when in the Hudson Highlands, late in spring, white splashes of dogwood spark across distant landscapes of new green.

Set Course for Gibraltar

Commanding on the high seas and in crowded shipping corridors on its first commissioned deployment, a new ship, of a new type, with a new crew, is not easy. All the more so when the destination is war. Rensselaer was cautious because—although the way was open—the weather was coming in, the sea was already agitated, and some of the sailors had, as he put it, a deficit of experience. "Stand by your lines," came his amplified voice over the 10MC. "All right," he said, unamplified, and then once again held down the microphone button. "Cast off bow spring line." The sailor next to the bow spring line remained immobile. "Cast off bow spring line," Rensselaer repeated, wondering why his order hadn't been executed. Still, the sailor didn't move.

"Is he deaf?" Rensselaer asked Movius, the XO. The command had echoed off the buildings next to the wharf.

"He's new," Movius said. "Maybe he thinks he's on the bow line."

Rensselaer went back on the 10MC, the communications channel appropriate to this evolution. "Sailor most forward." The sailor turned to look up at the bridge. "You're on a spring line, the bow spring line. We have no bow line. Cast off your line." He did.

"Cast-off breast lines." It was done, lively. And then, "Cast-off stern lines." As the ship slightly cleared the wharf, Rensselaer commanded, "Shift colors," and the national ensign was run up the gaff, although it would not be there for long, as it was late in the day. "Left ten degrees rudder, indicate two and a half knots." The bow moved slowly to port. The inner harbor had no current, and the wind favored the maneuver. "Rudder amidships. Indicate three and a half knots." They began to move ahead. When they reached the passage north, Rensselaer commanded, "Hard right rudder, steady at three and a half knots." *Athena* swung to starboard, her stern moving to port. Then, before the bow hit the centerline of the passage, Rensselaer commanded, "Left ten degrees rudder." *Athena* straightened. "Rudder amidships, indicate five knots."

As they cleared the harbor and headed for the gap in the Bay Bridge-Tunnel, they increased speed. The ocean wind began to flow over the deck. You could almost see it, and it hardly ever stopped. Eventually, you came to expect it, and when it wasn't there, you could hear your heart beat. They cleared the gap, and soon Fort Story disappeared off the starboard side. The command was given to increase speed to thirty knots. Rensselaer had approved the course the quartermaster (the navigator) and the XO had set for Gibraltar, ordering that it was to be followed electronically as well as plotted by hand on the chart table every hour, and checked with sextant and chronometer at noon each day and two times nightly whenever the stars were visible. "Verify as well with RDF and depth soundings," he had said. "I want all methods recorded on the chart. I know the GPS is almost infallible, but I want to see how everything aligns. It's good practice if something goes wrong.

"In regard to sextant and chronometer, you'll like it. You'll see. They aren't as precisely accurate as the electronics, but you'll come close, which means you'll have agency, you won't be just a passive receiver. There's something wonderful about using a sextant. If you catch a fish and roast it over a fire you yourself have made, it tastes better than if it's served to you at a fancy restaurant. That's because, without effort, enjoyment is corrupted into nothing."

The distance to Gibraltar was 3,840 miles, which at thirty knots would take four and a half days. But due to wind, currents, and the possibility of heavy seas, and thus allowing for an effective speed of twenty-five knots, they would reach the Strait in five and a half days. Thence to Haifa to refuel—the high number of naval vessels transiting the Mediterranean necessitated replenishment at an expanded range of ports—through the Suez Canal, the Red Sea, the Arabian Sea, and to the Gulf, although this had yet to be formally communicated to the crew.

Rensselaer spoke to everyone aboard via the 1MC (the one-main circuit), which spread universally throughout the ship. It was his first general communication at sea. "This is the captain. Move from condition five to condition four. No email or telephonic personal communications, EMCON otherwise normal. Watches will be manned per posted bills and standard practice. Absent heavy weather, I'll address the crew at the first opportunity in daylight. There's bound to be some confusion at the outset. If you have a concern, speak to the chiefs, the XO, or me, in that order, save for emergencies when the chain of command may not be appropriate. You'll know when that is if it happens. I'll remain on the bridge at least through the evening watch, or possibly until the heavy weather subsides. Chiefs, double your reporting. Captain out."

*

At any moment, hundreds of thousands of vessels are at sea, from super-tankers and immense Panamax container ships to warships, small yachts, battered trawlers, and flimsy junks. In day after day of emptiness without sight of another, each will have been seduced to believe that the sea is empty and clear. And yet hundreds of thousands of courses will cross, even if seldom at the same time, as they are traced from port to port. Wariness of collision must be exercised not merely at the bow but abeam and astern, and though a whole lifetime on the sea may pass without a close call, the sense of another ship bearing down in the darkness or from fog and gray rain must be cultivated and maintained. Even in the empty quarters of the oceans, which should be the most relaxing places on earth, one must forever be alert.

The bridge on *Athena* would thus be continually as professional as it was now, but perhaps not as tense as on this, her very first watch, as night approached in challenging weather and through the heavily trafficked sea-lanes converging on Norfolk. Lack of visibility while navigating causes physical exhaustion, and for an hour the rain transformed the windows into nauseating lenses uncorrected by windshield wipers at even their maximum speeds. Then the rain stopped and the wind pressured remnant drops across the glass and into oblivion, as if the ship were in the drying phase of a carwash. Ahead was a low ceiling of black cloud with down-ward, tornadic-looking funnels and continual flashes not of white but of golden lightning in what appeared to be short, almost curly strikes from the bottoms of the clouds to the horizon. Above the dark clouds a peaceful-looking, luminous screen of white was flushed with pink. They were not yet out of the OPC Weather Area, from the Baltimore Canyon to Cape Charles Light, and not even one hundred nautical miles offshore.

The captain and XO glanced at the approaching storm and went about their work. The XO circulated among the stations, checking radars, plots, meteorological instruments, depth soundings, communications. Rensselaer made regular inquiries on the various MC circuits, and frequently polled the lookouts. When not thus engaged, he wrote in the log or on the chart, recording so many readings and observations that it was hard to believe the only thing happening was otherwise uneventful forward progress. The bridge was hushed and darkened except for quiet, formal commands and responses, instrument glow, and dim red lamps that were still hardly visible due to lingering natural light.

Josephson, a newly commissioned ensign, approached Rensselaer to ask if the funnel clouds and lightning were a threat. "They seem to be passing, sir," he said, "at great speed, and should be behind us in fifteen or twenty minutes."

"Probably so," Rensselaer replied.

"Then calm sailing, sir?"

"It doesn't work that way."

"Really? It looks like it. The background looks clear—well, white—and unmoving. Won't it be tranquil once the black clouds pass?"

"What do you think makes that wall of white?" Rensselaer asked. "Cloud? Fog? Haze? No."

"Sir?"

"That's rain, Mr. Josephson, so packed and driven that it looks like a white wall. The sea is now southeast at seven feet, wind twenty-two knots. Soon the lightning clouds, which are mostly dry, will have passed over us with much drama. Then the peaceful white curtain will hit *Athena* like a cannon. The sea will run from fifteen to twenty feet, the wind to fifty or sixty knots. You won't be able to see anything. The ship will rise in the air until you think it'll somersault backward, and then it'll plunge like a diving submarine. The waves will cover the foredeck, slamming into us with tens of thousands of pounds of water weight, which is why we tie down with welds, turnbuckles, and steel. Which is why I gave the order to inspect the tiedowns, secure outside doors and hatches, and make sure no one is topside.

"I could be wrong. We'll see."

A minute or so later the first strike came out of nowhere and hit an undistinguished patch of sea. It was near enough to rattle the bridge windows, within a second of the flash, with a report like a cannon blast. Other strikes followed, as random as the flashes of fireflies.

Rensselaer took a step forward, then turned back a little toward Josephson and the helm. "Somehow at home the mountains seem to soak up the lightning and thunder. Not on the sea. The strokes can be so close you feel like you're between two cymbals."

"Home is on the Hudson, sir?"

"Yes."

"There are mountains there?"

"Beautiful mountains." Rensselaer addressed the helmsman. "Helmsman, stay on your mark. Lighter touch. When she swings, she'll want to swing back. All she needs is a little help."

"Aye sir, lighter touch."

Rain began to bang against the windows, in huge, wind-propelled drops.

*

The captain had neglected to mention the groaning bulkheads, decks, and superstructure; the feeling of gravitylessness during twenty-foot drops through the air before the bows found water again; the blasts of wind that held wiper blades still and caused their motors to grind as gears moved against gears that had been stopped; and the alarming sound of the screws half out of the sea.

Lightning strikes that had been nearby as the dark clouds passed over now were directly astern, but jagged branches of light remained impressed upon the eyes long after the bolts of lightning had vanished, each an addition to an electric forest of ghostly dead trees, their former lives the color of the sun.

Then the storm passed, night fell, and *Athena* cleared the convergence zone close to Norfolk, where shipping lanes were compressed together for entry from all points. The sea ahead was open and calm, as if having passed through a barrier in space and time *Athena* had entered the anteroom of another world.

At 2200, having skipped dinner to remain on the bridge, Rensselaer went to get something to eat.

"The XO has the con," he announced.

"Aye, sir, I have the con," Movius answered. Rensselaer went below. He knew he would have to get used to trusting the ship to others even in the first hours out.

Athena had a tiny wardroom, but as the refrigerators were in the crew's mess, Rensselaer went there, took out a ham sandwich and a Diet Coke, grabbed a bag of potato chips, and sat down across from Di Loreto, who, upon Rensselaer's appearance, rose and stood at attention. "As you were," he was told.

"Captain, sir, I can awaken the cook."

"Absolutely not. He has to get up to cook at the close of midwatch."

"Too bad you missed dinner, sir: steak and spaghetti."

"This is fine. Uh . . . Marine Mammal Specialist Di Loreto?"

"Sir?"

"Why are you here alone? You're not eating."

"I didn't want to stay in my rack, sir."

"Soon it'll be lights out."

"Yes sir. Then I can go back."

"Did something drive you up here? You're not studying, or writing a letter. You're just sitting there. What's going on below?"

"Nothing, sir."

"Nothing?"

"Yes sir. It's nothing. It's just that they're doing something that makes me uncomfortable."

"Spill it."

"They're watching a pornographic movie, sir."

"You don't have to watch it, do you?"

"No sir, but I have to hear it."

"And why does that distress you?"

"My fiancée, sir. She's a woman. I get upset when I think that people would treat women this way. I can't explain it exactly, sir. It's like when people would make jokes about Lucy, saying they wanted to . . . violate her, sir. Or put her in a tuna salad. She was better than they were."

"I understand. Go back to your quarters. This meeting never took place. When I finish eating I'm going to make a surprise inspection. You, too, will be surprised. Am I clear?"

"Aye, sir."

The last thing Rensselaer wanted was to come down hard on his new crew the first night out. But the best soldiers were those with the strongest ethics in service of the highest purpose. Clear and unfettered sight, unburdened by corruption, was necessary in combat. Not only that, but from the perspective of the Iranian Revolutionary Guard Corps, a warship in which such corruption was endemic would be deserving of defeat, and although their perspective was not his, Rensselaer didn't want to give them that.

The IRGC could not know that some of the *Athena*'s crew had been watching a pornographic movie, but he would, and in the most subtle, unchartable ways, this might influence his decision-making, his feeling for battle, and his confidence in the justice of action. Every impulse told him to do what he did next.

After he finished his sandwich, his potato chips, and his Coke, he took his time in going below, and then stood for a moment at the entrance to the crew's quarters. Inside, everyone was turned toward a laptop across the screen of which passed flesh-colored patches to the accompaniment of an almost comical faked orgasm. Rensselaer cleared his throat. The sailors turned, panic arose, the laptop was slammed shut, and someone called out, "Attention on deck!"

Men jumped from their berths or rose from where they were sitting, and stood at attention. He let them hold position for longer than usual, began to leave, and said, "Carry on," with more than a hint of skepticism. They relaxed, but remained standing and motionless.

"You know," Rensselaer said, turning back, "before Nine-Eleven, the hijackers went to Las Vegas to watch nude dancing, and, maybe, consort with prostitutes. A lot of Americans thought this was to have a last fling before death. It wasn't. It was to allow them the justification for killing, in their view, corrupt and sinful non-believers.

"They treat their women like cattle, it's true, but they're onto something in regard to us. Let me ask you, not aggressively, but kindly, I hope. . . . Y'all"—he picked this up in New Orleans; Katy, too, said it sometimes—"have mothers. Some of you have wives, sisters, including little sisters, and some—I know—young daughters. Would you like them to be in a movie like that?" he asked, pointing to the closed laptop.

"These women are all daughters. Some are sisters, wives, mothers. Once, they were little girls. Okay, something happened to them, so now they sell their bodies. The golden rule of the New Testament—do unto others as you would have them do unto you—was lifted from a different formulation in the Hebrew Bible: do not do unto others, as you would not want them to do unto you. It's less proactive, and presumes less.

"I can tell you, that even if you don't know it, this kind of thing lowers your value to yourself in your own eyes and makes you less confident in your own defense. Perhaps, though it may not be much, enough to tip the balance in a closely run fight. That wouldn't be good, would it?

"The people who in not so many days we may be fighting believe that they're pure and we're impure. Purity before combat was the rule in ancient times, and has been ignored in the scientized West. Let me assure you that impurity of any kind will weigh upon you in a struggle even if you are unaware of it.

"When we confront those bastards who would kill us, we'll know what they think of us, and we'll know who we are. It's important, gentlemen, that we know they are wrong. It's a mystical but undeniable element of the fight. It's part of staying alive. Really."

"Yes, sir," someone said.

Rensselaer let some moments pass, and then bluntly added, "There's a moon out tonight."

For a moment, they thought he might be mad, but then he went on. "Would it be against Navy regulations to throw garbage overboard?"

They were beginning to cotton. "It would, sir," someone said meekly.

"It would. But would it be interesting to see how moonlight makes an interference spectrum across a DVD? In regular light you see a rainbow, but would you in moonlight?"

"I don't know, sir."

"That's a worthy physics experiment," Rensselaer stated. "And, as you know, DVDs are famously slippery, especially in the wind."

"Yes, sir."

"Carry on."

After he left, there was silence during which everyone looked at one another in unfeigned shock. Then they went topside into the moonlight and the wind.

*

Morning on the first day at sea was auspicious as *Athena* swifted through almost flat waters in a world of blue. Better than completely still waters, they rose and fell like gentle breathing, and the crew not on watch had slept that night with the constant song—if it can be called that—of waves meeting the ship. The color blue is the mariner's happiness, for so much of one's time on the sea is gray. This was one of those blue days between giant weather systems visible on computer screens and from space as their white pinwheels swirl like global cotton candy.

A passenger on a cruise ship or liner cannot fail to be impressed by the sameness of the sea. Flat and featureless, it is torturously unrelieved for days and weeks. But for the mariner, especially in the Navy, this is not so. Civilian maps of the undersea are detailed enough, but undersea warfare has necessitated military maps of astounding detail, for this is one of the ways submarines navigate. Thus, for the officers and bridge watch of *Athena*, the Atlantic crossing had waypoints and features that in giving character to their journey made it far more measurable and tolerable than were it just another species of partial sensory deprivation.

Nearly every foot was charted and identifiable, but they would be pleased the most as they glided above many great "seamarks." Departing, they had passed over the Albemarle Shelf Valley and would continue, in the Western Atlantic between the Sohm Plain and the Bermuda Rise, on to the Washington Canyon, and then the Hudson Valley. The latter was indeed the Hudson Valley and, although hidden in the depths, the same feature of the earth's crust as that in which Rensselaer had grown up amid apple orchards and whitewater kills that tumbled down to the river. After the Hudson came the Carstens Valley, and then *Athena* would sail just south of the Mytilus Seamount. The Picket Seamount would be left behind. Then across the Newfoundland Plain, over the Iberian Basin, north of the Ashton Seamount, between the Tagus Basin and the Tagus Plain, over the Lagos and Faro Canyons, and into the Strait of Gibraltar.

Prevailing westerlies would speed the ship entirely to its advantage until north winds sweeping the Atlantic edge of Europe necessitated a vectored course into the busy sea-lanes leading into the Med. What with wind, weather, light, and storm, and the continual activity and watchfulness over the ship and its functions, the passage was carefully worked and richly observed.

At 0900 during the forenoon watch, Rensselaer ordered all engines stopped and all hands on deck. The bridge watch stayed in place behind him, but they could hear every word as he addressed the crew, who had crowded on the starboard side, the younger ones sitting somewhat precariously on perches to which they had climbed, like the sailors clinging to every horizontal surface of the *Missouri* during the Japanese surrender in Tokyo Bay.

Some captains are menacing, some aloof, some too friendly, some too drunk on their pasts and their futures to see clearly what is in front of them, and a very few, in the dry Navy, drunk. Rensselaer's manner was that of a much older man, whose velocity of speech was slowed and compressed by experience and sorrow. But surprisingly for a man who had no children, it was paternal.

"You've seen the P.O.D., the watch bills, and the various supplementary schedules. I don't have to tell you that every day you'll be busy until you sleep. I'll be brief, so that you can return to your tasks.

"The weather and the sea are now ideal, but where we're going will be even bluer and brighter. The deck will be so hot sometimes that it'll burn your feet through your shoes, and the light will assault you. Although you'll think you might, you'll never quite get used to it.

"Were we a larger ship we'd have no need for cross-training. The various departments on destroyers, cruisers, and carriers have little need for it. There's no reason that engineering and combat systems should be on a command track, or that SWOs on that track should immerse themselves in other specialties to the point where they lose competency in ship handling and overall command.

"But we're different, and because we're different, we're going to train until exhaustion. When shells are slamming into the ship, the decks are slick with blood, your wounded shipmates are screaming in agony, the officers have been killed, and the smoke is thick and choking—if all this should come to pass—I want you to be able to do automatically that which will keep you alive, keep the ship afloat, and keep her fighting. So we'll drill in flash gear even in unbearable heat. We'll know where every single battle lantern is kept not only in our own spaces but everywhere. We'll load and carry ammunition almost in our sleep. We won't just shoot into the sea when we practice, we'll put out targets, hit them, and keep score. Every man will become adept at fixing a breach, driving a wedge, putting out a blaze, and placing a tourniquet. I want us to be the fastest, the most accurate, the most automatic, the most disciplined and yet the fiercest fighters you can imagine. That's how we'll stay alive, throw back the enemy, and animate the courage and best traditions of the Navy. Those, if we're lucky, will flow into us and give us strength, illuminate the great and good parts of honor, and connect us to the American sailors who came before us. When you fight on the sea as they did, you'll bring them back alive inside you, a rare and joyous thing that makes the world seem close to just.

"And we're almost sure to fight not only on the sea but on land. You may not have signed up for that, but war modifies all contracts. Half the ship's crew apart from the SEALs should expect to become naval infantry. Those left on board will have to do twice the work and must be prepared to operate outside their specialties even in the event of no casualties.

"Now, you may ask . . . who signed up for naval infantry, of which the United States, having Marines, has none? No one. And you don't have to do it. You can volunteer or not. It won't be held against you if you don't.

"And you may wonder what it's all about. We're likely to go ashore, a lot more than once, and the force we'll need has to be greater than our six SEALs if we're going to do it right and survive. Normally at Bahrain we home port ten PCs and four minesweepers. Now they're fully engaged. I don't know the present order of battle in the Gulf, but I imagine that we've got a line of destroyers and cruisers to protect Saudi oil facilities, and carriers close by in the Arabian Sea to join the airpower we've surged to Al-Udeid, A'Dhafra, and Saudi and Kuwaiti bases.

"The Gulf now sees constant combat. Most of the major Iranian surface combatants have been sunk, but Iran seems to have an unending supply of shore batteries, small craft, mines, and missiles. We're not going to the Gulf per se."

This struck everyone as odd, and it showed in their faces. Some of the bridge watch turned around to look at Rensselaer's back, as if to ask, *What?*

"Our job, because we have more speed, more weapons, and can stay on station longer than the other PCs, is to scrub the Iranian coast from inside the Strait of Hormuz at Bandar Abbás, around the southwest corner of the Iranian landmass, and three hundred miles east, almost all the way to Gwadar in Pakistan.

"This is a wild, poorly surveyed coast. We don't know exactly everything they have there, but we do know that there are anti-ship missiles, raiding craft, and garrisoned bases. To reduce the distance for our aircraft to get to their area of operations, the carriers and their screens are not that far out to sea. The screens are not as heavy as they should be, and even if they were, there's no question that we would take the fight to the threat.

"We'll be alone and will attack, by sea and by land, numerous bases, some heavily defended. Because of the scarcity, we have six SEALs rather than the nine we should have. So you'll want to learn and practice as much as you can. Harden yourselves like SEALs, know how to handle wound trauma, how to operate your weapons as if by second nature, and otherwise prepare in every way for what lies ahead.

"God willing, the war will be over by the time we get there, but, in war, God seldom seems willing."

*

Many hours of planning and scheduling made it possible to coordinate training, work, and intervals of programmed rest. Although every last one of the crew had volunteered for Rensselaer's naval infantry, fifteen were selected on the basis that, if necessary, their jobs could be done by others. The engineering department spared only one man, weapons operators other than gunners spared none. Most of the enlisted crew who customarily served as officer of the deck would remain on board, with the understanding that in the absence of those men who were allowed to volunteer, watches would be lengthened even beyond what they might expect in combat.

The quartermaster would remain, as navigation to rendezvous points had to be precise for exfiltrating landing parties. Movius, the XO, would have to stay on board, which disappointed him mightily. He didn't know that Rensselaer intended to lead every shore engagement, which was entirely out of the ordinary, but so was Rensselaer. During his cock-up in the Oval Office, he had thought that if he were president he would be duty bound, contrary to sense as it might be, to go with the first wave of troops into any battle to which his decisions might lead. It seemed only just, and even while he was speaking with the president he was thinking about this. He knew of course that he would never be president, because, among many other things, leading troops into battle as president was exactly what he would have done.

In the privacy of his small cabin, he told Movius of his plans to go ashore. Movius tried to dissuade him: Rensselaer should be in overall command, from the ship. It was important that the captain stay with his ship for many reasons, including an attack at sea. No captain should risk himself unnecessarily. He was much older than, and might be a burden to, the younger, fitter men. He had done his time, he had fought many battles. It was almost a duty to give way to others.

As Movius spoke, Rensselaer listened and was able to hear in the background the SEALs on deck as they began to instruct their new charges. His eyes fixed on the shelves above his desk, skipping over dozens of naval books and reference volumes, and landing upon a section he wondered if he might ever be able to touch: Tocqueville, *De la Démocratie en Amérique*, a fat French dictionary, a Bible, the collected poems of William Butler Yeats, those of Emily Dickinson, and a textbook of economics, a subject in which he deemed himself—and all others—highly deficient. When he read Emily Dickinson he was transported to the austerity and quiet of nineteenth-century, rural Massachusetts, neither far from nor more wintry than the Hudson Valley. So saintly, pure, and austere was she, that reading her was almost a religious exercise.

When Movius finished, Rensselaer, who hadn't paid that much attention, said, "Those are all excellent arguments, perhaps irrefutable, but they don't outweigh the fact that I'm going to have to send kids, and some family men, ashore, where more than a few of them may die. If I'm still alive, I'm the one who'll have to write the letters and visit the families.

"I won't be able to do that unless I take the same risks. If *Athena* were a destroyer or cruiser, I'd stay, but she isn't. Almost half the crew will be ashore, and you're overqualified in every way for command of a PC, so what I'm doing is not irresponsible."

"I understand. But—"

"No. Just answer this question: if you were in my place, what would you do?"

"All right," Movius said, relenting. "I suggest, then, that you do some refresher training, and let the SEALs tire you out a bit."

"That was my intention from the start, and once things run smoothly, I will."

"And, sir?"

"Yes?"

"I think I should tell you that I overheard a discussion among some members of the crew. It was a kind of argument about whether or not you were going to get us all killed."

"What did they conclude?"

"They didn't. But they did seem to take very seriously the need to train, and a few were of the opinion that it was just the opposite: you were the kind of CO that would help them stay alive."

"That's what I intend to do."

*

The next day, word spread below to come on deck. The engineering watch could not. *Athena* was sailing through and amid an agitated cloud of shearwaters, spectacular birds known mainly to seafarers. They migrate from one end of the earth to the other, forty thousand miles of flight in a year. Upon seeing a shoal of fish, they fold their wings and hit the water like bullets, streaking their lines thirty and forty feet down, a kind of rifle fire into the sea.

The sailors were awestruck as birds in their hundreds plunged into the waves. The ocean was clear blue, so the underwater trails were visible. Birds shot into the water, swam a bit, then emerged to take flight, all very rapidly, coming dangerously close to each other. Their abilities in air and water, the distances they traveled, their speed, and their grace were almost beyond belief.

They lived more than half a century, flying millions of miles, surviving where a man would die in a few minutes. They sheared the wave crests, taking energy from the air. And their name—descriptive to a T, onomatopoeic, and beautiful—was perfect. Every sailor on *Athena* who saw them was elevated, and would never forget.

*

In a feat of organization, the fifteen chosen volunteer auxiliaries to the SEALs—to whom Rensselaer referred as "The Chosin Reservoir"—were run through an NSW training pipeline integrated with their watches, meals, and rest. The six SEALs manned six stations, rotating so that they themselves could train in all of them.

A volunteer would start with a six-mile run on one of the treadmills, which was set to measure his progress at each session, advancing by degree until he could run the distance at a constant speed of ten miles an hour. Some would not make that benchmark, but all would improve immensely.

The second station was weaponry. Holworthy began by stating, "Remember, in shooting, weapons disassembly and assembly, and doing things in sequence, slow is smooth and smooth is fast. When you rush, you drop things, you miss, you fuck up. When you jerk, you waste energy and time and things don't align—a magazine doesn't insert until you're forced to wiggle it; a round isn't fully chambered; a knife not fully grasped falls from your hand; it takes two tries, or more, to get your pistol out of the holster. Things like that. Go slow to begin with, and get smooth. Fast will come as if by magic: don't push it."

Each sailor practiced assembling and disassembling an FN 5.7 pistol and an M4 automatic rifle. He learned sighting, ballistics, fire discipline, etc., and he threw live grenades into the sea so as to get comfortable with them—as most people, understandably, are not. This was very dangerous on the ship, which could be badly damaged if someone dropped a grenade that the instructor then failed to throw overboard. Despite his instruction, one sailor panicked at the pop when the handle of a grenade was released, and dropped it. The instructor SEAL tried to kick it overboard, but it went instead into an angle plate. Racing against the six seconds, three of which had passed, the SEAL dived for it, grabbed it, turned on his back, and with one and a half seconds left, threw it backward over his head. It traveled about fifteen feet out and exploded just after it hit the water. He stood up, fetched another grenade, and said to his ashen student, "Try again."

When they took apart their M4s, Holworthy guided them through each step. The last was the most sensitive. "If you don't hold the ejector down when you remove the pin, it'll jump out and you may lose it and its tiny spring. Without the ejector, the size of a vitamin pill, or just the spring, the size of a sesame seed; or the pin, the size of a grain of wild rice, the M4 is dead. You're supplied with extras, but don't take them for granted. You can lose them, too—in the dark, as the ship pitches or a truck drives rough, or when someone starts shooting at you when you're cleaning your weapon."

Station three was calisthenics. SEALs are good enough at calisthenics to banish the pride of professional athletes. On *Athena*, they started with warm-ups that deceived their students into thinking of yoga and dancercise. Then they were pushed to and beyond their limits. For example, they were asked how many pull-ups they could do. Most said they didn't know, and then struggled to do four or five. Their instructor then told him that when he finished with them they would have to be able to do forty. Between other sets he would have them at the pull-up bar until they hurt so much they thought they would be permanently disabled. That would be the concentration one day, and the next day it would be something else, including weights, rope climbing, and if the opportunity arose, a mile swim.

The fourth station was where they received instruction in ambush tactics, infiltration and exfiltration, wound trauma procedures, land navigation, hand signals, radio and sat-phone, and specialty phrases in Farsi and Baluchi: *hands in the air, drop weapons, get on the ground, who else is in there, no talking.* The sailors were grateful for classroom instruction after their near-death experiences during calisthenics.

The fifth station was marksmanship, a science and art. The science is procedure, the art is the ability to still the body and the mind. The weapon is hot, excitable, and noisy, but the shooter must be as calm as the surface of a mirrored lake. And above all, he must be practiced. They shot thousands of rounds, as did the .50-caliber gunners and the SEAL snipers. Initially it was extremely difficult, as the floating targets and the ship were constantly and separately in motion even when the ship was dead in the water. But this was good, because they learned to hit moving targets, three-quarters of the battle.

The last station was CQC, close-quarter combat: offensive and defensive, hand-to-hand, with knife, rifle, rock, and wall. Walls are the most underappreciated of weapons. Present at almost all combats—although, in some, rock formations, trees, or vehicles stand in their place—they are an anvil that by means of relative motion can be made to function like a very heavy hammer. The sailors would practice, in alternation, and for an hour, only two moves each session. The SEALs said that was how you made them second nature. "You've heard of muscle memory?" O'Connor asked. "There's no such thing. The memory is in the brain, which tells the muscles what to do. If you practice a move a hundred times a day for a hundred days, you'll never have to think about it. It'll be automatic and fast."

The intense training integrated with regular watches made everyone so tired that when given the opportunity they fell asleep instantly, dragged and pushed into a heavy, blessed darkness from which, to their amazement, they awakened as if just born, full of energy and eager to beat the records of the previous day. Not the chiefs, who were older. But the young ones, moving toward their highest potentials, became different people. And they enjoyed every breath of this new life.

HOLWORTHY

Movius and Holworthy were assigned to cabins smaller than Rensselaer's and large enough only for a bed and shallow closets and lockers. Dressing and undressing, they banged into the locker doors, the base of the bed, and sometimes even the ceiling. At least in their tiny retreats they had privacy and the white noise of highly efficient ventilation. They didn't suffer the comings, goings, snorings, and thuds of sailors in racks above and below them, but could get a secure and undisturbed sleep in *Athena's* cradle endlessly rocking.

With the North Star to port over a gently rolling sea, Holworthy retired to his cabin, more than pleasantly exhausted. He shed his clothing, hanging it on hooks placed high enough so that they would not gouge the scalp of even the tallest sailor scrambling to dress in the dark. As he often did, he ran his hands over his arms, pinched his sides at the waist, and lifted his right arm to feel the tense musculature at the shoulder. He passed inspection, and no wonder, as he had done twice as much exercise as those in the two PT groups he had led that day, and run not six miles but twelve. He never let himself go.

Rensselaer was like this, too, but decades older, no match for Holworthy, who figuratively was forever cocked with a round in the chamber. SEALs had downtime. Not Holworthy. Even when he first joined, the SEALs had nothing to teach him in regard to readiness.

Unless he has the discipline to will himself to oblivion, it is hard for someone never unprimed for battle to fall asleep. Almost every night, Holworthy had to get himself past certain memories and speculations that monopolized the dark. He had tired himself out. The roll of the sea was conducive to sleep. The steady whoosh of cool, fresh air made the tiny cabin seem unconfined. He switched off the light, reclined, pulled his cotton blanket comfortably up to his sternum, felt his nakedness against the sheets, and closed his eyes.

He knew, however, that sleep would come only after hours of turning and thrashing over and over again in his mind the dominant memories, images, and emotions that had been with him almost all his life. A problem without an answer can repeat its questions and tortures without end. He tried, as always, to banish it, and, as always, he failed.

*

Amid West Texas fields still khaki and beige, trees budded but unleaved, and streams almost winter-cold, a schoolhouse sat in the warmth of bright sun as a spring wind whipped the flag and knocked its halyard and metal buckles against an aluminum pole. The wooden building without an ounce of steel was sheathed in worn shakes as brown as a horse's coat. It was two storeys high, with a sloped, shake roof. Since the 1920s, it had held classrooms for grades one through five, and was fronted by a playground and flanked by a patch of woods leading down to a brook.

On the second floor, the third-grade classroom was reached by a windowed stairway that led directly outside. Among the eight-year-olds sitting attentively at their desks were the Holworthy twins—Holworthy and his sister, Alice. Like Holworthy, she was blonde and blue-eyed, and as lovely as a child can be. Miss Daniels was their teacher. At age eight they wouldn't have known, but she was sixty-seven. She had straight, unkempt, almost shoulder-length white hair, thick glasses, and hands strong enough so that in her frequent and inexplicable flashes of temper she was capable of picking up Holworthy, carrying him to the back of the classroom, and throwing him into a closet, with the command to stay put until he was sorry for what he had done, which most of the time—if not all of the time—was nothing.

Miss Daniels, who always wore a tweed suit with a brooch, seemed to have it in for the Holworthys, who didn't know why, and, in the way of children, never told their parents of her obsession. But all the children were aware of her dazed, confounded look, and that sometimes she would trail off in lessons and stare straight ahead, mouth slightly open as if she had caught sight of something terrible. She would yell at them for no reason, especially at Alice. And no one knew why, perhaps not even the teacher herself, although when she lost her temper and screamed at Alice, sometimes charging at her desk, she would suddenly stop herself and retreat into her look of terror and confusion.

On a spring day that Holworthy would never forget, their father was going to pick them up after school and take them fishing. Because it was windy, and because to get to the river they had to walk through burs and brambles, their mother had put Alice's hair in a single gold braid, which fell to the middle of her back. When Alice came into class that morning, Miss Daniels had said only, "A braid." The way she said it was disapproving. But this was how she was.

After lunch, when the children had returned from sandboxes and swings, they had reading. When it was Alice's turn to read a paragraph in an old book about taking a sleeping-car journey, Miss Daniels asked, "Why did you braid your hair?"

"My mother did."

"All right, why did *she* braid your hair?"

"We're going fishing."

"You're going fishing," Miss Daniels repeated, her anger rising. "What does braiding your hair have to do with fishing?"

Frightened of what might come, Alice said, "By the river."

"By the river. By the river. Yes," Miss Daniels now almost shouted, "we know that fish live in water. I asked you why you braided your hair!"

"My mother did!" Alice shouted back, her voice rising in fear. Holworthy piped in, "It's because—"

"I didn't ask you! I asked Alice. Now. . . . " She was standing directly in front of Alice's desk. "*Why . . . did . . . you . . . braid . . . your . . . hair!*" She banged her right hand on the desk, and then drew back, shocked at herself.

By this time, Alice was crying uncontrollably, but still seated. Miss Daniels returned to the front of the class, stood in silence for more than just a moment, and then looked at Alice with such fear, confusion, and sadness that Alice stood, pushed back her chair, ran to the French door that led to the stairs, hesitated, and then the only sound was that of her feet on the steps, and the outside door opening and shutting.

Five minutes passed in silence as the students uncomfortably tried to read in the books opened before them. Agitated and not knowing what to do, Holworthy turned in his chair and was about to go after Alice, when Miss Daniels took a few steps forward, seized his shoulder, and shoved him down in his seat.

Eventually she resumed the lesson, and then started on the next one. He had no idea what it was about, and as Alice failed to return, the hours passed in an agony of indecision. She was probably sitting on a swing or in a sandbox, and certainly she was upset. He should comfort her. But he couldn't leave. Though Miss Daniels wasn't at all big, compared to him she was a giant. At three o'clock, his father would arrive and take him and Alice fishing, and everything would be all right.

What if Alice were not all right? He oscillated between determination to go after her and what he felt was his cowardly fear of running out of class in open defiance of Miss Daniels, who had not only thrown him into the closet but more than once lifted him from the floor by his ears, and swatted him as she threw him. And, he thought, what would it look like if the two Holworthys had misbehaved that day? They might be thrown out of school, and his parents would be very angry.

*

The bell rang at three o'clock. Without retrieving his lunch box and his jacket, he ran down the sunny, wooden stairs. Smiling and totally unaware, his father was waiting. Holworthy scanned the empty playground.

"Where's Alice?" he asked, obviously alarmed.

"What do you mean? *She hasn't come down,*" his father asked. "Isn't she up there?"

"No."

"Are you sure?"

In tears, Holworthy told his father what had happened. His father quickly scanned the playground, and then charged upstairs, Holworthy close at his heels.

"Where's my daughter?" his father demanded, so threateningly that it froze the room.

"She ran out of class."

"When?"

"After lunch."

"You didn't go after her?"

"I called out."

"No you didn't. You're a liar," young Holworthy said.

His father grabbed the teacher by her tweed suit so hard that the brooch fell to the floor. "You call the police immediately and assemble the teachers to search for her. If you don't," he said, trembling with anger, "if you don't. . . ."

Then he broke away and flew down the stairs, Holworthy following.

"Where might she have gone?"

"I don't know. I thought she would be in the playground."

"She's not. We'll look there," his father said, already breaking toward the woods. "Two and a half hours! Keep me in sight."

Calling her name continuously, they entered amid the trees. Holworthy remembered that Alice's hair had been braided, and he thought it was good that she wouldn't have tangled it in the newly greening briars. It was even somewhat exciting to be on this mission, helping his father, who had decisively taken command. If his father were there, nothing was to be feared. It was even more exciting when he heard the siren of a police car. Miss Daniels would be scolded. His father would see to that. It was great that she had been so afraid of him.

To the rear, teachers and police entered the woods, calling for Alice. It echoed and echoed. As he approached the stream and saw her, he heard his father and the others calling out. Her dress and underclothes were on the ground nearby, a corner of the dress caught on a bramble vine as if hung deliberately. Her skin was white as he had never seen it, her body bruised and bloody, her eyes and mouth open as she lay on her back as if staring at the sky.

He could have saved her. He didn't.

The Classical Sea

Unlike the vast Atlantic, the narrower Mediterranean offers frequent and changing views of islands and coasts, and is well endowed with subsurface features even if it is shallower and they are therefore less dramatic. *Athena* would pass through the Alboran Sea close to the Spanish coast, then hew to the African littoral all the way to the turn at Tunis. Then she would sail east-southeast, between Sicily and Malta, through the Ionian Sea and over the Hellenic Trough, south of Crete, above the Ptolemy, Pliny, and Strabo Trenches, north of the Herodotus Basin, and into the Middle East at Haifa.

Five days after she had put forth upon the open deep, *Athena* was gliding over swells (though sometimes lifting and dipping, with minor suction on the lift and a crushing of foam on the dip) as the sound of the Slave Chorus from *Aida* came over the Rensselaer-financed sound system. Of many kinds of music, this seemed most appropriate. Born of the Mediterranean, in dry, clear air, under a cloudless sky and strong sun, its rhythmic cadences elided ineffably with the roll of the sea.

In his cabin at midmorning, Rensselaer checked the weather at the junction of the Annaba and Tunisie forecast areas. Nothing to worry about. As he was doing this he thought he heard the faint strains of something other than *Aida*. Sometimes air catching on a metal edge, or a bulkhead vibrating in resonance with an engine or auxiliary motor, can sound like distant music, so he dismissed it and went on to review cables and reports. He then noticed a persistent yaw as the prow and stern oscillated rather more than a degree from side to side. It was so slight that someone with less time at sea might not have been aware of it. He put down his pen and looked up at the telltale. He was right. *Athena* would move a degree or two to port, then to starboard, and so on. He knew that this wasn't a result of high winds, because winds high enough to pressure the ship even slightly off course would have driven swells deep and high enough to make a substantial pitch, and the pitch was still gentle.

The faint music grew steadily louder. Listening closely, he detected a beat, and then a backbeat, and then what could only have been words.

Thinking that maybe the SEALs were using their own music for calisthenics, he went out on deck, where he saw that almost the entire crew had assembled on the port side. He looked toward the bridge. The bridge watch appeared to have drifted to the port side bridge wing. Anyone who had a binocular had pressed it to his face.

Sometimes, especially after long periods at sea, crews would behave this way on account of whales, a foreign warship, a tall ship, or the spectacular passage of an American carrier strike group. Realizing that the alien music came from off the port beam, and taking a few steps farther, Rensselaer saw an enormous yacht, bigger than *Athena*, from which the music was now booming. Running parallel with and a few knots slower, it was perhaps three hundred feet away on an eastward course into the Strait of Gibraltar.

Seizing a binocular from a boatswain's mate (who had been too absorbed to salute), Rensselaer read *Naughty Girl, London,* just before *Athena* drew past the point where he would not have been able to see the *Naughty Girl*'s transom. And then he saw what had magnetized his crew: a dozen people were on the *Naughty Girl*'s starboard side, brightly illuminated in the sun. Half were men, even the fat ones, in absurd, thong-like, European "bathing suits," and the other half were women, all of them young and variously slim or semi-voluptuous, also in thongs, some topless.

The women were lithe and tan, they held drinks in their hands, and a few of them were dancing to the lurid rock music, coyly and otherwise aware that they had taken momentary command of an American warship. To any sentient being it was clear that given the safety of three hundred feet of open water they were teasingly offering themselves to the sailors, who were painfully tortured—and enjoying it. The opera could no longer be heard.

The yacht was of a different world—loose, unthinkingly rich, soaked in pleasure and release, and entirely out of reach of everyone on *Athena*, most of whom were unable to turn away. An attractant so strong, this boatload of heroin in the sun drew every atom of their bodies.

"Who owns that boat?" a sailor asked Movius.

Without missing a beat, Movius answered, "Princess Olga, famous for her parties, her jewelry, and her magnificent balls."

Amidst the laughter that ensued, Rensselaer stepped forward. No one was aware that he had entered. Even the OOD and the helmsman were looking chiefly to the side, with breaks to check ahead, their eyes fixed on the bikinis or abridgment thereof. Rensselaer cleared his throat. All turned—"Attention on deck!"—and saluted, but their eyes darted right back to port.

"I have the con," Rensselaer said.

"The captain has the con," the OOD confirmed.

"Helmsman, increase speed to fifty knots," the captain commanded.

"Increase speed to fifty knots, aye, sir."

Within seconds, like a sprinter from the blocks, *Athena* gained enormous speed and left *Naughty Girl* in her wake. This was Rensselaer's way of restoring discipline and a sense of mission to his small company, asserting dominance over *Naughty Girl*, and affirming the dignity and seriousness of his ship.

Nothing more was said, and the crew probably had not imagined the desire flaring within their captain as well. Like them, he might have lost himself to the attraction of the women's bronzed bodies in the sun, on an almost blindingly blue sea, beyond the jurisdiction of nations, beckoning in the heat. But leaving the yacht behind brought its own satisfactions—the wielding of power, the acceptance of duty, the love of Katy, and the wish to return home. Later, Rensselaer told the XO, "I looked her up in the registry. *Naughty Girl* belongs to Ian Carmichael, a hereditary peer who sits in the House of Lords. English aristocrats, including most royals, are decadent twits who fuck like bunnies and live like barbarians because others clean up the messes they make. But as far as I knew when I took the con, it belonged to Princess Olga, known for her magnificent balls, so that had nothing to do with it. It was just that someone had to look ahead, and I guess it was me."

As soon as *Athena* had sufficiently separated from *Naughty Girl*, the lovely strains of the Slave Chorus reasserted themselves and mated once again with the smooth Mediterranean swell.

When *Naughty Girl* was no longer visible astern, and a sense of forward urgency had been restored, *Athena* slowed to thirty knots so she could make Haifa without refueling. Although they had not even begun to meet the tests of combat, and had not yet felt the full powers of the classical sea, much less of the waters off Arabia, they felt a sense of mission and history. The relatively shallow Mediterranean has an endlessly deep story, a life of its own. To fight in this sun, and on this sea. . . .

Athena and her little company pushed east against the track of the sun until, ahead, the great pillars came into view. Port and north was Gibraltar, Europe massively expressed as if recoiling from the immensity of Africa. Starboard and south was Jabal Musa in Morocco, the African gate, rising from the sea and taking on various shades of blue. With Europe to the left and Africa to the right, they glided forward. Jabal Musa rises almost three thousand feet from sea level. White clouds flow down its arid, blue sides cut with crags, valleys in beige, and scars of off-white. The northernmost emissary of the world beyond, all the way to the Southern Ocean, it seemed of such height as to lighten into the near nothingness of the clouds scudding over its summit.

*

At dinner, the day still bright, the officers assembled in their tiny wardroom. Training and watch routines were now running as intended, and this was the officers' first formal meal. Over coffee and dessert—a chocolate mousse and *gaufrettes* more suitable to a flagship and that any sensible person would have thought far beyond the capabilities of a cook on a PC—Rensselaer began the first of many discussions, remnants from the nineteenth and even the eighteenth centuries, when officers were highborn and expected to be comfortable in a Georgetown or Beacon Hill drawing room. It was much less formal now, but still a proving ground for those who were assumed to value virtue and knowledge, where civilized discourse, professional or otherwise, was required. The universities only imagine that they have a monopoly on such things.

"Gentlemen, on a PC we're lucky to have a wardroom even if it's not that much bigger than a closet. We have no silver, no swords, no credenzas, no sideboards, no awards. What we do have is a space in which to separate ourselves in satisfaction of the unfortunate but necessary task, contrary to every democratic impulse, of maintaining separation from the crew."

"Sir?" Josephson, the new ensign, asked, not because he didn't know.

"The Chiefs are old enough to be your father, Mr. Josephson, and you have to show them due respect. You'll seldom give them direct orders. Rather, you'll say, 'I think we should . . . ' 'Chief, will you . . . ?' 'Let's . . . ' 'It's time to . . . ' Only when in combat, or when time is of the essence, or when following well-worn paradigms such as getting underway or docking will you give them direct orders. They know more than you do. But you have command. Were you not to maintain some distance, their age and experience would sandblast away the now fragile authority into which you have yet to grow, and then where would you be?"

Josephson smiled somewhat painfully.

"The same goes for the crew. Many ratings are farther along than you. Command must always be firm, always respectful, always confident. You need an artificial means to pull this off, especially when you're young. Distance. Custom. The wardroom."

Movius added, "It can't help but be a class system. The only thing that maintains it is willingness and faith. If we don't uphold it, they won't either. You really have to practice it, or it'll evaporate right in front of your eyes."

"Sadly," Rensselaer seconded, "he's correct. It doesn't comport with the way we've been brought up as Americans, at least if you're not some kind of stupid snob, of whom there are plenty."

"Who?" asked Marchetti, the weapons officer, wanting to lead his CO into interesting but perhaps fraught territory.

"They exist by the millions." Rensselaer paused and then went on. "I love America, I miss it, I wish I were home. But do you know how many people have sprung up whose sustenance is to feel that they're superior to everyone else?"

"Certainly," Marchetti said. And then, wanting to be entertained, "Specifics, sir?"

Rensselaer obliged. "People who think they're better because they drive a fancy car, live in a fancy house, went to a fancy college. I spent four years at Harvard getting a Ph.D., and I can tell you, they think they're better than everyone else—*in the whole world*, except perhaps for Oxford and Cambridge. And you wouldn't believe how many of them are actually idiots and glorified clerks. People who think manual labor, and therefore the people who do manual labor, are below them. People who think that people like us, and police, and firemen, are just suckers who put their lives on the line because we're too stupid not to."

"So why do we then, sir?" Josephson added. "We should all know. We should be absolutely clear."

"You tell me."

"To defend the Constitution, sir, to make a more perfect union."

"To make a more perfect union, Mr. Josephson?"

"Yes, sir, that's what the Constitution says."

"Tell us what that means, exactly."

"Well, we've got the Constitution, but then our job is to make the country more perfect in fulfillment of it."

"Is that what they taught you at . . . ? I've forgotten."

"William and Mary, sir. And in high school."

"They still teach U.S. history in high school?"

"Mine did."

"What is the union? Give a definition."

Somewhat puzzled, Josephson said, "The United States, America, our country."

"So we're supposed to perfect our country, and Lincoln fought to perfect our country."

"Yes, sir," Lieutenant Velez, the COMMS officer, confirmed, coming to the aid of his junior.

"No."

"No?" Movius asked.

"No. The high school, and William—and Mary—were incorrect. The union is not the country. Neither the framers nor Lincoln would have agreed with Mr. Josephson, although they would have certainly appreciated his service," Rensselaer added wryly.

They awaited further explanation. A spoon stirring sugar into a china cup made a rather tense, bell-like sound. Rensselaer said nothing, letting the tension build, because he knew that if he said nothing they would think he was a bit out of his mind. And because they didn't know him, they did fear that he would leave the subject hanging.

But he didn't. After a rather torturous minute (in silence, awaiting an answer, a minute is a long time), when the officers feared for the rest of the voyage, he said, "Contrary to uninformed opinion, the union is not our country, and never was a country; is not people or a people; is neither institutions nor territory nor even a government. As Hamilton, Madison, the Framers, and the people themselves understood it in 1789, when they spoke of a more perfect union, and as Lincoln knew, the *union* was the relationship and agreements among the states that allowed them to come together to form a country.

"The difficulty lay in accommodating the disparate interests, cultures, economies, and histories of the colonies. Our early history was always threatened by centrifugal forces, which is why Adams observed that the Articles of Confederation were more like a treaty than a constitution, and why the Continental Congress was called a congress, not a parliament.

"The union is the mechanism that enables the states to accommodate each other's interests and come together in the federal structure that has *become* a country. Read *The Federalist* and see. *Union* is an abstract noun, and perfecting the union is perfecting the relationship between the states rather than the people or institutions within the states and, subsequently, the country. It has nothing to do with the Marxist dialectic that has lured people to believe that human nature is perfectible and can lead to the 'new man.' How much time has been wasted and blood shed for theorists and tyrants on their missions of perfection? But, yes, Mr. Josephson, we do what we do to defend the Constitution, and would die for it, as in fact we may. And we do what we do to defend that which we love and that which is worthy of love even if it is not our own."

"A complicated subject, sir," Movius said, "for any wardroom. Even on a carrier, with silver, stewards, and early American furniture."

"Those are wonderful things, it's true," Rensselaer added, "but, here, we don't need them. Our situation will be more than enough to augment the qualities of thought and action."

*

Rensselaer was concerned that his wardroom instruction might have been preening. He had spoken as if in a high-numbered graduate seminar in which a certain fraction of the participants were themselves professors. There, the as-yet-uncertified doctoral candidates fed nitroglycerin into their engines in an all-out effort to speak eloquently, show mastery of the subject, and hide the fact that they were desperately auditioning for jobs. Even though at the time he had a job, in the Navy, and was being paid handsomely as he studied, Rensselaer himself had fallen into this—it was the spirit of the place—and had pirouetted with the best of them, speaking in well formed paragraphs and careful to exclude any of his idiosyncratic Western New England dialect in favor of a more standard English. Sometimes in the midst of this competition he would be overtaken with embarrassment and shame, and flush as red as someone undergoing a medical emergency. The authenticity and honesty of this never failed to attract fine women, who knew that calculating, manipulative men do not blush.

When he returned to his cabin after his disquisition on the Constitution he blushed like a space heater, as if Katy were right there, gently and without a word reprimanding him for having shown off in front of his officers. So, with the caution of someone who had suffered justified reproach, he started his first letter to her, which was written as if she and the women who more than once had silently reached out to him across seminar tables were one. That is, she and they had the magical quality— confined to women perhaps because they are in such need of it given the rougher nature of men—of loving-forgiveness.

"Dear Katy," he wrote.

"I'd very much like to tell you where we are, what we've seen, and what we do, but I can't. Of the various levels of EMCON (electronic emissions control), we're now operating in perhaps the lowest, but we have mail censorship. I get to censor my own mail, and could myself censor the crew's mail or assign it to an officer, but we're such a small ship that I didn't want anyone to have that kind of knowledge of the others. So although mine goes straight through, the rest will be reviewed off ship by someone who doesn't know us.

"Patton was able to tell Beatrice, his wife, where he was, by saying, for example, 'Where we saw the ducks.' This wouldn't have gotten past the censor, even though it didn't give his position away, but he could do it because like me he could censor his own communications. There the resemblance stops, and I wouldn't do what he did, not only because it would violate my oath, but because we didn't see any ducks and on the open sea there are no ducks to see.

"My reportage must be limited, but there are certain specifics that will clear the bar.

"One of them is that day by day I've been learning the lesson—which applies to us and perhaps to all who love one another—taught by a coura- geous and brilliant being the size of a freckle and the weight of a few specks of dust. Like a politician's, the brain of this being is so small that you'd need a microscope to see it.

"But unlike a politician, my tutor is much smarter and of better character. He's a light-colored, almost translucent spider with legs much thinner than a hair. He may have joined us in New Orleans or in Norfolk, I don't know, but he's made his home inside a glass-fronted cabinet that holds a fire extinguisher and an axe. There's no reason to have a glass front on a ship of war, but somehow this one has it. I have no idea how it got there. It's the only one. It's mounted on the mess deck, near an outside door. There's a gap where it's attached to the bulkhead. Flies get in, and so does the wind. The spider can survive for a long time on one fly, but the gap that allows the fly to enter also channels bursts of wind when the outside door is opened, and the wind attacks his web.

"I'm not going to repeat the famous lesson of Robert the Bruce, who watched a spider in his prison cell fall and patiently climb again and again. Rather, a different lesson. When the complex web (it's a wonder: three-dimensional, a thousand elements) breaks, rather than rushing to rebuild it to its original complexity, the spider takes deliberate steps to shore up what's left, and then he is content with it, knowing that it's stronger than what came before. The wind has shown him what is strongest, and he sticks by it.

"So many people, as they're worn down by the world, lose everything in an attempt to re-create what once they had, or wished for, rather than shoring up what they have at the moment. Somehow we found the wisdom of that spider, and in middle age have come close to the perfection we couldn't reach even in youth. What a surprise it has been, how exciting, reassuring, and enjoyable. I keep on falling in love with you, and I don't think it will ever end.

"That's only an expression. It will end, and we know that, but, you know, think about it, on still nights wolves will still call in northern forests; snow will sweep across summit crests in glassy chains; the gem of the sun will never cease to glide across the sky; or waves break against unknown beaches; or grasses wave in the wind; and the whales will breach and sound. Until the sun burns out, life will never die. What could be a greater comfort? Although I have no solution to and no comfort for missing you.

"Except perhaps that we both believe that the quality of love is such that it springs over even the last great wall. I used to think that the candles lit in commemoration allowed the dead to speak in the dance of flame, and that the flame's gyrations were the struggle of a voice that no one could hear as it called out to no avail. Now I have a different view. I think they are heard. I think now that this is not as naïve as I once would have thought, and although I have no proof but only faith, I believe that the quality of love is such that once truly liberated it cannot be forced into any kind of confinement, and that somehow we will always be together.

"Only faith, only love, can lead to such a belief, for which all great art is an insistent hint and all beauty a model of what's to come. This doesn't comport with the traditions of the Navy. We're trained out of faith and into proof. We're trained to be suspicious of many forms of perfection. Round numbers, for example, are said to be untrustworthy, a sign of someone's guesses, or fudging.

"That is, it hardly comports with the traditions of the Navy except when burying someone at sea, when work, pride, and conscious effort pale before the unknown that reduces us to supplicants of hope and faith.

"What have I done? I don't want to be serious in this way. All I want is to hold you. This is my last deployment. I see every mile and every inch of the ship's progress however convoluted it may be, as distance covered on a course back to you. There's so much to look forward to (including never ending a sentence with a preposition).

"I hope my letters get to you, and yours get to me. There's no guarantee. We don't have vertical replenishment, and mailbags are always getting rerouted and missing the ships for which they're intended, especially as we have few port calls and those we have are subject to change.

"Stephen."

*

Their orders were to get to the Gulf with dispatch, but *dispatch* is not a precise term. They had to weigh the urgency of reinforcing the Navy in a war that was grinding on longer than many had thought, against the necessity of arriving in a tight and ready ship. They didn't want an engine problem that would take weeks to fix. So that, and conserving fuel to make it all the way to Haifa, capped their speed except in short exercises. And for morale as much as physical training, they had two swim calls in the Mediterranean, one in the Malta Channel and the other south of Crete.

In both, the sea was calm, the sun piercing, all-encompassing, its infrared felt in insistent pulses. In the Malta Channel they swam a mile. South of Crete it was two. The air above the water was hot and dry, the world below—and the sky—sapphire blue. Both swim calls were held after sailors not on watch had spent an hour or two moving ammunition, of which there was a great deal, to stock the magazines and load watertight storage containers on deck with various mixes of type. After such heavy work in ninety-degree heat, it was easy to get the men in the water—except for one, a gunner's mate named George Washington, who was quite fearful, and inquired of Movius if it was safe in regard to sharks.

"Sir, I'm from New Jersey, and a hundred years ago there was a great white who swam up the creek and ate a coupla kids."

"Mr. President," Movius said, calling him what everyone else did, "virtually no one gets eaten by sharks in the Mediterranean. Remember those girls in bikinis? They had a swim platform on their yacht. If *they're* not afraid, why should the father of our country be afraid?"

"You're sure about that?"

"I'm not, but the captain is. He's going in, too."

Rensselaer swam the mile, and as he did he thought of Katy swimming. She swam every other day, alternating it with running. In a bathing suit, she was breathtaking. And then, off Crete, he swam the two miles, and he thought of Katy again, picturing her at the pool—lithe, light, serious, and strong, looking so beautiful as she concentrated upon her laps and speed.

*

One evening not long after the swim call, Rensselaer addressed the crew as a whole for the second time, the lookouts and bridge watch hearing him while attentive elsewhere. The sun was casting a golden light upon the east, and the sea, lightly breathing, its surface smooth, was rolling but not breaking.

"I know you want to hit your racks, so I'll be brief. Not too brief. Our days are tiring, as they should be. We repeat things over and over, a thousand times over, so that they'll become part of you by the time we're on station. And the watch and training bills are complex and demanding. But you've done well. Master everything we exercise, until its practice isn't a burden and it's as fast as it can get. As your instructors have undoubtedly told you many times, slow is smooth, and smooth is fast. With time, smooth gets faster and faster.

"We've done okay with naval customs, but on station they'll be abridged. And given that we should train like we fight, we'll abridge them starting now. I appreciate your salutes the first time in the day you see me. Drop them. We're too small a ship. It wastes time, because, as you know, I'm everywhere. And if I or another officer goes ashore with you in combat, that venerable habit could cost us our lives. From now on, no need to come to attention unless it's expressly called for.

"Do your jobs. Practice overkill. Before you sleep, think things out. Envision your weapons and your actions. We'll push you hard, and then you should push yourselves harder. And know this: before battle, if we can help it, you'll have had the opportunity to rest. There are two things in combat of which you can never have enough—sleep and ammunition. We have one more day until we get to Haifa, refuel, and take on provisions. In Haifa you'll have ten hours liberty. That is, those of you lucky enough not to have pulled work detail. Enjoy yourselves, relax, and don't get into trouble. If you fail to rejoin the ship when we cast off, you'll get to know the Chesapeake brig. Tomorrow, push hard. By morning we'll be anchoring in Asia, in a country that's been at war since its birth. Like it or not, you'll be representing the United States. Carry yourselves modestly and with dignity."

*

The next day started with sparkling mist at sunrise, when the whole world, in deepened color, seemed lit as if by the special lights of a jeweler's case. Soon enough, in a fiery sun north and east of Egypt, the crew sprinted into the last day of its training. Given the gunfire of the .50-calibers, miniguns, the MK-46, and the M4s, as well as the SEALs' sniper rifles and machine guns, one would think they were already at war. In honing their accuracy, they exhausted thousands of rounds of ammunition. Even so, they would be left with a greater load than any PC, and would take on even more at Djibouti after transiting the Red Sea.

Not a moment passed when one group or another was not firing, practicing close-quarter combat, doing calisthenics, attending classes, calculating firing solutions, launching and recovering the RHIB, maintaining equipment, or standing watch. Taught and oppressed by common tasks, they came to know one another quickly.

The intensity of training encompassed all disciplines, but some examples might be illustrative. When not on watch, every sailor of the landing force—the volunteers of which had been winnowed down to twelve—carried his M4 all the time, so that it became almost part of him. He was given a little plastic bag with three sets of the tiny extractor, pin, and spring necessary for the operation of the M4 bolt and so easy to lose, and would carry them in a pocket. He had field stripped and reassembled the weapon over a hundred evolutions, the last twenty in total darkness. He was then trained in advanced marksmanship, combat reloading, fire discipline, and squad tactics. He fired two thousand rounds at moving targets. In close-quarter combat, he was taught the sequence of moves required to kill an opponent armed with a knife, and these were repeated, literally, a thousand times. Because of that, unlike so much else he had learned, he would never forget.

Everything was accomplished with similar urgency and intensity, and when the sailors collapsed into their racks they fell into a deep sleep within seconds. But it was a wonderful sleep, because they knew they were doing exactly what they should have been doing, and they had the satisfaction of giving it all they had.

*

Although they had not seen that much of its coasts, something about the Mediterranean spoke strongly even to those who knew little of its history. If land could speak or chant, every foot of its shoreline would have an incident to recall or a song to sing. Though no physical explanation could possibly be forthcoming, the quality of the water and the air, and above all the light, communicated indelibly that here civilization was born, God appeared to believers, and the stories of the West took shape with such power that they have continued to echo as if ongoing. And it was appropriate to the waters of the seas within this sea—the Tyrrhenian, Adriatic, Ionian, Mirtoan, Cretan, Aegean—that a ship named *Athena* glided upon them.

Looking up at the stars, which seemed to lurch across the sky back and forth as the ship rolled, the smoke from its stack dirtying for a moment air as sharp and bright as crystal, even the simplest of sailors was moved by the persistent radiance of so much that had come before.

HAIFA

Two hundred miles off the northern coast of Israel, they detected a small UAV droning slowly at five thousand feet. Apparently as soon as it had had a good look, it banked to the north and disappeared. Twenty minutes later, an Israeli F-16 flying thirty feet above the water roared past, fifty yards off the port beam, with only a slight dipping of its wings lest they catch the swell. Then it climbed almost straight up, its tailpipe clearing the surface by about five feet and blasting the sea into foam. Rolling to level flight upon completing its loop, it returned east.

"They don't fool around, do they?" Movius asked rhetorically.

Hesitating briefly while wondering what his Jewish XO might be feeling, eventually Rensselaer replied. "No, they don't. They never did."

"You mean the *Liberty*?"

"I suppose so."

"But the *Liberty* . . ." Movius began.

Rensselaer stopped him. "I understand. It was a war for their survival; the *Liberty* looked like an Egyptian ship; they warned us and everyone else away from the war zone; and they broke off the attack and offered aid. We've killed vastly many more of our own in friendly fire, thousands actually, yet we find it hard to accept that someone else can do it. It's just a question of being in or out of the family. I believe them, but I can't help being reserved."

"Are you reserved about the Brits?" Movius asked.

"Apart from being descended from the Dutch—Britain wrested the Hudson Valley from us—no."

"In the Revolution they fought us a lot harder and meaner."

"True, but it was two hundred plus years ago."

"The *Liberty* was half a century ago, and it wasn't on purpose."

"Mr. Movius."

"Sir?"

"I agree. Take yes for an answer. What's more, they're our allies, and for a very long time now we've been fighting the same enemies."

They slowed to twenty knots so as to arrive at I.N.S. Haifa just after dawn. At 0500 the next morning, as the stars had begun to fade, they saw a light in the distance and dead ahead. Rensselaer was summoned from his cabin. After announcing that the captain had the con, the officer of the deck told him that they had made contact with a *Shaldag*-class patrol boat from the I.N.S. 914th Patrol Squadron, and that it would escort them in. "They're not much for formalities, although I suppose they were correct enough. The commanding officer goes by Rav-Seren Hanok. A Rav-Seren, I believe, is a lieutenant commander. Hanok, a first name."

"Very well. Hailing frequency." With microphone in hand, Rensselaer hesitated before depressing the switch. "What's the name of the vessel?" he asked.

"They just said Eight Forty-One."

"I.N.S. Eight Forty-One, this is Captain Stephen Rensselaer of United States ship *Athena*, PC 15. Rav-Seren Hanok, thank you for your escort. Kindly guide us in."

"You're welcome. No worry," was the reply.

"Do we need a pilot?"

Rensselaer heard, "I don't think so," in heavily accented English. "We are two very small guys. No problem. Just follow me."

The Shaldag, which was not even half the size of *Athena*, loitered in wait, and, just after *Athena* passed it, turned and came up behind her, like the F-16 that had thundered off the port beam. Everyone on deck and on the bridge of *Athena* stood at attention and rendered passing honors, although not only did they not play the *Hatikvah*, Israel's national anthem, they had no such music aboard for any country, and it would have been ridiculous. Among other things, the sound of the Shaldag's engines was tremendous and would have drowned it out. The Shaldag, 841, was heavily gunned for a boat its size, but with neither missiles nor torpedoes.

The five sailors visible on its flying bridge and deck wore army fatigues and helmets. Though 841 was a much smaller craft, the bow gun was similar to *Athena*'s.

Without coming to attention the Israelis gave quick salutes. Then they sped up and rooster-tailed ahead as if to impress with their great speed.

"Oh really?" said Rensselaer. "Full ahead."

The helmsman repeated the command as he pushed the levers, and *Athena* lurched forward, knocking some people off their feet. In short order, it shot past the Israeli boat, approaching sixty miles per hour. A sailor on the port bridge wing was heard to say, "Un-fucking-believable," and once *Athena* reduced speed so 841 could pass it and take the lead, the Israelis were seen to be smiling. Over the hailing frequency came, *"Kol hakavod l'chem."*

"What the hell does that mean?" Someone on *Athena's* bridge asked.

"Who knows?" was the answer.

It meant, "All the honor to you."

*

As the sun rose behind it, Mount Carmel appeared dark and not as high as it actually was, but when the light increased and revealed the shape of houses and office buildings all the way up the steep slope, the scale became apparent. When *Athena* was close in and then beyond the breakwater, thousands of lights were seen briefly before either they were switched off or, as the sun crested the eastern part of Carmel, they were overpowered in its light.

The Shaldag escorted *Athena* to her berth and turned back out to sea. On the wharf were half a dozen Israelis, the American naval attaché, and a woman ostensibly from the embassy's political section. She was as purposefully attractive as, in Rensselaer's experience, female CIA officers with official cover often were. The waiting Americans and an Israeli naval officer crossed the brow and were piped aboard by one of the chiefs while four sailors stood at attention as sideboys. After that, nothing was formal except that the Israeli was an *Aluf-Mishne*, a captain, his rank commensurate with Rensselaer's. He had three gold oak leaves on each of his shoulder boards, so that, in American terms, he looked like a triple lieutenant commander.

The first thing he said after he introduced himself—as Tzvi Rechtman—was, "Look, you have ten hours, so come to my house for dinner tonight. I'll get you back to the ship on time." Rensselaer could only accept. The American naval attaché, a commander, then explained the provisioning and taking on of fuel. Trucks would arrive with pallets flown in from the U.S. to the Ramat David Air Base, east of Haifa, and the I.D.F.

would provide a supply of fresh food. A fueling barge was already pulling alongside.

When everything was arranged, including work parties, security parties, and liberty, Rensselaer, the naval attaché, and Patricia, of the "political section," went to the wardroom as the Israeli captain stayed on the quarterdeck and began a conversation with Holworthy.

"Do you want anything to eat? Coffee?" Rensselaer asked them.

They declined. The attaché opened his attaché case and took out a sealed manila envelope. "Put this in your safe."

"What is it?"

"New orders. You're not going to the Gulf."

Rensselaer was disappointed. "Are you sure?"

"Yeah."

"Why haven't we received them directly?"

"I don't know. It's kind of a joint thing." He glanced at his colleague.

"Joint or not, it should come through channels," Rensselaer said.

"Maybe it will, but evidently this is a joint thing with CIA. It came from Langley and the station chief in Jerusalem gave it to me. I don't know what's in it and nor should you until you pull out."

"But *you* know what's in it, don't you, Patricia," Rensselaer asked rhetorically.

"Maybe."

"So why can't we discuss it?"

Enjoying the whole thing, Patricia replied, "What if you get kidnaped today and you spill the beans? CIA is just what the Navy thinks it is. A bit off. They make a big thing of secrecy—way overboard." She found this amusing.

"We're not taking on any of their personnel, are we?" This had a seductive double or triple meaning.

"No," the attaché said. "I don't understand it, either. You're a naval ship, obvious to all eyes. It's probably just a normal pre-assignment but they've dressed it up, perhaps out of habit."

"If our not going to the Gulf is so secret, how do you know?"

"It's so secret that the station chief, in forwarding it, said to me, 'Here, give this to your guys on the *Athena*. They're not going to the Gulf.'"

"I can't open it now? In the Gulf War we were tasked by CIA, but never on a ship. And when they did it, it wasn't so great."

"You can't open it," the attaché said, wagging his finger, "until Christmas morning. It's the Navy. Get used to it."

*

The first to be released on liberty was Movius. Rensselaer figured that since he was Jewish and had never been to Israel, he should be allowed as much time as possible. He would have done the same for a crew member of Jamaican origin in Kingston, of Latvian origin in Riga, and so on. The chiefs would supervise the loading, and Rensselaer told the XO that he would fill him in on the briefing Rensselaer was to receive that morning from the Israelis.

"Do you know anyone here?" he asked Movius.

"Not in the whole country."

"Rechtman should have invited you, too."

"He did."

"That's good, even if it's not exactly according to protocol."

"As *they* might say, from protocol they know nothing. I'll see you there."

Everyone on liberty wore whites. Haifa was a navy town, and merchant seamen were common as well. Although they would never do this in Alexandria or even Istanbul, here it was safe. Rensselaer headed to the briefing, walking fast down the long breakwater. To his left were a busy harbor, and a city climbing up the mountainside toward a pure blue sky. It was rapidly getting hotter, and to the right of the breakwater the sea surged and receded, perfuming the air with the scent of minerals and life as waves swept to and fro stroking the seaweed-covered rocks.

In a building on the base, Rensselaer was escorted into an austere classroom where he took a seat facing the blackboard, which was actually green. After a few minutes, a middle-aged man with three bars on his shoulder came in and apologized for being late. "The cows were making trouble," he said. "They always do when I have an appointment."

"The cows?"

"Yes. To milk them."

"You milk cows?"

"In the morning, yes. If you don't, it's very bad."

"Navy cows?"

"No no. Kibbutz cows. I'm a *miluimnik*, a reservist. I had to go home because a cow went completely *mishuga*, and he broke the machine, which is I'm the only one who knows how to fix him."

"The machine."

"Yes."

"What is your rank?" Rensselaer inquired. "Your insignia are unlike ours."

"*Seren*, lef'tenant. I'm a reservist in *modi'in*, intelligence."

"And you're a farmer."

"I live on kibbutz, and everyone has to do many kind of work. I'm in charge of autonomous systems."

Rensselaer's expression gave away his puzzlement.

"We make things for the military and self-driving vehicles. It's mainly software and servomechanics."

"How did you learn to do this?"

"Here, and I studied in America—with Rechtman in fact, who you will see later. Same year, Caltech, doctorate. I love Pasadena. My English is not so good for a while, except for technical things."

"Oh," Rensselaer said.

"So, would you like some juice, some coffee, cookies, a Coke?"

"Thank you, I'm fine."

"Okay. So. You must take precautions when going through the Canal. You must have guidance."

"We do."

"But since the war started, things change every day. We help the Egyptians, as everyone know but don't say, in ISR. As you probably hear, *Ansar Bayt-al-Maqdis* has become Islamic State Sinai Province, and with the start of hostilities in the Gulf all Islamic State cells everywhere activated to the highest degree.

"The Egyptians are sending assets to the Gulf, and they are busy on their western borders with Libya, and on the Gaza border, in their cities, and even Aswan Province. What used to be their bad security in Sinai is now more bad. Insurance rates for transiting the Canal are now very hard. Some ISSP have rockets, others just RPGs and machine guns.

"The Sinai is very big, they seem to know when surveillance is over their head, so they move at night, make holes to hide in, sometimes right in the banks of the Canal. They even pretend to be Bedouin. They have tricks. Depending upon the management of your convoy when you go through, the hundred and ninety-three kilometers at eight knots will take from ten to sixteen hour.

"We advise that you man all guns and lookouts, port and starboard, the whole length. It's not likely to come from the western side, but it could. The Egyptians react after the fact, so if you are attacked you will have to do your fighting by yourself. The Canal pilot will be telling you as you approach areas of past attacks, but attacks could happen even in Port Said or Ismailia. An American warship is a big target. Questions?"

"The last attack?"

"Yesterday, fourteen kilometers south of Lake Timsah, heavy machine guns and two RPGs against a Maersk container ship, no casualties. If we pick up anything while you or anyone is in transit, we relay it to CENTCOM, and you will hear—without attribution."

"Okay. Thank you. Is that it?"

"Is it what?"

"I mean, is there anything else?"

"No, not really. Going back to the ship?"

"Going to see Haifa."

"My recommendation?"

"Shoot."

"See the Hadar, see the Technion—I teach there and at Haifa University—good ice cream at the zoo, sit in the late afternoon near the top of the Baha'i Gardens, and then have a nice dinner at Rechtman's, which is close. If you walk the whole way, you will be tired."

"How high is the hill?"

"Five hundred something meters. Some people, they can't do it. But, for military, not difficult."

*

The SEALs, being SEALs, stuck close to the water, walking west roughly along the shore until they got to a little beach in the Haifa neighborhood of Bat Galim, daughter of the waves. The sea close to shore was rocking in the wind and green in the morning light. To the wonderment of the ancient retirees who, like clockwork, came to this beach every day, the first thing the SEALs did was put on their fins and swim out into Haifa Bay until they could no longer be seen.

Israeli naval commandos never came in a group to the beach at Bat Galim, and these were foreigners. A white-haired octogenarian who had been trying to do pull-ups told the group of grandmas sitting half-submerged at the edge of the surf that, for reasons of national security, he was going to inspect the things the swimmers left behind.

"Americans," he announced after his inspection. "You don't have to worry."

"Who's worried?" asked one of the grandmothers.

"That's what you say!" the old man said, and went back to the pull-up bar, where he did . . . one, and called it a day.

Several miles out, in lovely water just the right temperature, amid crests that sometimes were brushed white by the warm wind, the SEALs headed for a container ship anchored in the bay and awaiting entrance to the port. When they reached it they took turns going hand over hand up the anchor chain until they reached the hawsehole, and then descended, arm muscles burning, far enough so that they could drop into the water and stay clear of the projection under the bow. When this was accomplished, they swam the several miles back to the beach, got an enormous lunch from a stand on the street, and sat down at a picnic table to eat.

The sun was extraordinarily hot, but they were situated so as to be in the wind.

O'Connor said, "The hawsehole was too far from the railing. We couldn't have boarded."

"Grappling hook," said one of the SEALs in a short interruption between him and his sandwich.

"We didn't have a grappling hook. I'm thinking, what if we had to do it this way?"

"Something to ponder," Holworthy said, "although I don't see another way."

"Ask the captain," another of the SEALs proposed.

"Why?" Holworthy asked. "You think he's magic?"

"No, I think he's weird."

"I'll let that pass."

"But he is."

"You don't want it to pass? Why?"

"He says weird things."

"Yeah," O'Connor added. "He does. He references things that no one knows about, because he's old. I'll give you an example. You know that skinny blond kid who looks like he's fifteen? They were making fun of him because he threw a bucket into the sea and the line pulled him from amidships to the stern, where Halloran here grabbed it and pulled the bucket in. The captain saw this and went to see what had happened."

"So, by this time," Halloran told the others, "everyone was making fun of the kid.

"Someone says, 'He doesn't have the brain to know not to rope a bucket into the sea at thirty knots, or the balls to pull it in if he does.' And another guy adds, 'And he had a lot of dating problems in high school.' So then the captain chimes in and says, 'Yeah, carbon for teens.' Everyone looks at him blankly. 'Sir?' someone asks, and the captain says, '*Carbon—for teens. Dating,*' laughs, and walks away."

"Okay," O'Connor allowed, "they never heard of carbon 14. So what? That's their problem."

"He should have explained," the insistent SEAL pressed on. "And it was lame anyway. You don't just walk away. That makes people think you're touched. And, then, some sort of message came in: I don't know what it was. He reads it, tears it up, and says, 'Fuck you. Toast my pretzel.' That's not normal."

"Look," Holworthy told him. "Maybe that was an expression when he was young. I don't know. When we've been on PCs, or even DDGs, there was no one of his rank, or if on a larger ship there was, we were never that close to him. They're human, you know. And, being old, he knows things we don't and we know things he doesn't."

"Like what?"

"Singers, movie stars, video games. He told me he's never played a video game."

"He hasn't?"

Holworthy shook his head in confirmation.

"Commander," another SEAL said, very soberly, "he's a prude. Remember the bikinis? What's wrong with looking? You think he's gay?"

"He has a fiancée."

"A man."

"No, her name is Katy."

"Maybe it's a man named Katy. On his planet, birds bark and dogs sing."

"Yeah?" Holworthy said. "On your planet, birds vomit."

"Has anyone ever seen her? He has no engagement ring."

"Moron, men don't wear engagement rings. And do you know how many thousands—tens of thousands—of men have died because of the glint of a watch or ring?"

"He could take it off."

"Not everyone wears jewelry. Do you wear jewelry, Stocker? Earrings? A nose ring? You should wear a nose ring. It would make it easier for the farmer." Stocker was built like a bull.

As if it were a competition, O'Connor added even more soberly than Stocker, "Still, Commander, you've gotta admit. . . ."

"I do admit. He's a wild card. I'll keep watch."

"Meaning?"

"Just that this is my team, and I'm not going to get anyone killed because of stupid or crazy. That's not in the deal, never was."

No one said anything. There was nothing further to be said.

*

Rensselaer ascended the almost eighteen hundred feet of Mount Carmel, and then hundreds more as he went up and down on the sides of the hills, looking at the recommended areas and academic institutions before he had ice cream near the zoo, and then walked to the promenade that overlooks city, bay, gardens, and sea.

He took immense pleasure from the unfamiliar way things presented themselves: views, streetscapes, a patch of evergreen forest framing the sea, a torrent of rosebushes tumbling over a fence. The glowing blue of the sea seen from high on a hill in north light was tranquilizing, hypnotic, and reassuring.

Little was left of Ottoman or Mandate Haifa. Now the predominantly modern city stretched for miles around the curve of the bay, which in the deep, north light held dozens of huge ships riding at anchor. As high as if flying, he looked out from the promenade and saw not only the whited metropolis below but the spectacular descent of the gardens. All along the coast were beaches and parks, and he had a clear, port-beam view of *Athena* resting beautifully, he thought, in her berth.

In the hour before he was expected for dinner, he sat still amid the flowers, mesmerized by the radiant blue spreading out before him all the way to Lebanon. The Mediterranean as it embraced the city was like a cool breeze comforting a fever. He would bring Katy to this spot when the war was over. After climbing Mt. Carmel and walking the hills they would be tired and would sit on the very bench he was sitting on, and look outward, lightly touching, breathing slowly, without a word. That is, were he lucky enough to return from this, his last run. It was time to stand down. She understood even better than he did, though she was younger and not ready to cross into the part of life that—although the young cannot know it—is the period of reflection necessary to reconcile and judge the action-driven years that precede it.

The stresses, dangers, and disappointments he had suffered had led him first to search for answers the way physicists search for a unified field theory, and then to conclude that there weren't any. That is, until he fell in love with Katy and discovered that she was the answer, plain and simple, inexplicably. Almost hypnotized by the exquisite blue light, he imagined her face again and again, never tiring of it, and he saw her moving—her stiff but explosive walk, because in a sheath dress and heels she was so strong and straight, and could hardly contain her power and energy. For a full hour he thought of her, he pictured her, he loved her.

Then, with a bit of arthritis, he rose and walked one street down to Rechtman's house, which from the road seemed like a pillbox, because one entered over a concrete bridge to a single-storey, block-like building. But this was only the top floor of a house of three levels set into the hillside. Every room and several terraces afforded a great view and the sense of safely floating over everything.

Before he had turned onto the little bridge, he had noticed a girl moving toward him. Now she came up behind him. She was in a gray uniform, and she wore a dark hat. In American terms it would be called an overseas cap, but it was felt, far more substantial, and rigid. It's rakishness would have made any woman look beautiful, as she was anyway because it's difficult not to be if you are a young woman of twenty, and for her it would have been exceedingly difficult. On the hat was a silver badge, and on her blouse above her rolled up sleeves were three white bars.

"Air Force?" he asked.

"Yes. You don't have to ring the bell. I know who you are. Rensselaer. I know before my father."

"You did?"

"Yes. I have the key." She began to open the door. "I work at Ramat David. We sent the F-16."

"And you knew my name?"

"We were expecting you, you know."

"And who are you?"

"Hava," she said, shyly.

As soon as the door opened, they were swept up by Rechtman, his wife, two beagles, and a boy of about eight who then found Movius at the door and added him to the group, which, as Rensselaer discovered when he looked toward the terrace, included Patricia, standing at the rail, drink in hand, alone.

"The dinner is made," Mrs. Rechtman said. "We just have to go to the kitchen and serve it to ourselves. But Hava, bring some cookies and juices."

Only cookies, seltzers, and juice. No liquor was about, and none was mentioned. It seemed to have been largely left out of the culture. And dinner was a fusion of Eastern Europe and the Levant—matzah ball soup, *hummus be-techina*, lamb, and roasted potatoes. No wine, just seltzer. And for dessert, moan cake, and tea in glasses.

Whatever the formula, it made for easy conversation. Apparent to all except the little boy was the undeniable attraction between Rensselaer and Patricia, of the kind that consumes business travelers and men and women on deployment, and can so often make them forget whom they love. Patricia—red hair, green eyes, statuesque, and young—had fallen with Rensselaer into a reciprocal cycle of intensifying signals as pleasurable and irresistible in their touch-and-go as anything physical that might come after. But Rensselaer had determined to lash himself to the mast. Movius, however, was totally smitten with Hava: almost, Rensselaer thought, to the point of desertion. Nor was she uninterested, although she was almost painfully more contained.

Seeing this, her mother said, "Hava was born in Pasadena. She has an American passport, and when her service is over she got already in and is going to Caltech, like her father."

Movius nearly expired. (Rensselaer would not know the full reason until much later.)

"What will you study, Hava?" Rensselaer asked. Very much aware of her extraordinary charm, he felt a glow much like paternal love.

"Physics," she answered. "I try to make the right decision. Everything here is, underneath, so serious. So, you do your best."

"Yes," Rensselaer said. "You're always at war. No safe place."

"That's true," Rechtman added. "In the full light," he pointed out the window, "you can see Lebanon. Nasr'allah has two hundred thousand rockets, and the only thing between them and this room is air."

"Even though we're going to the war," Movius said, "it's not the same for us, because we can go home, where there is no war. Our families are protected."

"It's not so bad," Hava said, almost as if to comfort him. "It makes you feel very alive all the time."

At that moment, Movius really fell in love, and although it was hardly a sure thing, he knew he would do everything he could to get back to her.

Everyone could sense this, now even the little boy, and, not least, Hava herself. After they left, Rensselaer, Movius, and Patricia stood in the street at the end of the Rechtman's little bridge. Patricia said to Rensselaer, her gaze isolating him from Movius, "The Israelis have a disdain—allergy? I don't know—for alcohol. Embassy parties here are cheaper than almost anywhere else, even in Arab countries where they come to the embassy to cheat. All they want here is seltzer. So, anyway, I'm staying at the Dan Carmel. There." She pointed. "Would you like to have a drink?"

"I would so like to," Rensselaer replied, "but I've ordered"—he had done no such thing—"my XO to lash me to the mast, because we have to get underway."

"At least that's a compliment," Patricia said.

"Absolutely. Maybe someday I'll run into you at Langley."

"Langley? Oh no, I'm a political officer."

*

As the captain and his XO approached *Athena* they heard and felt her engines at idle. Brash lights illuminated the wharf and the black water. "You like her, don't you," Rensselaer said.

"More than that."

"I think she was deeply affected. You're going to come back to her, aren't you." It wasn't a question.

"If I can. I've never seen anything like that—her charming, outgoing yet shy femininity, framed in a military uniform offering enough of a contrast to heighten her beauty, while giving rise to great admiration for a girl in such circumstances. I don't know. I've never been as knocked over as I am now. I can hardly breathe. In that rakish overseas cap, with the sterling silver badge, she has me forever."

"Would you leave the Navy?"

"There are more things in life than the Navy."

"I wish I had known that."

After the brow was pulled back, but before they cast off lines, they made sure that everyone was on board. Then they concentrated on the complex maneuvers and commands for getting underway. Slowly moving through the harbor, the lookouts and deckhands who were in the open air felt the particular sensations of a Mediterranean port at night—the way the lights reflect on the water, sound echoes against stone, and scents rise from a slowly turned wake. This time they had a pilot, who transferred to his launch somewhere between Bat Galim and Stella Maris as *Athena* headed southwest 240 degrees to Port Said. As the dark of the sea reclaimed the ship, Israel's lighted coast disappeared.

Though *Athena* was primed and ready in a fairly relaxed Condition III, everything was going so smoothly it felt like a yachting cruise. Approaching Port Said, readiness would be increased, and going through the canal and thenceforward they would maintain a full Condition III at the very least.

Finishing the second dog watch, Rensselaer returned to his quarters for the night. After preparing for bed, but still dressed, he sat at his desk and took out a picture of Katy. Unbeknownst to her, he had taken it as she was waiting for him at the streetcar. Then he switched on the golden light of a little incandescent lamp above the built-in desk, and without getting up from his chair reached to the safe and opened it, first with a key that only he and Movius carried, and then with the combination. He took out the manila envelope with his new orders, and closed the safe. Although of course he could not know for sure, the involvement of CIA led him to guess that *Athena* was going to be tasked in an evacuation, an assassination, perhaps a raid on a surveillance post somewhere in the Horn of Africa or on Socotra—something, as such things tended to be, messy, dangerous, of no doubt dubious legality and inconclusive, but necessary.

So it was with some dread that he broke the seal, pulled out the orders, and began to read, at first sitting back but then moving forward and placing the papers on the desk as if in recognition of their gravity.

When he finished reading, he aligned the pages neatly, stared at them, and read them again. Then he slowly placed them on the desk. Simply put, without great luck or divine intervention *Athena* and everyone aboard were to be sacrificed. But were he to state it that way to the crew, the likelihood of survival would be greatly diminished. He dared not show anything but confidence—the steadiness of which would give them the best chance of coming out alive and returning home.

III

The Sun off East Africa

Alone on the sea, in the Suez Canal, or hard by the desert, they were shocked by nearly overwhelming dimensions and colors: whether of the vastness of the oceans or the gold and white sands over which viscous air danced on the horizon. Isolation in space made for isolation in time. Their past lives were overshadowed by the infinities they sensed and the thunder of the sun. The flag stretched in the breeze, vibrating enough to sing. How wonderful and strange to be young and on the sea off the deserts of Africa, from which the wind blew hot and dry. How wonderful to be in such a place, at twenty, without knowing what lay ahead.

THE FIRST BATTLE: SINAI.
AND THEN THE RED SEA

Early the next morning a few hours north of Port Said as a shimmering sea lifted and lowered *Athena* on three-foot swells, no other ships were in sight. When the watch changed, Rensselaer ordered a full stop and assembled the crew, even engineering, called up from obsessively tended spaces bathed in the whine of turbines.

"Given Russian acoustic assets," Rensselaer announced, "and in the most unlikely but still conceivable event that we may be sitting over one of their subs, I didn't want to use the 1MC. I have a lot to tell you. We may be attacked as we go through the Canal, anywhere from Port Said to Suez." After summarizing for them the briefing of the previous day, he went on. "Before we enter the Canal, we'll move to Condition One. The fifties will shift to port or starboard as dictated by circumstances. Most of the time, armament will be heavier on the port side, but we'll keep two fifties and a minigun to starboard.

"It may seem a bit much that we'll be at general quarters while the merchant seamen on ships forward and aft of us are playing checkers and drinking beer, but we're a ship of war. As such, we're not only a richer, more prestigious target, but, now, an active part of the Canal defenses. Notwithstanding issues of sovereignty, our passage is, de facto, a patrol. The watch bills and P.O.D. reflect this and will be posted shortly." He looked over at the XO.

"Ten minutes," Movius said. Everyone heard.

Rensselaer continued. "First, I want to clarify something about the enemy with whom we're at war. It appears from conversation on the mess deck that some think we're at war with the Arabs. We are not. We are at war with the remnants of ISIS, Islamic terror groups, and others who are mainly Arabs, but Iranians are not Arabs. They are, by and large, Muslims, but they're neither Arabs, Indians, nor East Asians. They're Indo-European, and they come from that often neglected part of the world between the once great empires. In ancient times they were themselves an empire, the easternmost power known to the Greeks, and a perpetual rival. It's been a long time since they stretched from Afghanistan to the Mediterranean, which is what they've done now. Americans generally are unaware that, perhaps insanely, Iran has world-conquering ambitions. Thousands of years ago they fought the Greeks even off Athens, and the Greeks took the war to them. It seems that we're repeating that. Just so you know, that's who we're fighting. *Athena* versus the Persians. Nothing new under the sun.

"Some specifics. We're going to stop in Djibouti to take on stores and top off—loading mainly munitions, some food as well. Only supply parties will be leaving the ship. Our stay will last about three hours, if that. You won't share anything I'm about to tell you with anyone there, no matter what his rank. Is that understood? It's crucial."

Everyone nodded.

"We're not going to the Gulf."

Everyone groaned. There was much shuffling.

"At least not yet. We've been given a more important job, one that we may not have the opportunity to do, and that, if we are lucky enough to try, is something from which—I feel obligated to tell you—we may not walk away, even if some of us may swim. If you survive it, you'll remember for the rest of your lives." The crew listened intently. How could they not?

"Before I had even thought of going into the Navy, I wondered what it would be like for a general to sacrifice a certain body of his troops so as to save the rest. Somehow it didn't occur to me that admirals and the civilian command authorities might have to do the same. This has fallen upon us. I agree with the order, I'd give it myself, I would never get over having given it, and I intend to execute it. I intend as well to succeed, and to preserve the ship. No doubt that will be difficult."

Other than the idling engines below and the occasional splash of a wave against the side, there was silence. He went on.

"By now there's a giant armada deployed in overlapping operational boxes in the Arabian Sea beyond Iranian air and missile range. If my experience is a guide, ship movements within those boxes are precisely timed so that where they overlap they maintain maximum distance between carrier strike groups. Things are heating up in Korea and the South China Sea, so we're stretched really thin. Still, we've got four carriers just outside the Gulf, including the *Ford*. These are well defended against anything the Iranians have deployed.

"We've sunk ten of their twenty-one submarines. They keep coming, and we'll keep sinking them. Thus far, our screening forces have managed to intercept all missile shots. But if they can sink a carrier and kill thousands of sailors in one blow it'd give them an immensely strong hand. So that's what they've been trying to do.

"Russia has developed a hypersonic, maneuvering, anti-ship missile. NATO calls it SS-N-Thirty-Three. Russia calls it Tsirkon. It can travel at Mach eight: that is, somewhere around five thousand miles per hour, depending upon altitude, temperature, and I don't know what. It's fast and its maximum range is five hundred and forty nautical miles. I don't have a clue about the warhead, but at Mach eight the kinetic energy alone might be enough to sink or disable a large ship. Because the damn thing goes so fast it's enveloped by a plasma cloud that absorbs everything on the electromagnetic spectrum, making it invisible to radar.

"Our shipboard defenses can't handle anything even vaguely like that. Anti-ballistic-missile systems can, but not if it's flying low, in air, on a flat trajectory. So if a Tsirkon could get within five hundred nautical miles and link into some form of intermediate guidance—terminal guidance is built into the missile itself—it could possibly sink a carrier."

"Do they have the missile?" a chief asked, raising his hand *after* he spoke.

"Not in Iran. But the Iranian frigate *Sahand* has spent the last year upgrading in Murmansk, hidden in a shed so we wouldn't see it from our satellites. What we do know is that the three-inch gun on the bow was removed and left outside in the snow, which is the kind of thing Russians tend to do—leave stuff outside in the snow. And when the *Sahand* sailed from Murmansk it had a box-launcher—which, to preempt the wits among you, has nothing to do with either launching boxes or box lunches—mounted in place of the gun: four containers sized properly for the Tsirkon.

"Before the war, *Sahand* was shadowed after it sailed out of Murmansk, first by us, then by the Brits, and then by a French sub. It made a refueling stop in Algeria and then doubled back into the Atlantic and south. The French sub followed politely until the Cape of Good Hope and then turned around, losing it. The deal was that the U.S. would pick it up at that point, but by that time we needed everything we could spare in the Iranian theater and to deter China and North Korea. We had deployed a sub from Seventh Fleet, but needed the French to extend their pursuit for two more days around the Cape. Put it this way: they were never disturbed by Iranian nuclear weapons, and there are big demonstrations against the war all over France. They said no go to the IO."

A young sailor asked, "What's the IO?"

Rensselaer replied, "Think of the song."

"Sir?"

"'Old McDonald had a farm.'"

"Sir, I don't understand."

"That's okay. In naval parlance, the IO is the Indian Ocean. And the *Sahand* slipped away into the IO. As you well know, the Indian Ocean is many thousands of miles wide and long, with much of it empty of shipping. Because there's nothing in the southern half but freezing seas, no islands to speak of, and as it's not suitable as an SSBN bastion, it's not surveilled.

"Not only is it outside normal satellite coverage, but because the Iranians set up a sleeper cell that at the beginning of the war took out a key ground station, even with re-tasking we've lost the ability to look at the Southern Ocean. Our satellites are so heavily tasked that none would have been sent to scan that area anyway. Nor would it be at all sensible to detach major surface ships to run around doing the same, or to fly P-8s or Tritons, except as follows:

"A picket line of three Aegis destroyers and various aerial surveillance assets will be spaced just outside the range of the Tsirkon relative to the carriers. That is, a sparse two-thousand-mile line roughly from Cochin in India to Ras Hafun in Somalia. One Triton UAV and one P-8—they can't spare others—will survey the area directly south of them. Not a bad plan, but because it leaves a lot to chance Washington wants more. So, how will it get more? That's where we come in.

"*Sahand* has to refuel somewhere on the coast of East Africa. CIA has people in every port, but it's also possible that *Sahand* will meet a tanker or a barge out at sea. We have a handle on all the tankers now in the area, there being so few because of the war, the spike in insurance rates, and the closure of the Strait of Hormuz. It's possible however that a small tanker or barge will sally from some East African port without our knowledge.

"We don't want to weaken the picket line by sending a major surface combatant down there, because in fact the *Sahand* may already have refueled and may be somewhere in the open sea heading north. And why waste a major ship on a low-probability search? So they're sending us. If our intelligence picks up *Sahand*, we sail right at it to confirm its position, engage it, and at least slow it down so our more capable assets can close in from their widely spaced positions. If necessary, we are to sacrifice ourselves in inflicting to it as much damage as possible.

"Given the capabilities involved, doing so will be something you can liken to knowing when orchids bloom. You can't. At least I can't. But then again I don't know anything about orchids, and I do know how to fight a ship, although it's been a long time since the Navy fought a purely surface battle without air support."

He paused, recognizing that he and the crew had crossed over yet again into a state very different from the one that preceded it, and were that much farther from home. Still, the terrible odds excited him as if he were young.

"Now . . . ," he said, "now comes the pertinent question. What about the *Sahand*?"

The crew, too, was ready to fight. There they were, on the ocean, with no visible home shore to soften their desires. It was as if they were in a different time, their fathers' time, the time of their fathers' fathers, and perhaps all the way back to the unknowable beginning.

Someone said, "Fuck the *Sahand*!"

"Well," Rensselaer commented, "that'll be as easy as impregnating an elephant. But since that's what the chiefs do on liberty, maybe they can show us how." This went over rather well, but only because of the tension.

He resumed. "At twenty-five hundred tons, *Sahand* has six times our displacement and five times our complement. The bloody thing carries a helicopter, and even with its main gun removed for the Tsirkon, it has a forty-millimeter and two twenty-millimeters, six torpedoes, and, here's the rough part, eight Qader missiles. They won't waste the Tsirkons on us, but the Qaders have a four-hundred-and-forty-pound warhead, advanced guidance, and a range of at least a hundred and fifty nautical miles. I need not tell you what would happen if one of those warheads struck us amidships. It would blow us in half, and each half would go down in a minute or two. Other than the hip pockets, we don't have BPMD for a sea-skimming missile like that. And if the helicopter is in the right quadrant, it certainly has the range and altitude to spot us, set the missile on its initial course, and even provide terminal guidance if it stays beyond the range of our Stingers."

From behind him, Ensign Josephson asked, "Captain, sir, how the hell are we going to defend against that, sir?"

"Mr. Josephson asks how the hell we're going to defend against *Sahand*," Rensselaer returned. "First, whereas we can't ignore the facts, we don't have to be defeated before we fight. How could thirteen fractious colonies have ever thought they could defeat the world's most powerful empire? They took it one step at a time, they didn't let fear cloud their judgment, and they didn't give up when that seemed the only sensible thing they could do.

"The Qaders need guidance. There's a roughly one-in-three chance that the helicopter would be in the right sector. There's a chance that it would miss us even if it were. How reliable is the *Sahand*'s helo? How much can they afford to fly it in regard to fuel and engine wear? Far from their Tsirkon launch range, outside the war zone, will they even fly it at all? Or will they save it for when they begin to close? How accurate and reliable are the Qaders? We don't know.

"And that's just one part of the equation. It doesn't take into account what we ourselves might do."

Holworthy raised his hand and asked, in a negative, perceptibly bitter tone, "And what might we do, Captain?" In translation: *This isn't a SEAL fight. Why are we along for such a ride?*

Rensselaer chose to ignore the translation. "Mr. Holworthy, we're a United States ship, and like the *Constitution* when it took on *Guerriere*, or the fleet forces at Midway, we will take on a superior enemy and not stand down. That is *what* we will do. As to how we will do it, I'm working on it. That doesn't mean I have nothing. It means I have something."

The crew might have been unsettled had Rensselaer looked anxious, or caught, but he forced himself to seem confident and, inexplicably, happy. "Dismissed," he said.

In the SEALs' quarters even before *Athena* began to make way, Holworthy said to his men, "I didn't sign up to take a Disney cruise around the fucking Indian Ocean. If we go against the *Sahand*, we're just along for the ride.

"Americans are dying in the Gulf. Why are we held back here, doing nothing? By what authority are we made to just sit? We can help to win the war and save lives. Christ, I want to get out there!"

Soon *Athena* was making for Port Said, prepared to be drawn into the other worlds of the East, of battle, and all the things that link one war to another as if the procession of history between the wars were only a dream.

*

During the approach to the northern terminus of the Canal at Port Said, Rensselaer had left a glowing young Josephson as officer of the deck and returned to his cabin, where he sat lost in thought. Facing a David-versus-Goliath problem, he had neither sling nor stones. Even if upon his sighting of the *Sahand* the Air Force could spare a bomber, it would arrive too late.

That was assuming that he would see *Sahand* before it saw him.

Bombers with the range, either in the U.S., at Al-Udeid, or on Diego Garcia, were fully absorbed in the Gulf, where what they were doing was crucial in advancing the battle and protecting the fleet. What the *Sahand* would or could do was not yet clear. With tankerage, carrier-launched F-18s and F-35Cs would have the range, but would arrive too late to save *Athena*. She was going to assume the classic role of scout: invaluable and expendable.

At a knock on the door, Rensselaer opened a binder on his desk so whoever it was would not assume he had been doing nothing. It was Holworthy, who saluted upon entering, which, his having seen the captain several times that day already, he need not have done, even if Rensselaer had not suspended saluting in general.

"Have a seat," Rensselaer said.

"Thank you, sir."

"Why the salute, uncovered, when we no longer salute?"

"It's your cabin, sir."

"Doesn't matter. What's on your mind?"

"May I speak freely?"

"Please do."

"Sir, my detachment is irrelevant to a pure naval battle on the open sea."

Rensselaer answered, "*Athena* was hardly constructed for a pure naval battle on the open sea. We're a patrol craft best suited to the littorals. So, we're in the same boat."

"At least *Athena*, even if unsuited, would be serving a purpose, whereas my men will be entirely useless."

"Would you like me to drop you off in Yemen or Somalia so you can run around hunting terrorists, and then I can pick you up on the way back, if we have a way back?"

"No, sir. Leave us, if it's approved, at Camp Lemonnier, where we can catch a transport to the Gulf."

"But then, if we survive the mission, and are sent to the Gulf, I'll have no SEALs."

"What I mean to ask, sir, is would you object if I myself request it?"

"You're goddamned right I would. You're in the Navy, Mr. Holworthy. You don't just leave a ship for better pickings. We have a tradition of infantry and special forces aboard ship. You know that."

"Yes, sir, they're called Marines."

"Notice any Marines around here?"

"No."

"While we're in the open ocean, that's your job."

"With all due respect, we aren't of any use in a naval battle."

"You sure about that?"

"I can't imagine. . . ."

"Maybe you can't, but maybe I can."

Holworthy stared at Rensselaer, his expression suggesting that he thought Rensselaer had nothing.

Rensselaer understood what Holworthy's eyes were saying, so he replied, "This isn't poker. I'm not bluffing and you're not calling my bluff. I cannot, however, discuss what I'm thinking—with you, or anyone else."

"Not the XO?"

"Only with God."

"With God. You'll discuss it with God."

"At this stage, it's the only thing that's appropriate."

"Why?"

"Because it will require His intervention."

Holworthy didn't know quite how to take this, but he was told to get back to his duties, and he did. The captain was not unhappy. They were SEALs. They wanted to fight. And they would.

*

Although *Athena* had priority through the Canal and would not have to convoy, she still had to wait for a short time amid the gaggle of ships off Port Said before a gap opened behind the last to go through before her. From the line of low buildings and palms along the shore, a wooden rowboat made its way toward the ship. As the boat's double-set oars rhythmically propelled it forward, some of *Athena*'s guns were politely trained upon it, and Rensselaer was alerted.

Those on deck looked lovingly at the wood. After living with metal, plastic, and glass, upon water never ending, they saw wood, especially old, weathered wood, as magical and comforting. At sea there are no green ramparts of pine and fir along a distant ridge, or the intoxicating scent of lilacs after dark.

Two *fellahin* were at the oars, and at the bow was a kind of colonial dandy, in horn-rimmed sunglasses and a white linen blazer with a Yale crest on the breast pocket.

"Gimme a fuckin' break," Holworthy said, sighting this triumph of non-invisibility. "Boola fuckin' boola."

"Boola boola?" Rensselaer asked, binocularless.

"Yup."

"Who is it, William F. Buckley? He might as well wear a CIA cap."

"That's what I thought."

When Boola Boola came aboard, clearly relishing having, spook-like, come in a rowboat powered by natives, Rensselaer took him to his cabin. There, over lemonade and Famous Amos cookies, of which Boola Boola devoured fourteen, he referenced his employer.

"Really!" Rensselaer exclaimed. "I never would have guessed."

"How so?"

"A Yale linen blazer, and Hermès sunglasses? Didn't they teach you anything at Camp Perry?"

"I'm under official cover at the embassy in Cairo, political section."

"You're in the Sinai now, you're not T. E. Lawrence, and it's dangerous. Just sayin'."

"That's exactly why I'm here, to warn you that you may be attacked from the east bank, where ISIS and God knows who else are active."

"From whom does this intelligence come?"

"I can't say."

"I can't say either, but it comes from the Israelis, they told us at Haifa, and we're ready."

"There are scores of navies around here, and these guys can't tell the difference between one warship and another. They won't necessarily attack if they don't know what you are. But they're sure to if you're American. So it might be a wise idea not to run with the flag."

"I beg your pardon?"

"Perhaps you should lower the flag."

"I understand," Rensselaer said, drawing it out, "that, working in foreign hellholes, you have to sneak around. Not that you do, apparently. But this is an American warship. We don't lower the flag."

"Even if it means advertising that you're a prime target?"

Rensselaer nodded.

"That you might lose some of your crew?"

Rensselaer nodded again. "They would agree."

"Or that you yourself may die?"

"As many have before me. It's part of my job, believe it or not, it gives me a kind of joy, and believe it or not it dispels the fear of death. The Islamists think Americans are no longer capable of such things."

"They do."

"They're wrong."

*

With priority, soon after the Canal pilot came aboard, *Athena* glided past Port Said and slowly made her way south, when Rensselaer gave *Athena*'s first war order, "Unpin the fifties and make ready to repel attacks from shore and small boats."

The pilot, a rotund Nasser, mustache and all, was professional, friendly, and quiet. For reasons of security, some consoles on the bridge had been covered, and it was strange to see the Americans in helmets and body armor while he was in summer clothes, including powder-blue slacks and a sort of Egyptianized Hawaiian shirt with colorful zigzags rather than vegetation. This was fitting, as *zigzag* may have come from Zagazig, a city in Lower Egypt. Rensselaer knew this, but kept mum so as not to expend his captain's pedagogical allowance on something so inconsequential.

The pilot took note that on *Athena*'s port side four twin-barreled, .50-caliber, mounted guns, three in a row slightly forward of midships and one aft, were at the ready. The 30mm chain gun also pointed east, and at any one time two sailors were manning the 7.62 miniguns, and two SEALs were on deck with sniper rifles.

"The pilot said to Movius, "I don't think anyone will shoot us. They don't like when people shoot back."

"Not even ISIS?"

"*Daish*? Maybe. They are very, very crazy, but it doesn't happen every day."

"Every other day?"

"No. Now with the war, maybe once in ten days. The Army has been killing them."

By 1600 they were halfway through. In the thinned traffic due to the war, they saw no ships either forward or aft, just blinding white and yellow dunes to the east, and the azure water of the Canal rippled by winds that had come all the way across North Africa. The heat was such—110 degrees in the shade—that standing watch in body armor without either fainting or hallucinating required a great deal of strength and many breaks in the air-conditioned interior. The steel decks were so hot they had to be cooled with water now and then, and the radiant heat from sand and sun was numbing.

In a near-hypnotic state, the sailors watched the dunes as they seemed to float by. Half-asleep, they came awake whenever they saw an Egyptian patrol or a group of Bedouin, the latter all in black, sometimes with a camel or two but more often with a herd of goats, walking along the crest of a dune. When the dunes and the artificial banks that once had been the Bar-Lev Line were low, they saw deep into Sinai, sometimes all the way to the mountains. Rising air blurred images, carried others from beyond sight, and made the mountain ranges seem to undulate.

A fragile strip of civilization, the Canal was a silk thread laid across ten thousand years of history in a landscape that had never changed. The vastness and emptiness of it, with colors intense enough to wound the eyes, had been witness to struggles from the time of Abraham to the October War. And Bedouin from the biblical era and before were separate from all and lived as if time did not exist. The women, only their eyes visible, wore bells on their foreheads, like the bells that hemmed the robes of the priests of the Tabernacle. They walked across the sand in a strange way, shuffling but very fast, their feet bare.

At 1638 precisely, on top of a high dune to the east, a dozen or so men—no one had time to count them—crested the rim, dived to prone position, and began firing rifles, light machine guns, and RPGs at *Athena*. She answered immediately with thirteen gun barrels, firing thousands of bullets and shells.

Rensselaer nearly leapt to the port bridge wing, where a minigun was firing. "Take careful aim," he commanded over the 1MC. "Take careful aim," because he could see many shots kicking up sand far below the enemy, just as the incoming fire, directed downward from the lip of the dune, including RPGs, was poorly sighted, and frothed-up the water between the ship and the bank. But he went unheard over the merciless noise of eight .50-caliber barrels and all the other guns firing at once.

He stopped the minigun from firing and insisted that the sailor aim slowly. Two SEALs on deck with Barrett .50-caliber sniper rifles were calmly picking off the men on the dune, of whom less than half were still firing. Someone shouted, "RPG!" They could see it coming for the bow. It hit, but it was a dud and it bounced away.

A moment of silence brought little relief. Velez, from COMMS, who had paused firing his twin-fifty, felt a burning pain in his left arm. His right hand slapped it as if reacting to a bee sting. Then he noticed that the fingers of that hand were slippery and hot. Even at this point he understood that, no matter the pain, he had suffered only a graze. Upset that his blood was staining the deck, he kept on firing even as the corpsman, who had appeared as if from nowhere, bandaged the wound. "Stay still," the corpsman yelled over the sound of the gun, "just for a minute, so I can wrap this, goddamn it." Velez kept on swiveling the mount and moving around. "Stop it! Will you just stop for a second?" the corpsman ordered.

Velez stopped, turned to him, and said, "Do you realize what's going on here?" That gave the corpsman enough time to do what he had come to do.

Rensselaer called into the bridge, "Full astern."

The helmsman repeated, "Full astern, aye sir," and then, belatedly, the XO announced, almost under his breath, "The captain has the con." *Athena* slowed vigorously enough to make some sailors almost lose their footing, and then she backed to bring her guns broadside once again to the attackers. The first contact had been a surprise, and the ship was a little past the enemy, so the guns had to be brought to bear at an increasing angle. But after reversing and then coming almost to a stop broadside of the assault, all gunners on deck and ready, the massive firing seemed totally out of character for such a small, sleek ship. The many barrels, from the 30mm to the SEALs' sniper rifles, mixed with grenade launchers fired almost straight up to mimic mortars and strike behind the dune. Thirty-millimeter shells and high-explosive, .50-caliber-machine-gun shells struck below the crest and made fountains of sand and shrapnel in the air.

The dune curved broadly at the top, affording cover of only six inches or so of sand depth three or four feet in front of the attackers. Heavy shells and the 7.62s went through this, slowing somewhat but not enough either to bend their course or significantly lessen their striking power. It was as if the assailants had placed themselves in a shooting gallery, and it was over in less than a minute. Those of the enemy who may have been left alive were nowhere to be seen, and after the cessation of fire everyone felt a deafness and ringing in the ears.

"Report casualties," Rensselaer ordered. Each station reported in. Velez had been grazed in the arm. After a bullet had tangentially hit but not penetrated his helmet, a man had been knocked unconscious but was now recovered.

"Damage control." A searchlight had been shot out and there were multiple but inconsequential bullet holes, although a full inspection had yet to take place. No water was coming in. They couldn't immediately test all the electronics and instrumentation, both because of its complicated nature and because the pilot was on the bridge, but there was no visually apparent major damage.

According to protocol, the pilot had radioed-in his report of the attack, and by the time Rensselaer went to visit the wounded an Egyptian F-16 roared from a mile or two back across the Canal and the dunes. In another ten minutes, helicopters appeared in the distance.

Lieutenant Velez was from a tiny town, in New Mexico, where the only water was underground "What were you doing when you were hit?" Rensselaer asked.

"Firing a twin-fifty, sir."

"Who took over?"

"No one. I kept firing."

"To be noted."

"No big deal," Velez said. "It was a case of to be or not to be."

Everyone returned to his station. The guns were reloaded and ammunition boxes replenished. When the watch changed, and even at the evening meal, little was said. Although the term is too strong and imprecise, the crew had been blooded, were now bound more closely, and in some ways were now wiser than philosophers.

As *Athena* moved on, the Egyptians may have taken stock of the dead. If not, those who had been killed and left behind were erased forever from the world. The people who might remember them would not be informed of their deaths, and would eventually follow as the blood and the bones of the fallen disappeared in sand and sun, their only benediction the wind. As night fell and *Athena* approached Suez, the great desert lay in darkness off to port.

*

At a steady 40 knots after Suez they would reach Djibouti in less than 30 hours. With 6 to 15 miles of sea on each side down the 200 miles of the Gulf of Suez, they reverted to Condition III, and in the Red Sea, with 50, 60, or 70 miles of sea to port and to starboard, they had planned to relax somewhat, because their radar and visuals would alert them in good time to any surface threat. Still, they would be ready for general quarters even as they kept up their drills.

Their relatively high speed was necessary to bring them on time to the assigned area of operations in the Indian Ocean, and they had a long way to go after topping off their tanks in Djibouti. Many of the crew had been to the Persian Gulf and more than a few had cruised the Indian Ocean, but in the Gulf they had always been close to base and had mostly worked with other ships of Fifth Fleet. In the IO they had made transits in carrier strike groups or amphibious ready groups, virtual floating cities with thousands of Americans, fast food, internet, and convenience stores. *Athena* would be alone, unaccompanied by a Burger King or his Dairy Queen.

As expected because of the war, both the Gulf of Suez and the Red Sea were almost entirely empty of maritime traffic. Perhaps an astute economist could have extrapolated this into market effects and made himself rich, but for *Athena* it was yet another immersion in the spell of the East. Although no one who had participated in the engagement in the Canal felt guilt or regret, everyone, even those who had been below in engineering, was haunted by the inescapable fact that they had killed. They had been trained to do so, they were defending, and they had had no choice, but it went against their desires, sensibilities, and how they had lived theretofore—especially in regard to the men at the guns, who had seen their projectiles rip into a man and blow him apart. Perhaps had they quickly returned to Norfolk as if on a short deployment in the Atlantic their altered states would have been subsumed in the familiar and they would have more easily forgotten. But now they were coasting down the Red Sea, and the alien landscape mated with the changes within them in ways they had never imagined and could not and did not express.

Rensselaer was on the bridge, scanning the sea through his own, non-Navy-issued, Nikon binocular, which magically made things clearer, better defined, brighter, and more colorful than when seen with the naked eye. The Navy-issued optics were more powerful but less luminous. He dropped the Nikons to his chest and pivoted to Buck Lanham, the quartermaster. "Approaching the chart table and looking over the plot, he said, "We can't follow that course, straight down the center."

"West of center, sir," Buck said.

"I understand, closer to Egypt, just like a tanker making time. Why are there no tankers here, Mr. Lanham?"

Lanham had semi-bucked teeth, so everyone called him Buck. He had long since given up on protest. "The Strait of Hormuz is closed."

"What about the ones that left port beforehand, and container ships from Asia?"

"I don't know."

"Because they're taking the long way around, past the Cape of Good Hope. The Red Sea is too narrow and shallow, the Bab-al-Mandab so constricting, that a sub thirty miles on either side would have targets fed to it as in a shooting preserve."

"Don't we have ASW there to stop that, and close off the Red Sea?" Lanham asked.

"Our ASW has gone to hell since the Cold War, and everything we've got left is in the Gulf or screening the task forces in the Arabian Sea."

"Why would Iran waste a sub in the empty Red Sea?"

"Why wouldn't it spare one for the Red Sea in hope of catching a tanker, a container ship, or, better yet, an American naval vessel? Or maybe there were some, or one, already here or in the IO, unable to pass our cordon at the Strait. It doesn't matter. We've got to stay off the sealanes and zigzag a bit. Submarines are different than the *Behshad.*"

"The *Behshad*, sir?"

"For years the Iranians anchored a big cargo ship, the *Saviz*, near the Bab-al-Mandab to keep track of tanker traffic and naval movements. The Israelis hit it badly enough so that the Iranians replaced it with the *Behshad*. When the war started, we told them to move it. They didn't. One of our F-15s from Saudi Arabia; two two-thousand-pound bombs; no more *Behshad.*"

He addressed Movius. "As unlikely as it might be, it would be embarrassing to take an Iranian torpedo. XO, double the lookouts and require surface scanning for torpedoes. Be prepared for flank speed and extreme maneuver."

"Aye, sir," Movius replied, "we sure as hell can do extreme maneuver," and got to the order without confirming it by repetition. It was too long for that, and they were far enough into the deployment that often, other than to the helm, confirmation of commands wasn't always necessary.

Everyone on the bridge could see in Rensselaer's expression that he was reproaching himself for his negligence, which, had he not caught it in time, might—if only at the outside—have been catastrophic.

With a new course having been coaxed randomly and capriciously from Lanham's head—at one point he spun around and placed his finger on the chart, eyes closed, to set a waypoint—they came close to land most of the time. Already having upped their readiness because of the potential submarine threat, now, closer to land, they had to be prepared for small boat attack as well.

The change in course meant that they would arrive at Djibouti and, subsequently, on station, roughly fourteen hours later than planned. They had to cover the guns and periodically sweep sand off the decks, because with zigzagging they came so close to the mountains of the Hijaz in Saudi Arabia, and to the arid wastes of Egypt, the Sudan, Eritrea, and Yemen, that it was as if they were sailing on land.

The wind kicked up at Al-Qusayr on the Egyptian coast. Only eighty miles inland, the Nile curved eastward, but from the Red Sea one could spy only sand, yellow and white rock, and the occasional opening of a wadi that beckoned to the interior without promise of anything but desert—though only two camel-days west the Nile flowed with ease and, having passed the cataracts, nothing to wake it from newfound contentment. Wind descends at evening from rapidly cooling deserts to displace warmer air over the water. As night progressed, masses of cold air from the Egyptian desert to the west and the Hijaz to the east met and rose over the Red Sea, lifting the warmer air toward the stars, which, through its undulating lens, appeared to be panicked, flashing like sequins and jumping like fleas.

This was the spectacle above as *Athena* made south, speeding over the Daedalus Reef, coming within a mile of Ras Banas—in Egyptian territorial waters, but no one was watching—and then heading 120 degrees east so as to drive toward Saudi Arabia while missing St. John's Island by a hair, deliberately, because submarines shy from islands and reefs. Twenty miles off the Saudi coast, *Athena* increased speed to forty-five knots at a heading of 190 degrees south. Soon after, they saw the sparkling lights of Jiddah, and within a very few minutes it was possible to see, they thought, the distant lights of Mecca, with a hint of the dawn coming up behind them.

It was cold enough that the sailors on watch outside wore deck jackets. Facing the sea, each of them felt a loneliness freighted with neither pain nor regret. *Athena* seemed very small in a world infinite in extent, full of clear air and empty spaces: a world of great chances to be taken and wondrous things to see. Something that had begun opposite Gibraltar as they skirted the coast of North Africa—building in the Mediterranean, solidified at Haifa in the Biblical Levant, accelerated during the battle in the Canal, and now permanently impressed as if by Khartoum to starboard and Mecca to port—was the sense that however much they might battle and strike, their agency was not their own. Instead, they felt carried forward, apart from their will as much as they now felt part of the sea, the land, the sky, and the stars.

By 1100, where between Eritrea and Saudi Arabia the Red Sea begins to narrow, the sun was again kiln-like. The farther south they went, the more careful they were, hugging the desolate coast of Eritrea and slipping between the many former Italian islets, until twenty-five miles north of the Bab-al-Mandab they accelerated from the thirty knots to which they had slowed among the islets and made flank speed to the narrows: the twenty miles of sea between Africa and Arabia, an ideal spot for a subma-rine lying in wait. On high alert, they raced across the water. In the excitement of G-forces and forward momentum, the sailors had to hold on as *Athena* leaned port and starboard like a speedboat, tossing spray, challenging balance.

At evening Djibouti was in sight. But before they were safe in the harbor they stayed on watch, for the submarine danger, as unlikely as it was, would not subside until, hunting for *Sahand*, they were far down the littoral of East Africa.

*

On a small ship, news and opinion spreads instantaneously and osmoti-cally. Rensselaer was not surprised that yet another officer plagued by doubt and wanting to be constructive knocked on his cabin door. In this case it was Lieutenant, Senior Grade, Marchetti, *Athena's* weapons officer. He was earnest in general, and now especially so. Rensselaer usually related to earnestness with a silence by which to encourage doubt, thus cultivating objectivity in a young man suddenly seized by a brilliant idea.

Marchetti took a seat. "Sir, given that we'll be outgunned—guns *and* missiles—by *Sahand*, I don't know if it's possible to prevail without either support from the air or another vessel. I've done the analysis using the Hughes Equations, and it's clear we're at a decisive disadvantage, to say the least."

"What are the Hughes Equations?" Rensselaer asked, deadpan.

Marchetti was shocked. "Captain Hughes, sir."

"Yes, I know, Wayne Hughes, but I'm not familiar with his equations."

Marchetti was somewhat alarmed. "Everybody studies them in systems analysis. The Hughes Salvo Equations, sir."

"My postgraduate training wasn't in systems analysis. The last time I did that kind of thing was at the Academy, before you were born, and most likely way before Captain Hughes derived his formulas. But, okay, what are they?"

Marchetti happily leaned forward in his chair. "In this case, if delta A equals, parenthesis, theta sub beta, small alpha, beta sub two, large beta, parenthesis, divided by small alpha sub one, where large beta two is the number of *Sahand*'s missiles that are operable, and theta small beta is targeting ability assessed as point seven, then. . . ."

"What the hell are you talking about?"

"Sir, if you run the equations, it means, sir. . . . May I speak freely?"

"Of course. Speak freely."

"It means we're screwed."

"Marchetti."

"Sir."

"You've read Clausewitz."

"Yes, sir, I have."

"Sun Tzu, Corbett, Mahan, Hughes . . . ?"

Marchetti nodded.

"How do you think those guys distilled war into the maxims, concepts, and equations that they did?"

"By observation."

"That's right. They didn't read them in a rule book. They distilled them from their experience and observation."

"Right."

"And for whom?"

"For everybody, sir."

"No."

"No?"

"No. Not for everybody. For the majority of people who, like them, experience and observe—in real life, and in study—but who, unlike them, are incapable of coming to the same conclusions. Strategy and tactics are in essence metaphysical. You either have it or you don't. Most soldiers and sailors don't. They have to follow the rules. But the rules are inexact, so they often lead to trouble and defeat when those who can do nothing but follow them are faced with variations they don't cover. You see?

"People who do have it are actually repelled by rules—by the inexactitude and rigidity. You can follow Sun Tzu and Clausewitz and the rest. Or, you can be *like* them."

"Are you saying, sir, that you are like Sun Tzu?"

"No, I'm saying that I'm like Attila the Fucking Hun."

"Attila the Fucking Hun?"

"Did you ever see crows driving away a hawk?"

"No, sir."

"I've seen it many, many times. The hawk is a raptor, with talons and a sharp beak. He can dive like a Stuka. The crow, well, the crow is a crow. But in concert they never fail to drive away the hawk."

"With all due respect, sir, we're not in concert."

"I know. We're not even a crow—more like a mockingbird. Except for the Harpoons, for which we have insufficient long-distance terminal guidance, vis-à-vis the *Sahand* we're outgunned and outranged."

"That's my point, sir."

"Right. That's why we've got to be like Attila. . . ."

"The Fucking Hun."

"Yes."

"Fierce and ruthless?" Marchetti asked.

"Not at all. That wouldn't save us or sink *Sahand*."

"Then why?"

"Attila was no theorist, and the Hughes Salvo Equations are inapplicable here. Why? Because—read them—the Hughes Equations assume a rough equality between forces."

"I thought you didn't know the Hughes Equations, as you weren't a gunnery officer and they came around after you were at the Academy."

"Pedagogical license."

"But . . . Attila?"

"Ah. Attila had the stirrup, and his enemies didn't. With the stirrup, his archers could make quick turns on their horses, hands free. They could fire backward while turned in the saddle, aim more surely, gallop faster, stop suddenly. His advantage was the stirrup, and how it was used. We've got to find our stirrup.

"I'm saying, Mr. Marchetti, that if when I say fire you are able to put our missiles and guns on target as ordered, we'll make the best of it. We're not going to get air or fleet support. That's the whole point. That's our challenge."

"So, what are you going to do, Captain?" Marchetti asked, with the wavering doubt in which the young instinctively approach the old as the young come into the power of their prime and the old lose their grip. Rensselaer didn't hold this against him. For other reasons, his eyes narrowed somewhat as he spoke.

"The stirrup, Mr. Marchetti, the stirrup. I'm going to find the stirrup. Then I'm going to put *Athena* in harm's way, and fight her as of old. I'm not going to worry that we're outmatched, and I'm going to sink the goddamned *Sahand.*"

Marchetti was a good and skillful officer, with a superb temperament, but, a little shaken, he reported this conversation with the captain to his fellow officers. Very rapidly and with poetic license, it made its way around the ship: "The captain says he's Attila the Fucking Hun."

*

At the pier in Djibouti Port, trucks were lined up as Rensselaer had requested of Fleet, and the transfer of fuel, ammunition, and foodstuffs began immediately. After the frustratingly slow process of tying up, Rensselaer and three men—Josephson; Di Loreto of Marine mammalhood; and Holworthy, intimidating of aspect and demeanor—approached an Army truck from which ammunition was being off-loaded.

"Who's in charge here?" Rensselaer asked.

"I am, sir," the driver, a corporal, answered.

"I need to borrow your truck."

"I'm sorry, sir, but we're ordered to off-load this ammo and return to camp."

"Take it off the truck right now and put it on the ground."

"Sir, I don't have the authorization to do that. I could call in but I don't know what they'll say." While he was speaking, Rensselaer made a quick circle around him, quick enough that the corporal turned his head first to the left as he spoke and then to the right, without moving his feet. He wondered why Rensselaer had done this, and why Navy men were sometimes as strange as space aliens.

Rensselaer said, "Is that"—pointing beyond the corporal—"*your* hundred-dollar bill?"

The corporal turned. A brand-new hundred-dollar bill fluttered on the ground. He seemed dumbfounded. Seconds passed. "Yes," he said. "I believe it is."

"Take us to wherever we can get things like camouflage netting, tarps, wood, spars, and metal buckets," Rensselaer commanded as, after the ammunition had been removed, he climbed into the truck's cab.

"What?"

"Lemonnier has everything in the world. We need camouflage netting, tarps, spars, wood, and metal buckets," Rensselaer repeated.

"You do?"

"We do. Do you know where we can get them?"

"What are spars?"

"Like a pole or a boom."

"Like in construction?"

"Right, a light cross-member or beam."

"Okay." The corporal set his mind to it and off they went.

As they drove through Djibouti and into Camp Lemonnier, Josephson said, "It's like the crappy parts of Los Angeles except there aren't any homeless people and everyone has short hair."

"Not the girls," the corporal replied.

"No. Not the girls."

"Some of them."

"Yeah. Some of them."

They pulled up to a giant warehouse, which the corporal said was the Army's version of Home Depot. "You can probably get anything here," he announced.

"And rope," Rensselaer said. "I forgot rope."

"Go for it, sir," the corporal said, not quite sure if he were dreaming.

Inside, they faced a fearsome barrier of clerks. For someone of Rensselaer's temperament, it was better to face the Iranian Revolutionary Guard Corps than a phalanx of U.S. Army supply clerks. He approached the easiest-looking one, a young fellow who seemed like a better mark than the older, cannier, and likely unpleasant ones. Whereas the danger they promised was the years they'd marinated in the (to them) sex of bureaucracy, his was that of entry-level stupidity. Rensselaer took a chance.

"Yeah, we have all that," the clerk replied to the spoken list. "I need your requisition papers and approvals."

"No time. Emergency."

"I can't do that."

"Lives may depend upon it."

The clerk smiled. "I've heard that before."

"And what did you do?"

"Nothing."

Rensselaer pursed his lips and prepared another approach.

"Oh yeah?" said the clerk.

"What you mean, 'Oh yeah?'? I didn't say anything."

"You coulda told *me*," the clerk followed.

"I could have told you what?"

"I don't know. Whatever."

Now it was Rensselaer who was dumbfounded. After a moment, he covertly dropped another hundred, and asked, "Is this your hundred-dollar bill?"

"What hundred-dollar bill?"

Rensselaer pointed. "That one. The one on the floor."

"Nope," said the clerk.

"Are you sure?"

"I am. I don't think it is, because I dropped three hundreds."

"Crap," said Rensselaer, "and tell me, don't you address officers properly?"

"Not the Navy. I can't read the insignia. As far as I know, you're Sinbad the Sailor. Everything will be on loading dock eight in about fifteen minutes. The only wood we have is a million pallets around back. You're welcome to them."

For the lower-ranking warehousemen it was strange to see officers eagerly loading a truck. On the way back to the port, Rensselaer inventoried what they had: twenty artillery camouflage nets; twenty large tarps; one thousand feet of one-half-inch manila rope; twelve large metal buckets; four twenty-foot aluminum poles; and two freight pallets.

Unhappy to begin with about being trapped on *Athena*, Holworthy continued to suspect that the captain was not entirely sound. The others wondered as well. Di Loreto had no problem about questioning Rensselaer.

"Sir, do we really need all this stuff?"

"Do we need porpoises?" Rensselaer replied.

Unaware of Di Loreto's prior service, Holworthy was now actually alarmed. He repeated the question skeptically. "*Do we need porpoises*, sir?"

"Ask him," Rensselaer said, meaning Di Loreto.

"Do we need porpoises?" Holworthy asked Di Loreto as the truck bumped along at high speed.

"Dolphins," Di Loreto answered.

"I don't understand," Holworthy stated, feeling as if maybe he had been drugged.

"Why would you?" Rensselaer asked rhetorically. "You're a *SEAL*!"

In response to Rensselaer's delight in this, Holworthy just widened his eyes.

When they pulled up to the pier they called in a work party and everything they had taken from the warehouse was on board in five minutes. The other loading and refueling had been finished, and men were already in place at the cleats and bitts. Ten minutes later, after the officer of the deck—in this case Movius—had moved from the quarterdeck to the bridge, and the commands had been given (ease the spring lines; slack number two; check the steering line; cast off all), *Athena* made her way into the late afternoon, and by dusk was deep along the Gulf of Aden. Her course was straighter than in the Red Sea, not because the submarine danger was that much less but rather because Rensselaer decided that it was late enough that she now had to hurry along even if at greater risk.

He noticed a change in the young sailors manning the guns. Some had been afraid, but now they were so taken up by their surroundings that they felt only joy. Coming into theater, everyone aboard could feel what was ahead. It heightened their senses and their thoughts, so that they saw things anew. When properly sung, the Navy Hymn rolls like those great and powerful waves, high and deep, that are yet smooth enough not to break at the crest. To those whose lives are on the sea its music conjures images of the oceans. Now, with the world sharpened as if in a fine and magical lens, for some of *Athena*'s crew the smooth and rolling swells conjured in their hearts and minds the sound of the song itself.

KATY'S LETTER

Two hours out of Djibouti, a great stir arose. The crew were alerted to the discovery of a massive bouquet of daffodils flooding from a stainless-steel pitcher on one of the mess tables. The mystery astounded them as if they were apes. Whence had this come? Certainly not from Djibouti's scrub desert, and there were no greenhouses at Camp Lemonnier; and no prim, sunny, bay windows.

Had they been airlifted from the States? Taken on recently at Haifa? Grown in a secret, hydroponic enclosure at Lemonnier? Many theories proliferated, some ridiculous, none satisfactory. Though in the sea air the daffodils wilted after two days, when first they appeared they were the color of Vermeer's yellows and so new and heavy with water as to be almost tumescent. Every theory pointed to Rensselaer, but he admitted nothing and seemed as puzzled as everyone else. Eventually, speculation was abandoned and the search for causes forgotten. Thence forward, in reference to anything inexplicable, the crew would say, "It's like the daffodils."

"Captain," Josephson said as the sun was setting over Ethiopia almost directly astern. Pinafore was at the helm, listening intently. "When the sun sets here, it's as if time is speeded up." Then he was silent.

Rensselaer looked at him the way one would look at a clueless child. Josephson's features were so finely delineated, his appearance so young, that he could have been mistaken for a fourteen-year-old. Everything about him expressed his newness to the world. "Are you on LSD?" Rensselaer asked, deadpan.

"Not to my knowledge, sir, but look."

The sun was indeed racing to the horizon. Rensselaer didn't need to look. "Have you ever been in these latitudes?"

"Eleven degrees? No sir."

"Neither have I, sir," Pinafore volunteered.

"What's the farthest south you've ever been?"

"Norfolk, sir, Williamsburg," said Josephson. "Or, I don't know, Los Angeles? It was just Disneyland, and I was so young I didn't know where I was."

"Chicago," said Pinafore.

"Well that's not true, Pinafore," Rensselaer told him. We boarded in Norfolk."

"Norfolk is south of Chicago, sir?"

"It is, quite a lot. Now, we're twenty-six degrees south of Norfolk. If you went twenty-six degrees north of Norfolk you'd be somewhere in the middle of Hudson Bay, where the sun sets really, really slowly."

"It does?" Josephson asked.

Everyone on the bridge had an ear cocked to this conversation. "It does. Tell me why?"

"I don't know. Why would it?"

"You were in NROTC?"

"Yes sir."

"And they didn't do navigation and geography?"

"They did, but no one talked about the sunset."

"It's like this, Josephson. Every time a wheel rotates, the rim has to cover a lot more distance than the axle, right? Figure that the earth is like an apple. Stick a skewer through it and have it rotate around the skewer as the axle. If there was a skewer with a thickness of, say, a penny, at the North and South Poles, skewering the earth, it would take twenty-four hours for a complete revolution to cover . . . what, the three-quarters-of-an-inch circumference of the penny? Meanwhile, at the equator, it takes the same twenty-four hours to cover the twenty-five thousand miles of the Earth's circumference there. So at the North Pole, at the skewer, the earth is revolving at less than a millimeter an hour, but at the equator, more than a thousand miles an hour. The higher the absolute speed, as you get closer to the equator, the faster the sun seems to set."

"That's neat."

"It is. Josephson?"

"Sir?"

"In your off time, read through *Dutton's Navigation and Piloting*. And, Pinafore?"

"Sir?"

"Take a look."

"Aye sir. Will do."

"If you have a question, ask the LT."

"Which LT, sir?"

"The quartermaster."

Buck Lanham made a face.

At this point, Movius came onto the bridge to start his watch. He began to salute and then caught himself. Rensselaer took the 1MC. "This is the captain. Officially or not, we're in a war zone, and we're now really done with saluting. We've tried. It's a hard habit to kick. Now I repeat, I say again, I emphasize, no more saluting. This will be posted on the watch bills, but make sure your shipmates who may now be sleeping are made aware of it." His eye caught something in the corner. "Stand by.

"What's that?" he asked.

Several people said, "Mail, sir," referring to a large canvas sack resting against the bulkhead. It had arrived during the foraging expedition.

Rensselaer went back on the 1MC. "I'm happy to tell you that we got the mail in Djibouti. Pick it up at COMMS at the end of your watches, not before. When you turn in, be ready for general quarters—drill or otherwise. Captain out."

Clicking off the 1MC, he turned to Josephson, the officer of the deck until his imminent relief by the XO. "COMMS to the bridge."

Josephson repeated this into the 1MC, and went about his duties.

Soon, Velez came onto the bridge. "Mr. Velez," Rensselaer said, "take care of the mail, and message CENTCOM and AFRICOM. *'Athena* in the Gulf of Aden. Where is *Sahand*?'"

"Directly to CENTCOM and AFRICOM, sir?" Velez asked as he wrote down the message.

"Yes. Whereas I don't know about the other commands, they have liaison with CIA. CIA is watching the ports, and we received our orders through the embassy in Jerusalem rather than through normal channels. I could see a message lost forever in the stovepiping."

"Please verify, sir," Velez asked, holding out the message he had written.

"Message is correct. Transmit."

"Aye sir." Velez left, hoisting the heavy canvas sack onto his back.

Eight bells sounded the end of the second dog watch. "XO," Rensselaer commanded, "darken ship. Tomorrow, weapons check (all weapons, down to pistols) and long-range practice with the thirty. It's time to start using the telescopic mast. I want to calibrate the visuals and make its use routine. Note this on the watch bills and in the P.O.D. And the SEALs are getting too parochial. I want them participating and aware of what the ship is doing. They're a separate nation, but they're also sailors, which they tend to forget. I did, once. They have to be reminded of the unity of mission and command.

"We now have to worry about pirates. In the dark even with night vision it'll be hard to tell the difference between a pirate skiff and an Iranian fast-attack craft. If the radar shows anything moving toward us at high speed, call general quarters. If I haven't arrived and they're within small-arms range, warn'em once. If they persist, blow them out of the water."

Movius nodded. Before the captain left the bridge he announced, to the incoming and outgoing watches, "The XO has the con," and the new watch began.

*

Before he turned in, hoping for a letter, Rensselaer stopped at COMMS, waiting at the door while Velez finished his transmissions. The mailbag lay in the corner, still unopened. Velez finished and swivelled in his seat. "I had to mess around a lot to send to AFRICOM. Never sent to them before, but I managed."

"What's that?" Rensselaer asked, referring to a kind of tiny cargo net hanging from the ceiling and bulging with equipment.

"The sat-phones. Commander Holworthy asked me to keep them here. In the past he's had trouble with corroded contacts, and we have the best environment for electronics." Indeed, he was surrounded, bulkhead to bulkhead, with complicated electronics and blinking lights. "He wants the batteries at a hundred percent."

Rensselaer nodded.

"Captain, I can go through the mail real quick to see if you've got anything."

"No," Rensselaer said, "it'll wait until I'm done with what I have to do tomorrow. Get it to the crew first."

*

Encouraged by the captain's instruction about the sunset, after dinner as *Athena* ploughed south in a rolling swell coming broadside from the east, Josephson sought him on the bridge.

"Do you know where I can find the captain?" Josephson asked Movius, who had the con. Movius just pointed up. The captain was on the open bridge, where he often went in the evening to survey the ship from stem to stern. Though *Athena* was rolling, Rensselaer wasn't grasping a rail.

"Captain, sir. Request permission to speak."

"You're already speaking."

"Then to speak further, sir."

"Speak further, Mr. Josephson."

"It's really moving up here, sir."

"Not that much more than on the bridge, but this is exactly what we were talking about."

"Sir?"

"There's more roll up here than on the enclosed bridge. The higher you go from the center of gravity, which serves as the ship's axis, the greater the distance for every movement. Just like the apple with a skewer in the middle, or a bicycle wheel and hub. A five-degree pitch and ten-degree roll up here might lift us however many feet forward and aft, and take us however many feet to port or starboard, but the top of the mast will move much more. An imaginary line deep into the universe would move trillions of light-years in the seconds it takes us to move to and fro, or left and right."

"But that's not why you came up here, is it?" Rensselaer asked, looking not at Josephson but at the fading light over the sea.

"No sir."

"What then?"

"Sir, I wonder if I might ask you for career advice. It's kind of a mystery to me."

Rensselaer smiled. "Me? It's obviously a mystery to me, too. I'm a captain assigned to the job of a lieutenant commander. For me, every minute of this deployment is supposed to be humiliation and reprimand."

"Yes, sir. I know about that. But is it?"

"No."

"I didn't think so, sir. So, the advice, which I think might be invaluable, is—why?"

"I'm impressed. That's exactly what you should know. Because, in fact, I'm neither punished nor disturbed. Why? I was never ambitious except perhaps for a brief period when I was in love with a girl whose family were social climbers and they thought I wasn't good enough for her, so

I tried to prove them wrong. That lasted only as long as she did. I knew even then that you can't engineer your path unless all you want is frustration. For everyone who plots an ambitious course and succeeds, there are ten thousand who suffer continual unhappiness and failure.

"I just tried to be involved in things that interested me, and I worked hard—because I liked it. Opportunities arose and promotion came as a result of that, not because I had a design. I'll retire as a captain. Coulda been a contender, an admiral. Things interfered. But it was never my aim to be either, just to do my best at what I loved, and, when that was not available, at what I was assigned to do, like this.

"If you cease to think well of yourself because you shine in the eyes of others, but, rather, do whatever it is you do out of interest and delight (and discipline), such a great burden will be floated from your shoulders as you cannot imagine, and the world will appear as wonderful as it is to a child.

"So, what interests you?" he asked Josephson.

"You mean, what I would like to pursue?"

"What do you read about, think about?"

"Actually, distributed lethality, maximizing the punch of every combatant, even the smallest."

"Perfect for where we are right now."

"And fleet design, new weaponry, new concepts."

"All right. Study that intensively. Read everything you can, take notes, engage with it until you can write about it. And then write. It will be satisfying in itself, and if you do well and publish, opportunities will likely arise. Keep at it. That's how it works. And when you're fully absorbed in something that's deserving and worthwhile, you don't have to worry about career."

"What did you . . . ?"

"Deterrence strategy. That's a deep pool: history, psychology, cultural comparisons, game theory, physics, operational art, weaponry of course, geography, weather, economics, politics, bureaucratic politics, organization theory. I didn't think for a minute about promotion. I was far too busy even to know that time was passing.

"Josephson."

"Sir?"

"Work hard, be interested, be a good dog, and don't chase rabbits."

"Yes, sir."

"Dismissed."

*

When Rensselaer was back in his cabin and ready to sleep, he took out Katy's picture and stared at it the way soldiers and sailors stare at the pictures of the ones they love who are distant at present and will be perhaps forever—something they take into account whether they are aware of it or not. One discovers either that he is numb to the image and his heart is cold, or that his love has deepened to the point of exquisite longing. The features in Katy's photograph that others may have found imperfect—her inimitable physical sharpness, and the tension communicated even in a still photograph—he found painfully beautiful.

The next morning, Rensselaer allowed the OOD to keep the con even with the captain on the bridge, because he was in and out as he supervised the weapons checks. Gunners' mates were cleaning, lubricating, and otherwise preparing their weapons, and mixing ammunition loads for various scenarios. Missilery was a different story—mostly electronic, calibration, exercising data links, checking for moisture where it should not have penetrated. Even though the decks were crowded, the SEALs were out in the open, maintaining their arsenals all the way down to scabbarded knives. A weapon must feel like it is a part of one's body, so that it will do what it is intended to do with no more deliberation than one devotes to one's legs when walking or running.

Back on the bridge at midmorning, Rensselaer said, with an amused expression, "Up periscope," and the telescopic mast was raised. The OOD asked if what the captain wanted was to test the visuals even into the sun, to which the reply was, "Absolutely."

First they looked at the telescopic mast's radar. Counting atmospheric effects, the direct picture wasn't that much different from the more powerful lower radar. Then they switched to visual. Someone said, "My grandfather told me that for a long time all they had was black-and-white TV." As he looked at the monochrome picture, he marveled. "I wouldn't have watched it if it was like that."

"We had one when I was little," Rensselaer said. "You get used to it." Then they began the test, using their electronic maps and GPS to make precise determinations.

The air held very little haze. With a powerful binocular on the open bridge above, Rensselaer made out a feature of land, a crust-like projection of rocks that jutted into the sea—five miles, as measured on the electronic chart, between the rocks and *Athena's* exact position determined by GPS. Then he descended to the enclosed bridge and zoomed in with the camera at the tip of the telescopic mast. Visible to him ahead was a village tucked into the rolling terrain and completely undetectable from standard height. He marveled at how people could live on the sand, with only occasional scrub here or there, everything baking hot and dry, and nothing inland but desert.

The village was called Ceelayo. Each house had a walled courtyard. There were no streets, just paths, but there had to have been water there, although it certainly didn't look like it. Not that far from the sea was the mosque, identified on the electronic chart as the Masjidka Ceelayo. He could see it clearly. "What is the position and distance of the mosque," he asked the OOD, who was at the electronic chart.

"Eleven degrees, fourteen minutes, forty-three seconds north, and forty-eight degrees, fifty-three minutes, thirty-five seconds east."

"Calculate the distance from our position on my mark." A few seconds passed. "Mark."

The OOD worked the keys, and a line appeared on his colorful screen from a spot on the sea to the mosque in Ceelayo. "Ten point seven three miles."

"Nautical?" Rensselaer asked, almost skeptically.

"Nautical."

"Precisely in statute miles?" He already knew, more or less.

"Twelve point five."

"That's more than we got in trials," Rensselaer said. "I don't understand. We're fully loaded and not riding high in the water."

A rating stepped out onto the port bridge wing, and, craning his neck and shielding his eyes, stared at the telescopic mast. Returning, he announced that it had extended more, and was moving around like a sapling.

"They stiffened the mast with an electronic block that keeps the end-shaft deeper in the next-to-last shaft," Rensselaer told everyone. "The block has failed, and the mast is now taller."

"Yes sir," the OOD added, "and we don't see the greater movement, because of the image stabilization. Shall we attempt to fix the block, sir?"

"Leave it as it is. 'Our indiscretions sometimes serve us well, Horatio, for a divinity shapes our ends, and praisèd be rashness for it.'"

By far the oldest person on the bridge, Rensselaer assumed that they would know this was Shakespeare, but none of them did, for their generations had been taught other, lesser things. The language he had used, and his calling the OOD Horatio, left them silent and tense. They didn't think to inquire, because they didn't know enough to suspect. Instead, the story would spread throughout the ship, where it would be received, as gossip so often is, as if it were the finest delicacy. It was in fact a lot of fun to think that the old man was slightly off his nut.

*

In midafternoon and more than one hundred miles east of Ceelayo, the XO was taking a break on the mess deck, where the snacks were, as opposed to the wardroom, where they weren't. Although he had an ear cocked for any call that might require him, he was deeply absorbed in Adam Smith's *Theory of Moral Sentiments*. To the right of the book on the stainless-steel table were a plastic bottle of very cold Diet Coke and a large pile of cookies.

Seeking the cool, dry air, Holworthy walked in, his shirt soaking and beads of water on his face. "What's that?" he asked Movius.

Although Movius was the XO, they were both lieutenant commanders, equal in rank. "*Theory of Moral Sentiments.*"

"I mean the cookies."

"Oh. Special Oreos, vanilla outsides with chocolate inside. You have to request them."

"From who?"

"From Oreo. If you order enough they'll make specialty batches. We took them on in Djibouti. Don't ask me why the Navy ordered inside-out Oreos for Djibouti."

"Where are they?"

Movius pointed to a bin on the counter. Before long, Holworthy was sitting opposite him, twenty cookies piled into stacks of ten, like rounds in a magazine, and an ice-cold Diet Coke already condensing on the outside. "What's the point of a Diet Coke with high-calorie cookies?" Holworthy asked rhetorically.

"Why add insult to injury?" was the reply. "And a lot of people, including me, think Diet Coke is wonderfully dry, even more than Champagne. It's genetically determined. Don't tell the French."

"At birth?"

Movius looked up. He made sure his tone was not condescending. "Before birth."

"Right."

Movius, who thought SEALs feasted too much on their PR, went back to his book.

"What's going on with the captain?"

A question like that was not to be taken lightly. Movius closed the book and looked up. "Meaning?"

"He called the OOD Horatio. He said he has to talk to God. He had us chasing around for camo nets, metal buckets, and rope. What was *that* all about?"

"What are you suggesting?"

"I'm not suggesting anything. You're the XO. I think it's normal for me to report that my men, who thought we were going to the Gulf to do what we were trained to do, feel like they've been kidnaped to sit out the war fucking around in the Indian Ocean with a guy who's got one foot in the grave and maybe the other in the funny farm."

"Maybe he's got one foot in the grave, but the other's dancing, and anyway it wasn't the captain's decision. You know that."

"I'm not saying it was. I'm just commenting on the morale of my detachment. They're pissed off."

"You too?"

"Maybe."

"What do you want me to do about it," Movius asked, "give them hot cocoa and safe spaces?"

"No. They want dangerous spaces. That's the point. There's a war on. You've got a bunch of racehorses down below, and they're stuck in their stalls. I feel obligated to let you know that."

"Very well. I know it."

Very well is the phrase of a superior who has received information or a request from someone of lower rank. Movius had employed it to end the conversation, assert his higher position as XO, express his disapproval, and indicate that he would neither take action nor sympathize. Then he returned to his book.

But when Holworthy left, cookies and drink in hand, the XO closed the book and stayed in his seat. There was no point, he decided, in telling the captain, for Holworthy's complaint lacked sufficient substance.

*

At evening, rounding the tip of the Horn of Africa at Cape Guardafui (on the old charts, *Geez Guardafuy* on the new), *Athena* turned south 176 degrees so as nearly to graze Ras Hafun, a small headland protruding almost directly east. Behind this cape for many miles were immense dunes that, like waves, had been driven south by the north wind. The same wind had given *Athena* an assist, but now the air had begun to flow from the cooling desert, gently, because it was early, and to the east. At three or four in the morning it would be strong enough and dense enough to vector the north wind to the southeast, its force dissipating only five or ten miles from shore. Farther out, it would be largely spent.

With few and necessary exceptions, *Athena* had observed radio silence since exiting the Canal. There had been no radiotelephony or Internet uploads from the very beginning. Now she exercised thorough emissions control. EMCON meant no radar, no uplinks. It was early in regard to *Sahand*, but as no one knew where *Sahand* was, they had to take into account that it might appear at any moment. The strain of EMCON was enormous, as no radar meant the only way to avoid collision with craft not themselves emitting radar was by sight and hearing, and as the desert in the Horn offered little except scrub for goats, the wretched villages on the coast survived by fishing and piracy, so the waters were fairly crowded with radarless skiffs. Lookouts were doubled, and no one slept quite enough.

One thing that electronic silence and weeks away from the Internet succeeded in accomplishing was to return the written letter on paper to the elevated, magical position it once held. Rensselaer was the only one old enough to remember the tidal force of the traces of a woman's perfume on a letter; the charm, intelligence, and seductiveness of her handwriting; the excitement of holding in one's hand an envelope and pages that had been held in hers. He was the only one old enough to remember reading a letter many times over, and each time feeling slightly different longings, reassurances, or fears. Now the crew had begun to be educated in this, and he was about to be re-educated. His duties finished, the respite in his cabin was compromised only by the fact that, like everyone else, in anticipation of general quarters, he slept in his clothes.

Katy's letter was the last Velez had surrendered, as the captain, with so much to do and by his own order, had been the last to get his mail. It was on elegant but plain stationery—cream on the outside, a Tiffany-blue envelope lining, cream papers, hand-addressed and -written, with a floral stamp. And, yes, her perfume was strongly apparent, so much so that he spent a few minutes before he opened the envelope breathing in deeply to catch the scent, eyes closed. Then he opened it. Just the hand-writing was as seductive as anything by which he had ever been seduced.

"Dear Stephen," it began, as one would expect.

"Forgive me for not being good at letter writing. In the days when we did, I was too young and needy. When the family was together, we did not, of course, write letters. My children don't write now. I don't mean just to me; they stopped that a while ago. I mean in general. Now it's all Internet or texting or other useless, fashionable means with infantile, baby-talk names like Bish-Bosh, Wombat, Crinkle, or Winka Dink.

"So I'm not exactly Jane Austen. And there's so much Jane Austen going around that a lot of women now imitate her in what should be simple letters—'Pray you, Captain Rensselaer, I should blush to acknowledge. . . .' A new associate wrote me a note flavored like that. I called her into my office and said, 'Are you out of your mind?'

"I'm really not good at letters. Add to that, I'm a tax lawyer, educated over the years to write like a vending machine or maybe a very insensitive chainsaw. Enough with excuses.

"I'm back in New Orleans now—I was in California, and will get to that later. The heat, humidity, and penetrating sun have slowed everything down here, as usual. People are as lazy as hell, and drink, and have sex (not me), because it seems to make sense and they can't do much else. Please note that in that regard I *really* miss you, and (without putting into the written record anything that might embarrass me), as I lie in bed or sometimes even when I'm just reading, the object of my affection and the enabler of my action is you and just you.

"This year, perhaps because of the excellent timing of the rains, the vegetation is astounding. Flowers are so ripe with color that in bright sun rather than fade they dazzle the eye. If not for weed wackers, hedge trimmers, and illegal immigrants, the Garden District would be as swal-lowed by vegetation as a Mayan temple. I can't run outside, so I have to use treadmills—with people watching cable news on either side of me—but mainly I swim a lot, and I think you would be pleased by the shape I'm in. That's an invitation.

"A bunch of us had to go to L.A. last week at the emergency request of a big movie studio (I can't tell you the name of it, but it begins with *W*) that was thinking of selling itself to China. This involved contract law, international law, Chinese law, tax law, investment banking, and God knows what else. We weren't the only team. The Four Seasons in Beverly Hills was filled with lawyers. The deal was stupid and greedy. In fact, I knew that solely because of China's current investment policies it wouldn't go through, and it fell apart in a week. Meanwhile, we billed more than a million dollars, not counting the considerable five-star expenses, including a corporate jet that we had to charter because they had to have us out there immediately. Then, when we got there, they put us off and we spent two days by the pool.

"When we met in conference at the studio, about thirty people were sitting around the giant table, and we all had name placards. Our secretary, who calls me Katy, the only secretary at the firm who calls me Katy, because she looked up my high-school yearbook online, used it on the list of personnel. Somebody must've read the handwritten *Y* at the end of Katy as a *Z*, because my placard said 'Katz Farrar,' and everyone called me *Katz*, which broke up our people, and needless to say, me. The president of the holding company at one point turned to me and said, 'Katz, what do you think?' I couldn't stop laughing. He must've thought I was an idiot, who, to boot, had the first name *Katz*. I don't think they'll ever hire us again, and the whole thing will only reinforce Hollywood's prejudices about the South.

"Of the partners who, entirely inexplicably to me, will not leave me alone, the one most besotted, Roger, was along on the trip. We check into the hotel, and low and behold, our rooms are next to one another and there was a door between them. I thought this might not be a coincidence, so I took my suitcase downstairs and changed rooms. At dinner a couple of nights later, I heard our managing partner (who also has an interest in me, I think. Maybe I'm crazy) ask Roger, 'Why were you banging on my door last night?'

"'*Your* door?' Roger asked in reply.

"'Yes, *my* door.' He wasn't amused. It took Roger about a minute to figure out an answer, during which he pretended all that time to be fighting one lousy piece of sushi.

"'Well,' he said, 'I guess it was because your television was so loud.'

"'It wasn't on,' was the answer. 'It was four in the morning. I was fast asleep. I don't watch infomercials.'

"'It must have been coming from the room on the other side,' Roger said. And then, stupidly, almost endearingly, he gave himself away, saying, 'Sorry. That's *your* room?'

"It didn't stop there. The night before we left, we all met in the bar, to make a wrap as they say out there. But it was so noisy that no one could hear anything, so we decided to go out to the garden. But there was an Orthodox Jewish wedding in the garden with about four hundred people, so we trooped back in and found a room off the lobby—in which, by the way, the rugs are so plush they might as well be part quicksand, and everything else is marble shining beneath perfectly focused light.

"We did wrap up, about two scotches later for the men and one glass of Champagne for me. We were done and everyone was leaving when Roger, now on his third drink, asked me to summarize what I had said to one of the studio's in-house lawyers about offshoring. The way he put it, I couldn't really refuse.

"As soon as everyone was gone he said, 'So, your beau is in the Navy.' He talks like that—*beau*. He's from here."

"'How do you know?' I asked.

"'Angela Jowet, the paralegal, saw you on a bench in a park somewhere, with a naval officer. You were in his arms, she said. Your eyes were closed, you were smiling, and she thought you looked like you were in heaven.'

"'I was,' I answered.

"'Well, now I understand about the two-hundred-foot yacht,' he went on, as if he had caught me.

"'Yes, Roger,' I answered, perhaps a little testily, 'and don't screw around with it or me, because it has big automatic guns and missiles and it can blow your shitty little sailboat to Mars.'

"It's not so easy to dissuade a rich, drunk guy who has a crush on you. He found my response irresistible. 'Katy,' he said, 'I love you. I've loved you since you first walked in the door. First sight, and it's only grown stronger, and they want you to know that I'm here for you, and will be here for you, should you . . . now and in the future.'

"I said, 'Who's *they*?'

"He was so drunk. He said, 'I mean I.'

"So this is what I told him: I said, 'Roger, I'm flattered, but you've got to understand one thing. I love him, and it's the kind of love that, by the grace of God, you can find after you've really messed things up when you're younger, and been cast down, and you think it's all done and you'll be lonely for the rest of your life. Then someone comes along and you have all the excitement of falling in love when you're fifteen, but, unlike when you're fifteen, you know—and he knows—all those things that can poison, deaden, and destroy love. And amazingly, wonderfully, you also know that they're absent. You know the way is clear forever. You've never loved anyone like this before, and that's it. It's enough to carry on even if one of you dies first. You've arrived. You've got it made. That's how I feel about my naval officer. There'll never be anyone else.'

"He knew there was no bravado in what I was saying, no strain, just the truth. To his credit, he bowed his head, and said, 'I'm glad for you, Catherine, and sorry for myself.' He's a good and civilized man, and had you not shown up I might have married him out of expediency and lack of hope.

"But you did show up. And I'll tell you, when you left I cried, but I knew that no matter where you are, whether on the sea or close to shore, and no matter what will happen, we'll always be together one way or another. Bank on this, even should you doubt, or should you be in the fight. And when you see an evening star rising at the edge of a placid, waveless sea, know that it's true.

"If our letters cross, or if we forget the exact details of one another's faces or bodies, or the precise sounds of one another's voices, the love is still unbreakable. It's the kind of love that even if unexpressed is like those little particles that at the speed of light shoot effortlessly through ten thousand miles of dense rock, untouched and unmarred. Forgive my imprecise physics. I can't adequately express what's in my heart.

"Oh, and I forgot. This morning I heard a dove: very early, very close. Usually, it's not until evening.

"Love,

"Katy."

Off the Horn of Africa, in the Indian Ocean, with the desert rapidly cooling to the west and its great sand dunes even now cold to the touch, the captain of the *Athena* turned off the light in his tiny stateroom, and lay back in the dark.

THE SECOND BATTLE:
GENERAL QUARTERS

The weak are attacked by the strong and the weak alike: the former exploiting their advantage, and the latter seizing their best chance. Had *Athena* sailed in a squadron or larger group, or had she been the size of a destroyer or even a frigate, she probably would have been undisturbed in the Canal and been able to round the Horn of Africa and steam south without incident. But she was small and she was alone.

In the middle of the evening watch, tranquility reigned. At about 2200, *Athena* was crossing a calm sea with only the slightest swell, steadily putting distance between herself and Somalia, not because she shied from any coast but because her exactly due south course meant that in relative terms Africa pulled to the west. The moon was about to rise, but now the darkness was compromised only by starlight. Port, starboard, and stern lookouts and the bridge watch had night-vision binoculars. For 360-degrees 'round they saw nothing. Not only had the war suppressed maritime traffic, but they were outside the customary sea-lanes.

The one-third of the crew standing Condition III watch felt a pleasant equilibrium.

Physical exercises had been over long enough for everyone to have recovered, they were just past the stimulative jag of the evening meal, and not yet made tired by the hour. The only challenge was that everything seemed to be in perfect order, the sea a uniform block of coal-black yet to be painted by moonlight.

Not surprisingly, the sailors turned inward. Between scannings of the empty sea, the lookouts retreated to their thoughts and desires, and the bridge watch were occupied by the many available distractions. The steady monitoring of instruments is not merely commendable, it is entertaining. Hours pass quickly when monitoring even the smallest changes in depth soundings, course, speed, engine parameters, electrical usage, and radar and GPS plots. At the edge of what had recently been a heavily pirated area, despite EMCON the radar was switched on every ten minutes in short pulses that swept the horizon and then ceased. Awareness of the changing seconds in latitude and longitude (although in regard to longitude *Athena* was steady as she goes), occasional variations in the sea and air temperature, and the bells every half hour, braid the many strands of time into a river that provides the same satisfaction and pleasure of a real river as it flows.

Thus every officer and rating on *Athena*'s bridge other than the helmsman (who served as lee helmsman as well) moved in slow procession from instrument to instrument. Some were more closely tied to their stations, and the most mobile was the OOD, the one responsible for everything, who on this watch was Movius, the XO. He took evening watch as much as he could, because he enjoyed it.

A few minutes after five bells—which, as they struck, everyone counted on his fingers so as not to allow confusion in the reading of gauges and displays—the radar operator called out, "Officer of the Deck," who, a few feet away, turned to him, "radar, surface contact, bearing one eight zero relative. Thirty thousand yards, target angle zero, zero, zero, three vessels line abreast and closing slowly."

As Movius moved to the radar console, he said, "Size of return?"

"Very small, sir. Boats."

"Keep the radar up."

"Aye, sir."

The radar screen and all its scales and numbers were reflected in Movius's eyes. "I would say the distance between them," he estimated, "is about five hundred yards."

"I concur."

"Their speed?"

"Thirty-five knots more or less, sir."

Movius, who knew *Athena*'s speed, checked it anyway. Thirty knots. He summoned the captain.

In less than a minute, Rensselaer was on the bridge, carrying helmet, body armor, and life jacket, all of which he dumped in a corner. The captain went right to the radar, saying, "I have the con."

"The captain has the con."

"When did you hook on to the contact?"

The radar operator looked at the screen. He had marked the contact at first sight. "Less than two minutes ago, sir."

"Have they broken formation or changed course even slightly during that time?"

"No."

Rensselaer was silent for a moment. "We can outrun them, of course, but there's no need. XO, sound general quarters."

"Aye sir, general quarters." Movius seized the 1MC mic, activated the klaxon, and said, calmly, "General quarters. All hands man battle stations, assume Condition Zebra. I say again, general quarters. All hands man your battle stations. Assume Condition Zebra." The klaxon continued.

The sailors who were sleeping rolled out of their racks with displeasure, some drowsy enough so that they tied their shoes poorly and as they rushed to their stations they heard the clicking of laces feebly lashing the deck. Everyone thought that, although it seemed too early, *Athena* might have found *Sahand*. This was the cause of anxiety, as they knew *Sahand* could easily destroy them. Now, unlike as in the Canal, the sudden call to general quarters was met with much graver determination. Within another two minutes, all battle stations were manned, compartments closed as required, and the ship almost ready for combat as gunners removed tarpaulins and fed ammunition into the breeches of their guns, and weapons officers woke up their controllers and links. It was still pitch-dark, although if one looked where the moon was about to rise one might have seen the slightest hint of an orange line so faint that no one might yet vouch for it.

Staring at the screen as if it were a revelation, the radar operator announced, "Captain, radar. Surface contact. Bearing one, eight, zero, range eleven thousand five hundred yards, speed forty knots, closing."

Rensselaer commanded, "Extinguish all navigation lights; raise the telescopic mast." The sound of the motor raising the mast was heard over that of the engines, the wind, and the sea cleaving off the bows.

"Shall I go to infrared, sir?" Rensselaer was asked by the rating who had executed his last command.

"Affirmative."

"Infrared." The rating worked a joystick to turn the elevated camera 180 degrees, and then he increased magnification.

Mid-screen, the dividing line between ocean and sky served to separate shades of black, with the upper half lighter. About an eighth of the way below the line, three white smudges, maintaining separation, were bouncing slightly up and down. They were delineated more sharply on their sides than on their tops, which seemed indistinct, fuzzy. "What you see on top is probably masts, people, or some sort of weapons mounts," Rensselaer said. "Let's wait awhile to determine if they were following our lights."

Athena then went through weapons checks. Every station and every weapon except the Harpoons was queried and checked. The .50-caliber gunners reported their ammunition loads. The radar operator called out the contact's information every thousand yards less between the *Athena* and her pursuers. At five thousand yards separation, Rensselaer said to the XO, as well as to everyone within earshot, "They're following our wake. The bioluminescence we stir up must extend back at least fifty miles. Let's check that, and make sure it's not just a coincidence. Helmsman, left standard rudder, steady on course one, four, zero."

"Left standard rudder, steady on course one, four, zero, aye sir." *Athena* turned toward the southeast.

"Increase your rudder to left full, steady on course one, two, five."

"Increase my rudder to left full, steady on course, aye sir. My rudder is left full, coming to course one, four, zero."

At just the right moment, Rensselaer ordered, "Rudder amidships."

"Rudder amidships, aye sir."

Athena came slowly, smartly to course one four zero, and held. Without maneuver-board calculation, she could only have done so if the order had been given at precisely the right moment, the result of many years' experience. To the younger members of the crew, it was a mystery that without calculation the course had held absent adjustment.

Rensselaer then ordered *Athena*'s speed increased to forty-five knots. When the pursuers reached the spot where *Athena* had turned southeast, they turned as well, and their change of course made clear that they were following the wake.

"Quartermaster," Rensselaer ordered Buck, "plot a course on the maneuvering board so that we know when to turn due west, out of visual to our pursuers, and proceed to a distance so that we can intersect our present course two thousand yards behind them."

Buck summarized the command and went to the maneuvering board. Rensselaer told the radar operator to do the same with ARPA, so that the one might be compared to the other. While this was occurring, he got on the 1MC. "This is the captain. All hands. Increased speed may cause you to think we're running. We're not. We're maneuvering. Have your sound talkers ready."

The sound talkers, a voice-powered telephone system, would not likely be needed, but the suggestion that *Athena's* power might be knocked out told the crew that, in fact, they were not running.

The maneuvering board and ARPA solutions were closely identical. Rensselaer, Movius, and Buck checked them over and agreed upon their accuracy. From that point forward, *Athena's* speeds and courses were predetermined. She soon made a high-speed turn due west to two seven zero, heeling over—unlike a motorboat—to port. There she changed speeds and made another fast turn, this time to the northeast, four zero, again heeling to port. Neither turn was quite fast enough for the stern to skate. Proceeding at the specified rate, she crossed one four zero perpendicularly and swung to it, now finding herself, as the moon rose, two thousand yards behind the three contacts that were still following the remnant glow of her wake.

The three craft gave no sign that they knew the ship they followed was now following them. "Close to a thousand yards," Rensselaer ordered. When they had, he said, "Let's take a look." He turned around the camera on the telescopic mast so that it faced forward, and as he peered at the screen others on the bridge looked ahead with regular optics. The moon was now bright enough so that all ships were faintly illuminated.

"They're bouncing up and down a lot, so details seem to disappear, but do you see what I think I see?" Rensselaer asked Movius.

"Something mounted on each bow."

"Looks like a gun. Kind of thick. Reminds me of a harpoon gun. Thick and stubby. But it's not. I think I know what it is."

"What?"

"A *Malyutka*—what we call a Sagger—wire-guided, anti-tank missile. The Middle East is saturated with them, and there's no steel on *Athena* they can't go right through. Given the ordnance we have on deck and below, that's a problem if these guys are hostiles—although I don't see why Somali pirates would want to have such heavy weapons, or, for that matter, tangle with us. But we have to assume that they do."

He addressed the gunners' mates and weapons officers. "Lock onto the center boat with the MK-46 and be prepared for them to break formation. Lock one Griffin onto the boat on the port side. Be ready with the MK-46 to slew to the one on the starboard side and be prepared for them to scatter and come about."

"Center and then to starboard, aye sir."

"Griffin to port, aye sir."

"Helmsman, be ready to execute my commands even if they seem counterintuitive."

"Meaning, sir?"

"Meaning if they don't seem to make sense."

"Aye sir."

The mood on the bridge was tense but excitedly eager. "Mr. Velez, put me on every hailing frequency known to man."

Rensselaer looked ahead as he spoke into the microphone. "This is the United States ship *Athena*. Attention three small vessels on course one, four, zero southeast, three degrees, ten minutes, fifty-six seconds north, forty-nine degrees, fifty-four minutes, twenty-seven seconds east. Over."

No answer. Nothing. The boats continued as before. Rensselaer repeated his message. Then a crackle, and the sound of high-pitched outboards. A panicked voice came in over the sounds, shouting, "*Min ayna!*"

"What the hell does that mean?" Movius asked.

"It means 'From where,'" Rensselaer answered.

"You know Arabic?"

"Language elective in graduate school. Be ready." He clicked on again. "We are *behind* you, sir." Saying this gave everyone on *Athena*'s bridge immense delight. The gunner and the missile officers were locked on target. Nothing happened.

"If they're pirates," Movius said, "they'll break off. They're not going to try to fight a warship."

"That's true," Rensselaer agreed, "and we can't take them on without provocation, but stay ready."

The bridge watch relaxed a bit, expecting to stand down. Suddenly the three boats broke formation, turned, and came at high speed directly at *Athena*.

"Why are they doing that?" Movius asked no one in particular.

"Nine hundred yards . . . eight hundred . . . seven hundred," came the count, slowly and steadily. All weapons were now easily in range, but no one had fired. A bright flash came from the center craft. Several voices at once yelled, "Rocket! Dead ahead, bearing zero zero zero!"

"Fire at will," Rensselaer replied, calmly. Helmsman, steady as she goes."

"Aye sir, steady as she goes." Like a huge tracer bullet, the rocket came toward them extremely fast and passed on the starboard side one hundred yards clear.

"They probably were never told that you have to fire a thousand Saggers before you can be accurate," Rensselaer announced.

The Griffin was away, lighting the decks and superstructure in yellow and white. It seemed to have a mind of its own. Before it found its target, the pounding of the 30mm MK-46 deafened everyone as it spat out twenty-five rounds in thirty seconds. The center craft turned to and lay dead in the water, but the other two kept on. Then the one to port launched its bow-mounted Sagger, and an instant later exploded in a huge fireball. Now lacking guidance, the Sagger jerked up and down, left and right, did a rapid backward roll, and plunged into the sea.

"Head straight for the craft to starboard," Rensselaer commanded.

The helmsman winced. They could see very clearly the men aboard and the Sagger in the bow. "Gunner's mate, engage."

The gunner's mate hadn't time to reply as he fired. This time, the starboard craft exploded—not just because of the high-explosive munitions that had struck it, but probably because its large gas tank had been hit.

"Why didn't they fire?" someone asked.

This was inappropriate at the moment, but Rensselaer answered anyway. "I don't know. The Sagger is ineffective at ranges less than a thousand yards, but they were probably unaware of that. Who are they?"

They closed on the center craft, the one still afloat, closely enough so that now they heard bullets pinging against *Athena*'s hull and superstructure. Three or four hit near the bridge, making everyone duck.

"Left fifteen degrees rudder."

Athena turned broadside to the center skiff, from which, not even one hundred yards to port, half a dozen men were firing AK-47s. "Fire at will," Rensselaer announced over the 1MC. Six .50-caliber barrels and the port minigun opened up at the same time. In just a few seconds, thousands of rounds shredded the skiff and the men in it. One spread his arms and went overboard backward. Most were hit and simply disappeared below the gunwales, and when the boat was further smashed apart, the bullets made their bodies move as if in seizures. Then all was quiet.

"Hard right rudder. All engines stop." *Athena* swung gracefully around. When he wanted to stop the swing, Rensselaer told the helmsman, "Meet her." The helmsman complied.

If you look at a bright window from an otherwise dark room and then shut your eyes, the image can linger for a long time, fading like an impossibly fast sunset. Much like this, the painful sound of all the guns remained, ghostlike, after they had stopped, and rather than being just the absence of sound, the silence was heavy.

Off the starboard beam, wreckage bobbed in the moonlight—plastic jugs, wood, a body that hadn't yet sunk. Forward and aft, small fires burned on the oil-calmed surface, weakening into flickers. The waves slowly pushed the wreckage of the center craft toward *Athena* until it was only a few feet away. The RHIB had launched to check for survivors even though everyone knew there weren't any. Had there been one, they would have treated him kindly and tried to keep him alive. No one was comfortable about having killed. Quite the opposite. It weighed heavily upon them, especially because the fight had been so unbalanced in their favor.

After Holworthy was back and reported no survivors, Rensselaer was called to the starboard side amidships. The XO followed. A body, floating half submerged, was bumping gently against the side as if wanting to come aboard. "That's no Somali," Rensselaer said.

"How do you know?" Movius wondered.

"I don't know about you, but I've never seen a fat Somali. And that would explain the Arabic."

"Shall we fish him out?"

"I suppose we'll have to see if there's anything on him. Don't take him on board. If we do, we'll have to have a burial. Just see if there's anything in the way of intelligence."

They didn't take him on board, but raised him with boat hooks just enough out of the water so they could go through his pockets. Then they lowered him back into the sea, and perhaps because air had been expelled from his lungs when he was raised, he sank gently and disappeared.

His documents were in Arabic. Rensselaer held them and read slowly. "I had no idea you knew Arabic," Movius said.

"I can't order in a restaurant or ask how old someone is, but I can translate diplomatic documents and political speeches. It's been a while."

"This guy is Ahmad bin al Walid Mussalam. These are passes and ID from Islamic State in Iraq and the Levant: that is, ISIS, *Daish*. His nom de guerre is *Saif-al-Maghreb*, Sword of the Maghreb. He's probably Moroccan." Rensselaer opened some folded papers. "Here it is. He's a company commander in the *Jaish Abnaa'ul Khalifa*, the Army of . . . something . . . of the Caliphate. They weren't pirates at all. We'll have to dry this stuff out and send in a scan as soon as we're in an EMCON break. What's in the pouch?"

Movius opened a small but thick pouch, and removed a packet of wet, U.S. hundred-dollar bills.

"How many?"

"I don't know. It's five inches thick."

"Okay. When it dries, you, I, and two others will count it, write an affidavit, seal it up, and I'll put it in the safe. It's a prize of war, so it belongs to the Treasury. I feel like John Paul Jones. My guess is that we've got anywhere from thirty to fifty thousand dollars. Maybe if we get back home in one piece we'll get a bonus. I've never dealt with this kind of thing, although in Iraq, in ninety-one, a lot of guys did, and not by the book. You can bank on that. They did."

*

They set out again, due south. Rather than following the coast of Africa south-southwest, they were aiming for a position equidistant from any of the port cities on the continent and on Madagascar and various other, smaller, islands, where the *Sahand* might take on fuel.

Not until morning were all the guns cleaned, the magazines reloaded, the logs and reports filled out, the money counted—$37,400—and regular watches resumed. Everyone had been up for a long time, and some would have to stay up until the afternoon watch. Rensselaer summoned the whole crew yet again. As they all were awake, it was an opportunity not to interrupt anyone's sleep.

The sea was almost calm. A light breeze was enough to have a cooling effect in sunshine that had yet to intensify into the punishing glare of midday. "You did well," he said. "You did very well. No heroics, which is good: no wounded, no dead . . . among us. But let me remind you that the two engagements we've fought so far have been with far inferior enemies. Yes, they could have killed any number of us, or possibly have sunk the ship, but that wasn't likely.

"If we catch the *Sahand* it'll be different. We'll be the outmatched inferiors. It's one thing to go into a fight with all the advantages on your side, another if the enemy has them. To put it bluntly, if we catch the *Sahand* and you want to live, we'll have to do far better than our best.

"That said, I'd like to apologize to you for at times skipping the forms of address during last night's battle. It was only because of the urgency."

This left the crew rather stunned. Josephson, who hadn't yet learned to be cautious, spoke up, his question amplified for all to hear. "Captain, sir, is that a joke, sir?"

They were stock-still as Rensselaer hesitated before he answered. "No, although I suppose it could have been. But, no. The form of commands is very important not only in making sure that they're properly given and properly understood, but to emphasize day in and day out that the highest ranks are not dictators but subject to the same system and restraints that all must obey. In civilian life outside that system, we're all equal, so it's important as we work to know that we have a part almost as if in a play.

"If I'm the king in the play and you're soldiers, you know damn well that in real life I'm not a king and you're not my subjects. Necessity puts us on this stage and in the end only courage and efficiency gives us real rank. Offstage, we're Americans, equals, which is why when onstage we must play our parts ceremoniously—so as to be able to effect the division and not forget that it doesn't extend to life in general. That's what I meant."

Slightly east of and parallel to her previous course, *Athena* moved south as the forenoon watch began more quietly than usual while so many of the crew slept after the quick battle. Their dreams were likely not as peaceful as the sea, which was greenish blue, rolling with increasing swell, and sparkling in a rising wind.

Movius

During the night after the second battle, someone skilled in sign-painting had written—surreptitiously and in ten-inch letters along the curved steel soffit elevated forward of the RHIB—*We're Not in Kansas Anymore*. It bound the crew together as much as had had the battles, and beautifully prepared them for what was to come.

A few days later, due south in search of *Sahand*, Rensselaer, Movius, and Holworthy were on the bridge in a rare coincidence of the three senior-most officers standing together during a lull. The horizon was empty, as it had been all day except for the sighting of a battered Chinese fishing ship heading east-northeast, perhaps laden with a catch from the cold waters near South Africa.

Out of the blue, Movius asked, "Captain, why are you in the Navy?"

"Are you suggesting that I leave?"

"No, sir. Just curious."

Rensselaer decided, after a moment, to answer the question. "I grew up not that far from West Point, which for a kid in my high school was El Dorado. Everyone wanted in, and we thought we had an advantage because we were locals. But West Point was so popular I figured I'd have a better chance at the Naval Academy, and I did. I was young, and, like a duckling imprinted with the image of its mother, the Navy became part of me as I became part of it. And you?"

Movius deflected, asking Holworthy instead.

"Nine-Eleven," Holworthy answered. "Somebody has to be the tip of the spear. There are people who do horrible things, and the world needs to be protected. We can't be like them, but someone has to strike them down even if the people we protect don't know the difference between us and them."

"As famously stated," Rensselaer said, "even if some of the sheep don't know it, there's a difference between the wolf and the sheepdog. And what is that, Mr. Holworthy?"

"The sheepdog doesn't eat lamb."

"I don't know about that, but he has no lust for blood. Speaking about lust for blood, XO, you started this. What about you?"

"It's a long story."

"You can't bug out now," Holworthy told him.

"Okay. To begin, my father was a postdoctoral fellow. . . ."

"Where?"

"M.I.T."

"In what?"

"Theoretical physics."

"That kind of explains you," Holworthy was pleased to interject.

"Maybe. His eyes were bad, and he wore bifocals. Not long after I was born, he was coming down the main stairway of the Boston Public Library. The difference in the bifocals must have thrown off his depth perception. I guess he stepped into the air. He tumbled headfirst down the whole flight. It was so bad that after many surgeries he was left blind, and, the best way to say it is, childlike: sweet, simple, appreciative, and not at all talkative. So, a guy with a doctorate in theoretical physics ended up as a news dealer in a downtown Boston office building. He was able to get there and back on his own, and he could handle the little business he had—newspapers, a few magazines, candy, and soda, which he called *tonic*.

"There's not much money in that—he died eight years ago; the injuries didn't help—and my mother was a violin teacher. What really killed us is that people would give my father a dollar and tell him it was a five or a ten. Or they would just take things if no one was watching, or take two or three papers or candy bars and pay for one. When they substituted bills, he could come home with negative proceeds and not even know it.

"We didn't go on welfare, but we ate a lot of potatoes and pasta. When I was in high school, I would sometimes go downtown to pick up my father, and a few of those times I saw people steal from him. That's when I learned about the legal system. The same guy who gave my father a dollar bill, told him it was a five, and got back four-fifty and a paper, sued us for assault—what else could I do when he kept going with the money?—and got five thousand dollars. It killed us.

"M.I.T. gave me a full ride, but not only was it not quite enough, I couldn't help out at home as much as I had, and I had to give up one of my jobs that added to our income. I'd never thought of going into the military. I didn't think I'd fit in."

"You don't," Holworthy said.

"None taken," Movius responded.

"But obviously you did . . . go into the military. Why the Navy specifically?" Rensselaer pressed on.

"A strange accident. My father used to listen to tapes for the blind. The Library of Congress sends them to you for free, and you can get almost anything."

"Right," Rensselaer said. "C. S. Forester? Patrick O'Brian? Herman Wouk?" He was going to say Tom Clancy, but Movius cut him off.

"Jack Benny."

"Who the hell is Jack Benny?" Holworthy asked.

"That's what *I* said," Movius went on, "so I looked him up. He was a Jewish comedian, very famous in his day, born in the nineteenth century, died in the seventies of the twentieth. When I looked him up, there was a picture of him in spats, puttees, a Dixie Cup, an ammo pouch, and a nightstick. He was in the Navy in the First World War.

"It struck me. I could go to M.I.T. and get paid for doing it. Maybe I should have done a comparative analysis and considered the Army and the Air Force, but thanks to Jack Benny I went right into NROTC. At that time, they wanted mathematicians for ASW, and later I had some billets there until ASW was completely kneecapped in the budgets. Now they have a need for A.I., and after the war they're going to pay for my graduate studies. At least that's what they say. Guess where," he asked Rensselaer.

"Where?"

"Caltech."

"Where that girl, Hava, is going."

"Yup."

"How's your vision?" Holworthy asked.

"That, I inherited from my mother. Twenty-twenty. Like a hawk. And as you can imagine, I'm careful on grand staircases."

"Your mother still living?" Rensselaer chanced.

"Yes, and, thanks to my salary, well taken care of. My sister's, too. She just got promoted. Public affairs in the Pentagon. One if by sea, one if by land."

Then the three broke away to attend to their duties, Rensselaer vigilant but relaxed, Movius distracted by thoughts of the past, and Holworthy, as usual, like a bow string.

The Wardroom and the Water Spout

Until the latter half of the twentieth century, naval officers could without any discomfort whatsoever avail themselves of the wardroom. The tradition began when boys attending Ivy League schools (which were not called by that name until the middle of the twentieth century) had their own slaves or servants, and when officers had cabins with mahogany furniture while sailors slept in hammocks temporarily attached to the overhead. Eventually the formality of the wardroom began to seem like a play acted out. The more time passed, the more class distinctions seemed unnatural even in light of necessary command distance.

Athena's wardroom was so small the only furniture other than a simple dining table and chairs was a remarkably narrow sideboard along one wall, over which hung the ship's emblem. Several tiny spotlights in the overhead had burned out, and there were no replacements of the right type, so to illuminate the windowless space a lamp had been placed at the center of the dining table. It made things more intimate, although in regard to intimacy the close quarters were more than sufficient.

Movius to the captain's right, the other officers in no particular order. With *Athena* moving uneventfully south in the Indian Ocean, the officers had finished their dinner and were about to have coffee and dessert—a Sacher torte that by some miracle the cook had been able to bake, fill, and ice.

"Anything to report about crew morale?" Rensselaer inquired, of everyone.

"There was a little fight, a scuffle," Movius reported. "One of the crew, no point in naming him, said to another, 'What's it like to get up in the morning to the smell of frying bacon and realize it's you?' This precipitated a physical response, but nothing serious."

"Anything else? Mr. Holworthy? Why are you smiling?"

"Two nights ago," Holworthy answered, "the guys were a little punchy. Someone said something when the first watch was trying to get to sleep, and someone else told him to shut up. Then someone told *him* to shut up. And on it went, including that somewhere in there it became, 'Shut up, dog,' and 'Shut up, cat.' This went on, I swear, for half an hour at least."

"You didn't stop it?"

"No, sir. I was enjoying it, because it was so nuts. So did they."

As Velez cut a large piece of the Sacher torte and flew it to his plate, Rensselaer said, "Mr. Holworthy?"

"Sir."

"Are you happier with the fighting now that we've had two engagements?"

"No, sir."

"Really? It hasn't been that long, and we're headed for a third and potentially rather daunting one."

"With all due respect, sir," Holworthy said, "these are naval battles. We're neither naval infantry nor Marines. There's a war, and we're not doing what we're trained to do."

"Which is?"

"Kill the enemy, sir, and eliminate his capacity to fight."

"You're in the Navy, Mr. Holworthy," Rensselaer said. "One of the important differences shared by the Navy and the Air Force as opposed to the Army and Marines is that our task is almost exclusively to eliminate platforms rather than men. True, in doing so, men are killed—that's for sure—but it isn't the object, and only chance determines the human toll."

"In the same way, Captain," Holworthy countered, "the Army, Marines, and the NSW community's first object is maneuver, not body counts."

"That's correct, but to accomplish that, the target is men, unavoidably. That's why, as you just volunteered, you're trained to kill."

"Are you saying that's wrong, sir?"

"Yes, I am. It may be necessary, as it often is, but of course it's wrong. We kill to survive, but that doesn't make killing right, just as we kill animals to survive. . . ."

"Unless you're a vegan" (which he pronounced, with a short *e* and a soft *g*, *vehjan*, O'Connor interrupted, trying to take some of the tension from the air.

"That's right, Lieutenant," Rensselaer said, "unless you're a *vehjan*, you kill—or benefit from the slaughter of—animals. To survive, but it isn't right. Many things we do aren't right. We're imperfect."

Hardly concealing his agitation, Holworthy continued the argument. "Captain, I heard, and I don't know if it's true, that one of the tests Israeli naval commandos must pass is to be put in a dark closet with a dozen cats, and in just a few minutes wring the necks of all of them."

"Who told you that?" Movius asked. "A naval commando or a cat?"

"I heard it in the States. Some guys, perfectly capable in every other way, just can't bring themselves to do it, so they get kicked out, because, if you can't kill cats, how can you kill a man? You know, Movius, Jews are very sensitive: they all play the violin."

"Even babies," Movius replied, adding, "You think I'm kidding?"

"Your point, Mr. Holworthy?" Rensselaer asked. With the tension somewhat diffused, his question was more in the spirit of discussion.

"That if you have qualms like that, you may not do well in our job. You may hesitate in pulling the trigger, meaning that the mission may fail, and lots of us will die."

"Or an innocent kid may live."

"There's a fine line."

"There is. That's why old men like me, who were once young men like you, are here to caution you and temper your enthusiasm."

"But, sir, as untempered as that enthusiasm may be, it can be the difference between living and dying."

"I know. I'm just telling you what eventually you'll learn. Battle will come to you, you don't have to seek it."

"I respectfully disagree, sir. It's proper for us to seek the initiative, and to strike first."

"Of course, when engaged. But to yearn for engagement . . . ? Mr. Holworthy, have you been on a battlefield?"

"I've been in battle."

"I mean after large formations clash, or on a ship that takes major hits?"

"No, sir, not on that scale."

"Even on a small scale it isn't something you want to see. Think of a death in the Middle Ages: in the cold, in the dark except for perhaps a tallow lamp, with filth and the smells of suppuration, vomitus, urine, feces, no anesthetic, shrieks of pain, unmitigated fear. That's what a battlefield is like when there's no medivac and you're out of morphine. It's not the Mayo Clinic."

"I've always thought, Captain, that if I fight hard until the end I'd be too busy to die that way."

"If you're lucky. But things change when five AK-47 slugs carve a line across your stomach. You don't always die fighting. And sometimes it takes a while."

"You've seen that, sir?" Josephson asked.

"I have seen that."

Movius ended the silence that followed by saying, "Gentlemen? Can I say that? The coffee and tea are getting cold."

And then everyone ate cake.

*

Holworthy was incensed, and, with a growing contempt for Rensselaer, dreaded another meal in the wardroom. He told O'Connor, and then his men, that the captain's softness, his indecisiveness, and perhaps his age were not only depriving them of their opportunity to achieve their potential in the war, it was putting them in danger. "I have no confidence," he said, "that he'll seize the initiative and strike before we're struck, or that he'll fight hard enough. Yeah, he was a SEAL. Yeah, he earned the Navy Cross. But that was then. Between then and now he's had years in graduate school, and on staff—which is like running a fucking hotel—and three decades of aging."

"Is there a single admiral who isn't like that?" O'Connor asked him.

"No, but that's the point. You don't want an admiral, or a captain, commanding a PC. You need high confidence, no doubts, some recklessness, and a lot of testosterone. He doesn't fit the bill. He's the old guy who drives a Buick to Denny's for the early bird special."

"Okay," said O'Connor. "There's nothing we can do about it. Enjoy the French toast."

"I'm going to talk to the XO again."

O'Connor recoiled. "Oh no, no no no. Just don't. If you go to him a second time. . . . Do you realize what you're saying? Promise me that you will not do that."

"I'll have to think about it."

*

In midafternoon, the winds were crossing and strange, and a waterspout suddenly appeared a few degrees off the port bow a mile or so ahead. The helmsman asked Rensselaer, who had the con, "Should I alter course to avoid it, sir?"

"No."

Josephson, who was the OOD, said, "Captain, it's bearing right for us."

"Right."

"Wouldn't it be wise to run perpendicular to its line of travel?"

"No."

"Sir?"

"You'll notice that it stops. And it sways this way and that way and sometimes backs up. It's not really headed toward us, Mr. Josephson. It looks like it because we're headed toward *it*. It moves analogously to Brownian motion; that is, with equal probabilities that it will lurch in any direction. The winds are highly variable, so to the extent that they're strong enough to influence it, they add to the unpredictability.

"Right now, if held, our course would put us a quarter of a mile from its present position. It'll be about four minutes until we reach that potential intercept. The waterspout is moving at about five miles an hour. That means that if it goes directly for the intercept it could reach it in three minutes. In four minutes, it could move, theoretically, a twelfth of a mile beyond that, or a total of roughly eighteen hundred feet: the radius of the circle in which it may travel randomly to any point. The area of that circle, πr^2, is about ten million square feet. The footprint of the waterspout is about five hundred square feet. The chance that we would collide with that footprint in the ten-million-square-foot cantonment in which it can move in the time specified is one in twenty thousand.

"So it's probable that we can continue course and speed and we won't encounter it. And if it looks like we will, we can easily make an end run, hardly altering our course, as we can go twelve times faster than it can. Were we under sail it would be different."

Rensselaer turned to the helmsman. "Steady as she goes, one-eighty."

"Aye, sir, steady on course one, eight, zero."

"Did they teach you that at the Academy, Captain?" Josephson asked. "We certainly didn't get it in NROTC."

"No, they didn't say anything about waterspouts, as far as I can remember."

"Where did you learn it, then, sir?"

"I learned it by watching waterspouts."

"Oh."

The waterspout, which seemed to hold its distance, was greenish gray. It shed seawater, like a fountain, and it shone in the afternoon sun.

In the passageway, just before Rensselaer repaired to his cabin, Movius asked in a low voice, almost a whisper, "What's going on with Holworthy? Like a dog on a chain, he's held back, but he seems to be lunging toward insubordination."

"I don't think the chain will break," Rensselaer answered quietly.

"Really?"

Rensselaer shook his head dismissively. "A wayward mind entranced by dreams and incapable of transcending itself can be overruled by experience. Whether or not you call this wisdom, to see self-limitation and error overcome is one of the joys of existence. It's called growing up. We'll see if Holworthy does or not."

*

By evening the weather had changed radically. Rensselaer, Movius, and Holworthy were once again on the bridge not long before the late sunset of high summer. Holworthy was the OOD, but by virtue of being there Rensselaer had the con, and Movius was as usual doing extra work, in this case recalibrating instruments to make sure that in the near-equatorial waters some magnetic anomaly or sea sprite hadn't thrown them out of kilter.

To the west-southwest, a most extraordinary heavenly scrim, mesmerizing the three officers, had descended courtesy of the clouds, light, and setting sun. In a band conforming to the horizon, the sea was the darkest blue it could be before turning black. Closer in was a layer of sea much lighter in color—navy blue—and the chop, with, however, nary a visible whitecap, made it look like crêpe. Immediately above the horizon was a belt of glowing gold leaf, uneven at the top where falling rain—some of which reached the sea and some of which did not—painted the sky in a kind of semi-charcoal. And above this were successive layers of darker and darker blue until the topmost layer of heavy cloud somehow whitened. All in all there were eight bands of luminescent colors in a tranquilizing scene enlivened by the gold leafed horizon.

Rensselaer said, "The color of the sea looks like the dark, cool blue of the sea off the Greek isles, or a blue crêpe dress I saw on one of the most beautiful women I've ever seen, at the embassy in Paris."

"What were you doing at the embassy in Paris?" Movius asked.

"I accompanied Admiral Johnson to talk to the French about their SSBNs."

"How old was she?"

"Couldn't have been more than thirty. Maybe thirty-five. Nothing is as charming as a Frenchwoman. They've got that one all sewn up, and, I guess, a lock on the most magical indigo."

"Did anything come of it?"

"Oh no, I was married, and besides, even had I not been, she was some sort of princess, and to most people like that, with my rank in a room full of admirals and ministers of state I was probably as easy to ignore as a doorman."

Looking out—they were all looking out, astounded, and the helmsman found it hard to keep on course—Movius said, "It's like a Rothko. Unbelievably so."

"What's a Rothko?" Holworthy asked.

"A painter," Movius told him. "All his paintings are just like what you see ahead. As if he's reporting from beyond death."

"Not the pastels," Rensselaer said. "I don't like his pastels."

"True, not the pastels, but what he can do with red, maroon, blue, and black."

"I don't get it," Holworthy said.

"When you look at them," Movius went on, "they still the soul. The guy has been to heaven and he's been to hell. Supposedly it's abstract and theoretical, but I don't think so. I never thought so. I think they were illustrations."

Not long after, the light dimmed to almost nothing and the bands of color unified. Then lightning broke out, heavy rain swept toward *Athena*, and as the windshield wipers struggled to sweep sheets of fresh water from blurring a vision of what lay ahead, the spell was broken.

THE THIRD BATTLE: *ATHENA* VS. *SAHAND*

Two days later, deep in the Indian Ocean and off the trade routes and sea-lanes, they were over the Somali Basin, sailing toward the northern edge of the Mascarene Plateau, in almost virgin territory devoid of anything that might appear on the surface other than porpoises and dolphins. Placid, green seas by day rolling gelatinously smooth, emerald, and slick, turned miraculously blue at night as luminescent sea creatures lit the translucent waters. And all the way to the horizon, the sea was glossed in the kind of azure one might see in a Technicolor cartoon. They were eager to hunt the *Sahand* despite the forbidding overmatch, and anxious to face it if they could find it. For no particular reason, they were sure they would.

On the empty sea it was hard to believe that they were at war. Where once were heard the arresting noise of ten thousand rifle bolts rammed shut, ten thousand hoofs pounding a field in headlong charge, or the chest-shaking sound of tanks, their engines unlike anything in civilian life, now the dominant sound of war was the roar of fighter planes rising from desert strips or swooping in from above. But not on *Athena*, alone at sea, with none of the basso profundo of mass formations, tanks, or planes. The sound of her engines was ever present but not overwhelming. What the sailors would remember were the almost musical sounds of the wind as they accompanied the loneliness of patrol.

In the middle of the afternoon, *Athena* came to a stop and was allowed to drift in a two-foot swell caressed by a light breeze. Without the wind from her forward motion, it became almost unbearably hot on deck. Over the 1MC, Movius announced, "Lieutenant Di Loreto and Chief Pisecki to the captain's quarters."

Five foot seven, Pisecki was 190 pounds of muscle that seemed as hard as stone. He had a thick, red-brown mustache and a heavy beard that even though he shaved twice a day was always apparent. His eyes were blue and set amazingly far apart, and no one on the ship or perhaps anywhere else had ever seen him in other than an inexplicably high state of energy and cheer.

"Close the door behind you, gentlemen, and take a seat." Rensselaer had brought a second and third chair into his tiny cabin. It was tight.

"Sir," Di Loreto said.

They sat facing one another, Rensselaer's right arm and Pisecki's left resting on the built-in desk, and Di Loreto packed uncomfortably into a corner. Rensselaer went on the 1MC, stretching the coiled cord farther than normal because of his unaccustomed position at the desk. "All hands, this is the captain. Very soon, Lieutenant Di Loreto and Chief Pisecki may require your assistance. Make sure that you render it efficiently. Do not hesitate, balk, or gawk. You may think they're out of their minds. They aren't. They will be executing my direct orders. If you're puzzled, translate your puzzlement into usefulness. Captain out."

From stem to stern, *Athena*'s sailors turned to one another in silence, and with facial expressions alone communicated skepticism and astonishment. Their widened eyes, slightly raised cheeks, and slightly open mouths, said, *What?*

"Frank?" Rensselaer asked Pisecki.

"Sir?"

"You had time on the Coast Guard's tall ship, didn't you?"

"Yes, sir. Six months on the *Eagle*."

"You're our marlinspike sailor."

"I'd like to think so, sir."

"And when you were on the *Stennis* you were in . . . ?"

"Underway replenishment."

"And the lieutenant is highly skilled at mechanical improvisation. This should be easy for you, then." Rensselaer paused to organize his thoughts, and then spoke slowly. "Rig taut lines from the topmast to the stern and the prow. Halfway between the peak and the stern, set up the spars we got at Lemonnier, like a mizzen mast. Fashion three appropriately proportioned 'sails,' and set up a sheet and pulley system so you can run them up as jib, mainsail, and mizzen.

"For each of the buckets we took on, fill a gallon jug with half diesel fuel, a quarter lubricating grease, and a quarter cooking oil. Fill the buckets with kindling from the pallets. Suspend some of them and put others on deck, everything away from ordnance, with the jugs of fuel, and a flare or two for lighting each one. I want the guns, radar, rockets, and RHIB covered with camouflage netting or tarps that can be pulled off as fast as a magician pulls a tablecloth from under a set table. I suggest that you make them such that they can easily break in the middle. It just occurs to me now that that's maybe how Gypsy Rose Lee managed. She was before Velcro, but not before snaps."

"Sir?"

"When we clear EMCON, Google her."

He continued, "Have everything ready to go so that the sails can be raised, the tarps placed, the buckets lit, in just a few minutes. The faster the better. Can you do this?"

"I don't see why not, sir," Pisecki said. "It's not like cross-decking explosives."

"I'll leave it up to the two of you. If you have a problem, come to me."

"We're going to be a Q ship, Captain, aren't we," Di Loreto said.

"Yes, we are. A lot of the crew won't know what that is, and they'll wonder what we're doing. Let them. I want to see how it looks before I announce it and we drill, if we have time."

"Shall we start immediately, sir?"

"Yes. And work through every watch until you finish. Though we've heard nothing further about *Sahand*, she might be bearing down on us as we speak."

*

Neither Pisecki nor Di Loreto let on, each of them giving orders with a poker face and communicating neither opposition nor enthusiasm. The crew, however, had the perpetually entertaining and increasing enjoyment of thinking that the captain had really gone crazy. They were apprehensive of serving under his absolute authority, but delighted that his erratic orders reduced that authority, thus elevating them. Needless to say, thinking that he profited, Holworthy enjoyed this the most even as he was tortured by it. The crew hadn't wanted to think as they now did of Rensselaer—for he had been an excellent captain—but they couldn't avoid it. It was strange enough when they set up and rigged the buckets, and put in place the "masts" and sheets. But when they ran up the sails they had stapled and sewn together, they began to get really nervous.

By the time the tarps were placed, the sails had filled with the rising breeze to the point that *Athena* moved south-southeast at two or three knots.

"Goddamn," said Roberts, a deckhand, head upturned to the billowed sails. "The captain must have a gallon of scotch hidden in his cabin."

"You think he's just nuts?" asked another.

"I don't know," Roberts answered, still peering in wonder at the sails. "It's not as if we're low on fuel."

"Maybe he's a member of the Sierra Club."

*

Next, Rensselaer met with the XO, the chief engineer, and Holworthy. They were apprehensive.

"I want the three of you to coordinate the following as rapidly as you can. Chief, I want you to improvise extra gun mounts on the port and starboard sides. I don't care if you have to weld, bolt, clamp, or glue, but I want it so that we can move *all* our firepower cross-deck from one side to the other. That is, four more fifty-caliber mounts, one each on both sides amidships and astern, one more minigun mount on each bridge wing, and a grenade launcher mount on each side."

"We don't have the steel for that, sir."

"Improvise. Strap'em down if necessary. Figure it out."

"Mr. Holworthy, how many anti-tank rockets do you have?"

"Six."

"How many M4 grenade launchers?"

"Six."

"How many sniper rifles?" Rensselaer knew—he was just taking inventory.

"Two."

"Light machine guns?"

"Two."

"I want you to establish positions on the port and starboard sides for you and your men so that you can fast-break from one to the other, with weapons distributed so that whatever combination each man has, he can quickly switch either opportunistically or in response to orders. Ask for a volunteer to take position way up top, with one of the sniper rifles, an anti-tank rocket, and a light machine gun, as well as his M4 with grenade launcher. That will be the most exposed position on board—only a volunteer."

"No problem. I'll do it." As if the supports had been knocked out from beneath his satisfying conclusions, it pained Holworthy to be asked to do the kind of thing he wanted to do.

"It's extraordinarily exposed. It could be rough."

Holworthy shrugged his shoulders.

"Appreciated. XO?"

"Sir."

"A lot of drilling's going to happen on short order, and we may not have much time.

Everyone will be bumping into everyone else; no way around it. Start now even before the new mounts. Have them lay the weapons on deck if the mounts aren't yet ready. I want to be able to move everything from one side to another in two minutes or less. Start now."

"Now? Right now?"

"Right now. Drill general quarters, and organize it. Then arrange with Di Loreto and Pisecki to give them the men they need to man the canvas, ropes, and buckets. Right away."

*

For two days, they drifted—and sailed very slowly when the sails were raised—in the almost calm, abandoned spaces, as if they were the only ship, the only people, in a world of nothing but water. Still, and paradoxically, activity on deck was furious. A few scuffles broke out as the SEALs and sailors fought for space and right-of-way, and there were a dozen cuts and blood blisters as guns were lifted off their mounts, rushed across the deck, and remounted.

They worked so hard and so long in humid, oven-like heat that they were frequently punchy, and that was when, particularly among the ropes-and-canvas detail, pirate talk began. Pisecki barked out tall-ship nomenclature—which they quickly learned—to which they responded by saying, "Aye, me hearties!" or "Skull and bones to the top gallant, God save the Queen!" He let them, even if they seemed drunk, because they were having a good time as they strained every muscle to beat his stopwatch while simultaneously being as piraty as they could be. The SEALs thought the sailors were idiots, but SEALs often think that non-SEALs are idiots, despite which they are almost universally forgiven because they are SEALs, the tip of the spear, forgivably crazy. Now everyone seemed crazy.

By evening of day two they could shift the heavy and formidable armament from one side to the other in slightly less than two minutes. The canvas could be raised in a minute, after which the deck crew stood by the buckets, flares in hand. That night, with the exercises mastered the normal watches resumed and the stars came out with neither diesel smoke nor wavy air to mar them. It was as if, alone on the ocean, without main engine noise, *Athena* had slipped back in time to the beginning of the world.

*

Rensselaer was on the bridge. He thought of Katy in her tight, tan, sheath dress, her skin the same hue but lighter, and—given her age—not flawless, but glowing. From the side, with her reading glasses and her usual penetrating expression, she was formidable, with an attractiveness that emanated from her intelligence and power.

He had always loved to engage with her on these terms, and could understand why at her firm she was so desired. You could sit across a table from her, discussing anything, even tax law, and her face, her speech, what she did with her hands, and what she said and how she put it ... these alone were an almost violent, overwhelming, all-powerful seduction. She would pull off her glasses and turn full face toward him, and her particular beauty—the idiosyncratic perfection of her features, and her soft searching look—would combine with all else about her almost enough to knock him out.

This kind of memory could be repeated over and over again not with diminution but amplification. And so the captain of *Athena* was lost in them as his ship drifted silently over the ocean lit by an almost full moon. Then he was interrupted by Velez.

"Message, sir." Velez's tension and excitement awakened from their reveries everyone on the bridge.

Twice, and slowly, Rensselaer read the message. Then he nodded, and after a moment or two spoke to the XO and the others present. "This is a long, coded message within a Fifth Fleet coded message. Fifth Fleet hasn't read it. How did you read it, Mr. Velez?"

"I used a package of one-time keys, Captain, for communicating directly with other command authorities when naval channels are inoperative. Although it came over on Fifth Fleet it was encoded to fit the Fort Meade CODEMCON for CIA. I tried it and it worked."

"It did. It's directly from CIA. No reason not to share it with the Navy unless CIA thinks Iran might have a door into Navy COMMS. If Iran did, and they read this, we could never catch *Sahand*." He summarized the message.

"Soon after dark last night, *Sahand* slipped into a bay in Madagascar to refuel from a barge. All the lights were turned off. Three hours, then she was gone." He looked up. "I'm continually surprised by where our assets pop up all over the world. Do you know who Martin Gilbert was?"

This seemed odd. None of them did.

"He was a great Oxford historian, the biographer of Churchill. The day after Nine-Eleven, two suits showed up in his office and spread dozens of eight-by-ten black-and-white photographs across his desk, pictures of him and his students at his lectures in the seventies. He was astounded. They asked if he recognized a kid in a number of the photos. No, he didn't. Why? he asked. The kid was Usama bin Ladin. Who the hell was taking those pictures, at that time? Why? And how did they do it without detection? That's what I mean.

"Okay, not by coincidence, the next morning a light plane took off from Mayotte, on a course to Antananarivo, the capital of Madagascar. This is a relatively well used flight path, and wouldn't merit attention from maritime traffic below.

"It was our plane, with our people, and it intersected *Sahand*'s course, which by triangulation before, over, and after the intercept, they were able to fix as a heading of twenty-four-point-five-seven degrees north-northeast, point of origin, these co-ordinates." He read them. "Buck, go to work."

Lanham had already bent over the chart table. The line he drew went straight to the section of the Arabian Sea where the Fleet and the carriers were stationed. He announced what he had found.

In response, Rensselaer said, "We can only assume that to get to the launch point for the Tsirkon in a semi-ballistic trajectory originating four hundred nautical miles from target, *Sahand* will be moving as fast as possible. You know how these people think—not that we ourselves wouldn't."

We sank the original *Sahand* in the Tanker War of eighty-eight. They're losing the war, and now they may have all their eggs in one basket. For them, everything might depend upon the *Sahand*. Take out a carrier or two to avenge the namesake and hit the Great Satan.

"Mr. Lanham, get us on their track as far distant from the carrier-groups as is consonant with both our and their maximum sustainable speeds."

Buck used both the chart table and electronics. It took only five minutes, and he checked it over several times.

"What have you got?"

"The safe point of intercept, assuming an even greater speed of which *Sahand* is capable, is three degrees, thirty-eight minutes, thirty-five seconds north, and fifty-three degrees, thirty-seven minutes, fifty-one seconds east. I left some wiggle room, but that latitude and longitude are the exact intercept of *Sahand*'s unmodified course."

"How far are we from intercept?"

"Two hundred and ten-point-six-three miles nautical directly west."

"And how long after we get there at forty knots until the *Sahand* might show up?"

"It depends on how fast they go—roughly a day, a day and a half."

"XO."

"Sir."

"Wake up the engines. We've got some slack, so set Mr. Lanham's course to the intercept at *thirty-five* knots. I don't want to sit at the intercept too long and get nervous. Double the watches at twelve hundred hours tomorrow, when we'll move to Condition Two."

"Sir?" Movius asked. "On a PC?" Condition II, a heightened state of readiness just below Condition I—general quarters—was not by the book for a smaller vessel.

"It's warranted. The *Sahand* outpunches us. By all rights, to win, even to survive, we should be a much larger ship, to which Condition Two would be entirely appropriate."

Everyone aboard who was not asleep could feel the turbines muscling up and the swing of the bow as *Athena* turned east, steering by GPS, inertial navigation, compass, and, as if to confirm all this, a star that caught and kept the helmsman's eye.

*

As *Athena* moved toward the intercept, Rensselaer went to the engine spaces and queried the engineering chief. "I should know this, but I don't. In an emergency, how fast can you go from cold turbines to full power?"

Almost as if he fancied himself a SEAL, the chief had quite a non-regulation beard, which Rensselaer had ignored. "It depends on how long we've been cold, or, better, how cold we actually are; if we want to monkey with the fuel mixture; and if we want to accept some degradation in a less-than-gradual startup. I mean, no one really knows, but I like to think that cold metal at full speed is not good in terms of future fatigue."

"Let's say we've been cold for a day. . . ."

"You're certainly not going to get colder than that, unless you have to calculate for ambient temperature."

"And the fuel mixture is set for maximum volatility. . . ."

"Then you can't get, initially, maximum rpm, but you can soon after."

"Okay. And with my permission, in writing if you want, you can degrade the gears, because if you don't we'll likely be sunk anyway."

"A rough estimate, with those parameters?"

"With those parameters."

The chief thought. "Mind you, it's not exact, but if we're on standby and ready to go, I think that with this power plant and in these conditions I can get full power to the AIMs"—the advanced induction motors—"in two minutes, give or take ten seconds. How does that work for you?"

"Better than I thought. Even assuming that *Sahand*'s sonar operators are alert, by the time they notice, fix, confirm, and then notify the bridge, depending on how far *Sahand* stands off, it'll be too late."

"For us or them?"

"Them."

"Sir, I don't know what you've got planned, but I hope it works."

"So do I."

Rensselaer briefed the crew in two groups so he could do it in the mess while keeping the ship almost fully manned. He spoke without bravado, as what he proposed was hardly guaranteed to succeed.

"Does anyone know what a Q ship is, or, was?" Several hands went up.

"Boatswain's Mate Alford?"

"In World War One, the British equipped freighters with concealed naval guns. When a commerce raider approached, panels would drop along the sides, and the British ships would blast the hell out of them—especially subs."

"Exactly. *We* . . . are going to look like the burning, disheveled wreck of a sailing vessel. We can do that. We're small enough. *Sahand* will see neither our armament nor us until we drop the tarps. Then we'll use everything we've got in carefully controlled sequence to try to disable and then sink her."

"What's the catch?" Rensselaer was asked.

"You really have to ask? The catch is that if we haven't in fact calculated the correct intercept and we're sitting there dead in the water, we'll have to move to engage, and they'll hear the signature of our engines. They almost certainly don't have it on record, but in this empty quarter it'd stand out and they'd be alerted. The catch goes on: even if we're sitting smack on their course and they're not interested in investigating, or are too disciplined to be distracted from their mission; if they stand too far off even if they do investigate; if they see through our stratagem; if we have to chase them in order to fight them and they can launch their missiles at us from range; even assuming they don't sense the trap, if our tactics and saturation fire are insufficient; if their crew consists of more naval regulars than IRGC and they're appropriately manned; if their weapons are properly functional; if they're lucky, or we're unlucky. . . .

"A hundred things could go wrong, but I couldn't think of anything better to try in the face of a ship many times our size and with much heavier armament. At least we'll be able to pinpoint its position, which will be valuable in itself and all that's expected of us."

"Captain, sir," a rating asked. "Why don't we just report and hightail it?"

Rensselaer was appalled. "In the Revolutionary War," he said, "with just a few ships, we fought the greatest sea power that had ever existed, and we won some extraordinary and unexpected victories, once even beaching a sloop and dragging its cannon up a hill to defeat a far larger vessel befuddled by the trick. You can sink a sloop, but you can't sink a hill. Though the world and Americans themselves think we can't operate any longer at a disadvantage, victory at a disadvantage is in our blood, never forgotten, and still and always the greatest prize."

Then he heard, barely, a voice in the back of the assembled crew. "He wants to be an admiral."

"The hell I do," Rensselaer snapped. "I'm retiring after this deployment. I'd be retired now but for the war. My job is to keep you alive, but it's also to sink the *Sahand* so that others may live. Pray that *Sahand* doesn't take a smoke-shrouded, drifting vessel in tatters for a U.S. Navy combatant ready to spring."

*

The night before the expected battle, Rensselaer had a dream the likes of which surprised him. Floating in darkness in the air over the sea, without the oppressions of either gravity or pain, he looked up at the stars. But what he saw was not cold, distant, silver-white light, ethereal and detached. Every single star had vaulted over light-years of distance to show its true self, a roiling, orange, red, and white giant of ceaseless nuclear detonations, roaring like the fire in a forge. A trillion trillion stars, pulsing and hot, that even after the dissolution of humankind, much less Rensselaer's unnoticed part in it, meant that if not life then motion, purpose, and a kind of passion would outlast human vanities, in quantities unfathomable and for time illimitable.

No matter what the outcome when they met *Sahand*, and no matter should he and the others perish, the fires of the world beyond would burn and the heart of everything would beat. Morning broke with a surprisingly cool and dry breeze, rippling the water enough so that the rising sun was reflected by uncountable flashing diamonds, as if a shower of burning stars had landed on the sea. *Athena* was all business. Very few of the men spoke. The training had stopped, and preparations for battle were everywhere underway on the busy decks.

She faced south, her unique periscope raised, the sailor staring at the monitor trying not to doze, when something that electrified him appeared on the screen. "XO!" he screamed. "Look at this! What the hell is this!?"

Movius nearly jumped to the monitor. There, its image waving as if elasticized, was the *Sahand*. It was, however, floating not on the sea but in the air, five or six ship-heights above the water.

"Is it the system?" the sailor asked. "I mean, how stupid is that?"

Movius didn't answer, but summoned the captain to the bridge. And Rensselaer came at a run. As soon as he saw the *Sahand* floating in the air, he asked the OOD, "Did you download the NIMA calculator?"

"Yes sir."

"Bring it up."

It was up very quickly. "Running, sir."

"Input the variables. . . ." Using as a scale *Sahand*'s height from the waterline to the tip of her mast, Rensselaer placed a rule against the screen to determine approximately how far above the water the image appeared to be. Then he followed with a few numbers, and after pushing a button the OOD announced, "A hundred and five nautical miles, sir."

"That's a gift," Rensselaer said, "a great gift."

"Sir," the sailor could not restrain himself from asking, "what's going on?"

"Fata Morgana," Rensselaer answered.

"Fata who?"

"Ducting." The distance meant he didn't need to hurry, but Rensselaer compressed his explanation nonetheless. Though *Sahand* would not arrive for hours, he was eager to start taking advantage of what had just happened. "Fata Morgana is another name for Morgan le Fay, a fairy enchantress and the half sister of King Arthur."

The rating failed to suppress a nervous laugh. Then he repeated what the captain had just said: "A fairy enchantress and the half sister of King Arthur?"

"It's the name given to a physical phenomenon called ducting, a product of the refraction of light. You've heard of mirages?"

"Yes sir."

"A mirage is an inferior refraction, meaning that something above the horizon appears to be below it. The Fata Morgana is a superior refraction, when something at or below the horizon appears to be above it. Sometimes if conditions are right you can see cities and mountains many hundreds of miles distant. From San Diego you can sometimes see San Clemente Island, sixty-five miles away." Then, mainly to Movius and the OOD, "It's more or less impossible that it happened in reverse, either visually or electromagnetically, enabling *Sahand* to see us. Unlikely this gift of God was offered to them as well, even though they think they've cornered the market on Him. Soon, though, they'll pick us up on their radar. Let's get everything into place. Shut down all machinery. Total EMCON. Don't drop a wrench or bang your head. Nothing. Rig for quiet."

"Yes, sir."

"They're almost right on the line and only slightly east of it. Slowly and quietly—we have the time—all weapons to the port side. Camouflage up. When that's done, general quarters, voice talkers, ballistic protection, medical prep. Make sure there's extra ammunition port *and* starboard. Make the Harpoons ready to fire. Assume Condition Zebra. We'll get it done one thing at a time, silently. Shut down the MC until the first shot is fired."

He slowed himself deliberately, and was quiet for a moment. "Even though they've stripped the seventy-six-millimeter gun, they've got a forty, two twenties, six torpedoes, eight Qader missiles, and a helicopter. Let's hope they don't launch it to suss us out, because if they do we're done."

Somehow he seemed to know that they wouldn't, although he did not know either how he knew or why they wouldn't. Sometimes in battle a magnificent and intoxicating chain of luck arises. One can feel it as intensely as a wound. Confident that his orders had been assimilated and would be carried out, Rensselaer said, "Go," and they did.

*

Knowing that in a few hours they might be dead, maimed, wounded, or adrift and doomed to starve or drown, the crew had the concentration of mind and movement in which things are done with speed and grace and not much talk: the intensity almost seemed to say that this was real life and all else was illusion.

Quiet, brief commands raised the camouflage and nets aloft until even from fairly close *Athena* was unrecognizable—no longer a tight, clean warship but a messy, disorganized hulk. The pulleys had run smoothly and the lines hadn't tangled. Other than the softly spoken orders and the occasional click of fittings and closing of breeches, the only sound was that of the wind, and of waves slapping the hull more like the rapid oscillations of a lake than the muscular pounding of the ocean.

"I hope their radar isn't advanced enough to read our steel and jagged projections as a warship," Movius said to Rensselaer.

"I don't know about their radar, XO," Rensselaer answered, watching the transfer of weapons starboard to port, "but my hope is that we're small enough and close enough to the water that they'll take us for a fishing boat. And why would a coastal combatant be out in the middle of the IO all alone? Let's say they did make us for what we are. They've got to figure that they could take us quite easily, so if we're on the way to their launch point, why not put another feather in their bonnet?"

"Because they'll concentrate on their mission."

"A lot of people can't resist taking a pawn."

"Not good chess players. And they invented chess, didn't they?"

"Yes," Rensselaer said, "but we invented the corn dog. Top that."

The sailors on deck wondered somewhat nervously why the Captain and XO were laughing, but were comforted and somewhat amazed to see all the firepower that was now concentrated on the port side. *Athena* was a small ship, the smallest in the Navy but for the fact that she was a step up from her sister Cyclones. She didn't appear lethal, but something extraordinary was falling into place behind the nets and tarps. Port-facing, three 7.62 miniguns—two on the bridge wing, one bow-mounted on the RHIB—were each capable of firing 6,000 rounds per minute, 18,000 combined, at 300 per second. They didn't have this much ammunition to match for long their rate of fire, but the initial intense blast of so many NATO rounds would be suppressive, mutilating, and terrifying.

They weren't able to transfer the starboard hip-pocket to port, so the one on the port side, their only defense against incoming, sea-skimming missiles, would have to serve. The six, double-barreled, .50-caliber Brownings were theoretically capable of, collectively, 12,000 rounds per minute. Though a rate rather than an achievable salvo, the thousands of rounds of armor-piercing, explosive, incendiary, and airburst ammunition could drop a paralyzing curtain of steel and flame across the deck of any ship. Two grenade launchers, now port-mounted, could fire, collectively, at a rate of 700 rounds per minute, out to a range of a mile. Four sailors manned Stinger antiaircraft missiles they were to fire point-blank. Rensselaer had earmarked four of the remaining Griffin missiles and one of the Harpoons to be fired upon his order.

The six SEALs had at their disposal anti-tank rockets, light machine guns, and the two .50-caliber Barrett sniper rifles. Holworthy was already concealed up top, tied in so that if he were hit he would not fall. He would use all his weapons but concentrate first on eliminating bridge personnel with the Barrett.

The biggest gun was the radar-and-optically-directed 30mm chain gun: 50 rounds per minute of either explosive, armor-piercing, incendiary, or airburst ammunition. The chief, gunners' mates and Marchetti, the weapons officer, had carefully planned the load-outs and firing sequence for all weapons, to be modified as much as possible to meet changing circumstances, but no one in the midst of a battle was going to revert to the painstaking and time-consuming process of arranging rounds on a belt. The problem was partially soluble due to the plethora of guns, quite a few of which were loaded primarily with one type of ammunition, and could simply hold fire when it was not advantageous for them to participate.

Every man on deck, Holworthy in the yards, and the commanders on the bridge had ballistic armor and helmets. Corpsmen and damage control parties stood by their equipment. Watertightness was set. The mess stood ready for the wounded, saline and plasma already hanging on poles clamped to the laminate tables where the enlisted men ate, now like beds, with pillows at the head. And when all was ready, they waited. *Sahand* would be less than an hour away. They could almost feel her coming, and they hoped she would not launch her helicopter but rather come to take as close a look as possible.

*

Rather than encouraging of anxiety, the wait proved calming, as having done everything they could, they wanted to get on with it. "What are you thinking?" Rensselaer asked his XO as they peered from the bridge, knowing that the optics on the periscope would first show *Sahand*.

"Hava. I've never had opium, but when I think of her I imagine it's like opium. The goodness and life that radiated from her, and the contrast of her military uniform and her femininity, just killed me. I can't get over it. Hey, she's going to Caltech. She's as mature as a grown woman, and as enthusiastic and fresh as a girl. All I want is to be worthy of her so she might consider me."

"I think she may have come to a similar conclusion."

"Really? You think?"

"You didn't see that the two of you locked onto one another with a billion volts?"

"I tried to hide it."

"She did, too."

"What about you, sir, what were you thinking?"

Rensselaer lifted his binocular and scanned ahead. "You know, the older you get, the weirder you get. So it's not a fair question."

"I answered mine."

"All right. I was thinking about doors."

"Doors."

"In New Orleans sometimes it was so humid that the doors swelled, and to open or close them you had to attack with your shoulder and the full weight of your body. You'd think that, having been doors all their lives in New Orleans, they would have learned."

"You're not afraid, are you?" Clearly, Rensselaer was not.

"Would it help?" was his answer, betraying absolutely no fear, as there was no fear to betray.

If or when Movius would rise to command, this—*Would it help?*—would be the lesson he would most profitably recall.

*

After the midday meal and prayers on the *Sahand*, the captain had been on the bridge not ten minutes when he was told of a radar contact dead ahead at fifty-five nautical miles. He took note, assuming that by the time *Sahand* reached the reported position the contact would be many kilometers distant, even were it a slow-moving fishing boat. After a quarter of an hour, the radar operator called the captain to his monitor, which showed that the contact, which lay almost exactly athwart *Sahand*'s course, was not moving.

The captain asked what the radarman could deduce from the signal, and was told only that it suggested a ship the size of a trawler or even a dhow, and that the return was strong enough to indicate that it was constructed of steel. The captain told him to report in another fifteen minutes.

Fifteen minutes later, with distance shrinking, the contact remained unmoving as it sat neatly astride *Sahand*'s plotted course. The first officer proposed to dogleg around it. Without responding, the captain moved to the port side of the bridge, close to the windows. His pressed uniform, carefully trimmed black beard, and tense manner were nothing like Rensselaer's impressive but relaxed bearing. For the captain of the

Sahand was like someone who had been hurt and never gotten over it. He was perpetually alert, and perpetually reckless. With the consuming aggression of someone aggrieved, something in him made him always want to strike.

His order was spoken, the Farsi equivalent of *Steady as she goes.* Agitated by fear and opportunity, he maintained his rigid bearing, but the officers noticed that his speech was clipped and angry. Tension spread across the ship.

Ten nautical miles from *Athena*, a lookout high in *Sahand*'s superstructure reported a sighting at relative bearing 358 degrees. Having decided to investigate, the captain ordered two degrees to port and all hands to battle stations. Although it was done with urgency, it was nonetheless the urgency of a drill, for no one really thought it was anything but a precaution. All weapons came to the ready, but with no expectation that they would be used.

Though the captain knew he would be approaching port side to port side, he felt no need to cross-deck any of his armament, as Rensselaer had done. Not for a trawler or a dhow. Certainly it wasn't a warship, and for sure not an American warship, which would have been moving fast, locking on its firing radars, launching a helicopter or a UAV.

The first officer said he didn't like the way things felt—or that the ship sat motionlessly on *Sahand*'s course. Again he recommended avoiding it. The captain received this as an insulting challenge to his courage and judgment. He told the officer that what lay ahead was almost certainly a fishing boat, and that, whatever it was, they could deal with it.

Sahand plowed ahead without altering speed, and at their weapons and consoles the men were thinking of other things.

*

Twenty minutes before *Sahand* would come into sight, so as to let it see a column of smoke on the horizon, Rensselaer said, "Light the buckets," a highly unusual command, and possibly unique.

Along the decks, sailors lit flares and pointed them into the buckets, which immediately sent up volumes of black smoke. When the buckets were steadily burning, the flares were thrown into the sea, hissing once and finally.

Two of the buckets were hoisted, one a third the way and the other halfway up. The early smoke from all of them immediately fouled the nets and tarps, painting them in random patterns convincingly like either the works of abstract expressionists or the products of destruction, if indeed there is a difference.

Not long after, *Sahand* was visible on the horizon, moving fast. Rensselaer passed his next order through the sound talkers so that everyone who had them could inform those who didn't. "Fire only when opportune, and, I stress, *only* after I give the order for the first salvo. Until then, stay quiet and concealed."

At three kilometers, the Iranian ship cut its engines and glided forward, losing speed with the drag of its hull and stilled propellers. In sight was a burning hulk shaped unlike anything anyone on *Sahand* had ever seen. Brown and black, obscured by smoke, it was shaped like a sailing ship and it did have sails. Had *Sahand* been off *Athena*'s port or starboard beam, *Athena*'s length would have made clear that this was not so. But from directly ahead, foreshortening prevented the observation that the masts were not high enough for a sailing vessel of *Athena*'s proportions.

Sahand's captain told his officers that despite the unthreatening appearance of the vessel in their path, he didn't want to get too close. Rather, they would send a boat to reconnoiter. The order went out to launch a RHIB. As the deck crew swung their RHIB outboard on its davits and the boarding party transferred, their ship had come almost to a stop about fifteen hundred yards from *Athena*.

On the sound talker, Rensselaer spoke to the engine room. "Are you prepared to go to full power on my order?"

"Aye, sir. On your order."

"Spare nothing when you do. Hold. Hold."

The RHIB from *Sahand*, with a flak-jacketed, helmeted complement of eight, was lowered toward the waterline. On the bridge, quite naturally, all eyes were on it as it descended, and no one was watching the curious wreck ahead. When a boat is lowered, fascination is magnetic.

Although he couldn't count on it, Rensselaer knew this. When the RHIB was three-quarters of the way down, he ordered, "Full power." Quietly at first, *Athena*'s turbines began to turn. As they advanced to maximum rpm they made an indismissible whine, but not the throbbing of diesels one would expect at sea, and although on *Sahand* they heard it vaguely, they thought it might be from *Sahand* itself, or the sound of a distant commercial airliner, the sight of which is tantalizing to sailors on long and difficult deployments, who imagine the comfort and luxurious destinations of those above. As *Sahand*'s diesels were still throbbing, its sailors and officers who tried to place *Athena*'s faint hum could not.

When Rensselaer saw that the generators were at full power he commanded, "All engines ahead, flank. Helmsman, steady as she goes, rudder amidships."

With the highest horsepower-to-weight ratio the Navy had ever built, *Athena* could reach top speed in less than a minute, a miracle for such a fast and relatively large ship. The resistance in air of the canvas and nets slowed her down, but, reaching almost sixty miles per hour in that time, she closed on *Sahand* in about fifty seconds.

In the first ten seconds, no one on *Sahand*'s bridge was looking. In the next ten seconds, someone did look, and called out. In the following ten seconds, everyone had a great deal of trouble assimilating what was happening. The disheveled, smoking wreck had accelerated at a rate they had never seen a ship attain. After forty seconds, as *Athena*'s camouflage was collapsed and dropped, *Sahand*'s officers began shouting commands. But not until *Athena* was practically abreast were those commands sufficiently coordinated so as to make sense. The first order was to engage the engines. The second, to bring in the RHIB. The third, for the RHIB to cast off. The fourth—to the gunners and weapons officers—to fire. They, however, were not fast enough. Before *Sahand* could let off a single shot, *Athena* had come to a point-blank firing position and Rensselaer gave the order to open up. Then, as he was about to pass by *Sahand* at high speed, he ordered *Athena*'s engines into reverse to slow her down.

The first shot was Holworthy's. Because of light reflecting from its windows, he couldn't see into the bridge, so he took his sniper's shot at one of *Sahand*'s sailors manning a machine gun at the rail, and killed him. Then he used his own light machine gun to rake the bridge windows.

By this time, every one of *Athena*'s guns was firing. The noise was a weapon itself. Twelve .50-caliber barrels firing explosive, airburst, incendiary, and armor-piercing shells tore into the decks, bridge, and mounted weapons on *Sahand*. Stinger missiles were fired point-blank at the superstructure. Holworthy aimed his anti-tank rocket at a point just below the bridge, guessing that it might penetrate into a weapons-control space. It hit, and exploded within.

Miniguns poured such a high volume of 7.62 slugs across the decks and into the bridge that it was as if *Sahand* were subsumed in an immense swarm of bees. Hundreds of grenades burst above the decks and against the superstructure. The 30mm chain gun fired 40 rounds that slammed into *Sahand* at the waterline before *Athena* cleared its stern and resumed full speed ahead.

In less than a minute, *Athena* was a mile off *Sahand*'s stern. The Iranian ship was issuing not just smoke, as had come from the oily buckets on *Athena* before they had been tossed into the sea, but sheets of flame that were ballooned now and then by explosions. As the over-pressure from the detonations pumped air into the burning vapors and pushed them into yet more air, the colors of the flames changed from orange to yellow to white before they contracted back to the fires whence they had originated.

Sahand had not fired even one shot, and was in such distress that Rensselaer, looking astern, was sure she would surrender. He was about to make radio contact when he saw *Sahand*, now slowly underway, turn to starboard. On her starboard side, sheltered in the lee of *Athena*'s assault, some weapons had survived, and *Sahand* was about to fight.

Two Qader missiles rose from her smoke-obscured decks. Seeing this, Rensselaer ordered flank speed ahead. Seconds later, he called for chaff, and the chaff cannons shot a spray of shiny streamers and confetti that bloomed and sparkled in the sunshine like fireworks at night. Then he ordered hard left rudder to the stops. *Athena* slid into a nearly right angle turn to port, heeled over as if to capsize, and straightened back up at full speed. The action was so quick that, relying on the good sense of the helmsman, he had abbreviated the standard commands and simply said, "Bring her over to port at flank speed."

The first missile homed to the chaff and plunged into the sea. The second made a quick turn, almost echoing *Athena*'s skate, only sharper. They saw it coming. Again Rensselaer ordered hard left rudder to the stops, at full speed. The Qader was evidently not built for such a fast ship at such close range. It could not adjust, and exploded close to *Athena*'s starboard beam, sending shrapnel across the decks. One of the bridge windows was blown out, slamming down Josephson. Lacerated by shrapnel and shards of metal and glass, he bled profusely. On the main deck, a SEAL was hit, as were two sailors, one standing ready for damage control, the other carrying ammunition. Speight, the ammunition carrier, was blown overboard, a tremendously heavy belt of .50-cal rounds garlanded around his neck, his legs severed from his body and flying ahead of him as he tumbled into the white froth of the turn.

Rensselaer had no time to take any reports, for at least two of *Sahand*'s cannons were firing at *Athena* as she headed at high speed toward the Iranian ship's starboard beam. "Fire the Griffins," he ordered. The weapons officers had been waiting. Three Griffins ascended simultaneously and headed toward *Sahand*, which had no functioning chaff to launch, and was not at all agile enough for evasion.

Even before the Griffins struck, Rensselaer ordered hard right rudder at full speed and let *Athena* make a 180-degree turn to starboard, running from *Sahand*, before ordering rudder amidships.

"Are we far enough to launch Harpoon?"

"No sir! We need another mile."

"Ready to launch?"

"Ready to launch."

Rensselaer looked back as the Griffins exploded on and against *Sahand*. He called for damage and casualty reports. As they began to come in, Marchetti, the weapons officer, reported that Harpoon range had been achieved.

"Launch Harpoon."

When it launched, the Harpoon made *Athena* roll a little as the missile roared upward.

With movement that appeared to be immensely purposeful and determined, almost as if it were conscious, it arced toward *Sahand*, climbing to perhaps a thousand or two thousand feet. Everyone on *Athena*'s decks smelled its fuel. It then jerked, and plunged down at tremendous speed, striking its target amidships and centered. In the first second, nothing happened. But then the Harpoon's 500-pound, high-explosive warhead detonated in the interior of the ship.

As her magazines blew, *Sahand*'s midsection appeared to jump from the water, leaving bow and stern behind. This broke her in half, and she went under so quickly those on *Athena* who were watching found what they had just done so difficult to assimilate that, matching the sudden silence after *Sahand* disappeared—as if it had never existed—they were struck dumb. Such a large ship, and now nothing but a flat sea and gently drifting debris.

*

Battles are not always over even when they're won. The greater a breaking wave, the fiercer its undertow. There was neither celebration nor relief as *Athena's* crew worked and assessed with almost the same urgency they had had going into the engagement.

Rensselaer called again for damage reports. The wounded men had been carried to the mess, where the corpsman and one of the SEALs who was corpsman-trained were working to save them. The hull had been breached below the waterline in two places.

"What have we got?" Rensselaer asked over the 1MC.

A panicky voice answered, "Two holes a few feet below the waterline. We can't stop it. It's flooding like crazy."

"Pisecki to the breach," Rensselaer ordered, believing that if the flooding could be stopped, Pisecki could stop it, and if Pisecki couldn't stop it, no one could.

Anyone in Pisecki's way would have been flattened as his speed times his mass in the passageways and on the ladders made these places dangerous. When he arrived at the bakery stores compartment, where the water was coming in, he ordered, "Kill the switches, tell the captain two hundred gallons a minute, and seal the doors."

The eight men of the damage control party followed through immediately, with a hollow feeling of terror when they heard the closing of the dogs on the doors. They would seal the breaches or they would die. One of the holes was the size of a dinner plate, the other twice that big. "Where're the fucking screw plates?" Pisecki yelled.

"There," a sailor answered, pointing to the water, now about three feet deep beneath the holes. With the switches killed, only the emergency lanterns provided light. The plates were not visible. Pisecki dived down. He stayed underwater for at least a minute as the level inched higher. Then he surfaced, a patch plate in each hand.

"It's impossible to press it against the inflow," one of the sailors shouted. Everything had to be shouted.

"We do it or we die," Pisecki told him, handing off one of the plates and moving toward the bigger breach. As he went he called out, "Pump to the maximum." They were, but the pumps could only do so much.

At first the thick stream of incoming seawater would push Pisecki and the men who followed him back almost as many steps as they took. When he got into a position from which he could try to put the clamping mechanism into the hole so its bar would slap against the outside of the hull and the plate could be screwed into place, it was as if he were balancing on a tiny ledge. Every movement had to be carefully accomplished so his weight was in perfect opposition to the inflow, or he would be swept back. And because his range of movement was so restricted, much of the time his face had to be submerged in the stream of water and he couldn't breathe. To get a breath, he had to move slowly and, while maintaining his balance, momentarily exit the stream. He would emerge, his hair and mustache shedding streams of water, take an enormous breath, and then disappear in the silvery inrush, all the while maneuvering the hundred-pound plate.

It was so difficult that he thought his lungs would burst or his heart stop. He said to himself over and over that although it seemed he could not do it, if he wanted to live, he had to do it. So he found himself pushing beyond any strength he had previously known, while holding his breath and balancing precariously. Blinded by the water, he worked not by sight but by feel.

Then, in the darkness, half smothered, he heard the crossbar grip the outside of the hull. He turned the screw as much as he could, came up for air, and went back to turn it some more. Five minutes, ten breaths later, and the plate began to clamp against the inner surface of the hull. Then he ordered a young seaman to tighten it, and the water stopped.

He had dropped the other plate, so he dived for and found it, and repeated his actions, this time with much less strain, sealing off the smaller hole more easily—as the column of inflowing seawater was small enough and the breach positioned so that he could place and clamp the plate, breathing all the while.

When he finished, the water was up to his chest, but then again he was quite short. He asked if the 1MC was working, and the sailor answered in the affirmative, handing over the mic. Pisecki held it for a while, and then, having almost caught his breath, the water still dripping from his hair, clicked on.

"Damage control to bridge."

"Bridge."

"Inflow contained, positive outflow with pumping. Will weld plates fast to make completely watertight."

"Well done," was the answer.

Left up in the rush, the telescoping mast had been severed by the missile blast and propelled into the sea, followed by the main radome. Though the rest up top, including Holworthy, had been spared, *Athena* was scarred by shrapnel and stained by oil smoke. Tarps and nets had now been thrown overboard, but the ship still looked a wreck. However, weapons, engines, and most systems were intact.

Rensselaer called in Velez. "Break EMCON to send to Fifth Fleet, CENTCOM, and anyone who was messaged about *Sahand*: "*Sahand* sunk at three degrees, thirty-two minutes, five seconds north, fifty-three degrees, thirty-seven minutes, fifty-one seconds east. *Athena* underway, major systems intact, attending to wounded and searching for K.I.A. overboard. Will look for *Sahand* survivors next. We have casualties. Advise immediately as to nearest medivac facility and, as *Sahand* survivors may be located, brig."

Rensselaer ordered an Anderson turn and summoned all unengaged hands on deck to search for Speight, although everyone knew his body wouldn't be found. Legs, with no hollow spaces, would sink and never rise. Head and trunk would have sunk as well, as the lungs filled with seawater, and the ammunition belts would have carried him into the blackest deep. *Athena* would cover the area ten times, mostly to honor him in searching the small patch of sea where he had disappeared, and as an obligation to his family. In answer to Movius's query, about when to search for *Sahand*'s survivors, were there any, Rensselaer said, "They'll wait until we're sure Speight can't be found."

The officers hardly knew Seaman Speight. Twenty-three years old, in the Navy since eighteen, unmarried, with a chipped front tooth, freckles, silver, wire-rimmed glasses, and a slight build, he was known for having pronounced *antiques* as *antikews*, a fondness for swimming, and for being harmless, unremarkable, uncomplaining, easy to please, and liked by the chiefs. But no one knew his heart.

As the ship moved back and forth over the search grid, Rensselaer went to the mess. Martin, the damage-controlman, wounded and still in his fire suit, lay silent and dazed on one of the makeshift beds. The two medics were standing next to Josephson, having done what they could. They turned to the captain, and one, indicating Martin with a quick lift of his head, said, "Concussion, maybe cerebral hematoma. Gotta get him to a hospital."

But they said nothing about Josephson. When Rensselaer approached, he winced, and said, "Jesus Christ. I didn't realize."

"We brought him down here real quick. You couldn't have seen."

"What is that?" Rensselaer asked, looking at Josephson's neck. The left side was open, part of the thyroid was visible, and two clamps were resting across his neck so as not to hang their weight on the two halves of his severed left carotid artery.

"How can he live?" Rensselaer asked.

"The other carotid artery is untouched, as are the two vertebral arteries, we think. But he's gotten worse. We're not microsurgeons. If we try to sew it up, it won't work."

"Can you clamp down both parts of the artery on a tube linking them?"

"We don't have a round clamp, or a tube."

"We must have hose clamps small enough," Rensselaer said. He went over to the 1MC. "This is the captain. Engineering, bring small hose clamps, all sizes, to the mess, on the double."

"What will we clamp the arteries to?"

Rensselaer had no answer, but he felt stress close to that of combat— in fact, more so, as in combat the key to survival was to banish stress, and he had always managed that. *Slow is smooth, and smooth is fast.* As his eyes swept the room he was mentally inventorying the whole ship. And yet that became unnecessary when he hit upon the drink machine. Next to it was a cylindrical container of drinking straws. He dashed to it and brought one back. "They're plastic, thank God, the larger kind. They're supposed to be phased out."

"It's still small," the SEAL corpsman said.

"What else are we gonna do?" his colleague replied. "He's getting plasma. We can get whole blood into him."

"He's fading. You know it."

"Okay." Turning to Rensselaer: "Captain?"

"If he's going anyway."

A chief arrived with a box full of small hose clamps. They found two of the right size, opened the straw, cut it down, and dropped it and the clamps into a glass of alcohol. "We need a screwdriver, Chief, for Christ's sake. How the hell are we going to close the clamps?"

The chief rushed off.

One of the corpsmen took Josephson's blood pressure. "He's in shock. Almost gone." The chief arrived with a handful of screwdrivers. The corpsman picked a screwdriver and swished it in the container of alcohol.

They worked fast, gloved and masked, first spraying the open wound with antibiotic and applying coagulant to the capillaries. Then they opened the clamps and partially closed them over each section of the artery before gingerly inserting the straw into each, inching the rubbery artery up until it was within a few millimeters of the center. They slowly tightened the hose clamps, careful not to tighten them too much, until the straw began to deform, and then loosened them until it returned to its proper shape.

"Okay, let's see." They opened and removed the surgical clamp on the brain side, and very gradually opened the heart-side clamp. They could see the blood as it started to flow through the straw. "It's working."

When the surgical clamp on the heart-side was removed, the blood pushed through the straw. Just a little came out from the heart-side juncture. They put a drain in near it and began to sew up the wound.

"We can give him blood to make up for what drains, Captain, but even if the contraption holds, if we don't get him into a real hospital . . . " and here the corpsman shook his head, aware that even though the patient was unconscious, there was no telling what the unconscious could know.

Again Rensselaer went to the 1MC. "Captain to COMMS. Urgent message to all controlling commands. We need medivac, highest priority. Get it out with our position." Velez repeated the message. Rensselaer had heard him typing even as he spoke. "Do you need me for anything else here?"

"No sir. We've typed the blood and we're on it."

"I'll be on the bridge."

*

When Rensselaer reached the bridge, Movius asked how they were down below.

"Martin has a bad concussion, Josephson's touch and go. What search evolution are we in?"

"Seven."

"This is the captain," Rensselaer said on the 1MC, abandoning his sound talker, which he had forgotten he was wearing. "Commander Holworthy to the bridge."

Soon thereafter, Holworthy showed up, his head bandaged. "It's nothing," he said, "just a little piece of the Qader."

"Launch the RHIB and go back to the *Sahand*'s flotsam and see if there are any survivors. Be armed and take restraints. We'll start for an evac point when they assign us one."

"Yes sir. How hard shall I look?"

Rensselaer thought. "As soon as we get the evac point, we're out of here at full speed. That's your window."

It was remarkable how quickly the SEALs were ready and the RHIB hit the water, as if they had not only drilled this again and again—as they had—but as if they had habitually dreamt it in full detail. All the small movements seemed jointless, flowing together, like the water of a fast stream, inseparable and indivisible.

While still sighted from *Athena* as almost a small dot, the RHIB had been gone for ten minutes and *Athena* had just finished the tenth evolution when messages came back from Fifth Fleet and CENTCOM. Medical evacuation was not possible for Mogadishu, the nearest port, as all assets were deployed to the Gulf. However, ESB-3, the *Puller*, one of the strangest and most welcome vessels of the Navy, had just cleared the Suez Canal and would rendezvous with *Athena* at 13°, 04', 60" N; 51°, 29', 50" E in the Gulf of Aden just south of the Alula-Fartak Trench, 595 nautical miles north-northeast of *Athena*'s current position. This was not that much farther than Mogadishu. At maximum sustainable speed, it would take about sixteen hours to get there. That is, in a cooperative sea, for which every man on *Athena* prayed in his own way.

The *Puller*, an expeditionary support base on its way to the Gulf, had a fully equipped surgical module, a brig, and the potential of receiving, refueling, and relaunching a V-22 to evacuate casualties to Lemonnier, thence to be medivaced to Landstuhl in Germany, and then to the United States.

Buck Lanham was setting the course for the rendezvous—straight up and between the Horn of Africa and the little island of Abd al-Kuri—when he was interrupted as *Athena* made her last pass in search of Seaman Speight. The ensign was lowered to half-gaff and *Athena* briefly slowed to five knots. All hands turned to the sea and saluted the shipmate who, someday, in one way or another, they would follow. And then they left him to eternity in the deep.

*

Never out of sight of *Athena*, Holworthy, O'Connor, and three other SEALs in the RHIB motored through the slick and debris left by *Sahand*. Oil covered several acres and calmed the sea until it was almost flat, with only deep waves of long periodicity, as if the whole ocean were gently rising and falling. The water was green and black. Detritus here and there—an empty plastic jug, pieces of wood and insulation, cloth, garbage—easily caught the eye.

Among this were floating bodies, facedown and limp. And then there were the living, whom the SEALs pulled out of the water at gunpoint and immediately restrained with plastic cuffs.

They were nine all told, ratings of some sort, and two officers, distinguished by their insignia. It was puzzling to Holworthy, as one set was black and gold, and the other black and green.

The man with the green and black, which matched the colors of the water, had tried to remove his shirt as the RHIB approached him. Known for decisiveness, the SEALs—in this case O'Connor—fired a burst near him to get him to stop. He didn't. The RHIB closed, and O'Connor slapped him on the side of the head with a paddle, reached down, and yanked him into the boat as if he had been a sardine. The Iranian was at most five-foot-three and 125 pounds, and O'Connor, one of the bulls found in every SEAL team, was six-foot-eight and 250 pounds of muscle. Dazed by the blow and his sudden ascension, the Iranian officer nonetheless was admirably defiant. It was clear from his eyes and the taut muscles of his face that he would keep fighting, so they knew to watch him.

Athena did not head directly to the RHIB but in a line offset to the west. This told Holworthy that she was on course to make for the evac point. His complaint heretofore was that *Athena*, and therefore he and his men, had suffered a lack of action and purpose. Now, from a distance, he was almost awed by the little ship. Already it had been involved in three combats, it had taken casualties, and it had sunk a far larger and very important vessel. And it would be off to somewhere else, with men to save and prisoners to hold and interrogate.

Holworthy had the sense that things were hardly over, that *Athena* would be engaged more than he had ever thought, that she would find enemies and enemies would find her. For the first time on the deployment he felt enveloped in an almost mystical purpose, even as it was unknown to him. As she came into view, battered, smoke-stained, but still fully capable, her ensign a bright shock of color snapping in the wind she generated at speed, she seemed entirely different. Perhaps this came from viewing her whole and from afar. For, apprehended from without, she was graceful and strong, and although she was a new ship, she now had the scars of age. Vectoring the RHIB to meet her, he felt as if he were returning home.

*

Still forging ahead, *Athena* slowed for the RHIB, which sidled aft and bumped her stern ramp. After an exchange of signals, it shot forward and skied up the ramp, its propeller rising in pitch as it turned the froth of *Athena*'s immediate wake. The Iranian prisoners were impressed by the speed of this operation. The capture of the RHIB, the slowing and then increase of *Athena*'s speed, the orders, and the acknowledgments, were all of a piece and so quickly completed that it was like the closing and locking of a rifle bolt.

Prisoners were taken beneath an awning amidships. There, one by one, they were stripped of their oil-soaked uniforms, treated for superficial wounds and burns, given Navy BDUs to wear until their clothes were washed and dried, and then they were shackled. To keep track of their ranks and identities, the uniforms had numbers pinned to them, matching the numbers etched on the shackles.

All this proceeded under the guns of the SEALs. Di Loreto welded two eyebolts onto the deck, after which a chain was run from one to the other, and each shackle chain padlocked to it so prisoners could be removed individually for treatment, to go to the head, or for interrogation. When this was completed, Rensselaer appeared. He looked at them dispassionately. He was all business, and other than that they could not assess his attitude.

"Does anyone speak English?" he asked.

The one who had tried to rid himself of identification, said, "I."

"Are you the ranking officer?"

"No."

"Him?" Rensselaer asked, pointing to the next man. Their clothes were for the moment laid out in front of these two, the gold and black naval insignia their only identification.

"You don't speak English?" Rensselaer asked the ranking officer, who stared ahead uncomprehendingly. Rensselaer then astounded his own men by asking in the languages themselves if the naval officer whom he addressed spoke Arabic, French, German, Italian, or Russian. He didn't, so Rensselaer turned to the one who spoke English.

"Please tell your people that as prisoners of war you'll be treated according to the Geneva Conventions. We have no room for you below, but will do our best to attend to your needs while you're on deck. You will be adequately fed and clothed. We'll try to keep you cool during the day and warm at night. We hope to transfer you to a proper brig in less than a day."

The English-speaker nodded. "What is a brig?"

"Jail." Rensselaer looked at his uniform and read the Farsi nameplate, pronouncing it in Arabic. "Atash Farrakzad."

"Farrokhzad," he was corrected.

"Farrokhzad," Rensselaer replied politely. And then, to Holworthy, "Mr. Holworthy, when the uniforms are washed, bring them to me."

"Aye sir. I'll make sure the officers' are done first."

"Very well."

Rensselaer went back to the bridge. *Athena* was now at full sustainable speed on her northward course, and Josephson was still alive, attended continuously in shifts, while the crew and prisoners made do with MREs so Josephson wouldn't have to be moved from the mess.

*

On the now quiet and partially shattered bridge as *Athena* was sailing for the Gulf of Aden, Rensselaer studied the newly washed uniforms of the Iranian prisoners. Relaxing EMCON, he was quickly able to see from open sources on the internet that Farrokhzad was in fact the senior officer—he had lied: what a surprise—and the regular naval officer to whom he had pointed was clearly subordinate. Farrokhzad had green shoulder boards with black sleeves, upon which were three yellow-and-green rosettes. That meant he was a Guardian Colonel in the NEDSA, the IRGC Navy. Rensselaer then consulted the classified networks to further his understanding, after which he ordered the uniforms returned and Farrokhzad— who had been given the number *six*—brought unshackled to the wardroom.

As O'Connor had experienced directly, Farrokhzad was quite a little fellow, with coal-black, piercing eyes, and a neatly trimmed beard. His anger was unconcealable and irrepressible. Seeing this, Rensselaer told the sailor guarding him, "This guy has a bug up his ass. If he attacks me, shoot him. If he attacks you, I'll do the same." (When the prisoners had been taken aboard, all officers had been issued sidearms.) Turning to the Iranian, Rensselaer asked, "You heard that?"

Farrokhzad smiled with contempt. "You think I'll take over your ship?" He looked about. "Your boat?"

"Is that supposed to be insulting?" Rensselaer asked. "My boat, you may recall, sank your ship. And, yes, were I in your position, I would be working on that."

"You can waterboard me, or kill me," Farrokhzad stated, for he had certainly thought it out beforehand, "but I will tell you only name, rank, serial number—as you say."

Rensselaer shifted in his chair and listened with pleasure to the steady hum of the generators and electric engines driving *Athena* through the waves. "We won't kill you," he said. "And we can't waterboard you. Where would we get the water?" He glanced at the bulkhead, communicating that, outside, they were surrounded by ocean. "And we don't have a board. I was waterboarded in training. I'm not going to be overwhelmed with guilt because you brought up waterboarding, if that's what you had in mind.

"Also, your serial number is of no concern to me, and as you've seen, I know your name even if I mispronounced it."

"You know Arabic. Good for you. You don't know Farsi."

"I do know, however, that you are a *Sarhank Yakun.* . . ."

"*Sarhang-e Yekom.*"

"I stand corrected. *Sarhang-e Yekom*, a *Pasdaran*, Guardian Colonel in the NEDSA. I know that your father was one of the terrorists. . . ."

"Patriots."

"We're speaking English now . . . terrorists, who seized our embassy in nineteen seventy-nine. You were a boy, but you must've been proud of him."

"I still am."

"Yes. Taking diplomats hostage, an old Persian tradition. You studied engineering in Birmingham."

"Electrical engineering."

"Which is why your English is so good, and why, I would warrant, that you were on the *Sahand*. For the Tsirkon. Not only to supervise and possibly direct its deployment, but because the NEDSA—and by that I mean the *Pasdaran*—wouldn't want the regular Navy to take credit for such a prestigious weapon, and, had things worked out, the sinking of a carrier—or two carriers. Who was in charge, the captain, or you?"

"The captain is dead, and he was a fool."

"I see. You were entirely focused on the mission, and were driven half mad because the captain didn't bypass the trap we laid for him."

"Naval habits."

"I have them, too, and would venture that you would have taken over the *Sahand* by force had you enough *Pasdaran* aboard. But you didn't, did you?"

Although Farrokhzad said nothing, Rensselaer could almost see in his eyes not only the replaying of just what had been described but the longing for a different outcome.

"You don't want to talk about it. Why? Do you think I'll glean enough so I can sink your ship? You know, I've already done that."

"For why? So you can attack my country?"

"We attacked your ability to make the nuclear weapons and ICBMs with which, even though you don't have them yet, you threaten us and our allies, very clearly, daily, almost on the hour. What the hell did you expect?"

"It doesn't matter. You'll collapse from within because you are corrupt, racist, and degenerate."

"We are corrupt, you're right, but only about a tenth as corrupt as you. I guess that in some respects we're more degenerate, which I don't like either, but we don't treat our women—more than half the population—like slaves who must be hidden lest their very being corrupt the virtuous. And racist? Once, but look around. A fifth of my crew is black.

"You know what I tell every one of my crews at the outset? I tell them that I'm partially color-blind. I am, which is why I couldn't fly—I wanted to. I say to them that I can't tell the difference between navy blue and black. They get it, and it's true in both senses. We get along fine, we're brothers, and we bring that home."

"You speak so much to get me to speak, but I give no information," Farrokhzad ventured, "because, as you and I know, little bits of harmless information can combine in a mosaic. Don't forget, we have the art of patterns: we weave carpets. We have been at war with you for a thousand years, and you're too stupid to know it. We say it, but you don't hear it."

"I hear it."

"Then you are an exception. You countrymen are deaf. The war may continue for another thousand years, and only one thing is for sure: we will win. Oh yes, you love your machines. You are so good with machines. You see, you have the clock, but we have the time."

"That really, really sounds like an advertising slogan. You should work on Madison Avenue," Rensselaer told him. "And as far as what you say, I wouldn't bet on the outcome."

"I would. America can fight only when it does so from the air, with machines, and against a weaker enemy. You don't have the strength or will to sacrifice or to win. As things level and you have no great advantage, you'll run, and die."

"Really," Rensselaer asked rhetorically. "From what do you think we've sprung? Before we were Goliath, we were David. When the layers of corruption, riches, and ease have been blasted away, that's what we really are. At the heart of every American soldier and sailor is the willingness to take on superior forces and prevail. You haven't even begun to see us fight. In taking on *Sahand*, every one of my crew was willing to die. Every one of my crew was focused, determined, and brave. Don't misinterpret us, for when we awake and when we unite, your hopes, your ambitions, your dreams of conquest, will, like *Sahand*, sink to the bottom of the sea.

"*Athena* is just a little ship, but she's taken forth the souls of her predecessors in battles great and small. It's true that Americans fail to see how the Navy, hidden by distance but nonetheless in the bright light of the other side of the world as they sleep, embodies the spirit and courage of the America they sometimes forget. And Colonel, if I were you, I'd pray that you'll never live to see us fight without restraint."

"Do you think," Farrokhzad asked, "that you've come even close to crushing my spirit?"

"No. I don't care about your spirit. Be as spirited as you like. You're chained to my deck. I merely stated the facts. And I can imagine exactly how you'll feel when you and your men are swallowed by the brig of the *Puller* and brought close to your country in an enemy fleet. Your spirit may not be crushed, but you will suffer, as I would in your place. Would I have it any other way? No. But am I sorry for you? Yes, I am."

Afterward, alone in the wardroom, Rensselaer felt the rhythm and thrust of *Athena* moving forward. Nothing was certain, he thought, and when nothing was certain, all was alight.

*

Not, of course, for the Iranians, who were enraged by their defeat. Their hands were free, but although they could sit, stand, or lie down, they couldn't move about. Furthermore, they objected strenuously to the MREs. Farrokhzad was silent on this matter, perhaps thinking that it was below his dignity to complain, but he did translate the protests.

In return, the XO addressed the prisoners. "We have a gravely injured officer in the mess, which because of that is inoperative. Everyone on board is eating MREs and only MREs."

"They're garbage," the naval officer replied through Farrokhzad.

"They're food, so they tell us. They may not be what you're used to eating or to your taste, but we're not thrilled with them either. Maybe when you're transferred to the *Puller*, a Michelin chef will cook for you. Meanwhile, suck it up." This didn't translate well to Farsi.

Number three, who was as perpetually angry as Farrokhzad but primitive, coarse, unintelligent, and chunky, shouted something in Farsi, jerked his chains, and tried to throw the MRE overboard, but, because he was stupid, to windward. It stopped short in the air, pieced apart, and fell back over the deck.

"That's unfortunate," said Movius. "You should clean this up, but I can't let you loose." He summoned a sailor, who brought a high-pressure hose and began to wash down the deck. As the last of the macaroni and cheese cleared the safety lines, Movius said to the sailor with the hose, "I believe that in discarding his meal this gentlemen—that is, number three over there—partially soiled his clothing." Nothing was visible on number three's uniform. "Why don't you help him get clean?"

"You mean . . . ?"

"I certainly do, Ollie," Movius said, imitating Stan Laurel.

"Aye sir." He turned the hose on number three and kept it on him for a minute or two. This was perhaps not in the spirit of the Geneva Conventions, but perhaps not such a major infraction on such a hot day.

*

As a steady, cold breeze moves through a winter forest in a gentle current, subdued light and lack of life give rise to peace and tranquility. Where once the undergrowth teamed with insects, and birds had hopped and sung in the branches, the plants have lost their color and mass, and the animals are gone.

So it is on the sea beyond the continental shelves, off the trade routes, out of sight of land, in blue water with very little life in it, and the sea floor lightless several miles below. In these seemingly never-ending, open stretches it seems appropriate that death can elide with life smoothly, with neither shock nor pain.

The Navy corpsman climbed to the bridge. Approaching Rensselaer, he stood at attention, covered. He saluted. Though uncovered, Rensselaer stiffened and returned the salute. Everyone present became still. "Captain," the corpsman said, "Lieutenant Josephson has passed."

Rensselaer exhaled, briefly closed his eyes, and answered, "I see." A long pause followed. Then, "We have ice. Soon we'll meet up with the *Puller*."

"Yes, sir."

"Gather his things, respectfully."

"Yes sir."

"After we transfer the prisoners, Lieutenant Josephson will leave the ship, with full honors. XO, you have that?"

"Aye, Captain. Yes sir."

"Very well. Carry on."

And, of course, they did, as soldiers and sailors have done since the beginning of time. Soon the mess was reopened, and regular meals resumed, even on the table where Josephson had died.

"Anyone want grief counselors?" a machinist's mate asked as he entered the full mess.

"Yeah, I do," a rating replied. "As many as possible."

"Why?" someone asked.

"So I can kill them, that's why. When someone dies, you're supposed to feel grief and suffer, aren't you? These grief counselors, they go all over the place and counsel people who never even met or were aware of the people who died. One fake to another. Gimme a break. What's next, massage oils and rose petals in the bathtub?"

"That's enough," Pisecki barked. "Josephson died here, for God's sake, on this table. Shut up. As long as he's aboard, you'll eat in silence in this mess. Out of respect. Is that clear?"

*

Josephson had died just north of Abd al-Kuri Island, an uninhabited, mountainous desert with, on its eastern side, perhaps the world's wildest and finest beach. To mollify Holworthy, in a moment of weakness not long after they had departed Lemonnier, Rensselaer had considered leaving a few SEALs there on the way south, to observe traffic, as on occasion irregular forces were ordered to do. But he had decided then that rather than mollify Holworthy, he would keep him down.

The rendezvous point with the *Puller* wasn't far, and, arriving first, *Athena* waited. The *Puller* was out of sight but in radio contact. Eventually they saw her to the west, and she came even with *Athena* at dusk, although in that latitude, as Josephson had learned, dusk is so short it hardly exists. With the lights of the *Puller* blazing despite wartime conditions, her vast superstructure, hollow and beamed like a box-girder bridge, was cast in flares and shadows. A brow was extended from a door in the side and fixed to *Athena*'s main deck. As a gentle swell moved the two ships up and down at different rates, the hinged brow tilted slightly one way and then another.

The Iranian prisoners were escorted over the brow and to the brig in the *Puller*, which would take them very close to their own country, but then to the United States. They were bitter and depressed. The huge ship into the darkness of which they were swallowed seemed like an alien craft from another civilization, which, for them, it was.

A gray metal coffin was carried to *Athena* by a detail from the *Puller*. This was a sad thing to see, sadder than struggle, sadder than blood. It disappeared below. Josephson's body was placed inside it and the flag draped over it. Six of *Athena's* crew in dress uniform carried it slowly to the brow and set it on deck. After a long silence, Rensselaer spoke a few words.

"Our shipmates Speight and Josephson are no longer with us—Speight committed to the deep, lost except to God. And Josephson, who will go home. Neither of these men is unique in death. They are still very much like us, and we are like them: it's only a matter of time—however long, however short. If upon gazing at this coffin you feel a gulf between you, the living, and him, one of the dead, remember that our fates are the same, and he isn't as far from us as we may imagine.

"At times like this I question our profession. I question the enterprise of war. And then I go on, as we shall, and as we must. In this spirit we bid goodbye to Ensign Josephson, to whom you might have been brothers, and I and the chiefs, perhaps, fathers. May God bless and keep him."

Then the captain read the 23rd Psalm, a salute was fired, and Josephson's coffin was lifted to the shoulders of its bearers and slowly carried into the depths of the *Puller*. When he died, he was very young.

IV

Spinning on a Compass Rose

Like a lion that watches from a cane break or from the dark as you sleep, the sea strikes when it wishes.

In the Navy, You Can't Always Get What You Want

When the *Puller* started east on course for the Gulf, the lights on its grid-like superstructure sparkled like the lights of the Eiffel Tower when authored in gold. And then they began to go out, one group at a time. Long familiarity with the heavy steel switches on lighting panels meant that, as they watched, *Athena's* crew could almost hear the slap as these were thrown open. Soon, the *Puller* was just a dark shape, and eventually its stern light became a star light, and disappeared into the distance as the curvature of the earth took it below the horizon.

Left becalmed in the Gulf of Aden, *Athena* turned in the confused currents as listlessly and perforce exactly like its compass rose. Rensselaer and Movius had documented in great detail *Athena's* positions, actions, and casualties. The story was in the logs and in multiple reports filed as she had made to meet the *Puller*, after which she awaited further orders.

Every time Rensselaer took many steps forward in the estimation of the crew, he seemed to take at least a few back. They thought he was strange—different, anyway. And he certainly was different. He had no knowledge of spectator sports, and could neither make nor even understand the football analogies so often used in the military to clarify a proposition. And although he withstood the assault of certain kinds of what he termed the "non-music" chosen by the crew to enliven their workdays, even if he sometimes chose rock and roll that appealed to them as well, he liked classical music, something outside the experience of most of them.

Becalmed and waiting, they heard him over the 1MC. "This is the captain. What you will hear next over the music system is something really extraordinary: Beethoven's Fifth Piano Concerto as played by Glenn Gould, Leopold Stokowski conducting."

A seaman coiling line looked up at another and said, "What? Is this Earth?"

"Think of music not as pictures in the mind, but rather as a whole new world: without associations, captivating and sufficient unto itself, the way mathematicians describe mathematics. Music can transcend human capacities, and briefly take us with it to another realm, perhaps the one where, in this case, Beethoven conceived it. The Gould recording does this, somehow, like no other. Let it move you in the purest sense. Captain out."

"Yes," someone opined disrespectfully, "to lunch." Some, however, understood very well, and Movius had several opportunities to defend him when Movius was slyly questioned about what had happened. The little concert was irrelevant to naval warfare, but not at all to the magical abstractions of the sea—its dimensions, its colors, the chorus of the winds, the musical timing of the waves and the cadenzas falling from their breaking crests. And that was the point. It had an effect, because even the coarsest sailors had a relationship with the sea.

*

All U.S. commands were busy and stressed. Requirements changed by the hour and sometimes the minute. *Athena*, an afterthought of the fleet, much less the Navy, waited not for hours but for days. It seemed clear that she would be ordered either directly to the Gulf—the Holy Grail of the SEALs and, after the crew had been blooded in the first engagements and victory over *Sahand*, everyone else's desired destination. But the ship was battered and low on stores, having received just a token amount from the *Puller*, which had to hurry on. The periscope contraption had been knocked out, as had the search radar and several antennae. The port bridge wing window was gone; bullet holes had peppered the aluminum superstructure; the temporary repairs below the waterline held but were not confidence inspiring; the oil smoke had made the ship look like a tramp; though Martin had fully recovered, two crew members were dead and had no replacement; fuel and food were 60 percent exhausted, and the decks were stained with blood and oil.

Much could be made whole and replenished at the end of the supply chain that stretched from Seventh Fleet in Asia all the way to the armada in the Arabian Sea, which was why the Gulf was still a possible assignment. A quick run to Lemonnier in Djibouti would be even more efficient in terms of repair and resupply. It was conceivable that *Athena* would be ordered to Haifa, Naples, or even home. In sinking the *Sahand* on her maiden deployment, *Athena* had assured a place for herself in history. She had already been awarded a commendation, and no one doubted that a jangle of medals would follow.

Without orders, *Athena* could only drift, her bow pointing alternately and slowly toward one destination or another: the Gulf, Lemonnier, Haifa, Naples, home. And then the new orders came through.

*

Poker-faced, Rensselaer read them, and seized the mic. "This is the captain. Our orders have arrived. The war in the Gulf and Russian provocations in the Baltic continue to mean that the Western Indian Ocean has not a single allied warship—except us. Meanwhile, because we are beaten up, and because we're small and undervalued, the war can do without us, and we're to patrol from the Gulf of Aden north of Somalia southward all the way to Mombasa, to suppress an expected surge of piracy.

"If a replenishment ship passes nearby, we'll replenish. If not, we'll head back to Lemonnier or another port when things run really low. Even without incident, boarding parties may get busy in the next few weeks, and, absent the unexpected, training will resume beginning with the morning watch tomorrow.

"We were supposed to be the sacrificial lamb that slowed and pinpointed *Sahand*. Instead, the lamb killed the wolf. When you recall this in your old age, my guess is that a slight smile will accompany both a surge of pride and a touch of sadness. As your commanding officer, I thank you and I congratulate you. Now we'll head south and get back to work. Captain out."

He turned to the quartermaster. "Buck?"

"Sir?"

"Use the databases to calculate the center point of all pirate incidents off the Somali coast in the last year. Assign attacks within six months a double weight, within three a triple weight, within the last month quadruple weight. Chart a course to that point. We'll run there and then drift to save fuel."

Once more he clicked on the 1MC. "This is the captain again. With the death of Ensign Josephson, Chiefs Rodriguez and Holt are going to serve frequently as officers of the deck, and Seamen Washington and Placa will fill in to assume the duties the chiefs cannot therefore perform. LT Di Loreto will also resume talking to dolphins as long as we are not engaged in combat. In case you didn't know, that's what he does at the bow, which may be why *Athena* is blessed by the sea. Carry on. Captain out."

They turned south and steamed into the darkness. As usual, the stars over the seas adjacent to the desert were as crazily bright as they are in winter in the wilderness or at the poles. Though they seemed as cold as diamonds, their hard light when taken in was comforting and warm. Somehow, much like a loving embrace, it calms the heart. Rensselaer returned to his cabin and slept. As the ship rolled and pitched ever so slightly, he dreamt of Katy. At times he missed and desired her so intensely it was physically painful. In the dream, she was in New Orleans, in a garden, among flowers and patient greenery. Athena herself could not have been more beautiful and wise than Katy Farrar.

And that night, awakened by thunder, he eventually went out alone on deck and looked to see distant lightning flashes striking the sea. They illuminated the dark undersides of the clouds that had spawned them, so that momentarily the clouds looked like mountains. All the way to the horizon, patches of squall-darkened sea appeared and disappeared with each bolt of lightning.

*

When they reached the center point of the piracies—something that existed only in mathematical abstraction—they halted over it and once again started to train as they had on the Atlantic and in the Mediterranean. In the hot sun, they did their best to clean oil and soot from the superstructure, to inventory and maintain their weapons, write new watch bills, and scrub the blood off the decks. Presiding over an *Athena* as restored as possible while alone and at sea was the flag, a shock of bright and unsullied color floating above the gray, battered ship. Despite the fascinating colors at sea, it was yet a fact that the eye was arrested by this striking ensign as by nothing else.

Athena sat upon the calculated center point both as bait and like a spider that—as if versed in operations analysis—sits at the center, the maximally advantageous position on its web. As busy as everyone was with training and repair, for several days and then a week out of action they had the opportunity for rest. Hardest at work was Velez and his striker, Ivoire, who had to man COMMS without cease, listening to a multiplicity of channels and monitoring many sources of intelligence. Everyone felt strengthened by the past combats. They felt an attraction to and yearning for battle, with full knowledge of the risks and dangers and yet none of the anxiety they had experienced in the beginning. As *Athena* drifted, in their impatience for action the sailors were now almost like the SEALs.

In the lee of the desert on one of the nights of flaring stars, Rensselaer returned to his cabin for the eight hours of sleep he had earned by exhausting himself during the day. As usual, he laid out his BDUs so as to be able to dress in seconds when called. No reading: there wasn't time. No thinking upon a problem to be solved. He looked around the tiny cabin and, knowing that the ship was ready and armed, switched off the lights, lay back, and closed his eyes.

Half dreaming, half awake, he saw *Athena*'s statue atop the Acropolis, her golden spear-tip a second sun glistening over the sea and visible from afar to mariners. Like a lighthouse in daylight, it was a modest but persistent signal of warning to the florid, ambitious Persians. Though thousands of years had passed, the once seemingly remote and legendary wars of Greeks versus Persians—West versus East the fleets of two separate worlds clashing on cloudless summer seas—had once again arisen as if they had never ceased to exist. Though as a boy on the Hudson, Rensselaer would not have dreamt that his life would lead him to this, here he was, in the shadow of *Athena*'s diaphanous robes.

It seemed perfect and satisfactory that such a woman would be wielding a spear that captured the sunlight and shot its beams all the way to Sounion. As if confirmed by the near divinity of dreams, she seemed the answer to all things. Taking comfort from the imprecisely remembered lines that Lucretius had devoted to Venus, Rensselaer fell asleep as if in the presence of Athena, who "beneath the gliding stars of heaven, filled with her presence the sea that bears our ships, and governs the nature of all things that come forth into the shores of light."

But hours later he awoke in distress, his heart pounding, his body moist with sweat despite the coolness of his cabin. He switched on the lights, dressed, and went on deck. Though he had fallen asleep in near bliss, he had been assaulted as he slept by something he had known for a long time but only now had struck as if a fatal blow.

It was a simple thing, and not at all unusual but nonetheless astoundingly grave. His line, which had started at the very beginning of life, would come to an end with him. He was an only child, as were both his parents. He had not even distant cousins of whom he was aware. His first wife had borne him no children. Nor would Katy, and Katy it would be. So, with him, the progression of millions of years would stop dead. It was as if everyone before him had been tossing a ball back and forth, ten billion times, and he was the one who would drop it.

The papers, the paintings, the letters . . . his decorations, photographs, and sword . . . would be burnt, sold, or buried in landfill. All the material things in which his identity had found an echo would either rot or be scattered into the hands of strangers. Even were a perfect record of a life accessible to anyone but God—every second, every thought, emotion, and impulse, every struggle, idea, and act—it would not do justice in other than a divine eye to their infinitely complex interplay with the ineffable soul. As everything would eventually disappear, were that divine eye absent, everything would then be nothing.

The OOD asked of the others on the bridge who was at the bow. It was the captain, he was told by a sailor who had lifted a night-vision binocular to his eyes. Everyone was silent, until the OOD said, "Let him be," and they resumed their duties.

COMPAGNIE NAVALE FRAISSINET

Well before Rensselaer met Katy when he was in New Orleans fitting out *Athena*, the Marseilles director of the Compagnie Navale Fraissinet, as he often did, had lunch one day in the Old Port. Headquarters in Paris had been swallowed by a huge German conglomerate that, emphasizing Fraissinet's tanker and bulk carrier fleets, was undecided about its cruise business, which operated three 150-passenger specialty ships out of Marseilles. The director feared that despite the recent program of steering other than French holiday-makers his way, the Germans wanted to get rid of his ships so as to concentrate upon their core business. This, as well as the fact that he was now working for Germans, was the cause of ever-increasing resentment.

But because the spring sun was out, the colors were bright, the sea opalescent, and his bouillabaisse excellent, he was momentarily untroubled by his troubles. While tearing apart a baguette, he felt a very, very slight movement of air across the bridge of his nose. Looking up, he saw a butterfly passing before him so closely that he thought it would collide with his face. It made him smile. This caught the eye of a woman at the next table, who thought his smile was directed at her. Shy by nature, he could never have managed such a self-possessed and confident expression had he merely willed it himself.

She returned his unwitting flirtation with a look so hot and easy that he felt a kind of jolt. Like him, she was about forty-five, and her chest and firm cleavage was freckled and dark with sun, for him a sign of maturity's slow sexual burn, which he found irresistible. They began their affair almost immediately. It was exclusively sexual, and because both were married it could take place only in hotels. Because she was wealthy, he felt constrained to carry on in the top establishments and to give her gifts he couldn't afford. And because he had trouble understanding that Germans were actually people, he felt no guilt in appropriating from corporate accounts to support his trysts. Increasingly obsessed with her almost savage eroticism and the bronzed and freckled bosom that contrasted magnificently with his gift of a turquoise and silver necklace arrayed upon it, he embezzled to the point where the theft was almost as exciting as the illicit sex that made it necessary. The cruise subsidiary was doomed anyway.

But these were Germans, and they had German accountants. As German accountants inevitably and ineluctably would, the German accountants sensed that in Marseilles the figures were not always right. So, not surprisingly, the German accountants scheduled an audit. Relatively panicked (he was so far gone anyway), upon realizing that he might go to jail the director put his affair on hold and concentrated upon a scheme to refill the accounts before the German accountants arrived.

After visiting Australia, French Polynesia, and India, the ship *l'Étoile Océanique*, carrying 124 passengers and 52 crew, had made its most recent stop in the Maldives. Scheduled to come straight home through the Suez Canal, it was diverted to a safer route around the Cape of Good Hope so as to avoid the hostilities in the Middle East. The much longer route and many more days at sea necessitated tremendous fuel, labor, and provision expenses, which would make the voyage highly unprofitable.

So, for a bribe of €5,000, the provider of fuel in Cape Town would return sub rosa an advance payment of more than €100,000 and keep his fuel, receipts all in order. Nothing on the receipts was marked "Cape Town," but only the worldwide bunkerage company that fueled all Fraissinet ships. This was enough money to make the director's embezzlements whole, and then some, and with luck no one would know, not even German accountants.

It required, however, that *l'Étoile Océanique* come through Suez so as not to need the extra fuel that would have cost what the company would now unwittingly pay the director in Marseilles. So he ordered the captain to avoid the area of conflict in the Arabian Sea, dip slightly south into the Indian Ocean, and then sail north along the coast of East Africa to the Gulf of Aden, the Red Sea, the Gulf of Suez, and the Canal.

The captain protested with one word: "Piracy." To which the director replied, "All you need do in the limited area where piracy has been more or less completely suppressed is turn off your transponder, extinguish lights, and proceeded at maximum speed so as to limit your exposure. If you bring the ship around the Cape, this line, struggling for its life, will go out of business."

The captain replied, as a sort of compromise that was nonetheless meaningless, "Will spoof A.I.S. where appropriate." That is, he would manipulate his Automatic Identification System transponder to indicate a false position, which was equivalent to going dark, as no one, pirates or otherwise, would know the true location of his ship.

Thereupon, unbeknownst to its passengers, senior management, or the maritime and naval authorities, *l'Étoile Océanique* would loop south into the Indian Ocean and then turn toward the Horn of Africa.

*

l'Étoile Océanique's passengers were mostly middle-aged or retired: you had to have some money to take such a cruise, even if you got it by saving all your life. Nonetheless, it was in only the lower middle range of luxury. For example, the director had won promotion to director by coming up with the idea that the dining room should be as close as possible a reproduction of a Parisian bistro, with food to match. The savings on plush furniture and decoration, haute cuisine, and overly numerous waiters cut the catering budget in half, while the passengers enjoyed the satisfying mean between excessively luxurious and insufficiently good food. People were more relaxed about coming to dinner, they put on less weight and fewer airs, and they had less indigestion. Three seatings tended to sort themselves out into cliques, age groups, and character. All in all, because *l'Étoile Océanique* was small and offered two classes separated only by the difference between a cabin porthole and a larger, rectangular window, the passengers experienced none of the discomfort common to ocean liners with a dozen different levels of privilege.

Separated by as many characteristics as one can name, they were united in sharing the same elemental circumstances on board. The aristocrats among the passengers were several infants and half a dozen toddlers. Unlike most cruise ships, *l'Étoile Océanique* had no nursery or children's programs. Parents stayed with their offspring, and their children basked in the love of the many old people who felt in their presence an inner glow worth more than a thousand prescriptions.

Next in age, and touching in their awkward loveliness, were six French *lycéennes* chaperoned by one Madame Eugénie, of brittle, blonde hair, icy blue eyes that somehow seemed not to see anything, and so much pale makeup that a moon lander might have alighted softly and soundlessly on her face. On their spectacular school trip, when not in port the students passed the long days at sea obsessively occupied in their assigned summer reading: *Don Quixote, War and Peace, The Red and the Black, Crime and Punishment,* Dickens, and a dozen other titles, none of which was famous for brevity.

The girls found chairs in the lounges or chaises on deck, and were still for hours as they read themselves into the kind of trance impossible for arthritic older people who could not hold the same position for half an hour, much less a day. These girls, with whom it was hard to engage in conversation because they were always reading, had the charm and sincerity of youth, especially a girl named Sophie, with red hair, blue eyes, braces, and such tender affection for the characters in her thick tomes that she could often be seen in a chair, with the ocean streaming by, its light glistening in the tears that filled her eyes but seldom dropped.

Five or six young couples, unmarried but on de facto honeymoons, broadcast both unwittingly and unknowingly in every movement, glance, and smile that they spent their waking moments in their cabins, attending to sex. Most of the other passengers old enough to understand this treated it with a combination of irritation, amusement, and contempt. None with envy, for in the case of anyone who had at one time been thus transfixed, it seemed only as enviable as the exasperating stages of late adolescence.

In random portraits of some among the 124 souls, the eye might light upon several dozen retired couples from all walks of life, the slow bearers of gray hair, aging bodies, and fashions that had played out, returned, and played out yet again. They were a United Nations of Europe: mainly French but also Swedes, Poles, Slovaks, Italians, and Germans.

In addition to five widowers were four Swedish bachelors, former postal workers who never associated with anyone else unless, when drunk, they fished among the reefs of widows. And among the widowers was one tall, gray-haired, inscrutable, and lean older man who never spoke to anyone at all, carried a binocular hanging from a neck strap, seemed to be ex-military, and, unbeknownst to anyone else, was taking the cruise his departed wife had wanted to take and never could. He spoke to her silently, describing everything he did and everything he saw. In one sense, he was the most engaged and active of them all. His companion, whom he knew so well, was always with him, as close as if two souls could inhabit one body.

The widows, too, were fishing, with no luck. None of them wanted a drunken, retired, Swedish postal worker, all were vainly besotted with the tall, handsome binocular widower, and, as if to console themselves, at dinner they wore ridiculous gowns and were almost as made-up as Madame Eugénie. Their costuming was a nightly spectacle: a floor-length white taffeta gown trimmed with billows of white lace, topped with a white taffeta turban in the center of which was a green frog-brooch; a purple-sequined gown so low cut that one could see the hefty widow's extremely substantial bosom rolling with the movement of the ship; and so on. People were shocked, and yet the widows, shamed and saddened, could not but persist.

No one failed to marvel at a middle-aged, fat, bald, badly dressed Argentine and his young, very short and slight Brazilian Adonis-who-was-anything-but-an-Adonis, who walked in a very peculiar way that made him look like he was being continually bitten by horseflies. The two of them fought continuously and seemed perpetually embarrassed, the Argentine because he could have only a midget who walked as if stung by horseflies, and the midget because he was bought by someone so fat, bald, and badly dressed. It was strange when they passed, fighting in hostile undertones, but after a while no one gave them a second thought.

And then there were Martin and Petra, he a French Jew, she a gorgeous, statuesque German who had gone to Paris specifically to marry a Jew so as to assuage her guilt about the Holocaust, which she had neither committed, aided, nor abetted. Though an intellectual and a scientist (a chemist), Martin, at six-foot-four, was a physical match for his wife, being athletic and gentle, which she loved no end. They had been lucky, amazed, and delighted that the love they had for one another had nothing to do with either the Holocaust, her guilt, or their differences. That they had accidentally fallen into a kind of paradise radiated from them as it often does from such rare couples.

The captain was a Dane, the officers were French, and except for a few French waiters the crew was Filipino—very polite, obliging, hard workers who lived lonely lives at sea far from their families. Sometimes the people they served were kind and approachable, sometimes they were awkward, sometimes cruel. But they all disappeared, replaced by a new set as indistinguishable to the crew as the crew was indistinguishable to them. For most of the Filipinos on board it was exquisitely difficult when the ship neared the Philippines only to pass them by.

*

The passengers hadn't been informed either of the plan to sail around the Cape, its cancellation, or the dip into the Indian Ocean to bypass the Arabian Sea. The southward detour meant that they were off the major sea-lanes and saw no other ships. Sea life in the open ocean was of a much different character than that of the coastal waters in which they had spent most of the cruise, and the position of sun and stars made the ship's course seem unnatural and skewed. To varying degrees, each passenger, even if he did not know it, felt tugged left and south toward the part of the world's open oceans least trafficked: the southern Indian Ocean and the cruel Southern Ocean itself. Whereas the Arctic is a largely frozen sea circled by land, the Antarctic, land circled by ocean, is its polar opposite. And the Southern Ocean is so cold, stormy, and unwelcoming that the world has been forced mainly to ignore it.

Although as it veered south-southwest *l'Étoile Océanique* would not fall too far south, where it was winter, still, nothing but open sea lay between them and the Antarctic. Many of the passengers experienced, albeit dismissible, a sense of dread. Day after day, nothing was in sight, the sun rose and set where it shouldn't have, the electronic positioning chart outside the main dining room was "out of order," and the captain no longer attended dinner.

For the French girls, the discomfort was intensified perhaps because most of them were now reading *Crime and Punishment*. The widows and widowers grew even more depressed, and soon the retirees followed. The sexually obsessed younger people and the Filipinos were oblivious of everything, the former being too hot to be intelligent, the latter always busy, and resigned to being carried hither and thither across the world with neither say as to or care about where they were going.

In addition to dread, the captain and his officers felt the nauseating fear that comes when one persists in following a course one knows is not merely dangerous but also unnecessary, avoidable, and wrong.

But perhaps the most remarkable sensibilities belonged to Martin and Petra. On the second night of altered course, after they had returned from dinner and sat for a while in their cabin watching the empty ocean run by, he turned to her and said, "I don't know why . . . I have no idea why, but something is terribly wrong."

"Yes," she replied. "Exactly. I feel the same way. Something *is* wrong."

*

One of the kitchen workers, whose job for eight hours a day was to debone chicken, was a Filipino from Jolo, the center of Islamic piracy and terrorism in the Philippines. He was anything but friendly with his Christian compatriots, and his hatred of their unbelief had combined with both his resentment of his lowly position and his deep hurt that, unlike him, they were relatively happy. He kept largely to himself and spoke only when spoken to.

Middle-aged and pudgy, he had left behind a large family including a younger brother who drifted in and out of Abu Sayyaf, the Jolo terrorist body that, pressed on land by Philippine forces, had turned to kidnaping, of a most violent sort, at sea. *l'Étoile Océanique*'s chicken deboner, who had signed on using the decidedly non-Muslim name Jesus Magalap, knew that he was installed in a particularly rich target. But the ship neither went close enough to Philippine waters nor stopped in a port within reach of them in time to share intelligence with his brother. Nor did it follow a course that he could communicate with certainty.

When the war broke out, however, and the ship was on its way to the Maldives, the diversion around the Cape was planned and the catering staff apprised of the need to take on stores in Cape Town. Magalap, thus alerted, made a point to learn the course. Although he did not know of the cancellation of the first diversion and *l'Étoile Océanique*'s new and secret directive to come through Suez, he volunteered to take lunch up to the bridge, and there, in chirpy, friendly tones, he asked an officer to explain where they were going. Happy to oblige, the officer took him to the chart. Focusing upon one waypoint within reasonable reach of the Somali coast, Jesus Magalap memorized the coordinates and the time, and chanted these to himself as he rushed to his cabin to write them down.

In the Maldives, while the ship was tied up in Malé—a parti-colored city of low high-rises stuffed onto a lily-pad islet dangerously close to sea level—Magalap went to the post office and called home. Speaking very fast in his local dialect and using slang and abbreviations, he was able to convey to his brother the coordinates, the time of arrival, and an idea of who was on board *l'Étoile*. By the time he got to the six French girls it had been almost as if, singing of the twelve days of Christmas, he was talking about red hens, turtledoves, and a partridge in a pear tree. After his brother noted what he had said, Magalap hung up, walked through pastel-colored neighborhoods to the mosque, and prayed. Then he returned to the ship, where, pregnant with anticipation, he was now happy. His whole life and his career at sea had pointed at a violent dénouement. Only in that would he find relief from the torture of waiting for the worldwide supremacy of Islam. The violence was both to speed things up and to punish the unbelievers for having slowed the triumphant march of the faith.

He had no confidence that the phone call to his brother would bring results, but he had done what he could. In doing his duty, he had been good, and he enjoyed that he had appealed to allies far more powerful than the many on board who were more powerful than was he, so much so that most of them did not even know or care that he existed.

*

Martin and Petra kept to themselves not because they were besotted and intoxicated new lovers but because they were comfortable with being alone together. And like the young French girls, they were deeply absorbed in their reading.

"Being on a ship is strange," he said to her shortly after they had returned to their cabin for the night. "It's like the optical illusion that you see one way and then another. You have weeks at sea with nothing but water and sky for three hundred and sixty degrees all the way to the horizon, and at night you can see stars billions of light-years away. What could be more expansive than that?"

"And yet," she finished for him, "one is confined to a small vessel, all the smaller for the limitlessness outside, in a small cabin, with a small bathroom, and a short bathtub. At least for us."

"That's what I mean. Which is it? Neither and both. You go back and forth, as in the optical illusion."

"And the vibration," she added. She was speaking in German, he in French; sometimes they switched, and it was ever alluring. "It never stops— the forward motion, the sea slipping away, the hypnotic slap of the waves. It'll be nice when we get back to our garden. I miss Paris as never before."

"Too late to save anything if the weather's been dry. The grass will be so high there might be pheasants in it."

Not everyone may agree, but in a sleeping car in the Alps or on a ship at sea the rocking motion, repetitive sound, and great volumes of pristine air make for a deep, black, sound sleep that no anaesthesia can match. But such rest is nonetheless interruptible if the unconscious mind senses a primal threat.

At four in the morning, hours after the ship had turned onto a northward course three hundred miles off the Somali coast, Petra was awakened by a thud. At first she thought Martin had rolled out of bed, but he was fast asleep beside her.

Then she heard another thud, and a metallic slap against steel. She looked toward the window (they had paid for the larger cabin, with a rectangular window rather than a porthole), where she saw two lines moving left to right, right to left, vibrating with strain. They reminded her of musical instrument strings. Then she saw a person in dark clothes climbing up them using what she knew from her time in the mountains were called ascenders. Window cleaners who work on skyscrapers use them, but it was a strange time to be cleaning windows.

She woke Martin. "What is that?" she asked, looking at the window. When his eyes focused, he saw the ropes. Immediately alarmed, he held his reaction in abeyance. Probability suggested that it wasn't a boarding. So, staring at the window, he waited. Then another form appeared, once again a man in dark clothing, going up. Now both Martin and Petra froze, sensing that their intuitions had been correct. Something terrible was about to happen. When the man's rifle banged against the window, they knew it was so.

As they dressed, Petra asked if they should pull the fire alarm.

"No, that'll get everyone out of their cabins and on deck. They'll"—meaning the boarders—"probably pull the fire alarm themselves. We've got to alert the crew somehow, and hide."

"How?"

"We'll find a place—it's a big enough ship. I'll warn them, and come back to you, if I can."

Then they heard muffled gunshots. She was terrified, but she retained her self-possession.

"Now they know," Martin told her. "We have to hide. I hope the captain has had the good sense and opportunity to get rid of the passenger and crew manifests." As they sped through the corridors and down the stairs, he thought that there was always so much that should be done that isn't.

Many decks below, a wide central corridor went almost from bow to stern. Off this were the kitchens, storage, and crew quarters. On this level, near the main elevators and stairwell was a double row of dressing rooms for the always impeccably clad waiters, who had to turn out in what looked like highly starched, organ-grinder's-monkey uniforms, some even, according to rank, with a pillbox hat. Three of these rooms lay on each side of the hall stub leading to starboard. At the end of each row was an electrical closet. The doors were numbered with edged plastic strips that slid into aluminum holders. The same signage identified the electrical closet, only on this, written in red, with the symbol of a lightning bolt, were the words *High Voltage*, followed by an exclamation point. Martin switched the signs around.

Leaving Petra inside a dressing room that was now identified as an electrical closet, he went to the kitchen nearby. Deep below decks, he was unable to hear the submachine-gun fire above.

As he was looking through the kitchen, the fire alarm sounded. He sped up so much that he hardly knew what he was grabbing: three boxes of water crackers, a Gouda the size of a small loaf of bread, a foot-long knife, and some apples in a net sack. Forgetting that there was a water tap in the dressing room, he opened a huge refrigerator door and was confronted with fifty magnums of Champagne. He took one, and raced back.

Once inside, he and Petra threw the steel bolt on the door and, in the flattering, warm light cast by a fixture over the mirror, came to grips with their refuge. Behind the bolted steel door were a sink, a toilet, a typically short nautical bathtub, a chair, and a small counter. With no assurance they would remain undiscovered, at least they had done the best they could.

*

Ten men in each of three skiffs had approached the gaily lit ship, its lights glittering in gold as it crossed their path, and tied up to it by means of goatskin-covered grappling hooks noiselessly heaved onto the rails. Later, the boats would be made fast to deck cleats and towed astern on both sides of the wake.

It took a while for all thirty to come aboard, but long before they deployed their full complement they stormed the bridge. Bursts of fire were directed at the radio room, followed by the wholesale smashing of equipment with the steel butts of automatic rifles and submachine guns.

In his cabin when he heard the gunfire, the first mate correctly placed it in or near the radio room. Under the impression that NATO's Operation Ocean Shield and/or the EU's Operation Atalanta still deployed assets locally in Combined Task Force 151—though in fact only *Athena* was present—he pointed his satellite phone out an open porthole and, with the press of a single, pre-programmed button, called NATO Maritime Command HQ in Northwood, UK.

An efficient operator with a lovely voice received his call and report of approximate position. "Just one moment, please." When she came back on the line, she said, "Your reported position, in the Seychelles SRR, is in conflict with A.I.S. data. Please clarify."

"We spoofed it." Then he gave her the real position as best he could.

"What is your verification signal?"

"I don't know. It's on the bridge, I'm in my cabin."

"How many attackers?"

"I don't know. I'm in my cabin. I heard submachine-gun fire."

"We have no other distress signal."

"I believe they've destroyed our communications. I have a sat-phone."

"All right. Sit tight. Don't do anything that will bring harm to your passengers. Cooperate as much as possible. We will immediately notify the appropriate operators. Anything else?"

"No."

"We're on it. Communicate if you can. Good luck."

When the first mate put down the phone, even without knowing that the only naval ship off East Africa was only a small, battered, coastal patrol ship, he felt the hollowness and fear of being completely alone among an unpredictable enemy.

*

At 0421 during the morning watch, following procedure, Velez took a message to Pisecki, the OOD. Pisecki asked him to deliver it to the captain. Awakened by the kind of knock that meant something was amiss, Rensselaer swung his feet from his rack and, without turning on the light, went to the door. Velez's expression told him that he would not be able to go back to bed. At first he bumped, and then settled into, his chair, hitting the desk light switch as he did. In what to his eyes was bright glare, he read once, and again. Seizing the mic of the 1MC, he ordered the OOD to summon the XO and Holworthy to the bridge, and then dressed.

Once on the bridge, he didn't have to wait long while Movius and Holworthy read the message just as carefully as he had.

"Commander," Rensselaer said addressing Holworthy, "now you've got something in your bailiwick."

Holworthy seemed already to be planning, and Movius said, "We've got two conflicting positions, one a hundred and fifty-six nautical miles southeast of the Seychelles, as reported by A.I.S., and the other—"

"Wait a minute," Rensselaer interrupted, and ordered Pisecki, the OOD, to summon the quartermaster.

"The other," Movius resumed, "according to the mate's sat-phone estimate, is approximately three hundred nautical miles east of the Somali coast and, given the heading, presumed to be moving toward the Somalia SRR. What are we to believe?"

"The mate said they spoofed the A.I.S.," Rensselaer stated. "It's reasonable that they would. And it's probably gone dark now that the ship is seized. Anyway, he's called for help at that position, and there is no call from near the Seychelles. We'll go with the mate."

The quartermaster arrived. "Sir?" he inquired.

"Buck, we have a piracy. A small, specialized cruise ship, French registry, last reported position zero four, forty-one, four point two north, fifty-three, zero nine, twenty-six point zero nine east; heading, fifty-two degrees. It looks as if originally the ship was trying, just as we did, to slip between the Horn and Socotra. But if it's pirates they'll direct to the coast. What does a ship like that make, eighteen knots?"

"That sounds right."

"We're close enough. Plot an intercept course slightly to the north of the last reported position."

Velez arrived just as Buck Lanham went to his charts. "Another message, sir. Fleet."

Rensselaer read it. "Okay," he said, and read to all who were within earshot.

"'Reconnaissance only. Take no action. French ships will depart Toulon at ten hundred Zulu Time to relieve you. Repeat. Take no action.'"

"Of course," Rensselaer added, "reconnaissance is an action, so the order is contradictory and ambiguous. We should be at the intercept before the end of the forenoon watch." Looking at Holworthy, Movius, and Pisecki, he said, "Let the watches change normally, and then make ready for general quarters. This is different from the *Sahand*. With the *Sahand* it was a fight. Here, it'll be all negotiation and maneuver. So look lively, but expect to hold your fire."

*

After the fire alarm had been sounded on board *l'Étoile Océanique*, every passenger other than Martin and Petra had responsibly reported to life-boat stations, with children in bathrobes and adults in various states of dress. There, they were shocked to discover two dozen armed men, none of whom spoke any European tongue, and who—with angry shouts in impenetrable language that in its deep, rapid-fire, guttural sounds seemed both primitive and threatening in itself—herded all of them at gunpoint into the main salon. Though perhaps had it been sung gently or spoken by a woman, their speech might have been beautiful, when they spoke it was as if it had been howled by jackals.

On the bridge, four black-clad leaders forced the officers into a corner. Their chief, who had lost an eye and whose remaining one was fierce and inflamed, spoke in good English and ordered the captain to provide both the passenger and the crew manifests.

"We threw them overboard as you approached," the captain said.

"You did not. Bring them now, or I will immediately kill ten passengers."

The captain judged the man by the way he spoke, his one eye, and the way he carried himself. Unlike the fishermen-pirates of whom the captain had heard many stories from other mariners, the leader was completely confident, cold, in control of himself, and calm. He spoke quietly and those who heard him were sure he would carry out the threat. So the captain nodded, and, escorted, went to fetch the manifests.

Once these were supplied, the chief gave them to one of his men. He then ordered another to divert the ship, steering a course that he supplied, at fifteen knots. Then he marched the captain and his officers to the main salon, where the passengers and the rest of the crew were surrounded by more than two dozen men wielding Kalashnikovs, Uzis, and M4s. Many of the boarders carried grenades, and for good measure two were clad in suicide vests. Other than the leader and his lieuten-ants, all were Somalis.

Magalap, the kitchen worker who had provided the intelligence to his brother, was afraid to appeal to the hijackers in front of the crew, should the hijacking go wrong, so he stayed quiet, waiting to declare his loyalties less conspicuously. He moved to the front of the crowd, hoping to be able to separate himself off when the opportunity presented itself.

To quiet the murmur among the passengers, who despite their fright still lived within the illusion that they could speak and speculate, the chief fired a burst into the overhead. Plaster and fiberglass, some of it fine dust almost like snow, rained down in silence.

The chief was terrifying. No one aboard had ever directly encountered such a person. His remaining eye, doing double duty, seemed to be constantly and voraciously in motion. As evil people often do, he smiled broadly after everything he said, as if what he said, upon which the lives of the passengers, their wives, husbands, and children precariously depended, was miraculous and wonderful. It was as if he expected them to be grateful for his every word, while at the same time he made clear that they were nothing, and meant nothing, and that he was their supreme lord—which, for the moment, he was.

With each utterance followed by his crazed smile, he said, "Welcome. I am *Amir-al-Bahri*," which meant Emir of the Sea, or Admiral, and was the Arabic origin of the word in English and other languages, "Kaysar Hadawi, deputy to Sheikh Abdul Qadir al Mu'min, *rais* of the *Wilayat-a-Somal* of the Islamic State. As such, I have jurisdiction over you, and have taken command of this ship." He smiled so broadly and for so long that it was as if he had just informed them that their every wish had been granted.

"The ship will sail under a new flag." He motioned, and the black flag of ISIS was spread out by two of his men. In large white letters on black was written in Arabic (here simplified without the case endings), *La Allah Illah Allah*, or, there is no Allah (God) other than Allah. In black letters within a white circle, it read, from top to bottom, *Allahi rasul Muhammadu*, which was sensible only if read from bottom to top, *Muhammadu rasul Allahi*, Muhammad is the prophet of Allah. Perhaps it was preferable to order the words in reverse so that Allah would not be relegated to the bottom.

Among the passengers was a retired Swiss hydrologist who knew Arabic. He ached to ask why the sentence was inverted, but he dared not, because he knew that sometimes questioning—much less disputing—even a diacritical point in Arabic could call down a sentence of death.

The leader went on, and the more he spoke, the more he terrified. "I was educated at Saint Antony's College, Oxford. So you will listen to me. You see?" And then the smile. "We expect complete obedience. Any infraction will be punished with death. In the corrupt West, death is feared and hated. Among believers, it is a friend. It is loved." His eyes glinted like the colorless sparks off flint. "As death is nothing to us, it is less than nothing—which would make it positive, yes? A minus times a minus? Especially if it comes to unbelievers. I will show you."

He pointed to a gray-haired, older woman who had the misfortune of standing in the front row, and beckoned her toward him. Her husband, who was even older, perhaps in his late seventies, held her back and stepped forward in her place. "No, not you. Her."

She hesitated, but then did as ordered. "You must obey," said Kaysar Hadawi. He withdrew a pistol, and, very quickly, as if swatting away a fly, shot her in the forehead. As she fell back among the gasps of the crowd, her husband lunged at her executioner, but was slammed to the floor by one of the guards. "Did I say you?" Hadawi asked quietly, holding his smile. "No. You must obey. Now, sit. If you move again, I will kill ten people. Everybody sit."

They all sat, most of them immediately, some rather slowly, but then, after catching a displeased look from the guards, with awkward dispatch. Some took seats; others sat directly on the floor. "We will match your passports to the manifest. If anyone is hiding, he will die. Please be kind." His last sentence was inexplicable. The body of the woman he had executed was left bleeding on the floor in front of her despairing husband. Although he was still living, he was dead.

*

Neither Martin nor Petra had heard the shot, but they understood that were they to be found they might be killed. "It depends on who it is," Martin said. "If they're fishermen turned pirates, they may not hurt us. But if it's ISIS or As-Shabab, they may."

"ISIS or As-Shabab would rape me, wouldn't they?" she asked. "Probably."

"They'd do it in front of you, then kill me, then kill you."

"They do that, yes. They would probably keep you for use." She was horrified. And she was shocked but perhaps encouraged by how calm he seemed. "Listen closely," he said. "We can't afford emotion or fear. What we have to do is make it so that they can't harm us. At first we have to hide. But if that fails, we fight. Don't be afraid. If you master your fear, you won't suffer. Even physical pain will remain outside you. We have to survive. That means you have to banish all fear, even of death. Not only is it possible, we have no other choice."

She nodded.

"There's a problem," he said, almost disinterestedly. "The changing rooms lock from the inside, and have no keyholes. The electrical closets lock from the outside, and they have keyholes. If they look, will they note that—because of the way we changed the signs—they'll be able to open all the changing rooms except one, which will require a key? That was a mistake. I'll change it back."

He opened the door a crack, listened, and dashed out, quickly switching signs. Then he returned, his heart beating fast.

"Will they even check?" she asked. "Will they even be able to read the signs in French? Will they come? Would they force the doors?"

"We can't know what'll happen, but if they don't search, or they don't wonder, or they can't read French, or they haven't got the manifests, we may be able to stay here for a long time. And if not, as they say in Arabic, *wa i'la, fa'la,* if not, then not."

"How do you know *that*?"

"I went to Algeria once, for a week."

*

Things were quite different on *Athena*, a warship bristling with guns and missiles. Every man was armed with a personal weapon, each SEAL with an arsenal. They had trained hard. They had been blooded in three battles and had prevailed against far greater force. And they had been away long enough that, as they were steadily hardened by war and the sea, home and family had receded. At least for now, their souls had turned into the strange souls of soldiers—who assume that they will fight without fear for the rest of their lives, and that they will be apart from other men, in a world of its own with laws and time of its own. Veterans of combat, they would always think of it as the elemental reality to which they could at any moment be instantly thrown back, and that everything else was a dream.

Without knowing what awaited them as they sped to intercept *l'Étoile Océanique*, they approached it at a fast clip over the waves. At the calculated intercept they saw nothing, and began a search grid. A sailor was posted as high on the masts as he could go, and from the bridge they scanned with the surviving surface-search radar, which ordinarily was used mainly for identifying land features when coming into port or navigating among islets.

On board *l'Étoile*, Hadawi had demanded to see the A.I.S. early on, with the idea of turning it off (and then, for good measure, shooting it). Not trusting the explanation of the navigation officer, he actually read in the manual and was quick enough to see that it was reporting a course near the Seychelles, many hundreds of miles to the south. "I have read your manual," he told the navigation officer, a slight, bespectacled young Frenchman. "Why is it reporting our position inaccurately?"

"We spoofed it," was the answer.

"To avoid us?"

"Yes, you could say that. To avoid people like you."

"But we have no way, in our little boats, to read it."

"We didn't know that, so perhaps it was pointless."

"It was, but not now. I was going to destroy it. Why do so if it falsely reports our position? Leave it on. If anyone tries to alter it, I'll kill him. We are not primitives. We speak your languages. We can read your manuals, and we can use your machines, with which you would mislead us, to mislead you. Your navies, if any are left that have not gone to the Gulf, will try to find you near the Seychelles."

Kaysar Hadawi, however, did not take and could not have taken into account the young redhead at Northwood. On her lunch break she sat alone in the cafeteria, thinking about the calls she had handled that morning and dutifully passed up the line. It was now in the hands of officers trained to deal with such things. But as she was having tea and biscuits, something struck her. She inhaled quickly, stood, and, without finishing, rushed to the control center.

Approaching the officer in charge, who had recently relieved the one to whom she had reported, she presented her idea.

"I'm sure that's been done," he said, superciliously.

"But you said you're sure it has been done, not that it has been done."

"Are you suggesting that Commander Whately doesn't know his job?"

"No, sir, but what if it didn't occur to him?"

"Well, it occurred to *you*." This was demeaning, very much on purpose.

"Nevertheless, may I check?"

"Check if you wish, but I suggest for your sake that you contact directly the American ship *Athena*, to which the incident report pertains. If you go through channels there may be unpleasant blowback. Here." He handed her a folder with *Athena*'s direct link written in longhand at the top of the cover.

Very shortly thereafter, if not half than a third of the world away, Velez summoned Rensselaer.

"Mr. Velez?"

"A radio call in the clear, Captain. There's a woman on the phone." At first, Rensselaer felt a jolt, thinking it might be Katy.

"Who?"

"Someone from Northwood."

"Patch it over."

"I have to be careful. I don't want to lose it."

After a while, it worked. "This is Captain Rensselaer of the *Athena*."

"Captain," the lovely voice said. After weeks at sea, it was a delight to hear. "This is Northwood. Given the immediacy of the situation, I was asked to contact you directly. Are you aware that *l'Étoile Océanique*'s A.I.S. didn't go dark, and is still functioning, as it was before the seizure, but that it was spoofed?"

"I knew it was spoofed, but I assumed that it had gone dark after the seizure."

"No one has told you?"

"No. I've just been informed of where Fleet believes *l'Étoile* might be."

"Well, then. It continues to send. Given that we may know a former real position because one of its crew reported by sat-phone, you should be able from the A.I.S.-reported movements to calculate its exact whereabouts by using the reported position as the baseline. I can read you the A.I.S.-reported positions including those in real time so you can superimpose its relative movements and pinpoint it, if you wish. This was not relayed to you?"

"No. And you're doing this in the clear?"

"I haven't the time to go through channels. Let's hope for the best. We're on a sat-link with a narrow reception footprint, and although it isn't encrypted it requires a validated handshake for every burst."

"I know. Okay. Go ahead. Please read the positions to Lieutenant Velez, and stay in touch with him. Thank you. Your voice is beautiful."

"I'm blushing," she said.

"You should get a medal. Here you go." He switched back to Velez.

Turning to his officers and Chief Pisecki, Rensselaer explained the situation, and said, "As soon as Velez gives us the relative coordinates, we can plot a course straight to target—thanks to an English girl who sounds like she's eighteen."

Movius said, "Athena," and soon the hunter's course was set.

*

L'Étoile's radar was higher off the water than *Athena*'s, and Hadawi was using it. When it hooked on to *Athena* he sent a man aloft with a night-vision binocular, and not long after, he knew he was being followed by a warship.

On *Athena*, the man tied in awkwardly aloft hadn't yet seen *l'Étoile*, but as he wiggled in discomfort, trying to relieve the pressure of his harness, he inadvertently awakened his walkie-talkie. Not long after, everyone on the bridge heard, "The pines against the blue, and the wind whistling through them." Then there was silence.

Rensselaer replied, "Seaman Kelly, are you talking to yourself, or was that a message of strategic import?"

"Sorry, sir. I was thinking of . . . land."

"So do we all."

On *l'Étoile*, Hadawi stood at the binnacle and stared for a while into the black glass dome of the compass. Then he said, "Stop engines and turn on the lights."

Seaman Kelly had been slowly scanning to port. When his night-vision, at 12 power, slewed to zero degrees relative, he exclaimed over his channel, "Jesus! Dead ahead! All lit up like a Christmas tree!"

From the bridge, one could see only a pinhole of gold light upon the horizon. Everyone lifted his binocular and watched as one golden flash after another appeared to rise from the black of the sea until the ship was entirely visible, dead in the water, rocking slightly and throwing off light.

"Sound general quarters," Rensselaer commanded. "They must want to talk. Hailing frequencies." He clicked on his mic. "This is the United States Navy. The USS *Athena* is on your stern. Identify yourself."

Hadawi heard. One of his lieutenants began to bring him a mic, but he refused it.

"I say again: this is the United States Navy. Identify yourself." After a while, Rensselaer ordered, "Maintain speed, come to hailing distance off their port side."

The helmsman repeated the order and asked for an exact distance.

"Three hundred yards," Rensselaer answered.

"Three hundred yards off her port side, aye sir."

When *Athena* slowly pulled level with *l'Étoile*, seeing no weaponry other than Kalashnikovs and RPGs in the hands of the bandit-like guards posted on deck, Rensselaer ordered engines full astern. The propellers churned the sea into white foam two or three feet above the surface. Then the engines were stopped, and *Athena* came to rest.

Through the hailer, Rensselaer demanded identification yet again. To see more clearly, he had stepped onto the starboard bridge wing. Hadawi remained out of sight as he answered. "I am *Amir-al-Bahri* of the Islamic State, Kaysar Hadawi."

"I can see your flag," Rensselaer said, calmly. "What are your demands?"

"We have no demands."

"Very well. Then we are prepared to take aboard the passengers and crew."

"Then, Captain," Hadawi answered, "whom shall I kill every hour until all are dead but the women to be sold?"

As this echoed across the water and sank into the hearts of the passengers and crew crammed into the main salon, Rensselaer had to pause. "Tell us your demands," he repeated, as if he hadn't heard what had just been said, because he could think of nothing else to say.

"I say again," Hadawi returned, deliberately mocking the naval parlance, "we have no demands. We need not ask anything. It will take about a week to execute them all, and in that week we will command the attention of the world. Every unbeliever will imagine himself in the place of his brothers and sisters, every hour, as they kneel for the executioner's sword. And if a ship greater than your little boat arrives, and its intent is to storm us, I will kill them all at once."

"What do you want?" Rensselaer asked, impatiently.

"Just what I have said. You may be instructed to buy time. You may have it. I give the world a week in which to watch the executions."

*

Immediately, for Hadawi had given the order by hand signal as he was speaking, passengers and crew were herded onto the promenade deck. Trying to take note of individual characteristics, weaponry, and dress so as not to register anyone twice, Holworthy counted the armed men. Pressing a binocular to his eyes, he dictated the details to O'Connor. The hijackers were everywhere. He logged twenty, and had to assume there were more.

As the hostages assembled, the body of the executed woman was carried out by two of the terrorists, one grasping her wrists, the other her ankles, and swung back and forth to get momentum before she was cast over the railing. Her head bumped the teak top rail, and this made her body turn. After she hit the water, arms trailing and splaying, she disappeared.

"What can we give you to stop the executions?" Rensselaer asked over the hailer, observing, as did Holworthy, that two terrorists among the hostages wore suicide vests.

Hadawi responded with alacrity. "We have yet to show you. For all you know, she may have died in her sleep."

"I believe you, Mr. Hadawi: you don't have to show us."

"*Admiral* Hadawi."

"Admiral, then. You are in control. We understand."

"Let me deepen your understanding."

"Admiral, I will of course report everything, but in wartime, given operational secrecy, I doubt that my superiors will convey it to the press. No one will know. You need not execute anyone."

"Your problem, Captain. We'll leave one or two alive to tell the story. If your citizens are kept in the dark now, so much the better for us. For when they find out, they will force your government to send soldiers to fight us, which is what we want."

"Then give us the ones to be spared," Rensselaer said.

"Here is what I will give you," was Hadawi's answer.

Many of the men on *Athena*—among them Rensselaer himself, Holworthy, and most of his SEALs—were no strangers to the butcheries of combat, having witnessed the incineration, tearing up, and shredding of friend and foe. They had seen as well the corpses of massacred civilians that had been bulldozed into pits and left unburied. But none had experienced what they were now forced to witness.

Among the hostages, two rows back and previously inconspicuous, was a young French family. In her early twenties, the mother, who was diminutive and very pretty, wore a jacket slightly darker than her auburn hair. The color, Rensselaer noted to himself, despite increasing helplessness that he determined not to show, was Roxburghe, a word for which until that time he had had no use, but now would stay with him for the rest of his life.

She held her baby in her arms. Ten months or so, perhaps a year, the baby was dressed in blue and white. No one on *Athena* could make out the baby's face, and later they would thank God for that.

The guards parted the crowd around the mother and child, which made her husband leap in front of them. Not a big man, he was the match for his wife, and in general when people saw them many thought the child would grow to be diminutive, too, and this they took as a sign of fineness and delicacy to be admired and protected.

Though the father was courageous, the guards easily threw him aside and brought his wife and baby into a cleared space near the rails. The words "No, no," and "Oh God, no," were repeated many times on *l'Étoile* and on *Athena*, some silently, some very quietly, and some aloud. One of the terrorists commanded the mother to kneel. She did, bending her head protectively over the baby.

Now Magalap decided to come forward and announce himself, and leapt away from the stewards toward Hadawi, as if the stewards would have held him back. Seeing this, one of Hadawi's men fired a burst from his rifle into Magalap's chest. It was all so matter-of-fact that they turned right back to the mother and her baby as if nothing had happened.

As if from nowhere, a sword appeared. It was long and slightly crescent, with a green handle from which hung brown cords. The father broke from the guard restraining him and charged the man with the sword. A burst of fire was made to hit him in the legs and lower back, deliberately so as not to kill him. In physical agony, he struggled to move to his wife and child, but could only flail. *Athena*'s officers could see through *l'Étoile*'s white rails that a black-clad man knelt by the mother and held his arms out to receive the baby. Slowly, she complied. Even from a distance on *Athena*, where everyone had almost stopped breathing, it was possible to feel the mother's despair.

When the man who had taken the baby stood, and as the mother watched, he drew a knife. What he did then made the sailors of *Athena* try to turn away even though they couldn't. And some of them, though they were far from home, in the company of men, and battle-hardened, simply wept.

As the dead child was tossed overboard, the mother and father became still. And as the sword was raised he tried to lunge, but to no avail.

When it came down in force and cleaved his wife's head from her body, he stopped forever, having come to his end, in utter defeat, wanting only to die. They unceremoniously tossed her body overboard, in two parts, and turned to him. Over five breathless minutes for the hostages and *Athena*'s crew, they watched him in his agony. Then, while he was still alive, they picked him up by his wrists and ankles, swung him back and forth, and threw him over the railing. And they did the same to Magalap, who had been trying to tell them that he was one of them but could not speak. His desperation showed in his eyes.

The hostages were herded back inside as the terrorists took up watch positions on *l'Étoile* while it and *Athena* slowly rocked.

*

"Chief," Rensselaer ordered a shaken Pisecki, "you're the OOD. Take her a thousand yards to *l'Étoile*'s stern, prow steady on. If *l'Étoile* moves, maintain that distance and let me know course and speed."

"Aye, sir."

"Mr. Velez?"

"Sir?"

"Wardroom. Pad and pen. XO and Mr. Holworthy: wardroom."

When the officers had taken their seats at the wardroom table, Rensselaer turned to Velez. "We don't have much time. Send this message to Fifth Fleet, to Northwood, and—jump the chain—the White House."

"I don't know how to do that."

"I'll tell you how to go encrypted straight to the military advisor to the vice president."

"They'll kill you for that," Holworthy said.

"They keep trying. I don't want to get gummed up in the command structure as everything slowly percolates up to the top—where it's going to go anyway—a day and twenty-four dead later."

He dictated his message, had it read back, made a few corrections, and sent Velez off, saying, "Mr. Velez, be right there for the response, bring it to me immediately, and don't read it."

"Don't read it, sir?"

"Avert your eyes, fold the paper, I don't care, do whatever you have to do. Don't read it."

"Aye, sir."

Rensselaer spoke calmly and with concentration. "We've got forty-five minutes left to the next execution, which I doubt we'll be able to prevent, although I'll offer again to negotiate." He turned to Holworthy. "I've been over it, and I see no way in. Tell me something I don't know."

"I can't. They've got at least twenty men, probably quite a few more out of sight. They're at the railings, sometimes in pairs, all around the ship. Approach with the RHIB and they'll hear us all the way out to here. If underway, they'd hear or see us long before we could make fast. If they continue to drift and we swim, given the sentries, there's no way to board surreptitiously. Even if we could parachute to the sundeck, by the time we got to the hostages the suicide vests would blow. The only way to prevent that would be to appear from the inside and shoot the suicide bombers, but we can't walk through steel. We don't even know the layout, not having a plan of the ship. Maybe we could get one, but it wouldn't make much difference. I'm sorry, Captain."

"XO?" Rensselaer queried.

"Offer again to negotiate. That can't hurt. Do it immediately. When turned down, which almost certainly will be the case, steam just out of sight. Deploy the RHIB to go a little closer so they can't get away from us, but with the RHIB unseen close to the water and us apparently gone, they may calm down. They want attention. Maybe they won't kill unless they have an audience. Hadawi seemed to enjoy sparring with you. It could be worth a try."

"He did take a lot of pleasure in that," Rensselaer said. "That may be a way to get to him. We'll make another offer, deprive him of an audience, and await instructions."

They returned to the bridge, made their offer—which was not even acknowledged—then moved east and eventually out of sight, leaving the RHIB to watch *l'Étoile* from a distance, unseen.

*

Two hours later, Velez ran through the passageways with a folded printout. "I didn't read it."

Rensselaer did, but only to himself. It read, "Track commandeered ship until arrival of French forces. Manifests show no Americans on board. Assist French command only if requested. Take no action independent of task force arriving four plus days. Restore communications through regular channels only." He crumpled the paper and shoved it into his pocket. "Mr. Velez, send this message."

"Through regular channels?"

"No. As before."

"Ready."

"I say again." This was uncommonly rude, and Rensselaer knew it. "Hostages to be executed every hour. French task force will arrive too late. Request permission to engage should opportunity arise."

The message was answered almost instantly. Velez came running with it, folded as before. It read, "Request denied," and it was signed by the CNO.

"Velez. Send this: 'Is USS *Athena*, American ship of war, commanded to ignore its obligation to aid mariners in distress? By what authority if so? Clarify.'"

"Sir, they're gonna kill you."

"So I am told. Mr. Velez, you are ignorant of their message, do you understand? And therefore you cannot offer an opinion in regard to my reply."

"Okay."

"Send my reply."

It didn't take even ten minutes for the answer to arrive. As Rensselaer unfolded the paper, he said, before reading, informed by the rapidity of the response, "They must be in the Situation Room, as they should be. The SECNAV and the president will be kicking themselves."

"Why?" Movius asked.

"Because they put me here. I'd love to see their faces." He read the reply to himself: *Await further clarification.* "They must be talking to their lawyers, the Secretary of State, their political people. They don't know what to do. Neither do we. But they're . . . they're just the worst, so far away from what America once was. We've got a simple issue here. These bastards are executing innocent people. If we can strike, we should. The French will arrive too late."

"What's going on?" Holworthy asked. What do they say?"

"Essentially nothing," was the answer. "They must be deliberating. So, at the moment it's apparently up to us. And we're paralyzed."

*

At 0300, Rensselaer was summoned to the bridge. Hadawi was on the hailing frequency. "If you are within range, at zero seven hundred, pick up ten I will spare. Then you must depart and not track us."

"Will comply," was Rensselaer's immediate answer.

"Starboard side," Hadawi said.

"Your British English is impressive," Rensselaer said. "Perhaps we should speak more."

"You want to establish rapport. Very transparent. But I will tell you that I learned English in the excellent universities of the West, where I saw that your people are cowards and weak of mind. When we tell them that we will exterminate them, they apologize to us."

"You haven't yet plumbed the depths of the West," Rensselaer asserted.

"We shall see."

"Yes, we shall. At zero seven hundred, I'll send the RHIB."

"No. We will take them to you in our boats." Hadawi clicked off.

"I don't like this, but we have to do it," Rensselaer said. "At zero six hundred, sound general quarters and bring us two thousand yards starboard of *l'Étoile*. For now, steer for her at three knots, hold position when she's fully in sight, and call in the RHIB."

Over unbreaking, almost oily-smooth swells, *Athena* moved toward the glow on the horizon that soon turned into a jewel-work of golden lights, quite different from the harsh glare of stern-facing floodlamps as the RHIB sped over *Athena*'s wake and into its berth.

"Spacious Endurance" (Really?)

No one in his right mind wanted to be in Washington on that merciless, glaring weekend when it seemed as if a giant DeVilbiss humidifier was spraying hot, wet air over the city. Exhausted tourists took suffocating steps as they waddled along avenues the lengths of which they had tragically misjudged. Establishments with air-conditioning were passionately sought ice islands adjacent to sidewalks like barbecue grills.

The White House, however, was nicely cooled. With the president in residence, anyone of ambition was at work, especially now in wartime and crisis. The president, who privately likened Camp David to a "1920s resort for Polish meatpacking workers," preferred to stay at 1600. That meant frequent trips to the Situation Room. That, in turn, meant passing through what he called Piccadilly Circus, the West-Wing business end of the White House, at the entrance and exit for the people who did the work—from photographers' assistants to the secretary of state. When the president had to go through it, he passed large numbers of staff who wanted to see him and to be seen by him or by the important people, their bosses, who were always careful to walk some steps behind him unless he wanted to engage them in conversation. Even then, they made sure not to get ahead of him other than to hold open a door.

The Secret Service officer who sat at a little counter at the entrance seemed very much like a British Empire policeman standing on a raised traffic island in the middle of a frantic third-world intersection. He greeted and checked—if only glancing at badges or familiar faces—everyone who came in. Elevators and stairs dead-ended here, and the way to the Navy Mess and, beyond it, the plebeian mess, led off parallel to the Situation Room entrance. The Situation Room itself was flanked by a warren of staff, support, and video conference rooms.

Now, even in the dead of a summer weekend, black SUVs were lined up outside like loaves of overdone pumpernickel, and the Secretaries of State, Defense, Homeland Security, the Army, the Air Force, and the Navy, plus the Joint Chiefs, the National Security Advisor, the DNI, and the DCI were waiting at the long table, with select deputies who attended them backed up against the walls like footmen and footwomen. It was lunchtime, and the "circus," as the president called it, was packed with people on their way to the plebeian mess. But a path opened for him, and he was swallowed into the very rooms he hated most, because it was there that no matter what he said or did or didn't do, someone was going to die (or maybe many, many someones), and, no matter what he said or did or didn't do, one way or another he was going to take a hit.

The vice president was already there, his military aide (a Navy captain who unbeknownst to anyone was Rensselaer's classmate at Annapolis) standing in back of him. It was understood—it *had* to be understood—that in a room so full of people of such high rank and occasional or feigned expertise, only that which concisely forwarded the stream of business could be spoken. If everyone pirouetted, the meeting would last five days, so pirouetting was strictly forbidden. Showing off meant keeping other people not only from critical business but, later, from baseball, baths, and beer, so it was the kiss of death. Except, of course, for the president, who, if he wished, could speak for hours and numb the most powerful collection of behinds in the Western Hemisphere. Sometimes he did this, sometimes not. Especially on hot summer weekends his short attention span was further shortened because he knew that, hidden in the hedges, the White House pool was powerfully close and sparkling in the sun.

As an accurate sign of his irritation, the first thing the president said upon entry was, "Who left the vice-presidential seal up on the wall? I'm the president. *He*," the president stated, pointing at the vice president, "is the vice president. When I'm in the room, my seal goes up. Not his. His down, mine up. Got it?" An aide rose to make the switch.

And then the president, clearly in a foul temper, asked, "Why the crappy furniture? These chairs must be from the Eisenhower Administration. Okay, they're new, but I mean nineteen-fifties style. And the five-legged base is the kind of thing that would support an elephant. Why does the table bow out in the middle? That just takes up space. The ends, where I sit, are narrower. Why is my end narrower? Is it assumed that I have less stuff than someone who works for me? No corporate office would be a tenth as clunky, and this is the goddamned White House."

No one was expecting this, and the room was plunged into oxygenless silence. Then the National Security Advisor spoke up. "That can be fixed, Mr. President."

"Is that an answer to my question?" the president returned, angrily.

"No, sir."

"Does anyone have an answer?"

Only the vice president had the standing to speak. "Economy."

"Right," said the president. "Economy. Just like Jimmy Carter's sweater. Dignity, not luxury. You!" He barked at a bespectacled twenty-something kid sitting away from the table.

"Sir!"

"Answer the following question."

"Yes sir."

"Am I the king of Saudi Fucking Arabia, or am I not the king of Saudi Fucking Arabia?"

The kid was too frightened to speak. Two generals flanking him said quietly under their breath, "Not. Say not."

"No, sir," the kid said, still terrified. "You are not the king of Saudi Fucking Arabia."

"Right. That's the point. That's why we have crappy furniture. Napoleon wouldn't have had crappy furniture, but I'm not Napoleon. This is a democracy. All I am is an employee of the people. That's all I am. Right? Yes. That's all I am. Now, let's get on with it."

*

First came detailed situation reports on the war itself: how many targets were hit and of what kind; how many planes lost, people killed; the expenditure and accessible reserves of munitions; enemy transport and communication links broken; shore batteries eliminated; small attack boats and larger vessels sunk or remaining.

The president said, "If we know how many this or that are remaining, they should be hit. The only this or that, that should remain should be the this or that, that are unknown. That's what I want to see." None of his subordinates was sure of what he meant, but they pretended that they were.

Then came distillations of Iranian communications garnered from intercepts of the Supreme Leader down to walkie-talkie transmissions between corporals and privates. Everyone was watching Russia and China. Russia could use the American engagement as a pretense to move against the Baltic Republics. China could let the dogs out (assuming they hadn't been eaten) in North Korea, or create an incident in the South China Sea.

In addressing what China and Russia might do, the National Security Advisor said, "One can never be sure, but China and Russia know that the invasion of South Korea or the Baltic Republics is more of a concern for us then Iran's blockade of the Gulf. They know that, having destroyed Iran's nuclear capabilities already, we would let Iran ride while we transferred all our assets to their primary AORs. To boil it down, they understand that those are primary, Iran is secondary, and we would act accordingly."

"What about our allies?" the president asked.

In close concurrence with the National Security Advisor, who nodded as his rival spoke, the Secretary of State straightened in his chair enough so that his seersucker suit made an audible crinkle. His bow tie twitched along with his Adam's apple. "They are, Mr. President, in various states of approval and protest, depending upon their internal politics and electoral calendars. Japan is solid and distant. The Five Eyes, or rather the four others, are with us. France is with us but must downplay it at home. Germany is trouble as usual. Eastern Europe solidly in our corner. Scandinavia against us—what else is new?"

"The U.N.?" asked the president.

"What would you expect? We use our veto, and we try to bribe—excuse me, incentivize—and influence the multitudes of weirdos and dictators in the General Assembly."

It took more than an hour to get through all this, with reports on the economy, markets, and U.S. public opinion, but as the doves (birds, not a faction in the administration) began their marvelous afternoon songs in the White House shrubbery and on the Old E.O.B.'s hidden ledges that had not been bird-spiked, elongated silences seem to signal that the meeting was about to come to an end.

The president thought so, hoped so, and started looking from one person to another to confirm it. But there is always one more thing.

"Mr. President," the National Security Advisor said. "There is one more thing." The president took in a deep, disappointed breath.

"We have a situation in the Indian Ocean off Africa, sir. ISIS has commandeered a cruise ship with several hundred aboard, executed some in a most brutal fashion, and will execute one every hour."

The president was visibly shocked. "American citizens?"

"Not as far as we can tell from the manifests, if they're accurate."

"American Registry?"

"French."

"Then let France take care of it. They have the capability."

"Yes, sir, the French are on their way from Toulon, but it will take several days, meaning scores of executions."

"That's horrible," the president said. "But what can we do? Do they need a plane or something?"

"No sir, but one of our ships is on scene. We left a patrol coastal in the vicinity to take care of the pirates, but this is ISIS, and the circumstances are different. We've ordered it to await the French. It's only a small ship, sir, and there's little it can do."

"So what's the problem? I don't want to get sucked into something like this when we're in the middle of a war. It's too much."

"The complication is that the captain of the *Athena* points out that it's the obligation of mariners to come to the aid of a ship in distress."

"Not if it's impossible. Right?"

"Captain Rensselaer believes a way may open."

"Captain *who*?"

"Rensselaer, sir."

"Him? Again?"

"Yes sir."

"I thought we got rid of him. I thought he was banished to New Orleans. Wasn't he banished to New Orleans?"

"He was," the SECNAV interjected. "He was sent to finish the *Athena*. He did, and when the war broke out he took her to the Gulf."

"He's a captain, right? What's he doing with a little boat?"

"He was restricted to that command."

"Who did *that*, for Chrissake!" the president asked, ready to pounce on such stupidity.

The SECNAV hesitated, but had to answer. "You did, sir."

As much as everyone wanted to, no one laughed. "Don't tell me what I did or did not do."

"Yes, sir."

"My days here are numbered," the president said, "but we've got an election coming up, and I want the vice president, our glorious nominee"—he hated the vice president—"to carry on for me."

The vice president nodded. His expression was somewhat like that of a Pekinese thrown into the back of a limousine. He was more or less forbidden to speak more than a few words in the presence of the president unless bidden.

The president continued. "This is just one more trap that we can't fall into. Rensselaer. When I used to run at Fort Bliss back in the days when I could run, sometimes a giant mosquito would follow me for five miles and bite me twenty times: undoubtedly Rensselaer's first cousin. Order him to stand down and wait. And I don't want this to be part of the war in the Gulf. When the history is written, I don't want whatever's happening with ISIS in the Western Indian Ocean to be included. It will mar the narrative."

"It is a part of the general effort, and falls under Operation Prevent Armageddon," the Secretary of Defense was obliged to state.

"Wall it off. Call it something else."

"Do you have a suggestion, sir?" the CNO asked.

"I don't know. That's not my job, obviously. It's your job."

*

After receiving his orders to stand down and await the French, Rensselaer understood nonetheless that having agreed to accept the ten hostages even were it to mean defying a direct order, he could not suddenly refuse and thereby condemn them to death. In the burst with the order, he had also received notice that *Athena*'s activities had been sheaved from the main war effort and renamed, and he knew exactly why.

He explained this to the crew over the 1MC, and, with obvious contempt, announced the name of the operation into which *Athena* had been shoehorned.

A dozen men in the mess, looking at the overhead, heard this and reacted. "Spacious Endurance? What the hell is that?" someone asked.

"It's one of those stupid names they make up in the Pentagon. Maybe they employ some idiot just to do it and pay him a hundred grand a year."

"Or maybe they subcontracted to a branding company for a coupla million."

"We could do better."

"Yeah, we probably could."

A blizzard of names followed as they ate. "Dynamic Mongoose," "Vital Junkie," "Discombobulated Haberdasher," "Succinct Worm," and "Spaced-Out Doorman." Someone came up with "Portuguese Wombat" and "Pretentious Bazooka." This was followed by "Narcoleptic Bus Driver." And, finally, "Crazy-Assed Police Chief," "Intellectual Rooster," "Insincere Brazil Nut," and "Irresponsible Monkey." There was much mirth among the men in the mess, which served to refresh them when they resumed their duties.

On the bridge, Rensselaer said to Movius, "Spacious Endurance. I can picture it now, some family getting the announcement: 'Your son has died in Operation Spacious Endurance.' Despite their grief, I can see them saying, 'What the hell is that?'"

THE FOURTH BATTLE: *L'ÉTOILE OCÉANIQUE*

Sometimes in the early morning the sea, caught sleeping and lax, is a temple of light, as lucid and shining as a gem. At 0630 a light wind played upon the sunlit waves, now and then blowing a few drops of spray from their crests, but not enough to raise the general humidity. In the relative cool before the heat would press down, *Athena* steamed toward a point two thousand yards off *l'Étoile's* starboard beam. Velez arrived on the bridge with yet another message he had faithfully not read. General quarters had been called at 0600, and the ship was ready for battle, although in the circumstances battle seemed less than likely. The weapons were manned and, arrayed along the port side, the SEALs had their bipod-supported rifles at the ready.

Rensselaer unfolded and read the message. "Await French forces. Per direct presidential order, *Athena* is expressly forbidden to fire upon or board *l'Étoile*. Detailed clarification forthcoming pending decision of National Security Council. Stand by." He put this, like the previous messages, into his pocket for later destruction so as to make sure no one aboard would be tied to his decisions.

As *Athena* lay motionless at a distance from *l'Étoile*, even with high magnification no activity was visible on the passenger ship. The skiffs had disappeared from *l'Étoile's* stern tow, and *Athena's* officers presumed that one or more of these would be used to ferry the hostages.

"Why would they do this," Movius asked, "unless it's a trap?"

"Because these ten people will eventually speak to the press. ISIS wants the story to get out. On the other hand, if one of those skiffs is packed with explosives it could be the end of us. Everything has to be at the ready, including the big gun."

"Even if it kills the hostages?"

"They'd die anyway. We'll stop the skiffs at two hundred yards and send out the whaleboat to deal with one skiff at a time, and keep our snipers focused on the terrorists. Everyone going out has volunteered. ISIS, too, will have their weapons trained—a Mexican standoff."

"Why didn't you include me in making this plan?" Movius asked.

"You were sleeping, and I wanted you fresh. Would you suggest any changes?"

"I concur with every element, but it's dangerous. For the hostages, for the whaleboat crew, and the ship. And I'd have liked to have been the operational commander."

"I want you here, ready on the order to move us out as fast as possible."

Rensselaer then spoke into his sound talker. "If I give the order to fire, and *only if I give the order to fire*, the big gun, the fifties, and the port mini will open up upon a skiff I identify if it suddenly accelerates, has failed to stop, and/or is nearest *Athena*. Again, fire only upon my command." He thought he was finished, but then he said, "And remember the *Cole*."

They waited. 0700 passed, 0715, 0730. The sun had long risen on their stern, and with the now diminished breeze it was hot enough that everyone was already dripping wet in their helmets and body armor. The gunners had towels with which to wipe near their eyes so that sweat wouldn't sting and blind. The stocks and grips of the SEALs' rifles grew wet in their grasps. But everyone held his position, and the cook brought bottles of chilled water, warning each man not to toss the empties overboard, a strange concern given the circumstances, even if garbage floating on the sea is especially ugly.

As noted in the logs, at 0742 the prow of a skiff cleared *l'Étoile*'s stern, followed seconds later by the appearance of two other skiffs rounding the bow. They oriented toward *Athena* and moved slowly over pleasantly undulating waves with neither chop nor spray. Two of the skiffs were buff-colored except where they were worn white at the gunwales. The third was a cross between terra-cotta and red. They moved in unison, three abreast, and looked like the ship-shaped blocks of a war-college exercise in the days before computers.

Rensselaer, Movius, and Holworthy studied this little flotilla through stabilized binoculars. As the skiffs got closer it became clear that each of them held three hostages and four terrorists. Each hostage stood in front of a terrorist, who was belted at the chest and waist to her or him—five women and four men. Another terrorist piloted the skiff at the stern, and all the terrorists had AK-47s.

The whaleboat was deployed from *Athena*'s starboard side. Slowly and non-provocatively, it rounded *Athena*'s stern, heading toward the skiffs.

"I don't get it, XO," Rensselaer said, worried. "Why are the hostages deployed as shields? They know that we understand that if we blew their guys out of the water they would massacre the captives on *l'Étoile*."

"Maybe they're going to fire on us, or rush us like the *Cole*, and they want human shields so we don't pick them off."

"It doesn't make sense. The guys running the boats aren't shielded. I don't want to hit the hostages, but I don't want to be hit." He went on the hailer. "Approaching boats, stop at two hundred yards." Then he said it in Arabic, using meters, and again in English, using meters.

"XO, are we set to move out at maximum acceleration?"

"On the order, sir."

At two hundred yards, the skiffs cut their engines—they had understood—but they glided another fifty yards or so before they stopped. The whaleboat approached very slowly. Rensselaer briefly scanned it before slewing quickly back to the skiffs. Watching the skiffs intently, he spoke to Movius. "Why is Velez in the whaleboat?"

"He volunteered."

"He was supposed to man COMMS."

"His striker volunteered, Ivoire, but he's just a kid, so Velez took his place."

"I understand, but Ivoire isn't as skilled, and I don't like the fact that Velez is in danger.

Half the crew are just kids."

"I know."

Reacting to what he saw beginning to happen on the water, Rensselaer ordered over the hailer, "Whaleboat, hold position. Boats from *l'Étoile*, does anyone speak English?"

No reply came from the boats. Lined up abreast, with three sets of hostages belted to terrorists standing motionlessly and saying nothing. Close up, the terrorists looked both bizarre and threatening even in wooden boats with outboard motors, no armor, no weapons to speak of, and the guns of a United States warship trained upon them.

"Speak up," Rensselaer said, his words blasting across the water and carried by the wind.

In the same instant, someone in the whaleboat shouted over the radio, "RPG!" The nine men behind the human shields lifted RPGs from behind them. The whaleboat crew had seen the pathos of the hostages, who were pained such that they seemed to know they were going to die. Some of the women cried. Some had a beatific look, as if, in their last moments, they were bathed in love. And some were defiant and angry. There is no single way to die.

Shouldering the RPGs, all the terrorists aimed for the bridge. The second the whaleboat's warning had been assimilated, Rensselaer and Movius simultaneously ordered the helmsman to make flank speed, and *Athena* began to move.

In perhaps the quickest, most sorrowful decision he had made in his life, Rensselaer ordered, "Snipers take your shots." As *Athena* leapt forward, shots rang out. Three of the RPG-wielding terrorists were hit, falling and taking their hostages down with them. One of them pulled the trigger on his launcher as he went down. The flash of the rocket exhaust burned him and his captive and started a fire in the skiff, and the grenade went straight up.

To the deep, deep, everlasting regret of the shooters, the hostages were hit as two of the terrorists were killed. But one terrorist remained standing, although the woman to whom he was tied slumped almost enough to drag him down.

Before *Athena* drew out of the 150-yard effective range of the RPGs, five of them—anti-tank, armor-piercing, rocket-propelled grenades— were launched, not counting the one that went straight up. Three were wild, missing the ship entirely. One hit the lifelines between the rear superstructure and the RHIB, severing a cable on each side and exploding over the sea to starboard. But one made a direct hit, piercing the superstructure at COMMS and, as it was designed to do, bursting a millisecond after.

Athena then passed out of range, and on full power the whaleboat turned away from the skiffs. The terrorists held their AKs at the heads of the remaining hostages, and, faster than they had come, they sped back toward *l'Étoile*.

Athena came about to pick up the whaleboat as damage-control parties rushed in their fire suits and breathing apparatuses to the conflagration spreading from COMMS. All the electronics and hot electrical lines meant that the firefighters were restricted to halon and foam. The fire was intense enough to melt the aluminum bulkheads that enclosed COMMS, which meant that it was more than 650° Fahrenheit. Probably much more, and given that aluminum conducts heat at four times the rate of steel, to hold such a high temperature while the heat was rapidly conducted away, the source had to be significantly hotter. And the spectacular conductivity meant that the fire was quickly spreading to other compartments.

Pisecki calmly ran damage control, and when he had ordered all his parties to the right places he left his post and went to lead. Knowing that the whaleboat would have no problem catching up, Rensselaer ordered *Athena* to run with the wind at wind speed so as to deprive the fire of additional draft.

Black smoke and sheets of orange flame shot from the superstructure as the fire party confronted the blazes directly. After the exhalation bursts of halon and foam, white dust spread all over the ship. Commands and reports came as calmly as charges into the fire were fast and combative. In fifteen minutes, the flames were no more, but an acrid chemical smell would linger for the rest of the deployment.

While the captain stayed on the bridge, the XO went to report damage. Movius's own cabin was destroyed, as was Rensselaer's clothes compartment, which abutted it, and COMMS was gone. "Ivoire is dead," Movius reported. "He's unrecognizable. There's nothing left of COMMS. It's all melted. The deck plates are covered with solidified metal, and plastic that's still bubbling."

"What's left?" Rensselaer asked.

"There's nothing. I mean nothing."

"Even to salvage?"

Movius looked around. "Some steel racks, now bent, but everything else melted and disintegrated."

As Rensselaer watched the skiffs disappear behind *l'Étoile*, trying not to be dispirited, he said, "Get Seaman Ivoire into a body bag. We'll do our best to bury him decently when we get a chance.

"Chief Pisecki." There was no immediate answer. "Chief."

"Sir."

"Bring in the whaleboat."

"I'm already at the davits, sir."

*

The death of Ivoire hit the *Athena* harder than would have the loss of any member of the crew—Movius, Rensselaer, or even Pisecki, who was the most fatherly to the young. Only when Ivoire was gone did everyone understand how much it had been their honor and responsibility to protect him. They had been not as sharply aware of this while he lived, though they did sense that somehow they had formed a ring around him, happy that he was in the center. What they had thought of as merely liking him and enjoying his presence was something else. It was that in his presence they felt lightness and joy. The quality to which they had responded was holiness.

Whether he was aware of this or not, and no one could venture more than a guess, he never showed that he was, or used his effect on others to exercise any kind of power, or to capitalize on the regard in which he was held.

He was about thirty, and had been in the Navy for only a few years. From the low country of South Carolina, he had gone to Catholic schools and Georgetown. Though he easily could have been an officer, he chose not to be, and was never unhappy about being subordinate. Among other things, without exception, everyone with authority over him had known immediately that in the higher and more permanent order of things he was in fact superior. He had the quality of making hierarchy disappear— something that even in the Navy was deeply respected.

Once, Ivoire had just entered the mess deck when another young Southerner, who was white, was saying, "Well, that's nothing. I was on an LPH port visit to Kingston, and they got all the Afro-Americans out on deck so the Afro-Americans onshore watching would say, 'Hey! America's just like us!'"

"Tommy," one of his friends said—they had all seemed strangely frozen, and he had wondered why. "Tommy?" He cleared his throat.

Tommy turned around, and there was Ivoire, a foot and a half away from him. Tommy reddened with embarrassment and shame. When Ivoire gestured to him to come closer, Tommy thought he was going to be punched, and he would have accepted it. But Ivoire just said, "Tommy, the 'Afro-Americans' onshore were actually Afro-Jamaicans." Then he smiled, and he put his arms around Tommy, and any racial prejudice that might have been hanging around in Tommy just disappeared, at least at that moment. You could feel it, almost see it, part from him and fly away. Later, Tommy had said, "When he did that . . . when he did that . . ." and was unable to go on. Ivoire was the heart of the ship.

They assembled at the bow, the most unencumbered space on deck because in high seas water would have to wash over it with the least obstruction. Some stood dangerously near or even straddled over the anchor chains. Because every man was still vibrating from the fight and making ready to fight again, the ceremony had to be short.

The captain spoke: "Those of you who may not have known before have learned on this deployment how, when familiar with and accepting the prospect of one's own death, feeling is cut off when others die. We think, well, that's our job, too. When the soldier is old and many years have passed, deep upwellings of emotion will come, but not now. Now we look on, without reflection or broken hearts, and we keep going. There's satisfaction in that, and also honor to the fallen.

"In time, everyone is forgotten. You're young now, but your body will fail. You'll be pushed out by those who arise in your place. Fashions will appear that you'll neither understand nor countenance. All currencies and standards will change. As others are enmeshed in the struggles of the world, you'll be thinking of the silence amid the stars. Ivoire is there now. He was our brother. We loved him."

Rensselaer then read the Lord's Prayer, and what was left of Ivoire's body, encased in vinyl and wrapped in the flag, was committed to the sea. By custom, the flag remained, and was carefully folded.

The sea there was three miles deep. As his body fell into the depths, within sight of *l'Étoile* and in waters where the fourth battle had unfolded, *Athena* realized belatedly, though perhaps not in full, what she had lost, and consonant with her new blackened and torn port side, she was a different ship, and that much farther from home. The crew was now not merely comfortable with death and expecting it, but, although perhaps inexplicably to some at a far remove, comfortable in seeking it.

*

"I was supposed to have stayed in COMMS but I didn't want Ivoire to go in the whaleboat," Velez told the captain. "It should have been me."

"You couldn't have known."

"It'll be with me for the rest of my life."

"For some things there's no cure. You just live with them, that's all. What have we got in COMMS after the damage?"

286

Before Velez could answer, the port lookout reported from the bridge wing that *l'Étoile* was getting up a head of steam. Rensselaer acknowledged and turned back to Velez.

"We've got nothing, sir. No links, no transmission, no reception. The only thing that's left are the five hand-helds because they were with the SEALs. That's it."

"Their sat-phones?"

"The sat-phones were charging in COMMS. They're gone."

"You can't fix them? Just one?"

"You can't even see them."

"What about COMMS on the bridge?"

"Back-shorted. They're more or less melted inside."

"Can you construct something?"

"Maybe an orange juice can and a string. That's about it. You'd need many factories to make a piece of equipment that can do the job of what we lost. Sorry."

"So, apart from the hand-helds. . . ."

"They have maybe a few hundred miles range in absolutely ideal conditions."

"Sir," the OOD said, "*l'Étoile* is moving west and increasing speed."

"Keeping in mind the height of *l'Étoile*'s mast, we'll follow from beyond the horizon, tracking the wake in daylight and following the disturbance of bioluminescence at night. I'll be in the wardroom. Mr. Holt has the con."

*

Aboard *l'Étoile*, believing that with their little wooden fishing skiffs they had won a naval victory against an American warship, the terrorists were as elated as the hostages were downcast. To cast them down further, purely out of malice, Hadawi seized a middle-aged woman from among them, forced her to kneel, and, as she cried, decapitated her.

They wanted to inflict as much suffering and terror as they could. They didn't fully indulge their imaginations and enjoyments and massacre everyone, only because they were not ready to publish to the world until they had taken the hostages inland among the wastes and crags of the Somalian desert, and because they were preoccupied with controlling *l'Étoile* and fending off an assault—though not from *Athena*, which they had written off.

It was true that after taking so many hits *Athena* now had neither spit nor polish. She was blackened and stained with oil smoke and the smoke from her own fire in COMMS. The window glass and frame that had killed Josephson was replaced with plywood, which gave *Athena* the air of an abandoned tenement. Salt air had already begun to rust the scars on the steel hull where shrapnel from *Sahand* had stripped the paint. The superstructure was punched with holes and stove-in at COMMS, where a round opening gaped. Under the waterline, she was patched, and the national ensign was in shreds. Rensselaer kept it flying. He could have replaced it, but he and the crew loved and respected it too much to betray it on account of the damage it had suffered as they had fought under it.

Despite sinking the *Sahand*—which may have been the most important single action of the war, perhaps saving the carriers in the Arabian Sea off Iran, in a battle no one would have thought *Athena* could win— Rensselaer counted himself a failure. He suspected that unless *Athena* was withdrawn, much fighting and dying remained, and as *Athena* was the only American warship in the area, he doubted she would be pulled out. He had lost three of a crew of less than thirty, and although he had been forbidden to board *l'Étoile*, he could not foresee abandoning so many innocents to their deaths. Any effort to save them might mean a costly, cross-deck battle as of old.

In that circumstance, he would lose many good men. Whatever his own fate, by disobeying direct and emphatic orders he would be held responsible for, and indeed would be responsible for, the deaths among his own men and the hostages executed in the assault or killed in cross-fire. Should *Athena* assault *l'Étoile*, his only honorable way out after having done his utmost to keep the casualties down and save the hostages would be to be among those killed.

Waiting for Movius and Holworthy in the silence of the wardroom, he rested his hand on the highly polished table and pictured himself in the grave or in the deep, as the world, and Katy, too, carried on without him. When those who had known him were themselves forgotten, his existence would be unregistered except in a few strokes of ink here and there, which meant nothing to anyone and upon which, with no reason to linger, no one would. The only thing left, the only worthwhile thing at all, since the beginning and all the way to the end, was to love, and to do right.

Movius and Holworthy arrived and took their seats. They knew messages they had not seen had come in. These would be the only armature for sound recommendations in regard to what might lie ahead.

"What are our orders, sir?" Movius asked. "Everyone's on edge."

"XO," Rensselaer said, "I'll be quite surprised if we ever get back to normal."

"What *are* our orders, sir?" Holworthy asked, his skepticism in regard to Rensselaer having returned—despite the action Holworthy had relished—because he knew that Rensselaer was concealing the messages.

If Rensselaer told them, they could be held to account, so he didn't. He suspected that if it came to it they and the rest of *Athena's* crew, like him, would choose to disobey. They had seen the atrocities on *l'Étoile*, and they were good men. "Our orders," he said, "are to await orders."

"And since we cannot receive orders . . . ?" Movius asked.

"We proceed according to discretion."

"Whose discretion?" Holworthy asked.

"Mine. I want your advice, but the decisions are mine alone. Until Marconi, that's the way it used to be. The Navy's traditions and command structures were designed for exactly the kind of situation in which we find ourselves now. Those traditions should see us through. Although we don't know if aboard *l'Étoile* they're doing what they promised, we have to figure that every hour we lose one and perhaps more. Before the French get here a hundred will have been murdered. Buck extrapolated *l'Étoile's* course and speed, and if that holds, they might make landfall and the hostages might be taken inland in twenty hours or less."

"Why would they do that when they have them on the ship, where they can better see what's coming?" Holworthy challenged.

"Because on land they can disperse them, disappear, and elongate the crisis. If they're all together on the ship, one assault and it's done, and perhaps many of the hostages would be saved. That's what I'd do were I in their place—take them into the mountains and stretch the executions out for months, to keep the whole world horrified and helpless."

"We'd send in teams to stop them."

"If we could find them in however many groups they might splinter. And everything's in the Gulf now, so it would be late, or never."

"It would be easier for us on land, until they were divided up, anyway," Holworthy concluded. "But meanwhile, we lose twenty hostages?"

"If we go in now," Movius said—Rensselaer had long before come to the same conclusion—"we could lose them all."

"So we let the twenty go," Holworthy said, numbed and resigned.

"We do," Rensselaer confirmed, his tone the same.

"What if they change course, or go dead in the water again?" Movius asked.

Rensselaer answered, "At that point we might have to go in."

"It's going to be a very hard twenty hours, sir," Holworthy said.

"It is."

"I can speak for the crew, I think," Movius said. "I've talked to a lot of them individually, I've heard them talking, and I've spoken to the chiefs. After what we saw, they want to fight. It's not that they're angry. Yeah, they're angry, but it's deeper than that. Anger dissipates. They're beyond anger."

Rensselaer nodded in agreement, but, still, he was almost overcome by the crosscurrents of responsibility and consequence. Attempting to rescue the hostages might doom them all and many of his men. Forgoing the attempt might—it was likely—doom them all and leave a scar for life upon everyone on *Athena*. Disobeying the sense of the order, if not its explicit command, would mean his disgrace. That, however, would pale in regard to the disgrace of watching hundreds of people led to slaughter. Although concealing the orders from everyone would protect them from courts-martial and even reprimand, acting would expose them to the risk of dying.

He understood simultaneously the burden of high command and how that burden could be borne only by distance from both the situation and its consequences. This was a luxury the CNO, the SECNAV, the Secretary of Defense, and the president—insulated by stages, dealing with matters of flesh and blood translated through many steps into abstractions—had to have so as to enable such decisions as now fell to Rensselaer without the slightest luxury of separation.

"If they hold their course," he said, "we'll pretty much know where they'll make landfall. In that case, we can put extra fuel in the RHIB and do a covert reconnaissance out ahead of them. Does that seem sound to you?" he asked Holworthy.

"That sounds just right to me. They've had the initiative up 'til now, and that's been hard to bear. It's time we took it back."

"Then make your preparations."

*

With *l'Étoile* dead in the water, even deep below decks it was possible to hear the staccato tapping of automatic weapons fire, screams from above, and the distant, muffled thud of RPGs. As of yet, no one had set foot in the short hall off of which the dressing and electrical rooms were arrayed. Though they might be found at any moment, as the hours dragged on and nothing happened, Martin and Petra felt more secure.

The last meal they had had was far more salty than what they were used to, which made them correspondingly thirsty. In their confined space, it didn't take long for them to see a little sign above the tap, which said, "Non-Potable Water." Unlike what was supplied to the passengers, it was saltwater with a taste of petrochemicals, as were the water in the tub and the line that fed the toilet. They had to drink, and they had only Champagne.

"We wouldn't be at our best if they did find us, would we?" Martin asked. "I'm so thirsty I couldn't take just a sip, believe me. And if they saw even the empty bottle, being Islamist terrorists, it probably wouldn't be very much to our credit."

"It would be more dangerous to go out again," Petra said. "Is there a high water content in cheese?" Then she said, "That's stupid."

Because they were somewhat punchy, this made them laugh, suppressedly.

"Petra, if we don't drink, the dehydration will make us drunker and weaker than if we do. I should go out."

"No, don't. We may die anyway, so why not die with Champagne while it's still reasonably cold?"

"After a moment's consideration and the exchange of exactly similar, sad, and yet defiant looks, he popped the cork. As the mist from the bottleneck settled, they listened hard. Nothing. And then they drank. They were so thirsty they drank the Champagne like water, and it was a magnum. Soon extremely relaxed, they lost their fear, and between the two of them it didn't take long at all to finish the bottle. It was a Jean Lallement, a small and little-known house but a most excellent Champagne, and it completely did them in.

*

Many decks above them in the main salon, the terror had not subsided, especially as no one had been properly fed.

Not long after *l'Étoile* had steamed away from what Hadawi took to be the incapacitated *Athena*, a sense of triumph spread among his troops. They had succeeded, the world would know, and they held the upper hand over the paralyzed great powers. This was unfortunate and tragic for the younger women among the captives, especially the six French *lycéennes*. For they and women who seemed under forty were separated from the rest and herded into the bar. The doors were shut, and then, by rank order, Hadawi's soldiers chose the women they wanted.

Somehow, almost inconceivably, Madame Eugénie had blended in with her girls and moved with them to the bar. Hadawi's men thought it amusing. When the first of her trembling girls was chosen, Madame moved between her and the man who had selected her. "*Non!*" At first, he laughed. Then, in one quick movement, like a boxer, he swung the butt of his rifle at her head, felling her instantly. He took the girl, and the others took the other five, Sophie last, perhaps because of her braces.

All the women were forced into individual cabins. The young and the old, the obvious virgins prized not for their youth, delicacy, and innocence but merely because in some ancient and obscene code virginity itself was seen through a horribly distorted lens as a reflection of the quality of the man who violated it.

The other passengers well understood what was happening. Some were close enough to the accommodation corridors to hear the pleadings, screams, and sobs. These women and girls were variously wives, girl-friends, mothers, and daughters. The terror they had felt was now replaced by a deep, all-encompassing blackness.

*

On the lower deck that ran almost the whole length of the ship, and which, unlike the areas accessible to passengers, was austere—no wood paneling, carpeting, incandescent lighting, or paintings, as on the upper decks—Martin and Petra were recklessly drunk, and, like all drunks, spoke more loudly than was necessary.

"I have a theory," Martin said.

"What's your theory?" Just saying this gave Petra pleasure, and it shone from her blue eyes.

"My theory is that alcohol, whatever it does—and I know what it does, chemically, biochemically, sort of, as much as can be known about the brain and all that: I'm a chemist—has an effect beyond what science can show."

"Oh, really?"

"Yes."

"And what is that?"

"I think—and it may not really be *think*, but sense—that alcohol cancels out the learned." He pronounced this as "learn*ed*," when he meant only *learned*.

"You mean people?" she asked, wrinkling up her nose and squinting in disdain, because of the way he had said the word.

"No, I mean the things we have to learn so as to exist in the material world. As with drugs, canceling that out gives a glimpse of the spiritual world. Of course, that's a bad idea in the material world—to which we're—you could say confined, limited, sentenced—because it's so unhealthy, and because you can't bring anything back from it into the sober world. But it's true, and it makes death acceptable because it shows you what's beyond."

"It does."

"It does. But I don't recommend it."

"Indeed. We don't live that way."

"We don't. Why would we?"

"We wouldn't. Why should we?"

"We shouldn't."

"But I must say that it makes sex more spiritual even if annoyingly anorgasmic," Martin said.

"Not for me."

"I know. It also means that, though I'm impaired, I'm going out, because I know that death is one with life."

"I know. It also means that I'm going with you."

"No. That's too much."

"I see," she said, "I do. I wouldn't, otherwise, but now I'm so tolerant."

"I'll go. And I won't be afraid. I have a connection to the eternal, to God. I can't lose." He was very drunk.

It never would've happened without the magnum of Champagne, but he left, and the door clicked shut. He was fearless, and she feared nothing. And he was angry at being a Jew, 1942-style, but he was also perfectly confident that he could take down any enemy—Nazis, Hitler himself, anyone.

He went back to the huge, multipart, empty, industrial kitchen, hoping to encounter a hijacker. But he didn't. In complete relaxation and delight, he assembled a stock of foods: many bottles of Perrier, baguettes, *jambon*, *crudités*, cookies (especially chocolate), canned and smoked fish, more cheese, a container of sliced roast beef. It was too much to carry back in one trip, so he took as much as he could, gave it to Petra, and returned to the kitchen once again. Still fully intoxicated, he saw a huge dumb-waiter-like apparatus almost the size of an elevator, and was so curious about it that he seemed to forget the circumstances. It was an incinerator. Oblivious of any threats, he was magnetized by the detailed instructions, and read them carefully, with, somehow, more enjoyment than one might expect to be gleaned from incinerator instructions.

This *appareil* directed high-temperature gas jets as hot as multiple acetylene torches at whatever was weighing upon its spring-loaded steel grate, turning refuse into gas and ash. When the ash fell through the grate and the weight upon it lessened, the jets would cease. Until then the temperature was like that in a blast furnace. A mushroom-shaped green button turned it on; a mushroom-shaped red button turned it off.

A very clever way, Martin thought, to dispose of garbage at sea. Even wet garbage such as meat scraps would be reduced to ash, which would then be environmentally and responsibly discarded in the ocean: just fertilizer. "Nice," he said to himself. But, then, hearing a passageway door close, he instantly became slightly less intoxicated even if not enough to make him fear, and not enough to scotch the desire to meet up with one of the terrorists despite knowing that in his drunken relaxedness he would not be at his physical best.

Casting about, he searched for a weapon. Nothing. The knives and cleavers were in a different bay. How he wished he had a cleaver. He realized that part of his difficulty in delivering the first load of food and water to Petra was because he had drunkenly kept the empty Magnum bottle in his hand. And it was still there. He looked at it, and smiled.

Then he calmly stepped back behind a partition and awaited the footsteps coming toward him.

"Oh my," he said to himself delightedly. "Here he comes."

And it was so. Appearing was a fierce-looking, bearded terrorist who carried an automatic rifle. He was horrible to behold. Dressed in black, he had the dead, empty eyes of a man without a conscience, he was muscular, and he smelled of sesame oil. But he was not nearly as big as Martin, who also was muscular, and who had been made fearless by Champagne.

Holding his rifle, the terrorist stepped forward. All the decks he had searched had been empty. Expecting nothing, he had grown quite careless. Martin was behind him, and could easily have hit him on the back of the head. But Martin was so happy that he wanted to do it in a different way, so he said, "*Bonjour!*"—which made the terrorist turn, startled, right into the magnum that smashed against his forehead.

"Excellent," said Martin, totally nonplussed. "You did perfectly." He didn't know whether he was addressing himself or the terrorist.

As if no one else might come along—though the man he struck had, in fact, been wandering about the ship, looking for him and Petra, there was no one else—Martin stripped him of his weaponry and rested it on one of the stainless-steel islands. Then he dragged the unconscious man over to the incinerator. Opening the dumbwaiter-like door, he hoisted the limp head up to the edge, where it stayed because the chin caught on it. Then he grabbed the waist and eased the body in, feeding the legs after it. "*Bon voyage, Nazi,*" Martin said. He closed the door, and pushed the green button. Though the man was still alive, he was unconscious, and he would be dead before he could awaken. The incinerator would turn off when the ash was so light the rising grid tripped a switch.

Martin looped a belt of magazine pouches around his shoulders, slung the rifle, an American M4, gathered up the remaining food, and returned to Petra. When the door was shut he said, "Petra, I killed one of them. I incinerated him. I did. I actually incinerated him. No one knows what happened, we have food, we have a rifle and ammunition, here we are, and I couldn't have done it without Champagne."

*

L'Étoile had not varied course since *Athena* had begun to trail her straight-as-steel wake and the luminescence she cut through the water. From this, Buck Lanham was able—as even a yacht club novitiate would have been able—to place landfall at a small village on the Somali coast, unknown to the world and straddling a feature that had barely made it onto the map: Ras Hagar. The term *ras* denoted a headland or a cape, and at Ras Hagar there was hardly such a thing, just a minor bump out into the sea, slightly north of the village, and a concrete pier slightly to the south, built long ago by the British or Italians. The chart actually said "Built by either Britain or Italy, pre-1950."

This was likely because parallel to the pier at the southern end of a beach a little over a mile long and five hundred feet at the widest, a wadi led through a three-hundred-foot-high escarpment into the interior and was used as a road. Another wadi, to the north, was wider but steeper on the sides and impassable to vehicles.

Had it been accessible to European vacationers, the beach at Ras Hagar would have been prized for its whiteness, its expanse, and the double lines of surf arising from the Indian Ocean's African shallows. But it was 190 miles south of the Horn of Africa's tip, in unrelieved desert controlled by Somali warlords, pirates, and the Somalian province of ISIS. The fishing/piracy village there consisted of between fifty and one hundred one-storey, mud-brick huts, a small mosque, and not much else.

These were loosely clustered near the outward passage at the southern wadi, just north of a large salt pond created when the surf crested a narrow strip of beach between it and the ocean. The pond had probably been born of the effect of the pier, which, between pond and village, jutted seaward, intercepting the surf's eternal attack upon the land. Piracy here had been unsuccessful, as all but one ship had been retaken before it could make land, and that small ship, a Kenyan coaster loaded with cattle, fetched a ransom of only €50,000. The village had reverted to fishing and was unable to support half its population, until ISIS took over and stimulated its economy with infusions of blood-and-oil cash from the Levant. Although not happy with the new governance, people came back. Western intelligence agencies had no idea of the new regime, as surveillance had ceased after the diminution of population. On *Athena*'s chart, 9° 02' 4.5" N, 50° 35' 21" E was marked, "Semi-populated fishing village."

A little more than half a mile up the coast, the land shallowly bent inward before projecting into an almost de minimis salient: Ras Hagar. Behind this, after speeding wide and ahead of *L'Étoile*, Holworthy and his men beached the RHIB and camouflaged it as best they could with nets, and mats of washed-up, dried seaweed. The escarpment there was far more gradual than the one high over the village, and at a little past midnight they began to ascend by the light of a quarter moon.

In addition to his own weapon and eight magazines of ammunition, each SEAL carried a 125-pound pack. This near-one-thousand pounds of collective supply was not as much as it might seem. Ammunition, grenades, three Claymore mines, and water made up the bulk of it. The rest was filled in by food, clothing, two hand-held radios, camouflage netting, shovels, and, because the ground in the Middle East was so often hard and rocky, a pick, or rather, half the head of a double-headed pick—eight pounds just in itself. They didn't know how long they might have to stay should the RHIB or they themselves be discovered. Thus all the ammunition, water, and food.

The night wind was coming off the land, which had cooled precipitously in the trick deserts play on those who don't know them and are caught shivering in the cold. Nonetheless, the SEALs began their climb unprotected, for they knew that though the rise would be only about three hundred feet, they would be soaking wet after carrying a total (including their own body weights) of almost three hundred pounds up a crumbling slope that necessitated two or three steps when otherwise just one would suffice.

They were in territory about as empty and isolated as possible, and yet every five minutes or so they would stop, listen, and scan with night vision. Not a single one thought it necessary, but on the off chance that their enemy was more competent than estimated and had posted a picket line, they took all precautions—and the periodic if short rests enabled them to move faster when they climbed. In daylight the cliffs would be ocher, the desert beyond, khaki and buff. The air was so cold that there was no scent, but in beating sun the rocks and sand themselves would have a scent, and the scrub of the desert, too, though its faint perfumes were as sparse as the water it retained.

When the SEALs came over the top of the bluff, they were very hot, but then, in the wind, they were shivering and dry within a minute or two. They put on their sweaters. No one could resist the wonder of where he was and what he was doing. But this elation would vanish after a day half-buried under camouflage nets in 120-degree heat as the wings of flies made the only breeze. Now, however, between unending desert and unending sea, they stood beneath a dim moon and the stars. Not a single earthly candlepower served to lessen the glow of the Milky Way in this place that had not changed since the beginning of the world. They were there as timeless soldiers and raiders, divorced from all they had known, comfortable with physical deprivation, strain, and death. They hardly recognized themselves. But in the cold, crystal wind coming off the desert, they were glad to have come.

And then they set out to hump south on the plateau, half a mile in, on a track parallel to the sea. Moving fast on level ground, they stopped only every ten minutes. In the first break, they took off their sweaters and had water. Then they came to the north wadi, descended, ascended, and broke again, this time with chocolate and water. They virtually raced across the last mile and a half to their observation point above the village, where they arrived at 0330 and dropped their packs.

Without an order from Holworthy, they automatically spread out into a perimeter while he scouted for a place to dig in. They were three hundred or so vertical feet above the village at an eroded place along the bluff where landslides had settled in an angle of repose. Probably the village had grown up there because it was safe from further rockfall. Which is not to say that the slope was gradual. And that it was littered with sharp rocks made its top an ideal defensive position, although to the south, on the plateau, the remains of an abandoned settlement could be used against them as cover for weapons of sufficient reach. There was nothing they could do about that.

As Holworthy and the others knew from exercises and real life, fighting your way up a steep rock slope is almost the worst thing you can do. It isn't just that the enemy has cover and a nearly perfect view, but that your every movement must struggle against gravity as it simultaneously puts you in hostile sights. And then, courtesy of rocks and scree, his every bullet becomes shrapnel. A machine-gun burst of a hundred rounds in a few seconds will send a thousand shards in a stinging, sometimes deadly cloud. The SEALs didn't worry about a frontal assault up the slope, and in the other directions they had excellent fields of fire. They placed their Claymores to the south, where a flank attack might originate.

Then they dug in right at the edge so that with their scopes they would be able to see everything, and yet to see them one would have to be less than thirty or forty feet away. They took note that there was no reason that anyone would be up near their position, not even goatherds, as there was neither scrub nor a path. Five slept while one listened and scanned.

*

The morning sun rose bloody at the edge of the sea, climbing fast according to its near-equatorial privilege. It yellowed just as fast, awoke the village, and then settled into the blazing white with which until just before it set it would punish this entire quarter of the world.

Holworthy and his men were completely on their own, with *Athena* still out at sea, no air support, medivac, or long-range communication. The nearest American forces were 550 miles south near Mogadishu, unaware of their presence. "We might as well be on the moon," Holworthy told them. "No running to mama."

No one knew Holworthy's story, so if he had emotions it was hard to prove or imagine. When he was made, it seemed, everything was poured into competence and efficiency, with emotions left begging. As the sun rose, he got to work.

The radios could sometimes range two hundred or more miles, especially if transmitting from a height. Although even with the SEALs at three hundred feet above sea level and the receiving hand-held on *Athena's* bridge thirty feet above the water, the ship was not yet close enough for line-of-sight transmission, Holworthy was fairly confident that he would get through. The likelihood that ISIS would break the encryption was almost nil, but the radio direction finder presumed to be on *l'Étoile*, or a simple set in the village, could give away the reconnaissance.

Normally, Holworthy would have communicated via uplinking to a satellite, which after shufflings here and there, probably even back to the U.S., would downlink to the ship, the only interception possible being from within narrow and vertical transmission columns. But with the sat-phones destroyed he had to transmit horizontally. As far as RDF, he realized that he might even be picked up by American arrays in the Med, or similar Russian installations he knew not where.

Thus he worked hard to keep his transmissions exceedingly brief, and had arranged with Velez to bypass normal voice-to-voice etiquette. He wrote down his report so he could say it fast and then click off. After an hour of close observation, he composed and rehearsed it like this: "Dug in commanding position three one five degrees northwest village sixty-three one-storey mud-brick from high waterline to fifteen hundred feet back. EST two hundred civilians, twenty armed men Kalashnikovs. Two possibly Russian one-oh-five-millimeter towed guns directly north and south of village at ten feet back of high water, ammunition two piles each gun, seven trench lines various lengths in village, two machine-gun emplacements visible. Possible sandbagged HQ three structures south of mosque, dozen black flags, two dozen vehicles scattered, stores stacked on probably functional pier. Sea condition two, offshore sandbar, weather clear." It was essential that *Athena* know where the SEALs were dug in so as not to fire upon them.

His transmission began with "E2C to base. Record this transmission." After a second, Velez said, "Go."

Holworthy sped through his report in thirty seconds followed by, "Out."

Velez had recorded it. He then made a transcription and brought it to Rensselaer, who said, "Doesn't mince words, does he?"

"No, sir. Would you say they're expecting us?"

"I would say that, yeah. But they don't know us."

What Holworthy had left out was the feel of the place. Before the sun rose, dozens of muted fires had appeared among the huts. Fuel was so scarce that these were just large enough to heat water for rice and tea, and although they blazed for a minute or two they quickly settled into red spots like cigarettes in the dark, and then were further muted as pots were placed upon them. But the scent rose in the still air, for the breeze was in stasis, cold air from the desert having ceased spilling over the plateau, and warm air yet to blow in from the sea. The smoke calmed the SEALs as if they were bees. Something very lovely and kind there was about woodsmoke in the small, subtle doses that sweetened the air.

As it got light, the SEALs counted people as best they could, and then averaged out their estimates. When the light was dim enough to see a laser dot but bright enough so that it would not be as conspicuous as in the dark, Holworthy took the range of the two artillery pieces, their ammunition stores, the trenches, and various landmarks in the village. He then sent two men out several hundred feet in each direction along the cliff line and had them mark firing positions with some stones, against which he ranged with the laser.

For forty-five minutes, he used a calculator to triangulate the exact distances from each of the SEALs' firing positions to each of the targets. The discrepancies were not great, but given that in regard to the village every shot was 500 yards or more, the more exact the ranging the better their chances of hits with their three M4s, one Remington 700, and the Barrett .50 they had carried up for Holworthy.

Each man had his role and his ranges, as well as a clear understanding of hand signals, procedures in case of attack from the flanks, the routes and methods of withdrawal, the firing order, and a clear instruction not to fire too close to civilians, especially women and children, even if it meant forgoing a legitimate shot.

"Can you figure it, sir? They prepared to defend, but they did it so badly."

"Not for them," Holworthy answered. "Their traditions are unscientific, and they don't have the history we have of infantry fighting. I'd say that for a bunch of terrorist bastards they've done quite all right."

"Except. . . ."

"You want a list?" he asked, peering through his scope as he spoke. "Their artillery is on the beach, not up here. Are you kidding me? They don't even have spotters or lookouts on the bluff, much less a perimeter to keep us out. The guns aren't dug in. Neither is the ammunition. They haven't laid any mines—see people walking all over the place, everywhere? They haven't marked out any fields of fire, or arranged anything. They should have had buoys out in the water to range the artillery. I'll bet they haven't had any gunnery training either. You can't just point and shoot an artillery piece. And then, I don't know about these guys, but most of the insurgents I fought don't aim their weapons. They use them like a hose. Their shots go wild and they burn through their ammunition so fast that in a manner of minutes they can't do anything but run away.

"Don't get me wrong. It's not the rule. A lot of them are trained, and there can be marksmen among them, but in general they lack fire discipline and precision, and they think that emotion adds to their effectiveness—like what you see in the movies when the hero is mad and he jerks the pistol forward to help the bullets hit harder.

"We try to stand our ground methodically, intently, and without emotion. They scream a lot when they fight. Except for when we communicate, we fight in silence. Are you worried?"

"No, sir."

"Good. Don't be. I don't know what the CO is going to do, but *Athena's* got a lot of firepower should we need it, and to be behind the enemy, on high, unobstructed ground. . . . If we engage fully, it'll be their worst nightmare."

Their preparations made and the message to *Athena* delivered, the SEALs settled in to endure the heat of the day, sleeping when they could, and savoring the relatively cool wind as it arose from the sea, because by noon both the wind on the desert and the wind over water would be almost unbearably hot. From the village below they heard the occasional tinkling of metal, children playing, the sound made by rickety doors as they were slammed shut by the breeze, and of course the call to prayer. It was the latter that told American soldiers each time they heard it that they were in another world, which they would never change.

Everything down below was surprisingly busy, and yet the fishermen did not take out their boats, but, rather, pulled them back far from the sea. Soon, the SEALs were discovered, but only by flies.

V

The Desert

In a letter that would not be mailed for a long time, one of the sailors wrote, "We are about to go into the dessert."

The Fifth Battle: Ras Hagar

L'Étoile and *Athena* were five hours from Ras Hagar, which by further and more precise extrapolation had proved undoubtedly the landfall, when Holworthy's south picket reported a large dust cloud at the picket's four o'clock. It rose from the wadi road at a rate that indicated fast-moving vehicles. The SEALs were roused. Even though their positional advantage could be nullified by a large contingent of enemy, they would stay to fight any number, because to surrender was to die.

Soon enough, a line of more than twenty pickup trucks sped into the village down below. Several men previously unseen by the SEALs emerged from the largest building and fired shots into the air. At first the SEALs thought this was celebratory, but it was a signal. People emerged from their houses en masse, carrying bundles, tools, and children. As if they had done it before, they quickly climbed into the trucks, and after ten minutes, when the only remaining figures were armed men, the trucks drove back to the wadi, and the dust cloud moved south and west. Holworthy reported this in clipped fashion, as before.

When apprised of it, Rensselaer conferred with the XO, Marchetti, and Kenny Larman, the gunnery chief. "The question is," Rensselaer announced, "do we speed ahead of *l'Étoile* and destroy the village when it's lightly manned, with no hostages as shields? Clearly, they want a hardened, defensible position in which to disembark and hold the captives. We could deny them that. Your views?"

Marchetti said, "Yes. Otherwise it would be infinitely more difficult—or impossible—to do so without harming the hostages. And we can do it much more easily if the strongpoints aren't fully manned, assuming that a hundred-and-five-millimeter shell or two doesn't score a lucky hit on us before we can take out their artillery. Or, they may have an anti-shipping missile."

"No report of that," Movius said.

"It could be hidden," Rensselaer stated, "but those are the risks we take."

"We should go in, Captain," Larman urged, in agreement with Marchetti. "XO?"

Movius shook his head. "No."

"Why not?"

"If Hadawi sees that his strongpoint has been destroyed he could do at least two things—kill all the hostages and escape inland, or turn back out to sea, continuing to use the ship as the strongpoint."

"But if he has the fortified village, with the hostages as shields, how is that better?" Marchetti asked.

"Granted, only slightly. They'd be fixed in position, and if the French get here they, and—who knows—maybe the U.S., could manage a land assault surprising enough to save them. It's been done."

"But assuming that they continue the executions," Rensselaer said, "by the time of the assault, if ever, most would be dead."

Movius answered, "There's no clear path, sir. You have to decide, working in the dark. What does your gut say?"

Rensselaer lifted his eyes to the overhead, tilting back, and then straightening. "It tells me to prepare and wait on events. We shouldn't get ahead of ourselves, figuratively or otherwise. How does that sit with you, Chief?" he asked Larman.

"I understand, sir."

"But when and if we do go in, I want to pour a Niagara of gunfire on those positions. Like the *Sahand*, but more so."

"That's what we're working on, a broadside heavier than even against the *Sahand*."

"How?"

"Cutting and un-bolting the starboard stern fifty, the starboard grenade launcher, and moving them to the port side; maximizing the loads; straining the barrels; using all the remaining Griffins and the Harpoon; maybe, after the first barrage, getting close enough to shore to use infantry weapons with grenade launchers. And the SEALs' light mortar that they left behind."

"Wonderfully not by the book," Movius said.

"Sir," Larman said, "we've been on our own since we left Little Creek. They pushed us out here like this and expect us to work miracles. The book my ass."

"As the CO, Chief," Rensselaer addressed Larman, "it would be inappropriate for me to agree with you, if, indeed, I were to disagree with you."

"Yes, sir."

"Carry on."

*

Every one of *Athena's* crew had clearly in mind the executions on *l'Étoile* and was fixed on striking back at ISIS, though even after a little time the horror was abstracted and petrified to a degree that it could be borne. But for the passengers and crew of *l'Étoile*, fear and despair were as live as an electrical current. Unless they slept—knowing to what they would awaken, it was hard to sleep—they experienced continual terror. They could feel it taking years off their lives just as surely as they could feel their rapid loss of weight occasioned not merely by having little food, but by an unceasing tension more taxing than physical exercise.

The only people on *Athena*, *l'Étoile*, and the bluff above the village who were not fairly clear about what was happening were Martin and Petra. They had heard gunshots and screams, but as far as they could be sure, other than the man whom Martin had killed no one had yet died, nor might anyone. Knowing that most piracies ended in ransomings, they tried to reason out the best course of action. Like Rensselaer, they had several uncertain choices, but unlike him they were even less guided by knowledge of the facts. That Martin was grounded in the scientific method and Petra an academic historian, they found, offered little to no advantage.

"If they discover us with this weapon they'll know that we—I—killed one of them. Surely they'll kill us then," Martin said. It was as if he were teaching a class at Paris Sorbonne, where he was an adjunct while working at Sanofi, the drug company, on preserving drugs in tropical climates.

"On the other hand," Petra said, "if we give up the weapons we'll be helpless, and if they intend to kill us, why not take some of them along?"

"And what if they don't intend to kill us?"

"I have to say," she said—her bravery was vital and vivid—"that I'm enraged about being a captive. Maybe it's worthwhile to die fighting, to show that we aren't slaves or sheep."

"That's spectacular, Petra, and it makes me love you all the more. You are magnificently barbaric. But don't we want to calculate our chances and live?"

"Martin, keep the gun."

Martin thought about this, and agreed. "You're right. Maybe we'll die, but to hell with them: we're not sheep. We'll take them with us."

*

Had they come to a logical, safe, quiet decision, it would anyway have been countermanded by what happened next. While they were finding their courage, one of the hijackers had been unable to suppress his lust for Sophie, who had been taken and raped by another. He wanted her. Her red hair and her youth worked upon him, especially since he was very ugly and his head was shaped somewhat like an eight, with a pronounced cerebral swelling; his beard was dirty; and he had never been wanted by any woman, even within the constraints of the system in which he believed, in which what the woman might want was entirely immaterial. He knew his position.

So when the rapes were ended by order of Hadawi, he wanted nonetheless to take Sophie for one more, and he tried. When the sentry at the door to the corridor that led to the deserted cabins stopped him, he crossed the room, with Sophie—numb and hardly alive—in tow, and approached another guard, who was standing at the door leading to the areas below decks: the kitchens and crew quarters.

"No," the guard said. "By order."

"Here," the man with the swollen skull and dirty beard told him, proffering a fistful of money. The guard took it, and Sophie was dragged down the stairs to the kitchens. She made no protest. It was as if she were in a dream.

Once in the central corridor, he sought a more private space, took her to the hallway where the crew's dressing rooms were, and threw her to the floor.

Hearing the first instance of someone intruding on their refuge, Martin cocked the M4 and released the bolt. "You know how to use that?" Petra asked, quite aware that these might be her last words.

"I was in the army."

"A cryptologist."

"They trained us on rifles like these."

Something took hold of Sophie, and, instinctually, she began to fight. Her attacker threw his weapon down and knelt beside her, grabbing her arms. She struggled and cried. The sound was unmistakable.

Martin pulled the door inward. He saw the ISIS terrorist kneeling in front of Sophie, pulling at her underwear. He saw the Kalashnikov beyond. And he pulled the trigger on the M4. A single round only. The bullet went straight into the heart, after which the eight-shaped head flipped backward and to the body's right, taking the would-be rapist and killer cleanly off Sophie and depositing him conveniently on his back. The only blood he would shed soaked his shirt and magazine carrier, and because the bullet had failed to exit, not a drop went to the floor.

Petra went to Sophie, enfolded her in her arms, and rushed her into the changing room. "Stay there," she said, and closed the door. "Lock it."

Martin removed the ammunition magazines from the vest-carrier and placed them in one of the empty changing rooms. He picked up the body under the arms. Petra lifted the feet. "No scuff marks," Martin said as he led, backward, to the kitchen. They moved as fast as they could.

As he stuffed the corpse into the incinerator opening, repeatedly casting glances down the wide hall, he said, "This is getting to be a habit." Being German, Petra took his statement literally.

"Do you mean putting bodies in an incinerator?" she asked.

"It's a joke."

"How can you joke at a time like this?"

"Because I'm not German."

"I don't understand."

"Of course you don't." After he pushed the green, mushroom-shaped button, the jets of flame began to roar.

They ran back. Martin retrieved the ammunition he had stored, they knocked at their door and told Sophie who they were, and, once in, locked it quickly after them. Martin washed the blood off the magazines and dried them. Picking up the Kalashnikov, he saw that the lever had been left on automatic and the rifle was loaded and cocked. "Very dangerous," he said, handing it to Petra. "Be careful. All you have to do is pull the trigger and it will shoot. If they come before we decide what to do, we'll have to fight. We've killed two of them already. No mercy for us."

He turned to Sophie. During the cruise, he and Petra had said that they would love to have a daughter like her. Just the sight of her reading in one of the lounges or on a deck chair filled them with the benevolence that an as-yet-childless couple feels when at the dawn of parenthood they encounter children. "What are they doing up there?" he asked.

Her eyes seemed glazed. Martin and Petra realized that she hadn't said anything in the minutes she'd been with them. "Sophie?" he asked. "Are you okay?" No answer. "We have to know, so we can decide what to do. It depends on what's going on above. Are they treating you—apart from this"—he gestured at the lower half of the door—"well?"

Emotionless, she said, "They cut off people's heads. They throw babies into the sea. They raped all of us."

After a long pause out of decency and shock, he had to continue. "How many are there?"

"I don't know. Twenty or thirty. They execute one of us every hour."

"What was all the firing about before?"

"There was an American ship. It couldn't do anything. Now it's gone."

"What can we do, Martin?" Petra asked.

"This is as good a hiding place as any. If they find us, we'll fight. Then we'll find another place deeper below decks. Or we can wait for night, go on deck, throw a life raft over the side, and jump into the sea." He turned to Sophie. "Can you swim?"

"Yes. They hit Madame Eugénie with a rifle, and she never got up. They just left her there, and then, after a while, they threw her from the ship. No one said anything, because we no longer speak."

*

When during the regular scan of the horizon with his binocular Holworthy saw a vague black stain in the otherwise intensely blue sky, a disturbance of the consistent azure not even as strong as a light, accidental, pencil stroke, he kept on returning to it until he could see that it was smoke carried on rising heat in wavering air. He alerted the others. Not long after, as if straight from a geography book, the mast was visible just over the horizon, and then, slowly, the all-white superstructure of *l'Étoile*. Holworthy informed *Athena*.

On the bridge of *l'Étoile*, Hadawi ordered the Danish captain to state the ship's maximum speed.

"Twenty-three knots."

"Possibly more?"

"Why?"

"You don't ask. You answer."

"Depending on wind, current, load, type of fuel, and disregard for the engines, maybe twenty-six."

"There," Hadawi said, pointing to the reddish cliffs ahead. "Ras Hagar. Twenty-six knots."

The captain said, "If you want to try to dock at the pier on the chart we have to begin deceleration now. It would be impossible at twenty-six knots."

"I said twenty-six knots."

The captain hesitated, but then called for maximum speed. Queried from the engine room, he confirmed that everything was out of his hands.

As the SEALs watched *l'Étoile* racing to the coast, Holworthy said, "She's going to run aground. Unless she turns now, she's. . . ."

Gaining speed, *l'Étoile* never veered from a direct perpendicular to the beach just north of the village. ISIS soldiers ran to the pier and shot into the air.

"Please allow me to warn the passengers and crew," the captain requested. "We're going to crash."

"No," Hadawi said. "If they're hurt too badly to move, we can shoot them."

The helmsman looked anxiously at the captain, and the captain said, "Steady on." Given the situation, he was rather nonchalant. When one is fairly certain one is going to die, nonchalance takes on a different character, and seems like something it would have been wise to embrace long before.

*

The SEALs were amazed to see the massive *l'Étoile* pick up speed and push on toward the beach. Though they didn't stand, they raised their heads higher than before, knowing that every eye in the village would be focused on the oncoming ship. As they watched it cleave the waves into white foam thrown from its bows, they forgot to breathe. Even when a ship or a ferry is so mishandled that it bumps its prow against a dock, it almost always does so slowly. At flank speed, *l'Étoile* had not the slightest hesitation.

First, she skidded over a sandbar a hundred feet out from the beach, slowing from twenty-six knots to perhaps twenty, and then her bows were raised as she hit the beach itself. The keel slowed and stopped her, but not until she was a third of the way out of the water. The sound of sand and scree scraping against her steel sides roared up the cliff face like thunder. Her seventy-two-foot mast bent forward and collapsed over the forecastle. The lifeboats broke from their davits, some falling into the sea near the stern and then pushed shoreward by the surf, some resting at crazy angles on deck; some even flew through the air and landed on the beach. A spark-filled cloud of black smoke was belched from the stack along with the sound of an explosion muffled by the spaces between the engine room and the outside air. As the propellers tried to turn, and did, a little bit, the SEALs heard the grinding of metal.

"The propellers can't disengage," Holworthy said. "Cut the goddamn engines." Flame issued from the stack, and didn't subside. Horns, klaxons, and fire alarms sounded. The fuel lines had ruptured, and diesel fuel was sprayed at high pressure in the engine spaces.

After a while, the first of the hostages appeared at an opening in the side, about twenty feet from the ground. The still-intact accommodation ladder was lowered by the crew, and it almost made it to the sand, its platform coming to rest five feet above. The hostages were herded down these stairs at speed. Though too many crowded the hanging structure, it held. When they got to the bottom, they were forced to jump. Though most were old, they were at gunpoint and they jumped. About one in three of these limped or were helped away, one in five or six fell to the ground, and everyone was hit by the rifle butts of angry, nervous guards who treated them, including children and aged ladies, like cattle.

As flames issued from the upper decks, the wind blew smoke against the ocher cliffs and into the otherwise blue sky. "Sir!" a SEAL yelled. "Starboard side, toward the stern."

Holworthy looked through the scope on his Barrett. Three figures were running on the promenade deck. Two were women, a blonde and a redhead, their hair ablaze in the sun. One of the women, and an obviously European, very tall man, had rifles. What to make of this?

As far astern as they could get, they went to the rail. A number of life rafts had been inflated automatically after they were thrown into the sea during the grounding. The three figures mounted the rails. "Cover them," Holworthy ordered.

The SEALs took aim. As they clicked their scopes into proper range it sounded briefly like a field of crickets. All of them saw two captors burst onto the promenade deck. "We fire, we give away our presence," someone said, compressing the words.

"Take aim," Holworthy said. "My decision." And a quick decision it had to be when the captors stopped and raised their weapons at Sophie, Petra, and Martin as they climbed the rails.

"Fire," Holworthy commanded. The shots were simultaneous. They dropped the two men and echoed off *l'Étoile*, over the village, and back up the cliff. "Shit," said Holworthy. "Cover."

Martin, Petra, and even Sophie were surprised by the shots. Before they leapt, they looked back and saw the two terrorists fall as if they had shot themselves. But with no time to wonder, they threw themselves out into the air forty feet above the sea. Holworthy was the only one who peeked out. He watched them hit, swim a fair distance, and climb onto a raft.

Everyone was on the port side of *l'Étoile*, marching the hostages and crew to the village. The raft was on the starboard side. As soon as what looked to Holworthy like a father, mother, and daughter were on it, they found paddles and worked furiously to gain and clear the small promontory, namesake of Ras Hagar, far behind which the SEALs had hidden the RHIB.

"Watch the village and the gunmen to see if they've spotted us," Holworthy commanded. "I'll cover the raft and the beach north of the ship."

As Holworthy kept his eye on the beach, he heard, "Commander, a bunch of guys are looking up here and pointing. We've been made."

"Not good," Holworthy said. "At least the family seems to be getting away." And they were. They rounded the promontory unnoticed. "Do we have—"

He was interrupted by the cry of, "Dust cloud in the wadi."

"So soon?" Holworthy said, thinking that the trucks were coming onto the plateau. "We missed them while we were watching down below."

The same kind of trucks that had moved the civilians didn't turn toward the SEAL position but sped from the wadi into the village, enveloped in white dust that mixed with smoke from the burning *l'Étoile*. They had brought a hundred or more men armed with infantry weapons, including dozens of RPGs projecting upward like bee stingers.

Dismounting, they were met by the soldiers already there and those from the ship. After a great commotion—chaos, really—the hostages were fully loaded onto the trucks. It took no more than fifteen minutes, and then all but nine of the vehicles—two of which were "technicals," one with an antiaircraft gun and the other with a large recoilless rifle mounted in back—drove into the southern wadi.

A hundred and fifty men were left. The SEALs saw that many were arguing. That is, until Hadawi appeared with his officers and the disputes

312

stopped. He deployed about a hundred to the artillery, the technicals, the huts, and the trenches. Standing among the roughly fifty left, he turned toward the cliff, and pointed.

"That's it," Holworthy said. "They know for sure. Drop him, get the others as well as you can. Careful shots. Save ammo."

The clicks returned, and the SEALs fired at the ranks around Hadawi. Holworthy aimed his .50-cal and hit the man next to him. Because ISIS uselessly returned fire they were exposed long enough so that the SEALs killed about ten. But Hadawi disappeared, and the forty men left ran toward the wadi. While they were yet exposed before they rounded the ridge on the wadi's north side, the SEALs dropped another four.

"How far out are the Claymores?" Holworthy asked when the firing stopped.

"As far as we could."

"How concealed?"

"As best we could. The ground's hard, and not much scrub."

He turned north and called his men in. "Redeploy and take ammo." The two SEALs who had been north moved south and west and took cover behind shallow folds in the terrain. Their line extended about fifty yards, matching the spread of the Claymores.

Holworthy called in to *Athena*. "E2C to base."

"Go," Velez responded.

"They made us. We can talk in the clear now. The hostages and civilians were moved inland on trucks. The village is occupied by a hundred men, and an additional thirty or more are on their way to assault us. They've manned the trenches, huts, and artillery. We'll try to keep them from the bluff, but we may call in targets up here if we're pressed. The village is a free-fire zone. Repeat. Free-fire zone. No civilians. The ship is grounded on the beach. A couple of hostages escaped on a raft, so watch that you don't plow into them. Where are you?"

"We see the ship," Velez said. "Keep your heads down. We're coming." Everyone on the bridge heard this. *Athena* was already at battle stations, in condition Zebra, all set to fight. A single battle taught more than a dozen drills, and this would be the fifth. No one was nervous.

"Helmsman increase your rudder to left full, steady on course two-twenty," Rensselaer ordered.

"Increase my rudder to left full, steady on course two-twenty, sir." *Athena* turned southward.

Then Rensselaer: "Rudder amidships."

"Rudder amidships, aye sir."

Athena straightened.

"My rudder is amidships, sir."

"Steady on course. Increase speed to thirty knots."

"Steady on course, thirty knots, aye sir."

After ten minutes that seemed like hours, Rensselaer commanded, "Be prepared to come about to course forty on my order."

"Aye sir."

Two miles south of the salt pond and only several hundred yards out, Rensselaer ordered, "Helmsman come about, right full rudder to the stops."

As *Athena* leaned over and skidded its stern, everyone aboard knew the battle was about to begin.

"My rudder is right full to the stops, sir."

"Steer course forty."

"Course forty, aye sir."

Athena straightened once again.

"My rudder is right full, coming to course forty, sir."

"Rudder amidships."

"Rudder amidships, aye sir."

In a few moments, *Athena* stopped even the slightest swing and the needle was right on 40 degrees. "Steady as you go."

"Steady on course, sir. Checking course."

"Increase speed to forty-five knots."

"Increase speed to forty-knots, aye sir."

Athena shot ahead, at first lifting slightly out of the water. Rensselaer went on the 1MC. "This is the captain. We're making our first pass. There are no hostages or civilians near the target. Free fire, but find your aim."

Everyone was surprised, but not that surprised, when over every loudspeaker and bullhorn on the ship, turned all the way up, they heard Wilson Pickett and "Land of 1000 Dances." All the fight in them was focused by the music, which banished fear entirely and choreographed every movement so that not a single one was wasted, out of place, or awkward. It took them from themselves as if they were Celts amid a hundred bagpipes. The gunners, grenadiers, and mortarman were amazed and delighted. As the rhythm and the beat syncopated perfectly with the waves, the wind, and the motion of the ship, their senses heightened and aligned. They were very far from home it is true, but suddenly everything that was home flooded into them. They knew who they were. They felt their history. And as *Athena* passed the salt pond, her crew was alight as perhaps they had never been in all their lives.

Not having seen *Athena*, the artillery crews on the beach were unaware of her until from beyond the salient south of the salt pond they heard the deep rumble of her engines and the unmistakable sound she made at high speed through wind and waves. They had been smoking, making tea over a little fire, and looking straight out to the horizon.

As soon as they understood that a ship was approaching from the south, they started to move and yell. The flimsy tripod dangling their kettle was knocked over into the sand. Both crews struggled to pivot their guns southward and, at the same time, depress the barrels to a flat, point-blank trajectory. The loaders and the men trying to turn the azimuth wheel were screaming at the men pivoting the guns, because as the guns turned it was hard to load and to change the azimuths. Getting ammunition into the breech and both adjustments were vital, and both groups understood this, but couldn't work together. The pivoters came out with less in the end because the loaders insisted that they stop so a shell could be rammed into each gun.

Athena appeared, and, as Rensselaer had planned, the sun was in the eyes of the artillerymen, who, before the ship moved into their firing window, had about fifteen seconds when all they could do was wait. Unfortunately for them, the first of *Athena*'s guns to find its own firing window was the MK-46 30mm mounted on the bow. In those fifteen seconds before the southernmost artillery piece could fire, the 30mm pumped out eleven airburst rounds, perfectly aimed and ranged in anticipation that the first task was to silence the artillery. Hundreds of shell fragments rained down upon the sand, the guns, their crews, and the ammunition. The northern gun crew, however, had largely escaped.

The fragmenting shells had made the beach look almost the way it might have looked in a rainstorm, except that the shrapnel was much heavier and forceful, and pushed eruptions of glittering sand toward the sun. The men were pressed down and killed silently, and the metallic sound of the rain of projectiles hitting the guns was heard all the way up the bluff. That is, until the MK-46 gunner aimed directly at the ammunition dump, which exploded with flame, sound, and overpressure that both swept through the village and knocked down the other gun crew. Bravely, because, like good soldiers throughout history, and perhaps being in a real battle had cleansed them for a moment of whatever it is that makes terrorists terrorists, they got back on their feet and managed to get off a round competently aimed at *Athena*. It struck the stern right below what would have been the RHIB's midships, and blew the steel apart above the waterline, severing a high-pressure hydraulic feed to the rudder and setting the hydraulic fluid on fire.

In the few minutes it took Pisecki to reach and choke off the line, pressurized fluid was sprayed into the wind, and it burned in a red-orange plume thirty feet high and almost as wide. The .50-calibers at the stern had to be abandoned. One of the sailors manning them was slightly wounded. The other gunners dragged him forward out of the fire as .50-caliber rounds began to detonate.

From shore, it seemed to anyone unfamiliar with the strength and redundancy of a warship that *Athena* was fatally afflicted. Her appearance was such that ISIS in the trenches, thinking the battle over, climbed out, raised their weapons, fired in the air, cheered, and danced. The gun crew that had scored the hit was stunned at its success, and froze in pride.

The next minute and a half, however, would prove this a mistake. *Athena* was not seriously damaged, not insofar as her capacity to fight, and as she passed broadside, all her guns except the two blown .50s in the stern opened up copiously and full-throated. The noise had to have been heard deep into the desert and out to sea. It was a shock not only to the enemy but to *Athena*'s crew itself and the SEALs on the bluff: ten .50-cal barrels firing theoretically at a collective pace of 10,000 rounds per minute, but actually at about half that, or 70 rounds per second; the MK-47 blasting out 50 rounds per minute; the miniguns sweeping the village with 100 rounds per second; the mortar lobbing shells that whooshed-in every ten seconds, and the grenade launchers in a single minute dropping 600 grenades over the trenches and huts.

Smokeless powder or not, Athena was shrouded in a white cloud. Hot brass, the shell casings, began to pile up on the deck. If they hit a gunner's neck, lodged between his shoe and his foot, or, worse, between his neck and his collar, he would be burned and carry the scars for the rest of his life. But he wouldn't stop firing. Even sailors not on deck had to plug their ears lest they lose their hearing, as Wilson Pickett, most uncharacteristically, sang in silence. All the firing from the port side actually pushed the ship slightly to starboard, not quite uniformly, forcing the helmsman to steer a minor vector to remain on course. It was impossible to hear the rain of enemy small-arms fire pinging against the ship, but it pockmarked everything. No one was hit, no bridge windows broken, but afterward they would count more than 150 fresh holes and dents.

When *Athena* came about, Rensselaer scanned the battlefield with his binocular. He couldn't see everything, but he did see scores of bodies, the two wrecked guns, and shattered and smoking buildings. No one was moving, because, not yet under assault, the SEALs on the bluff picked off anyone who did. The SEALs were dumbfounded at the result of *Athena's* single pass. None of them had ever witnessed naval gunfire support.

Rensselaer saw that, though draped with bodies, most of the technicals were intact, if windshieldless, and one had been blown on its side and was burning. He ordered *Athena* to slow to five knots, the gunners to remain at the ready, and Pisecki to report damage. Pisecki did. The rudder lines were redundant, and *Athena* would have no trouble steering. The port-side stern above the waterline was blown apart and blackened, and looked like hell. The ramp for recovering the RHIB was completely out of commission, so when the RHIB came back it would have to be towed. But *Athena* was still fighting. Rensselaer took the hand-held and called Holworthy. "What have you got?"

"That was unbelievable."

"One pass," Rensselaer said. "I thought it might take ten. Report."

"The village is done for. About twenty escaped to the wadi. Everyone else is dead or wounded, although if you land, you'd better pick your way carefully as you clear."

"What about you?"

"We have yet to see them. They may not know what happened to the village. They wouldn't, I expect, so they'll press the assault. We may need fire support. We left the mortar."

"I know: we used it," Rensselaer said. "We'll try to do better than a mortar. Give us the coordinates when you're ready. How're your batteries?"

"They're okay. We're going to have quite a fight up here, I think."

"We can dock and send up a shore party to hit them from behind."

"Probably not necessary, and the village hasn't been cleared. Why do you think they wanted to defend it so badly?"

"So we couldn't follow the hostages into the interior."

"You think they're dumb enough to think that ships go on land?"

"No, I think they're smart enough to know that we're crazy enough to get off the ship and chase them down."

"Are we?"

"You are, and I certainly am."

*

Rensselaer was still holding the hand-held when Holworthy's message came through not that long after they had last spoken. "They're here, at least fifty of them, coming from the southwest and the wadi. They're moving slowly, leapfrogging from cover to cover. They've actually got an antiaircraft gun—looks Russian—mounted on a technical. They passed the abandoned village, where it might have concealed itself, and are heading toward us. I guess they want a closer shot, which is stupid. Lots of RPGs, at least two heavy machine guns. There are a lot of Somalis, but foreigners, too. Chechens and Uzbek-looking. Some are Europeans for sure. It's like the United Nations of shitballs. I'd appreciate it, when the technical gets into firing position, if one of your Griffins pays it a visit. Over."

"Do you have a functioning designator?"

"Affirmative."

"We're ready. What are the coordinates?"

"Hold on. He's still moving. Slowing." Holworthy put down the radio, determined the coordinates, and came back on air. "Given the terrain and how we're being approached, the center of the box would be nine degrees, two minutes, twelve point two eight seconds north, and fifty degrees, thirty-five minutes, eleven point zero six seconds east. Send it our way if you can. Once I see it, it'll see the laser."

"Repeat the coordinates."

Holworthy did. "Confirm."

Rensselaer read back what he had. "Right."

"On your command," Rensselaer said.

"Yes, sir. And can you cover that area, upon request, within a radius of three hundred yards, with airbursts from the thirty mil?"

"I'll order a firing solution. Let us know when you want it."

"Soon. We are"—he watched as scores of men and the technical approached—"rather outnumbered and outgunned."

One of the SEALs asked, "What's gonna happen, Commander?"

"What they usually do with the technicals if they can't find sufficient cover is charge at full speed. That's what the gunner's shield and the steel plate over the windshield are for."

With not a shot yet fired, the approaching force stopped. An order was given. They dropped to the ground—even those on the flat with no cover—and began firing. The SEALs (who had been waiting for them to come even closer) fired back, with the Barrett .50, a light machine gun, and two M4s, all careful shots. Next to Holworthy as he fired were the radio and the designator. When he turned to them, first he called for the 30mm. The thump at 50 rounds a minute was heard seaward, and the shells exploded in the air above the assault force, which had no protection from the bursts above.

"Go lower," Holworthy spoke calmly into the radio.

"We can't, because of the trajectory," Rensselaer answered. "Is it having an effect?"

"Not as much as we need, but keep it up."

"Right."

"The technical is moving." The antiaircraft gun on the technical began to fire, throwing up huge sprays of rock and earth in front of the SEALs' positions, then adjusting so as to walk the rounds in to target. But the fire was inaccurate as the truck bounced over the rough ground.

Despite the noise of scores of rifles and the exploding 30mm shells above, the technical was close enough to the SEALs that they heard the gunner's shouted command—unintelligible to them—to stop so he could zero in on them.

"Give me the Griffin," Holworthy shouted above the firing, into the hand-held.

It is always surprising to see how fast a Griffin launches. Larger missiles seem almost to move in slow motion, initially so much so that one wonders for a fraction of a second if they will fall over, or if the huge cloud of orange flame that arises from the vertical launch module will spread over the whole ship. Not the Griffin, which leaves its launch box with the speed of an arrow leaving a bow, and then speeds up faster than a fighter jet making a pass over the ship, climbing almost beyond sight, and bears down with shocking rapidity upon its target.

The first of *Athena's* four remaining Griffins launched with its characteristic whoosh. Holworthy kept his laser on the technical, which was firing toward him and raising geysers of red earth and dust. He worried that the thick dust between him and the technical would diffuse the laser. But he knew that, given the speed of the Griffin, he would not have to worry long.

Almost like a bird of prey, the missile saw the laser dot on the technical and dived toward it with unhesitating, suicidal speed. If nothing else, it was decisive. And it proved accurate as well, homing exactly to the dot, which then disappeared as warhead, propellant, and the technical's anti-aircraft rounds and gasoline tank exploded, blowing the pickup truck, its heavy gun, the driver, and the gunner twenty feet into the air while simultaneously separating it into three or four big pieces and hundreds of little ones. For a moment, all firing stopped.

Then it resumed. The SEALs and the bombardment had already killed half the assault force, but those who remained pressed on. The closer they came, the easier they were to hit, but their high rate of fire had already wounded two of the SEALs, and they were closing rapidly on the SEAL farthest inland.

"I need another Griffin," Holworthy shouted into his hand-held. "Launch!"

Up it went, and he put a laser on the small group threatening his right flank. The missile exploded in their midst, flattening what was left of their bodies in a circle around the point of impact. "Another one," Holworthy said, and another was launched. It knocked out yet another group. Now the rest began to retreat, and the SEALs dropped them, firing carefully and accurately, even with the machine gun. As about ten survivors came together at the beginning of a little ravine, they took cover and began ineffective fire at the SEALs. This surviving force was shaken, and their marksmanship, perhaps never properly developed, was extremely poor.

Nevertheless, Holworthy, seeing that they had grouped together and that bullets were still whizzing by him, called for one more Griffin.

"The last one," Rensselaer said. "Are you sure?"

"Yeah. They're still shooting at us."

"Ready?"

Marchetti nodded.

"Launch."

The Griffin killed everyone remaining, after which, as the SEALs tended their wounded and took stock, they "heard" the after-battle silence that rings in the ears.

Its shore party fitted out and loaded up, *Athena* prepared to dock. As she made a careful approach, Rensselaer said to Movius, "What the hell year is this anyway? It might as well be nineteen forty-four, or the Battle of the Somme."

*

After *Athena* docked, the air was different. Where the sea mates with the land the scent is fecund and particular. Like the scent of a fresh-water lake in the last weeks of July, its signature is neither sweet nor foul but strong and unique: wet sand and rock, plants, seaweed baking in the sun.

The gunners stayed at their stations as the shore party prepared to clear the village, and the whaleboat went to retrieve the RHIB. Nothing stirred, but nothing ruled out hidden survivors, snipers, and traps. The SEALs descended the slope, their heavy packs weighing upon them. They could have come around by the wadi, but they didn't want to pass all the dead. The battlefield was still, and had any of the enemy had a chance to live, *Athena* lacked the resources to care for or imprison them. Although Rensselaer had spoken only to Holworthy about what might follow, somehow it was generally assumed that everything had to be husbanded for the campaign to find, fight for, free, and evacuate the hostages, and to keep them and *Athena*'s crew alive. To leave to die even those who moments before had been trying to kill them was a terrible thing, so the SEALs chose not to know of survivors. Because they saw no evidence of movement, they believed there weren't any. They hoped not.

Their first priority was the more than 150 passengers and crew of *l'Étoile*, especially the women and children now somewhere in the interior and at the mercy of medieval psychopaths so violent and depraved that the sheltered populations of the West could not for long hold in mind the depth of their conscienceless cruelty. The men on *Athena* had no such luxury.

When Rensselaer told Movius that Movius would stay behind and in command while Rensselaer led the shore party, Movius said, "You're also going to go inland, aren't you?"

"Yes. We've been long on the deep blue sea, and now it's time to chase down the Devil."

"With all due respect, it makes no sense. Holworthy and I should do that while you stay in command. It's your ship."

"You're an SWO and you haven't had infantry training or experience. You can't really tell Holworthy what to do, and I can. Besides, if it's my decision to do this, I have to go. Only those who volunteer. What would it look like if everyone gets killed and I'm on *Athena*, doing paperwork?"

"They'll think you're grandstanding."

"They can think whatever they want, and I may never know it anyway, in which case, tell Katy I love her."

"Now I know her first name. But that's all. How am I supposed to tell her."

"You'll see in my things. If I lay dying I'll be thinking of nothing else but her, because I have nothing else but her. Until then, I can only focus on the tasks at hand. That's what affords us the best chance of survival. No one should be a hundred percent a soldier—except in battle, when no one should not be."

A younger man might have decided more easily. War and everything like it appears differently with each advancing decade. The French word for retirement is *retraite*, retreat. The fight goes out of you as you age, and then the only means that allow you to continue until the light goes out, too, are the lessons of experience. But these are limited as to how far they can carry you, and Rensselaer had drawn them down so much in the recent battles that he wondered if they would still serve him.

*

The twelve infantry-trained volunteers waited in full battle dress on the quarterdeck. Outfitted the same way, Rensselaer came down from the bridge. "All volunteers, is that correct?" They answered that they were. "Checked your weapons?" They had. "Full kit, meaning extra magazines, two grenades, blood stop, bandages, morphine?"

"Yes sir."

"All right. You can shoot and you can fight. Don't forget that. You've had infantry tactics only in theory, but by the end of the day or sooner you'll get the hang or you may be dead. Don't shoot the SEALs; they're on our side . . . kinda. For all intents and purposes, you're now Marines. Follow me, spread out, move carefully from cover to cover, and use all your senses and then some."

He led. They moved one or two at a time, running from one defensible position to another, always backed up from behind. At first, in clearing the huts, every kicking-in of a door or pulling back a curtain was terrifying. But upon learning that most were deserted, attention turned to their squalor, the smell of open latrines, the relics and evidences of deep poverty. The SEALs cleared the western half of the settlement while the shore party took the eastern. Both worked northward. Not a shot had been fired until, halfway in, machine-gun and RPG fire erupted from the large building that was evidently the enemy HQ, and which straddled the two sectors.

They were all pinned down at once. Rensselaer used the radio to call Holworthy. "Have you seen the back of the building?" he asked.

"We have. No windows or firing ports, just a blank wall."

"Clear approach?"

"As far as I can tell. I'll take care of it. We didn't use the Claymores."

Heavy-machine-gun fire came from the sandbagged HQ, cutting channels in mud-brick walls and paralyzing the shore party. But two of Holworthy's men, covered by the rest, walked undetected to the back wall. One cupped his hands and gave the other a leg up so he could pull himself onto the roof. Once this was done, the Claymore they had brought was passed up and put face down on the portion of the roof above the firing ports. As the wire was run back and down, an RPG was fired from inside and collapsed a wall near where Rensselaer's sailors were crouching.

The SEAL on the roof, one of those who had been slightly wounded, lowered himself, and he and the other one ran the wire to Holworthy. Attaching the wire to the detonator, Holworthy said, "One good turn deserves another," turned the handle, and pushed it down. The roof blew in and the rear wall and a side wall collapsed outward. Into a cloud of dust that blocked any view of what was left inside, the SEALs shot two grenades and two blasts of automatic-weapon fire, then waited in silence until the dust sank or blew away. No one inside was still alive. In fact, only some body parts—a leg with the boot still attached, a helmet still holding a head, but no one wanted to check—were visible. The roof had buried most of everything and the grenades had done the rest.

SEALs and shore party resumed their progress through the village. It was so hot that all their uniforms were soaking wet and sweat ran down their faces. Despite the unlikely chance that anyone might still be in hiding after the surprise from the HQ, every breach was as tense and almost as draining as if someone within would detonate a suicide belt and blow everyone to hell, because at each house this was still possible.

At the very last hut, Rensselaer kicked in the door. Inside, it was deserted but for things: an empty sardine can hosting a crowd of flies, a wooden bed frame without even the webbing that may have supported a mattress of some sort, a wicker broom from which half the bristles had broken off probably long before. "At least we didn't find a doll," Rensselaer said.

"What do you mean?" Pisecki asked, but then caught himself. "Oh, kids."

The village was clear, but sentries were posted on the cliff tops, and gunners on *Athena* manned their stations and kept watch on all sides. Now and then casting a glance at the darkened ruins of the village, the crew worked through the night to prepare the little expeditionary force. Only by first light would they part with it and take *Athena* to safety offshore.

*

That night, Rensselaer dreamt that he was a matador, though not dressed in a matador's ancient and, to an American, incomprehensible costume of tights, pompoms, and silly hat. He had no costume, or, if he did, he was unaware of it, as the dream played out solely from the matador's eyes. He saw the bull not as spectators do from a safe distance but from a few feet away.

The bull's nostrils were wide and flaring, and because of visible moisture, grayer than his black nose. Condensed vapor came from them when the bull snorted. His eyes were active, changing, calculating, burning with anger. Head and horns were bent, the muscles of the neck unyielding. It was clear that the bull would do nothing but fight to the end. The distance between the horns was narrower than the width of a man's trunk.

Rensselaer knew the bull would charge, and that he himself wouldn't run. The bull hurtled forward. Rensselaer, too old, too stiff, and no longer light enough for such acrobatics, was hardly athletic enough to grasp the horns and, like Minoan youth, vault over the animal's back. He took the blow. The horns pierced his abdomen on each side and he was lifted into the air as if he weighed no more than a sheet of paper. Powerless and in exquisite pain, he watched the world blur around him, and felt the velocity of the bull as it approached the wooden wall of the arena. Rensselaer's blood, driven by the wind, blinded and choked him.

Gasping and covered in sweat, he awoke. After switching on his desk lamp he stared at his cabin door until his pulse and breathing returned to normal. In the shadow of the lamp, the cabin door was as black as a bull.

The Sixth Battle: Somalian Plateau

It took a lot of rushed planning to prepare the expedition, as well as all the shop spaces on the ship and the many skills of its chiefs, ratings, and officers. They didn't know what they would face in the interior, how long they would remain, and if indeed they could track the hostages. Just about everything was as uncertain as it had been since the beginning.

Surveying the preparations from the open bridge, Movius spoke his piece to Rensselaer. "It's my responsibility as your XO to remind you that hostage rescue is notoriously difficult for many reasons, including that the first rule of hostage-taking is to move them around. We've already gone way out on a limb. If we fail?"

"We fail. It's like what Casals said at ninety when he married a woman of twenty: 'If she dies, she dies.' No matter how well it goes we're bound to lose some and maybe all of the hostages. No matter how well we fight we're bound to lose some of us. But it can be done. Remember when Boko Haram took several hundred schoolgirls and all we managed was a pathetic tweet campaign, 'Bring back our girls'? What happened? Nothing. But we could have done it."

"They disappeared deep in the forest."

"We had a UAV base within range and even if we hadn't we could have sent a Global Hawk, a Triton, or a U-2, not to mention tasking a satellite. Meanwhile, you set up a base and immediately bring in special operators: twenty, fifty, a hundred, whatever it takes. They're always ready. It's what they do.

"The reconnaissance flights fly so high no one below can hear or see them. They scan vast areas optically and with infrared. Hundreds of people moving across the terrain can be picked up optically. In jungle cover, infrared will sense their cooking fires: they're not carrying MREs or Power Bars, but rice and flour. They have to cook. Even the smoke can be seen. We knew where they started, their maximum speed, how much time had elapsed, and the direction in which they headed. It wouldn't have been that difficult to track them.

"You find them, watch them, and extrapolate their course. The planes take off. At the right place the advanced teams make a HALO jump and steer to assembly points. They surround the target and use speed, flash-bangs, sniper takedowns. And then the rest of the force in helos goes in to secure the hostages.

"The helos and V-22s come to a landing zone and take everyone home. We could have done it. We chose not to. We could have protected the Vietnamese boat people from the Thai pirates. We chose not to.

"Here"—he gestured toward the land—"we don't need to parachute in. We'll have vehicles, and we have a ship as a base. The problem is numbers. I'd like to have two platoons or a company, but we have what we have."

Five diesel trucks were available for use. Others had either been hit too badly, were in poor shape mechanically, or were gasoline-powered. The village's gasoline storage tanks had been blown up in the assault, and the diesel tanks punctured. Diesel trucks could run on *Athena*'s turbine fuel, which would be taken from *Athena* and carried in plastic jerry cans, of which the village had a seemingly unending supply. Water and fuel would last for a combat radius of three hundred miles and five days out.

Pisecki and Di Loreto supervised cutting the antiaircraft gun from one of the technicals. It and the heavy recoilless rifle were not the kind of weapons they needed, and the guns were spiked so ISIS could never use them again. Replacing them on the technicals were the two miniguns from the bridge wings, and the two grenade launchers. The ammunition and grenades for them, as well as ammunition for infantry weapons, were spread evenly among the trucks, along with food, water, medical supplies, cold-weather gear, and whatever else they thought they might need. They didn't put all of one thing on any one truck, lest it be hit.

During the skirmish on the cliff top, one of the SEALs had been too badly wounded to go. He wanted to, and had helped clear the village, but had then collapsed. He almost cried when left behind. So they would have one SEAL per truck, plus Rensselaer, who despite his age still counted as a SEAL. The twelve SEAL-trained crew brought the complement up to eighteen. Pisecki—who looked more like a SEAL than Holworthy, in that Holworthy was thin and Pisecki was more or less a cage fighter—made nineteen, and they took the two sailors who manned the grenade launchers as well.

These twenty-one men rode four per truck, with Rensselaer's truck carrying five, including Holworthy accompanying him in front. Di Loreto was left on the ship, but two of the twelve were mechanics under Pisecki, and they took tools, tires they found in the village, and patching kits improvised from *Athena*'s stores. One of the SEALs was trained as a corpsman. One of the twelve SEAL-trained crew was the Stalker UAV operator. They jammed a Stalker's bulky cases into the trucks, sacrificing days of supplies on the theory that the UAV's twenty-five-mile sacrificial range would save them more than it would make them do without if they could locate their target in such a way that they could cut across the track they were about to follow and thereby reduce the distance traveled, or even arrive at the apparent destination of their prey before it did. Also, although rain was unlikely, high winds might wipe away the hostage convoy's tracks over certain terrain, leaving *Athena*'s expeditionary force with no way of following except to observe from the air.

One of the SEALs asked Rensselaer, "Sir, how are we going to take back a hundred and fifty people in five trucks?"

"They have twenty trucks or more. We have fuel enough for ours. We can consolidate what they have left in their tanks. We have siphons. We can jettison supplies. We'll figure it out."

"What if they split up?"

"Either we split up as well, or we deal with them in sequence."

"I see. What if their track disappears?"

"The Stalker. And if we get nothing from it, we go blindly where we guess they might have gone—until we have to turn around. No one says we can't fail."

*

Having showered and eaten breakfast on *Athena*, their uniforms newly washed, the trucks fully loaded, and the air relatively cool, they set out, putting distance between them and the ship just as surely as it moved offshore. They caught a last glance of her as they climbed the south wadi, following the deep and unmistakable tracks of the score or so of trucks they were chasing.

After a few hours of bouncing about and suffering surprising jolts, they were also nauseated by the trucks' rolling and swaying in the sand in a way much different from the way that *Athena* moved through the sea. Although everyone fought hard not to show it, they were land sick as well as literally dripping wet in the 110-degree heat. Traveling at about the same speed and in the same direction as the breeze, they had little benefit from it. The floors of the vehicles were slippery with sweat. It stung their eyes and left white salt stains on their uniform shirts. When there was a gust of wind, it lifted sand and dust of various colors that stuck to their clothing, hair, and faces. Within a few hours they were bizarrely colored ochre, gold, and brown, except for the areas shrouded by their driving goggles, which in contrast made them look like they had egg whites for eyes.

Despite constantly spitting out sand and grit, they were parsimonious with their water, and yet careful not to drink too little. For 360 degrees 'round all they saw was sand; scrub; flat-topped, low trees in clumps here and there; and cloudless sky. They didn't realize it, for this was known only to Rensselaer, but without authorization they had invaded a country of sorts, even if it was a failed state in which U.S. forces were operating elsewhere. No one except those left on *Athena* knew they were there, and no one would—or could—bail them out. They had no idea how many men they would have to fight if they found what they were seeking, on what terrain, against which weaponry, in what conditions, or for how long.

Via GPS they did know exactly where they were, but only in terms of coordinates. The map they had was a nautical chart at a scale of 1:250,000, showing merely forty miles inland and that in sparse detail. Beyond the forty-mile strip, they might as well have been on the moon. Their only reassurance came from the belief that they were doing what was right; their only comfort from knowing how well armed and prepared they were; and their only pleasure from being soldiers completely on their own in a place forgotten by the world.

*

The going was slow because sometimes they crossed deep sand into which the tracks they followed seemed to disappear, but then after careful observation they would pick them up again. In midafternoon they came to a crossroads. They stopped, gave the trucks a rest, drank some water, and gathered around the spot where two rather well worn roads intersected at right angles.

"How do we know that they didn't go left or right?" a sailor asked.

"You tell me," Holworthy said.

"I don't know, sir."

"Because there are no curved tracks. A truck can't make a perfect ninety unless it's on a turntable. They went straight. But they stopped."

"How do we know that?"

"Look at that shit over there."

The sailor looked toward the horizon, where Holworthy had pointed. "Sir?"

"Look lower."

"What is that?"

"That, sailor, is exactly what I said it was."

"Shit?"

"Right. And because you win first prize, you get to go over there, count it, and tell me how dry it is."

"How dry it is? How will I know?"

"Figure it out," Holworthy said. "Observe, orient, decide, act."

"Sir, with all due respect, is counting shit relevant to my rating?"

"With all due respect, if you don't do it, it will be relevant to your rating for the rest of your enlistment."

As the sailor left, he said, "Join the Navy, see the world, and count Somali turds." But when he returned they knew by his unorthodox report that the convoy had passed less than a day before. In other words, *Athena*-force was going faster and catching up. Five or ten more miles in, they saw why. All along the track they had observed small, rusty petrol cans of the size that in the U.S. would hold paint thinner. Even in these vast distances the habit of gas by the liter hadn't been broken. Some had been discarded long ago, some of the new ones perhaps by the hostage convoy. But there were also freshly oil-soaked patches and oil-covered, discarded engine parts, showing that at least two ISIS trucks had had mechanical trouble. As they were not left behind, they had been repaired, which obviously had taken time. The afflicted vehicles had no doubt also slowed the convoy even before they broke down, and perhaps they were slowing it still.

One thing they were able to conclude was that the hostages were no longer being executed every hour. Had that been so, they would already have come upon a dozen bodies. This was encouraging, until at around six they saw ahead what they thought was a rock pile or a low tree. Heading west-southwest, they had the sun in their eyes. But as they came very close they realized that they had come upon a dozen bodies on the side of the track, some piled, most headless. No effort had been made to spare women or children.

This was devastating, and it only amplified what they had learned Ras Hagar when the whaleboat went to retrieve the RHIB, and the sailors had seen a raft bobbing a mile out. They took the RHIB and brought Martin, Petra, and Sophie aboard. The debriefing had been particularly difficult, and in *Athena*'s sick bay there was nothing other than antibiotics with which to deal with Sophie's rape. Neither could they could test for sexually transmitted diseases or pregnancy. She would have to wait. But, still, she was in a far better position than the rest of the passengers and crew of *l'Étoile*. Martin, Petra, and Sophie were treated as if they were a family, and, indeed, Sophie clung to Petra like a small child.

When Rensselaer saw that two of the bodies in the pile were those of adolescent girls, he was as puzzled as he was horrified, for he assumed that they would have been kept for other purposes. Perhaps they had tried to escape. It was impossible to tell, and there was no use speculating. Nor was there time to bury the bodies, which were left behind. Without the right tools for such hard ground, it would have taken too long even for twenty men.

*

They moved along steadily, following the track of their prey. It was easier for them, in that the captors had had to find a path amid the rocks, bushes, and scrub, and all the pursuers had to do was hold to it. Now and then, Rensselaer or Holworthy would call a stop to examine things that had been discarded: food wrappers, cigarette boxes. The cellophane wrappings of German cookies told him that they were not tracking the wrong vehicles.

If not as difficult a drive as that of the terrorists, it was hard to bear in the great heat and glaring sun. Slowly moving, winding about umbrella-shaped trees and clumps of bushes that all seemed the same, put Rensselaer and the driver who had relieved Holworthy (who was trying to sleep in back) in a semi-hypnotic state. To break it, he asked the sailor, whom he hardly knew, where he was from.

"Katy, Texas, sir."

"That's right. I remember from your record. It's a very nice name. I've always loved it. It's feminine, cheerful, and strong. The kind of woman in whom you know you'll never lose interest."

"We like it, too, but it's not named after a woman but the initials of the railroad or something."

"Still, every time you say it. . . ."

"You get used to it. Other people like it a lot, too. It's different from what they think—although I let'em think what they want. It's not a little town in the middle of rangeland, with cowboys and cattle."

"No?"

"No. It's kind of like a suburb of Houston. One side of it is still farm-land, but the other has a billion houses, malls, you know."

"So, you don't have a horse and a lever-action Henry?"

"No, sir. Never been on a horse, and I've got a Winchester Seventy. We've got a water park, you know. That's fun. It was the old carrier docked in Corpus Christi that got me interested in the Navy. Because it's in the middle of the country, people think Texas is just a lotta land, but we have a big seacoast. I wanted to be on the water." He looked out at the desert ahead. "Ha!"

*

Whether the natural effect of the chase, their eyes growing more expert in following the track, the driving that became a rhythmic process of avoiding obstacles, or their adaptation to the unrelieved terrain, they moved faster and faster until they were racing, until their speed itself built in them a greater and greater desire to catch ISIS, at whom their anger mounted as if with the heat. Now all they wanted was to close with and fight Hadawi and his little army.

Desert dotted with flat-top trees and scrub eventually gave way to reddish and black sand; ridges impassable to vehicles other than through geologically ancient channels worn in the rock; and featureless flats along which they sped, their eyes fixed on a horizon wavy with heat. Increased speed gave away the gradual ascent of which they had been oblivious when moving more slowly. Now they could feel it, and before the pursuit was over they would rise more than three thousand feet above the sea level to which they were accustomed. There, unlike on the ocean, the air was dry, slightly cooler in the day, and truly cold at night.

Now that they were moving faster, so as not to choke on the thick clouds of dust raised by vehicles in line, they spread out in a shallow V, like a cavalry charge. There was something really magical about forging ahead so aggressively, and though no one brought it up they wondered if their resolution would falter if they were just to stop. Now, however, because of their strange, velocity-induced confidence, they had no fear whatsoever.

But at the opening of a huge defile of black cliffs through which wound a sandy roadway in some places only twenty feet wide, they halted. It was a perfect place for an ambush, and if Hadawi had any sense at all he wouldn't have ruled out being followed. So Rensselaer had his force pull back far enough from the cliffs to be out of RPG and machine-gun ranges, and there, waiting until dark, they slept in the heat, or tried to, leaving only one sentry to keep an eye on what was ahead.

At dusk, they roused themselves, ate, and drank. Then they drove closer, and sent two patrols of five men apiece up onto the plateau, one on each side of the cut. By the time the patrols found themselves on top of the escarpment, the stars had come out and the wind had come up. They had to move cautiously, as the ground was riven with cuts and folds where an enemy could hide. The patrols picked their ways across the rock for half a mile, rising and falling almost as if on petrified waves, and they found nothing.

Leading the western patrol, Holworthy radioed back that it was okay to come through. They would stay on the heights until the convoy cleared the defile on the north side, in case the enemy had taken position below, where even with night vision the men up top could not see clearly. In that case, both combatants would be deadlocked in the narrow space until the two patrols would arrive above to catch the enemy in a triple crossfire.

But the defile was empty and the scouts descended the face of the escarpment. Once they had rejoined the convoy, it set off again, slowly, but not that slowly, as the tire tracks they followed were sharply illuminated and cast in shadow by the trucks' low beams.

*

They halted the next morning because they felt that the enemy was near, and after carefully calculating times, speeds, and distances, they guessed that it had to be so. They secured their position behind a natural barrier of boulders and trees, and put together and then launched the Stalker. At first they flew it to the rear, where it spiraled and spiraled into the clear sky until it reached its maximum altitude of twelve thousand feet. The operator announced this to Rensselaer. "We're at the max, sir."

"Can you push it higher?"

"Not really. It strains, makes more noise, and uses more fuel beyond that altitude."

"Is that maximum altitude with a full load of fuel and standard payload?"

"It is."

"In the climb, we've reduced fuel weight, right?"

"Right."

"We have only the imaging payload."

"That's correct."

"And we've got desert thermals of upwelling air, right?"

"Yeah, we do."

"Keep spiraling, go higher."

"Aye sir."

The Stalker climbed to fifteen thousand feet, where it was impossible to see from the ground, and, depending upon updrafts and downdrafts—in the morning it was riding on updrafts—impossible to hear.

Rensselaer, Holworthy, and the operator concentrated upon the display. The camera panned around, covering from its altitude a much larger space than necessary, so the magnification was increased to narrow the area of investigation, enabling them to distinguish features on the ground with far better resolution. Ten minutes passed.

"There," the operator said. He zoomed-in at a mass north and ahead of the Stalker. They could see clearly that it was a collection of low build-ings and a fortress of some sort (almost undoubtedly a relic of the long Italian dominion) on a rise overlooking the desert around it.

"How many trucks do we count?" Rensselaer asked.

They all counted, and although Holworthy said twenty-seven, the oper-ator and Rensselaer saw twenty-six. "Close enough," Rensselaer declared. "Save as many images as you can. Don't move the Stalker too close. And note the coordinates."

"They're stamped on the images, sir."

"Right."

When they had saved in the operator's laptop the detailed and comprehensive pictures of the objective, they brought the Stalker back first in a long, power-assisted glide, and then, with the engine out of fuel, in a silent descent from ten thousand feet. Before it bumped to a landing, they had their intelligence. The fortress was seventeen miles ahead. Four technicals were arrayed to cover the four quarters of approach. No trenching. Two heavy machine guns were mounted on the parapet of the fortress's decaying tower. The two largest buildings had two guards stationed in front of each one. The other structures had none, and armed men moved freely about. No pickets were outside the area or on the track that led to it. And no civilians appeared in any image.

Rensselaer and Holworthy looked at one another. "It's gonna be a problem," Holworthy said. "It wouldn't be easy even if there were no hostages, even if our whole complement were SEALs or Delta."

Rensselaer nodded. "True, but I'd be willing to bet—we have no choice but to bet—that no guards are permanently stationed inside those two buildings. That means, if we can take out the four in front, we've got the hostages behind cover, and then we can hit everyone else hard."

"I worry about the technicals, and the guns in the tower," Holworthy told him.

"That you deal with in the same way you fight someone who's coming after you with a stick. You get close in. It'll take covert movement and good timing."

"No kidding," Holworthy said, more apprehensively than when, charging across the desert, he had been high on forward motion, the steady pace, and the light flooding into his eyes.

Rensselaer replied, "We've got until nightfall to get it locked down."

*

First they studied the aerial shots of the village, and, with no printouts possible, converted them to a schematic map drawn on a 2x2 square of canvas tarpaulin. Using elevation readings from the imagery, they lined-in ten-foot contours that showed the settlement rising only twenty feet or so above the plain after a climb of little less than a mile on an almost negligible slope of half a degree. Nonetheless, the fortress tower's height of approximately thirty feet would give sentries posted there unobstructed views across the desert. The fortress was the easternmost building. To its west were the two large structures—one perhaps a mosque, the other indeterminate—in which the hostages seemed to be held. Separating fourteen smaller houses from the larger structures, the desert track ran between them before looping around to join the main route westward. A technical was stationed east of the fortress, one just south of the village along the road, one north along the loop, and one west on the road as it led out. The photograph showed no one manning the large guns in the truck beds, as the gunners and drivers had undoubtedly taken refuge in the cabs' shade. Trucks purely for transport were scattered everywhere, offering so much cover that the tiny village mimicked a dense urban environment.

Rensselaer, Holworthy, and Pisecki—the three in command—and O'Connor and the three noncom SEALs, gathered around the map, which was held with stones against a strong afternoon wind blessedly not strong enough to blow sand. Little is as troublesome as sand in the eyes, throat, ears, nostrils, gun barrels, machinery, engines, food, and everywhere else.

They had drafted two copies of the map so they could draw on the first to make the plan of assault and move to the fresh sheet as it was refined, changing or abandoning lines, arrows, and time notations as necessary. One of the SEAL noncoms protested. "This map," he said, "differs from the other one. The fortress is too far to the right."

They looked at him in disbelief until Pisecki broke the news. "You're right. Ya see, we don't have a copy machine. I would've taken it to Kinko's, but the nearest one is seven thousand miles away. It's probably right next to a Starbucks. Would you like me to bring you a triple mocha, nonfat, iced latte, or an iced grande with nutmeg shavings and chocolate shit?"

The noncom SEAL replied, "Oh."

Then they got back to business. In the last iteration, the complicated and demanding assault plan was fixed, calling not merely for performance but luck. The SEALs' ear-budded communication equipment had been destroyed as it, like the sat-phones, had been trickle charging in COMMS. The only way to know which phase to activate in the assault would be by precisely following the clock, which meant that each task, such as taking out the technicals, the sentries, and the machine guns in the tower, had to be successfully completed within the time allotted, something that demanded a perfection of timing that seldom was achieved.

Much more likely was that, as Holworthy put it, when gunfire awakened the enemy force after a stealth takedown had failed, everything would get totally fucked-up. After all, the SEALs, the only ones trained to kill stealthily, and none of them necessarily a master of the technique, had to eliminate eight men manning the technicals, who would no doubt be inside their truck cabs even if, as hoped, they were asleep; four sentries guarding the two hostage cantonments; and the machine-gunners on the tower. Almost certainly, they would not succeed in doing so silently, in which case they would have to fight fifty men or more, and the plan would be useless save for fallback general orders tailored to broad contingencies.

The initial plan, studied, recited, and repeated for hours by everyone across all ranks, would have been of great benefit to Hadawi had he labored to imagine himself in Rensselaer's position and map out what Rensselaer might do. But Hadawi was more a political than a tactical commander, and he operated less according to foresight and calculation than by drawing upon emotion, commitment, daring, and faith that everything was so much in the hands of God that his impulses of the moment would carry him through. He and those like him truly believed— at the very root of their being—that too much thinking and planning demonstrated a lack of faith. For them, a signal virtue was the ability to jump into the darkness, trusting in Allah. Impetuousness was therefore a sign of holiness, and it revealed to others and themselves the absolute reliance upon the divine to which saints and martyrs are commanded. Thus, other than posting the technicals, the four sentries, and the machine-gunners in the tower, he had given no orders and made neither plans nor preparations to counter an assault.

Although Rensselaer could not know this, and certainly would not rely on it, at a gut level he sensed it, and thought it might be a salient factor of battle that would allow him to confound the odds. One way or another, he had no choice and was compelled to try. To stretch the point, it may be said that he and Hadawi were somewhat the same in that he was relying upon God to have caused Hadawi to rely upon God even more so. And such a thing was not unusual in war, for prior to battle the outcome is known and decided only in heaven. Some may scoff at this, but no doubt only because they have neither waited for a battle's beginning nor survived its end.

As *Athena*-force discussed and assimilated their plan, in the village three men, one of whom was some sort of commander, walked past the guards and entered the easternmost hostage building. In the dim light, they shone flashlights at the women, who had been moved against the east wall. The women raised their hands to shield their eyes from the light, partially covering their faces. It didn't matter. The commander picked out three of them by moving the beam of his light up and down their bodies.

As they were being taken out, two men—a husband, and a boyfriend—lunged from where the men had been herded, and were shot. When they fell, they were dispatched with shots to the head.

Numb with terror, the three women were walked across the compound. It was very cold. Among them was one of the French schoolgirls. She hadn't had time to put on her shoes and was struck by how cold the sand was beneath her bare feet.

*

Although the attack would commence at 0400, *Athena*-force spent the evening positioning, checking their weapons, going over the timing, and then trying to get some sleep. At 0130 they synchronized watches, after which Rensselaer briefly addressed them.

"This may be the most difficult and perhaps for some the last thing you will ever do. You're doing it for others, for principle, for decency, and, in essence, out of love. Our actions and imperfections will always be with us. It's impossible to kill a man, no matter how evil he may be, without a perpetual debit to one's own conscience and a trespass against God. Anyone who tells you otherwise is blind to himself and the world. But we take on such a burden so that those at home need never bear it, nor even understand that for the sake of the innocent we protect, we accept the stain.

"If you have doubts, think of what they did on *l'Étoile*. Whether or not we're remembered with respect or at all, whether in the next hours you live or die, know this: even if known but to God, to do what is right will be permanently engraved on the walls of time. I'm at a loss to explain it, but I think that today of all days, up in this high desert, we bear witness to the tens of thousands of American sailors forever at the bottom of the sea. May they smile upon us. Good luck, carry out your orders, have no fear, and fight like hell."

*

At first the problem had seemed insoluble. The two trucks that Pisecki and his men had fitted with miniguns and grenade launchers had to enter the compound immediately after the sentries and the technicals had been neutralized. Then, in coordination with the assault, they would drive between the cluster of houses where the troops were bedded and the larger buildings where the hostages were kept, delivering a fierce broadside from the east, while *Athena*'s naval infantry (as Rensselaer called them rather than Marines, which seemed less exact) enfiladed from north and south.

If, however, *Athena*'s weapons trucks would be brought close enough to open fire when needed, the sound of their approach risked alerting Hadawi before actions dependent upon stealth had begun. If they were not close enough, it would take minutes to arrive, during which time the alerted enemy could form into defensive positions even were these slapdash and unplanned. Although ideally the sentries and the technicals would be eliminated in silence, if this proved impossible the plan of attack switched to accommodate early discovery, in which case as well the gun trucks would have to be close.

With camouflage netting, no moon, and great care, the trucks might remain unnoticed stationed only a quarter mile south. Through pitch darkness and over churned sand at maximum speed of forty mph it would take approximately twenty-five seconds to reach the village. Assuming the trucks could remain undetected at such a distance, this was workable. But how could they get so close without being heard?

The three purely transport trucks stayed five miles from target. Then, one at a time, the gun trucks moved up at idling speed in first gear so they wouldn't stall out and traction was assured. When they had reached the two-mile distance from target, they went ahead in the same fashion after Rensselaer had gone to the quarter-mile point to monitor the wind.

Cold, dense, night air flowed toward the coast, in this case crossing the village from about 350° North to 170° South. But sometimes, as if catching its breath, it ceased. So Rensselaer sat on the ground, starlight giving away the black contours of the buildings only a little north of him, and waited for a gust in the right direction. Then he would stand to make sure that he was not in thrall to some odd cross-current on the ground. Then it was back down, so as not to give himself away by blocking the stars on the horizon, and, with a simple "Go," on his hand-held, he would signal the movement of one gun truck at a time in first and with half a dozen men pushing it so if it hit uneven ground it wouldn't have to strain and make a louder sound.

In this way, when there was wind to carry south the little noise they made, the gun trucks were brought up close. Chillingly, the engines of both trucks shut down with a backfire that made everyone cringe. But the trucks were not detected, and were positioned facing the target, ten yards apart so as not to combine their masses and block the starlight, the only way anything could be seen on such a dark night.

Before they had set out—in fact, many times that day—the three commanders had said to the men, "For God's sake, whatever you do, don't turn on the lights or honk the goddamned horns." And they had prayed that when the engines shut down there would be no backfire, as, in fact, there was.

Waiting for the rest of the assault force to catch up, Rensselaer whispered to Holworthy, "Apparently Hadawi doesn't have a searchlight. There's no way something on these trucks wouldn't glint."

"Maybe he does."

"He hasn't used it."

"Maybe that's the point, and he's smarter than we think, and he'll turn it on intermittently and not according to a schedule."

Rensselaer was worried. In daylight during the first of several inspections he had required that all wristwatches, wedding rings, other jewelry, and anything that might glint be moved to pockets and wrapped so as not to clink. They would have enough trouble keeping their weapons and ordnance silent. "What the hell, sir," a sailor had protested. "I swore to my wife not to take off my ring. If I take mine off that means she can take hers off, and who knows what she'll do, sir."

"She won't know."

"Yes she will, sir. You don't know her."

"Still," Rensselaer told him, "wouldn't you prefer that your wife screw every acrobat in the circus than that you come home dead?"

"No sir."

"But I would."

"Sir, you aren't married."

"I'm talking about *your* wife. Your wedding ring could get us all killed. Besides, they closed down the circus, so don't sweat it."

"Yeah," said someone. "And that means that all those acrobats have nothing to do, and you know how dangerous that can be."

"Enough," Rensselaer said. "I'm sorry I brought it up. No one should worry about unemployed acrobats. You all know what you have to do."

As they waited near the gun trucks and focused on the village for signs of movement, the rest of the force approached as quietly as they could, separated, like the trucks, so as not to block too wide a field of stars.

*

One man stayed with the transports, sitting in a truck carrying mainly ammunition and medical supplies. With the onset of firing, which would be audible even farther south than he was, he would race to a predetermined point and await orders. With his truck partially or fully unloaded, if he and two others were no longer needed for fighting they would go back to fetch the other trucks.

Fully assembled, they were twenty-one, as follows: a driver, a gunner, and a grenadier in each gun truck; six SEALs, including Rensselaer and Holworthy, and the rest of the "naval infantry." At 0200, those not manning the trucks moved out.

Five naval infantry looped very wide and east around the fortress so as to be able to approach and take position from the north. Five approached from directly south. The SEALs divided up into two teams to take out the technicals. Rensselaer would eliminate the east technical and then position himself with the Barrett east of the tower to kill the tower machine-gunners when they popped up, as undoubtedly they would. For his shots to clear the parapet the trajectory had to originate from a relatively far distance, but with the Barrett's night-vision scope he had a very good chance of a hit at an even greater distance than required.

SEAL team north would hit the north technical as SEAL team south hit the south technical. At this point, if firing broke out, both teams would rush to the hostage impoundments and shoot the sentries from wherever they had good probabilities of hits. The goal was to prevent the sentries from entering the buildings to execute the prisoners. In thinking about this, Rensselaer had banked that, first, Hadawi had not necessarily issued such an order; second, that it might not be the sentries' natural reaction; and, third, their first impulse would be to hold their ground and defend their posts.

If, as intended, the north and south technicals fell without a sound, the SEAL teams would make their way as slowly and stealthily as they could to the hostage impoundments, where they would kill the guards. With the very first report, the minigun-and-grenade trucks would rush north, with grenades hurled into the village on the go. As Hadawi's troops exited their sleeping quarters they would be faced with grenades falling like hail, the crossfire of ten automatic weapons, torrents of bullets from the miniguns, and whatever the SEALs at the entrances of the impoundments might contribute. Left out at the beginning would be the west technical, which, to get into a firing position, would have to loop north or south, during which time it would come under fire from night-vision-equipped troops invisible to it in the dark.

Working precisely by the clock, the attack elements set out at different times so as to arrive at their various positions simultaneously. All of them had to cover the last quarter mile or so, more than 1,200 feet, crawling slowly across hardscrabble, thorns, and rocks. Their heads had to be down, and they had to be almost absolutely silent even as the two-inch thorns stabbed them all over, including in the testicles, as if, they thought, deliberately. After almost two hours of this in some cases, they then had to go into battle.

No one, least of all Rensselaer, expected that the attack would conform perfectly either to the main plan or the alternatives nested within it. Attacks of more than embarrassing simplicity seldom if ever do, and this one would be no different.

*

Though they set out last, the five infantry south of the village arrived before any others, at 0345. Spread out so as to be less visible, they were still close enough to communicate. On the left wing, to the west, one of the sailors, Monroe (which he pronounced *Mon*-roe), an engineman from Los Angeles, was initially shocked and alarmed by something moving toward him from his right. Beginning to slew his M4, he realized that it was Gunner's Mate Lester Minorkis, who had actually crossed over the man immediately to *Mon*roe's right, forcing him to shift to Minorkis's previous position.

"What's going on?" *Mon*roe whispered, alarmed.

"I wanted to finish our conversation."

"Are you out of your mind?" *Mon*roe asked in as disturbed a whisper as one could make.

"They can't hear us if we whisper."

"Shhh!"

"They can't. The wind's coming from the village at least at five miles per hour. There's no way."

"Finish it *after*."

"One or both of us might be dead."

"You're crazy. Go back."

"No. They can't hear us, and we've got more than ten minutes."

"Oh God," *Mon*roe said. "What?"

"When we were making our own pancakes...."

"What?!"

"On the ship."

"That was...."

"I know, a long time ago."

*Mon*roe was stunned into silence. On the one hand he wanted to kill Minorkis, but, on the other, he really wanted to know what in their current situation Minorkis could possibly want to bring up about when they were making their own pancakes, which was before they passed Gibraltar.

Minorkis continued, quietly even for a whisper. He was right: the wind was such that no one even twenty feet ahead of them could have heard. "I wanted to tell you that I used to cook short-order."

"You did tell me."

"Yeah, but I didn't finish. My parents have a Greek diner. They're Greek."

"I figured that."

"From the time I was five, I worked in it. Before the Navy, I was super expert at short-order."

Doubting his sanity, and thinking that perhaps he was in a dream, Monroe asked nonetheless, "Then why didn't you become a Navy cook?"

"I wanted to do something else. What I was about to tell you, and I couldn't because then we had the drill for general quarters, and then I forgot, but now I remember, is that short-order is like just what we're about to do now—infantry fighting."

"I draw a blank."

"For one, the pressure never ceases. If you cook badly, or the eggs aren't done as requested, or the orders are late, or confused, the restaurant goes down. As you're struggling with an order, five more come in. If you run out of something and you have to get it, everything goes to hell, and things may burn or get cold. If you drop something on the floor and you're honest, you have to start over. You're going so fast that if, for example, you're buttering toast and you get butter on the plate, you have to get a paper towel and clean it off. In that time, something may boil over. Then you're really screwed. You have to handle your tools like your rifle: know how much ammo is left in the magazine, quick tactical reloads, good aim, rapid target engagement. People are yelling at you—'Where's my order?' 'The customer wants more fries,' 'Where's the pickle,' 'Not enough.' People bump into you. You don't have a second to yourself. You have to go with the speed and the rhythm or you're finished.

"You see? Just like combat. Short-order. Get lost in the rhythm. Surrender to speed. Think of nothing else."

"Okay, Minorkis," *Mon*roe said. "I got it."

Minorkis pulled his watch from his pocket. "Have to get back. Five minutes."

"Minorkis."

"Yeah?"

"No sane person could be your friend."

"I know."

*

The south technical had to be taken out lest it destroy *Athena*-force's gun trucks with its Russian double-barreled antiaircraft gun—the kind with cones at the barrel tips, as on the pom-pom guns of the Second World War, to contain flashback that would make aiming difficult. As Holworthy's south SEAL team crawled toward it, the cab lit up and the passenger door opened.

The SEALs stopped dead and pressed their bodies into ground literally covered with flint, which was hardly accommodating, although more so than the thorns, some of which were still embedded agonizingly in their flesh. Fearing that the whole operation would be forced to start before the appointed time, Holworthy and his partner watched the man who got out walk around the back of the truck. They could barely see him, but they didn't want to use their night scopes because to do so they would've had to raise their rifles, which might have made noise.

A match flared as the man, who had moved to the truck's south side to get out of the wind, lit a cigarette. Thereafter, the little red-orange beacon of the cigarette, moving in an arc, hesitating in his mouth as he drew in a puff, riding back down in his hand, announced his position.

"Get back in the fucking truck," Holworthy said to himself under his breath. But no, the man came forward, until he was ten feet in front of them. He was smoking and looking out toward the horizon.

Holworthy whispered to the other SEAL, "Get the one in the truck," and started to raise himself. But the cigarette came down in an arc once again, and, still staring out at a horizon beautifully littered with very bright stars that seemed to ride just above the ground or even to touch it, their target began to sing quietly in the Arabic scale of the *maqam*, repeating with considerable variation and changes in tone the phrase, "Yappa, yappa, yappa," or "Yabba, yabba, yabba," or somewhere in between the *P* and the *B*, skillfully, sadly, and, to Holworthy, no stranger to the Middle East, familiarly.

"Go," Holworthy whispered as he himself rose and bounded toward the singer, who became aware of him not even a second before Holworthy's left hand covered his mouth, and the knife in Holworthy's right sliced his neck, severing the carotid arteries. There was some noise, but no clattering to the ground, as Holworthy lowered his victim slowly in the few seconds before death. And the wind was up, blowing south, taking sound with it.

This afforded Holworthy's partner the opportunity to approach the driver, who was still in the truck and who had heard nothing to alert him, as if the SEAL about to knife him was the one who had gone to smoke. It was so dark even with the fantastic starlight of the desert that the American was just a form. He casually knocked on the window, and then opened the driver's door from the outside. Thinking that his gunner wanted to tell him something, the driver was in no way alarmed.

With great and shocking force, he was pulled out of the cab and dispatched exactly as Holworthy had dispatched the gunner. The only sound was the driver hitting the ground and air escaping his lungs as he did. Even before he was dead, Holworthy had arrived. They closed the driver door quietly so it wouldn't bang in the wind, and moved toward the hostage impoundments, no longer crawling but walking fast and quietly, with three minutes left until 0400.

*

North SEAL team was late in approaching the north technical because the east technical had moved to where the road to the village turned west. North and east technicals were now separated by a few yards, and the four men manning them were gathered around a little fire in the stretch between, talking while fussing about a pot on the embers. Anyone standing watch at four in the morning on a cold night, whether on a ship or in the desert, is driven as if by an irresistible force to drink something hot. Chocolate, too, has been for more than a century a staple for sentries.

In their arduous training and continuous exercises and operations, SEALs become almost telepathic. North team said not a word, and yet each of the two understood the problem exactly. There were too many enemy to go quietly, especially as two of them had slung weapons and were standing. Grouped around the fire, they may not have been alert, but their placement meant they had a view in every direction.

Were they to be eliminated, it could be only by gunfire, and there was no way to tell what effect this might have on the rest of the operation. Were they to be ignored, their vehicle-mounted heavy guns might extract an unacceptable toll or lead to defeat. The two sets of guards at the hostage impoundments had to be taken down simultaneously, which was perhaps not possible for only one team. South team would wait for north team. Meanwhile, north team now would have to wait for firing to erupt before hitting the technical crews. That is, nothing would happen, time would drag on, and the chances of discovery would increase.

A civilian might find it hard to believe that the options above would clarify between the two SEALs without a word spoken. That, however, is exactly what happened. And it took just a look for them to decide upon what to do, which was to strike the technicals and run to the impoundments. If they had had adequate COMMS they would have assigned the infantry to the crews and gone to meet south team, but the infantry was too far behind and east of them, there was no way they could reach them, and they were novices.

So north team raised their weapons, and with their night scopes drew their beads on the technical crews. They knew to shoot the two on the left and the two on the right according to their own positions, and were close enough for head shots. "Ready?" one asked.

"Ready."

"At two seconds."

Two seconds passed. Two accurate shots rang out simultaneously, striking the leftmost and rightmost man, both of whom were instantly killed. In the second and a half of paralysis before being able to process what had happened, the other two froze in place. The triggers were squeezed, and the second two collapsed. In the short time in which one could see that they were down and probably dead, the SEALs rose and began to run.

They tossed a grenade in the bed of each truck and didn't look back as six seconds later the explosions sounded behind them. Sprinting, they ran east and curved south to the impoundments. The road was as loose as beach sand, for it had been churned up by ages of traffic, not least camels. At Little Creek or Coronado, the SEALs ran on sand, always on sand, and if anyone had to ask why, this was why. Two men in the midst of many times their number of enemy were sprinting under heavy loads in cold desert air and in the dark, beneath an immense, moonless sky burning with white stars. Even in combat they could not help but to be constantly aware of such an all-enveloping sky.

*

So he might walk rather than crawl, in Rensselaer's transit to his position east of the tower he had given it a wide berth. It was not because of his rank or his age that he chose not to crawl, but because of his rifle: that is, the Barrett .50-caliber that he carried in addition to his M4. With scope, sling, and chambered magazine it weighed almost thirty-seven pounds. The additional ten-round magazines added almost twelve pounds. Crawling with it, its ammunition, and the M4 all slung across his back—sixty pounds of steel—was not only a nightmare, but the almost five-foot length of the Barrett meant it would knock against the M4 and the ground when it moved from side to side. Which is why Rensselaer went wide, so he could use the Barrett's carry handle, making less noise walking than by trying to slither across a field of flint. He had expected to take out the east technical, but he saw quite early that it had gone. Still, so as not to alert the enemy, he kept the village at the planned distance.

Being upright in things physical just as in things moral made one more visible and a better target, so he had to keep a lot of distance between himself and the enemy. Though his path was much longer, because he could walk relatively fast his timing allowed for arrival simultaneously with the others. That he was farther out was of little consequence given the ranges for which the Barrett was designed. Dispatching an ISIS terrorist in Afghanistan, its record kill at 2.2 miles was an outlier, but striking a vehicle a mile distant was ordinary and expected. Rensselaer took a position between a quarter and a half mile from the tower.

He set up the rifle, steadying its bipod amid the rocks, deploying the monopod at the butt, laying out the magazines so he could choose the kind of round he would use: ball for personnel and unarmored targets, or high-explosive, incendiary, armor-piercing. Should he be discovered, his M4 was accessible just to the right of the Barrett. He lay in place as comfortably as he could, waiting for 0400.

He didn't know the name of the little settlement to the west. Perhaps it didn't have a name, or it once had had a name but after it had been abandoned no one remembered what it had been called. Everything was so similar to so much in the Middle East as he had experienced it. Cold, clear, winter air. A tapestry of stars in a show so bright and sharp that one could see by their light. Hard, cold, rocky ground. A long view over desert to the dark shadows of unlit buildings silent in the still air. Or, seen from a distance, a fortified town or base with a perimeter of electric lights, resting like a diamond necklace upon the dark and rolling landscape.

It was so beautiful, for being fundamental, harsh, and unforgiving, that he had almost forgotten where he was, until north team's gunfire rang out early. Awakened by this, for some reason, perhaps the vagaries and delusions of the night, the machine-gunners in the tower thought the assault was coming from the east. The one facing west moved his weapon to join his mate on the eastern-facing parapet, and there, without any kind of aiming, the two guns began to fire into the darkness, hose-like, as if they were watering a patch of garden or painting a wall. The idea seemed to be to do the job by making a lot of noise and covering a lot of area. This, Rensselaer had concluded long ago in his reflections about why such people didn't bother to aim, was an extension of the battle cry intended to terrify and demoralize opponents, despite the modern consequence of excessive expenditure of ammunition.

It was always possible to be killed by accident, and the sounds of thousands of slugs smashing into rocks and dirt was all around him. But he calmly put the cross hairs on the parapet wall at the level where he judged the left machine-gunner's center of mass would be. In this, Rensselaer was half blind, but only half so. The guess could not have been off by that much.

When a .50-caliber round exits the Barrett, it does so like a shell leaving an artillery piece. No one ever gets fully used to it. As hundreds of rounds are pushed through them, the twin fifties fixed on ships or vehicles make much more noise, but they're mounted on steel that transfers their force to the mass of the deck or vehicle bed. With the rifle, the force is transferred to the man and his sore shoulder, and each shot feels like the salvo of sixteen-inch guns. He engaged the trigger. The Barrett jerked back like one of the guns of the *Missouri*, and its projectile, meant to pierce steel armor and brick walls, went through the mud parapet and struck the machine-gunner, who was toppled backward—not with the absurd, acrobatic body toss of the movies, but with a force equal to the force of the Barrett's recoil minus the power the projectile had expended in piercing the mud-brick parapet. It was enough to push him over, with his heels as hinge.

The other gunner paused in firing, trying to assimilate what had just happened. He stared at the hole in the parapet, wondering if it had already been there. But he failed to do what he should have done: move off-center from his gun and out of sight. In the instant as he wondered, another round exited with an immense shock from the Barrett, supersonic even when it hit the wall. Striking the second gunner on his right side, it twirled him around, and as he banged into the north wall, he died.

Immediately after the shot, Rensselaer had begun to gather his equipment. He stood, grasped the Barrett's carry handle, and started running toward the tower. As he ran, he heard cascades of gunfire sounding to his left, to his right, and ahead. With firing all around, when Rensselaer reached the door of the tower he threw in a grenade. In the dusty aftermath of its explosion, he entered and, as if expecting to find an infantry squad within, tensely climbed the stairs to the roof. No one opposed him, and the two sentries on the roof were dead. In a dreadful but necessary act, he shot each one to make sure—how horrible to fire into the corpses of men he had killed—and then he set up the Barrett on the tower's west-facing parapet.

*

Upon hearing the premature fusillade, south SEAL team had dropped prone and fired at the guards in front of the impoundments. The four guards were stock-still, looking northwest toward the sound of north team's volley. The SEALs took aim and shot them. Taking the right, Holworthy dropped one and hit the other one multiple times as he started to seek shelter inside the south building. But he got in, and he had his weapon, which was what they had most feared.

The other SEAL hit the two guards at the north impoundment and put them down without ambiguity. Then he and Holworthy ran forward. "Secure it," Holworthy ordered, gesturing toward the north impoundment. He himself reached the south one and charged in the door. He almost shot a Filipino steward who had taken the wounded guard's gun from him and, not knowing how to fire it, had beaten him over the head.

The steward dropped the gun and raised his hands. "He's dead, sir. I hit him, sir." Indeed he was. Holworthy checked, and then glanced around. A candle burned in a holder on the shelf on the back wall. It was the only light, and all he could see were the faces of people in the first row of hostages. They were dirty, and the stench was hard to bear. Holworthy didn't know it, but two half oil drums were in the corner, a jury-rigged latrine. It seemed as if a thousand questions were asked of him at once. He didn't understand a single one.

"United States Navy," he said loudly. "Move to the sides!" He gestured with his arms. "Move to the sides!" Then, a few feet in from the door, his heels nearly touching those of the dead guard, he lay on the floor, opened his bipod, took a spare magazine from its pouch and placed it to the left of his rifle, a grenade to the right, and, assuming that the other impoundment was now similarly protected, waited for whatever might come.

What worried him most was an RPG fired from directly in front. He would try to shoot the grenadier before he took aim, but it would be extremely difficult to make out anyone in the dark. Which was better, to scan a narrow field with the rifle's night scope, or take in the whole field at once, trying to detect a disturbance in the darkness? He chose the latter.

*

Just as north SEAL team's premature fire had set Rensselaer into action, the two infantry squads followed suit. South infantry advanced at a run, tossing a grenade into the south technical to make sure it was neutralized, and dropping to the ground a few hundred feet beyond to cover the south flank of the village. North infantry took responsibility for the north flank in the same fashion. By the time they had taken position, *Athena's* gun trucks had arrived on the road between the village and the impoundments.

Holworthy was frustrated because the gun trucks hadn't stationed themselves, as they were supposed to have, to block and protect the doors of the impoundments. Only he, Rensselaer, and Pisecki had radios, no one on the trucks. The drivers by this time were underneath, their rifles pointed toward the village, whence came scores of men, running in crowds and firing wildly.

The order had been, except for miniguns and grenade launchers, and unless faced with a tight cluster of enemy, to use scopes, single shots or, at most, bursts of three, and the order was followed. As ISIS soldiers rushed out of the houses, often firing uselessly without acquiring targets, they were shot individually by the ten infantry, the four SEALs, the two drivers, and Rensselaer on the tower. As soon as groups of men were visible as they altered the texture of the darkness, the miniguns raked the village, and the grenade launchers blasted it with the effect of artillery.

In a very short time, almost two hundred grenades exploded amid the huts. It sounded like the end of the world. Many of the walls shattered. Some came down, and when two or three grenades would find their ways inside through the gaps or a doorway, a hut seemed to explode outward.

The slaughter was a punishment for what ISIS had done on the decks and in the cabins of *l'Étoile Océanique*, at the execution site in the desert, and in truth all over the world. Hadawi hadn't suspected that from a small, battered ship such a force could follow him so deep in, that it would dare to do so without air support, that it would find him, and that it could marshal such murderous fire. After all, he had had half a hundred men, give or take, four technicals with heavy guns, and two heavy machine guns, all on the high ground in open desert.

Scanning the darkness quickly became impossible for Holworthy when the assault opened and thousands of muzzle flashes blinded him to any subtleties of shading. Nor would scanning through the scope be of any avail, as the continual flashes washed it out most of the time. Now he could cover only the spaces 50–100 yards directly in front of him, at most, and even those only partially.

At the battle's midpoint, one of Hadawi's men managed to take position next to a hut, aim his RPG at the open door of the south impoundment, and fire. As soon as the plume of his rocket bloomed, Holworthy shot him dead, and in an instant prepared to die himself, with only seconds to feel his despair that so many civilians would be killed along with him. As the rocket approached, he held his breath and his heart seemed not to beat. He hadn't time to warn of the RPG, and there was no place for anyone to go anyway.

As he waited to die, the grenade flew over him. He felt the heat and smelled the rocket exhaust. Then it hit the back wall. But because it was designed to make a hole in armor and explode after it penetrated, it went through the wall and exploded on the other side. In the enclosed space of an armored vehicle, the blast pressure would have nowhere to dissipate. But, beyond the wall, the charge burst in open air. So although fragments of RPG casing were embedded in the dried mud wall, nothing penetrated, and the overpressure was insufficient to knock the wall down. No one inside was even slightly hurt.

Just after that, as Rensselaer, high in the tower, was hitting one house after another with armor-piercing rounds, he saw through his scope the interior of a truck light up as its doors were opened. North team hadn't had time to destroy the west technical, and before north infantry could do so the enemy had gotten to it. Changing his focus and scope power, he saw two men get in. At first he thought the technical would move to the battle, but no gunner was visible in the truck bed, which held a large, single-barreled antiaircraft gun. And when the truck started to move, it went west. Guessing that Hadawi was in flight, Rensselaer adjusted his scope, loaded a high-explosive incendiary round, and trained the Barrett on the road west.

It was here that a shot could fly unblocked by the houses. As the truck reached a few feet to the rear of this point, he fired. But he had been unable to calculate properly the truck's speed, and he didn't know if Hadawi was in it. Because the distance involved made a flat trajectory impossible, the bullet would have to travel ballistically. With a flat trajectory, all he would've had to worry about was windage: i.e., the X axis. Ballistically, the Y axis came into play, and he had to calculate for distance. With the target traveling at an unknown, variable speed, only luck would allow this, and although he fired five rounds as the truck receded west, that luck was not to be his. After his last shot, he was stunned by silence, for it was the last shot of the engagement. Except for the moaning of the wounded and the steady rush of the wind, the desert night was once again quiet.

Now they would try to save lives rather than take them.

*

The aftermath was by far the worst part of the battle—the wounded and the dead; and the smell of burnt flesh, gunpowder, and spilled intestinal contents. At best, the odor would be partially carried away in the wind. On the sea it was different. The enemy would disappear under the swell, all his disarray and sadness buried in hushed ceremony. The casualties among one's own men were difficult enough to bear, but even then, burial at sea had the same finality, quickness, and decency as when the enemy ship gently vanished, leaving only silence and a puzzled conscience. The sea washed over everything, consumed everything, absorbed everything, equalized everything. Imperturbable, it quieted with ease the occasional violence upon its surface, and as if by magic reconciled the heart to the prospect of eternal sleep. But not the land, where bodies would lie and rot until they were buried not in deep, mysterious waters, but in graves so relatively shallow as to make impossible the comfort of forgetfulness.

Rensselaer now divided his men according to two equally important tasks. Half would look after the hostages and the wounded, the other half would clear the village to make sure no threat remained. He made it clear to the mopping-up operation that there would be no executions. They could fire only at remaining hostiles in or about to take action. Only one of the enemy resisted, and he was dispatched after he shot from beneath a truck. The total of half a dozen reports made everyone within earshot cock his head to listen, but then it was over. Three of the enemy gave up, fearfully.

No hostages had been harmed during the assault, although almost a score of them, mainly older people, were sick. They had gone without their medications, suffered nightly hypothermia, and been ill-nourished and under stress. A few had high fevers and were delirious. Flu and diarrhea were endemic, and even the young people were coughing and weak. The Filipino crew, young for the most part, tougher, their immune systems tutored on every inhabited continent, were in the best shape, and they were superb in caring for the sick. Foreseeing this state of affairs, Rensselaer had brought from *Athena* as much in the way of medical supplies as he could. The corpsman became a central figure, first in treating the combatants.

Both *Mon*roe and Minorkis had been killed. No one had seen it happen, but after they failed to report, they were found facing the village and shot in the backs of their heads. In the dark, someone had circled around south infantry and caught them unaware. Two sailors were wounded, both from rifle fire, one seriously though not critically, the other superficially, shot through the calf—entry and exit—and unable to move more than a few feet.

They would wrap *Mon*roe and Minorkis in sleeping bags and take them back, hoping that the trip would be short and that the large French ships, with morgues, had arrived. The corpsman and others turned to the hostages next, mainly distributing antibiotics, fluids, anti-inflammatories, analgesics, food, and instruction to the stewards.

It was tempting not to attend to the ISIS wounded, but reluctance vanished as their cries became more and more pitiful. The corpsman and volunteer assistants, including some stewards, did what they could with sutures, blood-stop, and morphine. When *Athena*'s crew and the hostages were ready to move out, the three ISIS prisoners who hadn't been wounded would be uncuffed and left with medical supplies for their comrades.

"We can't save them, take them, or execute them," Rensselaer told Holworthy and Pisecki. If the prisoners and some of the wounded live, God knows what atrocities they'll commit in the future, but we can't just kill them. That's the way it is."

"Yes we can, and you know it, but at least we can take one for interrogation," Holworthy said.

"We'd have to feed him and guard him, and we don't have the time or facilities to break him down. He won't be any more sleep-deprived than we are."

"I could break him down," Holworthy volunteered.

"Not when you're under my command, not in the way I think you mean."

"They kill us, we kill them, but we can't get tough with them?"

"Not unless the threat is imminent."

"The law?" Holworthy asked.

"The law. Sometimes, however, it's necessary to be civilly disobedient, so to speak. Don't quote me. But only then. Clear?"

"Clear."

Athena's crew, their weapons still with them, had nonetheless become once again more like sailors than infantrymen as they rushed around accomplishing various tasks. First, they assembled the fleet of trucks necessary to convey them, their stores, the hostages, the wounded, and the dead back to *Athena* and, they hoped, the French squadron. They lined up sixteen serviceable trucks and distributed all the fuel they could siphon and gather. Ten fifty-five-gallon drums of fuel had survived in a dump west of the village, and by siphoning and spreading out the supplies they themselves had brought, every truck had a full tank, and then there were the ten drums.

With preparations completed as the sun rose, they crowded everyone into the trucks, checked the village once again, and set out. The sailors marveled at how quiet the hostages were, and felt love and pity for the French *lycéennes*, who now moved like their elders.

The minigun-and-grenade trucks were last. Before they rolled out, the SEALs on them uncuffed the three unwounded ISIS captives and set them free to attend to their wounded and dying. The captives were bitter and contemptuous to the end. None could speak English, but they were able to make clear that they thought the Americans were weak for not killing them and their wounded. Their faces showed it, and the look in their eyes said that they would come after the Americans—all Americans—and would be stopped by nothing but death.

They were tied to each other as well as cuffed. "Unhook'em," Holworthy said. Under the SEALs' guns, they were freed. The SEALs mounted the truck, and as it rolled away their former captives spit toward them. O'Connor raised his rifle, then thought better of it.

THE SEVENTH BATTLE: HADAWI'S ARMY

In weighing whether to speed the trucks to the coast, thus jarring as opposed to making the sick and injured more comfortable but perhaps dooming them to arrive too late, Rensselaer decided to move as fast as possible. Sometimes the road was so rough that as each truck bumped over it the truck's back end would lift a few feet in the air, with the front wheels acting like a hinge or the forelegs of a bucking horse, and come down with the force of a battering ram. This was worse than when all four wheels became slightly airborne, as then the shock was distributed more broadly.

Halfway to the defile, a vehicle in the middle of the line used its horn to signal a general stop. Rensselaer and Holworthy both went back and found that one of the sick hostages had died. He was a thin, partially bald, white-haired old man whose skin even when he was alive had been as glossy as if it had been coated with varnish. An electrician from Strasbourg, he had been on the cruise with several fellow retirees and their wives. His wife now held his head in her lap as his former colleagues stayed near, not knowing what to say. "The union paid for the cruise," she said. "He had such a high fever. He was delirious, and he didn't know where he was. He asked me, 'Why is my bed going so fast?' I told him we were in a truck. He looked completely lost, and then he died."

They wrapped him up as well as they could, and she stayed with him, even as his body bounced when the truck went over rough ground. The French girls stared numbly at the horizon, and said nothing.

Not long after starting up again, Rensselaer and Holworthy heard the horn of yet another of the trucks they were leading, and once again called a halt. A sailor came running up alongside the column, and when he arrived he turned and pointed up.

"That ain't no bird," he said.

Rensselaer and Holworthy, squinting because of the sun, lifted their binoculars and searched. "A UAV," Holworthy announced.

"Can we shoot it down, sir?" the sailor asked.

"Too high," Rensselaer answered.

"If we had a Stinger?"

"No. It's just a little thing, probably made of plastic. They probably got it at RadioShack."

"You mean COMMS, sir?"

"No. RadioShack was an electronics store. Let's get going." They started forward again, and the sailor's truck picked him up at a run.

"They know we're going to Ras Hagar, so what does it matter?" Holworthy asked.

"We don't have time to launch the Stalker, so we don't know where *they* are. They're probably on the track. But if they're not directly behind us and rather off to the right somewhere, and they know our course and speed, they can plot an intercept. Which is why it matters."

For the next ten miles or so, they kept watch all around, hoping nothing was on their flanks or, somehow, in front of them.

When the defile came into sight, still low on the horizon and an hour away, the column swept wide and right to avoid one of the wadis that spread from the plateau into a dry delta. As they turned, Rensselaer—in the first truck, with Holworthy at the wheel—glanced to his right and, now that the column had veered, was able to see what had been directly behind it.

At first he thought it was a sandstorm. But the immense, reddish-yellow cloud didn't rise high enough and was not broad enough to have been a sandstorm. He judged it to be about fifteen miles behind and a mile wide. Ordering Holworthy to stop, he took out the Barrett and peered through its scope. At 14 power, it showed that the cloud was composed of separate pillars of dust raised by vehicles speeding along a wide front. He counted the pillars. By this time, Holworthy was standing behind him, looking in the same direction with his binocular.

"You see what I see?" Rensselaer asked.

"What?"

"Individual columns of raised dust."

"At this magnification it seems all of a piece."

Rensselaer put the Barrett back in its case. "It isn't. I counted. At least seventy trucks, moving at high speed. It's a whole army."

"Are you sure?"

"It's not the Good Humor man," Rensselaer replied.

"Now I understand," Holworthy said. "Hadawi was taking the hostages to a real stronghold. We didn't know that. In seventy or more trucks, he could have a thousand men."

*

The raised dust of *Athena*'s convoy was also a pillar in the desert, which Hadawi's army used as a guide, but it was different. In a narrow column, it rose higher and was yellowish white, because the reddish-colored particles were heavier, and fell back, while the lighter, more ethereal white dust climbed on thermals and shone in the sun like the mitres of light that slice the darkness of a great cathedral. *Athena*'s column could neither hide nor fade into the background, and would be allowed no peace. As he drove forward, Rensselaer thought this was much like the strategical role of the Navy—to see, to be seen, and to clash with the enemy in the clear, with neither forests nor mountains as shields. Taking fire for the sake of those whom he protected even when they were unaware opened up new worlds of lucidity and feeling, if only because an instant of nobility at the perilous edge could outweigh a lifetime of ease in the sheltered center.

"Keep up our speed," he said to Holworthy half an hour on, "and now and then arc to the right so we can take a look back." When they did this, they saw that Hadawi was gaining. "Snake back, go faster."

"We can make it to the defile," Holworthy said when he rediscovered the track, "but if this keeps up, there's no way we can get to Ras Hagar before they catch us. And we don't even know if the ship is there or the French have arrived."

For the tenth time, Rensselaer tried to raise *Athena* with his hand-held. "I can't get through. Not in the daytime, not on this side of the escarpment."

"But probably at the top," Holworthy said, "like last time. If they catch us before the defile, then what?"

"We die. Increase speed."

"If you want the hostages bounced out of the trucks."

"This will cut our time a little," Rensselaer said, "but swing right again, briefly."

"Why? That's crazy."

"I just have a feeling."

"You have a feeling?"

"Go right."

Holworthy arced right again. It was he who then said, "They've stopped." They had.

"They're praying," Rensselaer told him.

"How did you know?" Holworthy asked as he swung back.

"I looked at my watch. They have to get out of the trucks, find the right bearing to Mecca, and go through the prayers. We're going to make it to the defile. When we go through, we'll take a minigun and grenade launcher up top. Hadawi can be stopped in the narrow passage. Then he'll have to go around, which will take a few hours at least. I'll stay to do that, and try to call *Athena* from the rise."

"Good," Holworthy replied. "We can do that."

"Only one is necessary."

"You're wrong. The trucks can't climb the escarpment, but infantry can, and they'll be coming for you right and left. If Hadawi gets through he'll massacre everyone. Obviously, it'll take at least two to close the passage. Don't pretend otherwise."

"I can't ask you to do this, because there won't be a way back."

"Bullshit. We'll leave a truck on the other side with the key in the ignition and the engine running if you want." The part about the motor running was said in jest. "And when we've hit enough trucks to block the passage we'll get out of there."

"You think so? With a thousand men firing at us, and God knows how many technicals with God knows how many heavy weapons? Are you kidding? I'll be lucky if I can stay alive to cripple enough trucks to block the way."

"But you will leave one of ours for escape, right?"

"As a gesture. I'm not coming back."

"Then I suppose neither am I."

"Mr. Holworthy, this is a direct order. Take the column to Ras Hagar. A direct order. That's it."

"I'm not taking that order. What are you going to do, have me arrested? Shoot me? If I stay, I double the chances of stopping them. You can't court-martial me after we're both dead."

*

As their exhausts choked the passageway in gray smoke, they wound through the escarpment, then stopped at the other side. With almost every able-bodied man pressed into service, including the younger French crew and Filipino stewards, they rushed a minigun, a grenade launcher, the Barrett and the Remington, and ammunition to a spot on the escarpment over one of the tightest bends of the defile, with a view north to the plain and as much cover as possible left and right along the top of the rise.

The minigun and its tripod and electric battery alone weighed about 125 pounds. Although its 7.62 round weighed only about an ounce, three thousand of them and their links and containers came in at more than two hundred pounds. The grenade launcher and its tripod were lighter than the minigun, but the grenades themselves were very heavy en masse. And all would be left behind, spiked if possible. If Hadawi were to judge solely by the firepower that would be directed upon him, he might think he was facing not two men but a company.

Once in place in his firing position on the plateau, Rensselaer called *Athena*. The transmissions were spotty, but Movius heard. "We have . . . -s-tages. Will arrive . . . hours . . . -gar. Over."

"Is air cover available?" Rensselaer asked repeatedly, unheard. "Have French arrived?"

"What is your position?" Movius kept yelling in reply and in vain at his hand-held. Given coordinates and fire direction, he could have used the remaining Harpoon, but he didn't even know if Rensselaer was pressed or what the target might be if indeed there was one.

Rensselaer put Pisecki in command of the column. Pisecki took the order and said, "Aye, sir," certain that he would never see Rensselaer or Holworthy again. He had offered to stay with them, but he knew his greater obligation was to the column, and he left to rejoin it.

The mass of dust had risen again to the north, and was now much closer. Rensselaer and Holworthy set up the weapons and waited in the sun, hardly noticing its heat. After a while, Holworthy said, "What will you miss?"

"Katy. She's middle-aged, you know, just like me, but you can't see it. She's beautiful, strikingly so, and as I always say, sharp. That is, her appearance, her intelligence, her wit. And yet, despite all that, when she smiles she has the charm of a young woman, the sweetness of a girl. I was going to marry her. It's strange. I almost feel as if I have, that we'd spent many years together. That'll have to be enough. What about you?"

Holworthy thought. "My sister." It was all he said.

"What about your parents? Are they still living?"

"No. I'll be seeing them, too."

*

When Hadawi's brigade was three miles distant, its trucks, which from the escarpment and with the naked eye could now be made out individually, began to form into a column in preparation for threading the passageway. At two miles, this was half accomplished, and Rensselaer and Holworthy had gone prone and fitted their shoulders to the butts of their rifles, spare magazines of ammunition laid out to each man's left. They could only guess the ranges, but they were pretty good at that, having in Rensselaer's case trained over many years of watches in which he would sight a ship or a point on land, guess the distance, and then compare it to what the radar or the electronic chart said. And in its featurelessness the desert was much like the sea.

Loaded with high-explosive, incendiary rounds and aiming at the radiator/engine block of the two lead trucks, Rensselaer fired off his first two shots. Both were high but spectacular, exploding in the cabs and blowing them to pieces as the trucks veered off to the right and burst into flames. The trucks following them accelerated, thinking they had encountered RPGs and would close on and kill whoever had fired them. Of course, there was no one.

Instead, Rensselaer's close-on second shots, now that he had the range, were armor-piercing rounds that went through the radiator into the engine block of the truck in the lead, and then the one that replaced it. The first one veered off to the right and rolled over. As the next one's engine seized up, its wheels stopped turning, and the trucks immediately behind it, weighted with antiaircraft guns and following too closely, piled up in a huge wreck. But all the vehicles behind these hooked left and kept coming.

Once in range of Holworthy's Remington 700, drivers were picked off one by one, faster than Rensselaer could take the heavier shots from the Barrett. For both of them, the closer the column came, the surer the shots. Neither stopped until, firing on a flat trajectory and using the last of his ammunition, Rensselaer blew up two technicals from which heavy machine guns were raking the rock face, raining shards, every single one of which missed both him and Holworthy. They had directly knocked out more than a dozen vehicles.

Confident in his numerical superiority, Hadawi could think of nothing but to press on. With the object of luring what he called a Crusaders' army and wiping it out, he had assembled and trained almost a thousand men. His intention had been to surprise a rescue expedition and kill or capture every last man, executing those whom he captured together with the remaining hostages in a mass slaughter that would terrify the world. When an even larger relief expedition arrived, it would find hundreds of bodies, the carcasses of helicopters and vehicles, and decapitated soldiers and civilians alike littering the battleground and rotting in the sun.

His force, meanwhile, would have dissolved, and would remain inactive for a year with absolutely no communication, only to reassemble on a set date at a specified place to carry out the next mission. These plans had gone awry. The Western powers would now know the size of his army, and respond accordingly. The least he could do was to pursue, recapture, and execute his former captives. If not, the whole of his venture would fail.

Wanting desperately to get through the defile, he sent fifty men to ascend the gradual incline to Rensselaer's and Holworthy's right, and a hundred to the left on the other side of the divide. Counting on force, momentum, and his attacks from the flank, he assumed that he would break through, though it might be costly, and ordered his column to proceed into the defile. How many men could the Americans have left to block him? Had he known there were only two, he would have surely been more frustrated than he already was.

Both Rensselaer and Holworthy understood that in daylight, absent a muzzle flash against the darkness, Hadawi had not been able to ascertain where the firing had originated. Even so, they wondered why almost all of his effort was directed to the other side of the defile, on their left, and accepted this as mere luck in their favor. But when they heard the trucks below and moved to man the minigun and grenade launcher, they understood. A brightly colored flash of color, moving languidly in what little wind there was, astonished them at first. Far from them, on the other side of the gap, the American flag, it's deep red and pure white impudently visible against the absolutely clear sky, had been Hadawi's target.

"Pisecki," Holworthy said as he gripped the minigun, grateful for what Pisecki had done.

Just before Hadawi's lead vehicle reached the tight bend in the defile, Holworthy said, "And he knew we wouldn't leave it here either—if we get out." Then they opened fire.

The grenade launcher sounded like a mortar as it shot out its charges, but when these reached the floor of the defile among the trucks and on the truck beds themselves or on their hoods or cab roofs, the explosions— more than a hundred—echoed against the rock walls like a thunderstorm in the Alps. The cacophony was stitched together by bursts from the minigun, with which Holworthy poured several thousand rounds along the stalled column to suppress its defensive fire.

Between the grenades, the showers of minigun bullets, the explosions of gas tanks and munitions in and on the trucks, and the echoes and ricochets from the walls, the defile was turned into a deafening, flaming junkyard. It would have taken half a dozen tow trucks and bulldozers a day to move the wreckage, and Hadawi had not even an hour. The tires of the trucks burned, leaving wheel rims that dug into the sand, so nothing could roll. There would have been no traction for tow trucks anyway. Hadawi's force, with now only two-thirds of its vehicles and leaving behind many dead and wounded, would have to go around the escarpment, which would bring it an hour and a half south and require another hour and a quarter to follow the hypotenuse back to the line of travel. The battle itself, which was not over, would set it back at least another hour. So, in staying, Rensselaer and Holworthy had given the escape another four hours at least.

When it became clear that Rensselaer's fire was coming from the northeast side of the defile, Hadawi directed all his guns there, and, judging that his overwhelming numerical advantage made crossfire unnecessary, called his men off the southwest side, where they had been approaching the flag. Rensselaer and Holworthy turned their weapons toward the men advancing toward them from east on the plateau. Their grenades cut them down like cannon fire, and the minigun killed or wounded most of those who had not already fallen or been able to seek cover among the folds of rock. Only about twenty were still able to fight, and they were fifteen hundred feet away, pinned.

Hadawi's antiaircraft and machine-gun fire from the plain was useless. It shattered the lip of the escarpment but couldn't crest over it to hit Rensselaer and Holworthy. "Now we can get to the French," Rensselaer said. "I didn't think we could do it. I'll cover you while you go back, and then you cover me. Go." They leapfrogged, with the one left behind using his M4 to force any one of the enemy who advanced to find cover or get hit.

"I'm going to get the flag," Holworthy said.

"Are you crazy? Leave it."

"I can't."

Rensselaer knew there was a place where the defile was narrow enough between two overhangs at the top for a spectacular jump. "You can't clear that," he said as he fired off suppressive rounds. "Don't die for the sake of the flag."

"Right," Holworthy said, and took off at a run.

"Idiot," Rensselaer said into the air between him and the enemy, for Holworthy's idea of valor had now decided Rensselaer's chance of remaining alive. But Rensselaer was too busy suppressing enemy fire to dwell on this. Again their shots were undisciplined and badly aimed, as if their purpose was mainly to make noise.

Holworthy reached the narrows, put down his rifle, and shed his magazine carrier. He looked at the gap and realized that he had never jumped that far. Terrified, he half moaned and sang, and half grunted, in a concert he would never repeat. Thinking he was going to die for symbolic bravery, he pulled back nonetheless and set out at a furious run toward the rim. And as he was running he thought not of the flag, or his life, or anything noble to suit the end, but of Evel Knievel in the Snake River Canyon. Then he left the rim, flying, not knowing if he would make it. For, among other things, such as being shot at, the length of the gap, and explosions now in back of him on the plateau, the southwest rim was slightly higher.

His right foot landed on the edge, but the left foot did not, which forced him back. He bent his body forward to fight his backward momentum, and fell onto the rock, catching the upper part of his chest, his chin, his hands, and forearms. The rest of him was moving back and down. He clawed at the rock with his fingernails and his chin until both were bloodied and had arrested his fall. Then, mainly with the muscles of his core, he was able to pull himself forward and to safety. At first he couldn't move, and his abdomen seized into so tight and painful a spasm that it took five minutes for him to recover.

Even before Holworthy made the jump, Hadawi had realized that direct fire would do no good. He had no idea how many Americans were on the plateau, as the radioman with his northeast force had been killed and no one had taken up his radio. And he had no mortars or mortar-men. But he did have RPGs, hundreds of them, and he gathered several hundred of his men and evenly distributed them in a rectangle roughly 200 by 100 feet. Each one had an RPG launcher and five grenades. Hadawi directed them to point skyward at various angles, so the charges would travel upward in an arc and then come down on the plateau. These were the explosions that Holworthy had heard before he jumped.

As aiming them was only a guess and determining their trajectory only a prayer, they went wild, but there were a lot of them. At first, Rensselaer thought Hadawi had mortars, but then he figured it out. Some of the charges fell among Hadawi's own men, to what effect Rensselaer couldn't see.

Holworthy didn't have time to think. When he could move again, he ran toward the flag, leaving a trail of blood from the cuts beneath his chin. The flag was on a tent pole stuck into a crack. At first, because of the blood from his fingers, his hands slipped as he tried to pull the pole from the rock. Then he found purchase, and the flag came up.

Running with it in the sun and the wind, with powerful explosions coming from ahead, he was cast back into other wars in which things were different and yet so very much the same. He was magnificently aware of the sun, the air, the light, and sound. When he reached the gap, despite the flag, he was going much faster than during his first jump, and he flew across the open space, the flag stretched out by his forward course. Upon landing, he stayed upright. But then he put the flag down, not caring that it was on the ground—he had just risked his life for protocol, enough for that day—and took up his rifle to cover Rensselaer.

When Rensselaer heard Holworthy's shots, he fired a few himself and ran as fast as he could to Holworthy. Seeing the flag, and momentarily delighted, he was too busy to say anything but "Go!" They resumed their leapfrogging, this time amid the RPGs, some small fragments of which, or perhaps pieces of rock, hit them with a stinging spray that made them bleed in dozens of places. There were so many bullets, shell fragments, and rock splinters flying that Rensselaer thought he was like a bee in the rain, and could not imagine how he would get out alive. He thought, what happens when a bee is struck by a large raindrop? Does he fall to the ground? Does he get up again?

Near the beginning of the descent, but still high on the plateau, Holworthy said, "You go first this time." They couldn't see Hadawi's men anymore, but the RPGs were still hitting randomly all over.

"Okay," Rensselaer answered, and, seconds later, Holworthy looked back and saw Rensselaer on the run. They were soon to descend. It seemed good. But as Holworthy watched, an RPG came down close to Rensselaer's left, exploded, and lifted him into the air and sideways toward the edge— over which he flew.

Holworthy ran back. The RPGs were still coming, but no rifle fire. He looked past the edge. Forty feet or so below, Rensselaer lay face up, his body folded-in along the length of a V-shaped depression that had developed over the ages as a ledge had pulled away from the cliff wall. His mouth and eyes were open. Blood flowed in a pool from his head and multiple shrapnel wounds. He didn't move.

"Captain!" Holworthy yelled, with no response. "Stephen!"

Rensselaer was unreachable from above or below. Holworthy waited as long as he could, the RPGs still coming. Then he saw a dozen men advancing toward him. Once more, he called to Rensselaer. There was no question in his mind. Rensselaer was dead. So he slung his rifle, took up the flag, and ran down the slope to the truck.

From halfway down the eastern face of the escarpment, the remnants of Hadawi's northeast force fired at the truck as it sped along the track. The flag was stretched taut in the wind—a bright target that received not a single hit.

*

On the long drive to Ras Hagar, Holworthy felt regret and determination. Doing what he had been trained to do, he pressed on. At a very early age, his father had observed him walking in the rain, his head bent in the way most people bend into a storm. "You won't get any wetter if you walk upright," his father had told him, "but it'll teach you how to face life to come." From that day, Holworthy had been primed to be a soldier, although this had not been his father's intention.

When he reached the south wadi at Ras Hagar, knowing that the sea would soon come into view, he was elated. Yearning for the sight of the sea as the wadi opened onto it, he was prematurely relaxed when, as if from nowhere, machine-gun fire raked the sand in front of his truck. He braked to a stop and looked toward the top of the wadi. A hundred and fifty men were lined up, most standing confidently, some with anti-tank rockets beside them, almost all with weapons pointing at him. At first, he threw open the door in preparation for seeking cover. But there was no cover. It was almost dusk, and the sun was directly behind him, illuminating the small army and deepening the colors of its uniforms. He saw that the patches on them were tranches of blue, white, and red. The tricolor, the French.

Why had they stopped him? He put his hands up. Their weapons were still aimed. He turned only slightly and gestured toward the flag flying from the back of the truck. In the absence of a breeze it had embraced the pole to the point where it could not be made out unambiguously, and the sun was in their eyes. He called out. *"Athena*! SEAL!"

"Okay," they answered, and pointed their weapons down. Somewhat irritated, Holworthy got back in the truck and drove the last few hundred yards to the beach. The view didn't disappoint, as the blue of the ocean was deepened by the gold of the setting sun. Resting on the sea were three warships. It was as if home had come to embrace him. One was *Athena*, battered, dirty, and proud. And two were French; one an enormous dock landing ship, the *Siroco*, the tricolor flying (strangely, he thought) from the starboard stern corner; the other, the frigate *Guépratte*, its tricolor at the bow.

Though the lights of the three ships were suppressed by the rich light of the declining sun, still, they sparkled. Landing craft were motoring back and forth between the beach and the *Siroco*, and the village was crowded with trucks. Two French armored cars with anti-tank missiles guarded the end of the wadi, and even from a distance the infantry on the ridges seemed comfortably dominant and assured. Holworthy saw the hostages in lines waiting to board the landing craft. The wounded were already aboard *Siroco*. Martin, Petra, and Sophie had transferred to it immediately when it had arrived. From near where the RHIB was pulled up on the beach, Movius and Pisecki were running toward him.

"Where's the captain?" Movius asked.

"Dead."

Movius closed his eyes and briefly covered them with his hand. He asked, accusingly, "You left him?"

"He fell onto a ledge forty feet down. Even had no one been shooting at me I couldn't have gotten to him."

"We're going to have to get him," Movius said.

"Hadawi's got almost a thousand men between us and him."

Movius gestured to the swarm of French. "They've got helicopters."

"But will they?"

"We'll see."

"Where are our guys?" Holworthy asked.

"Except for Monroe and Minorkis, they're all okay. So are the sick hostages. The *Siroco*," he said as he pointed to it, "has a hospital aboard. Two operating rooms, forty-seven beds, surgeons, doctors, nurses—unbelievable."

"I have to see my men."

"Sure. Then we'll talk to the French commodore. If he doesn't give us a helicopter, we'll stay. We'll get the captain one way or another."

"What are our orders?"

"You don't want to know."

"I would imagine they're pissed."

"You would be right, but I've never felt better in my life, or prouder." Movius looked at his watch, and then at the operations on the beach. "The idea is to get everyone onto the ships by nightfall. *Siroco* is supposed to leave immediately for Djibouti. The Europeans will be airlifted home, our wounded to Landstuhl, our dead to Dover. The *Guépratte* will stay to cover, but I don't know for how long. With its guns and some luck, we could wipe out Hadawi. If they were Americans, they would stay with us. But we don't know about the French."

"If *Siroco* goes, what about the helicopters?" *Guépratte* was turned, bow landward, so that Holworthy couldn't see its stern.

"*Guépratte* has a helicopter deck, and a light helicopter on board, but they can't handle an NH90, their big helo."

"What *are* our orders?"

Movius smiled tightly before he answered. "Our orders . . . are to return to Djibouti immediately, as soon as *Siroco* gets underway. In Djibouti a relief crew will replace us and take *Athena* home."

"Immediately?"

Movius nodded.

"Not without the captain. But they don't know."

"They don't. And if they still insist that we leave immediately we'll have to get a good lawyer to parse what *immediately* means. You know, like what the definition of *is* is. But right now I'm in command, and given where we are and how we got here, I have some discretion and I plan to exercise it—even if it takes us a week to get him back and ten years in the brig."

*

The French commodore on *Siroco* spoke excellent English, which helped a great deal, as Movius and Holworthy spoke little French. He received them at dinner in a very American-looking dining room, with a counter upon which sat an expresso machine, condiments, and a glass-enclosed model of a fairly ancient brigantine. He wore the same workmanlike uniform as everyone else on the ship, with reflective material across the chest that caught the light from lamps recessed in the overhead, and which to an American suggested a skunk in the headlights. Holworthy quietly asked Movius, "Do they have skunks in France?"

Because Movius had donned his whites, he felt out of place. Holworthy had changed to clean fatigues, but his face and arms were blistered with sunburn and dotted with minor wounds that made him seem quite fierce. He and Movius were struck that, like a corporate worker bee or a White House staffer, the French captain wore a photo ID badge. And they marveled at the cleanliness and order of *Siroco*, which seemed to have not a single dent or streak of rust. *Athena* in contrast was as beaten up as Holworthy. The French ships were like fresh troops on their way to the line who pass the filthy, bloodied, silent veterans streaming back. Even though the veterans were once new, they can no longer comprehend what that is like. The lightness of being has been driven out of them unbearably.

The captain of *Siroco*, commodore of the French squadron, was bearded, bald, and heavyset. They were seated at a table for four, with tablecloth, flowers, and bentwood chairs.

"Our captain died," Movius began, "while staying behind with Lieutenant Commander Holworthy to delay Hadawi's troops at a narrow defile. Two men"—he paused—"versus perhaps a thousand with heavy weapons. He's still there. We need a helicopter to retrieve him."

"He's dead, yes?" the commodore asked.

"Yes."

"Even if we can get permission, it will be delayed. I'll explain later. First, we'll eat, then we'll talk."

Though U.S. Navy food is fairly good, it could not always be so on *Athena*, especially after provisions had run low. And it could not in any form compare to what the French had. Neither the water of the Île-de-France nor a brick oven nor the atmosphere and humidity of Paris were available here, but the bread was just as good, which deepened the mystery of French baking.

The commodore kept the conversation to a minimum as his guests, eager to get Rensselaer back, ate fast. Then they walked to a sitting room and sat on couches around an oval coffee table.

The commodore began. "What your captain did, *remarquable. Horatius Cocles sur le pont Sublicius.*"

"Exactly," Movius confirmed. "Horatio at the bridge. It gave the trucks four more hours to bring your people here."

"For which we are very grateful, believe me."

"We need your help," Holworthy said. "An RPG blew him off the escarpment into the defile, where he landed on a ledge about ten meters down. One helicopter sortie, that's all."

The commodore was deeply sympathetic. "I want to do it. But it isn't up to me. Let me explain. First, very soon, ISIS will arrive. Everyone is aboard except the covering force, who are on their way. As Commander Movius," which he pronounced *Muhve-yuz*, "knows, we will then pull offshore and observe. If from the beach and the village they fire at us, we have permission to shoot back. That is already cleared. If they don't, we cannot.

"I can't send out a force to retrieve your captain, even a small one, until I receive permission. The way things are, such an order will not arrive—if it does—until tomorrow at the earliest. And as we do not know if Hadawi has MANPADS—that is what you call them?"

"Yes, man-portable air defense systems."

"Probably your Stingers, we cannot fly helicopters over unreconnoitered territory in daylight. So tomorrow night would be the earliest."

"What are the chances, do you think," Movius asked, "for the go-ahead?"

"It's difficult to say. Our people are safe. The country and the world think the crisis is over—and it is. Everyone is relieved and has gone on to other things. Our civil authorities will not want to spoil the good result with the loss of an NH90 and its crew just when people are celebrating. And, then, France is and has been involved all over Africa since colonial days. We have both resistance and encouragement for this from other nations, and of course we ourselves are divided about it and always have been. We deal with it in two ways. First, there is the Foreign Legion, which tells the French that foreign mercenaries rather than Frenchmen are at risk. This trick we borrowed from the Romans, and it works. Second, we try to limit our involvements as much as possible.

"Here, we are authorized to retrieve the hostages, but once they are on board, the authorization is no longer, and we are forbidden to operate on the soil of yet another state in Africa—or, if you like, yet another anarchic territory in Africa. I will ask, and they will deliberate. All of France is grateful to *Athena*. You are quite famous there, you know, for the moment."

"We didn't know."

"Yes. The name of the ship has been a great help. It suggests to the French the classical world, beauty, and wisdom, none of which they associate with America. This week, they do, until they will forget. But of course I will request permission to retrieve Captain Rensselaer's body. Commander Holworthy," which he pronounced *Ole-vohr-tee*, "you can guide us?"

"I can."

"And if we go, you understand that although you will be with us, we will be in command."

"Yes, sir, I do."

"Good. Perhaps almost as much as you, I want not to leave him."

"We won't do that. If you can't help us, we'll find a way to bring him back ourselves."

"I understand, although, knowing your orders, I will make no comment."

A subaltern knocked, and was told to enter. He announced that the covering force was aboard, and the last ones in had reported that far to the northwest a dust cloud rising in the setting sun looked like it was on fire. The enemy would probably arrive in less than an hour.

*

Hopeful that the commodore's request would be favorably received, Movius and Holworthy returned to *Athena* as it and the two French ships moved offshore out of range of Hadawi's guns but hardly so far as to make their own weapons ineffective. After the RHIB was dragged up *Athena*'s damaged ramp and lashed down, resting on its side, Movius ordered general quarters. Though this time there was less urgency than previously, it was done on the double.

Soon, several score trucks and technicals burst from the south wadi and flooded into the village and over the beach. It was not quite dark enough for them to use their headlights, or for the gunners and officers on *Athena*, *Siroco*, and *Guépratte* to resort to night vision.

Movius, Holworthy, and Pisecki, who was once again the OOD, stood on the starboard bridge wing observing through their binoculars the puzzling, frenzied activity on shore.

"What are they jumping around for?" Movius asked. "There's no one there and nothing they can do. I don't get it."

"All passion, no reason," Holworthy added. "Look at it. They're insanely worked up, shooting in the air, shouting. They're literally jumping up and down."

Pisecki observed, "Notice, they're looking at *us*. Look at that guy to the left, near the technical—see him?"

The others slewed their binoculars until they did. "Yeah," they said, one after the other.

Pisecki went on, incredulously. "He's screaming himself hoarse, threatening us, pointing his AK."

"The bulk of this force are Somalis from Puntland and who the hell knows where," Holworthy added. "They're not, like Hadawi, educated Levantines with one foot in modern times. You're witnessing tribal warfare thousands of years old."

"The question is," Movius stated, "are they stupid enough to open fire on us with no effect except to allow us to open fire on them? Even though our lights are doused they see our silhouettes. They've got to know that we're out of range."

"I wouldn't bet on their geometry," Holworthy commented.

"Why would Hadawi be so stupid?" Pisecki asked.

"You've got to consider," Holworthy answered, "that to keep his men loyal he has to make them happy. And don't forget that Hadawi is someone who cuts off people's heads and throws babies into the sea. No matter how clever he might be, he is, by our standards, insane. You have to respect him only in the same way that you respect a cobra."

The captain of the *Guépratte* seemed to have a sixth sense informing him of the answer to the questions the Americans had been discussing, and as all waited and as the moon was just rising on a calm sea that lapped gently against the sides of the ships, he ordered his four-inch gun to slew landward in preparation for a broadside. Everyone on *Athena* heard the sound (a cross between grinding and whining) and turned to look. They understood the balance of forces, and were intensely curious about what might happen.

Five miles out, the ships were well beyond the range of anything on the technicals. Their lights were extinguished not because they needed to hide—they could have been blazing like those of the floating amusement parks called cruise ships—but rather out of adherence to the requirements for combat even if in this situation these were irrelevant and the little fleet invulnerable.

Hadawi, however, was not invulnerable. The *Guépratte*'s four-inch gun had a ten-mile range and could fire eighty rounds per minute. That is, from the unfortunate point of view of a totally unarmored infantry force on the receiving end, a thirty-pound high-explosive shell landing every three-quarters of a second. In addition, the *Guépratte*'s two 20mm cannons had just the range to target, and were capable of dropping albeit far-less-damaging shells but at the rate of twelve rounds per second. Fire control and direction were so quick and precise that it was possible to pick out individual trucks quite easily. But given the concentration of the enemy and the volume of fire, a general salvo was all that was needed.

Though Movius had allowed for a dash in, and running broadside as before, now the Americans would likely be only spectators held in reserve, which, given what they had done and what they were used to, was hard to take.

Instead of subsiding, the frenzy of Hadawi's troops swelled, feeding upon itself until thousands of muzzle flashes from AKs lit the beach like Satanic fireflies spitting sulfurous flame. Very soon the entire shore was covered in orange sparks. The whole of Hadawi's army was firing out to sea and to no avail. Within seconds of the chorus of AKs reaching its full volume, the heavy guns on the technicals began to fire as well. This was a different provocation, and was treated as such.

The commodore gave the order to fire at will, and *Guépratte* opened up. As its heavy shells hit, the span of their destinations both in time and space allowed them to overlap into what seemed like a continuous explosion further magnified by echoes from the cliffs. Village and beach were lit in yellow and orange light that illuminated not only the buildings and the escarpment but columns of heavy black-and-white smoke that had formed above the chaos in an immense cloud which reflected the light of explosions back upon their source.

In less than a minute, *Guépratte* had turned Ras Hagar into hell once more, this time more dramatically than ever. Hadawi's army had stopped firing. Anyone still alive ran for the few trucks that hadn't been hit, flew aboard, and raced toward the south wadi.

Observing this, Movius said, "I wonder if the *Guépratte* will drop some shells on the wadi to block the exit." Because the noise was so great, he had to repeat this.

"The trucks are escaping," Holworthy announced, and, rather more enthusiastic than Movius, blurted out, "Come on Frogs! Redirect!"

The French, however, did not. Perhaps they were too astounded by the power and effect of their barrage to act further. The firing stopped, and if anyone was left alive, by next light he would have limped out or he would be dead.

With the sunrise, the officers and crews of *Athena* and the French ships saw through their telescopes and binoculars the rubble of buildings, the burned carcasses of trucks, and scores of bodies lying on the beach. The vultures had not yet descended, but, higher than the cliff tops, thick swarms of them wheeled in the air.

VI

Lovely Appear

"Lovely appear, over the mountains. . . ."

Alone

The RPG that detonated against the rock floor fifteen feet to Rensselaer's left sent out a shockwave and sprays of shell casing. The purpose of the munition is not to kill infantry but to pierce armor. Though magnified by ricochets inside a tank or an armored personnel carrier, the shrapnel is secondary to the overpressure of the explosion. Except for a few small pieces that traveled close to the ground, most fragments were propelled away from the center of the charge at a forty-degree angle, and flew over Rensselaer's head. The blast, however, hit him full force, lifting him into the air and rightward over the edge of the defile.

With no time to think or fear, because the explosion was immeasurable to conscious thought, he perceived it nonetheless as if it unfolded in slow motion, and felt neither pain nor regret as he sailed over the abyss. The glimpse of stopped time was so comforting as to suggest perfect answers to questions that had not even been asked. Blown into the air, weightless, the world made soundless, he was aware of the complete death of his will, and he felt nothing other than intense relief, gratitude, and joy.

After a moment of gravityless suspension, he fell, back first, looking up into featureless blue. Forty feet down, he landed with immense force in the V shape of a ledge that, partially cleft from the rock wall, narrowed at its bottom. Every bit of air was pushed from his lungs, many of his ribs were cracked, and then the back of his head hit the rock, opening a gash in his scalp and rendering him unconscious. He soon regained consciousness but was totally paralyzed and could not breathe.

Despite the injuries, he felt no pain. Then Holworthy appeared, looking over the ledge and calling soundlessly. Rensselaer couldn't even blink to let Holworthy know he still lived. It was like a dream in which he knew ahead of time that Holworthy would conclude that he was dead and leave him there. Even if Holworthy knew he was alive, he would have had to leave him, to which Rensselaer had no objection.

After Holworthy left, Rensselaer waited for Hadawi. If they had no way to get him up from the ledge, they would just shoot him as he lay.

If they did have the means, they would retrieve and then torture him. But in regard to either possibility he felt perfect equanimity, and that he was the master of the situation, looking from afar in time and distance to events so minor in the sweep of time as almost not to exist.

They didn't find him. Thinking that, like Holworthy, he had escaped, they didn't look. He expected them to become very busy below as they took out their dead and wounded; retrieved supplies, ammunition, and guns; and cleared the passage. But no one came. As his hearing returned he heard Hadawi's army rush away, and like the men scattered below, not all of whom were yet dead, he was left in silence except for the occasional moans and cries of enemy wounded, though by 2300 the cold had silenced them forever.

At four in the morning the temperature would drop into the thirties. Even before midnight it was cold enough in the wind so that a sentry in such a situation who had to man his post without moving would experience hypothermia sufficient to dull his reflexes no matter how much he was bundled up in cold-weather gear.

Rensselaer's cotton fatigues were of little value against such cold, and wind accelerated by the constricted defile went right through them. He decided to curl up for whatever warmth it might afford. Perhaps if his back were pressed against one side of the V and his knees were lifted into his chest, even the rock would offer some insulation. At least it would block the wind, and in lessening his surface area he would slow the dissipation of heat. Of the many ways to die, cold was not high on his list.

He was afraid to move, because the effort might tell him that he was in fact paralyzed. Not having stirred for hours, he was now forced to try. First, he attempted to lift his arms. He couldn't. In fact, he couldn't feel them. He didn't know it, but their circulation had been compressed as they and the rest of him had been pressed between the sides of the V. *All right*, he thought, *maybe my legs aren't paralyzed*. At the same time that this seemed to him to be stupid—because if he were paralyzed from the neck down it would obviously include his legs—he tried to move them, and succeeded. He was able to lift them, one at a time, a few inches. It caused great pain in his ribs, something he actually appreciated, for it overrode the cold.

When he tried to pull his knees up to his chest and turn to the side the pain became exquisite, and he had neither the strength nor the leverage to do so. Perhaps if he raised his upper body. He tried this. The agony of his abdominal muscles and ribs, and the effect on his breathing, might themselves have stopped him, but these were the lesser part of it. His head was immovable. At first he attributed this to the medically dubious paralysis he suspected but began to doubt when, because of the movement of his legs, his right arm became un-wedged, and thus the pressure on the left arm lessened, and they both began to tingle as if they were Galvani's frog legs hanging pitifully on what would become perhaps the world's most famous length of wire.

"Well that's nice," he said, moving his arms and discovering that he could still speak. He almost forgot the cold as he entertained the possibility of having "paralysis of the head," if such a thing existed. It didn't sound right. Still, he couldn't move his head. Not only was it immovable, the pain in his ribs escalated when he tried to do so. He thought to move his arms up to it so as to "loosen" it. That didn't make sense, but he certainly had time to try. Thus, he spent the next hour or so moving his arms, little by little, more and more, freeing and restoring them, until, at about midnight, when he was numb and shivering with cold, he reached his head. He then tried to lift it with their aid. Nothing but strain.

Feeling about, he encountered a slick surface, almost plastic, and much smoother than the rock. Tracing this, he found that it merged into his hair. Then he realized that it was dried blood and God only knew what other fluid, which had soaked his hair as it flowed from a head wound or wounds that he could neither see nor feel, but which bonded him to the ridged and porous rock. Perhaps if he had pulled hard enough he might have freed himself. But he might also have opened the wound and bled out. Most of the bond was out of reach of his fingers, so chipping away at it was impossible.

He now understood that he was going to die like this, and that as he died he was going to be very cold. He had gone from blue to white, neither of which he could see. He had always feared being trapped in a dark compartment, the cold seawater rising until he drowned. At least that would have been quicker. Here, it would go slowly. It's one thing to be cold if you can move, and quite another if you can't. And then he remembered.

*

380

When very hard—some mistakenly said catastrophic—winters struck the Northeast in the seventies, Stephen Rensselaer was in middle school and poorly dressed for the cold. Manufacturing on the Upper Hudson had long since begun its precipitous decline, and his father, a foundryman whose trade was practiced in a nineteenth-century building in darkness periodically made orange by the pours of molten metal, was among the first to be laid off. He never stopped looking for another job, and never refused any work he could find. When the unemployment insurance ran out, the family eschewed welfare. Instead, Stephen's father cut and aged wood, rented a truck, and sold firewood in Manhattan for fifty cents a split, or the astounding price of two dollars per eighteen-inch log.

Given the time in the woods, the splitting, the aging, gas for the chain saw, sharpening the chain, repairs, renting the truck, fuel for it, tolls, bribing police and the doormen on Park Avenue for a parking space, and carrying up the wood, the price was not so inflated, but it astounded him nonetheless. On school vacations, Stephen sat in the back of the open truck to guard against theft while his father carried the wood into the service elevators. Were the load not that heavy, Stephen would sometimes take it. When Stephen was in school, his father had to pay the doormen quite a bit extra to watch the truck.

At Christmastime, in the cold, as he perched on the firewood piled in the truck, Stephen would watch people walking on Park, Fifth, or Central Park West. There was a visible difference between him and the boys his age whom he saw. They had better haircuts, and puffy jackets. Despite his wool sweaters and blanket-lined denim jacket, Stephen was always cold, and he shivered in the back of the truck. When he could carry up to the apartments, it took a while to warm up, so initially he held himself stiffly, and one could read the discomfort in his face.

On account of more foot traffic and firewood purchases on the west side of Park, the back of the truck was thus open to the north wind and shielded from south sun. On Fifth, there was no choice but to park in the same direction, though on the east side of the street. During very cold days, if the loads were too heavy for him to carry, he would really freeze as he stayed with the wood. His father sometimes let him carry a heavy load in several trips so he could warm up. And sometimes his father turned on the heat in the cab while running the truck just so Stephen could get some relief. Once, he was given a dollar and told to get a hot chocolate somewhere where he could get warm. He found a restaurant on Madison, but the hot chocolate cost $2.50, so he pretended that he had had it, and surreptitiously threw the dollar in with the money from the wood. In the apartments it was wonderfully warm, and he had never seen such beautiful rooms. He felt no envy (never in his life would he feel envy, ever: this was just the way he was) but only delight in the sudden luxury and ease of entering a curated, eleven-room apartment on Park Avenue, in the same way that were he to have seen a painting of Eden he would not have begrudged it to Adam and Eve. It was a different world, and when, once, a doorman had told him that the apartments in one building were "triple mint," he understood the meaning but thought the phrasing uncomfortably alien.

It was to these apartments that the boys in puffy jackets returned from their shockingly expensive prep schools in Manhattan or New England. From the relaxed way they walked it was easy to see that they were warm. A boy and his sister close to Stephen's age caught his eye one day when it was sunny and ten degrees and he was facing north. She was very pretty, and had a navy blue band in her blonde hair. Flowing from the bottom of her puffy jacket was the plaid skirt of a school uniform; from his, the bottom of a blazer.

They hadn't noticed Stephen sitting on the stack of wood in the back of the truck. "Hey," he called out. At first they kept walking, and then they paused. "What's in those jackets?"

"Goose down," the boy answered.

"They look really warm," Stephen said.

"They are, they really are. You should get one."

"I'll give it a try," Stephen told him. "Wanna buy some firewood? I cut it."

The boy's sister had pivoted slightly to her left and now faced Stephen. "Our fireplace doesn't work," she said. "There's a thing in front of it that blocks it up." He was quite sure that she looked at him with interest. As for Stephen, he could fall in love in five seconds flat, he often did, and he certainly did then.

"Okay," Stephen told them. "Maybe next year your fireplace will be unblocked."

As they departed, he began to dream of her, and of puffy jackets. Where he lived on the Upper Hudson there were hardly any down jackets at the time. When eventually he found one in Albany, the price was far too high. There was no way he was going to have anything more than what he already had. With the family food budget of three dollars per day, down jackets would have to wait.

That winter it was sometimes 32° below. Stephen discovered, however, that, just as the initial heat of summer gradually became tolerable, it was possible to acclimate himself to the cold. And just as, by February, cold days in October seemed in retrospect to have been quite warm, the secret was adaptation. He decided to try to teach his body to acclimate not automatically but according to will.

One Saturday early in March, when the next-to-last of that winter's Arctic fronts descended from Canada and brought very cold air in high, bright sun, it was nine degrees Fahrenheit and the land was covered with blindingly white snow. In a recent thaw, patches of the Hudson had swallowed the snow accumulated on them and re-frozen into glassy ice now unbroken because, on its way north from the Tappan Zee, the little Coast Guard icebreaker had yet to clear the stretch of river at Stephen's house.

He left for the ice at eleven. As he didn't have a watch, he took a white plastic kitchen timer, with red numbers and notches, which struck one loud bell after up to an hour of loud ticking. A little ways out on the Hudson he found a snow-free circle about fifty feet in diameter. At its center, he set the timer for an hour, and lay on his back.

Though he was somewhat out of the strong wind, it sought and found the openings in his clothes. In less than a minute, he felt the ice through the shirt, sweater, and jacket that now hardly seemed to exist. When he began to shiver, he sought to stop, but he had no idea how. Tightening his muscles and tensing as one does in the cold was ineffective.

So he tried the opposite. He relaxed, let out a breath, and delayed breathing in. This seemed to work, and he kept it up as it did, concentrating on stopping the blood flow to the surface of his body. Whether or not this succeeded, he felt as if he had divided himself into a surface that although it was cold little bothered him, and an interior, which was warm. He didn't shiver. His extremities and skin didn't freeze, but were as cold as they could be without doing so, in a kind of suspension. For a full hour he was still, and when the bell rang he rose on the ice, having taught himself something he had not even previously imagined. Now he would be able to sit in the back of the truck as comfortably as if he were in a puffy jacket. And although someday he might be able to afford a puffy jacket, he knew that he would never really need one. And long after, staying in the cold surf during BUD/S training at Coronado would be a lark.

*

Well past pain, on rock almost as cold as ice, Rensselaer felt nothing except within, where now he seemed to burn. This had never happened on the ice, for he had stayed only an hour. He knew that any great distress might confuse the senses in such a way, though it seemed too early to die. Trying hard to stay conscious, he went through his options. Because he was confused and disoriented by the cold, he would drift off to sleep, then awake later, having dreamt that he asked questions of Katy, or she of him. God, she was lovely, lovely, when first he saw her. The thought of her banished all pain, and the dreams seemed more real than that to which he awoke, until he hardly knew the difference. The questions were asked but never answered. They had to do with numbers, shapes, and lights. And in the dreams she was imperturbable, a savior, an angel.

Whenever he awoke, however, because of his study and practice of celestial navigation, he knew the approximate time. And he knew, therefore, that he was neither in heaven nor in hell. *This will end*, he would say to himself, and then drift off again, only to awake.

He reminded himself repeatedly that his choices were nonexistent. If no help came—and why would it?—he would have to risk opening the wound. If he succeeded in not bleeding to death, he would have either to climb forty feet up or descend much farther down. He hadn't been able to see below him, but for an hour in the light he had explored the way up, looking for a route he might follow despite his weakness and his wounds. The ridged but unbroken rock would be unavailing. In and out of consciousness, he discovered and rediscovered that he was going to remain where he was.

Each time he came to this conclusion he felt the relaxation, if not the comfort, of surrender. Then he would go through it all again and again, his only anchor to reality being the clock of the stars, which told him not only that morning would come, but when. And each time he came to and looked at them, he knew from the calculations he made that because his ability to do so was somehow intact, he was still there, he was still who he was, and he was still alive.

*

The first sign of morning was a softening of the black sky. Not that it was gray, or anywhere near blue, but that in their slight dimming the stars seemed to be receding into it, and then to become smaller until, not that long after, they vanished, the brightest among them appearing to sink upward into the gray. First to go had been the Pleiades, the weakest but, in their close embrace that made a smudge of light like that of a disappearing comet, the most beautiful. Of all the groupings, in their softness and sheen the Pleiades were the best.

Eventually all the stars were gone, it was not quite so cold, and the wind began to flow through the cut, south to north, as a warm breeze from the sea pushed like a tide toward the desert. This, too, told him the time.

A ray of sun, deep rose in color but as gently diffused as the Pleiades, struck a triangular outcropping above him on the other side of the cut. As it grew in intensity and the color changed, its faint blush stayed with him. The image was strong and persistent because it was so much like something he had seen long before, something forgotten until now, when, like remembered music, it arose from childhood.

He was far enough gone that he didn't know why he was there or how long he had been there. That he was dehydrated, feverish, internally battered and inflamed, concussed, and lucky to have emerged from shock, didn't matter. For having seen only briefly the roseate triangle, he felt only love and steadily growing tranquility. And this is why.

*

The Dutch Reformed Church to which the Rensselaers adhered was in a spare white building with tall, mullioned windows of wavy, antique glass; colonial brass chandeliers; and cushionless pews. That he was there on Sunday mornings was no more unusual than that the night was dark or the day was light. From his infancy, all that was said and sung left him not so much with understanding as with impression and feeling. As he had been born and simply taken into it, he felt the right to reject it, or not, even before he understood what it was. It was just there. He neither rejected nor accepted it, and then he grew very busy as he came into adulthood.

Now he was anything but busy, and in its brief appearance the roseate triangle brought him back to a winter morning when he was seven or eight, long before he had learned to overcome the cold by surrender to it, when it burned his hands with near frostbite, threatened his toes, and once nearly killed him. He was coming home from school, when the temperature dropped so precipitously and the wind grew so strong in a sudden blizzard that he could only crawl the last twenty feet to the front door, couldn't get up, and was able to pound on it only so softly with his gnarled, frozen hands that had the dog not alerted his mother he would have died at the threshold and been buried by the snow in less than half an hour.

The church was heated by a huge, tiled stove on the steps of which the children were allowed to sit as their parents shivered in the pews. From this somewhat elevated position, his back warm against the radiant tiles, Stephen looked straight west out the side windows and across the Hudson to the Catskills, their uninhabited eastern cliffs and peaks draped in the austere winter cloak of the Hudson Highlands—cold snow grayed at a distance by a plethora of black, leafless trees. Nothing is quite as bleak as the sight of this looming over an ice-choked river, even when the sun is shining, and especially when it isn't.

Early in the morning, when the stove had not been burning long, the first service had begun just before sunrise. The words of the sermon were interesting to Stephen in the same way that sledding down a hill might be, for the sensation, the patterns, the delight in understanding the meaning of the surface over which he passed without comprehending its depth. In the long run, just to hear the language and the tone was as productive as to grasp the import.

When the sermon came to an end, the minister turned to the choir. As an organ was too expensive and too big, the church made do with a piano. The choirmaster, a woman with blue-framed glasses and a bowl haircut, gestured to the choir and the pianist—another woman with blue-framed glasses and a bowl haircut, who Stephen thought had to be at least two hundred years old—and said, "Lovely Appear."

The lyrics—"Lovely appear, over the mountains, the feet of them that preach, and bring good news of peace"—made little sense to him. He had never understood all the biblical stuff about washing feet, which in a country where people wore shoes seemed rather odd. And that the focus of such a hymn, its music, its poetry, was on feet, seemed silly. What did not seem so were the image of mountains, especially as he stared at them through the windows, the syntax that archaically, mystically, and beautifully allowed the subject to follow the verb, and the very pleasure of the phrase *lovely appear.*

In his mind the dross was shed—that is, the feet, preaching, news, peace—and all that was left was the power of *lovely appear*, the image of mountains, the mountains he saw, and the music. It made a deep impression, for the rest of his life suggestive of the brick and iron of his childhood, the austerity, the love and the struggle, the hard times in the snow, and the unbreakable bond with his parents, who now as he lay on his back in a crag lost in a desert on the Horn of Africa, were long and forever gone, and whom he had always loved more for their vulnerabilities than for their strengths. It was their vulnerability that had led him to a life devoted to protecting even those who would never know what he did, even those who would condemn him while living free behind the battered shield that he and others would hold for their sake and for the mysteriously pleasurable sake of holding fast even unto death.

As a child, he had had no such thoughts, but was lifted by the words sung again and again: *lovely appear.* The chance that this impression might vanish was forever foreclosed when purely by accident the sun rose from behind the Berkshires and painted the triangular Catskill peak highest in the range with the diffuse and delicate roseate light of early morning. The snow reflected its rays like a glass-beaded screen, and as the hymn echoed through the church, atop the mountain it seemed that a cool fire burned, just as it would many years later on the prominence of desert rock above the ledge where he lay dying.

*

He was comforted by the balance of things, in the appearance of this sign reminding him of his early innocence. It was an emissary, he thought, signaling that between the beginning and the end he had been faithful, and his life had been coherent enough that he could now depart.

The Somalian desert, however, was not too well aligned with the Dutch Reformed Church, the thunderstorms of the Hudson Valley, or the workings of memory in Stephen Rensselaer's heart. If anything, asserting its vastness, majesty, and age, it remained arrogantly in contradiction. Were he to die here, he would have to die on its terms, not those imported or remembered.

And the first thing the desert did was flood his eyes with light, as the sun, now white, found a way into the passage and broke upon it like a wave. He was already feverish from his night in the cold and now this morning sun made him so much hotter. He was lucid enough to know that sweating would throw his electrolytes out of balance and stop his heart—if not that day, then, assuming he survived another night, surely the next.

The sky soon became the unique desert blue that in its high depths turns black. Gusts of wind sometimes blew sand over him and into his eyes. The sun seemed to be something living, with a will, as did the cliffs, and even the desert beyond the plateau, which, though he couldn't see it, he knew was there.

The rising, varying structure of the cliffs above, and the sun flashing against crystals in the rock, were like the lights, shapes, and muted colors of a vast city at dusk. So many times he had watched from a distance as the sun, rising or setting, had given life to a mass of buildings and bridges. He was often privileged to see this from the harbors of cities to which he had guided his ship at dawn or dusk. It could be so beautiful and golden as to comfort the deepest distress, for the sight of such a thing meant that the life of the world and the beauties that arose without deliberation or design would continue full force in his absence, their benevolent author lifting from him the anxious illusion suffered by so many that faith and justice rested solely upon their struggles and successes. In short, everything would be all right.

As time went on, he tried to think of Katy and was heartbroken that he could not, for now he hardly knew himself or who he was. By afternoon, without water, in 115 degrees Fahrenheit, he was only a component of nature, a thing like the rock, the sand, and the sun, all of which seemed to take on life inversely with his loss of it, until eventually he and they would be the same.

This was no tragedy, and he felt no fear. Rather, he experienced an increasing velocity. Each time he shuddered with chill in the immense heat, he thought he had reached the jumping-off point from which he would be pulled into the sun and stars. But, each time, he fell back.

The rock against his fingers was so complex, as he had never realized before—its grain, its plains, its ridges—that it seemed like a world unto itself. The heat, too, was no longer just one thing, but rather a thousand different emanations, each with its own message and voice.

Wind whistling against the rock ledges made him hear once more the wind in *Athena*'s rigging as it made a concert among her stays, her sharp edges, vibrating cables, and buckling sheet metal. It was hard to believe that in these voices that were singing a voice was not speaking. When trembling white lines of foam were scudding across the waves, if you held your mouth open only slightly the wind would seize your lips and speak for you. At times like that, listening to invisible forces and joining in, he wondered if in fact we are instruments of a will of which we cannot conceive, something always there, as if at the tip of the tongue, that takes benevolent delight in vanishing as we close.

Words were soon to leave him, and this he regretted. The last of them he heard as if spoken by wind and water, and saw as if written in the air.

In heartbreak and in memory I am fixed upon the ocean, always the ocean, to which everything flows as it returns in rivers and rainfall and through quiet coastal marshes where waves dance in the reeds.

This was beautiful, but not enough, and, even as he slipped, he knew it.

Katy on the Home Front

Because in the Garden District it has always been so easy just to do nothing, and because she could not know where *Athena* was, Katy had tried as best she could to wait in tranquility. But one windless, silent night, a thin crescent of bright moon appeared in the window and, of all the things in the dark of the room, aimed for her eyes. It seemed like a message, and from then on she was unwilling merely to wait.

Seeking news of Stephen, she came up with nothing. When he first deployed, she was simply blind. He was somewhere, presumably in the Gulf, and in the war reports she found no hint of anything he might be doing. Like previous Middle Eastern wars, this one dragged on until it migrated to the back pages of the papers. The Iranian nuclear infrastructure had been destroyed, during which some twenty-some American airmen had been captured and an equal number killed. It was assumed that, at best, the prisoners would be held a long time.

Apart from special forces raids along the Iranian coast and continual attacks on Iranian military assets and supply inside Iran, most of the war consisted of protecting Saudi and Kuwaiti oil facilities and keeping the Gulf and the Strait of Hormuz open for oil tankers. Air battles over water had been much in the news for a few days until what little was left of the Iranian Air Force was shot down and its bases completely destroyed.

Soon it became a war of missile defense, and air raids against the missiles that Iran seemed to have in endless supply. Every day, the sky would be streaked with their trajectories on radar and in smoke, and every night orange points of flame appeared among the stars, their targets oil terminals, tankers, or American naval vessels. Either alone at night or in daylight swarms, small Iranian boats, many on suicide missions, would attack the Navy. In the Gulf and the Strait, every ship was continually at general quarters, and the PCs were constantly on patrol or engaged. Two American destroyers and three littoral combat ships (known to PC crews as "fat, slightly-armed yachts") had been sunk, with hundreds killed. The PCs were nimble enough and of sufficiently low value to avoid being sought out, and to survive when they went on the attack, as they often did. None had been sunk after the first hours of the war, and their daily engagements were largely unreported. Among other things, embedded reporters had been assigned to larger, more comfortable vessels.

PC crews suffered individual casualties, but these were not identified as to where or how they took place. So, initially, there was nothing Katy could divine from the press. When *Athena* sank the *Sahand*, the Pentagon did not want to stress the threat to the fleet the latter had presented with the Tsirkon. Among other things, this would have brought into the open Russia's limited support for Iran, and the State Department correctly was of the view that were this exposed it would spur Russia to defend its posture by asserting it further, rather than, as it was doing, quietly letting it drop. The Tsirkon, after all, had been supplied and fitted to the *Sahand* well before the outbreak of war.

In the briefing about the *Sahand*, no mention had been made of any of this. The Pentagon spokesman merely stated that a major Iranian warship had been sunk in the Indian Ocean by an American patrol ship that though overmatched had employed superior tactics. Sensing a David-and-Goliath story, reporters asked for details, but the spokesman replied that operational secrecy meant he was not at liberty to supply them. With little to go on, they repeated what he had announced. It could be nothing other than a minor story, and they had called the American patrol vessel a *boat*, further muddying the waters.

Knowing something about this, Katy doubted that a patrol boat could sink a major combatant. Nor, given her long conversations with Stephen, did she place patrol boats in blue waters. She guessed that it must have been a PC, and, knowing Stephen and how he thought, suspected that it might have been the *Athena*.

But after that, nothing followed until the worldwide obsession with *l'Étoile*. Here were almost two hundred hostages, from countries not at war, held by the world's most savage and reviled captors. Especially the children, women, and old people, from the Philippines and half a dozen countries in Europe, every one a civilian, captured universal attention from the moment the news media learned of them.

The initial reports stated that a French naval squadron was on its way. Soon enough, word leaked out from many sources in Europe that an American naval ship had been the first to respond, that it had engaged the hijackers as they ambushed it in a faked hostage release, that it had been damaged, and that contact with it had been lost. All the American authorities could say was that they had no communication with the ship, and assumed that its ability to transmit had been damaged or destroyed. Attention then turned, as it could not but do, to the promised hourly beheadings.

Katy had no way of knowing for sure that the American ship was the *Athena,* for the Navy hadn't even identified its type, but despite this she became anxious and alarmed. Her work suffered noticeably, and she was impatient with others, actually saying to one of her well meaning suitors, who found excuses to talk with her simply because to him her presence was semi-intoxicating, "I told you before. We don't have to go over it again. Go away." Then, not even looking at him, her right hand moving as if to shoo a fly, "Out." And, to a delinquent middle-schooler she found smoking a joint on her front steps, "Get off my steps you little shit or I'll rip your lungs out." Not characteristically quite this blunt, she watched as he ran down the street as if chased by a bull.

One evening as she started to cook dinner she turned on a small television in the kitchen and saw that the hostages had been rescued, and Europe was celebrating the *Athena* and its crew that had fought fiercely at sea and on land. Many European governments and their peoples were especially eager to honor the ship, because, offended by and generally disapproving of the war with Iran, they were happy to amplify the rumors that an American warship had accomplished the rescue of their citizens by going against the express orders of the American government, and, it was said, the president himself, of whom the Europeans were proud to be ostentatiously horrified.

This was reported in the European press—whence came the news via the hostages' families and leaks from the French Ministry of Defense—as a *mutiny*. Much was made of the story that *Athena*'s captain and the commander of its SEAL detachment had stayed behind to slow an ISIS force of a thousand men. Horatio at the Bridge: the world lapped it up. No names were released, but soon enough the American press got wind that left behind were Rensselaer and Holworthy.

Caught between what everyone perceived as both a mutiny and an inspiring story of sacrificial heroism, the Pentagon had no idea which way to lean, and went into deer-in-the-headlights mode, saying only, "Due to operational secrecy and still-burdened channels of communication, we have no further comment except to say that *Athena* is afloat and in the company of the French squadron. Thank you."

A thousand questions followed the spokesman as he left the room.

*

Katy immediately began to work the phone, and got nowhere. The press conference had been taped earlier in the day and there was the time difference to boot. She reached only low-ranking night duty officers at the Pentagon, who, as usual, were extraordinarily polite and institution-ally unforthcoming. She persisted nonetheless, and was able to reach the Secretary of the Navy's duty officer, who at first put her off.

Then she said, "Look, I'm Stephen Rensselaer's fiancée and I'm a lawyer. I want an appointment with the secretary tomorrow or the next morning. I'm going to fly out of New Orleans tomorrow. He knows Stephen. Tell him that I'm like Stephen but more so. Tell him that if I can't see him and I get the runaround, I'll go to the press. There are a lot of them in Washington, you know, they're always hungry, and they'll be very inter-ested in what I have to say. You tell him that. No one will let me know if Stephen is alive or dead. And, if he's alive, you'd better be doing every-thing you can to bring him back. Have you got that?"

"Yes, ma'am, I think so. I'll tell him as soon as he comes in tomorrow."

"No. You tell him now."

"Would you like him to call you?"

"No. I want him to look me in the eye." Frightened that perhaps she had gone too far, she hung up abruptly, frightening herself even more, but it was precisely the right thing to do. Still, how afraid of the press would the Navy be? She was no politician, and didn't know. Then again, public opinion, already split and agitated in the midst of the war and the upcoming presidential election, was not something they could dismiss. Thinking she might have been out of control, which almost made her cry, she had a feverish vision of the nominating convention in a few days, and the candidate embarking upon a modern-day version of Theodore Roosevelt's, "Perdicaris alive, or Raisuli dead!" She was terrified in a way, but, symmetrically matching that, she was determined.

*

On the ride from Reagan to the Pentagon the taxi driver wanted to talk, and she didn't. When she had a trial in another city and was anxious and thinking of her case, she found that banter made her sick to her stomach. Northern Virginia and the District had rich rains that August. The trees were deep green and heavily laden with leaves now in their prime, the Potomac was running full, the monuments glaring white, the afternoon air hot and clear.

Enduring what seemed like interminable waiting in the Pentagon visitors' hall, she was then called up to the desk, and the SECNAV's office sent down her escort, who, like Stephen, was a captain. She was sad to think that Stephen may have had to escort visitors this way, like a glorified movie usher. In fact, he hadn't, and probably, because he hated working at a desk, he would have much enjoyed the walks.

Freeland rose to greet her, enchanted by how lovely she looked in her summer dress, which was sleeveless, navy blue, and tailored in France. She wore pearls. He could not help but show how visibly impressed he was by her beauty, severity, and dignity, which immediately changed his strategy for dealing with her. He had said to the captain escorting her, "When she gets here, I'll explain, and then you run her through the scuppers." Though this technique was tried-and-true, upon first sight of Katy he thought it might not work, and immediately came up with a different approach in case it didn't.

"Please," he said, pulling out a chair for her. They sat facing one another, his left and her right elbows resting on the conference table. The escort captain's eyes were drawn to her legs after she crossed them and her dress rode up past her knees. Freeland shot him a quick look that caused him to avert his gaze.

"What can I do for you?" Freeland asked. "Stephen was the most brilliant aide I ever had, but he's not exactly diplomatic. I was actually very angry at him when he ran afoul of the president—I'm sure you know about that—and thereby deprived this office of his considerable talents."

To which Katy answered, "He has more political sense than you may think, and his view was that you used him to shield yourself from the blow. If the president had gone along with your policy, you would have claimed credit. If it exploded, Stephen would get the blame. Right?"

Quite a long time passed. Freeland looked at the ceiling, grasped his jaw between the thumb and index finger of his left hand, let his hand drop, looked directly at Katy, and said, "Right."

"I'm glad you're being straight with me," Katy said.

He answered, "For that, anyway," and smiled.

"Good. Keep it up."

"I'll try. I'll try."

"I'd just like to know," she said, with emotion and seriousness that contradicted the construction of the language she had used—with the limiting *just*, the conditional, and *like* falling short of *demand*—"if Stephen is dead or alive, if you know where he is, and if and when you're going to bring him back. He's a hero in Europe. Some say he's dead. Some say he's alive in the Somali desert. What are you going to do?"

"Okay, let me explain some things. Politicians, and that's what I am, are by and large cruel and inhuman sons of bitches."

"I know that."

"Of course. Ever notice how they completely ruin their own families? There are notable exceptions of course, although not me," he said, wistfully.

She nodded.

"That they're narcissists, idiots, and egomaniacs is only a small part of it. There's a more universal, legitimate reason for their son-of-a-bitchness. It's because they're forced to make decisions in case after case in which they cannot take account of people on an individual level. You send people to war because sometimes you have to, and they can come back dead. Could be by the thousands, or millions. If you shy from such decisions, most likely there'll be even more suffering. So you try to do your best. Often it gets to you, but you keep going. You know how many sailors I've lost in this war, and how many more I will lose?

"As I said, or implied, sometimes I get emotional. But I have to concentrate—correction, all of us have to concentrate, because it's a messy, imprecise, collective effort—on winning the war as quickly as possible and with as few casualties as possible, the former having an immense effect upon the latter. Today just as every day, I'll get a report of the dead and wounded, not just in the war zone but all over the world: enemy action, accidents, illness.

"Yes, I know Stephen, but he's one of hundreds of thousands. The *l'Étoile* affair is primarily European. We're fighting a hot war on the other side of the world, in the Arabian Sea. Which is all to say, Ms. Farrar, that I actually don't know about Stephen."

"Then who does?" she asked, not quite ready to accept his explanation, but allowing for the possibility that it was true.

"Reports come in from dozens of sources. They tend to be stove-piped, because that's what happens when you have three hundred thirty-seven thousand uniformed personnel, half a dozen fleets, a hundred thousand reservists, hundreds of major combatants afloat, many more smaller vessels, research institutions, universities, health systems, retirees, a thousand fixed-wing aircraft, a thousand helicopters, a justice system, almost two hundred thousand Marines, forty thousand Marine reservists, five thousand armored vehicles. . . ."

Katy made no response.

"What I can do, what I will do, is have Captain Piro take you around to whatever offices are most likely to have that information. He's one of my best officers, he knows the best prospects, and he has carte blanche from me. That's the best I can manage. If we did this for everyone, this place would seize up in an hour.

"Larry, are you set?"

"Yes, sir," the captain answered. "It'd be my pleasure."

*

Even before they left the E Ring, Captain Piro felt bad for Katy. For one, her tense walk, which with each clop of her heels drew attention to her magnificent legs (at which he now allowed himself to steal quick glances) must have been painful, and he couldn't see how she would be able to make it through the endless ring corridors, of which the Pentagon has more than seventeen miles, as he ran her through the scuppers.

"Ma'am, do you have running shoes in that bag? Most women have them because of all the walking."

"I do."

She found a bench, changed her shoes, and then left the captain breathless as he tried to keep pace with her fast walking. They covered about four miles and visited a dozen offices, every single one of which, from public affairs through personnel, medical, and various combat commands, said they would get back to Katy through the SECNAV's office. Exiting Naval Special Warfare, Katy turned to her escort and said, "All right, have you run me through the scuppers enough?"

"How'd you know that?" he asked, taken aback.

"How do you think I know it?" she asked. "I share the same bed with someone who used to do your job."

"Oh. But he never did this. He did strategy and policy."

"I know, but he had eyes and ears. Take me back to Freeland. This has been unavailing. He knew it would be."

"Yes, ma'am," Piro said, thoroughly enjoying the prospect.

*

Caught up in the spirit of it, Piro walked her right in. Two admirals at the conference table stood in deference to her. This was a lovely thing, mainly lost in civilian society, and she appreciated it. Freeland stood as well, turned to the admirals, and asked, "Would you give us a moment?" They graciously assented.

Still standing, Katy and Freeland faced one another. She said, "We've run through the scuppers, and there's nothing."

Freeland looked at Piro, who turned his palms upward, pushed his head forward slightly like a pigeon, and protested, "She knew. Stephen."

"Mr. Secretary," Katy said. "We walked four or five miles, yes, but I have running shoes"—she looked down at her feet—"and I can run four miles in twenty-seven minutes. I'm as fresh as a daisy, and if you don't level with me, tomorrow I'm going to hold a press conference. Stephen, or, rather, what Stephen did, is now known throughout the world. Granted, the story will die, but it has at least a few days' life. The media will eat up what I have to say. Your choice." She hated to litigate, threaten, and be tough, but she did know how.

"All right. Sit down." They sat. "I was hoping you'd just go away, but you have leverage and you're not the girlfriend of an eighteen-year-old electrician's mate. The truth is, we really don't know." He looked at his watch. "But we're about to find out, maybe. *Athena* did a lot of extraordinary things on her deployment, things I can't divulge now."

"The *Sahand*?" Katy interrupted. She didn't know about the Tsirkon, but she did know that the *Sahand* was Iran's largest warship.

"Let me continue. *Athena* took a beating, but we kept her deployed because she was so goddamned good at what she was doing, and she freed up many ships. She was the first to respond to *l'Étoile*, but she had no authorization to do anything but wait for the French squadron. Instead, she got into a battle, her communications were blown out, she followed *l'Étoile* to port on the Somali coast, and Stephen followed the hostages deep into the desert. Usually it takes Congress, or at least the president, to invade another country.

"Stephen has always been too much his own man. We train the SEALs to exercise their initiative, but sometimes we train them too much, and Stephen, as you know, was not born to follow orders. Yes, he and Holworthy, the CO of the SEAL detachment, stayed behind and slowed a thousand men. Holworthy got out. Stephen was hit by an RPG and blown over a cliff to a ledge below. Holworthy got no response from him. He could be dead, he could be alive. We don't know.

"But, literally at this moment, Holworthy is guiding a French raid to retrieve him, and then we'll know."

Contrary to what he had said before about politics and politicians, and himself, Freeland softened, because Katy, bravely looking straight ahead, was trying to suppress tears.

"Let me tell you something about Stephen," Katy said, still suppressing. "Like everyone, he had his doubts, you know. About his profession, about his life. But he told me that, once, he was standing on the bridge of his first command, wondering if what he was doing was right. A sunbeam came through the bridge windows just before sunset, illuminating a bulkhead with extraordinarily clear, beautiful light—like the light, he said, of Rome's golden autumn, for which purpose Rome's colors of ocher and terra-cotta arose. That's how he put it.

"And he said. . . ." She paused to collect herself, and to look up, so as to remember it exactly. "He said, 'We have become a civilization that elevates idiots, prostitutes, and clowns. Am I still to defend it? Yes, for its principles. Yes, for what it was. Yes, for what it still may be.'

"If only the president who blocked his promotion and ended his career could be even slightly like that."

In agreement, Freeland smiled, but only slightly. He didn't want to burden her by adding that the people get the government they deserve, but it was what he believed. "Give us your number," he said. "We'll let you know as soon as we know, no matter what time. I promise. And I'm sorry. I hope he's all right, although you understand that the chances aren't great. What comes after . . . we'll table that for now. Where are you staying?"

"I haven't arranged that."

"It shouldn't be hard. Everyone's out of town for the convention, and the heat has discouraged the tourists. If you haven't heard from us by about midnight, which would be morning over there, call in, because it would only be because something's wrong with your phone.

"Captain Piro."

"Sir."

"Can you stay 'til we hear?"

"Yes, sir. I'd be happy to." He wasn't, of course, but his time with Katy was echoing pleasurably within.

"Let me know first, then I'll call Ms. Farrar," Freeland told him.

At the entrance to the Pentagon, another taxi pulled up. Always when she had worked in Washington, the clients had paid for the Four Seasons in Georgetown. It was the only hotel she could think of. Then, weak with exhaustion and not at all as fresh as a daisy, she was driven across the Potomac.

RECHERCHE ET SECOURS

As soon as the nearly equatorial sun had with its usual great acceleration fallen below the western horizon, a doctor, corpsman, Holworthy, and a dozen special forces from a platoon of *Commando Jaubert* boarded an NH90 helicopter resting on the *Siroco's* aviation deck. Six commandos at each side door went in and took their seats in less than thirty seconds, not because it was necessary but because that was how they did it when it was.

The *Commandos Marine* were at least as impressive as the SEALs. Their selection process, if not their training, was harder; there were fewer of them; and they spoke perfect French, even if not to the standard of the *Academie Française.* The doctor, corpsman, and Holworthy walked up the rear ramp. Although the medical personnel carried heavy duffels, the interior was already set up with an ambulance's worth of equipment, and body bags.

Holworthy had gone over a map with the pilots, but at their signal he would come forward to guide them on the approach. As the engine started and the blades slowly began to rotate, the doors were closed and the ramp lifted. Holworthy didn't know much French, and couldn't even get the gist of the various commands and responses. None went over the radio. Communication with the air boss on the ship was by hand signals exclusively.

When the engines were running smoothly, the helicopter lifted from the deck and sidled over the sea. Then it pointed its nose down slightly and gathered forward momentum and altitude as it flew toward the coast. As the helicopter cleared the beach on a night with no moon, Holworthy heard the command *assombrir*, meaning to darken. When the NH90 left the anchored ships, the sailors on deck followed the almost hypnotic red light under its belly and watched its dirty exhaust trailing into the distance. But as soon as the command was given, all external lights were extinguished and the interior grew as dim and red as a photographic darkroom. The light before a raid was always both comforting—in that it was calming—and terrifying, in that the dim red color was suggestive of blood and fire. Holworthy and his French counterparts had long been conditioned to see red light as a precursor to battle.

The helicopter flew at almost 200 mph, 50 to 60 feet above the ground. No trees or structures on its route were higher than that, and it could safely follow the terrain so closely because the pilots had night-vision helmets. The engines of military aircraft are more powerful than those of their civilian counterparts, and it is impossible not to feel the difference. Inside, the NH90 was functional and rough—webbing straps, drab partitions, racks, handles, folding seats, a cable hoist. And no one was so inexperienced that he was nauseated, as he might have been, by the helicopter's deliberate swaying and tacking to protect itself from antiaircraft missiles and ground fire, even if the latter would be largely ineffective against the NH90's armor. The desert below seemed empty but for a few wild camels visible to the pilots through their night vision goggles. As the beasts, stampeded by engine noise, loped along in the dark, the ghostly white tint given to them by the night-vision goggles made them look otherworldly, and its infrared caused their humps, the hottest parts of their bodies, to look like arc lights on legs.

After a long stretch, Holworthy heard, *"Zero minus dix,"* his signal to come forward into the cockpit. Soon after he arrived and donned a night-vision helmet, he saw the central escarpment in the distance, and soon after that he thought he could make out the narrow canyon that split it. With the announcement, *"Zero minus trois,"* Holworthy heard a chorus of rifle bolts pulled back and then the loud sound of their release and rounds expressed into a dozen chambers. Looking back, he saw the commandos lowering their night-vision equipment.

As Holworthy guided the helicopter to the spot where Rensselaer had gone over, it swept back and forth from side to side for about forty-five seconds, scanning for enemy. As far as anyone could tell, the plateau was deserted except for the bodies of the dead, which Hadawi had failed to retrieve. Spread about like boulders, some had died on their knees and then fallen forward as if praying, though not in the direction of Mecca. One was draped over his tripod-mounted machine gun. Everyone in the helicopter knew that when he got out, despite the night wind, he would have to deal with the stench.

As it was landing, the helicopter rotated 180 degrees after the CO of the special forces called out *"Treuil!"* ("Winch!"). Until corrected, the pilot had forgotten to land with the winch on the side facing the defile. At touchdown, the side doors opened and the commandos jumped out, racing to form a perimeter, some leaping over bodies. Followed by the doctor and the corpsman with a litter attached to a line playing out from the winch, Holworthy and the commando CO went to the edge. The French had agreed that Holworthy would go down, and he was about to. Already in harness, he clipped onto the cable. The four men looked into the defile. None of them had night vision, but they could make out the ledge below, and that a form lay upon it, absolutely still.

*

Rensselaer would not have felt the cold of night, just as toward the end of the day he hadn't felt the heat. He was beyond that. No longer on an alternately freezing and burning rock ledge in the desert of a country—a whole region of the world—that offered little but one kind of suffering or another, he was on a terrace with Katy. In the distance, snowcapped mountains were blindingly white. The terrace was surrounded by geraniums, roses, and evergreens. It overlooked a valley thick with pine, fir, and palm trees. Royal palms rose as high as cedars, and thousands of date palms showed patches of saffron where immature dates had begun to form in clusters. The sun was strong in a flawlessly blue sky, but a cool wind blew over Stephen and Katy as they reclined on chaises.

He had suffered the heat and the cold, but then, when suffering was over, she came to him and brought him to this place. It had been unnecessary to try as he had to will her into his mind's eye, when she was merely waiting for him to release. And when he did, he was with her, and in such equanimity that he was not even shocked by its perfection.

So little was left of Rensselaer by the time Holworthy reached him that the mythical twenty-one unaccountable ounces of his soul were just about to float up between the rock walls to be taken by the wind. Holworthy, the cable supporting him, and one knee on the ledge, leaned forward and put a finger on Rensselaer's neck. Expecting to feel cold, hard flesh, he was surprised to feel the heat of a high fever. The pulse, however, was so weak that in combination with the high fever it hardly promised that Rensselaer would live.

"Litter!" Holworthy called. It was lowered to him. He positioned it against the cliff face in preparation for rolling Rensselaer into it. This would be very difficult. First, he struggled to put webbing around Rensselaer's waist, and then clipped it to the cable, should Rensselaer slip from either the ledge or the litter before he was tied in. As Holworthy started to turn Rensselaer toward him, he found resistance from the head. "Don't fight me," he said. "I'm putting you in the stretcher." There was no answer. Holworthy traversed a foot or two left and felt around Rensselaer's head, which had stuck to the rock.

"*Médecin! Médecin!*" he called up, tilting his head back.

"*J'arrive!*" He heard, and the doctor began to rappel down on a separate line anchored in the helicopter.

When he arrived on Holworthy's right, Holworthy said, "His head," and pointed. The doctor pushed off from the ledge and sailed around Holworthy to examine Rensselaer.

"We have to get him quick," he said. Then, feeling around Rensselaer's head, he added, "I don't want to open the wound. I don't know if it's surface or not. But I may not be able to prevent." He took a suture kit from a pocket and extracted the thinnest thread. Then he carefully put the thread behind Rensselaer's head, and in a sawing motion used it to cut through the hardened blood. When he was done, he said, "Okay. Not bleeding," and he and Holworthy got Rensselaer onto the stretcher, strapped him in, and signaled above. The winch moved slowly, lifting Holworthy and the stretcher, which Holworthy kept level and away from the cliff face by planting his feet against the rock, walking up, and pulling the litter out toward him. Three men hauled in the doctor as he walked up the rock in the same way.

Holworthy was not even aware when the soldiers who had made a perimeter around the helo boarded it. As it lifted and tilted, the doctor and the corpsman moved Rensselaer from the wire litter to a more comfortable stretcher. They took his vitals, hooked him up to a monitor, and ran an IV into him. The doctor examined the back of the skull. "We clean, stitch, antibiotics, and it's finished. The fever may go with hydration. We have to X-ray, et cetera. He may have internal injuries. Spine, brain, hemorrhage." He put on gloves and glanced at the monitor. "He's already coming back a little."

The helicopter picked up speed and climbed. As it did, and all kinds of good things were running into Rensselaer's veins through the IV, he awoke. He saw the doctor, and then Holworthy. The first thing he said, in a hoarse, barely intelligible voice, was "Who are they?"

"French."

"The hostages?"

"Safe."

"You should have left me there."

"Why?"

"It was Eden," Rensselaer said, and then retreated back into the dream.

The Emptiness of Luxury

When Katy's taxi pulled into the drive of the Georgetown Four Seasons she hesitated to get out. And when she paid her fare and did leave the taxi, it was with a heaviness that made her immune to the comforts of luxury so carefully gathered there. Even at home she had no item of clothing as ebulliently starched as the uniforms of the doormen, porters, and clerks who greeted her. These same porters seemed wounded when she insisted upon carrying her own small bag, and, she thought, wearily, that they attributed this to a doctrine of feminism or equality, or a desire not to part with the tip.

She spoke to a giant young man who, after almost seizing her bag, stepped back when she held on to it, and looked at her, affronted and hurt. "It's not anything," she said. "I just want to carry my own bag. I'm not in a good way."

Rather than enjoying the carefully plotted elegance within—colors scientifically and artfully coordinated, a perfection of finishes, precisely engineered lighting, carefully determined architectural proportions, and flawless cleanliness, all of which were choreographed to impart a feeling of well-being—she felt a defensive tightening of her muscles, especially those of her core, which served to negate and dismiss the otherwise powerful effects.

She hadn't requested it, but they were attentive enough to put her in the room in which she had always stayed whenever work took her to Washington, in a corner overlooking the pathetic junction of the diminished C&O Canal and Rock Creek before, under a braided lanyard of overpasses and roads, they seeped together to join the Potomac. This time, it would be on her own dime, but she didn't care. And then she brought herself up, quite painfully, for not caring, as it was too much like when her parents had died, and in the process of returning home in the emergency, the spending of money went unnoticed. She wanted to be upset about what her stay would cost her, so she could feel that everything would come right in the end.

No one had died yet: it was okay, as one would normally, to think about money.

As she always did in hotel rooms, she arranged her things in the closet, on the desk, and in the bathroom, where she laid out her toiletries along one side of the sink in the order in which they would be used at night. Before bed, she would lay out the morning items in this fashion as well. And when she checked out, despite knowing that the maid would strip the bed, Katy would make it up so well that it would take a detective to ascertain that someone had slept in it. And she would fluff the pillows, clean the mirror in the bathroom, fold the used towels neatly in a pile on the floor, wash out the soap dish, bundle up the garbage, and leave a very generous tip accompanied by a note thanking the maid for how nice the room had been kept when Katy took possession of it. That was just the way she was.

After showering, and then combing out her hair, she dressed in one of the robes from the closet. As the heat of the day dissipated into night, she sat for such a long time watching the lights of Washington come on that her hair was dry when she finished. Contrary to what she had feared, sleep came immediately, it was deep and uninterrupted, and it lasted until nine the next morning.

Feeling stronger, if numb, she walked into Georgetown to have breakfast. As always, she ate like a health-conscious bird. Given her exercise, athleticism, diet, and self-control, Stephen had always said that she would live forever. As if girding for battle, she wouldn't, but there was something to his pronouncement. With her muscular strength and her frame, in comparison to most people she lived as if in lesser gravity. And although her walk, especially when she was in heels, was—or seemed, anyway— remarkably tense, she moved as if she floated unburdened by excess, unconscious of her body except of its strengths, its graces, and its pleasures.

As she stepped into the elevator on her way back to the room, her phone rang. But as she answered, the elevator doors closed and she was cut off. She looked anxiously at the screen. The caller was Freeland. Her room was on the top floor, and the ride up seemed interminable. She unlocked her door, threw her purse onto the bed, and, on her way to the window, pressed call-back. As she stood close to the glass, heart beating fast, Freeland answered on the second ring.

"He's alive. They got him. He's in the sick bay on one of the French ships. He's got some broken ribs and a superficial head wound, he's severely dehydrated and pretty worn-out from going back and forth between hypo- and hyperthermia, but no permanent damage as far as they can tell. The French are treating him like . . . I don't know . . . Ulysses, Achilles? He and the CO of his SEAL detachment held off a thousand enemy. A thousand! You can't ignore that. It's amazing, and it's not possible to downplay."

In the joy of the first few seconds as Freeland spoke, all the luxury Katy had denied she now felt flowing into her as if she were being lifted by water flooding a lock. Now she wanted to enjoy everything around her, from the million-count sheets to the marble halls, to the *pain au chocolat* and lovely-sounding china as it was struck by clinking silver. She wanted to walk on the deep, cushioned carpets, to hear her heels click on marble floors, or just to lie in the full sun, in a cool breeze, overlooking an Eden of pines and palms and flowering trees.

VII

Trial

How illusory our powers, vulnerable our agency, and fleeting our time.

Rensselaer in the Clouds

If not as good as French cooking, French medicine is yet excellent. But the combination of limited shipboard equipment, young and relatively inexperienced military physicians, and the press of civilian patients from *l'Étoile* made Rensselaer's initial diagnosis imprecise. In the C-17 on its way to Germany and the giant U.S. military hospital at Landstuhl, the medical team noticed his decline, and upon landing he was rushed into an operating room on account of a hematoma at the back of his skull near the brain stem, and persistent bleeding in his chest cavity from shattered ribs cutting into the surrounding tissue on his right side.

"What now?" he asked the surgeons just before he was put under.

To shift the ground, they answered with a question. "How do you feel?"

"Pretty good," he said, weakly, wanly, "actually, well, maybe."

"We have a little more work to do."

When he awoke he didn't know where he was or what had happened, and he hadn't the slightest idea of time. An attractive nurse—somehow, all nurses are pretty—told him who he was, where he was, the date, and where he had been.

He nodded. "I'm not quite there yet, but I remember. How long?"

"Since when?"

"Since I've been out."

"Overnight. You came out of anaesthesia fairly quickly, but then fell asleep. You slept through two trips to imaging."

"What'd they do?"

"They rearranged your ribs and put a plate in the back of your head."

"A plate?"

"A tiny one."

"So . . . a saucer?"

"More like a half-dollar. Why would you have been doing that kind of stuff at your age anyway, and with your rank?" she scolded. "Let me see your arm so I can check the IV."

"Necessity."

"If you say so. Now you can rest. Everything's okay. Just sleep."

He did. Days passed mainly in sleep. And when he had gotten his strength back enough to stay awake, his ribs killed him. He asked one of the doctors how long it would last. It would last a long time, the doctor said, but now that his neurological condition had reverted to normal it was safe for a narcotic. "Four days," the doctor said. "And that's it. We don't want to get you hooked."

They did, in fact, hook him up to a drip, and his pain vanished. After two days, a different nurse took over the morning shift and he thought that she had increased the concentration of whatever it was that now separated him from himself as if he were a disembodied spirit. He could still speak, so when she came to check on him he asked if she had upped the dose.

"No," she said. "No change. Just what's on order. What's your name?"

He told her.

"What day is it?" He told her.

"What's eight times eight divided by two?"

"Thirty-two," he replied instantly, certainly, and proudly. He felt as if he had just trisected an angle or proved Fermat's Theorem, although he wasn't quite sure what that was.

"You're right, and you're more sober than half the people in the officers' club."

He spent the next hour floating in air, eyes wide, and with hardly a reaction when an unknown captain walked into his room. This was not unusual. The hospital was full of captains—doctors of great learning and skill who were respected but never fully accepted as real Navy. This officer, however, was not a doctor.

"How are you?" he asked.

"I'm kind of like an airship."

"I see."

"Yeah."

"Are you okay to answer a few questions?"

Thinking that he was again going to be queried as to sums, Rensselaer said, "Sure." Then, remembering that the officer wasn't a physician, he asked, "What kind of questions?"

"I'm Dick Osborne."

"You're Dick Osborne."

"I am. I just have a few questions about what happened on station."

"You think?"

"It won't take long. A debriefing. I'll record it."

"I had no pens or paper. My head was smashed against a rock. I had no . . . I have to write it up."

"But you can't, and it's important that we have the information."

Truly at ease, floating in the clouds just below or perhaps above the ceiling, Rensselaer's reply was "Information."

Dick Osborne thought he had him. "What did happen?"

"Oh," Rensselaer said, longingly, "if I had time enough to tell." He seemed both amused and longing.

"You do. You have as much time as you want." The tap of a finger signaled the start of recording. "So if you would start from the beginning."

"The beginning. The beginning? Nooooo, not for a naval investigator who hasn't read me my Article Thirty-Ones, Dick Osborne."

Osborne said something under his breath, and then, "Would you like me to?"

"No."

"I can help you, really."

"Oh of course you can. Like a boa constrictor. What? You think I'm a lollipop? Morphine or whatever it is makes you high, it doesn't make you stupid, Dick Osborne. Can you stop at the nurses' station and tell them that I want to come back to earth, Dick. Okay?"

As Rensselaer watched Captain Osborne moving down the corridor toward the nurses' station, he laughed like a crazy person. Drugs.

*

By the beginning of October, though he had largely recovered, he was weak. He would take slow walks in the strangely deserted garden, and then return to his private room. Almost no one spoke to him, and he spoke to almost no one other than Katy. Every day. Hearing her voice on the phone was like falling in love all over again.

Most of the crew, he was told, had been dispersed. *Athena* was under repair at Hampton Roads. And he was not supposed to speak with anyone while his case was reviewed. He had read in the papers that DOD refused to comment on what the press called "the *Athena* Affair" until all the facts had been ascertained. Although this had no effect upon the gifts of flowers, cakes, and awards that arrived almost daily from many points in Europe, these in turn had no effect upon his situation other than to puzzle him.

He was able to sleep in a medivac C-17 as it crossed the Atlantic, in a far more comfortable bunk than on the best commercial flights. He was fresh, shaved, and alert when at 1530 he landed at Dover. As soon he left the C-17 he was escorted to a naval Gulfstream that shot off immediately, headed south, rose to altitude, leveled briefly, and began its descent to Naval Station Norfolk. The terrain was familiar and beautiful. The wild beaches and barrier islands, broad bays, reed-carpeted wetlands, and the patchwork of newly harvested fields made him feel safe at home, as if the plane were floating on waves of benevolence rising from a benevolent land, which he was sure it was—especially as the declining sun lit the breakers' white foam with a sheen of light gold.

As the plane decelerated on the runway, Rensselaer asked the rating who was his escort, "Am I going to *Athena*?"

"I don't know, sir."

A little plane when taxiing can turn surprisingly sharply and stop surprisingly short. This the Gulfstream did in front of the terminal. Its door opened, and Rensselaer walked carefully down the stairs, setting foot in America for the first time in months. Unlike any ground he had been on since, this ground felt solid and real.

It appeared that no one had come to meet him, something that for the Navy would be par for the course. Only one man was in the terminal, standing as if to greet him, but as he had a garment bag, Rensselaer concluded that he was waiting to catch a flight.

He was a commander, taller than Rensselaer, probably fifty pounds heavier, and ten years younger. He had big hands and thick fingers. He was tanned and his close-cropped, golden hair lay across his head, neat and flat. Square-faced and blue-eyed, he was the archetype of a British yeoman. He didn't take his eyes off Rensselaer, who walked past him and toward the exit.

"Where're you going, sir?"

"Actually, I don't know."

"Captain Rensselaer?"

"Right."

"I'm Frearson, your attorney."

"My attorney?"

"Yes, sir."

Rensselaer looked at the garment bag. "I must be in a hell of a lot of trouble if your briefcase is that big."

"It's yours. From *Athena*. Your dress blues. They were packed away below. The whites didn't make it."

"I know."

"You can put these on in the bathroom."

"Why?"

Frearson checked his watch. "In twenty minutes, the charges will be proferred."

*

On the ride over, Frearson said, "Look, I was appointed, but you can choose or add someone else, including a civilian attorney or another JAG. This is an important case. You might consider bringing in Gene Fidell, the dean of military law, and no relation to Fidel Castro, I think."

Rensselaer sized up Frearson. "Are you as solid as you look?"

Taken aback, Frearson answered, "I am."

"You know those things in railway stations, at the end of the track, that are engineered to stop a train that doesn't slow down enough? You remind me of one of those."

"Thank you. Can't wait to tell my wife."

"No doubt she already knows. Where'd you go to school?"

"Harvard College, and Harvard Law School. I know you were Harvard GSAS."

"So why the Navy? Didn't you pass the bar?"

"First shot."

"Then why not a firm? How did you rank?"

"I did okay. I was on *Law Review*, if you must know. Frankly, they were a bunch of pompous assholes. I clerked for a year and then enlisted."

"Something's not right here. *Harvard Law Review*, appeals clerk?"

"Yes."

"Then Navy JAG?"

"When I was in high school," Frearson told him, "I had my congressman's nomination to the Naval Academy. I chose Harvard instead. You yourself chose Harvard over NPGS."

"I did. Reputation, the first refuge of a scoundrel."

"I fell for that, too, but in the first week I saw a kid named Jim Scalzo coming down the stairs of Pennypacker. . . ."

"What's Pennypacker?"

"A freshman dorm outside the Yard, unknown to graduate students like you. He was in his NROTC uniform. He had his military classes at MIT. I knew I'd made the wrong choice. It was a dull pain, inside, almost like grief, and it took nine years to correct. What it comes down to is, whatever its faults, I love the Navy. I may be insane, but I really do."

"Do you win your cases?"

"Most of 'em."

"You cop a lot of pleas?"

"No, that's not winning."

They left the gray sedan, which then pulled away as they went into the HQ. As he climbed the stairs, Rensselaer was apprehensive for the first time. The officer who proferred the charges was a vice admiral, three ranks above him, which seemed unnecessary. The admiral was in someone else's office, and he sat rather stiffly in a starched white uniform with fewer ribbons than Rensselaer's, no combat designations, certainly not Special Warfare. Rensselaer had that above his ribbons, and the command-at-sea below them. The admiral had surface supply corps below, and command-ashore project manager above.

Rensselaer stood at attention. Frearson, also at attention, was several paces back and to the right. Other officers—none of whom, like the admiral, introduced himself and one of whom, presumably, was the prosecutor—flanked the admiral and stood in front of a bunch of flags. Rensselaer's impression was that he was facing something that looked a bit like a salad.

"Captain Rensselaer," the admiral said, his tone simultaneously questioning and disdainful, "were you not informed that in Virginia the switchover to winter uniform is on fifteen October?"

"No, sir, but I pretty much knew it."

"So why are you in winter uniform?"

"I don't have a summer choker, sir."

"You don't?"

"No, sir."

"And why is that?"

"It was in a stowage space next to COMMS, which took a hit and burst into flame. One of my crew died there. I wasn't thinking of my wardrobe at the time. Anyway, it was destroyed, sir."

"I see. I'm sorry about that."

"Sir."

"Mr. Frearson, have you been given a copy of the charge sheet?"

"No, sir, I have not."

"You should have been. Are you and your client prepared to hear the charges without notice, or would you like an adjournment?"

Frearson glanced at Rensselaer, who, without a sound, said it was okay. "We don't need an adjournment, sir."

"Very well. I'll read the charges. I don't know why I was picked: I'm trying to build a goddamned aircraft carrier." He put on a pair of half-round reading glasses, stiffened even more, and began.

"Captain Stephen Rensselaer, United States Navy: according to the charge sheet, form four fifty-eight, you are charged with the following violations of the Uniform Code of Military Justice:

"'Article Ninety-Four, Section one, b. two: mutiny by refusing to obey orders or perform duty, usurping or overriding lawful military authority.

"'Article Ten, improper hazarding of a vessel.

"'Article Eighty-Seven, missing movement.

"'Article Ninety-Two, failure to obey order or regulation.

"'Article Eight-One, conspiracy.

"'Article Eighty-Five, desertion.'"

"Desertion?" Rensselaer asked, amazed.

The admiral cleared his throat, simultaneously to confirm and to reprimand.

Again, but this time with a tone that indicated contempt for the accusation, Rensselaer said, "Desertion."

The admiral ignored this, and forged ahead. "Article One Hundred and Thirty-Four, the General Article. In this case, diverting a component of the Armed Forces of the United States, in time of war, to invade a territory with which the United States is not at war, thus subtracting from the capacity of the United States to wage war, and risking creation of another front.'

"I myself have in proferring these charges noted on the charge sheet that they include one or more capital offenses. Due to the nature of the charges, and by order of the commander in chief, you will, despite your rank and long service, be ineligible for the customary confinement to quarters or base, and will forthwith be placed under arrest and transported to Naval Consolidated Brig, Chesapeake, where you will be kept in isolation from other prisoners.

"Due to the scope of the charges, the fact that the alleged violations took place overseas, and the ongoing conflict in the area, a trial date has not been set, and will be determined only when the investigation of the charges has been completed.

"Counselor, do you or your client have anything you would like to say?"

"Yes, sir," Frearson responded. "In light of the—in the view of the Defense—unprecedented confinement order for the accused, a captain with a distinguished record and career, and in regard to the publicity and potential political nature of this case, can you confirm that the order comes from the commander in chief? That is, the president?"

"I can. It's in writing, appended to the charge sheet. You'll receive it with your copy."

"Does it detail the conditions of confinement other than to specify isolation, sir?"

The admiral shook his head. "No. Speak to the CO of the brig. They may have instructions. They may work according to their own protocol. Anything else?"

"I want to note again before my formal protest," Frearson said, "that given my client's record of service the conditions of his confinement are both highly unusual and totally unnecessary."

"Noted. Anything else?"

Frearson glanced at Rensselaer, who indicated no. "No, sir, nothing else."

Navy Consolidated Brig, Chesapeake

The new CO of the Navy brig in Chesapeake had decided that, as in Iraq, where he had served, it was cowardly not to patrol outside the wire. Here, outside the wire meant only a ring of thick forest and hayfields, then in one direction the Great Dismal Swamp, and, in others, farmhouses, more fields, and neighborhoods. Nonetheless, once in a while, lightning would strike a Marine, and with a rifle and a radio he would find himself walking gingerly through the woods, as cottonmouths (big ones) were hardly unknown near the vast swamp. It was customary for the low-ranking unfortunate assigned this task to head immediately east-northeast, where a huge hayfield fronted the forest and allowed much of the route to be walked in the open, safely apart from snakes, spiderwebs, mosquitoes, and thorns.

Twenty-year-old Marine Rifleman Lucas Merriman from northwest Nebraska waited in the trees at the edge of this field for a huge John Deere tractor to pass. As soon as it did, he walked out and followed it. But the farmer, who was towing a fifteen-foot, bat-wing brush hog, hogging down brambles and weeds at the edge of his hayfield after the third cutting, looked back a lot to make sure he was mowing as close to the edge as possible.

"Damn," Merriman said after the farmer spotted him, stopped, and throttled back his engine. But there was no way Merriman was going to retreat into the woods, even though in the first week of October they were far more hospitable in the clear air than they had been in the haze of summer. When the farmer got to him, he said, "I'm sorry, sir. I just hate to make my patrol through all those thorns and stuff: snakes."

In his mid-seventies but possessed of the strength of those who do heavy labor, the farmer said to the young Marine, "In these woods you don't have to worry too much about snakes. They don't like pine needles, you know." And then the sight of a Marine with the woods behind him prompted the farmer to volunteer, "I was at Khe Sanh."

"Sir?"

"Khe Sanh. The siege."

Merriman looked puzzled, so the farmer just sighed. "Since when do you guys patrol in the woods? Why would you do that?"

"A coupla months. We got a new CO who says you gotta know what's going on outside the wire."

The farmer turned, spat, shook his head, and rolled his eyes. "I'll tell you what's outside the wire: Burger King, Food Lion, Duck Thru, Sherwin-Williams."

He and Merriman then waited for one thing to lead to another, and when it didn't, the farmer said, "Are they all in there?"

"Sir?"

"I figured that's where they would be. Where else would they go?"

"Oh, them. I can't talk to the press."

"You can't talk to the press," the farmer echoed. "You can't talk to the press. Who do you think I am, Woodward and Bernstein?"

"Who and who?"

"Watergate."

"I've heard of that."

"Look," the farmer said. "I live here. You're standing on my field. I'm not the press, I'm your neighbor. This land's been in my family since before the Revolution, and I've been working it since I got back."

"From where?"

"From Vietnam."

"You were in the Army?"

"No, I was a Marine, like you."

"Yes, sir. They're in there, some of them. I really can't. . . ."

"They're heroes."

"Well, they're prisoners."

"Are they mixed in?"

"I really can't say, but, no. Sometimes we have two guys that did something, and they have to be kept completely apart so they can't coordinate their stories. I don't get it. Some of these guys were at Landstuhl for weeks. They coulda made up a story then."

"Maybe they don't have to make up a story," the farmer said, looking toward the trees.

*

In the movies, much is made of a cell door slamming shut as the signal and symbol of confinement. But seldom do cell doors make such theatrical noise and clatter. Rather, as if to parody an old song, they are sealed with a click. In fact, not only their openings but even their closings are a relief, as are almost any movement, living or mechanical, any sound, any change in the light, from what really burdens a prisoner. What oppresses him is the unremitting sameness of his cell, its unrelieved planes, un-textured finishes, nonexistent decor. A prison cell transforms time into torture. When pinned by the enormous wrestler of the state, you are broken in many ways before it forever recasts your life. While it is crushing the breath out of you, no matter how versed you are in the law, or how much faith you have in institutions, you understand that in one way or another it can hold you forever and it can take your life.

Rensselaer had never been imprisoned in America (he didn't recognize the legitimacy of an Iraqi prison) and had never thought he would be. Even at Landstuhl, as he came to understand that he might face charges, he assumed that during whatever proceeding he might undergo he would be confined to quarters. In fact, his tenant's lease was up in September, and he looked forward to moving back in. Katy would visit on the week-ends. The legal business—perhaps nonjudicial punishment, summary court-martial, or even court-martial—would stretch out for weeks or more, but only on weekdays. He would come and go on the Metro, and, carefully, because they were so expensive, buy things to eat at Dean & DeLuca, take long walks with Katy, and lie back with her in calm embrace.

He was wrong about that. Much intervened. The suspenseful and half-hidden drama of the *Athena* was such that in this, a presidential election year, the party conventions absorbed it like sponges. Two positions solidified, especially after one of the candidates did in fact mimic Theodore Roosevelt's "Perdicaris alive, or Raisuli dead" speech. The Republicans made the very good case that Rensselaer was an American hero as of old, that his bravery and initiative, even had it not resulted in the salvation of almost two hundred souls, was, if not correct, admirable: in fact, more admirable for being, though incorrect, a resort to first principles. They knew this would appeal.

The Democrats countered with the powerful argument that Rensselaer had defied his orders, hazarded his ship and his men, and invaded another country without the consent of the people, the Congress, the president,

CENTCOM, or even Fifth Fleet. The country was already at war, and the last thing it needed was involvement on another front on the disastrous ground of the Middle East or in the chaos of East Africa. To them, Rensselaer was a great danger, as he had done what Aaron Burr had only been accused of plotting to do: that is, with the purloined forces of the United States, privately invading another country.

Press access would have been highly inflammatory, so *Athena's* enlisted crew were assigned to distant ships at sea and instructed to be silent, and by exceptional order of the president the principals were imprisoned. Were they not flight risks, officers were almost always released on their own recognizance and honor, but as *Athena's* commanders were charged with high crimes—capital crimes—they were remanded into custody and kept isolated from each other. They didn't even know, although they speculated, that they shared the same brig in Chesapeake, which despite its name does not front the Chesapeake.

For Rensselaer, everything was confusing, disorienting, and not at all helped by his head injury. Here he was, wearing fatigues without rank insignia, arising at five in the morning, shuffled around according to schedule. In counseling, a perfectly nice woman wanted to know what his "issues" were. "I'm in prison. That's my main problem," he said, "and the word *issue* is not synonymous with *problem*, even if most people now think it is."

"How do you think you can make your life better?"

"By getting out."

"No, really."

"Really."

"I understand. But what bothers you now, that maybe we can work on?"

"Woodworking shop."

"How so?"

"How so? Well, I was going to be promoted: rear admiral, lower half. Then I was in blue-water naval battles. Then I fought on land. We lost good men, five of them. When I wake up, sometimes I still think I'm at sea or in the desert. And now? Now I'm building a wall-mounted cat ladder and gymnasium. I have no choice. I don't want to build a fucking cat gymnasium. The librarian chose a book for me, a more-than-half-century-old, Time-Life illustrated guide to the Mid-Atlantic states."

"How is it?"

"It's not exactly life-changing. I'm in the midst of a lot of important stuff and, you know, I just feel . . . I have a lot of serious charges, and here I am, next to the Great Dismal Swamp, building a cat exercise thing."

"Let me ask you what I ask everyone who sees me for counseling. What constructive advice would you give yourself?"

"I would say . . . remember that the harder you pull, the tighter it gets. Relax. Keep fit. Have patience. And pray."

*

Extricated from accomplishing the finishing touches on the cat gymnasium, Rensselaer was brought into conference with Frearson, who stood in a beam of autumn sunlight looking very golden in his khakis, his hair shining like metal and his skin roseate and tanned from a day at the beach.

"Where the hell have you been?" Rensselaer demanded. Since the charges had been read, it had been a week, with no sign of his attorney.

"Didn't you get my messages?" Frearson asked, upset that his client thought him remiss.

"What messages?"

"Every day, except when we went to the beach on Sunday—and even then all I thought about was the case—I've been working. What did you think? I went up to D.C. I've been researching opinions, filing motions. I told you all this, and that I'd be ready to speak with you today."

"I heard nothing. I've been in woodworking, and counseling." Then, under his breath, "Fucking cat gymnasium."

"Before concentrating on the facts of the case, I wanted to immerse myself in the nature and history of the charges. And to get as much political intelligence as I could. Let me be frank. Your case is stomach-turning. So many streams come together in it, and things are changing day by day."

"The *law* doesn't change day by day."

"That's right. Not the essence of the law, and the essence of the law is our best hope. But think of it as the goal, the room you have to fight to get into. Before you can do that you have to pass through a gauntlet. It's not supposed to be that way, but you've managed to get yourself enmeshed in the gears of both a war and a national election. No one can control the course of such things, and neither of them brakes for roadkill. The law isn't the only thing we have to deal with."

"Are you saying you can't handle it?"

"I told you, you can bring in anyone."

"That's not what I'm asking."

"Can I handle it?" Frearson repeated, posing the question to himself. He thought for a while. "Yeah. Everything rests on the composition of the board. But in the past I've been persuasive even with highly prejudicial officers, partly because I actually enjoy it. That is, rather than arguing with them, I try to entice them to follow me as I myself discover the truth. To be convincing, you have to convince yourself. When they see this they become involved and they can't help but shift to your side. Then you've nailed them like ten-pins, if you know what I mean."

"I do know what you mean."

"Let's proceed. First," Frearson said, "before anything, Katy."

"Katy?"

"She has to be warned about inquiries."

"She's got nothing to hide, and she's used to dealing with the government." Rensselaer then elaborated.

"You're sure?"

"Absolutely, but I would like you to tell her. . . ."

Frearson opened the notebook and took pen in hand.

"No. You don't have to write it down. It'd be better if you just repeat it from memory. Tell her that I love her more than anything else in the world, that I ache to see her, but not in prison. And not as I'm tried. It would throw me off just as surely as it would have had she been present during the battles. Tell her that I'll come to her in New Orleans when all this is done, that one day when she goes to wait for the streetcar, I'll be there."

"You know," Frearson began in a gentle, cautionary tone, "you can't—"

Rensselaer interrupted. "No. This is how we do it when we go into battle. We determine on victory and survival. We take the chance. We even elevate the chance, like Cortés burning his boats."

"The streetcar?" Frearson asked.

"St. Charles. She'll know. Katy Farrar."

"Her firm?"

Rensselaer told him.

*

"To begin," Frearson said, "'in the gross and scope' of it. . . ."

"*Hamlet*, scene one," Rensselaer crisply shot back, as if returning a serve in tennis.

"That's right." Frearson was delighted.

"When you argue a case, do you use a lot of Shakespeare?" Rensselaer asked, somewhat nervously.

Frearson smiled. "No, but I do use some, quite deliberately. If just one member of the panel knows it, it's a step in drawing him to my side. In my experience, it's more powerful than ethnic or racial sympathy, which a fair judge is rightly taught and expected to suppress, and which anyway you yourself won't get—we don't have too many Dutch admirals—but no one is yet obligated to suppress the pleasure of a literary allusion."

"I'm not Dutch, for Chrissake, I'm American. Fine. Go with Shakespeare, as long as you don't lard it up, in which case they might be tempted to imagine you in pantaloons and a codpiece, and we'd be done."

"I don't lard it up. I'm not your Cousin Vinny, who's going to show up in a maroon planter's suit."

"That would almost be worth it. But, go ahead."

"I've never had a case with such momentous and changing influences. Usually, by definition, courts-martial are about something that occurred in the past. Here, we're also dealing with present and future variables."

"Every fight is like that," Rensselaer told him. "I'm used to it."

"I'm not, but I am beginning to get the hang of it. What are we dealing with? First, the charges. I'm pretty sure I can blow five of them apart, and I suspect that they were added just to make more work for us and subtract time and effort—as they inevitably will—from the first and last: Article Ninety-Four, mutiny; and One Thirty-Four, the huge catch-all. Once we get the lesser brush cleared, these are what can hang you."

"Capital offenses."

"Only the mutiny. The General Article can't include a capital offense. They'll try to use it to amplify and add import and context to the charge of mutiny. Nothing's impossible, but not since Eddie Slovik have they executed anyone. I'm thinking that the worst you can get is life. And to go there they've got a lot of political headwinds. Of course, I'll fight the two key charges as matters of fact and law, but it hardly stops at that. I can argue unjustified command influence. That can go one way or another, especially given that we're dealing with the president—uncovering it at that level would be exceedingly difficult if only for the constitutional questions it would raise.

"We don't know who will be on the panel, except that they have to be admirals. Some may be careerists whose judgment is influenced by who wins the presidency and control of Congress. Some may be subject to pressure from one party or the other due to past conduct that has been overlooked deliberately so as to have a hook in them. That actually happens. Some may be SWOs who want to protect the Surface Warfare Community by making a scapegoat or an example of you, or, conversely, to protect themselves by acquitting you. Some may be aviators who see it as an opportunity to slow the drift away from carriers, or submariners who're jealous of the light and the fresh air you guys get. Who knows? What one hopes for is a panel of fair-minded, unprejudiced, experienced officers who understand how properly to apply the law."

"And who have read Shakespeare."

"And who have read Shakespeare. I've filed motions with the object of delaying the trial until after the inauguration. If Hartsfield wins, he may want to signal a reversal of his predecessor's policies. They do that, you know, and he has a lot to work with. If the vice president wins, he may want to signal continuance with, or departure from, the policies he's had to swallow and endorse for all these years as the president's fanboy. Did you see his interview last night?"

"No. Without a television, I find it difficult to watch television."

"Don't you have a dayroom or something?"

"I can't go there. Even when I build the cat thing I'm the only one in the shop other than the instructor. What did he say?"

"He touched upon you, although he didn't mention your name, and was very careful not to prejudice your case specifically. He's falling behind in the polls as fast as Hartsfield's pulling ahead. The administration is being hammered because the war is dragging on and the Iranians are spreading it via their proxies: the attack in London, car rammings in Jerusalem, the machine-gunning in Buenos Aires. Every American embassy all around the world has been heavily reinforced."

"And what's hammering Hartsfield?"

"Nothing. That's just it. He pretty much stays out of it, doesn't say much about the war."

"He supported it in the Senate."

"That's true, but now he's sitting back while everyone bites the vice president's ass. The vice president has no choice but to stick with administration policy, but he also has to mollify the critics. Unfortunately for us, he does that by condemning the proliferation of our forces into too many countries."

"How can he condemn that? He did it."

"They inherited it from previous administrations."

"They didn't change it a whit."

"True."

"He doesn't have a leg to stand on."

"You didn't see the interview," Frearson said.

"The *Athena*? That's his diversion?"

Frearson nodded. "A rogue operation that endangers us on a new front."

"New front like hell."

"While you were engaged it was. You diverted resources. You cost American lives. That's the story. And although you were only one PC, everything you did was highly amplified by the press all over the world."

"We saved almost two hundred people—from our common enemy."

"Not one American among them. It's playing quite well. The White House, SECDEF, and Fleet are committed. It's their story, and they're sticking to it."

"Why? It can't possibly be adjudicated before the election."

"Doesn't matter. Once they're committed, they're committed. Even should the V.P. lose the election he's going with it. He'd look worse if it turned out he was using *Athena* as a scapegoat, as of course he is."

"Have they gotten to the prosecutor?"

"No. He's not someone who can be influenced, and he's very capable. The press on their side is libeling you, by name. The implication is that somehow the *Athena* Affair is responsible for the war not going as swimmingly as promised, and that you went rogue when you were denied promotion."

Libel is difficult to bear, and this showed on Rensselaer's face. "How could anyone possibly believe that?" The question was naïve.

"Never overestimate people's intelligence," Frearson told him.

"Still."

"Have you ever been in a supermarket?" Frearson asked.

"Of course I've been in a supermarket."

"*Someone* reads those tabloids. Did you see the one with the fat kid floating in a life ring? 'After All These Years, Titanic Baby Found in the Atlantic!'"

"I missed that one," Rensselaer told him.

"Do you play chess, Captain?"

"I do. Sometimes I even beat Movius, my XO."

"Congratulations. Now you're a pawn."

The Glass House

Not that long ago, law firms were not quartered in crystal boxes comprising boxes of multiple office-building floors with internal and external walls of glass. Now, theatrically lit and scientifically ventilated, the slick, transparent spaces arrayed around floating staircases and airy atria coruscate from early in the day to late at night. If not privacy, the glass affords silence, and in a glass office one sometimes has the feeling of floating in an aquarium.

Katy understood that, a hundred years before, a law office would be as heavy as hers was light, with stolid Victorian or, were it to have been modernized, Edwardian furniture, and wood paneling, rugs, mantels, and hypnotically ticking tall clocks that could lull to sleep even an agitated ambulance chaser. But what would it be like a hundred years hence? When one of her now increasingly erstwhile suitors entered her office as she was entertaining this question, she had deliberately chosen to continue her determination to drive him away, so she greeted him with her musing. "Who knows?" she asked. "Maybe we'll hang upside down like bats."

This kind of thing was enough to keep them off. They said, "She's a great lawyer. Perhaps it's the stress." They knew that for a long time she hadn't known if Stephen were alive or dead. They knew that now he was imprisoned, and that his very case—which spoke to his actions, which spoke to his character, and thus to hers—was one of the things that, however small, had divided the political parties and become part of the nation's fate, and they were somewhat awed by her connection to it. The ones who had fallen in love with her longed for her as before, but now she was untouchable, in another realm, elevated and isolated so that her position alone was sufficient to discipline their desire. In fact, to slap it.

For Katy, the glass house was perfectly complementary to the suspension of feeling she tried to will upon herself. Her tax cases were mindless games that nonetheless demanded full attention and made time fly. Coming in the morning, leaving in the evening, anaesthesia in between. At home, the quiet and stillness put her into an easy trance—the ticking of the clock as if she had traveled back to the law offices of a century past, the rain steady and powerful but not quite as wonderful as when she had lain in bed with Stephen, or the heat outside even in the dark, and the orchids and the palms so beautifully patient, and now and then a gin and tonic just so imagination and memory could fly while she was perfectly still, and time went by.

Safe in the glass house, she waited. She had had the strength to wait as Stephen fought, and she would have the strength to wait now. The sound of the air-conditioning was Zen-like. The boats far below on the Mississippi glided silently but as smoothly as if keeping time to a waltz.

Then the receptionist's voice came over the intercom. "There's a Mr. Osborne here to see you."

"Mr. who?"

"Osborne."

"Is he counsel in the Winterich case?"

"No, he's in the Navy."

"What does he want?"

The receptionist disappeared and then was heard again. "He says he's sorry he couldn't make an appointment, but he's in transit from Washington to San Diego, and he's supposed to speak with you."

Katy hesitated, got her guard up, and said, "All right, bring him in."

It took a full two minutes to walk from reception down the wide alleys between the crystalline boxes. And though by the time Osborne and his escort arrived at Katy's door not everyone would have had time to prepare for all the possibilities, she was good at projecting scenarios. She hadn't been warned of the investigative techniques, because of what Stephen had explained to Frearson.

"They have a score of techniques with which they get information to which they're not entitled," Frearson had said.

"You really don't have to warn her," Rensselaer told him. "There's no more capable person in the world. She'll know immediately. She doesn't like it when, because she's a beautiful woman, people let down their guard. Don't ruin it for her by making it too easy."

"Ms. Farrar?" she was asked.

She sized him up. His countenance and manner were false. She would be tough. "It's on the door, you know, I'm sitting at the desk, and law firms don't have substitute lawyers the way schools have substitute teachers."

"But you are."

"I am, yes. Would you like a peanut butter cup, a miniature one such as you might get at Halloween? I have one a day, as a treat."

"Sure. One a day. They're fattening."

"That's not it. I can't gain weight even if I try, and I do love them. It's an exercise in discipline."

"Yes," he said. Now he knew he didn't know what he was dealing with. "So, I'm Dick Osborne."

"*Captain* Osborne." Of course she recognized the insignia.

"Exactly. I need to ask you some questions about Captain Rensselaer."

"You need to? What makes you need to?"

"They may help him."

"What else may they do?"

"I beg your pardon?"

"They may help him, and, if they don't, mightn't they hurt him?"

"I don't know."

"You still haven't answered my question."

"What question?"

"Whence your need?"

"I don't understand."

"Need. What compels you to ask some questions? Why do you need to ask them?"

"To find information."

"That's the result. What is the impulse that translates into need?"

"It's my job."

"So you were ordered."

"Yes."

"By whom?"

"The prosecutor."

"I see, the prosecutor."

"Yes. But facts are facts."

"You need not say that, Gertrude. It's self-explanatory."

"Gertrude?"

"A rose is a rose is a rose. Gertrude Stein. Friend of Alice B. Toklas."

He didn't know what the hell she was talking about, but he knew he wasn't getting anywhere, so he cut to the chase. "Do you have any correspondence from him? Letters, emails, voice mails?"

"Yes."

"I need to have copies."

"*Need* again."

"He's facing very serious charges."

"Yes?"

"These are necessary. You have a close personal relationship."

"Yes?"

"Will you please supply them? I have to see them."

She laughed.

"I can subpoena them."

"I can contest your subpoena."

"This is not going to help him."

"Nor will it hinder him."

"Was he in the habit of disparaging the Navy?"

"Of course not. He loves the Navy. He's given his life to it."

"Even after he was removed from the list?"

"Even then."

"Did he ever disparage the president?"

"Well, he was not especially fond of Woodrow Wilson."

"Would you rather," Osborne began to ask, resorting to his most powerful weapon, "answer these questions now, or later under oath?"

"Under oath," Katy told him. "That's the best thing about a trial, isn't it, better yet than the structural benefits of the adversarial system—to see people at their finest, who with no thought to their own interest sacrifice it and everything else in the sacred pursuit of truth. Testifying under oath is good for the soul. It purifies. I'd be grateful for the opportunity."

Osborne stared at her, his mouth slightly open, his tongue pressed against his lower teeth. There she was—gorgeous, with sparkling eyes, sitting in her glass house, the Mississippi flowing silently below her. "I'll tell you," he said, "the two of you drive me crazy."

"You've met Stephen."

"I have."

"And now you've met me."

Skirmishes at Law

Trial Counsel for the United States—in civilian terms the prosecutor—was Victor Beck. In grade school, to overcome the obvious disadvantages of being called Vic Beck, he sought to escape the pot by jumping into the frying pan, and named himself Skip. So what if people said "skip back," Skip was a popular name at the time and had seemed like a good fix. But why Skip Beck was better than Vic Beck was something understood perhaps only by an eight-year-old. Rarely problematical in the United States, *Skip* caused some difficulty when, after law school at Columbia, he worked on an M.Phil. at Oxford. In England, every time he introduced himself or was introduced, and every time someone read his name on a form or a list, people smiled. At Magdalen College's opening convocation, when his name was read out, the audience of several hundred laughed.

After the ceremony, he asked a random person why.

"Why would your parents have named you that?" was the reply.

"It's a sobriquet," he said, rather than *nickname*. After all, he was at Oxford. "Why not?" Laughing, the person whom he had asked walked away.

So he asked another student, a girl. Girls were nicer. They would take the time to explain. But she couldn't, because she was laughing. "Come on," he said, "tell me."

"Don't you have skips in America?" she asked.

"Of course. I'm one."

This set her off again. When she stopped, she said, "I understand. Come with me."

That was easy. Just starting university, she was eighteen, was very pretty, with red hair and green eyes. Their black robes flowing, she led him through a few streets in the heart of Oxford until they reached a construction site. Pointing to a dumpster into which a load of debris had just fallen and raised a cloud of white dust, she said, in her native Scot's brogue, because now she was out of earshot of her fellow college members, "There, that's a skip."

"Ahhh!" he said, "I see." And he fell in love with her. Now she was his wife. He had been saying, in effect, "Hi, my name is Dumpster," so he

432

abandoned it before he met her parents and before the wedding, in Edinburgh, as it would have been a problem had he not. Now he was once again Vic Beck. But that name didn't fit him either. One might think that anyone named Victor Beck would be a bully and a lummox with muscles of steel. Hardly. He was short, slight, and superficially delicate. So is a stiletto. Whereas Frearson was sunny, deliberate, slow to speak, and stolid, Beck was quick, cunning, dark, fast-talking, and fierce.

Perhaps because he was small of stature, he was fanatical about strength and fitness, and could fight like a Tasmanian devil, which actually isn't that fierce but has a fierce name, as opposed to the gently named honey badger, the fiercest, craziest animal on earth other than a White House correspondent. His energy jumped from him. Though he spoke fast, when he paused he elongated the last sound he had issued into a kind of hum, holding the space until he had decided that he had nothing further to add.

*

Because it was a capital case, the court-martial consisted of a military judge (an admiral) and twelve members. As each one had to be of a rank superior to that of the accused, Rensselaer found himself facing thirteen admirals. The president of the court-martial, a four-star known to everyone in the Navy and many beyond, was Admiral Porter. The others were three- or two-stars, nothing less.

If only for the near-kaleidoscopic flash of their decorations and gold-striped sleeves, the sight when they convened was stunning. An unused helicopter hangar at Naval Station Norfolk had been transformed into a courtroom both large enough to hold the press and spectators and secure enough to assure order. Because the ceiling was so high, a steel frame had been constructed upon which to hang lights in the otherwise preternaturally dim and cavernous hanger. The electricians found that it was easier to rent theatrical spotlights than to install what they called "high hats" on this frame, so that, not surprisingly, the effect was theatrical. Caught in the brilliant light from above, the flags and uniforms exploded in color. As the proceedings advanced in December and promised to continue into the new year, the lights provided more than enough heat, construction-site heaters went unused, and they would have been too noisy anyway.

That November, the vice president was defeated in his run for the presidency. Elevated instead was a Senate independent, Hartsfield, who was politically unclassifiable. He had drawn from the politics and ideologies of both parties while leaving behind their mistakes, idiocies, radicals, morons, criminals, and hangers-on, roundly condemning both in such logical and uninflated oratory that his election promised a sea change. When, after he became president-elect, people called him "Mr. President," he snapped at them that he was not the president and would not be until the twentieth of January.

That was a good sign, Rensselaer thought, the mark of someone who would act with probity. Frearson was not so encouraged. He said it was a good sign, yes, but the danger was that Hartsfield might be inflexible. These indications, however, were uncertain, especially as Hartsfield kept everything as close to his vest as had Calvin Coolidge—perhaps closer. The press went crazy. He was a prospective president who said little; who had never issued a tweet; who projected seriousness, depth, and dignity. It was a nearly unbelievable change, in that he was neither infantile nor senile, nor a crook, narcissist, or idiot.

*

When the court assembled for the monotonous dueling of preliminaries, in which the frustrated and silent panel of admirals had not even a minor part as most everything was left to the judge, they had little to do but form impressions. Two and a half Becks could fit into a Frearson. Frearson's fingers were bratwurst-like, his fingernails rounded and showing a lot of white. Beck's were thin and aerodynamic, the fingernails almost pointy. Frearson reflected the light. Beck absorbed it. When Beck spoke he leaned forward to convince and then leaned back as if his words were a wave that had broken against a seawall and would hit him on the rebound. When Frearson spoke it was as if he were speaking to an unseen judge or God himself, making an argument for its own sake and knowing that if it were true it would succeed regardless of tactics and theatrics.

Frearson's strategy was to do everything he could to delay and stretch out the proceedings so that the verdict would come down after January 20th. To the extent that the court's decision would be based on the political mood of the country, he aimed for the quiet period between old and new regimes, when previous fights had been deflated or at least paused, and new ones had yet fully to take shape. Very imprecisely, he thought that in the dormancy of winter, when all life was challenged, mercy and understanding would come more easily.

Christmas and New Year's became his allies as they brought everything to a halt. From the election to mid-December, he and Beck fought over technicalities, of which an unending supply existed. And in this, Katy assisted remotely, contesting Beck's subpoenas with a near-magical skill that convinced Beck and his assistants that actually getting her on the stand would be as delightful as sharing a sleeping bag with a porcupine. Beck said, "Call *her*? No way in hell."

On 17 December, Frearson took time off to be with his family, Katy was keeping her promise to Stephen to remain in New Orleans until the trial was over, and Rensselaer was excused from woodworking shop and counseling. A lot of guards got leave, and, due to their absence the prisoners spent more time in their cells and more time—in Rensselaer's case, alone—in their exercise yards. It was unusually cold, and it got dark very early.

One day at five o'clock, alone in his fenced enclosure, in the deep gray dusk just before the floodlights came on, Rensselaer heard a faint, familiar, almost crackling sound, like a cross of rain and wind. Not far to the east on the deserted beaches, the waves broke and the surf hissed ever so quietly as it was blanketed in falling snow. That was it. That was the sound, almost a hiss, steady and quiet, for over Chesapeake, which is not far from the sea, it was snowing. He imagined that on the beaches, though it was dark, snow about to die in the breakers would cast a strange white glow.

The First Cut

Trial commenced on the twelfth day of an atypically cold January. Spectators and press who had been kept waiting outside the hangar shivered for a long time even after they were seated. Usually at about the half-hour mark, one by one, they began to remove their coats. For the principals, who came directly from heated offices and conference rooms, it was different.

At first, preliminaries ruled, but then, on the fifteenth, even as the press thinned out to begin taking up position for the inauguration, Beck went on the attack. The lights were as hot and dazzling as a July afternoon.

"Your Honor," Beck said, addressing the military judge, "the prosecution would like to enter into evidence Exhibit Eighteen, an official letter of reprimand dated June the eleventh, nineteen ninety-one—"

"Objection," Frearson said firmly. "We're not trying that incident, which, decades ago, never even became a case. I move that the exhibit be stricken from the record." He knew very well that it would not be.

"Trial Counsel?" the judge asked.

"Your Honor, the prosecution recognizes that the subject we propose was never a case, and, not being a case, could not be tried then and cannot be tried now. It is, however, representative of a pattern of behavior enshrined in the record of the accused, which the prosecution will use to illustrate the accused's frame of mind preceding and during the acts for which he does now stand trial. Further, as the author of the letter of reprimand is no longer living, the prosecution would like to give the accused the opportunity to take the stand to clarify or rebut its content."

The judge said, "I'm prepared to sustain the objection, but I'd like to hear the reaction of defense counsel."

Frearson answered as calmly as if ordering in a restaurant. His body didn't tense, and he spoke to the judge without raising his head. "Defense withdraws the objection and my client will take the stand."

Clearly, Frearson, who smiled tightly and turned away from the panel so no one would see, had planned this. Beck looked like his bird-thin face had been hit by a timber. He turned to the assistant trial counsel as

436

if making an explanation, which was very much out of the ordinary in that he seldom shared anything with her other than the assignment of tasks. "Is he crazy," he whispered rhetorically, "putting his client on the stand in a capital case?"

"Apparently he is," she whispered, "or, if not, watch out."

"I don't get it. He may want to be transparent to appeal to public opinion, but this case will be tried according to law. I'm going to cut him to ribbons."

Rensselaer rose, took the stand, identified himself, was sworn in, and watched Beck, a copy of the letter in hand, glide up to him as if on wheels. Beck was going to go through all the questioning to establish that the letter was the one at issue, when Frearson, without looking up from what—to Beck's un-concealable astonishment—appeared to be a cross-word puzzle, said, "The defense is willing to stipulate that the letter is authentic, and pertinent."

Beck was a little unsettled, but he was used to the blows and fears of trying a case. Though Rensselaer, who had not been apprised of Frearson's strategy, was more than unsettled, he summoned the calm of battle, a state in which the memory of having survived other combat deliberately arises to command that the senses function uninfluenced by fear.

"Captain Rensselaer, would you be so kind as to read the court the body of this letter of reprimand from your commanding officer in the Gulf War?"

Rensselaer took the document with his left hand while crossing his chest with his right to retrieve a pair of tortoise-shell reading glasses, faux, of course, to protect the turtles, but plastic, which endangers them. He looked considered and thoughtful as he put them on and distanced the letter to bring it into focus. "'Eleven June, Nineteen—'"

"Please just read the body of the letter," Beck asked.

"All right. 'Lieutenant, J. G., Stephen Rensselaer and...'" He looked up. "Shall I say their names and ranks?"

"No. There were four of them, is that correct?"

"Yes."

"Under your command."

"Correct."

"Continue."

"'... attached to elements of the Second Marine Reconnaissance Company,' blah, blah, blah ..." This he said rather than completely cite the long unit name. "'... were hunting for Iraqi Scud missiles in the Wadi Al-Hazami when their unit encountered a fortified Iraqi position on high ground, blocking their advance. During the subsequent assault, Lieutenant Rensselaer willfully disobeyed, and caused the SEALs under his command to disobey, a direct order from his Marine superior officer. His actions might have endangered his unit, and his conduct is unacceptable, for which he is herein reproved.'"

"Captain Rensselaer, what does *reproved* mean?"

"Scolded, corrected?"

"According to the dictionary, 'to censure, condemn, reprimand, rebuke, blame, chide, and find fault.'"

"Okay."

"How many times did you receive the direct order that you disobeyed?"

"I really don't know. I would guess about three. The last one was as we were leaving, and the captain was screaming so hard I thought his head would explode. He was panicked."

"According to *you*, he was panicked."

"It was pretty clear."

"Maybe he was angry because you were disobeying him in the middle of a firefight? Is that possible?"

"Objection, leading the witness," Frearson said, somnolently.

"Sustained."

"I'll rephrase. Is it possible that he was angry because you were disobeying him in the middle of a firefight?"

"Yes. It is possible."

"How many times did he give you the order that you disobeyed?"

"Three, I think. I've said that."

"What was it again?"

"Three."

"Your witness."

Frearson rose, slowly. Neither the spectators nor the admirals moved a muscle. No one could imagine what this slow-moving, bulky, ponderous man might do to reverse the impression they had of Rensselaer.

*

"Well," Frearson said, followed by nothing but a long silence during which he looked around and scratched his left ear. Some people, including some of the admirals, briefly held their breath.

Frearson held up a document—two pages that his right hand had been holding against his thigh as if he had not meant to keep them with him when he rose. But he had. "Your Honor, this is the after-action report compiled by the staff of the Marine Reconnaissance Brigade of which the Second Reconnaissance Company was a component. I move to have it entered into the record after questioning my client."

"Objection," Beck called out. "Your Honor, we're getting far afield here. This is not the case we're trying."

Frearson merely smiled, and said nothing.

Both cunningly and restrained, the judge asked, "Trial Counsel, have you not, with all your might, led us here?"

"Not with *all* my might, Your Honor."

"I see. Objection overruled. You may continue, Counsel for the Defense."

"Thank you, Your Honor," Frearson said, this time hardly suppressing his smile. He approached the stand. "Now, Captain Rensselaer, here is the after-action report concerning the events that led to your reprimand." He read the date, identified the office, the command, the numbers assigned to the document, and then held it up for Rensselaer to see. "Have you seen this before?"

"No. I have not. I was interviewed, but so was everyone else who survived. I never looked into it."

"Why not?"

"The reprimand was correct. I disobeyed a direct order. I saw no need to challenge it."

"Were any charges pressed?"

"No."

"Were you reduced in rank?"

"No."

"Was your pay docked?"

"No."

"Was your next promotion on time?"

"It was. I became an SWO in nineteen ninety-three, and advanced in rank appropriately."

"I will draw from a summary of your naval career subsequent to the letter of reprimand, and ask that you correct what you see fit. To the surface fleet in nineteen ninety-three as a full lieutenant. Five years later to Harvard for four years, exiting with a doctorate—your thesis being on nuclear strategy—and promotion to lieutenant commander. In two thousand three, the Iraq War, commanding a patrol coastal. In two thousand five, promotion to commander, assignment as executive officer of a DDG. In two thousand seven, staff duty under Admiral Johnson, Director of Strategic Programming. Two years later, command of a DDG. Another four years, promotion to captain, a year at the Naval War College. Two thousand sixteen, command of an amphibious ready group. Two thousand eighteen, staff duty, assistant to the SECNAV. Is this correct?"

"Yes."

"Your Honor," Beck interrupted. The prosecution is aware that Captain Rensselaer has had a long naval career. What is the point of this recitation, which leads us even farther afield?"

The judge nodded, turned to Frearson, and said, "Counselor?"

"To show, Your Honor, that the defendant's *distinguished* career was not affected, as we might expect, by the otherwise serious charges in the letter of reprimand, as a preliminary to showing why this was so, which thus enlarges the scope of inquiry into the matter that the prosecution itself has brought up. With the court's permission, I will ask my client to read the report. It's not that much longer than the letter of reprimand, which it clarifies immensely."

"All right, Counselor, go ahead, but we can't spend too much more time on this."

"Thank you, Your Honor.

"Captain Rensselaer, will you please read from the body of the report, as you did previously from the letter of reprimand?"

Again, Rensselaer made the cross-body movement to retrieve his reading glasses, and again he looked considered, and senior. He began.

"'At zero four twenty, the four platoons of the Second split up to advance west toward known Scud firing positions scattered near the Wadi Al-Hazami. First Platoon, consisting of forty-two men and augmented by five Navy Special Warfare Operators, moved along the central track without incident. At zero eight hundred they observed the exhaust trail of a single rocket, and were able to hear it. Judging that it was approximately two miles ahead, they increased speed, but after a short distance found that their vehicles could no longer negotiate the trail, which had likely been eroded by recent rains.

"'Dismounting, they double-timed ahead, straining under the weight of their weapons and equipment. A launch complex—as far as they knew, for only later did they discover that several launch complexes were grouped together—was behind a steeply rising escarpment at the top of a roughly thirty-degree, boulder-strewn ramp. The summit overlooked and dominated the wadi they had been following. At the crest, an Iraqi force was dug in, and immediately began to fire at them with light weapons and mortars. The Marine unit commander . . .' Shall I say his name and rank?" Rensselaer asked the judge.

"Just the rank."

"'Captain—— decided that in view of the importance of the objective, a frontal assault was justified. The commanding officer of the SEAL detachment, Lieutenant J. G. Stephen Rensselaer, proposed instead that he take his men back to the vehicles and drive north for a short distance to a passable track that led to a point behind the fortifications they faced. Captain—— rejected this approach and ordered two squads to advance up the boulder slope. The first squad was able to move only fifty yards or so before it was exposed to withering fire from above. Three men were killed immediately, and two of the other three were wounded, one mortally. Against the advice of Lieutenant Rensselaer and the Marine noncommissioned officer, Gunnery Sergeant——, Captain—— ordered the second squad forward. The second squad advanced reluctantly, its chief motive being to aid the wounded and pinned-down Marines. Reaching them, they began to bring them back when, observing their movements, Captain—— ordered them to continue advancing up the slope.

"'Second squad, equally pinned down, in attempting to carry out the order suffered one man killed and another wounded. Retreating to the relative safety of the spot where first squad had taken shelter, they informed Captain—— that they couldn't move forward. At this point, Captain—— ordered squads three and four to move forward on the same line.

"'Observing the high reluctance of these men to carry out the order, Lieutenant Rensselaer proposed once again his plan of envelopment. According to the testimony here appended, Captain—— by this time had lost control of himself and was screaming, shaking, and at times incomprehensible. Lieutenant Rensselaer took it upon himself to order the

Marines to hold until he had cleared the ridge. As he departed, Captain——directly ordered him a number of times not to leave.

"'Lieutenant Rensselaer and his men returned to the vehicles, drove north in one of them, and discovered a navigable track that enabled them to round the escarpment, where they found themselves between the Iraqi blocking force and the launch complexes to the west. Leaving the vehicles where they could not be observed from either the missile sites or the blocking position, they made their way up the slope to the rear and on both flanks of the blocking force.

"'After almost an hour of approach, they were in position to attack. Only one sentry had been placed behind the blocking force, and, foolishly, he was turned away from the Americans and toward the backs of his own men, and he was combing his hair. Lieutenant Rensselaer eliminated him in silence.

"'At his signal, the SEALs opened fire from three directions. Though the Iraqis numbered more than a score of men, they were all facing east. The five SEALs laying down accurate automatic weapons fire killed nearly all of them before they could redirect their weapons. Two tried to escape, but, to prevent them from warning the missile sites, the SEALs killed them as well.

"'With the way clear, half the Marine platoon advanced with the SEALs, while the other half moved the wounded and the dead to an evac zone. Captain——, at this point described as unable to command, was also airlifted out. He was relieved of his duties and at this writing his case is unresolved. The mission continued successfully, and is described in the after-action report immediately following for this sector, beginning at twelve-hundred on——'"

"You can stop there," Frearson interrupted. The courtroom was silent. "Captain Rensselaer, how many men, and how many missions, did you save that day?"

Beck practically launched himself from his chair. "Objection! The witness is being asked to judge his own actions by volunteering a counterfactual speculation."

"Sustained."

"Redirect, Your Honor?" Beck asked.

"Keep it short. We have to get back to the case we're supposed to be trying, and after this, we will."

Frearson withdrew and Beck approached the accused. "Thank you, Your Honor," he said. Then: "Captain Rensselaer, no one doubts your abilities. I certainly don't. But let me ask you once again, did you receive a direct order that day?"

"Yes."

"How many times?"

"Three."

"Did you know that you would be able to eliminate the blocking force?"

"No."

"Were you aware then, and are you aware now, that in the military one does not refuse a legal, direct order issued by a superior officer?"

"Yes."

"And on that one day, how many times did you do that?"

"As I've said, three."

"Excuse me, say again. I didn't hear that clearly."

"Three."

"No more questions."

THE KILL

In a deceptively thick and plodding way, as if discovering at every moment something surprising that he had not known, Frearson convinced the court to hear the history of *Athena*'s deployment, from the Suez forward. Beck objected strenuously on the grounds of relevance, but Frearson was able to cite precedents going as far back as when, in English admiralty law, they were enshrined with quills. Though these had little standing, he won none-theless by referring to American law case-by-case, and the need to establish context. At first skeptical, the court surrendered to the thirty precedents Frearson cited in an astounding chant, without the use of notes, delivered completely deadpan to emphasize that the immense and obvious weight of his argument needed neither passion nor technique. Not all his citations presented convincing parallels, but collectively they were overwhelming.

What followed in the next three days was a masterful retelling of *Athena*'s vivid history. Frearson paced like a bear as he spoke, his tone and timing almost—Rensselaer thought—Homeric. Though no one knew it and yet everyone was magnetized by it, he spoke in meter half the time, and it was as if high above the lights in the helicopter hangar, waves were breaking and guns were firing in the darkness.

It was just a sea story, but as he told it the reporters forgot to write, Beck forgot to object, the judge forgot to interject, and the admirals were still, their breathing shallow, the images that Frearson recalled awakening in their own memories the stock of lifetimes and the indelible sense of the sea.

Beck had nothing to say about *Athena*'s first battles, but after Frearson moved the story far enough along so that in the imaginations of all present the white mass of *l'Étoile Océanique* rose above the flat sea and at dusk its lights sparkled with what Frearson called "French allure," the judge announced a recess, and a re-energized Beck leaned toward his assistant and, looking daggers at Frearson, whispered, "Story time's over, bitch. Now comes the law."

*

When they resumed, Beck said, "The prosecution calls Lieutenant Michael Velez."

Velez had been twenty feet from Rensselaer at Chesapeake for months, and neither had known of the other's presence. When, uncovered and on his way to the stand Velez passed his captain, he saluted anyway.

"Lieutenant Velez . . ." Beck said.

"Sir."

"You were the communications officer on *Athena*, is that correct?"

"Yes sir."

"How long did you serve on *Athena*?"

"From the time she was commissioned until we were relieved at Lemonnier."

"That's Camp Lemonnier in Djibouti?"

"Yes, sir."

"In that time, were you the sole person in COMMS?"

"No, sir. I was training Seaman Ivoire, the best man on *Athena*. We all thought so."

"And what happened to Seaman Ivoire?"

"He was killed when we tried to retrieve hostages from *l'Étoile*. I went in his place in the whaleboat to make the exchange, because I didn't want him to take the risk. But an RPG hit COMMS. It should have been me."

"This was as *Athena* was engaging *l'Étoile*?"

"Objection," Frearson said. "Trial Counsel has made a statement in the form of a question to lead the witness."

"Sustained."

Rensselaer touched Frearson's arm, and whispered, "Let him. Velez won't be led. Watch. You'll see."

Beck stepped back and then rocked forward. "I'll rephrase. Mr. Velez, was Seaman Ivoire killed while *Athena* was engaging *l'Étoile*?"

"No, sir. *Athena* never engaged *l'Étoile*, never fired a shot, never came alongside."

"Well then who killed Ivoire?"

"Hadawi's men, who had hijacked *l'Étoile*, and left it in their boats."

"Yes, we've heard about that. Let me ask you this, Lieutenant. If *Athena*'s crew took to its RHIB and its whaleboat and assaulted, in their boats, the crew of a nearby ship, wouldn't you say that *Athena* had attacked the ship?"

"Maybe. But I would not say that the ship had attacked *Athena*. Right? And Hadawi's men were not *l'Étoile*'s crew. When they were back in their boats and on the sea they were ISIS pirates. They fired at us first. We weren't any more engaged with *l'Étoile* than we were with the *Mayflower*."

The spectators laughed, and the admirals—most of them—smiled. Beck was not happy with this. "In your view, Lieutenant, is firing upon a ship's boats not engaging that ship?"

"They weren't *l'Étoile*'s boats, sir, any more than *Athena*, by virtue of floating on the same patch of sea, was *l'Étoile*'s boat. They were Hadawi's boats, from Ras Hagar."

The judge interjected, "Trial Counsel will refrain from arguing with the witness over what may or may not be definitions of law. Please confine your questions to what the witness may have seen, heard, read, et cetera. He is a witness, after all."

"Gladly, Your Honor. Mr. Velez, are you familiar with the following message, date-stamped and received by you aboard *Athena*? I'll read it. It's marked Exhibit Four A. 'Track commandeered ship until arrival of French forces. Manifests show no American citizens on board. Assist French command if requested only. Take no action independent of task force arriving four plus days. Restore communications through regular channels only.'"

"No."

"No?"

"No, sir."

"Did you receive this message? Let me put it this way. Until you took Ivoire's place in the boat, who received classified messages?"

"I did."

"Was he not cleared?"

"He was, but he wasn't quite ready, cryptologically."

"What do you mean by that, exactly?"

"I mean, he could do it, but it was like teaching someone to drive. You start on quiet streets, but when it's time to go home on the freeway, the instructor takes over."

"Fair enough. Would you, then, be the only person to decode this kind of message?"

"Yes."

"So you received the message?"

"Objection."

"Sustained."

"Is it likely you yourself received the message?"

"I'm sure I did."

"Why are you not familiar with it?"

"I didn't read it."

"Don't you read to make sure it's properly decrypted?"

"We do."

"Why didn't you read it, then?"

"I was ordered not to read it, and all the encrypted messages received from that one on. And then we completely lost COMMS."

"Who ordered you?"

"Captain Rensselaer."

"Why?"

"I didn't ask."

"Was this order irregular?"

"In my opinion?"

"In your opinion."

"Yes."

"Why didn't you ask about it?"

"If an order doesn't appear illegal or dangerous, we don't do that, you know. It's the Navy."

"I see. Immediately after that order, that is, Four A, you did send this one, Exhibit Four B, did you not? Please read it."

Velez read, "'Repeat. Hostages to be executed every hour. French task force will arrive too late. Request permission to engage should opportunity arise.'"

"Do you remember that one?"

"Yes. I sent it."

"What about this one, Exhibit Four C? 'Request denied.' From the CNO himself."

Velez shook his head.

"Please speak your reply."

"No. I was unaware of that one."

"Why?"

"The same reason. I was ordered not to read it."

"Did you deliver it to Captain Rensselaer?"

"I did. That one came immediately and it was short. I assume that was it." Frearson made no objection to the assumption.

Beck continued. "Please read the reply, Exhibit Four D, which you yourself sent."

Velez was beginning to get angry, and his annoyance, that of someone who is pushed and trapped, was discernible. "'Is USS *Athena*, American ship of war, commanded to ignore its obligation to aid mariners in distress? By what authority if so? Clarify.'"

"Please read this message in response, which you received but, as you say, were ordered not to read. Exhibit Four E."

"'Await further clarification.'"

"And, finally, Lieutenant Velez, the last message *Athena* received before its communications were destroyed, this one, Exhibit F, received by you and—if we are to rely on your previous testimony—not read, according to Captain Rensselaer's standing order. Is that correct?"

"Yes, sir."

"Did you see him read it?"

"Yes, sir."

"Did he hand it back to you?"

"No, sir."

"What did he do with it?"

"He folded it and put it in his pocket."

"Was that what he did with the other messages he ordered you not to read?"

"It was."

"Please read it."

"'Per direct presidential order, await French forces. *Athena* is expressly forbidden to fire upon or board *l'Étoile*. Detailed clarification forthcoming pending decision of National Security Council meeting. Stand by.'"

"Would you read again the first two sentences?"

"'Per direct presidential order, await French forces. *Athena* is expressly forbidden to fire upon or board *l'Étoile*.'"

"No further questions."

The judge looked at Frearson, who seemed bored. "Counsel for the Defense?"

"No questions, Your Honor."

Unable to hide his excitement, Beck stood. "Your Honor, the prosecution would like to call Captain Rensselaer."

*

For as long as he could after Rensselaer took the stand, Beck paced back
and forth in front of him. Somehow, successfully delivered in his expression and posture, was his assertion that Rensselaer was pathetic, repellent,
and dangerous. A prosecutor about to examine the devil might have
moved and looked the same way.

"Captain Rensselaer, do you need to have Lieutenant Velez's testimony
and exchange with counsel read to refresh your memory?"

"No. I just heard it."

"Is what Lieutenant Velez stated correct?"

"As far as my involvement, yes."

"Why did you order him to take the uncharacteristic measure of not
reading incoming messages after *Athena* had closed on *l'Étoile*? And are
you sure he didn't?"

"If I may answer the last question first?"

"You may."

"Once the messages are decrypted they're spit out of the machine. You
can grab them without looking. I can't be a hundred percent sure, but
I'm as sure as I can be."

"Why?"

"Velez has great integrity. Look what he did in trying to protect his
shipmate from danger. We had an excellent relationship. I believed him,
and he seemed confused by what was going on, which you would expect
if he hadn't read the incoming traffic.

"As for the first question . . ." Rensselaer glanced at Frearson, who almost
imperceptibly signaled his consent. "I wanted to protect the crew."

"From what?"

"This."

"Are you saying that you foresaw these proceedings?"

"I foresaw the possibility."

"Why?"

"A conflict was arising between what I was ordered to do and what I
was obliged to do."

"Obliged? Obliged by what?"

"By the laws of war, conscience . . . decency."

"Did you believe that the laws of war, conscience, and decency gave you freedom to disobey a direct order from the appropriate command authorities, and the commander in chief himself?"

"As you know, my plea is not guilty."

"To preface my next questions, I'll read from the messages you were careful to instruct Lieutenant Velez not to read, to protect him from . . . *this*. 'Assist French command if requested only. Take no action independent of task force arriving four plus days.' Do you remember that one?"

"Yes."

"'Await French forces.' Do you remember that one?"

"I do."

"'Per direct presidential order, *Athena* is expressly forbidden.'" He paused and emphasized. "'Expressly forbidden . . .'" he paused again, "'. . . to fire upon or board *l'Étoile*.' Remember that?"

"Yes."

"And this? 'Stand by.'"

"Yes."

"So now I will ask you, did you at any time assist the French command?"

"No."

"How far into the Horn of Africa, without any order whatsoever, did you travel to engage in combat with land forces?"

"Almost certainly more than a hundred miles. The trucks were primitive, and had no odometers. It can be calculated exactly, if one were to locate the village where the battle took place."

"More than one hundred miles over the desert?"

"I don't know if it was technically desert. It was dry and bare."

"How many villages did you attack?"

"Well, if I may garble Paul Revere, one if by land, one if by sea."

"Is Somalia a sovereign nation?"

"It's a failed state."

"I didn't ask that. Please answer the question. Is it a sovereign nation?"

"As far as I know."

"Are we at war with it?"

"No."

"Did you make war, in Somalia, deep in its interior?"

"Yes."

"Did you have orders to do so?"

"I did not."

"Did you have orders not to take action, to stand by, to await the arrival of the French task force?"

"I did."

"As you stated before, did you keep your crew ignorant of the orders you did have, to protect them from 'this.' That is, a court-martial?"

"Rensselaer took in a long breath. "Yes."

"No further questions."

THE CROSS

"Captain Rensselaer," Frearson said, once again with the slight fatigue of voice and stance that suggested he was unimpressed by the charges and thought he would have no difficulty refuting them, "I'd like to ask some questions about the orders you're accused of disobeying, as expressed in the messages Trial Counsel has been discussing. First, were you ordered to 'Take no action'?"

"Yes."

"Were you also ordered to track and monitor *l'Étoile*?"

"Yes."

"Is following a ship, surveilling it, and reporting intelligence in its regard, an action? Indeed, three actions?"

"Yes."

"Captain, were you ordered simultaneously to take no action . . . and to take actions?"

"I was."

"Which of those did you choose?"

"I chose the latter, to take action . . . actions."

"Could you have been faithful to both orders?"

"No."

"Now, you were also ordered to wait for the French task force. What did you do?"

"I waited for the French task force."

"You did?"

"Yes. I didn't resume my patrol. I didn't leave the area. I was there— rather, *Athena* was there—when the French ships arrived."

"Objection," Beck called out, irritated. "This is all a matter of semantics that have no reasonable bearing upon the charges."

To this, the judge responded, "Counselor, whether you like it or not, the law depends entirely upon, and would cease to exist without, words and their meaning. We learn this, if we do not already know it, in law school." He turned to Frearson. "Counsel for the Defense may proceed."

Frearson continued. "Not only were you ordered to await the French task force, you were ordered not to fire on *l'Étoile*, is that correct?"

"Yes."

"Did you fire on *l'Étoile*? Or, rather, did *Athena*?"

"No. I did not. Not a single shot. Once *l'Étoile* was beached, wrecked, on fire, and exploding, Commander Holworthy took out terrorists who were about to shoot escaping hostages, but *l'Étoile* was by that time scrap on land. And *Athena* herself never fired a shot."

"You were ordered not to board *l'Étoile*. Did you at any time board her?"

"No. Never."

"Not even after she was beached? Would it not have been prudent to secure her so as to make sure no terrorists had remained on board?"

"It wasn't necessary. Hadawi had offloaded and stockpiled various supplies while it was possible to retrieve them. By the time we got there, *l'Étoile* had begun to burn hot, and explosions within it were collapsing the decks. The fuel bunkers caught fire. It got hot enough to melt steel, and even had it not been, the smoke was so thick it would have been impossible for anyone to have survived. We sent no search parties. Everything was too hot for days, and much of the structure had fallen in on itself and been fused by the heat."

"So, what orders did you violate?"

"None."

"Were you not told to await the decision of the National Security Council?"

"I was, and I did, until our communications were knocked out and I could no longer do so. We were on our own, as in the days when command initiative was the rule."

"Not these days, with real-time communications?"

"No, not these days, but we had no communications whatsoever, and were thrown back to the era of John Paul Jones."

"Objection," Beck called out. "The defendant has no legitimate basis for comparing himself to John Paul Jones."

"Counsel for the Defense?" the judge inquired.

"Your Honor, he didn't. He stated that lack of communications threw his ship back to the *era* of John Paul Jones. That is all."

"Overruled."

"John Paul Jones or not, did you not disobey orders not to pursue the pirates inland?"

"No such orders were received."

"Ah, but that was not the question. Did you disobey orders not to pursue the pirates inland?"

"No."

"Oh," Frearson said. "That's right. No such orders were received, or, in fact, issued. Tell me, Captain Rensselaer, is it possible to disobey orders that were neither issued nor received?"

"I think not."

"So, what orders did you disobey?"

"None."

"Would it be possible for an officer exercising command initiative to exceed the limits upon it so grossly as to merit charges and punishment?"

"Of course."

"How?"

"In any number of ways."

"Such as?"

Beck did not object to Frearson's invitation to speculation on the part of the witness. He thought it could only be to the prosecution's advantage.

Rensselaer forged ahead, in Beck's opinion, courting damage. "For example, if a boomer captain—"

Frearson interrupted. "For the general understanding"—he meant spectators and the press—"what is a 'boomer?'"

"An SSBN, a ballistic-missile submarine."

"Right. Go on."

"If a boomer captain, cut off from communication and somehow able to get around permissive action links, were to launch a nuclear missile targeting Moscow—or, let's say, Paris—command initiative would be no defense."

"Given that you engaged," Frearson asked, "in heavy, casualty-rich, ground-and-naval combat in a country with which we are not at war, do you not think that, as in the example you just cited, command initiative would be no defense?"

"No."

"No? Why is that?"

"Your Honor," Beck interrupted, "as much as I enjoy Defense Counsel challenging the actions of his own witness, who is also his own *client*, I don't see where this is going."

"I'm asking the witness—my client, the accused—to explain his conduct regarding one element of the charges against him. I can break it down into smaller bits if the prosecution needs help with comprehension."

"I think this testimony is invaluable," the judge stated. "Proceed."

"Thank you, Your Honor," Frearson said. "Captain Rensselaer, will you explain why you think your action was justified by command initiative?"

"For reasons both positive and negative," Rensselaer answered. "First, on the positive side, unlike the example I offered, the effects were quite different. Millions of people didn't die and a nuclear exchange between states did not occur. Instead, those who did die were enemies of the United States, against whom the United States is or was engaged in combat in Syria, Iraq, and the Horn of Africa. And almost two hundred innocents, citizens of our NATO allies and other allied countries, were saved.

"Second, the region of Somalia in which we made our incursion is neither under the control of the Somali government nor itself recognized as a sovereign state. The United States has often invoked the right of hot pursuit, such as, during the Vietnam War, in Laos and Cambodia.

"Third, a great deal of precedent exists—historically at least: I'm not a lawyer—for the American Navy, when out of contact with command, to leave its ships and operate on land: in hostile countries, neutral countries, and ungoverned territories. Sometimes this has been successful, as in the Perdicaris incident, and sometimes not, as in the Eaton Expedition. Hostage rescue, as in the *Mayaguez* incident or in Iran, has involved the United States invading not ill-defined regions such as Eastern Somalia, but sovereign nations with which we were not at war.

"Those are the positive reasons for my conduct, completely aside from the moral and humanitarian imperatives in the absence of any other force or agency coming to the aid of the hostages."

"Did you have a negative reason, or, rather, a negative incentive for your decision?"

"I wouldn't call it an incentive, but, rather, the reasonable belief that had I not done what I did, I would have been culpable, I would have found myself in the Chesapeake Brig, and in this courtroom facing charges, just as I am now."

"Objection," Beck called out. "This is wild. The witness has crossed into the purely speculative and theoretical. He's way out of line."

"Mr. Frearson, I would tend to agree, unless you can re-frame your question."

"I will, Your Honor. Captain Rensselaer, did you have reason to believe that had you not exercised your initiative as you did, you would have failed in your duty and been subject to punishment?"

"I did."

"Was this reason mainly speculative, a product of your imagination?"

"No."

"What was it, then?"

"It was a case, in law, of command malfeasance in a situation closely parallel to the one here in question, a case that every line officer in command at sea is either familiar with or should be. In the absence of guidance, it weighed heavily upon me."

"And that was?"

"Captain Balian of the *Dubuque*."

"If I may anticipate Trial Counsel's objection, Your Honor," Frearson said, "I assume that every member of the panel is familiar with the *Dubuque* incident, but, whether or not to Captain Rensselaer's advantage, in describing its influence upon his decisions, it will illuminate his frame of mind at the time."

"Your Honor," Beck argued. "The accused's interpretation of the law is irrelevant and immaterial."

Frearson countered, "I will argue the law later. Here we have the opportunity for the accused further to disclose his motive. I would hope the court would be eager to assess motive in this case, especially since motive is so often unintelligible, shielded by constitutional privileges, or merely unknown."

"The court would," the judge said. "I instruct the witness not to opine upon the law but to state simply why, in light of the *Dubuque* incident, he chose to make the decision he made. Proceed."

*

Rensselaer glanced at Frearson, who, saying nothing, briefly lifted both hands at his sides, as if to say, *Proceed.* "How much latitude do I have in this, Your Honor?" Rensselaer asked the judge.

"I'm sure Trial Counsel will keep you in bounds," the judge told him.

Rensselaer began. "I haven't reviewed the incident, but it occurred while I was at the Academy, and was a topic of discussion in several subjects of instruction, and informally as well. We were all very much aware of it.

"As I recall, the *Dubuque*, an LPD with nine hundred Marines on board, was on its way to the Persian Gulf to assist in the tanker war. The *Roberts*—that is, the *Samuel B. Roberts*, a *Perry*-class frigate much like, I might add, the *Athena*—had hit an Iranian mine a few months before, and things were heating up.

"That was the time of the Vietnamese boat people. Somewhere in the South China Sea, the *Dubuque* encountered a broken-down junk overloaded with refugees. The engine didn't work, a score of refugees had already died, and they had run out of provisions and water.

"Of course, under Article Zero Nine Two Five, it fell upon *Dubuque* to rescue them, and because the boat people were well known and not unassociated with American foreign policy, Seventh Fleet had issued a specific order reiterating the duty to rescue.

"The *Dubuque* stopped, transferred stores and a chart, and that was that. The captain wasn't told that the engine didn't work, how many had died already, and that some of our sailors had repelled one or—I've forgotten—maybe two refugees trying to climb aboard, and left them floundering in the water. Evidently he was not aware of the actual number of refugees on the junk and that the provisions transferred were not at all sufficient, especially since some had been lost during the cross-decking.

"So we left them, and thirty-seven more died before the others were rescued by a fishing boat. They had begun to eat each other, and had they not happened upon the fishing boat, they all would have died. Now, the *Dubuque* was very big, and easily could have taken on the eighty Vietnamese even if they had to sleep on deck. Further, it had lots of launches and connectors, and it could have spared at least one boat and a couple of sailors to tow the junk to safety, even had that been unorthodox. But it didn't. And even though, suspectly, the captain was apparently unaware of crucial facts, he was court-martialed, convicted, and relieved of command.

"I assume that, as I said, had I failed to attempt to rescue the hostages—no other asset was anywhere near—I would have been convicted of dereliction of duty. That was the negative part of my decision, although I admit to having been so moved by the positive part to the extent that, had the negative part not existed, I would have done what I did anyway."

Beck rose. "Your Honor, given the latitude you've afforded this witness, I request a short redirect."

"You may."

"Captain Rensselaer," Beck asked, "the court is undoubtedly impressed by your devotion to Article Zero Nine Two Five, which lays out a duty to rescue those in danger of being, or of actually being, lost *at sea*. Do you know the difference between land and sea?"

"Yes, I know the difference between land and sea."

"Is Ras Hagar on the land or on the sea?"

"Land."

"Is a hundred miles inland from the Somali coast land or sea?"

"Land."

"Does Article Zero Nine Two Five oblige U.S. Naval forces to rescue people in danger of being or actually being lost *on land*?"

"No."

"Would you repeat your answer please?"

"No."

"No, you won't repeat your answer, or no it doesn't?"

"No, it doesn't."

"Are you sure?"

"Yes."

"Would you affirm your answer?"

"It does not."

"No further questions."

CLOSING STATEMENTS

By closing statements on January eighteenth, the *Athena* affair had become only an afterthought, detritus in the continually moving current of events. At one time an element of the election, its attraction had diminished the instant the new president was chosen, and was then further devalued, for Americans at least, by the complexity of a trial that unfurled without even a hint of sex. Europe, too, had forgotten. Since *Athena* had rescued its hostages, Europe had suffered massacres in Paris and Brussels, and the kidnaping, by Boko Haram in Nigeria, of a young French doctor and her beautiful children. This captured the imagination of the continent and held it for months, draining many barrels of ink and watts of electricity. Probably there had been nothing comparable since the ransoming of Richard the Lionhearted, who, though notably ugly and short, was at least a king.

As Rensselaer's court-martial had advanced, the press had thinned out. With neither cameras in the courtroom nor satellite trucks allowed on base, structural impediments to sensationalist coverage had existed from the beginning. The former JAGs that the networks had enlisted as talking heads were unanimous in their predictions that the facts pointed to the near certainty of conviction. Rensselaer's actions, they said, had simply been too extreme. Long ago, when the nation had been youthfully flexible, he might have been a hero like those who fought the Barbary Pirates. Not now.

In the First World War, the future general Patton had beaten an American enlisted man to death, with a shovel, for not advancing into enemy fire. By the Second World War, though Patton was relieved of his command for merely slapping a soldier, he was eventually put in charge of the Third Army. Now, a suggestive proposal to—or perhaps even a wink in the direction of—a female soldier could be career-ending. What then of going off entirely on one's own and using a surface combatant of the United States Navy to bombard and destroy a town in a nation with which the U.S. was not at war, invading its wretched interior, and engaging in numerous battles, all after clear orders not to take action? With nary an exception, the talking heads were of one opinion. That is, the experts without bodies said the verdict was in the bag.

For these reasons, the only member of the civilian press present on the eighteenth was a crime reporter for *The Virginian-Pilot*, who, due to the murder of two convenience store employees during a robbery in Hampton, was so impatient to leave that the whole time she was covering the closing statements her right foot tapped at high speed as if she were listening to boogie-woogie. The small remnant of national press present a few days before had decamped to Washington to cover Hartsfield's inauguration. In deadening winter, Naval Station Norfolk was gray and tranquil amid intermittent snows.

Once the vast reservoirs of retained heat in the nearby ocean, the Roads, and the bay had dissipated, Arctic air had no amelioration, and dusk on the seventeenth had seen energetic snow squalls. On the eighteenth, under the lights in the helicopter hangar, the huge press and spectator section held in addition to the *Pilot* reporter three sailors who had wandered in to get out of the snow, and not a single civilian.

The admirals in their two rows of six apiece flanking the judge were as colorful, if hardly as consequential, as the disciples at the Last Supper. To a man they were suffering the way one does when one has overshot a freeway exit and must drive away from the destination for ten or fifteen miles before leaving the road, re-entering in the other direction, and driving another ten or fifteen miles back. They knew they would be at a disadvantage were they kept from Washington, whence many of them had come and where everything was about to change. If they couldn't influence or even make contact with the new appointees to whom they would soon report, they would be at a severe disadvantage. Although they didn't tap their feet like the frustrated reporter, they were impatient to render their verdict and get back to work. When the judge announced that after closing statements the court would adjourn until the twenty-first, the admirals felt the blow as if from the *Yamato*'s 18.1-inch guns.

That is, all but the president of the court-martial, Admiral Porter, who outranked them, was senior, soon to retire, and so famous for his taciturn, laconic manner that he was ironically nicknamed Chatty Kathy. It was not unusual for him to chair a contentious three-hour meeting without saying a single word. When asked once by the President of the United

States to comment on his economy with words, he had replied, "No." All who served under him respected him so much it was like love.

So, the atmosphere was not pleasant once everyone had arrived, shaken the snow off caps and jackets, and taken seats. The lights hadn't been on long enough to heat the hangar. Before Beck was called to make his closing argument, Frearson turned to Rensselaer. "The lights haven't been on long enough to heat. It's cold and miserable. He'll have to make his argument while he's chilled and—look at him—depressed. I'm keeping my coat on, and by the time I get up the room will have warmed and the admirals will have awakened. What's also good is that the political pressure is in abeyance, and will remain so as they deliberate. And no matter what happens now, we can always appeal."

Rensselaer looked at him, and asked, with neither anxiety nor fear, "Do you think we're going to lose?"

"We've got at least an even chance, yes. Did you ever believe, when going into battle, that you were assured of victory?"

"Never."

"Well, here we are."

"The judge opened the session, sized up those before him, and asked, "Is Trial Counsel ready to proceed with closing arguments?"

*

Thin, eager, and despite an occasional shiver, Beck popped up like a fishing float. Rather than answering the question, he launched right in. "The prosecution," he said, his voice and his characteristically explosive physical movements slowed nonetheless, and to his surprise, by the cold, "is willing to admit that the results of Captain Rensselaer's private expedition using the Navy's resources were generally successful. But we ask the panel to consider two closely analogous examples. First: hostages are taken in, let us say, Denmark. Contrary to explicit orders to 'take no action,' an American warship in the North Sea bombards a Danish village and sends a raiding force to rescue them—successfully. So what? Isn't success overshadowed by everything else?

"Such as . . . integrity of command? The authority of the United States? Risk to American relations with other countries? That risk undertaken blindly and without the broader knowledge of higher military and civil authorities? The risk, in confronting the ferocious Danes, to the lives of American personnel, none of whom, presumably, joined up to serve under a privateer commissioned by himself and unconstrained by orders? The subtraction, again, in defiance of orders, of assets potentially in dire need elsewhere? For an American officer privately to invade Denmark would be unthinkable. And yet every consequence, every condition I have just outlined applies precisely, if on a lesser scale, to Captain Rensselaer's actions.

"I need not point out to this distinguished assemblage that although proportionality, degree, and result may be pertinent in sentencing, conviction requires—demands—only principle. It is binary. Yes or no. Black or white. Did the captain violate the law, or did he not?

"Consider a second and closely related hypothetical. What if every commanding officer of every ship in the Navy believed as Captain Rensselaer did?" Here, Beck paused, turned away from the panel, and then spun back around deliberately fast.

"No. Let me modify that. What if only half the commanding officers took their ships where they wanted, when they wanted, to do what they wanted? What if a quarter? A tenth?

"What if a precedent is set, so that in the future any officer might look back and conclude that if *his* objective is achieved, and *his* aims accomplished, he"—he paused—"or she, has license to make decisions and pursue objectives independently of his command, his government, his nation? I need not remind a panel of admirals of every naval officer's duty properly to interpret and manifest his commanders' intent, but without tortured reinterpretation, delay, rationalization, exaggeration, or excuse.

"In the past few weeks, we have been over the facts of the case, which speak for themselves, and, in being extreme, are unfailingly memorable. In fact, they almost jump out at you. I doubt that any of us present will ever forget them. The defense has hardly challenged a single one of these facts, relying instead and in almost every instance on a nearly irrelevant, often absurd, and—on this I congratulate them—highly creative interpretation of actions and deeds that to any reasonable trier of facts and law should seem to be nothing more than, if I may quote my five-year-old son, 'wiggling out.'

"In lesser cases, I've given longer summations. Even though this is a capital case, I'm comfortable with brevity. Given the facts and the law, I see no other choice but brevity. Out of probity and respect, I cannot say to you, 'You must convict.' That would be presumptuous. And I think you've heard enough from me. My voice is irrelevant and it is weak. The strong voice that I trust you will hear, echoing through conscience, judgment, and history, is the simple and clear voice of the law. The law that we did not make but to which, as a sacred trust, all of us are keenly obligated. I ask you, therefore, to heed that voice, and to convict."

"Is that all, Captain?" the judge asked.

"Yes, Your Honor. At heart it's a simple case," Beck said both confidently and sadly.

"Commander Frearson," the judge now asked, "are you ready to proceed with your concluding arguments?"

"Yes, Your Honor," Frearson answered, as slowly and calmly as if to contrast with Beck's jump from his seat. Bear-like, he extracted himself from behind the defense table and unselfconsciously ambled up to face the admirals.

They were magnetized by the difference with Beck. Frearson's big body, with not a whit of fat; his big head, with straight, golden hair covering it in a neat but generous military haircut; and his ruddy windburn testifying that even in January he had managed to be outdoors for hours each day, drew their attention and their respect. Unlike Beck, he spoke slowly, but with great strength; mildly, but with great confidence; and always in a deep, commanding voice, the gift of both his size and his natural authority.

*

"I thank the prosecution for its brevity. Why not? The prosecution's client is three hundred and thirty million people, the vast, vast majority of whom have never heard of this case in any detail, if at all—and are uninterested in it, and immediately unaffected by it. Like the prosecution itself, win or lose, they will go home tonight and eat their dinners just as on any other night.

"The defense however, has a different burden. For us, in this capital case, what is at stake? Life and honor are at stake. If the *Nimitz* plows over a swimmer at its bows, perhaps not even a seismograph on board would register the impact. That is what we have here: a dozen admirals, thirteen if you count Your Honor. I took the liberty during the trial of adding up your stars—twenty-eight. That's a lot of brass. And then, the

Navy, the DOD, the government, the nation: of far greater weight than just the *Nimitz*. We, therefore, do not have the luxury of brevity. I wish we did. To the prosecution, I say, congratulations on the lightness of your burden and its inconsequentiality to your client, who, I might add, has only benefitted from Captain Rensselaer's many years of service and his recent extraordinary actions, heroic actions, which, I will show, were not forbidden by law but, quite to the contrary, *mandated* by it.

"I have something more to say about the prosecution's brevity. The defense has no such privilege, because in a capital case, with the potential of a capital penalty, it is the defense's duty to strain to the utmost. To save a life. Just as one would stretch as far as one could, with an eye to and the hope of achieving the impossible—to save one's wife, one's child, one's fellow sailor or Marine, bystanders in danger, civilians, men, women, and children—the defense in a capital case is guilty itself if it does not exceed its own limitations, risk its own interests, and do everything it possibly can. All this by command of the sanctity of life.

"That we will do. And is that not exactly what Captain Rensselaer did?"

Anyone watching Admiral Porter and most of the other admirals would have seen an ever-so-slight lifting of the eyelids. Beck saw it, and it worried him. The crime reporter for *The Virginian-Pilot* had, unbeknownst to her, stopped tapping her foot. Now she was anxious about two things—getting to Hampton to report on the slayings, and having to leave, as she was assigned to do, in the middle of these proceedings. She felt torn, but she had no choice. She looked at her watch and took a deep breath, but she did not leave.

*

"Whereas the defense recognizes its responsibility to refute one by one the charges against the accused, we would like to point to overarching facts in regard to all of them. First, they have been amassed with unusual promiscuity: seven articles, some, in our understanding, inapplicable and even inexplicable, arrayed like lead soldiers and fired like scattershot with hope for a hit. Second, I'm duty bound to note before the court that these charges have come down during a presidential election in which the charges themselves have been an issue and the president himself has directly intervened in the details of the case, ordering the detention of Captain Rensselaer when clearly the captain is neither a danger to the public nor in any way a flight risk. What would he do that might endanger the public? Rescue hundreds of innocent civilians in Nashville or Grand Rapids? Where could he flee? Iran? Syria?

"A Navy captain with long and honorable service, he would ordinarily and at most be confined to quarters. That is how we do it. But not this time, when the charges impinged upon an election in which the president's heir and legacy were at stake. As you very well know, command influence can be attributed to officers far inferior in rank to any member of this panel. And command influence in courts-martial can rightly be characterized as—if I may, in following Trial Counsel's example, quote my own little boy—a 'no no.' But what do we have now, explicitly, even in writing? We have the President of the United States exercising command influence. This despite the law clearly stating that, if I may quote, 'No person . . . may attempt to . . . influence the action of a court-martial or . . . the action of any convening, approving, or reviewing authority.' By his unusual order, the president has signaled his presence and intent. Even the smallest signal from such a uniquely powerful source has undeniable impact and influence.

"As for the associated charges," Frearson said, with perfectly modulated annoyance and contempt that, while insufficient to cross into resentment or accusation, were highly effective in garnering sympathy for his irritation at having to suffer them, "Article Ten, improper hazarding of a vessel. Everyone on this panel will know that this facet of law applies to matters of navigation and piloting. *Athena* neither ran aground nor bumped into anything. Yes, in the battle of Ras Hagar she was brought into harm's way, but if the Navy is to charge captains for venturing into harm's way, even when disagreement exists in regard to the interpretation of orders, the Navy will be transformed into nothing more than a tremendously down-market cruise line with limited menus, gray ships, and no waterslides. You may wonder why the defense didn't move to have this charge dismissed. Frankly, we wanted it to survive so as to betray the nature of and motivation for all the charges.

"Article Eighty-Seven, missing movement. Yes, Captain Rensselaer was not aboard *Athena* when by his order his executive officer took her a few miles offshore of Ras Hagar, but *Athena* went nowhere. Unless one interprets movement as changing berths or anchorages, nothing was missed. And it is patently ridiculous to apply a regulation intended for sailors who don't show up because they are either drunk, AWOL, or in the clink, to a commanding officer who is fighting ashore while his ship awaits him in close proximity and clear sight of land. This, too, we failed to challenge, so as deliberately to preserve its absurdity as a point of illustration.

"Article Eighty-One, conspiracy. With whom, exactly, did the defendant conspire? In trying this case, Trial Counsel was happy throughout to stress that Captain Rensselaer kept his orders, his plans, and his intentions from *Athena*'s officers and men. If this charge is to stand it will perhaps uniquely establish that it is possible to conspire in secret only with oneself, lifting from future prosecutors the annoying burden of identifying co-conspirators.

"And then Article Eighty-Five, desertion. Really. Now, the court will determine whether or not—and I will show *not*—the remaining charges should apply. But are we to believe that a captain who repeatedly leads his troops into battle—against Ras Hagar, on the Somalian Plateau, holding off Hadawi's army—who achieves his objective, and who is both gravely wounded and victorious, is guilty of *desertion*?

"Considering the elements of the statute, Section (a) one, Captain Rensselaer did not go or remain 'absent from his unit, organization, a place of duty with intent to remain away therefrom permanently.' He did quite the opposite.

"Section (a) two. He did not quit 'his unit, organization, or place of duty with intent to avoid hazardous duty or to shirk important service.' Again, he did quite the opposite. The one element of the charge that may cast a shadow over his innocence is the question of 'place of duty.' I will clarify this, I think, rather unambiguously, in my general defense, but as this charge alone is a capital offense, the defense will address it later to make sure that the shadow is eliminated, so that the absurdity of the charge is exposed in full view. Again, how can a commander who repeatedly leads his troops into hazardous battle possibly be charged with desertion?

"I will address the remaining charges largely as one. They are differentiated for sure—mutiny by refusing to obey orders, usurping lawful military authority, Article Ninety-Four. Failure to obey order or regulation, Article Ninety-Two. And the General Article, One Thirty-Four, as formulated in this case: diversion, invasion, subtraction of military capacity in time of war, and risking the creation of a subsidiary front.

"We have addressed the technicalities. That is, the nature of the received orders, and the duty of a commander when in changing circumstances he is out of communication. We've argued these in such a way that here we need only refer to our points, which the defense is quite sure are so clear in the minds of the court that they need not be reiterated. What remains is the general defense, which is the strongest defense, and with which we will demonstrate, as stated briefly before—and not at all briefly in our brief—that Captain Rensselaer was obligated to do what he did, and that this obligation, superior in law and in morality, overrides any infractions, real or imagined, that may stem from it.

"To wit, military personnel of the United States are bound to adhere to the Second Geneva Convention, which states, *inter alia*, that in regard to those 'who are at sea and who are wounded, sick or shipwrecked,' its adherents are obligated to 'take all possible means to search for and collect' those very same, which the text then cites as 'shipwrecked, wounded and sick.'

"*Shipwrecked* means, as well as clinging to wreckage in the water, being cast upon a shore, as Robinson Crusoe was shipwrecked for a very long period. Not only Defoe hews to this definition, but Shakespeare— 'shipwracked upon a kingdom,' *Hamlet*—and Swift, whose Gulliver was 'shipwracked on the coast of Balnibarbi.'

"According to Article Seventeen, one, of Additional Protocol One of the Second Convention, the rescue of those it identifies as cited above is of such importance that anyone—I stress, anyone—'shall be permitted, *even on their own initiative*, to collect and care for the wounded, sick and shipwrecked even in invaded or occupied areas,' and, here I stress, 'no one shall be prosecuted, convicted or punished for such humanitarian acts.'

"Lest the court conclude that Captain Rensselaer is not on trial for the rescue efforts the Convention deems un-prosecutable, but for disobeying orders, a different and additional thing, I respectfully point out that according to the charges he is indeed on trial for the efforts themselves, and that the transmission of orders was curtailed very early on, throwing him upon his own initiative and interpretation of not only the tension arising due to what may, or may not, have been an order to stand down, versus not only the Geneva Convention but U.S. Navy regulation Article Zero Nine Two Five, Section one.

"This, American law, military law, *Navy* law, states: 'Insofar as can be done without serious danger to the ship or crew, the commanding officer or the senior officer present as appropriate shall: a., proceed with all possible speed to the rescue of persons in distress if informed of their need for assistance, insofar as action may be reasonably expected of him or her.'

"Now, much has been made by the prosecution of the supposed disqualification of Captain Rensselaer's rationale, license, and efforts to satisfy his obligations under both international law and U.S. Naval regulations, because of his operations on land. As we all know, this is the Navy. We have ships, and ships don't go on land." He glanced patronizingly at Beck. "That's true.

"However, a very large part of the Navy, including of course the Marines, is devoted to amphibious warfare. Our massive amphibious ready groups all over the world exist for the very purpose of warfare on land, and are expected to operate in combat zones that extend hundreds of miles inland from the surf. Nor is naval aviation confined to or based exclusively upon the sea. In recent decades, naval operations have focused upon—and naval personnel have served in, survived in, and given their lives in—AORs far inland, such as Iraq, and Afghanistan, which does not even border on the sea.

"Before she was diverted, *Athena's* original tasking was to fight in the surf zone and inland along the coast of Iran on the Arabian Sea. For that purpose, she carried a detachment of Navy SEALs—Sea, Air . . . *Land*. I submit that the fight ashore does not in any way remove his actions from what is expected of a U.S. naval mission, or alter the nature of Captain Rensselaer's obligations under law. As the court is aware, in the appendices to our brief is a list of scores of operations and incidents, from the Revolutionary War to the present day, of U.S. Naval personnel, whether Marines, SEALs, or sailors, operating extensively on land, over land, and inland, without incurring censure, prosecution, or even the batting of a judicial eyelash. That *Athena's* rescue efforts left the water should be of no relevance whatsoever and certainly neither the basis of nor the justification for any charges.

"I venture to say, gentlemen, that this case presents not a violation of law but the necessity of weighing the merits of conflicting laws and competing demands. It would be a lot easier if Captain Rensselaer had, under the Geneva Conventions or Naval Regulations, refused an illegal order. At issue however is not a conflict between what is forbidden and what is asked, but between what is required and what is asked. Even so, the 'asking'—that is, the order—was itself ambiguous. He was ordered both to take action and to take no action until a decision was reached, and then he was cut off, and thus the decision devolved upon him.

"The *Athena*'s crew watched as men, women, and children were slaughtered before their eyes. They were told of, and witnessed, a series of steadily carried-out executions, by the clock, one an hour. Put yourself in their place. Put yourself, more appropriately, in Captain Rensselaer's place. Aware of the possible consequences stemming from the ambiguities, stress, and uniqueness of the situation, he deliberately insulated his crew from even the knowledge of his decisions, to protect them and to take all the risk and responsibility upon himself. On the expedition landward, he took only volunteers, who, solely according to conscience and spurred by what they had seen, chose to follow him.

"One cannot say exactly, yet it is reasonable to assert, that the man on trial here today saved almost two hundred completely innocent lives, and did so in extended, valorous combat against a common and declared enemy of the United States, a savage and terroristic enemy against whom our troops are fighting this very day in the Levant and in, and here I stress, Africa itself, indeed in Somalia, not that far from where *Athena* took on the very same foe.

"I need not remind the distinguished members of the panel of the gravity and danger in naval warfare. Here at home, with our pressed uniforms and gracious customs, we may seem at times to be the attendees of a giant yachting party. But how that changes, and with such shock and speed, abroad and on the sea. This is recognized, but often in a manner that escapes recognition not only by the general public but by us as well.

"For example, in the custom of associating a woman with the christening of a ship as it is about to be launched. A very dainty thing, no? Mamie Eisenhower struggling to smash a bottle of Champagne against the steel? From what does that come? Well, it used to be wine . . . red wine. Why red? Because it served as a substitute for what in ancient times had been blood, the blood of slaves or captives who were tied onto the rails so the ship would crush them as it slid into the water. That is part of our origin, and knowing it should sober us in regard to the essentially tragic nature of our mission. We are engaged in what is an ultimately very sobering enterprise endowed with the capacity to

469

transform the very purest motives into quicksilver imperfections that escape classifications of law.

"Nonetheless, we have made our case for the legal imperative. There is also a moral imperative. In weighing the harm versus the good, you cannot avoid putting those two hundred lives on the scale against whatever theoretical harm might have come from the captain's decisive, courageous, and successful exercise of his initiative.

"We teach initiative. We encourage it. We stress that it is one of the things that enables a free people to survive in its struggles with lockstep totalitarianism. We have always heavily counted on it. And we admire it. No one denies that it comes with risk, but our lives on the sea teach us that risk is ever present.

"Not a single member of the court is unaware of the United States Navy's maxims in regard to each element upon which this case turns. Taken from the greatest figure in naval history, Admiral Horatio Nelson . . . well you know it by heart, but I shall quote it anyway: 'In case signals can neither be seen or perfectly understood, no captain can do very wrong if he places his ship alongside that of the enemy.'

"To preserve the blessings of peace and home, we go to war. And in war these very things are destroyed and we are taught their opposites. Yet that which we cherish cannot exist unless we are willing for a time to abandon it. Of the many tragedies of war not least is that he who does not return must die knowing both that he has lost and cannot regain the virtues he has fought to preserve.

"Some return unable leave the echoes of war behind, and are changed enough so that they no longer can embrace that for which they left to fight. Only the truly blessed—fortunately the majority—bend to war when they must, and straighten once more for home and hearth.

"Captain Rensselaer kept his men in the dark to protect them, yes, but also to allow them not to turn their backs upon their responsibilities. In his interpretation of his orders, he resolved ambiguities that his superiors failed to reconcile. Because he did, some of his men died, but literally hundreds of people were saved, families preserved, children freed to grow up.

"Like all of us, he and his crew were torn between the fire of the hearth and the flames of war. He took it upon himself to reconcile the paradox and contradictions of war and peace. He had no choice, for he was the captain, far from home, left to his own devices. There was no one else.

"I beg the honorable court to keep in mind that Captain Rensselaer reiterated in dangerous practice the great traditions of the Navy. He followed the highest laws to which we are devoted and in respect of which we are commissioned. And, gentlemen, he succeeded.

"I close with this. I see in my mind's eye a small American ship, six thousand miles from home, battered after multiple combats with the enemy, on station so long that its supplies are taxed, its aspect ragged, its crew exhausted. Alone and small though it is, it is the only warship at the edge of a vast continent. So much is it like the little ships of our Navy as it began, so cut off from communication, so long enduring, that it must call upon the virtues of that other time. Were the sailors of Odysseus magically cross-decked to find themselves upon *Athena*, they would immediately sense a common bond. Whatever your verdict, *Athena* and her crew will be remembered in the annals of the United States Navy for bravery, humanity, and for having done right. And may God bless them for that.

"I rest my case," Frearson said. Trying unsuccessfully not to show it, he was deeply moved. No one could tell if the long pause before adjournment was because the court was moved as well or had expressed its disapproval in silence.

VERDICT

When in that cold January there were no sweet showers as in April on the cape but it snowed as if the world were ending, pilgrimage between the brig and court became extremely difficult, as neither Chesapeake nor Norfolk, unaccustomed to three-foot drifts, had many plows. The brig itself was unusually quiet, not merely from the muffling of the snow in the air as it fell and on the surfaces it blanketed, but because intake had slowed, release had quickened, and quite a few guards had been granted leave.

To Rensselaer's surprise, he was allowed into the dayroom, which was almost empty. "Why?" he had asked.

"Your guys are gone," the guard told him.

"Who?"

"The other officers, your crew."

"Movius?"

"Yes."

"Holworthy?"

"Yeah, him, too. The officers and chiefs. Pisecki, he was a chief, right? It's hard to keep track, 'cause you don't have insignia. But officers and chiefs were the only ones in this block. They put them on a bus yesterday."

"What happened?"

"Charges dismissed, I was told, as a result of the facts of your trial."

"Where'd they go?"

"San Diego. Holworthy—he was a SEAL, that I know. He said the ocean's freezing this time of year even there, but he's going do a big swim and then walk up Orange Avenue to Dunny's and have burritos and beer. That make sense?"

"Very much so. Pisecki?"

"Flying him on a Greyhound out to the *Stennis* before it gets out of range. They offered him leave but he wouldn't take it."

"That's Pisecki. What about Movius?"

"The Jewish guy?"

"Yeah, the Jewish guy."

"I didn't mean it badly. I said that because he went to church on Saturday. I mean, they brought in a rabbi. While he was here, in the brig, I think he managed to get a gig at Caltech—teaching or studying, I don't know. Can you believe that? How could he do that when he was up on charges?"

"Two facets of law," Rensselaer replied. "Presumption of innocence, and chutzpah. Caltech is in Pasadena. Ever been there?"

"No."

"It's like the Garden of Eden. He's in love with a girl who's there now. She's formidable, beautiful, and charming." Rensselaer smiled.

"It makes you happy?"

"It does."

As Rensselaer sat in the dayroom, he had no desire to play Ping-Pong or watch television. Ping-Pong was out anyway, because the two other sorry prisoners present were playing some sort of children's board game. So he went back to his cell, where he strained to hear the falling snow, but could not.

*

The verdict would be handed down at 0700 on the morning of 20 January, allowing the admirals time, even in the snow, to rush to Washington for the inauguration. Accordingly, Rensselaer left Chesapeake at 0430, because of the weather an hour earlier than usual. No one was on the road, and it was dark all the way. Rensselaer thought it fitting that he was taken in the dead of night and in the cold. It was an appropriate antechamber to what might be the rest of his life in a cell, or even, as unlikely as Frearson had assured and history supported, execution. He was a soldier, who had learned in training and practice to keep his emotions in check even in the face of death.

They arrived early, no one was there, and the lights were off until his guards couldn't stand the cold and one of them found the electrical panel and threw the switches. Instantaneously, the world was filled with the glowing colors in the flags of the fleets and commands. And by the time Frearson entered, it was fairly warm.

"Are you all right?" Frearson asked. He himself was not, but he hid it.

473

"I'm all right."

"You're not worried? You don't look worried."

"Would it help?"

"We can always appeal."

"I'm prepared for the worst," Rensselaer said emotionlessly, "as I have been since I took my oath as a midshipman. After all, it's only a matter of time. Eventually, everyone sinks under the waves, but the sea remains untroubled."

The admirals filed in. Despite or perhaps because of trying to be expressionless, they looked grim. Only the principals were in attendance, not a single reporter or civilian, not even the crime reporter from *The Virginian-Pilot*, who hadn't made it in, because of the snow. Once, the *Athena* affair had seized the attention of the world, but no longer, for that was in the summer, and now everything was hushed in white. Rensselaer found this, keyed to the nature of things, promisingly just.

After the court was called to order, the military judge announced, pro forma, that the verdict would be handed down by its president, the senior and taciturn Admiral Porter. In appearance and in truth he was stern, kind, and—chiefly—wise. Responsible for this were not just his age and his character, but years of being tested day by day in action and decision. He was grayed, sad, tough, and, as much as he could be, in control of circumstances and himself. The admiral was exactly what Rensselaer had once hoped someday he himself might be were he to live as long. And then the admiral read.

"Captain Stephen Rensselaer, United States Navy, this court-martial finds you not guilty of Article Ten of the Uniform Code of Military Justice, improperly hazarding a vessel.

"Of Article Eighty-Seven, missing movement: not guilty.

"Of Article Eighty-One, conspiracy: not guilty.

"Of Article Eighty-Five, desertion: not guilty.

"In regard to Article Ninety-Four, Section one, b., two, mutiny by refusing to obey orders or perform duty, usurping or overwriting lawful military authority. And Article One Hundred and Thirty-Four, the General Article, in this case diverting a component of the armed forces of the United States in time of war to invade a territory with which the United States is not at war, thereby subtracting from the capacity of the United States to wage war, and risking creation of another front, the court wishes to make the following statement in view of the fact that violation of the first article is a capital offense.

"The court recognizes both the overall success of *Athena's* undertaking in preserving the lives and safety of the hostages, and the valor this called forth. We are sympathetic to the arguments of your defense counsel, respectful of your motives, and impressed by your skill. We found in our deliberations that every member of the panel could see himself in your place, and not a single one of us wanted to convict.

"However, admiration and desire aside, we felt compelled to consider, among others, two articles of common precedent. The first, adopted from the late Justice Scalia's Canons of Construction—to which I imagine defense counsel is not likely to object—is that words are to be understood in their ordinary meanings, assuming they are not specifically assigned other meanings within a specified context; second, that nothing is to be added to what the text states (*casus omissus pro omisso habendus est*); third, that the expression of one thing implies the exclusion of others (*expressio unius exclusio alterius*); and, fourth, that mandatory words impose a duty.

"The court, therefore, had to consider that the orders you received, to wit, 'Take no action,' and 'Stand by,' were valid and were to be obeyed.

"We considered carefully defense counsel's opinion that in this extraordinary case it was our task and duty to judge between the competing demands resulting from the confliction of valid laws neither of which necessarily trumps the other. In terms of setting precedent, we believe that this court is competent neither to make such a determination in general nor to apply it to this case alone.

"Further, we did not judge that it was necessary. What relieved us—indeed, prohibited us—from such an excursion was the precedent in law to which our sister service, the United States Coast Guard, adheres. A major part of their function, their history, and their experience has been the rescue of those imperiled at sea or shipwrecked ashore, and their doctrine is both very clear and exactly analogous to United States Naval doctrine and law, though ours is more fully developed in regard to fleet movement and combat at sea. Coast Guard and Naval vessels are obligated to accomplish rescues, but, clearly, and crucially, *unless otherwise directed by higher authority.*

"The logic of this, including as it applies to the actions here in question, is in view of this court highly compelling and sufficient to be exclusionary. The obligation to rescue, as expressed in every instance and imperative cited by the defense, was—in fact, in law and in deed—*accepted* by Naval command at a higher level than *Athena* and her captain. *Athena* was an organ within the whole, no less subject to the direction and discipline of higher authority than a boatswain's mate in a dinghy during a rescue would be subject to the order of the commanding officer of the vessel from which he had launched.

"The higher in the chain of command, the broader the view and the greater the knowledge of other demands, resources, and consequences. We hardly need say that the ships, planes, and special forces of both the United States and its allies were in the area and potentially available; that, once landed, the hostages were in the AOR of AFRICOM, the assets and plans of which *Athena*, especially as she was entirely without communication, could not have been aware. Nor could *Athena* have been aware of the needs and situation of American forces in the relatively nearby zone of conflict, or of the diplomacy involving allies, neutrals, and enemies.

To reiterate so as to be absolutely clear, obligations under the Geneva Conventions, Second and prior, and under Naval Regulations, Article Zero Nine Two Five, Section one—the court stresses—had been accepted and met by higher authority. *Athena*, as an instrument of that authority, was not entitled or privileged to carve out a separate justification for independent action.

"Therefore, the court has found that the orders, clear on their face, were binding. And therefore, in regard to Articles Ninety-Four, Section one, b., two, and the General Article, One Hundred and Thirty-Four"— here, Admiral Porter paused, some thought, with deep regret—"Captain Stephen Rensselaer, this court-martial finds you . . . guilty.

"Sentencing will take place here on twenty-two January at zero-seven-hundred. The prisoner will be escorted back to Naval Consolidated Brig, Chesapeake."

SNOW

In the Florida Everglades at the Rod and Gun Club, time had almost stood still except that in the passage of a century a small town had grown up around it, and it, like people, had gone through phases of dilapidation and restoration so that, similar to the case of a dowager well acquainted with plastic surgery, what had been there to begin with was hard to distinguish from what had been added.

Long ago, it had been so authentic as to have been almost as unbelievable as it was true: white clapboard, ceiling fans, dark furniture, surfeits of both liquor and wicker, fishing rods and hunting rifles carelessly resting here and there, Seminole guides waiting by their boats, fugitives and the famous daintily respectful of one another's privacy. Though much had changed, some things had remained the same, one of them being that, until the day of Hartsfield's inauguration, snow had never fallen. But then it did, drifting through the bayonet palms and melting into the black water of the Barron River. Not a lot, but it was enough, one of the old Seminole guides said, "to make everybody shut up." And a wag wrote on the blackboard announcing the restaurant's specials: "How hard these days / To fish with rod / And hunt with gun / But if it snows / You're really done."

No one had foreseen that a monstrous Arctic vortex would collide with an unusual northward charge of moist air from the Gulf of Mexico. When these crashed together over the Midwest, the storm they formed was much like the Blizzard of 1888, except that now the west wind and the jet stream went at it like a bulldozer, ordering it into a north–south line a thousand miles long and two hundred miles wide furious with snow and moving straight east at twenty-five miles an hour. The snow at the midpoint of the line was so heavy and incessant that in the eight hours during its passage over any location it left four feet of itself or more. Wind gusts up to sixty miles per hour drifted it at times into eight-foot swells.

Washingtonians remembered the derecho, the summer wind and lightning that had swept through on a unified front several hundred miles in length, darkening the sky and tossing up debris like a tornado, so that westward traffic on I-66 came to a stop as garbage bins and screen doors that had been lifted from the western suburbs pelted cars like hail. The Inauguration Storm was a similar shock, but of overwhelming, paralyzing white.

*

It was responsible for the coldest, shortest, least attended inauguration in modern history. Even Hartsfield couldn't hear his speech because of the wind shrieking past the lectern. Heaters were hidden inside, but so much snow was blown into them that they shorted out. Loudspeakers on the mall were blown off their poles. The West Face of the Capitol and much of Hartsfield's face itself were coated with snow and ice. It was so bad that in the middle of the inaugural address the outgoing president had leaned toward his successor and, in immense distress and perhaps not really according to historical protocol, said, "Speed it the fuck up, will you!"

And because no one was listening anyway, Hartsfield did speed it up, and was very much amused as he raced through the speech so fast that hostile commentators later said he sounded like Mickey Mouse. The parade up Pennsylvania Avenue was canceled, and the presidential limousine followed a snowplow to the White House, where for the first time Hartsfield sat alone in the Oval Office. A fire blazed as snow and wind banged against the tall windows. He wasn't at his desk, but in a chair close to the fireplace, which provided warm illumination as he watched the dim, bluish light outside and held a tumbler of scotch in his left hand.

His newly appointed chief of staff knocked and entered. "Mr. President," he said, for only the second time ever, "I guess an emergency declaration for, my God, everything east of the Rockies, will be your first official act."

"No," Hartsfield said, "my second."

*

Every single admiral on the panel had been trapped like a rabbit, confined by the snow to unprepossessing guest quarters and prevented by the closure of I-95 and the airports from shoring up their prospects in the infancy of the new administration. The base was on emergency power, and that evening they trooped through the snow to the *Eisenhower*, where the food was better. They would meet the next day to determine Rensselaer's sentence. In the *Eisenhower*'s wardroom they ate in silence rather than continue to debate their divisions in sentencing. They couldn't bring themselves to talk about it anymore, and knew that, at the last minute, they would have to have the judge guide them through the conflict.

To the south, in the deadly silent brig at Chesapeake, Rensselaer sat on the edge of his bunk, a blanket over his shoulders, summoning the stoicism that a soldier learns upon accepting that the currency of his profession is his life. The worst might come, but it was both his duty and his comfort to face it without even a twitch. How many times had he imagined oncoming death? How many times had he foreseen slow torture and how he would accept it, knowing that at its end he would be either dead or alive, but that he would be released from it one way or another.

Now, in the darkness, with snow blanketing the roof, the exercise yards, and the fields and forests beyond, he steeled himself. But when eventually he slept, he dreamt of Katy, and all this hardness was undone.

*

By the morning of the twenty-second the roads would be plowed and the runways cleared. But it was still the twenty-first, and glorious beyond belief. Half the country was covered in blinding, untouched white. Hardly anyone moved. The sky was so blue and the wind so cold that it was as if the nation had awakened at the South Pole. The press partial to Hartsfield had an almost universal headline along the lines of "Storm Over, A New Beginning." When the new president saw half a dozen such announcements peeking out from the tops of the folds of the leading papers laid one upon another on a mahogany table in the upstairs living quarters, he turned to his wife. "The more they gush, the harder we'll get hit later. Compliments are like a stretched cable. They snap back eventually, and can kill."

He picked up a phone on a side table, pushed a button, and said, "I want to see the Attorney General at ten this morning."

The answer was a simple, "Yes, sir."

Hartsfield put down the phone. Almost stunned, he said to Mrs. Hartsfield, "I just ordered the Attorney General of the United States to appear in my office at ten. And he will. I didn't ask. I ordered."

"You're going to have to try never to get used to it," she told him.

"How am I going to do that?"

"I don't know. I can't think of anything more corrupting. Don't be like those jerks who enjoy it. Check yourself at every instance. When you come out of this, whether in four years or eight, I want you still to be the man I married. The moment I see you enjoying your own power, you're going to catch hell from me. I mean it."

"I know you do," he said. And then: "We can even have sushi for breakfast if we want."

*

At 0430 on the twenty-second, Rensselaer was awakened. He dressed by the weak light of his desk lamp, and he, two guards and a driver left at 0530. It wasn't necessary. They got to base an hour early and sat in the car for forty-five minutes with the engine running and the heat on, until, still in the dark, they went into the helicopter hangar and, just as they had done when the findings had been announced, turned on the lamps. Frearson arrived shortly thereafter, ruddy from the cold. Sitting down next to Rensselaer, he said, "We're going to appeal. Don't despair."

Quite calmly, Rensselaer answered, "Correct me if I'm wrong, but was there anything in law or procedure that would favor, or even allow, an appeal?"

Frearson seemed taken aback. "Command influence, for one."

"You think that would be sufficient?"

"It depends. I'll go through the record of trial with a microscope. The courts are jealous of their independence and they hate pressure and interference above all. To put it in New York terms, they might want to whack the politicians just to send a message. Of course we'll appeal."

Their covers were on chairs next to them, but they were still in their naval great coats. As 0700 approached and the hangar warmed, Frearson said, "We'd better take off our coats. It would be a sign of disrespect to be wearing them during sentencing, especially you, as if you're just stopping by on your way to lunch."

They both stood at once and removed their coats, folding them so they could be placed on the chairs. And their covers—with the brims aligned and facing the dais—then rested upon the coats like birds settled on nests. Rensselaer's dress blues, adorned with a big rectangle of ribbons and the larger devices that spoke to his long and distinguished service, shone in the intense light from above, echoing the colorful flags.

O-seven-hundred arrived, but the admirals did not. Then 0710, 0720, 0730. "What does this mean?" Rensselaer asked Frearson.

Frearson shook his head from side to side, expressing perfectly both that he didn't know but that he was concerned. He was indeed concerned, because he imagined, though he did not let on, that a dispute had arisen in regard to the severity of punishment, including, at the outside, the death penalty. Just the possibility that at this late point the court was divided caused him to fear harsh punishment. "You can't tell," he told Rensselaer. "Maybe they're distracted by a matter within one of their commands. Maybe someone doesn't feel well. Who knows?"

But at 0735 they walked in, without their coats, and took their seats. Rensselaer felt waves of anxiety enough to unsettle his gut, alternating with a sense of calm sufficient to lower his blood pressure. But from his appearance, he was undisturbed.

The judge called the court to order, and said, "The president of the court, Admiral Porter, will now pronounce sentence." He turned to his right to listen to the admiral, the judge's duties over except eventually to close the proceedings.

As was his wont, Admiral Porter did not immediately begin to speak. He kept his eyes on the table in front of him, and smiled, which made both Frearson and Rensselaer lean forward in their seats.

"In fact, Your Honor, with all due respect," Porter said, "the president of the court will not pronounce sentence." Here, once again, he hesitated. The air was still, both inside and out. It seemed that no one breathed but Porter himself, who seemed tickled, a word no one would have thought appropriate to him but which now was exactly right. The judge was shocked, and, along with everyone else, he waited.

Finally Porter continued, with deliberate, almost teasing slowness. "Yesterday afternoon, just after the roads had been plowed, I, as president of the court, received the following documents from the Department of Justice, not to be opened or read until the court convened today. And as you may have observed, when the proceedings were called to order I did open them. I haven't read them fully, but to know what's in them you don't really have to. I shall read the first now." Here he paused again, deliberately, as if to see how long people would seem not to breathe.

He read. "'William A. Hartsfield, President of the United States. To all Whom These Presents May Come, Greeting: be it known, that this day, I, William A. Hartsfield, President of the United States, pursuant to my powers under Article Two, Section two, Clause one, of the Constitution, have granted unto Stephen Rensselaer, Captain, United States Navy . . .'"

Here, Admiral Porter looked up, and announced that similar documents were enclosed for each member of *Athena*'s crew charged, even if their charges had been dismissed. And then, after deliberately allowing everything to hang, momentarily gravityless, in the air, he went on.

"'. . . a full and unconditional pardon.'

"'For his convictions under Article Ninety-Four, Section one, b., two; and Article One Hundred and Thirty-Four, of the Uniform Code of Military Justice, of which he was convicted on twenty January of this year. And for any and all other offenses during the deployment of the United States Ship *Athena*, from Little Creek, Virginia, to its return to same. In testimony whereof, I have hereon signed my name and caused the seal of the Department of Justice to be affixed. Done at the City of Washington, this twenty-first day of January. . . .'"

Admiral Porter held it up. "Well, here it is."

Rensselaer was speechless, paralyzed. But more was to come. Porter went on. "I must say," he said, "and at risk of violating the customs of the court, that I find this not only extraordinary . . . but pleasing. Captain Rensselaer, you will be more than pleased, because the second document relating to you is a presidential commission. Captain Rensselaer, you have been promoted to rear admiral, *upper* half."

This stunned the court and not least Rensselaer himself. Among the Navy's 350,000 sailors were more than 3,000 captains, but only 60 rear admirals of the upper half. Though presidents can make and have made such promotions, they seldom do.

"Admiral Rensselaer," Porter continued, "you may be pleased to know that your XO and the commander of your SEAL detachment have also skipped a grade, and have been promoted to captain. The awards and decorations resulting from actions during *Athena*'s deployment, all of which were put on hold, will follow in due course, and you have been granted six months leave, from this day. Can you assimilate all that?"

"Frankly, sir, no," Rensselaer answered. "I need some time."

"Take the time. Meanwhile, I'll give the proceedings back to His Honor. Your Honor?" Though as surprised as everyone else, the judge preserved his judicial demeanor.

"Captain Rensselaer. . . . " The clerk of the court cleared his throat. The judge then corrected himself. "Admiral Rensselaer, you are free to go. Guards from the brig, remain to receive the release documents. The proceedings are now closed." He banged the gavel.

Rensselaer and Frearson walked out into cold sunshine that was not half as shocking to them as what they had just heard, and as they did, with one metallic bang of the heavy electrical panel after another, the spotlights in the helicopter hangar were extinguished bank by bank and forever.

Epilogue

POYDRAS AND ST. CHARLES

At Porter's request, the captain of the *Eisenhower* provided a launch in which Rensselaer and Frearson sped down the Elizabeth River on its west side so as to avoid the delays of passing honors, for now a blue flag with two stars was flown, a tremendous shock to Rensselaer after his imprisonment in the brig. Where the river divides, they veered to starboard into a vast forest of gray ships, dry-docks, skyscraper-tall cranes, and giant blocks of scaffolding, and the prow of the launch now and then knocked against small pieces of floating ice.

Most of the ships at the BAE yard were far bigger than *Athena*, and it took a while to find her, tucked in between two destroyers at the yard's west end. Despite having done so much, she was of such low priority that—unlike the other, larger ships the launch had passed, which were singing with the sounds of cutting and grinding, and illuminated by rivers of golden sparks and blue acetylene—she was alone and quiet, her wounds open and beginning to rust, her sides stained by black smoke, the tip of her topmast broken, the starboard bridge window that had killed Josephson still sadly covered with plywood, her weapons shrouded in canvas, her steel pockmarked by gunfire, and, of course, her decks and superstructure laden with snow.

"How tough she looks," Rensselaer said, "as if she's seen everything in the world and is so wounded and broken she needs to be buried."

"How bad is it?" Frearson asked.

"Don't let it fool you," Rensselaer said, "she's ninety-five percent ready, just a little rough on the outside. A part of me wants to take her to sea again."

"That's over," Frearson stated.

"I know. But I've never loved a ship as much. I hope that somehow she knows that. This was my last look, and now she's on her own. She'll be fine. There's something about her. She'll have no descendants, so her story alone will have to do. If there's a god of ships, or if God grants souls to them, then she'll live on, just like us."

*

When the launch returned to base, Frearson asked if Rensselaer wanted to stop at the Naval Exchange to buy new insignia: two stars now, for some the ambition of lifetime, and for Rensselaer, even with the aid of a deus ex machina, well-earned. No, he did not. If he had had civilian clothes he would have changed into them, he said, but he didn't, and being in uniform might help him get on a flight he hadn't booked.

"I can take you to Richmond International, Reagan, or Dulles," Frearson offered.

"No, Norfolk."

"There's hardly any traffic out of Norfolk."

"The big airports will be all tangled up with cancellations and pre-booked flights. Norfolk might be faster. It's a gamble."

"Where're you going anyway?" Frearson said, as if he didn't know.

"New Orleans," Rensselaer answered, for the pleasure of saying it.

The runway was empty and veils of snow sometimes blew across it. "This is crazy," Frearson said. "Planes are allergic to this place."

"You saw what happened today?" Rensselaer asked. Frearson nodded. "The air is still charged with it."

As they walked into the empty terminal, Rensselaer seemed perfectly confident. No one was at the counters. Of a man mopping the floor, they asked who was in charge. He pointed to a door. "You see?" Rensselaer said.

Frearson returned, "See what?"

They knocked. A woman appeared. "When's the next flight out?" Rensselaer asked.

"Not until this evening," she said.

"That's too late," Rensselaer told her.

"Oh is it?" she asked rhetorically.

"There must be something," Rensselaer insisted. "You've got that nice big runway. What the hell is it for?"

The woman looked at Frearson as if to ask, *Is he mad?* Frearson just shrugged his shoulders. Then she said, "Why don't you go to the base; they're ten times busier than we are."

"They usually don't go to civilian airports. I've got to get to New Orleans."

"You want to fly from this airport to New Orleans?"

"To wherever I can make a connection."

"The only flight out is this evening to New York. Except a United charter coming in from Bermuda."

"When?"

"Nine ten."

"Then where's it going?"

"Atlanta. But it doesn't take passengers."

"We'll see," Rensselaer said.

The woman was astonished. "Who are *you*," she asked, "Admiral Dewey?"

"No ma'am, I'm Admiral Rensselaer," he said—for the first time.

"That's not what I see," she insisted, looking at his insignia. It was a Navy town, and she knew.

"He was just promoted this morning," Frearson told her, almost like a child.

"All right. Ask if you want. They won't take you."

As it happened . . . the captain of the United flight had been a Navy P-3 pilot, and his co-pilot had been the captain of an E2-C. One of the stewardesses welcomed Rensselaer aboard. "We've been in Brazil and Bermuda, so we missed the storm. As we flew in, it was amazing to see everything covered in such deep snow. You must have had such a hard time getting here."

On the way to his seat, Rensselaer stopped, turned back to her, and smiled. "Yes," he said. "I did."

Sometimes, when music accompanies ordinary things, it brings out the music that is already within them. For example, a plane rising confirms—not just by the act of lifting into the air, but also—in the ratios and balances between its altitude, speed, and forward travel—relations that are musical in essence.

Frearson stood outside the terminal, in bright sun, the wind whipping the cuffs of his trousers, and as if in salute he shielded his eyes from the glare as he watched the plane race down the runway, increasing its speed until it gave itself to the air, rose up, and began a steady climb against a sky so deep and blue it pulsed against the eyes. The course of its travel and the line of its rise conformed like music to those underlying ratios of the heart that, though unseen, determine everything. And though unseen they leave their evidence in the fragile, quickly vanishing traces of friction when the world's heartbreak is met with love and courage. Rensselaer's flight rose upon the cold air as smoothly and steadily as a gull on the wind.

*

Anyone who thinks New Orleans is like the other parts of the United States has a lot to learn. Its elemental rules are very different from those it pretends to accept as they are imposed upon it from without. They may be suppressed from time to time, but like the Mississippi and the tides, they rise and they abide.

At Katy's firm—born of the arrogant impositions and pressures of the "human resources" department, fear of lawsuits, and work/life columns in the newspapers—every woman had to answer one question, even were she unaware of it: to what will you look in determining the course of your life? Sudden fashions that invade relations between the sexes, or the impulse as old as life itself to court, to love, and to unite? What will you risk, what will you flout, and what will you endure to do so?

Perhaps the answer would have been different in New York or Los Angeles, but this was New Orleans, where logic and intoxication were often indistinguishable. Oblivious of all the bright and current lines, Katy's suitors never ceased. They saw in her what Stephen had seen, and it was irresistible. All she had to do was speak, or turn and look at you, or change her expression, and it was endlessly electrifying, made even more so because she often doubted herself. When she did, her efforts at correction led to a mixture of magnificent daring and charming modesty, as if through mackerel clouds the sun were flashing light and shade.

She had rejected one suitor after another, but because she was so interesting, so alive, and so desirable, they persisted. Some came to resent and even hate her. But then they resumed. For her part, she was confused. Being honest, she couldn't deny their virtues and good qualities—when they had them. And yet they were as exasperating as mosquitoes or oversexed adolescent boys. She wished they would leave her alone, but had they left her alone she would have thought that maybe she had crossed a line of age that, despite strenuous effort and subterfuges so often marshaled in vain, cannot be re-crossed.

She had no idea that on this cool and very dark day in January, Stephen was on the way to her. A low ceiling of almost black cloud hovered over the city as if supported by the unusually dry air beneath it. Strangely, at noon, offices and restaurants turned on their lights.

Every day, she looked at *Navy Times* on the internet, but *Navy Times* had withdrawn its stringer from the trial, and there was nothing. No news was comforting in that it announced yet another day when the hammer had yet to fall. Normally she checked just before she went home, so that in case of bad news she would not have to be in the office, and with no news she could sleep well that night. But today, for whatever reason, perhaps the cool and the dark, or because she was spurred from within, she called up *Navy Times* on her screen at two, just after she returned from lunch. Perhaps it was because she found the brief she was writing, on behalf of a video game company, profoundly distasteful.

At first she skipped right over the headline near the bottom of the page, but then she returned to it. Though she had rapidly passed by the story, she'd seen enough in a second or less to know what it said. Absent its stringer at the trial, *Navy Times* reported from the day before: conviction on two counts. It was as if, internally, she had fallen twenty storeys.

At that very instant, one of her bow-tied, Brooks-Brothered suitors appeared beyond the glass. Though it was on business, she savagely waved him away. For a moment, she stared at her desk, out of focus, and then she remembered that Stephen Rensselaer was a sailor, a soldier, that he went into battle not knowing if he would come out. So, with tightened jaw and narrowed eyes, her breathing deep, she disciplined herself. She would wait to hear from him, or, the next day, read the news. The two counts were capital offenses. This was now very much her battle as much as his, the age-old task of women who without recourse to action must wait and bear the news.

Paragraph by paragraph, sentence by sentence, she continued with a brief. Her courage was as beautiful as she was. And somehow, though Stephen wasn't aware of it, in the magic of things unseen it would serve to weld them together even more than before.

*

At six o'clock, waiting for the light on the southeast corner of Poydras and St. Charles, Stephen worried that he had missed her. Perhaps she had already gone home, or to swim, or to a client meeting. The streetcar stop on the northwest corner was crowded, and she wasn't there. Usually, willing to pay the price of not getting a seat, she stood back on the steps that rose from the sidewalk to the elevated plaza, because she didn't like being hemmed in by groups of people.

The traffic light was long, and when he wasn't scanning north up St. Charles to see her approaching, he stared at the trees across the street. Their trunks were thick and dark, the ground around them dense with fern-like palms. He had yearned so much for this place, a symbol of what he wanted and what he loved, that in his memory the fence that cordoned off the trees and small palms from the sidewalk had been constructed of black, nineteenth-century wrought iron. He had seen it in his dreams and in the confused, effulgent darkness of nights at sea, when it is impossible to see, and the eyes create inchoate movement and texture out of nothing. He had pictured it so intensely that he even saw the rust where paint had become too old and worn to cling.

But the fence, though some kind of metal, was neither black nor spear-tipped but light-colored and of an unattractive, modernist design. He refused disappointment, and went with his memory, defiantly replacing what was there with what was better—to match the beauty of the trees beyond, of what he remembered, and of what could be. He wondered if he had done the same with his memory of Katy. He wondered if that of which he had dreamed so hard had been an illusion unfair to her and eventually heartbreaking for him. Then he crossed St. Charles, and waited, his eyes on the stop across Poydras.

He knew how hard she worked, that this was not ordinarily a swimming day, that she loved quiet and routine. Imagining again and again how she was when he had first seen her, he wanted now to be blessed to see her again in the same way—after so much, across oceans and seas, at such risk in far deserts under a different sun. And although he yearned for her such that he could hardly breathe, he hesitated for a moment, pondering if ever again he would be so close to the oceans and the stars that life and death seemed one and the same: lovely and exciting and easy to bear, full of light and silence in the eternal rhythm of waves in the oceans and in the air. The thing was, you couldn't grasp them in their immensity and abstraction, but only by hints and in longing. They were always alluring and always out of reach. But in a woman these disparate and ineffable qualities were made real sufficiently to create life. It had taken him this long, but with the help of *Athena* he had understood that Katy herself, and Katy alone, was worth all the blue oceans and all the bright stars.

Then he saw the yellowish light of a streetcar jerking left and right as it headed south. The group of people waiting re-formed itself in expectation. Suddenly, a crowd of children and their teachers came racing down the steps of the elevated plaza to join the office workers. He hadn't seen the school trip assembled there like a herd of gazelles. The streetcar would be packed, as it would already have passengers aboard when it arrived.

When it did arrive and opened its doors, no one got out. But among the first to get in was a figure unmistakable for her slim grace and elegance. She had been there all the time. Aware of the children, she knew that she wouldn't have been able to get on if she waited apart and on the steps as usual. She was in a crisp, white, form-fitting dress shirt. The sun was now occasionally breaking through the clouds, and just before she got on, her hair caught the sunlight.

At first, Stephen was going to dash across Poydras, but he understood that too many people were waiting. She disappeared inside. Three long blocks south at Julia Street, some people always got out. If he boarded there, he would be able to find a place to stand even if next to the driver.

He had no luggage, only, under his left arm, his greatcoat. Hoping that the traffic light was as long as it had been before, he began to run south toward Julia Street. Though it was cool and dark for New Orleans even for late January, it was hot every time the low sun cracked the clouds, he had been wounded, he was out of shape, and he was in his dress blues. Running was difficult and taxing. A block down, he took off his hat and held it in his right hand. Behind him, he heard the sound of the steel wheels on the track, so he picked up speed.

He was in no condition to run. The doctors had said that at his age it would take six months to a year to recover fully, and that he had to be especially careful about sudden, peak exertion. But there was no question in his mind, even though he could have let the streetcar pass and then walked to Katy's house, that he had to see her now.

He was thinking, *Oh God, when she alights I want to hold her forever, but how long can we stand in the street?* It didn't matter that people might stare at them, because all was left behind, there was only the present, which as if with an explosion of light took the place of past and future and had become everything for the first time in his life, which had all led up to this.

His vision began to blur, and his heart pounded unsteadily as if in protest. But he kept up and even increased his pace. Long before, he had made peace with the fluid and timeless sea, where comfort is unneeded and unknown. Long before, he had understood that even in a ship full of men, at sea one is alone; that only a heart that has been broken can be full; and that even in every kind of unforgiving desert there is nonetheless infinite love always speaking, always apparent, always appealing. So he kept on running, and would not give up.

Katy was in the seat next to the window on the right side of the car. On her left was an extremely large man who, without intending to, made it such that she was pressed next to the wall of the streetcar so as not to be pressed against him. She tried to read a law review article about video game cases, but her heart was hardly in it. Nonetheless, she took refuge in looking down.

Halfway to Julia Street, something caught her eye. A man was running along the sidewalk. Automatically, she looked down again, but then quickly turned her head to look out. He was in naval dress blues, and in his right hand was an officer's white cap. As if she were someone who has lost a love to death and imagines the sight of the lost one back from the dead, her heart leapt. But she caught herself, to avoid the pain of disappointment. This couldn't be. It simply could not be. Still, she turned to look back as the streetcar passed him. Unable to see him, she was left only bewildered, her pulse rapid.

When the streetcar stopped at Julia Street, and people squeezed down the aisle, with many *Excuse me's*, she was hardly breathing, and she didn't dare take her eyes from the front. Then Stephen, flushed and expectant, rose on the steps.

No one quite understood why this woman, trapped in her seat, was crying, or why the naval officer, a rare sight in New Orleans and breathing as if he had just run a race, kept on saying, quietly, "It's okay, it's okay," as she cried.

When the streetcar named St. Charles reached their stop, he went down, and waited. People filed past. She appeared near the driver, no longer in tears but so buoyant that she wondered if she would be able to descend the steps.

When she reached the second step from the bottom, he moved toward her, she took his hand, and she jumped down—like a young girl.